UB·

MW01600248

ETERNITY'S HANDMAIDEN

By R. Peter Ubtrent

Eternity's Handmaiden

Copyright © 2004 by R. Peter Buttner

All rights reserved. No part of this book may be reproduced or utilized in any form or by any means, electronic or mechanical, including photocopying, recording, or by any information storage or retrieval systems, without permission in writing from the publisher.
For information contact:

Prairie View Publishing
PO Box 45
New Carlisle, Indiana 46552
USA
www.prairieviewpublishing.com

ISBN: 0-9744-9917-X

First Printing 2004

For Genevieve, who always believed in me.
And for Jotykavi, whose friendship kept me sane.

I would like to thank my editor Lorri for her support and advice and for giving me the opportunity to publish my work. I'd like to thank Roger also for the great artwork and for his support and of course I'd like to thank my family, especially my mom and dad for their love and self –sacrifice during the hard years.

As a drop of water is to the storm, so is an individual to the collective: one such drop misplaced will matter little to the force of the aggregate. But how are we to know when that one drop, which we have misplaced, is in fact the basis for the aggregate as a totality, and in that misplacing rend the storm of its force? How are we to know how many drops can be misplaced before we bring eternity to an end and in that end bring life to a new beginning, coming full circle in that path of the consciousness which starts with that single raindrop? Perhaps that is why the gods, in their infinite wisdom, provided us with one who knows these things, who can, in her ever-recurring life, be aptly named Eternity's Handmaiden, and who knows which drops can be misplaced and which cannot.

--- from the sayings of Mahriso Pasha, Taoist monk, First President the United 0' Neill Colonies Federation.

*We must always keep the springs of laughter dancing in our hearts.
Otherwise tragedy will overwhelm and deaden us.*

PROLOGUE

The ice axe banged into the bullet-proof surface of the sheet, dislodging a chunk of the ghoulish white, transparent ice to fall into the raising wind gusts and crash onto the helmeted figure a good ten meters below, who hunched his shoulders and waited for the shower of particles to cease. Dr. Krishna Pratali securely imbedded his other axe into the ice, tested his placement with a tug, then kicked the front part of his crampons in and stepped up.

He grabbed another ice screw, a twenty-centimeter long and three-quarter centimeter thick threaded, hollow tube that would arrest any fall, and began the laborious process of working it into the rock-hard ice sheet.

He looked up at the lenticular clouds making their way across the face of the dark blue sky, then at the dark band building on the horizon and knew that they were running out of time. This mountain and these storms were not forgiving of mortals who dared challenge them.

This was Cerro Torre, which rose out of the Patagonian Andes like a halberd into the winter sky, defying those who attempted to conquer it.

On the southern tip of Argentina, the Patagonian Andes plunge deep into the heart of the great Southern Ocean, the narrow land-mass all that separates the Southern Pacific from the Southern Atlantic, all that stands in the way of the pounding fury of the storms spawned over the oceans, which tear their way around the bottom of the globe in unabashed vehemence.

The west side of Cerro Torre sits squarely in the path of these storms and

5

they frequently slam the mountain with punishing slashes of wind and rain, adorning the peaks with fantastic mushrooms of rime ice. They grow in wild and twisted shapes as if the sculptor were passionately insane. Each storm pounded the rock and in that pounding the twisted shapes evolved until their translucent grayish blue color capped the granite monoliths like gargoyles, an insurmountable barrier to the summit for those foolish enough to try.

These rime mushrooms sat athwart the main passages up and provided a dangerous challenge, not able to support a persons weight but forcing one to go around and in-between and making the ascent that much more difficult and spectacular.

It was why people chose this mountain ... and this time of year.

Krishna finished working in the ice screw. Although the temperature was well below freezing, he could feel the greasy sweat underneath his many layers of clothing, under his helmet. He rested a moment. For all the challenges Cerro Torre offered, he was glad that altitude was not one of them. With a peak at only 3102 meters, high-altitude sickness was never a worry. He could not imagine doing all this and having to lug around portable oxygen.

He looked out over the vast expanse opening up below him, the dark blue sky in stark contrast to the blinding white of the snow and ice, the dull granite gray and rustic browns comprising the rock they had chosen to climb on this particular trip and marveled at the freedom he felt at this moment. Although extremely dangerous, especially during the winter when only a handful of climbers had successfully navigated the vertiginous cliffs, it was the best way he knew to unwind after the last few months of concentrated work on the patients for which he was responsible.

As a neurosurgeon at one of the more prestigious hospitals in the world, Krishna's work involved one thing and one thing only: repairing the damaged brains of people who were nothing but anonymous faces. He had wanted to stick to pure research, stay in a lab somewhere and never have to deal with the human side of the profession. It had not worked out the way he had planned it. That youth-inspired dream, he had learned much to his consternation, would never have made it all the way to the reality train.

Life was not that straight forward or simple.

It was not that he didn't enjoy his work. The truth was far from that. He found the entire experience extremely challenging and the lives he saved made any qualms about pure research look selfish and ill conceived. But late at night when he had time to himself – which was so rare as to be almost

6

non-existent – he still dreamt of where his interests lay; the theoretical side of the work, the advances in neurosurgery that could be instituted to save even more lives, correct more of the mental problems facing so many people in the world these days.

Then there had been the sudden, tragic deaths just a few months ago of Kido Nakamura and Dr. Hart, two new acquaintances he had made at a conference recently attended. He had only known them briefly, having talked together for no more than five hours at the most and then they communicated through e-mails and phone blurbs that held more questions than answers, but they had somehow struck up a harmonious cord. Although they were all in completely separate and unrelated fields, the idea with which these two had approached him had been an awe-inspired break-through, a true revolution if it could be achieved. The ideas had been rumbling around in his mind ever since and he was determined, when he returned from this vacation, to make more time for the research they had intended him to accomplish.

They might be dead but it didn't mean that the idea had to die with them. If their totally revolutionary concept could be successfully implemented, it would be one of the most important advances in science, nay in humanity, since Newton and Einstein.

A thick Spanish accent floated up on the rising wind. "How long will you be admiring the scenery? We need to move along. We only have a few hours of sunlight left and either we reach the next ledge or we have a sleepless night here on the cliff face and I for one don't wish to sleep here."

Krishna shook himself out of his musings and looked down at his climbing companions. He smiled at them. He needed to stop all this idle daydreaming and get back to the work at hand. He looked back up at the imposing edifice, which rose like a wall of white before him and took stock of his next move. He concentrated on making easy, smooth swings with his ice axes as he slowly and methodically made his way up, twenty feet at a time, planting ice screws and securing their ascent to the sheer ice walls standing in their way to the next way point.

His calves quivered with exhaustion. His breath came in pants. It was tiring work to be sure and the sun, as it began to sink lower and lower, its slanting rays of light coming off the low fireball turning the rime mushrooms a caustic yellow, would not wait for him to rest.

Francisco worked his way past Krishna, thankfully, taking the lead and heading for the lip at the top of the head-wall and the site of their camp for the night. With the short, winter daylight and the bitter cold, they had spared rigging the usual umbilical cord of rope strung out behind them to secure their descent. They had decided early that it would take too long to rig the line and be too much of a dead weight hanging down below them for the security it offered.

They were all veteran climbers and this type of mountain required that they reach the summit as quickly and efficiently as possible, extra precautions would only hinder their ascent.

The climb had become so steep now that Krishna was forced to use only the very front spikes of his crampons, knowing that if he didn't reach the head wall soon, he would be too exhausted to go on. Hanging off this cliff face was not the best possible place to be when the storm hit. There was a storm brewing off in the Pacific he could feel in the frigid blasts of cold buffeting him with their telltale sign of power. They might have to wait it out in one of the rare huts lining the west side, boredom more of a threat at that point than anything else.

But first things first.

They needed to reach that ledge in short order.

He heard it before he saw it and knew exactly what it portended, though somewhere in his analytical mind he knew that the odds against it happening were astronomical. Had he had time to think about it, he would have found it odd how the human mind could create such esoteric thoughts and drag up such trivial data points at a time when it was facing possible extinction. Perhaps it was some form of survival technique.

He would not have time to contemplate the problem.

The warning from Francisco was more panic than caution and Krishna grabbed the line with his gloved hands, bracing himself for the sudden lurch of weight that he knew was coming.

An ice screw had failed, snapped in half like a toothpick.

Francisco swung free from the vertical for a moment, the loss of his support unexpected and sudden. He swung an ice axe into the gleaming white sheet but it merely glanced off to the spray of scattered ice particles glittering in the fading light like mini fireflies. Another screw snapped and Francisco plummeted down, his safety line like a useless tail.

As Krishna watched his companion come toward him, several thoughts flashed through his mind at once. First of all, it was almost impossible for one of the ice screws to fail like that. They were designed to the highest specifications and could support up to ten times his weight.

For two to break was unthinkable.

His second thought was about his family. Images of his beautiful wife and two small children began dancing before his eyes. Who would take care of them now? Would his employer continue to pay them benefits? Who would teach his son to play sports?

When the third and fourth screw let lose with a snap that echoed through his very soul, Krishna knew that this was it. Without the ice screws to secure them to the wall of ice and granite, gravity would work its unalterable ways and pull each of the climbers off the face to certain death on the jagged rocks below. There was nothing he could do to avert the disaster about to befall them and yet he felt a strange calmness come over him as if he somehow knew that it was all going to be all right, that everything would be taken care of and he need not worry.

The line went taut in his hands as the full weight of Francisco came to him. The rope burned through his gloves as he clamped down slowly, letting the tension build gradually so that the sudden addition of Francisco's weight would not pull him off also.

But his efforts were in vain, for with a loud pop, followed by a series of deafening snaps, the rest of the ice screws holding the team in place let loose and the company of hardy adventurers plunged down the three hundred meter cliff, their cries of terror lost to the screaming wind that had begun to assault the mountain peak with its merciless howling.

Their frozen, dead bodies would not be recovered for several months, the look of agony and shear horror etched on their faces a mute testimony to what had happened, a snapped ice screw taken as evidence of the tragic accident that had befallen Dr. Krishna Pratali and his climbing companions in their attempt to conquer Cerro Torre ... and themselves.

A trick of government is to make the people feel guilty.
Guilt must begin as a feeling of failure. Therefore,
failure must be easy to come by and provided for
readily by the government.

1

5 August 2085

The view from the office window was usually, in all respects, fantastic. The clear skyline allowed one to see for kilometers, the spires of the surrounding buildings receding off like majestic descending steps to the altar that was the tallest building of the city. Its soaring structure allowed for an unobstructed panorama of the city lying below like a foundation of stability. The architecture here emphasized the harmonious while interspersing with gardens and parks, making sure the city was not a great sprawling edifice of meta-structuring metropolises into which the old cities of Earth had been allowed to fester.

But this evening the view was gone, replaced by a low band of clouds hovering over the land like a leaden shield, dropping its mixture of nitrogen and water onto a humanity thirsting for so much more. The wind, high up in the storm where the tower pierced into the tempest like a lone brawler defying the gale, pelted the window with splattered drops of rain smearing and running along as if chased by the very hounds of hell.

The storm had come in unexpected, as most such storms still did despite the assurances to the contrary by those in the meteorological services, and had overwhelmed the tower in a barrage of wetness that now sent a chill wave of despair through the structure as if leeching into the walls and dripping on the inside like misplaced dew.

But the man standing inside, looking out into his own reflection, was oblivious to the force of the tempest outside striving to regain the surface of the planet from the virus that had infested it so many hundreds of thousands of years ago. If it could not eradicate man with his own stupidity, perhaps it could drown him out. It had happened once before to the betterment of the planet.

He was not tall by any means. Most would, in fact, call him short, but certainly not to his face. That would be a mistake never to be repeated again. His stomach – once had been firm and strong, washboard abs a part of the muscular frame that was his youth – was now a pouch of fat and intestines, sticking out like the proverbial Buddha in defiance of any to criticize. His face was round, the heavy bags under the eyes and sagging chin an indication that age had been more of a foe than a friend. Red speckles danced randomly across his cheeks, a sign, the doctors assured him, that his blood pressure was still too high. His lips were full, scarred from too many years in the sun, too many missed kisses in the bedroom. His stark white hair sat atop his head like a warning of experience, mocking the youth he had once held and in that mocking, turning bitter, that which had once been satisfied.

His three-piece designer suit, custom-made to his specifications from the finest material, looked neat and pressed, the jacket thrown carefully over one of the three heavy leather chairs gracing the dark and foreboding office. His bow tie was undone, the top button of his white shirt open to allow his ample chin waddle to dangle in all its fatness. He looked tired.

His whole demeanor was one of trouble and worry as he stared into the raging storm that was his reflection. He could certainly not say that life had not been kind to him. It had, in all honesty, been more than kind, bestowing more money that he could conceivably ever use and more women in his younger days than he could remember, their faces like so much clutter to a mind's eye become blind to a past he would rather forget. He liked his fancy clothes, liked the feel of the expensive fabric against his flesh and yet he could still vividly remember a time when he would have been happy to have one decent dress shirt to wear.

He smirked at the remembrance.

Strange how happiness, as defined by his youth, was just as elusive now in his older age as it had been then despite the fact that he had achieved all his planned goals before he was even thirty.

The genius he once was had set up shop in someone else's body at some time which he could not pinpoint and left him with the growing girth of his own obesity as a consolation prize. He was well aware how people looked at him now, how they saw only the superficial outside and chuckled at his inability to maintain the look that the magazines wanted everyone to see as normal.

But it was his eyes that most people would speak of after they had met him. If asked to describe him, most would have a general description of stoutness that was vague and nondescript, but all would have a comment on his eyes, which blazed away in their deep recesses like fiery green candles in a dark room, an unwavering brightness transcending his physical appearance, drawing people to him like moths to the flame, compelled with no known reason to want to talk and engage in conversation with this short, fat man.

And his conversation would be brilliant, filled with an intelligence that seemed lost in the body that presented it, that would seduce even the most abstinent of skeptics. He could hold an audience spellbound with tales of safari and the Outback, or attack without mercy those ideas and opinions he found disdainful and without merit. He had rarely lost an argument. But then, he had rarely engaged in one that he knew he would lose.

But none of that mattered.

What mattered now was the woman for whom he was waiting, the woman who would direct him to activate an asset he felt was better left alone. It was always the same. Those who used his resources never understood the price to be paid and rarely, if ever, knew what it was that they were asking of him. Unfortunately, that was not the case with the appointment for which he was currently waiting. She was well aware of what she did, every move of that delicate intellect planned and crafted until it stank of perfection.

And he hated her for it, for it was his resources that normally suffered under the demands of her ego.

She was already late, something he didn't tolerate. People who were late were people who thought their time far more important than others, their lives taking priority over the mere mortals who happened to infect their path occasionally.

There was a knock, like a rap on the door of decision, hard and caustic, echoing through the room and into his soul like a rattle of drums.

"Enter," he said in his gruff baritone, killing off the echoes of the rap in the shadows.

The door swung open on silent hinges and the tall woman strode in as if on skates, her jaw set firm and hard, her eyes uncompromising in their amber intensity. "I suppose you've heard?" she asked in a tenor rumbling about the large room like a peal of distant thunder.

"I have," the man replied simply, not having turned from his vigil of the storm raging out the window, seeing her reflection perfectly and deeming not to look at her direct visage for fear that a Medusan curse might befall him.

"Then, Dr. Cavalier, I think that your earlier conjectures were in error."

"Perhaps.... We shall see." He was not about to admit any error on his part. He didn't make errors

She threw a sheaf of papers bundled up in a tan portfolio, the words *Eyes Only* boldly stenciled in red, onto the shiny mahogany table. They slid halfway across before coming to a stop. "That's five now. The president doesn't want to wait for a sixth one. She wants you to do something, Vincent, and wants you to do something now."

The use of his first name made Cavalier turn to look at the President's Chief-of-Staff, to see the blazing eyes reaching out to him in the darkened room, the beautiful lines of her aristocratic face always creating a pang in his heart for the body laying beneath all that gruff exterior and fashion-designed suits, which fit her figure better than they should have been allowed.

He didn't turn to stone upon setting his eyes on her.

Would wonders never cease?

Claudine Maxwell was not one with which to be fooled. He was more than aware of that little fact. She had not, as was the common opinion, slept her way to the top with her dark-haired good looks and model-perfect body. She had earned her position with integrity and grit, honesty and determination, assets anyone who had worked with her for any length of time would have seen within moments. She was respected by those she served, feared by those who opposed her and oblivious to anyone else.

"It's always now, isn't it Claudine?" Cav said as he ignored the sheaf of papers on his desk starting to fall out of the portfolio as if wanting to be read, needing to be seen to validate their existence.

"She wants to know if they truly are accidents, if it's all just coincidental."

Cav smirked, then walked over to the built-in bar and pulled the top off of the crystal carafe holding a smooth, amber liquid. "Drink?"

"No time, thank you." She had not always been this frigid. He remembered well a time when she would have jumped at a chance to drink with him. But than that was before his genius had abandoned him and left him a disgusting bum of a man. "So what should I tell the President? She's going to want an answer."

Cav sipped the cognac with practiced ease, the liquid burning a path down to his stomach with a retribution he felt deep down. "They always want an answer, Claudine," he said as he topped his glass off and replaced the stopper to the carafe, the clink of the glass odd in the stillness of the room, the rhythmic ticking of the French clock on the mantle like a subconscious countdown. "But sometimes...," he stated as he walked across the room and back around to the window, resuming the vigil he had held before she had entered, "... sometimes the answers are not the ones that they want to hear."

A frowned creased her face.

She hated having to come here to talk to this man. The brief and explosive love affair they had so many years ago, in that other lifetime that was their youth, made it even more difficult, especially with the condition into which Cav had let himself fall. Although pity was something she sometimes felt for him, a loathing was usually the feeling she had when she thought about having ever been involved with a man who ran one of the most nefarious and clandestine operations in the world and looked like a poster boy for over-indulgence, gluttony.

But then he was the best at what he did and that made it necessary to come here, to talk to him, to have to pretend to find his company marginally comfortable. When he didn't say anything else, she cleared her throat loudly.

He turned his head slightly, caught the indication that she was becoming impatient and smiled a crooked, consoling smile reflecting back in the window like a ghost. "I'll have to see who's available at such short notice."

"No." The word was like a shotgun blast and made him wince inside. "The President wants your best. I think we both know who that means."

He nodded his head slowly as he downed the last of the cognac, the burning no longer hard and firm, the kick of the drink having already dissipated to his tolerance. "You do know that she's inactive." It was not a question but more of a statement, a hoping that the Chief-of-Staff would change her mind.

"This is considered an emergency, top priority, National Security at stake." Her words were like a litany of excuses.

He smiled again, his eyes flashing a warning. "It's always a matter of National Security, isn't it? When has it ever not been?" He turned his head to look at her again, felt his limbs begin to solidify into stone and went back to looking at her reflection. Reflections were somehow softer, more muted, as if only a part of the evil inherent in humans was displayed, the mirror not able or willing to tolerate the rest. "Half of them aren't even our citizens. We've plenty of others who can do the job just as well."

"Activate her, Cav," she said with a finality, ending the conversation there and then. She always was one to get the last word in, even if she had to say it on the other side of the door. "I'll expect a report on my desk within two days. No more," She turned on her heel and strode to the door, her tight, long skirt conforming to her firm body like a glove, the reflection in the window he watched making it difficult to see her as the President's highest advisor or the shrew that she had become.

She stopped at the door and turned to look at his back, a yearning for the man she had once known making a feeble effort to assert itself, then ruthlessly pressed it down, back into the long, lost echoes of the past she kept hidden away deep within. "We paid for her, so we'll damn well use her." She hesitated a moment, made certain that he didn't have a reply, then slammed the door shut on his solitude.

Dr. Vincent Cavalier watched the lightning as it played across the clouds in fingers of divine nimbleness, the vibrations of the thunder shaking the window ever so slightly and causing the wind-pelted rain to dance even more energetically across the panes. He lowered his head a moment, wondering what he had ever done in his past lives to deserve someone like Claudine Maxwell in his current life. He would have preferred to come back as a snail for any bad karma he might have accumulated over the years.

He threw his cognac snifter across the room, shattering it in a spray of broken dreams tinkling to the carpeted floor like so many wasted lives, the shards not even picking up the muted lights to sparkle.

This is the season of gathering cold, the fading memory of spring.
Light flows slowly through the woods, a light that you could harvest
like grain or scoop into your astonished mouth the way a bear scoops
honey until your bones dissolve and you can never return
to the life that you were living.
-- Tom Sexton

2

6 August 2085, 0535 hrs
Alaska

Alaska is a land of unforgettable beauty and uncompromising wildness. It's still a frontier, a last refuge for those seeking a life that does not hinge on the metropolises that seem to define so much of humanity. The vast, unspoiled stretches of frozen tundra and towering mountain, quiet stream and tumbling river, tranquil wildlife and dignified lakes of pristine reflection harkens back to what the Earth once was, once was before the advent of humanity and its supposed monopoly on intelligence: an intelligence that decimated thousands of other species for its own righteous pursuits and then apologized to an empty landscape of malls and condominiums.

But Alaska has held its own, an island awash in a sea of rising urbanization and suburban sprawl that defines the new generation more so than anything else, her untouched back-lands a suffusion of openness and magnificence for those bold enough to live with it. For one didn't capture such a land. Only those born of an ignorance bred in the mind-numbing back streets of urban chancre infesting the very vitality of life with its lesions of concrete and steel can be brazen enough to claim to be able to capture the land. Those who live in the solemn openness of the lake and the brook and the mountain know better, and see, in their temporal existence, an acceptance by the land of them.

So it was in the lone cabin that sat by the gently flowing stream and glacial lake, the first covering of virgin snow on the ground still months away, the stillness of the morning air chill in its embrace, the vivid hue of the wildflowers, robust in their vibrancy, covering the tundra like a patchwork quilt and lining the path to the open porch and the double French doors that was the front entrance.

The stream running behind the cabin was about six meters wide and first appeared from the valley out of which it ran as a broad, straight, transparent ripple, its bottom flowered with round stones varying in size from the small to the fist-sized. As it neared the cabin, the stream gradually swept left in a meander, the far bank undercut by the turn, the water turning ashen with increased depth, toppling birch and alders dipping into the current, the course of the stream making them tremble and bob as if bestirred by a breeze. The nearer the cabin the more densely the trees grew as the arch of the stream continued till in a thicket a lone, tall pine, the needle-less snags of the bottom third like ghost fingers in the shadows, stood tall in its solitude, a marker for the cabin.

A long pool hugged the near bank, either mysterious with ripples and waves giving it a depth it didn't have, or crystal-clear to its sandy bottom. Then the stream narrowed and, rushing in dark and strong, still deep in its latent vigor, met the caliginous lake in a tumble of water. Being a glacial lake, it sat dark and brooding, its depth unseen, the green rolling carpet that was the meadows running to its shore, spread between gray and brown hills.

But the meadows stretching out from either side of the stream and all around the cabin were anything but smooth. Close to the lake and running up toward the tundra the land was filled with tussocks, mushroom shaped grass mounds that are the stuff of Arctic legend. Narrow at the base and wide at the top, the tussocks are unstable to walk on; any step slightly off center and they would topple, sending the walker stumbling. Then came the tundra, a dry, spongy cushion abloom with a bouquet of wild flowers running the spectrum of the rainbow and beyond, to the lazy sound of the awakening insects filling the air with their acrimonious buzzing.

Finally, the meadows turned into talus, rocky and rugged, climbing higher and higher into the hills turning into the mountains whose snow-capped peaks stood like sentinels guarding the valley below. A mass of pine trees interspersing with birch and aspen colored the horizon, standing like a line of soldiers on the fringes, reaching into the distant haze with their strong earthly essence and towering tops of dark, woodland green, the light green of the aspen a dapple of glittering light within.

The cabin was large as far as cabins go, a two-story construct that had four bedrooms, an immense kitchen, a library and numerous other amenities the owner rarely used. There was a three-car garage, though it housed only two vehicles: a silver Range Rover that was a classic in its own right and a new personal VTOL (vertical take-off and landing) that was rarely used if ever, sitting idly under its cover as if shunned for its ability to bring the outside world closer.

Two dogs ran about the cabin, frolicking in the freshness of the morning, chasing birds and rodents and dandelion seeds discharging into the light breeze in a spread of snow-white spores.

Music diffused out of the open windows, light and airy, fitting the majestic backdrop of snow-clad peaks rising out of the morning mist like giants in slumber, awaiting the right time to rumble to life and re-awaken their kin. A single violin stood out, played with a passion that would have made any music instructor proud, backed up by an accompanying orchestra on disc, the sound traveling for kilometers across the flower-topped meadows of the long valley. But then the cabin had no neighbors within hearing distance and the animals of the land didn't bother to complain.

The music was by Strauss, *the Radetsky Marsch*, a powerful piece of eloquence that the female played with striking intensity, almost as striking as her lack of clothing. Naked as the day she was born, the female floated around the open den, eyes closed in concentration, a smile on her face that would have surprised the few people who knew her, had they been able to draw their eyes away from the body that was sleek and well toned.

Alexis Locke stood a good two meters tall and was exceptionally well proportioned. She had breasts on the small side of medium and never had a day's problem with their size regardless of the magazines and models who seemed to sport the fuller, larger variety and made everyone else who looked not as they looked feel guilty for a false inadequacy. She was very comfortable with her body, as any female who looked like her would be. Although she was sixty years old, she looked more like she was in her late twenties and felt about as old, a by-product of her genetic manipulation, which had dominated her life from the beginning. With a life expectancy of one-hundred-and-fifty years, she was still considered young by the day's standards and she didn't really care what anyone else thought. They weren't the ones living her life. It was not like she met many people anyway out here and that was the way she liked it.

Her dirty-blonde hair was short, reaching down to just below her ears and cut in a style exemplifying her attractive face to the fullest. She was tanned, a deep dark brown making her blue-green eyes that much more striking in their setback sockets, blazing forth with an intelligence stunning most who met her. She had a crooked smile that was rare to behold, the one planted on her face now unconscious and lighting her up like the auroras gracing the twilight sky in all their resplendence. Her nose was small and compact, her lips petite but well-formed, again against the custom of the day that had the models with their pouty looks making the men all weak in the knees.

Little to no makeup scarred the beauty she possessed like a natural aura. She didn't even have any make-up in the house, no foundation or eyeliner or smeared lipstick to mar what she saw as nature's own eloquence. But then she really didn't care much about any of that. It wasn't like she was hunting for a man to marry. Perish the thought. And if she really needed a sexual fix that her own cadre of toys couldn't satisfy, she always had the option of finding someone in the nearest town. Dumont, the local game warden and all around handy-man, stopped by every few weeks on his supply runs and they would curl up in each other's arms for a night full of passionate, unhindered, meaningless sex that certainly was not enough for her needs but was good enough while it lasted.

She could always fly into one of the bigger cities down south and engage in a night of sport if she really wanted – and she did sometimes with those few gentlemen friends she had acquired over the years, but it had been nearly five years since that urge had stuck her hard – but for the most part she was content with the way it was. She lived alone, though not really alone if one counted her two faithful dogs – Sasha and Argyle – to keep her company and the ever changing vista greeting her every morning out the large, plate-glass windows stretching up to the vaulted ceiling and allowing the full grandeur of the landscape to flood the room like a beacon from on high.

She had received numerous offers of marriage and had even had a child once – a child whom she had never known, having been forced to give it up at birth – but that was in the distant past, a past she was trying, with the solitude of the Alaskan frontier, to forget. Deep down, perhaps, she wanted to have a man around the house, someone other than the dogs to love and hold at night when the chill winters from the Arctic seeped through the eaves and the door-jams and under the covers like tentacles of nature's fury. But then men presented far more problems and needs than solutions and she

19

had found out, the hard way unfortunately, that men also had their fair share of fears and doubts that she really didn't want nor need.

She was a loner due to circumstances more than desire. In this world of satellite tracking, implanted tracking chips and constant surveillance, being anonymous and alone was not that easy. But she had managed, for the last fifteen years, to do it successfully. She was one of the few individuals nowadays, not living in one of the smaller developing countries, who didn't have a tracking chip implanted in her and that certainly made it easier to remain anonymous. The less people she had contact with the better, regardless of whether she was tracked or not. There were those out there who would like nothing better than to end her life in a heartbeat, or keep her around to do their own bidding, whether of an espionage or sexual kind.

She didn't want to contemplate either one.

The annoying chirp of the vid-phone made it through to her mind as she waltzed around the room, but she chose to ignore it. No one ever called her. She couldn't even remember the last time the phone had rung, so whoever it was probably had a wrong number and would go away soon enough. The phone, not fond of being ignored, chirped louder and this time the automated house system chimed in with its polite voice, telling Alexis that the vid-phone was ringing and asking kindly whether it should turn the music down so that Alexis could answer it.

Alexis' smile vanished in an instant as she stopped dancing and playing the violin and stomped her foot on the wooden floor, the mood of the moment and the flow of the music now gone. "Fuck it all to hell!" she shouted in her high, melodious voice making the swear words somehow sound polite.

The music stopped and the vid-phone continued its pressing chirps, anxious now that someone answer it. "Can't you take a message?" she shouted to no one in particular as she placed the violin gently down and strolled over to the message center, uncaring that she was completely naked and that whomever was waiting on the other end would get an eyeful when she stepped before the visual system. Whoever it was deserved it for interrupting her morning. "Isn't that what you're there for you stupid piece of shit!"

"It is a priority one incoming message, text only," the fully integrated house computer answered in that gentle voice brooking no never mind to its owner's hostile tone and manners. "I can not answer such a call."

She frowned as she hit the receive key too hard, cracking it, wondering what in the world this was all about. The last time she had received a priority one message was over fifteen years ago and she had regretted answering that one. She was certain that this would be the same.

She was greeted with a series and chirps and shrills and realized that she should have shunted the message into her computer system. With even more frustration, since she had forgotten that she wouldn't be able to read the incoming message until it was decrypted, she moved over to the monitor and waited, leaning on the table and fuming that her morning had been ruined before it had even begun. It was not every day that she got into the mood to play her violin and dance around naked. She certainly knew that she should do it more often just for the freedom it entailed but one sometimes didn't always think of such things at 0430 in the dark.

It only took a few moments for the computer to process the incoming message, but the date, time and single word appearing sent a chill through her bones and up her back, making the soft warmth of the morning turn ice cold.

Tuesday, 6 August 2085, 1500
Archangel

Her frown deepened as she erased the message and then all traces that it had even made it to her. It was what she had feared: a rendezvous. They would be by this afternoon to pick her up, take her away from her pristine Alaskan solitude and into a world that she had sworn off. Or so she had thought. She quickly learned long ago, much to her dismay, that one never left the agency. Its insidious fingers, like the very talons of death, were always there, ready at any moment to pounce and dig deeply, dragging one back into a world of intrigue and treachery, death and foulness filling her mouth with such a taste of shit that she almost gagged.

When she had left fifteen years ago, after forty years of faithful service, she had made it clear that she was done with it all, finished with walking in the shadows and killing in the darkness. But they had had other plans.

Especially Cav.

Just the very thought of the man made her cringe, her eyes blazing in an anger she had rarely felt since moving into this cabin, this life-style. That man had made her what she was and though she at times was grateful, those moments were rare and few and far between in the last few years. Mostly she just hated him with a passion. Hated him for creating her, for bringing her into the world for one purpose and one purpose only: to serve a government she didn't respect, much less wanted to live under.

21

She had been created as an automat to do the bidding of people like Cav, assignments they didn't want to touch for the stench it would impart to their sensitive fingers and so she had been sent in time and time again to change a government, to steal plans, to give double agents false information or to assassinate on order, like a trained dog for the pleasure of the master, and the master always changed, the agendas always changed and yet the killings always remained the same.

Well, that wasn't quite true. There was much to recommend the government under which she now lived, much to make it stand apart and above from the various other countries infecting the globe with their pretensions. At least here she could live her life in peace, as she wanted, dancing around naked in her house with all the windows opened if she so desired and not have a governmental agent come around and tell her to fall in line or else, reading off line after line of scripture or law that forbids everything but breathing, and even that under certain circumstances.

She walked over to the kitchen and poured herself a tall glass of orange juice, then glided back to the den and fell down on the cushy sofa and quietly drank while she watched her two dogs play around the house. They certainly had not given her much time to prepare. She looked at her watch: 0630. Not much time at all. Whatever it was must be urgent. But then it was always urgent to them. The president could break a nail and it would be an emergency.

She laughed to herself as she finished her juice and leaned her head back, closed her eyes. She would have to get a hold of Dumont and ask him to watch the dogs. No, that wouldn't work. His work forced him to be gone for weeks at a time and that would not do at all. He couldn't look after her two animals and still work. It was asking far too much.

Well, maybe not. He did enjoy her sex and perhaps he would be more than willing to look after them if it meant more for him. Better yet, she could set the automatic house system that would feed them and let them out and watch over things in general. Hopefully she would not be a long time away from the cabin. She smiled. She somehow knew that that was not the case here. When they used *Archangel* like that, it always meant that someone had screwed up and they needed her to fix it.

Sasha and Argyle came bounding in, tails wagging and tongues lolling, the pleasure in their eyes vibrant and real. She hugged them both and then explained, as if to a small child, that she would be leaving for a while and that they would have to be alone. They licked her face in innocent oblivion, then

22

found their way to the water and drank their fill in loud, splashy gulps.

She stood and put her glass away, then contemplated what she would have for breakfast, perhaps her last. These types of missions always held that high risk of her never returning, ending up a decomposing body in some field or forest or abandoned building for the maggots and rats to feed off. The very thought of what she had once done made her pause a moment as she watched her two dogs sprawl on the floor by the open double French doors. It had been fifteen years since she had done anything major for the agency. Fifteen long years wherein she had found the comfort and meaning of her life in the wilds and openness of her new home and she was not about to just lose all that to the whims of Cav or anyone else with a three line message. It had taken her all of five years just to get over the feeling that she was being watched, to get over the routine that had her inspecting everything every morning on the off chance that someone had planted an explosive device in her stove or poisoned her milk.

No. This time she was going to tell them that they could go to hell. She had given her all for forty years and enough was enough. They had no right to demand anymore of her, especially after such a long break away from the action. Though she was certain that she could jump right back into the game without so much as a breath of hesitation that she was ready, it had just been too long out of the loop and that made her feel slightly uncomfortable, a feeling with which she was not all that familiar. She would just tell them no. And whether they liked it or not, it didn't really matter. They certainly couldn't force her to do anything she didn't want.

She had to smile at that errant thought.

Everything's laughter,
everything dust, everything nothing.
Out of unreason comes everything that exists.
-- Glycon

3

6 August 2085, 2200
The White House

President Heather O' Rourke leaned back on the sofa in her private chambers on the second floor of the White House, sipping slowly on a margarita, the tangy taste of the salt on the rim mingling with the hardy punch of the tequila. She had made it extra strong this time, hoping to lose herself for the night and wake up in the morning with a fresh start.

But the knock on her door told her that tonight would not be the night.

The Secret Service Agent opened the door at her acknowledgment and asked if she wanted to see her Chief-of-Staff. The President nodded desultorily and Claudine Maxwell strode in with that purposeful look on her face always heralding trouble.

"So what's so important that you have to interrupt my one time alone in this hell-hole?" the President asked in mock irritation.   Heather was not one to forget people who helped her. Had not been for Claudine organizing and arranging her staff and schedule these last few years, she would have failed as badly as those critics of her election had prophesied.

Having unexpectedly ridden into the top office of the land on the popular support for her platform of staying out of all future conflicts in the Indian-Pakistani area – a completely opposite platform from the incumbent, who had allowed thousands of U.S. peace-keepers to perish in the holocaust that was the nuclear exchange of the Second Indian-Pakistani War – she had been

24

quickly and harshly criticized by the Washington Establishment for her lack of judgment when it came to domestic matters.

It had always fascinated her that so many people in America had simply forgotten, or perhaps chose to ignore, that over one hundred million had perished in the first nuclear exchange between those two religiously warring nations. Maybe it was because no Americans had been involved then. Maybe it was just because the numbers and the brutality of the event, occurring in a little under twenty minutes in totality, had forced the common person on the street to block out the tragedy in order to better cope with their daily lives.

Either way, Heather O'Rourke had never been one to let a little criticism affect her negatively. Over the years, she had convinced even the worst of her critics that she did indeed have a domestic plan that would work, given enough time and money and now, as the next election drew near, she was expected to win in a landslide, the first female president to ever win back-to-back elections. Perhaps this would finally bury the fiasco that had been Hilary.

Claudine walked over to the small bar where the blender holding the fragrant concoction sat and poured herself a glass. She took a healthy slug then turned to look at her old friend Heather, whom she secretly despised. "They picked Archangel up this afternoon. She should be briefed by early tomorrow morning." Her voice was harsh, with no introduction or hello.

The President took another sip of her own drink. If she could draw the alcohol directly into her veins, she would not hesitate to do it. "Do you really think that it's necessary to go to such extremes as this? I mean, it's not like the people killed were well-known scientists or anything. They weren't even the best in their respective fields and here we are spending taxpayer's dollars on an investigation. I think that you're over-reacting to this whole damn thing." Claudine walked over and sat herself down uninvited across from the president and stared at her, wondering how someone so naive and simple could have ever been elected.

A half-smiled crossed her face as she realized that the majority of people who voted for her were not much smarter and made decisions more with their emotions than with their minds. Claudine was certain that a majority of those who had voted for Heather voted for her legs and bust as much as for her platform, if they even knew what it was.

That was one of the many flaws with democracy, something that Claudine, were she the one in charge, would make certain was the first thing to change.

No more damn elections by the ill-informed populace. It was a waste of time. But until that time came, she would have to continue to play second fiddle to Heather O' Rourke, the prom queen from high school turned president whom no one in their right mind thought would ever win the election until that idiot of a predecessor had lost all those people in that stupid religious conflict over a piece of land that once was lush and beautiful but was now nothing more than a radioactive wasteland, as was most of Pakistan. What a way to loss an election. Moron.

But Claudine didn't plan on playing second-fiddle for long. "Apparently, the CIA thinks it more than a coincidence that they all were killed in supposed accidents," Claudine answered as she crossed her legs and leaned back, still keeping her steel-hard gray eyes locked on Heather. "I think it prudent that we use the assets that we have to the best advantage. Archangel was our best at one time."

"She's not even ours," Heather answered back roughly with a frown as she looked away from the intense stare of Claudine. There was something in those eyes that set off warning bells in her head. Claudine, despite her help and assistance along the way, was still a dangerous friend to have. "She belongs to that fat bastard Cavalier."

"And doesn't Cavalier work for us?" Claudine said with a hint of annoyance, finishing her drink with a last, long swig and placing the glass down on the coffee table a little too hard.

"Nominally," Heather said.

"It was government money that paid for the project and government money that sustained it, regardless of the concessions that those in your shoes back then gave to the agency seventy years ago. As far as I'm concerned, that makes her and everything else that Cavalier and his cronies come up with ours to do with as we please." She leaned forward and titled her head slightly to the side, an indication, Heather had learned, that Claudine was starting to get curt and impatient. "And unless you treat the agency with that in mind, they'll run rough-shod over this office and this country. I for one don't want to see that happen."

She held her stare a moment longer, then broke off as she leaned back and looked toward the window, the hot Washington august summer was more intense then usual, the humidity making any time spent outside a drenching experience. Even now, late at night, the still air was stagnant with the lingering daytime heat.

The president frowned. "Is she really that good to go to all this trouble to get her? I mean, living all alone on a Federal Game Reserve up in Alaska, isolated from everyone by her own accord? When was the last time she did anything for us? Certainly not during my tenure."

"No. She's officially retired, having put her forty years time in," Claudine said distractedly.

"Forty years?" the president said in shock, getting up to pour herself another drink. "She must've been one of the first produced. How old is she?"

"In her sixties, but what does that mean anymore? I'm told that they're expected to live to be one-fifty, making sixty not even half. If you saw her, you'd think that she looks like she's in her twenties. It's disgusting is what it is. I'd kill to have a body like that when I'm sixty." And she was not being dramatic. Claudine Maxwell was more than ready to kill a few people if it meant that she could look like Archangel.

"Starting to sag, are we?" the president asked with a hint of mirth as she walked over to the window and looked out over the city, her city, and its teeming, sweating mass of incompetent old men and drug-pushers.

"Not any more than you are, Heather."

Heather's smile faded. Claudine was far too free with her words lately. "What about the others? Why can't we use them? If this one has been retired for ... how long?"

"Fifteen years."

"Fifteen years?! I'm sure we can find someone else." Heather turned to look at her Chief-of-Staff, amazed that the self-appointed White House perfectionist would choose to go to all this trouble for someone who had been out of the game for fifteen years.

"There's no one else with her skill and experience level. She's the only one of the original group to have survived this long. The only one of the next three groups to have survived, as a matter of fact."

"She's that good?" Heather asked as she sat back down, grateful for the efficient air-conditioner in the building. She hated the heat, especially the sticky heat of the East. If it were possible, she would move the White House to Colorado for the summer where the air was cool and dry.

"She's that good."

"But fifteen years? Won't she be a little rusty?"

Claudine stood. "She's bred for it. I don't think it's something that one forgets that easily. It is part of her genetic code I'm sure. And besides, I've looked into it a little more than I should have. She could match any ten CIA agents with one-hand tied behind her back and the other hand covering an eye. Cavalier might be fat and slovenly now, but when he first initiated this project, he was the best at what he did. He was, literally, a genius. Anything that he created during that time would be better than anything we've ever seen." She walked to the door and prepared to leave, looking over the figure of the president and wondering if she could get Cav to do her one more favor. The thought lingered in her mind a moment longer than it should have before she dismissed it, though its echo still found its way into the recesses of her deviousness to be discussed later.

"What kind of back-lash can I expect to get from her activation?" Heather asked, not bothering to look at Claudine as she stood by the door, knowing the look that would be on the other woman's face and not in the mood for the condescending look that would be found there.

"It all depends on what she turns up. But I would think that this might just turn out to be the big one. Better prepare yourself for that old plausible deniability act."

"I don't want this to blow up in my face, Claudine," Heather ordered with a rare authority that she showed only occasionally and never before to her Chief-of-Staff. "Make sure that it doesn't." She turned now to look at Claudine and saw in her face a momentary look of disdain that was quickly replaced by a smile, as if the disdain were but a shadow that had momentarily, accidentally crossed Claudine's face.

"Of course, that's part of my job."

They stared at each other a moment.

"Good night, Mrs. President," Claudine finally said as she stepped out through the door and it closed behind.

Heather O' Rourke pursed her plump lips as she stared at the closed door. She had a bad feeling in the pit of her stomach that this was not going to work out at all in her favor. And it had been those feelings in the past that had kept her out of trouble many times. The last thing she needed was to have her landslide election next year become a fiasco.

And then there was Claudine....

We too often forget that not only is there a
soul of goodness in things evil , but generally
also a soul of truth in things erroneous.

4

7 August 2085, 0312 hrs

The VTOL Lear fought the high winds that buffeted it, tying in vain to line up on the landing pad atop the towering building standing tall and stable in the storm enveloping the city for the past three days. The monsoonal rains lashed the landscape as if God Himself were trying to cleanse the stench from the Earth. Business had come to a stand still, the high, sustained winds having knocked down power-lines all over the new city, throwing the majority of the homes of those poor souls trapped like lemmings into a darkness that was more than blackness, seeping through the closed doors and windows like a prehensile precursor of death.

The tall building blazed forth with its own power supply, the new fusion reactor built into the basement structure churning out its sun-like power with a consistency that was extraordinary, lighting up the building like a beacon through the baneful lashings of nature.

It was, however, little comfort to the pilot of the VTOL as he struggled to land his ship somewhat near the pad and not topple off the roof.   The passenger he had ferried all the way down from Alaska sat in the jump seat slightly back and between the two pilots, watching stoically the efforts of the two men to bring the craft home, the compensators whining their protest to the extreme abuse to which they were being subjected. She could have suggested a few tricks to make the landing easier, but decided that the male pilot probably wouldn't take too kindly to her presumptiveness. If she were in his position, she wouldn't like advice either at this particular moment. So Alexis just sat silently and watched as the blinking landing lights of the pad blurred through the rain on the windscreen, the wipers useless against the barrage of water, the electronic landing systems more or less useless in conditions far outside the normal range of operation.

It had been a long and trying flight and she was already seething inside with the fact of her having to come here. The last thing she needed was for the Lear to end up on the pavement below in pieces with her inside. But through an extreme effort of will she kept her mouth shut and just watched, wanting so much to tell the fool all that he was doing wrong but choosing to play the dumb female rather than give away any indication of her abilities. Fly-boys tended to talk at bars, bragging about their latest mission and Alexis didn't need her description circulating about the local haunts where who knew who might be listening.

But then perhaps it was all for naught anyway. No one attempted a landing like this in this type of storm. To have to bring her down in this gale was more than enough material for these two flyboys to make up all sorts of stories about her. When Cav said jump, most people around him usually just asked how high.

With a loud thump and a bone-jolting bump, the VTOL settled onto the pad and the landing crew hurried to secure it against the wind. Alexis made her way quickly out of the ship and to the main terminal, the hood of her light windbreaker over her head in a vain attempt to keep the rain off of her face. This was not the tropics and she had not expected this type of reception. As such, she had worn her old and faded blue jeans, the ones she had finally broken in so that they fit comfortably and snug, outlining her lower body in lines attracting the attention of most of the male members of the landing crew. She also wore a black t-shirt, covered with a plaid shirt buttoned halfway down to her waist, her hair in a quick ponytail and her cowboy boots clacking along the non-skid.

She was not expecting to stay very long. By the time she stepped into the all-too-familiar room, with its dark, tomb-like interior accented with heavy wooden panels and shelves and shelves of archaic books, she had shed the wind-breaker and held it loosely in her right hand, her hair wet, her mood foul. Memories she would rather have not recalled flooded her mind as her eyes involuntarily swept the office, the large, dark mahogany desk sitting toward the tall windows that shook and vibrated from the assault of the storm.

Several lamps were sprinkled about the room randomly. The light they emitted was dull and yellowish as if their radiance were limited to only a meter around them, useless for the most part in illuminating anything save themselves. An odor permeated the air, an astringency she could place as the cloying pungency of a cigar adulterating the air with its illegal stench of hypocrisy.

She had been very happy the day that the filthy, addictive, cancerous drug had been outlawed, along with their smaller cousins, cigarettes, to the chagrin of several large companies who had gone bankrupt to the loss of hundreds of thousands of jobs.

The large chair behind the desk that had been turned away from her swiveled to reveal the corpulent figure of Cav, the dull glowing ember of the cigar sticking out of his face like a cancerous growth.

"What the hell is this all about, Cav?" she launched at him before he even had a chance to remove the stinking trash-heap from his mouth and speak. "And put that damn thing out before I do it for you." She stood with hands dangling down at her side, relaxed, her eyes burning in the dusk of the room like twin candles of dread.

He smiled, though it was hard to see through the dim lighting, and removed the cigar. "Nice to see you too, Alexis," he said in his thick voice carrying across the room with a depth suiting the body well. He pulled open a drawer and snubbed the cigar out in it, then slowly closed the drawer back up. He hit a switch and the silent whir of re-circulation fans began to clear the air of the foul stench.

"We have an assignment for you," Cav said as he opened another drawer and pulled out a disc.

"No fuck," she shot back, advancing on the desk and the man in menacing steps.

"No need for such foul language, Alexis." He slid the disc across the table and she stopped it with her hand as it reached the edge.

"Cut the crap, Cav. I don't appreciate being pulled from my home and my dogs after fifteen years of inactivity." Her tone was harsh. She was not about to be played by this man like he had done for most of her life. She had paid her dues and didn't need him or his assignments anymore. "What's so fucking important that you needed to reactivate me? It must obviously be huge, because I didn't hear a God damned peep when the Indians and Pakistanis decided to irradiate the Kashmir valley again!"

"Relax, Alexis," he said with that slick smile still plastered on his face as if plastic surgery had made it permanent. He was well aware of her explosive temper and her anger. And he didn't blame her one bit for her anger toward him and the system that had abused her most of her life. "Would you like a drink?"

She stared hard at him a moment, then walked over to one of the numerous over-stuffed leather chairs and sat in it. "You know I don't drink, Cav. Just get to the damn point so that I can say no and go back to my cabin. I had a fishing trip planned this weekend and I don't want the worms to dry-out."

Cav rose out of his chair and made his way over to the bar, the increase in his size since she had last seen him making her eyes widen.

"Well, haven't we gone to shit."

His smile wavered slightly. "And you're looking as lovely as ever, my dear," he intoned in all sincerity as he poured himself a cognac. "Still running twenty kilometers a day?"

"I never ran twenty kilometers on any day, Cav. Cut the chitchat and get to the damn point. I don't like it in here and you know it."

He walked back over to the desk and sat on it, producing a creak from the legs that didn't sound all that healthy. He picked up the disc she had discarded on the table. "Okay. Put this disc in that machine over there and scan the files while I tell you about it." He threw the disc at her and she caught it deftly in one hand.

"Why? I don't want to do it, whatever it is, so why go through the routine?" She stood, holding the disc like it was diseased. "Whatever it is, I'm not interested. Capiche? NO."

Cav didn't stir from his position on the desk, just stared at her as she stared at him, the beauty he had created striking a cord in his heart. He had forgotten how volatile she could be and how utterly charming when she wanted. He would have to play this one so very carefully. "In the last six months, five people have been killed in what the local authorities have deemed as tragic accidents."

"And this means what to me...?"

He smiled again as he took a sip of his drink. This was as difficult as he had suspected. "Humor me, okay Alexis? Listen to what I have to say and then, if you still feel like you don't want it, I'll let you go."

She smirked with an arched eyebrow. "Let me go, Cav? Apparently you've forgotten what it is that I can do." She looked at her reflection in the window vibrating with the fierce winds outside, the rain dancing across as if on drugs.

His reflection stood out in the murky haze also and she saw him for a moment as the man she had once known, thin and trim, a genius who could be the biggest son-of-a-bitch she had ever met and the most important man she ever knew, ever loved. Then his over-sized body blurred back to the reflection that was reality and she sighed inwardly. "Okay, Cav. But I'll tell you right now that you're wasting your time and mine."

"That's fair enough," Cav said as he moved over to the computer terminal closest to her and inserted the coded disc. The screen came alive with the picture of a young, attractive woman.

Alexis turned from the window and looked distractedly at the image. She could tell that the woman in the photo was Ukrainian. She could see it in a heartbeat, the distinctive lines and clear blue eyes under the short-cut mantle of natural blonde hair a clear give away.

Cav moved back over to his desk and leaned on it again, taking another sip of his drink before he started to speak. "Ykaterina Godonov, PhD. Thirty-five years old. Born in Kiev. Genetic researcher with a firm in Minsk, assigned to Galileo Prime on Mars two years ago to work on simple gene splicing. Nothing special about her work or her. Killed on 21 December 2084 in an explosion in her lab, caused, the local authorities claim, by a malfunction of a heater coil and faulty wiring. Burned beyond recognition. Very messy. Had to use dental records for identification."

"Faulty wiring on Galileo Prime?" Alexis asked as she sat down in front of the monitor and looked at the un-interesting life of this ordinary scientist. "I find that hard to believe."

"Yes," Cav said with a smile, happy she had caught on to that little fact and that he had at least sparked her interest.

The picture on the screen switched to another woman, oriental, older, not nearly as attractive, rather plain looking. "Kido Nakamura. Age forty-two. Born Osaka. Software designer for a small company in Osaka. Worked for the company for almost twenty years and had a few accomplishments, but mostly worked de-bugging other people's programs. Games usually. Died on 3 March 2085, the victim of a random shooting in a restaurant. The local authorities claim that the restaurant was targeted for a robbery but something went wrong and she got in the way of a couple of bullets. Twenty-six to be exact."

Alexis raised an eyebrow. "That would kill most anyone several times over. Anyone else killed?"

"A waiter and the owner of the restaurant, but no other customers despite

33

the fact that the place was crowded." He finished his cognac and went for another, watching Alexis closely. He could see that the tension in her shoulders had eased considerably. It was a good sign. Maybe he could talk her into it. He didn't want to think about the alternative. There was no alternative.

The image switched to a young man who looked familiar to her somehow. He was handsome, his dirty blonde hair long and tied up in the back into a ponytail that was all the rage now among the younger upper mobiles who seemed to have infested most of the tech jobs. The smile on his face, from the obvious camping trip where the picture had been taken, indicating that the man enjoyed life from the point of communion with some happier state, which she had thought she had attained in Alaska.

"Alexander Hart, PhD. Age twenty-eight. Born in Seattle. Computer specialist for a firm in Boston. Worked on nano-technology and its incorporation into integral computer systems. Once again, nothing real special here. Was one of many working on the same simple procedures. Drowned while on a rafting trip on the White Nile on 26 May 2085, even though he was a competent swimmer. Matter of fact, won several medals when he was in his late teens and early twenties at Harvard. His body was chewed on by a few crocs before they could retrieve it. Nasty business that was."

"Lucky they retrieved it at all," she said quietly, almost to herself. She was beginning to see a pattern but held back any comment lest Cav think her interested.

The image changed again to reveal an older man, dark complexion, possibly African. "Mbombo Dumvo, PhD. Age Seventy-five. Born in Johannesburg. Lead engineer for nano-tech industry on *Stargazer I*."

She turned to look at Cav. "The O' Neill Colony?"

"Yes. I'm glad that you've kept up with the newer advances the last few years."

She narrowed her eyes, conscious of the intended barb at her. She decided to let him know exactly what she knew. "Fully operational three years ago, *Stargazer I* is the first of a series of O' Neill Colonies in orbit about the sun. Self-sufficient structures housing up to 20,000 people in an artificial gravity environment. Basically a large, rotating cylinder. Two more in the final stages of completion, three more in the initial phases." She eyed him a moment to make sure that he understood her own barb at him, then set her attention back to the monitor.

"Impressive," he said as walked back over to his desk and sat on it again to a creak of protest. A particularly vicious wind gust rattled the windows more than before and he turned to look into the darkness beyond the reflections, the black of the storm and the power-starved city below almost draining in its obscurity.

"I'm still on-line, you know," she answered back as she scanned the data of Dr. Dumvo and found it as uninteresting as the others. "Just because I chose to live in a remote area doesn't mean that I don't stay informed."

"I'm glad to hear that. It'll make this easier if we don't have to up-date you much on the latest advances."

She smirked again. She'd up-date him in a moment if he didn't continue with the presentation. The sooner he finished, the quicker she could get out of here and back to her cabin. This was all so much bullshit that it almost made her sick to think that Cav dragged her here for this. But then, since it did seem so normal and routine, she was slightly intrigued as to what it all meant.

Obviously, someone somewhere had a hair up their ass over this.

"Dumvo died of what is being called an `experimental mishap.' The authorities on *Stargazer I* are not known for their cooperation with Earth authorities and that was all that they would say. My informant couldn't get a better answer either and he's fairly well placed. They don't have many such incidents up there and I think it shook them up pretty badly."

The image changed again to another male, this time with the distinctive look of a Hindu from India, his large mustache black against his dark skin.

"Dr. Krishna Pratali. Age fifty. Born in Utter Pradash. Neuro-surgeon for a prestigious hospital in New Delhi. Killed while mountain climbing in South America, on a mountain he'd climbed several times before. Once again, not the best in his field, or even at his hospital. Rather average person overall."

The screen went blank and the disc popped back out automatically. She turned her chair so that she could face Cav. "So what's the connection between them?"

"As far as we can tell, there isn't one. That's one of the problems. None of these people ever knew the others, except for a possible brief meeting at a recent conference between Nakamura and Pratali and an obscure e-mail between Pratali and Godonov. Other than that, these people had nothing to do with each other. Most of them didn't even work in the same field."

She locked eyes with him a moment. There had to be more than this. "You're kidding, right?" she said with acid. "What moron decided that all these people were connected? Was this your idea, cause I know that you used to be smarter then this. This is crap. I can't believe that you dragged me all this way to look at this! You could have faxed it to me, for Christ sake!" She stood, ready to throttle the life out of him just for the presumption to get her involved.

"It was by order of the president, Alexis. This has an *Eyes Only* tagged to it."

She looked at him with incredibility in her eyes, the final piece of the puzzle falling into place for her. "That stupid Prom-Queen? You've got to be kidding me. The only reason she was elected was because the party bosses thought that they could get down her tight pants and have themselves a good ole time with her in the Oval Office, and I don't doubt that they do. There's no way that bimbo came up with any possible connection between these people. I'd be surprised if she even knew what a neuro- surgeon did."

Cav laughed. He couldn't help himself. Although he had more respect for the current president of the United States than Alexis obviously did, having met Heather O' Rourke a few times and been impressed with her range of knowledge, he realized that Alexis' opinion was one shared by many people.

"It's not funny, damn you," Alexis shouted as she stood with that inner rage. "I'll be going now and don't try to stop me. I don't want to hurt you, even though I do find you more despicable than ever." She started for the door, grabbing her windbreaker off the chair-back where she had dropped it off.

"It was the Chief-of Staff, Alexis."

She stopped in mid-stride and turned on him. "The bitch-queen of the White House? Now that I can believe. That woman gives the rest of us women a bad name. Didn't you fuck her once?"

Cav's jolly expression fell from his face like a landslide and he turned back to go to his desk. "I also happen to think that there's a connection here somewhere." His tone was now far more serious.

She noticed how he changed the subject off of his relationship with Claudine Maxwell and back to the mission. She pursed her lips a moment, ready to pry a little deeper into the wound she had opened, then changed her mind and allowed the man his dignity. Or what little he had left in that obese body.

Cav rummaged in his desk a moment, found the plastic bag for which he was looking and tossed it at her.

She caught it and took a look. "A broken ice screw," she said almost to herself. She opened the bag and pulled it out, examining it closely. "I've

36

never seen a broken one before. This happen the last time you tried to go mountain climbing, Cav?"

"Your humor, if that was what that was, has denigrated in the last few years. I liked you better when you were younger," Cav remarked dryly as he sat back down in his large chair.

"When you could control me, you mean," she replied just as dryly, putting the broken ice screw back in the bag, a feeling of deja vu suddenly sweeping through her. She shuddered a moment, a chill down her back.

"That ice screw came from Pratali's accident. It snapped in half like it was defective," he said, choosing to ignore her cogent remark. They had too much history behind them to fall into a tête-à-tête of insults. If he didn't keep on the subject, this discussion would break down into an uncontrollable rage of accusations and barbed words.

"Shit happens," she remarked as she threw the bag back at Cav. It landed on the desk and slid across, falling off the other side and onto the floor.

"Shit doesn't happen to ten of them at the same time," he answered back, his anger with her starting to grow. He guessed that she had always been this headstrong, but that because of his love for her he had never really noticed it. But now, after fifteen years apart, fifteen years of Alexis discovering what her life could have been like had he not interfered, her latent characteristics had risen to the surface and spilled out into his lap. He probably deserved every last insult.

She looked at him with a creased forehead. "Ten, huh? That's a little unusual." She moved toward him a step, her hands on her hips. "But I don't see what the hell this has to do with me. At the most, this is a simple case of some detective work that even the CIA can handle. And, if not them, then one of the numerous other agents that you have running around out there on leashes. This isn't worth pulling me from my home after all this time. Either you've lost your mind and Claudine is pulling you around by your penis again or there's more to this that you aren't telling me. Either way, I'm gone. I don't need this. I put my time in and this bullshit here isn't even worth my coming all this way. This is wrong, Cav. Very wrong."

He nodded his head a moment, then looked down at the floor. He was hoping that her natural curiosity would compel her to want to look further into this case, but that obviously wasn't going to happen. He would have to tell her. There was no other way around it.

She waited a moment for him to speak again and when he just sat there looking at his fat, sausage-like hands, she turned to leave.

She had the door halfway open when he spoke, his words echoing in her ears like a gunshot. "Dr. Alexander Hart was your son."

She turned slowly. She knew she had heard the words correctly, but they somehow didn't register fully. "I'm sorry. I must've completely misunderstood you because I swear you just said that Alexander Hart was my son."

"Yes, Alexis. After you gave him up, I kept an eye on him over the years. Dr. Alexander Hart was your son."

She closed the door and stared at him as if she could kill him. So many emotions boiled up inside her that she didn't know which one to concentrate on, didn't know anymore why she never killed this man many, many years ago.

It was not long before he felt the tightness in his throat and instantly knew that he had only a few moments to plead his case before she closed his windpipe down and crushed his larynx. "I've wanted to tell you many times, but I didn't think you wanted to know anything about him," he gasped as his hands closed around the invisible force at his throat and fell off the chair to his knees.

She walked up next to him and stared down with cold, steel-hard eyes shining with a light of their own. "Give me one good reason why I shouldn't choke the very life out of you like you deserve, asshole."

He gasped for air, the tightness increasing to the danger point, the invisible fingers around his throat like a vise-clamp. "Because ...you...haven't ...already..." he managed to get out before he fell to the floor, his eyes bulging in their sockets.

She stood over him a moment, then blinked.

The pressure ceased immediately and he inhaled gulps of refreshing air as he lay on his back. She walked away from him and over to the windows, the storm outside seeming to have increased in intensity beyond what she thought possible. If she didn't know better, she would say that they were in the middle of a typhoon. It was an odd thought to have at this moment when she learned that her son, whom she had been told was dead at childbirth had actually been alive all this time and now was truly dead in a freak accident. But then the human mind was an odd thing to understand and she was, by all accounts, still human.

It took several minutes before Cav regained his feet and made his way over to the bar and poured himself a drink.

"You bastard," she finally said in a voice icy in its hatred.

38

"You gave him up," he weakly countered.

She spun around with such fury in her eyes that Cav dropped his glass and it tumbled to the thickly carpeted floor, spilling the contents all over his pants. "YOU FORCED ME TO GIVE HIM UP!! YOU GAVE ME NO CHOICE, YOU SON-OF-A-BITCH!!! YOU TOLD ME THAT HE WAS DEAD!!!"

"It was for the best," he managed to say as he picked up the glass and tried to calm himself down. Although he had known that she was more than capable of constricting his throat like that without ever touching him, he had somehow never thought that she would do it to him. One should never underestimate the wrath of a wronged mother when it came to her children.

"The hell it was," she responded. "The hell it was." Her voice had lost some of the cold reserve, becoming more imbued with a tint of sadness that he seldom heard in anything she had ever said. "It was the best for you. The best to keep me working for you."

He poured himself another drink and gulped it down before she could turn on him again and force him to spill it. He was getting too old for this crap.

Alexis shook her head slowly. To learn that her long-thought dead son was part of a mission Cav was trying to get her to take was almost too ironic for her. She found it hard to believe that Cav would keep this from her. She looked at her reflection in the window and saw herself for the first time, the instrument that she was and realized with a growing knot in her stomach that Cav had been right in keeping her son's existence from her. She wasn't mother material and his world would have been filled with tension and unknowing. But that still didn't make being led to believe that he had died at childbirth correct or moral in her mind.

It was wrong and Cav knew it, else he would have told her a long time ago.

"You took everything from me, Cav," she said with a voice even and detached, a voice speaking more to the reflection than to the man who standing behind her, looking on ruefully at the woman he had created. "You took my childhood and my parents and my life .... And now my son." She lowered her chin to her chest and closed her eyes. "I've got no more to give, Cav. No more."

He walked up behind her, wanted to place a hand on her shoulder, hug her to him as he had done when she was little and give her the assurances that everything would be okay. But that was not to be. Those days had slipped into the wandering stream of the past long ago. He could not bring himself to touch her, to feel her pain and succor it, because everything was not going to be okay. This was the real world, a world he had, in his small way, helped to create with its death and murder and intrigues that people had thought would pass with time but that just grew more subtle as humanity grew more bold in its explorations of the mind and of space.

The world was not the wonderful place that those in the early part of the century had been so eager to make it out to be. It had turned darker in some ways even with the advent and possibilities that the O' Neill Colonies and the bases on the Moon and Mars entailed. And Alexis was one example of that darkness. Genetically designed from scratch for use as a multi-purpose agent who could do more than any before her, built for a world where normal humans could no longer cope with the evil slinking into every crack of every corner until a blackness filled the world making those who had known it before gag at the stench

She had become, over the years, more than anyone ever imagined and when she had gotten pregnant, had the audacity to become independent and free-willed, Cav had seen in her the ultimate truth of humanity. He had seen it and hidden it away from the rest of the world, deciding in a moment of clarity that the world was not yet ready for such a revelation.

She turned around and saw that he had been struggling with the thought of holding her and knew that the time for that had long passed. Memories as clear as if they had occurred yesterday clouded her mind, memories of her childhood with this man whom she had grown to love as a father and then learned to hate as a bastard when the terrible truth of her existence was revealed. She could feel the tears wanting to flow but knew that that reservoir had been emptied many, many decades ago. "I'll be leaving now, Cav," she said in hushed tones, aware that although one of the victims had been her son, she had never had one until this moment anyway, so what the hell did it matter? All she wanted now was her cabin and her dogs and her Alaska.

Cav didn't attempt to stop her as she walked out of the office, leaving the door open behind her. He knew that he had already asked more of her than he had the right to ask. Although she had been, at one time, his creation, she was now her own person and as she had so ably demonstrated, was not about to let anyone tell her what to do ever again.

He looked down at his desk and noticed that it was missing immediately. He made a quick cursory inspection but didn't find it anywhere obvious. A smile crossed his face as he sat down to compose his reply to Claudine Maxwell.

Alexis climbed back into the VTOL Lear and buckled herself in securely.

The storm had, beyond all possibility, grown worse and the pilots were not at all happy about having to fly in it and they voiced that opinion with low grumbles and muted phrases that her exceptional hearing picked up without any trouble, bringing a smile to her face to know that there were others in this crazy world tonight who weren't happy.

As the craft lifted off into the dark, brewing sky boiling with an anger bred of insolence, she felt the shape of the disc in her pocket and closed her eyes, oblivious to the violent shakes the Lear encountered as it clawed its way to altitude and out of the raging storm that was as much her soul as it was nature.

In late March with the days lengthening
It will come down from its snowy den to teach us one
more time that we have not bent nature to our will,
the stars don't tick to our winding.
--- Tom Sexton

5

8 August 2085, 0038 hrs
Alaska

   Alexis lounged back on her sofa, a soft, emerald green silky robe dangling over her body, the sash tied in a loose knot, a cup of hot chocolate cupped in her hands. The warm, alluring aroma of hazelnut rose up and mingled with the faint fragrance from the burning logs in the fireplace, which infused with the perfume of Mozart floating upon the tranquil air like a nocturnal mist. The night sky was lit up with the majesty of the aurora covering the sky in rippling sheets of red and green, dancing with their own life against the backdrop of the snow-covered peaks.
   It always amazed her how something as small as the energized particles of the solar wind which, having little to no effect by themselves, could, when working together, create such majestic displays of grandeur she was now enjoying, as if the sky itself were on fire.
   Her two dogs lay on the sofa on either side of her, curled up in peaceful sleep, the rigors of the day long past. Her computer system was still up, the VR system for data retrieval and manipulation still held in stasis where she had left it an hour ago. With the disc taken from Cav's office, she had absorbed every last bit of detail on her son, a son she had managed to push to the back of her memory and forget about but which now came forward with

42

a vengeance. The first item on her agenda when she had been dropped off at her cabin was to find the DNA pattern of the man Cav claimed was her son and match it to her own.

She had her genetic code memorized, one of the many benefits of her training and once she found Alexander Hart's code in the data she knew that Cav was telling the truth. He was her son. She had stared at the data for hours after that, at the face of the man she had given life, at the mundane routines of the life he had lived till she had it memorized, burned it into her consciousness like a brand of guilt. Most women would have cried, broken down at the cruelty of it all and wept tears for the son that they never knew.

But then Alexis was not like most women. Although she felt a pang inside, it was more related to the fact that someone had dared to take her son from her, had dared to act against her in such a way. Any feeling of loss, of a need to be comforted was trampled by her years of hard, stoic conception to the sins of the world and humanity in general and to cry now, for this singular loss, would be a hypocritical act she would not perform.

Having never really had a family to speak of, the closet thing to a father being Cav, she had never had the experiences of family loss before. She had, of course, lost partners during operations but that was different, a product of the circumstances that were her life at that time and thus not to be taken to heart. As a matter of fact, as she sat back and thought about it, her life running through her mind's eye like a broken projector skipping and jumping from image to image, she realized that she had never, in her sixty-five years, shed a tear in sorrow.

Never.

And that surprised her a little. Not that she thought it a bad thing. It had never occurred to her before to even think about it. Tears were for those who actually lived, who experienced life in all its agony and rapture and in that experience felt the sorrow and the pain and the joy making their lives worth living, that made them human. She was not one of those fortunate souls. She had lived life in a vacuum, in a shell of events letting her glimpse only that which it was felt she should know, that which was vital for the success of the mission.

It was not to say that she had never experienced life in all its fullness, but she had done it more as a spectator than a participant, someone who went through all the motions for a limited amount of time and then moved on to something else, to another reality, leaving behind what she had experienced as a post-mission debriefing in a dossier or a smoldering ruin in a dirty city, to be viewed from afar afterward and calibrated to make better use of her talents the next time she encountered the real world.

And now, when real life hit her square in the face, reached out with its ice-cold skeletal hands and seizing her heart in its vise-grip, she was beginning to see what it was like to really live and...

... It didn't affect her in the least.

Had she become immune to it? Was she truly unable to shed even one tear for a son she had thought dead at birth, for his death before he even had a chance to begin his life? Perhaps it was a defense mechanism, a sub-conscious blockage in her that didn't allow for such sentiment to get in the way of her mission. But there was no mission here, nothing to stop her from feeling that which all the other mortals living their lives in abject bewilderment felt when they experienced loss.

Maybe there was something wrong with her.

Or maybe, just maybe, this was just the way it was, her psyche immune from such physical and urbane thoughts. Maybe callousness had grown over her heart over the years and it was hardened, allowing nothing to penetrate. She was not all that certain that it was a good thing to have ... or even a bad thing.

It was during her sojourn through the life of her lost son and her own lost emotions that she had begun to look into the other people who had been killed, the others who had lost their lives in the well-disguised accidents. Within her VR interface she had set up a large board, a chart displaying all the connections she could make between the five people. There were not many. The very fact that Kido and her son had met at that conference on integrated computer systems and their application to higher-reasoning artificial intelligence told her little. She would have to look into that one closer, find out more about the field and ascertain whether there was a minute connection she was not seeing due to her lack of detailed knowledge of the procedures involved.

But the cryptic e-mail to Godonov, who was a geneticist, gave her a clue that she figured that bitch Maxwell had also seen. It had been the clue, Alexis was positive, which had convinced Maxwell that *Archangel* be used on this case. That had lead Alexis to look at the other two killed and their connection, if any. Although she could link Nakamura, Hart and Godonov to each other in a tenuous vinculum, the involvement of the other two, if there even was one, still eluded her immediate grasp. But she knew it was there. One of the things she could do well and that she enjoyed was piecing together puzzles that had little to no clues to their correlation, a mass of unrelated facts that would, if given enough time, coalesce into an integrated whole greater than the sum of its parts. She felt deep down that this was one of those problems, a conundrum that was worthy of her skills.

So it was that she found herself now on the sofa, drinking her hazelnut hot chocolate, allowing her mind to relax and possibly make a connection that her conscious self could not see, the temporal display of the aurora soothing in its regal splendor.

She felt it before she heard it, a disturbance in the air around her cabin that was not normal. Both dogs raised their heads in unison, low growls escaping as they searched for the source of the abnormality. Alexis, used to bears and the like coming around to her remote cabin and wanting to make it their own, leaned forward and set her steaming cup on the table, the marshmallows having already melted in a sporl of white.

"Computer, status of security system."

The house computer answered in its unemotional voice. "Perimeter security system deactivated as per your request."

Alexis was suddenly alert. She had not deactivated the system. "Computer, reinstate perimeter security system and bring interior systems to status `imminent.'" She stood and made her way quietly, quickly over to the paneled wall. Touching lightly, a shelf pulled out to reveal two small hand-held weapons. She grabbed one as the house computer responded to her commands. "Perimeter security system unresponsive. Interior security system set to status imminent."

The lights dimmed to near pinpoints of luminescent, allowing her acute vision to offset any intruder's plans. The outer doors locked and the pressure sensitive alarms on the windows came active, the small charges of explosives ready to turn any would-be burglar into a mess of shredded blood and flesh. Small, interior weapons came on line, ready to attack any individual not programmed into the software, which was a very short list.

The dogs jumped off the sofa and made toward the French doors, their growls permeating the air with anger. Only the flickering shadows of the small fire embraced the room, the muted light from the aurora adding a dull edge to the darkness. She closed her eyes and relaxed, settled herself for a moment, then reached out with her mind and scanned the perimeter of the cabin, searching, looking for the intruders that she knew were out there. Unless the bear mother and her cub had increased their technical skill level by a factor of a million and figured out how to disable her sophisticated security system, her visitors were human and that never bode well.

She found them quickly enough, though they were somehow muted, almost blurred to her mind as if they were coming in and out of her senses, of reality, as if they didn't belong, as if only a part of them were here in this temporal plane. There were three of them, working together as they swept in slowly, cautiously, expertly. Whomever they were, they were not the typical house-burglars. These people were professionals and that meant only one thing: Cav had to have sent them. Sent them to eliminate her, perhaps for the disc she had taken, perhaps for her refusal.

It didn't really matter.

Alexis quickly moved her obstinate dogs into the bedroom and closed the door. She didn't want them caught in the crossfire she was certain was about to erupt. With the agility of a cat, she climbed up into the rafters near the tall windows, lost in the shadows to all save those who looked closely. One of the numerous items she had picked up over the years was that most people when they broke into a house never looked up. It was just not a natural inclination to think of a threat coming from above, from the area where spiders lived in the dust-coated corners of the ceiling.

She waited, patiently, her weapon held loose and ready. She would need to capture one alive, to question. She needed to know why Cav had sent them, if he had sent them at all. It could very well be that bitch Claudine who sent these assassins to her cabin for Alexis' refusal to do her bidding. But that would mean that Cav had told her where Alexis lived. If so, then the president would shortly be without her Chief-of-Staff and Cav would be without a throat.

They entered the cabin quietly, stealthily. They stayed together, Alexis noted, and didn't split up. Whomever had sent them knew of what the prey was capable and had trained these three well. Had they split up, Alexis would have picked them off one by one. Of course, she was going to take care of them all anyway. It just would have been easier had they spread out. Perhaps there were others waiting outside her mental range, waiting for her to be flushed out. Perhaps these three were even the decoys, sent as cannon fodder. When Alexis had eliminated them she would relax, let her guard down and then the real attack would come. That would certainly be the way that Alexis would handle it.

They came into her observable range and she was actually surprised, a feat difficult to achieve. Not only were they mentally blurred but visually as well, as if they were shadows themselves, slinking along the walls with

46

weapons out, blackness against the black of the hallway, quiet, calm, confident. They seemed to waver in the air as if uncertain of their own existence, defying the molecules around them to support their solid shape. She narrowed her eyes and watched as they made their way slowly and with the utmost caution into the den. Their outlines were indistinct, as if melting into the very air around them, their lines vague. No features were visible, only a blackness that seemed to absorb what little light there was as if drawing it into their outlines to avoid detection.

She also noticed a shimmer in the blackness, a ripple like water disturbed by a slight breeze. She concentrated and projected, touching them with her mind.

They stopped short.

She pulled back immediately, shocked they had noticed, had felt her probe before she had even penetrated. They looked up ... and all hell broke loose.

There was a flurry of weapons fire, but not like she had expected. No bullets with fiery muzzle blasts came her way but rather darts flying through the air with incredible speed. She flew from her perch, swinging along the upper rafters, moving in the darkness and the shadows. She felt a prick and knew that she had been hit. She reached into herself and found the entry point, felt the lethal poison that would affect her in seconds. She identified it, broke down its molecular constituents and atoms, saw that it was beyond anything she had ever encountered before – and she had encountered all known poisons – and then began to break it down into its basic parts, to neutralize it before it did any harm. Within a matter of seconds the poison was gone, tore apart at the molecular level and negated.

But this changed things completely.

Alexis fired five quick, steady shots in the direction of the shadows, her aim accurate and deadly. The shots appeared to have little to no effect and she could distinctly hear the clink of her bullets hitting various places around the room, where she had not aimed, their energies spend.

She frowned as she moved again, a palisade of darts flying through the air like a swarm of locusts. She would have to do this the hard way. She would have to get in close and personal. She didn't like to kill others, to take away life that was precious to all, but there were times when it was necessary and though she might not like to do it, she had no aversion to it when there was no other option. And here, with these mysterious attackers, she was keenly aware that there was no other option. She even doubted that she would be able to capture one alive.

Well, let the games begin, she thought as she calculated her first attack and set it in motion, ditching the gun onto the sofa as she flew past. She realized her sight was slightly askew with the distortion these foes presented and so compensated her course. She connected with the head of one of her assailants, the sickening snap and crunch telling her, even as she landed and rolled behind a table, that she had killed him instantly, his limp body sagging to the floor like a sack of potatoes, the dart gun clattering to the hardwood, now useless.

Sparks and a distortion wave of some sort undulated over the body, then dissipated to leave behind a dead lump in black. It made Alexis suddenly realized that she had been seeing the intruders mentally, that they were invisible to the naked eye, a device of some sort camouflaging them like a chameleon, making their outline smooth into the surrounding blackness and shadows and making them for the most part invisible to the naked eye.

She didn't have much time to reflect on it as another dart found its target and she neutralized the poison quicker this time, knowing now how to defeat it. There was a flash of bare steel, a knife produced as Alexis swung in close, to nullify the range weapons and make her assailants fight close in. She deftly deflected the thrown weapon blazing through the air, the flicker of the firelight making it appear almost beautiful in its deadly flight. The music of Mozart began to rise to a crescendo, the silent moves of the humans appearing as if choreographed by a demented playwright.

Alexis rolled in and swept the feet out from under the nearest attacker, tumbling him to the floor unceremoniously. The other hesitated a moment, as if unsure what to do next, the stealth technology that they had counted on to counter-balance Alexis' natural skills apparently useless.

Alexis, however, didn't hesitate.

Decades of experience and a natural, inbred skill base made her react instantly, made her an efficient killing machine that didn't need to think to be successful.

She struck a rock-solid blow at the nearest attacker's chest, sending him sprawling back into and over the sofa, his gun flying out of his hands, the crunch of ribs echoing through the room. The assailant whom she had knocked down earlier jumped up, ready to engage in hand-to-hand combat, posed for a fight to the death.

Whoever these people are, Alexis thought as she shot a glance at the assailant on the other side of the sofa as he slowly rose, *they certainly are tenacious*. The attacker before her launched into a series of moves that looked familiar to Alexis but somehow seemed different, like a known play that has a few lines and blocking changed along the way. With a speed she wouldn't have suspected he had, the attacker connected a shot to her side that stung like fire. Alexis stepped in rather than back and engaged him in a series of hand moves blurring with a rapidity that was unnatural. The shadow man was forced to do his best just to keep up and then she landed an unseen blow to the side of his head that brought stars to his eyes. This was followed instantly with a kick to the chest collapsing his rib cage in a splinter of bones and sending him sprawling back. But he refused to fall. She eyed him a fraction of a second, a frown deepening her beautiful face, and finished the job, her jab to his nose driving the cartilage into his brain and ending his life in an agonizing instant.

Why had he not just sat down and played dead?

What a waste.

She was hit then from the side, the force of the blow sending her and her assailant careening into the wall, knocking pictures down to the sound of shattering glass. There was another flash of steel, the gunmetal black of the blade slashing at her chest. She blocked with her arms crossed, then kicked up into the groin area. Her foot encountered a hardness that was not his manhood and she realized that he had come prepared for that attack.

He gave her a sharp kick to the side and disengaged, then came at her again with two daggers, the blades blurring as he feinted. She analyzed the attack, found the weakness and exploited it. When he was but centimeters from striking, she fell back, kicking her legs under his and shoving her body past him. In an instant, she had spun around, grabbed his left foot from behind and twisted it to a bone-crunching angle.

The man turned with the pain and slashed down at her. She let go and rolled away, then kicked up and gave him a blow to his temple with her foot, felling him instantly. She moved onto him immediately, ready to give the coup de grace, but it was unnecessary.

He was dead, the same shimmer and dispersion covering his body for a moment then disappearing to leave behind a corpse in a black jumpsuit, the material of which was not even familiar to Alexis.

It was then that she noticed the vicious, concerned barking and growl of her dogs as they scratched at the bedroom door in their attempt to come to aid of their master. She would have to re-paint that door. She calmly stepped away from the dead assailants and opened the door for her dogs, who ran out in a rush of adrenaline and loyalty and went directly to the dead bodies, sniffing and growling and clawing until they finally realized that the threat was gone.

Alexis walked over to the table on which she had laid her hot chocolate. It had miraculously survived the attack and she lifted it up and took a sip of the still hot liquid. Her robe had come undone during the struggle and her naked body glistened with sweat in the subdued flicker of the firelight making a play of shadows on the vaulted ceiling. The music had subsided to a calm and eloquent Mozart piano concerto, somehow fitting for the moment of reflection.

Her heart beat barely above normal.

She took another sip and stood looking at the mess that the three assailants had made as they lay dead on her den floor. She frowned, then threw her head back to clear her mind. A pain began to make its way to her consciousness and she explored her side with her fingers. There was a wetness that was red on her fingers as she pulled them away and studied them: a dark, crimson speaking of a deep cut. She frowned even deeper as she finished her chocolate and walked over to the kitchen to put her cup in the sink, then ran water over a clean dishtowel. She took her robe off, disgusted that it was now stained with blood and slashed along the side. It wasn't all that easy to get these silken robes up here in the wilderness. It wasn't like Dumont carried them on his VTOL.

She immediately walked over to the laundry room and sprayed the stain remover onto the large blotch of blood, then threw it in the hamper, all the while holding the wet dish-towel to her side, hoping that perhaps in the morning she could find a way to repair the damage to the robe. She walked back to the kitchen and pulled out the med-kit she always kept handy for emergencies and examined the wound for the first time as she stood naked in the den with the three dead assailants still laying on the floor, the dogs still sniffing and exploring about.

It took a good ten minutes to clean out and seal up the wound with the skin-grafter, ten minutes wherein her anger began to build over the arrogance of Cav in thinking that these three could have taken her down. It had not, except for the interesting poison, even been a real challenge. The use of the new camouflage suits was something different, though, and as soon as she had finished with her wound, she examined the closet body to see what this new technology was.

She had heard nothing about it, nothing at all. That meant that it was military in nature, one of the handful of secret projects to which even she didn't have access. Whatever it was, it was compact and light, the fabric of

50

the suits worn an apparent integral part of the system. And it felt cold, almost frigid to the touch as if it had been cooled and yet she knew that after all the time laying there, the suits should have been closer to room temperature. The material also felt strange as she ran it between her fingers, as if at certain moments the fabric ceased to exist and her fingers touched each other, skin on skin. It would only last a fraction of a second yet it intrigued her vastly.

Had she not been able to see them mentally, been able to see their own mental projections as they looked for her, the system they wore would have been very, very effective. This was something that she might be able to use in the future and after looking over each of the three dead bodies, found the one closet in size to her and began to strip him.

She was quite shocked when she discovered that this man had breasts and thus was not a man at all. As she pulled off the face covering, she saw that it was a rather attractive female, young, with short-trimmed hair and a military look about her that confirmed her earlier assessment. But once again there was that feeling, that sense that they didn't belong here, in this dimension, as if they were passing between dimensions and losing cohesion as they did, becoming solid one second then ethereal the next.

She examined the suit for a moment after she had taken it off the now naked body, then rolled it up and placed it on the coffee table in front of the sofa. As she looked at it, she realized with a suddenness that was chilling that her sophisticated internal security system had not fired a shot at the intruders and thus had not recognized them as intruders. How could the system, which was the best that any military on the planet had developed, not have seen these people as attackers, not recognized them as humans and thus attacked them? "Computer, can you repair the perimeter security system?"

"I will send a worker droid to accomplish the task. It will take approximately thirty minutes," the voice answered her.

She nodded her head. At least the damn expensive computer could handle that chore. "Activate motion detectors and bear alarms, please." The last thing she needed now was for a bear family to smell the blood and come wandering over for a look.

"Alarms activated."

Alexis sat on the armrest of the sofa and stared at the naked body of the female attacker for several moments, trying to come up with a rationale for what she was feeling, seeing. There was something about her, something that didn't sit right with at all. She took the masks off the other two, both men, and saw the same wrongness on their surprised death-masks she had seen in the female, which she had felt when she had first scanned them. It was almost as if they didn't belong in this time. She memorized their faces and her feelings for later reflection.

Her dogs came up to her side and she petted their heads unconsciously as she stood and contemplated her next move. This attack put Cav's data, which she had been pouring over earlier, that had before seemed interesting but not all that promising, in a whole new light. There was something there. Something major. No one sent these types of people with this type of hardware to kill someone without a good reason and her refusal to accept the mission was not one of those reasons. Not even on a long shot.

It was something else.

She stretched a kink out of her back, then picked up the three foreign weapons and placed them in a bag, took one of the darts, placed a small cork over the needle-sharp tip and placed it in a small plastic bag. She wanted to get this poison analyzed. Next stop was her bedroom upstairs to change into the same clothes she had worn to see Cav last time, set the house computer to watch the dogs, sent a message to Dumont to please drop by as soon as possible and keep them company or even take them to his house, then carried the three bodies out to the garage.

She erased the files out of her computer system concerning the five killed people, as well as the data from the disc, put the disc into her jacket pocket, grabbed an orange and banana from the refrigerator and went out to the garage again. By the time she was finished, she was furious and it showed on her face. No one did this to Alexis Locke.

At least not twice.

Life unexamined is not worth living
--Socrates

6

8 August 2085, 1425 hrs

She had expected her anger to abate as she flew the thousands of kilometers to Cav's office, as it had always done in times past when she was particularly ticked off at him. She found it odd that she remembered the times when she was angry at him far easier than the times, if they even existed, when she was pleased with something he had done.

In fact, now that she thought about it, she really couldn't think of any time in the past, in her very long relationship with the man who had given her life, when she was not pissed off at him for something or other. Their relationship, if one could even call it that – and she was certain that their were legions of psychologists just waiting to evaluate their relationship and quantify it as typical for those so close – seemed to revolve around an antagonism that went beyond the mere formality of those who hate each other yet have to work with each other.

And yet, her anger had always abated, had always reduced down to a diffuse mélange of hate, which he joked at and she packed away for later analysis in a mind too filled with the hatred of others.

But this time it didn't.

Her anger seethed and churned inside her like a living thing, fed by the extra time she was given to think and reflect on what had actually happened back at her cabin early this morning and what it meant for the rest of her life. It was, of course, not the first time someone had tried to kill her. And it certainly wouldn't be the last, she was sure of that. What truly bothered her

53

was that it had happened at her cabin, her retreat from the world, a place that had, until now, been her own private reserve from the killing and the inhumanity that seemed to thrive on this planet.

And if she were honest with herself, having her solitude interrupted in such a callous manner was not even the bad part. It was the fact that they had known where to find her. That was a serious problem and it was what kept her anger boiling for the entire trip. The only one with that information – apart from Dumont, who didn't have a clue that she was not Morgan Trist, reclusive ex-author who wanted to be alone from the world – was Cav, and for him to have given that knowledge to someone else was unforgivable, especially when that someone else had tried to have her killed.

It was an unforgivable breach of trust and verdict on her life making her realize how easy it was for people like Cav and the president's chief-of-staff to write off others when their usefulness came to an end. There was the remote possibility that Cav had a leak, a bad leak and this was the first manifestation of that leak and it was possible that the leak originated with Claudine Maxwell. It was also possible that if frogs had wings they wouldn't hit their asses when they bounced.

Either way, she was determined to find the answer and at the moment, the only place to find that answer was in Cav's office, with her hands wrapped around his fat, greasy neck until his eyes popped out.

There was another problem.

She couldn't live in her cabin anymore.

That paradise, which she had thought perfect found along the banks of that river, between the mountain crags with their winter snows and summer flowers, was no longer a viable refuge for her. It was certainly to become a nonviable refuge for the animals who lived there in one of the last pure preserves on the over-populated planet. With the knowledge of where she lived out in the open – which was certainly going to be the case now that the assassin had missed and her life would have to be ended regardless of the original reasons -- she would be the target of any number of governments and other agencies who had been striving for her elimination for decades. She had finally found a place wherein she could relax, she could say was her own and not worry about missions and killing and danger.

That was now all gone as completely as the twig that falls into the swift moving stream and is eventually sent to the ocean to be forever lost in eternity. She didn't intend to be like that twig.

It was no wonder that her anger had not abated.

When the flight controllers informed her that she didn't have clearance to land on the upper pad due to the heavy rains crashing down from the black, laden clouds in sheets, she told them in no uncertain terms with a voice that could have made a blow-torch look subtle, that if they didn't allow her to park her VTOL on one of the upper pads, she would blast her own pad in the side of the building and park anyway.

This convinced them to let her land without any further conversation.

The heavy winds of the storm had more or less subsided by the time she set her VTOL down, but the rain seemed determined to assail the land below with a Noahistic fury. It made the loss of power that had occurred several days ago that much more dangerous, the flooding in the streets beginning to make life a living hell for those not fortunate enough to live in Cav's towering fortress of self-sustaining bull-shit. The clouds seethed and boiled at the altitude of the upper landing pads, ragged wisps of coal black water vapor curling around the tower and the antennas like forlorn ghosts lost in time. She didn't notice any of it. She stepped out of her ship to the disgruntled look of security, who stood around by the landing pad as if they seriously expected to make her go back in her VTOL and take off again. However, one look at her face made them all step back and allow her to pass, the naked dead body she dragged behind her a nuisance they didn't want to bother with and a problem they didn't want to even think about.

The door to Cav's office slammed open with a rush, the bolts on the hinges straining under the mental impact forcing it open from afar. The splinters from the housing of the locking mechanism flew in a wild spray onto the floor like a giant game of pick-up-sticks Alexis entered, ready to do battle, ready to deal with a cadre of assassins poised for her entrance, the dead body bouncing behind her like a toy in some black comedy. She heaved it forward and it slumped to a stop on the carpet.

Cav sat behind his desk, apparently awaiting her arrival. He had heard about the commotion concerning her clearance to land and her tumultuous exit from her ship. He didn't know what to expect from her, but he did know one thing: it was not about to be good. He had seen her in this mood before and knew what it portended.

"You fucking bastard!" she voiced indiscreetly as she reached forward mentally and grabbed him by the collar, lifting his fleshy, short body out of the seat and a good meter into the air.

Cav relaxed, well aware that he was powerless to stop or even interfere with whatever it was she had planned for him. All he could do was wait out her anger, wait till it abated and then try to speak to her reasonably and find out what went wrong this time and how he was to blame.

"You of all people should know that if you plan on killing me, you'd better do it right the *first time* because I sure as hell won't give you a second try."

His eyes widened, the look of utter confusion and shock on his face causing Alexis to pause for consideration. "What the hell are you talking about? Tried to kill you? Who tried to killed you?"

"Well let's examine this a moment Cav," she spit out with clenched teeth, her face a mask of hostility he had never seen so intense. "Since you're the only dumb bastard who knows where I live, I guess that narrows the field of eligible options down quite a bit, wouldn't you think?"

"I don't have a fucking clue what you're talking about, Alexis. Now let me down and we can talk about this. If someone is trying to kill you then we have a serious problem."

"You're damn right we have a serious problem, asshole!" She tightened the grip on his throat and slowly started to squeeze the life out of him, her earlier moment of pause gone now that he was starting his excuses.

Cav started to choke, clutching at his throat in a futile effort to alleviate the pressure and the pain. "Alexis ... I swear ... that I didn't ... know anything ... about this," he panted out in staccato burst of panting and choking.

She looked into his eyes, at the man she had once loved as a father and saw that he truly didn't have a clue, didn't know a thing about her attackers. Either that or he was putting on one hell of performance as she choked him to death.

She let him go and he fell to the floor with a sickening thud. She wished that she could look into his mind, could mentally probe him to be sure, but he was shielded from her, had always been for reasons she had never fully understood. It had something to do with a block put within her mind when she was created, but she had never had a real reason to pursue the truth before. Perhaps that was a mistake.

She discerned the hasty foot-falls of the security detachment running down the corridor leading to Cav's office and with a flick of her wrist closed the remnants of the door shut and sealed it against further intrusions. She needed to be alone with this man at the moment.

Cav pulled himself up with the help the edge of the desk and looked at Alexis with anger and bewilderment, rubbing his sore throat for the second time in as many days. He was not sure how to approach this out-burst, her use of force a new chapter in their relationship and a sign that things were not all that kosher between them. "What's with the naked female? Is this some new fetish of yours?" he asked, resorting to humor since he knew that he was completely defenseless where Alexis was concerned. That she had not killed him he took as a good sign.

The guards began pounding on the door demanding entry. Cav yelled in an irritated voice that he was just fine, simply storm damage and that there was no security breach or any need for their presence. They argued with him a moment, then disappeared back down the corridors when they were satisfied that they had covered their asses.

She looked down at the body, aware that his ill attempt at humor was all he had at the moment, then walked over to the nearest chair and sat down. "That's one of my attackers, Cav. They were all wearing this, which made them invisible to the naked eye and infrared." She threw the black suit onto the floor next to the body. He came around from behind the table and approached the dead body on his floor. She was still not convinced that he wasn't involved somehow. "So tell me Cav. If they aren't from you, then who the hell has this kind of hardware capabilities? Has the military now declared war against me?"

Cav inspected the body and the suit carefully, his practiced eye finding several interesting anomalies he was at a loss to explain adequately. After a good five minutes, he finally straightened back up and walked over to his bar, where he poured himself a stiff drink of bourbon. He threw it back down his throat, then looked over at the body again, then at Alexis. "How many were there?" He was furiously trying to figure this out, figure out who not only had the power to call in such a hit, but also had access to the sophisticated hardware and the location of her retreat. He was the only one who knew where she lived, who knew the details that would be necessary to plan and carry out such an operation.

"Three."

"Whoever sent them must not have known you very well," he said with a smile, imagining what they must have been thinking as she kicked their asses around the cabin.

"Oh, they knew me well enough," she said flippantly. "Perhaps not as well as they would have liked to, but they were professional and highly trained and ready to kill me without a hesitation. In fact, they basically fought to the death. I tried to take one alive but that was not in their mission briefing, I would suspect." She reached into her jacket pocket and pulled out the small plastic bag holding the poisoned dart. "They also used these." She threw the bag onto his desk. "Although I wouldn't protest if you killed yourself just about now, be very careful with those, especially with the tip. It's the harshest poison that I've ever encountered and we both know that I've encountered more than my fair share of them."

Cav walked over, picked the bag up and held it to the light. "I don't recognize the caliber or the make. I'll be sure to have it analyzed immediately." He narrowed his eyebrows at the device, becoming more worried with each sentence she spoke. "Do you need a clean-up team at your cabin?"

"I brought all the bodies with me as gifts for you." She stood and walked over to the window, her hands behind her back, the same rain drops as she had seen before when she was here earlier still running down the panes in their own little worlds, oblivious to the confusing problems of the mortals. She sometimes wished that she could be as free as they were, free to just fall where they may and heed nothing, be mindful of no destination or urgent needs. "They knew were I lived, Cav." She turned to look at him with intense eyes. "If you didn't sent them, then who did? And how did they know where I lived, who I even was?"

"I can't explain it, Alexis. But you have to believe me when I tell you that I didn't send them or know anything about their existence. I can't believe that you would even think that. You're like a..."

She held up a hand and the words stuck in his throat. "Don't say it, Cav, or I just might kill you anyway." Her eyes blazed with a vivid intensity. She didn't, at this moment, want to be reminded of all she owed him or how she once felt for him. Not now. She needed her anger to stay focused on the problem.

"Okay, I won't," he said quietly as he swallowed hard. "But however they found out where you lived, it didn't come from here. The only place that I keep your personal information is in here." He pointed to his head. "And I haven't told anyone where you live. Be serious."

"You told those two flyboys who you sent to pick me up, Cav. Remember them? It was just yesterday. Who else have you told that you can't remember?"

"What I told them was that they were to pick up my mistress from my cabin in Alaska," he replied with equal vigor. "They don't know shit about who you are or even what you are. And I had their nav-com scrambled when they returned so that no one else could back-track with it."

She looked at him from under her eyebrows. "You told them what? No

58

wonder they kept looking at me with those damn strange smiles and all that stupid laughter on the trip back."

He poured himself another drink and then knelt next to the body. "I seriously doubt they thought about it much at all. I have them bring me women all the time from around the world. Besides, they're hand-picked for my more confidential jobs and they've been with me for many, many years."

"Doesn't mean they can't be bought off. Money still goes a long way."

"Actually, yes it does. I'd have known about it if they were even approached. However, I will put someone on them right away to make certain. The only other thing I could possibly do is kill them, if that's what you're looking for to make you feel better."

"If it was them, then they already told, so killing them doesn't do any good. And it certainly wouldn't make me feel any better."

"No, I suppose it wouldn't at that."

"Cut the crap, Cav. This isn't funny. This is personal now. No one tries to kill me in my own home."

"And you actually thought that I did it. Amazing. After all --"

"Shut the hell up, Cav."

Cav spread the woman's legs apart and pointed toward her left inner thigh. "Did you notice this?"

"That she's a woman? Yes, Cav, I noticed that little detail. Are you that hard up that you need to look at dead women's vaginas?"

He looked at her a moment with humorless eyes, then placed his attention back on the woman's thigh. "I was actually referring to the tattoo here, on her inner thigh. Did you see it?"

Alexis moved forward to get a better look, her forehead furrowed. She didn't remember seeing any tattoos, but then she had not thought to disgrace the woman's dead body by spreading apart her legs. The tattoo was located where her leg intersected her hips on the inner thigh, partially obscured by pubic hair. It consisted of what appeared to be an omega symbol surrounded by finely drawn scribbles, which could be words. She recognized nothing of its origins and didn't even understand the scribbling.

But then the tattoo was not what was bothering her. She had missed detecting it and she didn't like missing details like this. Such things usually meant a great deal when the assignment was over.

He rolled her over in an attempt to look for any other markings but found nothing. "There's something strange about her. Like she doesn't belong. I felt it when I touched her body. It was far colder than a dead body should be

59

and there was some sort of electric field at play around her skin. Did you notice any of that?"

"Yeah, I noticed it alright. They were all the same. When they were alive, they seemed to almost move in an out of our three dimensions as if they weren't quite all here. I thought it was the suit doing it, but obviously that was a wrong assumption."

Cav rose on creaky knees. "I'll have my team do an autopsy on all three and maybe that'll shed some light on who they are and where they came from." He moved back over to his chair and sat down. "These aren't normal people."

"No shit, Cav. You can be so brilliant some times." She took a seat on the arm of a nearby chair, arms dangling loosely at her sides, staring at the naked female on the carpeted floor as if waiting for it to sit up and tell them all its secrets.

"I don't recognize the tattoo," he offered as he brought his computer interface on-line to search for the pattern.

"Odd place for it. Almost as if she didn't want anyone to know she had it. People only hide things there that they don't want others to know they have."

"Or as a sexual turn-on."

She eyed him severely.

"Don't look at me like that. I know plenty of women who have tattoos down there or on their asses which they think turn guys on, and to tell the truth there're plenty of guys who find that kind of shit a turn-on."

"This world is full of very sick people."

"You've obviously been away in Alaska a little too long."

A team of specialists dressed in white chemical suits come to the door and stepped in with a large bag and a gurney. They bundled up the naked female as if they did this type of work in Cav's office all the time, then left without saying a word or even acknowledging that there were two living people in the room.

Cav looked over at Alexis as the group left with their prize on the gurney. "You have to believe me when I tell you that I had nothing to do with this, Alexis. I don't work that way and you know it. I've no reason to have you killed at this particular moment. I need you."

She smirked at his candor. "So glad that you threw in that little caveat there, Cav." They stared at each other a moment before she spoke again. "I wish it had been you in a rather morbid sort of way."

He kept his eyes locked on hers. "Because then you'd know."

"Then I'd know," she answered curtly. "Now I don't have a clue who wants me this dead to send these clowns to my place. It's going to make accomplishing this assignment that much more difficult. Usually they don't start trying to kill me until after I start making inquiries."

He cocked his head slightly. "What assignment are you talking about?"

"Into the death of my son. I'm going to find the bastards responsible and tear them apart piece by bloody piece ... slowly."

A small smile worked its way onto his lips almost as if it were afraid to make its presence known. "Can I take that to mean that you've accepted the mission?" "It means just what I said, Cav. I'm going to find the people who killed my son. That's all. I don't give a rat's ass about anything you want or that bitch Claudine wants. This is personal now. No one attacks my family like that and gets away with it. No one." She leaned on the front of his desk with both hands palms down, looking him directly in the eyes, the hint of violence like a lurking shadow across her irises. "You better hope that nothing comes back to you, Cav. Because if I find out that you had anything to do this, anything at all, I'll kill you just as surely as I step on an ant."

He left the threat unanswered. He had, over the years, gotten used to powerful people threatening him on an almost daily basis. "And if you happen to discover a link between your son and the others, that would get them killed also?"

She ignored his question just as efficiently. "I'm going to need some support from you, Cav. You know the drill. I'll be down in the weapon's lab, so tell them to be expecting me." She turned toward the door and made her way easily across the carpet. "And tell your security goons to lay off, else you're going to have a lot more dead bodies laying around this place."

His smile widened, this time with the full expectation that she would see it and not be amused. She had accepted the mission, albeit on her own terms. But then with Alexis, there was no other way of having her accept a mission. "I'll let you know the minute the autopsy results come back."

"That would be nice." She opened the splintered door to leave, then turned to look at him one last time. "You'd better warn Claudine that her time on this earth is limited, because I know that she's involved." She left without waiting for a reply, leaving the door hanging open on one hinge.

Cav breathed a sigh of relief and leaned back in his chair as he downed the glass full of bourbon he had been holding onto for the past five minutes. He had almost forgotten how difficult it was to work with Alexis Locke. Odd that one would forget something so bad tasting. Maybe he had repressed it out of shear terror.

The side door to his office opened and Claudine Maxwell stepped out elegantly, the smile plastered on her face like a model's perfect nightmare.

"Shut the damn door, for Christ's sake," he spit out at her. "Do you want everyone to know that you were here? What if she comes back? Your secret services boys won't be able to do a damn thing for you if she decides that you're the bad one here and she's just a step away from making that decision."

She waltzed over to the door and shut it slowly, then turned to look at him with a bemused look, which spoke little for his concerns. "Very interesting. Your little experiment has a rather ambitious independent streak to her, doesn't she?"

He flung his bourbon snifter at her but his aim was far off the mark. "You stupid bitch!" he screamed at her with spittle flying freely. "Did you really think, in that grotesquely deranged brain of yours, that you could send three of your military flunkies up to Alaska and KILL HER?! Were you born that stupid or is it something you've worked on over the years?"

She chortled at him, looking over at the now harmless snifter lying on the carpet, the smell of its lost contents permeating through her own perfume. She walked over to the bar and poured herself straight vodka, drank it down in one gulp. "It would appear that this little mission is a little more important than you thought at first, wouldn't it."

"Fuck off, Claudine. Just bend over and fuck off." He put his hand over his forehead, could feel his pulse racing, his veins straining to pump the blood that his heart could barely circulate. He could feel himself sweating, like a sticky coating on his skin that should have warded off people like Claudine but didn't seem to be functioning properly.

She poured herself another Vodka and walked over toward his desk, aware that the man was close to a coronary. "Slow down, Cav. You'll give yourself a heart attack at this rate." She sat on the arm of a chair, her short skirt riding up high on her thighs and giving that tease of a glimpse at her nether regions women used to such devastating advantage. "If I didn't know better, I'd think that you were sleeping with your little experiment, the way you're carrying on about her. I don't remember you getting all this ... What's the right word? Emotional? Yes, emotional over the others and their ultimate deaths." She sipped at her second vodka like a seasoned professional.

"Don't fuck with me, Claudine."

She laughed again as she threw her head back and flared her hair out.

"Not a chance in the world of *that* ever happening again."

"Alexis is the last person in the world that you want to make angry. She will carry out her threat, you can guarantee it."

"Do you hear yourself? It's like a broken record." She sipped some more, staring everywhere in the room but at him. This was worse than talking to the president. At least that blonde bimbo had an excuse for being so ignorant. Cav had once been a genius. He had no more excuses. "Relax. I didn't send anyone to kill your precious little slut. I'm not that stupid, Cav, despite what you openly think about me."

"I sometimes wonder about that," he whispered to himself.

She finished her vodka, thought about getting more but decided that the warm feeling she was beginning to get was more than enough of a shield against his hypocrisy. "Why the hell would I, as you so clearly said, demand that she be assigned to this case only to kill her off? It makes no sense. Not even to a kid. Anyway," she intoned with a wave of her hand. "It appears that your little princess is going to take our little missions after all. Imagine that."

"Don't be so sure about that. And you damn well know her name. Why don't you use it?"

"Sure she is," she said as she wrinkled her nose at him, ignoring his plea. "She said it herself."

"What she said, had you bothered to listen, is that she's going to find the people who killed her son and hunt them down like the dogs they are."

She looked at her nails and realized that she needed a manicure. "Isn't it the same thing? When she finds the people who killed Dr. Hart, she'll have found the people who killed the others and case closed."

He looked at her from under his hand. Was she really this dense or just this arrogant? "It's not the same thing at all. But it really doesn't matter anymore. I think that the more she looks into this the more connections she'll make with the others and it'll become a puzzle she'll need to solve. It's the way she works."

"And that's different in what way?" She rose from her seated position elegantly and walked over to his desk, where she sat again, angling her legs just right for Cav to get an eyeful. She reached forward and grabbed a fat cigar out of the open box on his desktop. She rolled it under her nose, inhaling the aroma as she closed her eyes and imagined herself anywhere but here.

"It's different because finding the killers isn't the same as finding out why they killed them and who ordered it. It's them that we need to get at else they'll just keep sending in assassins until they achieve their goal."

She clipped off the end of the cigar and lit it, talking out of the side of her mouth as she did so. "Do you really think that there'll be more deaths?"

He said nothing for a few moments as the bluish cloud of smoke rose above her, enveloping her in a haze. He was finding it difficult to see what if anything he ever saw in her besides the great body. And even that didn't seem to entice him as it once did despite her efforts to the contrary. "I've a feeling that whatever this is, it's bigger and more wide-spread than even you suspect. If you didn't sent those people to kill her, then there's a third party at play here who neither of us knows about and they have access to some pretty sophisticated shit.

She smiled big as she pulled the cigar out from between her plump, sensuous lips and blew out a cloud of toxic fumes. "I like them big, Cav. At least you get your money's worth that way."

He closed his eyes and leaned back, wishing that she would just leave, perhaps even die. Yes, that would be nice if she were to just keel over and die right here in his office because then he could piss on her still warm corpse. "You might just get more than you bargained for with Alexis, Claudine, far more."

She slid the cigar back into her mouth with a twisting motion, her lips puckered up around it and her cheeks sucked in, the twinkle in her eyes malicious.

She certainly hoped so.

Science tells us how to heal and how to kill;
it reduces the death rate in retail and
then kills us wholesale in war.

7

8 August 2085, 2000 hrs

He found her sitting in a back office of the second floor of the extensive weapons lab, which he kept staffed around the clock. One never knew when a particular weapon might be needed at three in the morning. Her feet were propped up on some lowly engineer's messy desk, he having long since departed for his modest home and modest life. A glass of ice water rested in one hand as she read diligently a report on the computer screen

She didn't look up when he entered.

She didn't even acknowledge his presence. It was rather obvious that she was still angry with him and he let that pass for now. At least she was no longer choking the life out of him.

"They finished the autopsies," he said after several minutes of dead air between them, her eyes never once moving toward him.

"And? ..."

He moved so that he could see what was on her screen. Schematics for the new military proto-type of the Spec 5 double plasma cannon. Light reading to be sure. "Tap into the morgue's d-base. You're not going to believe this one."

She dutifully did as she was directed and soon was staring at a recorded feed of the autopsy, the typical dry, monotone voice of the primary coroner droning on about the typical Y-cut and the aftermath.

"Am I looking for something in particular?"

"Just wait a moment."

She looked at him then, her eyes shifting ever so slightly to take in his pudgy face with the chin waddle and the bags under his still intelligent eyes like lost candles in a burlap sack. A startled exclamation from the autopsy team brought her vision back to the screen and she leaned forward as she watched; not because it would allow her to see better but because it was one of those human traits to want to be closer to events transpiring before you, as if closer translated to comprehension and thus acceptance.

She ran her tongue along her teeth as she breathed in deeply at the startling events unfolding before her. The bodies were disintegrating at an astonishing rate, as if a switch had been thrown and time was suddenly marching forward at a year a second. First to go was their skin, turning into a grayish ooze and then disappearing altogether, next the eyes, tendons, muscles and finally the bones turning into a powdery ash, sitting on the examination table as if defying any to explain.

"What just happened?" she asked as she touched a few keypads and replayed the scene.

"Your guess is as good as mine. The autopsy team is still trying to recover. It was like your assassins never existed."

She watched it a third time, looking for she knew not what but looking nonetheless because there had to be an explanation for what had just transpired. Bodies didn't just disappear like that. "What about the ashes that were left over?"

"Nothing there to speak of. Human remains basically. Very *old* human remains."

"Were they able to get anything out of them?"

"DNA."

"Where?"

He pointed toward the relevant command and she immediately moved there, watching as the streams of code started to scroll along the screen. She punched a few more buttons and the VR system lit up, displaying the DNA in all its glory throughout the room.

She rose out of her chair and studied the sequences a moment, then looked at Cav, who was still sitting, a look of bewilderment on her face. "This looks like my code."

"Yes. It does."

She looked back at the floating information. "But how?"

"It's actually not your exact code, as I'm sure you can tell. But it does have quite a few markers which are dead-on identical and they're the ones that I specifically programmed into you those many years ago."

"So they're clones?" It could not have been said without more shock if she had tried.

"No, not technically, but close enough to worry the shit out of me. This isn't possible, what these three represent. The technology isn't here yet to do this in this way. Those three people should not exist."

She smiled, briefly. "They don't."

"Yes, well that might be true at the moment but they *did* exist." He stood, moved toward her and pointed at a particular grouping of genes. "See there? In the fourth and fifth sequence of the brain pattern?"

"They had the same abilities as I do." She looked at him. "Why the hell didn't they use them, then? I mean, why go to all the bother of cloning my better parts and then not train the clones in the primary skills specifically cloned."

"You're asking the wrong person. Speaking of that ..." He reached into his inner coat pocket and produced a small bag in which was the poisoned dart she had brought him earlier. He opened the bag up, grabbed the dart out and proceeded to prick himself in the finger.

"CAV?" she shouted as she grabbed the dart out of his hand and made ready to call the medics. She was well aware that the poison would react instantly to his system. But it didn't. She looked at him completely baffled. "You should be dead."

He smiled at her and put the dart back in the bag. "Lethal to you, yes. Completely harmless to me and anyone else on this planet." He handed her the bag and she studied the dart through the plastic. "Genetically engineered?"

"Perfectly." He took the bag from her hands and put it securely back in his inner coat pocket as if it were a treasured item. "It was designed to kill you and only you. Claudine Maxwell didn't order this. There isn't anyone on this planet with the technology necessary to create this. I've gotten close recently, but even then, I can only narrow it down to perhaps a hundred thousand people. But just one person? Not for decades, if not centuries. This is the perfect assassin weapon. You can put this in the water supply of the city where the target lives and it'll not only be completely harmless to everyone but the target but undetectable as well."

She leaned against the desk, staring at the far wall as she tried to process all she had learned in the last five minutes and she was having a hard time. "How do you know that no one on this planet has this tech? I mean, you're holding it in your hand so someone has to have perfected the technique."

"Impossible. If I haven't done it, then I would've heard about anyone else who did. This isn't just a back yard, personal computer type of job. Something like this takes billions of dollars and a research facility par excellence and any expenditure on that scale I would know about. The equipment alone would raise red flags from here to Nepal. No. Whatever this is, whomever these people are they're so far more advanced than we are that they could take us out in a matter of seconds if they were so inclined. But on the bright side, I'd say that we've caught our killers. You might not have to do much more investigative work after all."

She smirked at him. "I think you're jumping the gun just a little here. Those six deaths on that disc you showed me weren't sloppy executions. They were meticulously planned and carried out. If you've got a cadre of these people around with this technology, why even bother with the ruse? Why not just take the targets out the old fashion way?"

He pursed his lips at the suggestion. She had a point, but he felt that there was something missing. "Perhaps they didn't want to advertise they're presence."

"And the attack on me? What was that? An after-thought?"

"That, I think, was an under-estimation of your skill levels. Just because they can clone a majority of your DNA doesn't mean that they have a clue what you can do or how well you can do it. I seriously doubt that they expected that you could neutralize poison introduced into your body, otherwise they would have never bothered with this."

As if a sudden vision had come to her eyes, she stirred and looked up at him as if bitten. "How stupid of me," she voiced with a vexation born of failure. She shook her head at the obvious answer staring at her all this time. Fifteen years ago she would have picked it up immediately, realized her error early on and changed her thought patterns appropriately. She had been out of this game for far too long and this was the perfect sign of that.

"What?" he asked, aware that she was going through her ritual self-chastisement and would be lost to him for several moments while she tried to figure out why she had missed a particular salient point. Being a perfectionist was a backlash of the job at which she had once excelled and Alexis, as far as Cav was concerned, was the consummate perfectionist when it came to her missions, preparation and execution. If she missed something during a prep, even something minor that could be easily overlooked, she would beat herself mentally for hours over her supposed ignorance.

She stood and started to pace about the small room, hands in her hair, face a mask of frustration.

"For god's sake, Alexis, what is it?"

She stopped at the window, which had been closed off with a cheap plastic blind, and shook her head again. "They weren't after me. That was why they were so surprised when they found me there. I should've still been here, discussing this mission with you and not at home."

"That's a rather large leap, if you ask me. They did have the poison engineered for you and you alone. You don't carry something like that around if you don't plan on using it."

"In an emergency, perhaps. But I wasn't the target, Cav." She looked at him now, her eyes intense. "They were there for something else, Cav, perhaps even the information on the disc. Perhaps they're after the same thing you are."

"So then you're saying that these people might be trying to figure this all out also. I don't buy that. With the technology these people have, why would they even bother with something trivial like this?"

"Because, Cav, it isn't trivial. Whatever it is that you've stumbled onto here, it's a big one and it's biting back." She sat down again, heavily, running a hand through her hand and frowning at the computer screen that had reverted back to the information she had been studying when Cav had first entered the office. "The five people who were killed, did they leave behind any diaries or journals? Anything to indicate what they might have been working on together."

"No." He sat on the edge of the desk to a loud protesting creak. "That was one of the red flags that perked the interest of the intelligence community and thus me and Claudine. Any and all journals or diaries that they might have had are all missing, as if someone had systematically taken them. Computers were wiped clean, completely, of any relevant information that might have connected them. Even my boys can't recover any of it, at least with the machines that weren't blown up, like Godonov's. That one was a complete loss."

Her frown deepened. She could feel herself being dragged into Cav's world and she didn't want it. It was like a rock caught in a slide, moving along with the rest of the rocks but not wanting to move at all. But one thought continued to resonate through her soul and it was that one thought, which a day ago she would have scoffed at ever having, that drove her onward and made the rockslide she was caught in not all that bad. "Then it would appear that we'll have to do it the hard way and find all the friends and relatives, talk to them, find out what they know, dig down until we find the key to this bizarre tale."

"We?" he asked with an undercurrent of amusement as he looked down at his Buddha belly.

"That was a figurative statement, my dear fat little man. I'll be the one doing all the legwork. You'll be doing all the technical support."

He smiled, a broad look of triumph she didn't fail to notice. He had her aboard. "I'll of course supply you with whatever it is you need. Where do you want to start?"

She moved over toward the door, staring off at the far wall as she thought. Her mind-processes already far ahead of Cav's. She pursed her lips, looked down at the floor a moment. This was not going to be an easy mission. She still had no idea who the people were who were trying, very forcefully, to kill her and she knew that the attempt at her cabin was not the end of it. If anything, the next time would be even more forceful, perhaps even killing off any civilians who might be around her. They might not have intended at first to kill her, whatever their original mission, be it to find the disc or whatever, but her interference had put her life at the top of their agenda, she was certain of that.

She was the target now.

And if, as she was beginning to suspect, they had nothing whatsoever to do with Alex's death or the other four, then she still had to figure out who had done those killings and the motive behind them. This puzzle had more missing pieces than it had available pieces and she was beginning to get that warm feeling inside her.

This might just prove to be the challenge she had been looking for all her life.

"Alexis?"

She came out of her deep-thought and looked over at him. She noticed his eyes, saw the tell-tale glare of a typical male at her ass, her sleek profile, "Stop leering at me, Cav, before I break your fucking nose."

"I wasn't leering at you, my dear."

"Yeah, right, and that bump in your pants is a banana."

He looked down at his crotch, though he wasn't sure why, knowing before he even looked that there was no bump. "I don't find you attractive in that way, Alexis, and you know that."

She stepped out of the office and looked over the lab spread out before her in all its murderous wares, the numerous people working on better ways of killing people and then going home to their wives and kids and pretending to be caring individuals. It was a typical hypocritical office of human vanity. "Yeah, whatever Cav. Sell it to someone who believes." She looked back at him, having dismissed his pleas of innocence as the manure they were. "I think the best place to start is finding out all I can about that conference that my son" – *it still sounded so odd on her tongue, the word tripping over her deeply hidden emotions like a bear-trap set lightly* – "and that Nakamura attended together. I'll have to see after that. What I find out from that will most likely determine where I go next. I'm leaning toward Japan, but *Stargazer I* looks promising." She ran her hand through her frayed hair a moment, closing her eyes and realizing that she had not gotten but a few hours sleep in the last few days. "This might just take a while, Cav. Don't expect any communiqué's from me for a while, if at all. I'm still not convinced that there isn't a leak here at your little organization and I don't need to be advertising my movements to the people trying to kill me. Let them figure it out the hard way."

"I'll back you in whatever way you want to handle it, as I always do."

She was forced to smile at him. "Really? I seem to remember a different level of cooperation between us back then, one that involved a lot of you telling me where to go and what to do and how to do it and me just agreeing and doing it."

"Funny how time plays tricks on the memory."

She turned back toward the lab, a smirk marring her sculptured face. "I'll need someone to get my dogs and move all my stuff out of the cabin. It's obvious that I can't stay there anymore. And while you're at it, might as well find me a new place to live. Maybe a beach-view this time."

"Consider it already done. Anything else?"

She looked back at him. "This stays between you and me, Cav. The mission, I mean, and my acceptance of it."

"I'll have to tell Claudine, else she'll raise hell – "

She stepped forward and poked him hard in the chest. "Tell her and I'm off. Understand? Just you and me. No one else."

"Ok. You don't have to poke me so hard. It might be soft but it still hurts." He rubbed his chest where he was certain a bruise was already forming. "When do you want to leave?"

"Soon. I need to do a little more research before I even consider leaving, though. I've already got several orders in with the lab techs, so be a good boy and make certain that they get done quickly, huh?"

He rose to escort her out of the lab. "I'll make the arrangement, put a priority on it. What about transportation?" They began to walk toward the far elevator exit.

"Same as always. A multiple of covers, also. Plus clearance to pass through levels one and two if I need it. And tickets and official papers for a trip to both *Stargazer I* and *Galileo Prime*."

"CIA, NSA, or FBI?"

"Whatever is more believable at the moment." They stopped at the elevator and waited for the car to arrive. "Maybe a journalist would be good. Official government types seem to make people nervous now-a-days."

"You'll have a full set of identities within the hour, three different ones just in case. Anything else?"

"A sub sandwich, with meatballs." She smiled her famous crooked smile at him, aware suddenly that at the moment, Dr. Vincent Cavalier was the only friend she had ... and she didn't even trust him.

Cav smiled back. "My treat, my dear."

Consciousness is the mere surface of our minds,
of which, as of the Earth, we don't know
the inside, but only the crust.
--- Schopenhauer

8

9 August 2085, 0600 hrs

Cav entered the large corner office dimmed to a faint breath of light, the one source of illumination casting a pale cone of yellow over the prone figure present, her head laying on her crossed arms. The computer screen had long since turned off on its own and its black face stared out onto the dismal scene of dark rain clouds hanging low, obscuring all below in a haze of deepest depression.

The rain had stopped for the moment: the storm was only catching its breath, making ready for the next round of torrential rains to inundate the already saturated plains below. There had been no tropical storm warning given, the systems that had suddenly developed off the coast too quick to allow for people to prepare. And so they sat in their damp houses in their damp chairs, watching the water level rise higher and higher, flooding their dreams as much as their houses like the proverbial flood.

He watched her for several moments, a tight smile trapped on his lips. He was aware that she was most likely awake, that she could feel his presence, even if it was but subconsciously. If he had the foolish notion of attacking her in any way, he knew for a certainty that he would de dead before he could even get within a foot.

God, but he had built her well.

73

But a nagging feeling had started to grow in the pit of his stomach that he didn't like. It was a feeling of impending doom and he knew, like he knew that he had built her well, that it was directed toward Alexis. There was something about this whole conundrum presented that was beginning to stink and he had the cold feeling that he was seeing her for the last time, seeing that crooked smile and that twinkle in her eyes when she found something humorous.

It was almost like a premonition, warning him that there was more to this than what had been presented and that it would cost the lives of those he cared for the most, including Alexis. Perhaps unknowingly, this was the very mission for which she had been designed, had been created to under-take those sixty- five years ago in that anonymous underground lab, in that flurry of activity and nervousness that had eventually ended with her birth, her perfect birth marking what Cav took to be the beginning of his life and the ultimate culmination of his career. He had indeed been reborn that day, that less than perfect day when Alexis had entered the human race and given it a rude awakening to the future.

It had not taken Cav long to understand that the human race was not ready for her or her siblings. The entire project had been so secret that even the nurses and doctors who had such an important part of her early life had been unaware of her potential, of the plans that the brilliant young geneticist had for the whole brood of perfect people created in an idealistic furor of hypocrisy. They had known so little of the project and its implications that they had not even seen their deaths coming, like a sudden flu descending on a town of herbalists.

Erased was the official term used, a term which Cav had at first not even thought twice about but which had eventually haunted his dreams, both sleeping and waking, making him into, partially at least, the bulk of a man he was today. He saw the justification of the actions at that time, saw that they all had to go, the doctors and nurses and attendants who had never realized that they had signed up for a one-way trip to hell. But soon he saw the entire fiasco for what it was and saw in his decisions the monster he had tried become

Saw it in the mirror every morning.

There had been an accident. Another official term used for the destruction which had rained down on those caught unawares.

Most had not seen it as an accident but rather as the pinnacle of a nefarious plan of power and deceit hatched by a man desperate for attention from a world that had ignored him. Cav had for many years ignored them, ignored the words behind his back, the accusations of his colleagues and finally the secret senate hearings that had put the blame squarely at his feet for the brilliance that had gone wrong. He had fought tooth and nail to keep the project alive, to keep his dreams alive and keep the one viable child alive who, Cav was certain, would vindicate all his expenditures and his failures.

Even to this day he was unsure what really went wrong, what had caused the birth of a mutation unaccounted for in the genetic splices and alterations. But something had happened, something unforeseen and thus unalterable. It was in the fourth birth after Alexis, in a birth that had given rise to a monster. Not one, of course, like the movies liked to depict with horns and fangs and hair all over so that it looked more like a runaway mongrel than a human, but a monster nonetheless, a man who should never have been, a species so distant from Homo Sapiens that it was almost the creation of a whole new species.

It was a mind capable of so much, a body so perfect that it scared the very people who had asked for, no, demanded the very existence of the project and this exact proto-type in the first place. And in that panic over a creation that they themselves had helped to create, they had shut it all down, stopped the funds and the authorization as tightly as a spigot, lest the secret ever leak out and incriminate those in power who wanted to stay in power. It had been that birth which had lead to death of all of them, all the proto-types and the doctors and the nurses and any who might have had a hand in such a creation. It had only been Cav's brilliance that had saved him, the solutions in his mind, the prospects that they had him now by the shorthairs and could demand all sorts of devious weaponry from him. And in his supposed salvation came the salvation of Alexis, the only proto-type to ever survive to this age, to be used as she had been intended and even then it was but a sham.

Alexis was their tool far more than she ever was his love. He had led the illusion that he ran the projects, picked the missions and fought the powers that be over the way she was to be used. Yet it was not until far later, till almost forty years later, shortly before Alexis had gained an independence they could not any longer contain that he had finally wrestled enough power and money from them to allow for his own independence.

And even then it had been but a smoke screen, a brief respite that only allowed him to think that he somehow controlled his own destiny and in turn that Alexis controlled hers.

This most recent assignment was proof of that delusion beyond a doubt.

If he had any delusions that he had control over anything to do with Alexis and her existence, he was sorely mistaken. And it was that very loss of control worrying him now, putting into his stomach such a cold hand of balled up dread that he could vomit from it as if punched. He could feel it like a vise-clamp to his heart, squeezing mercilessly until his soul could take no more and he burst from his own hypocrisy.

He could still remember that cold winter morning, the snow falling like autumn leaves in a cool October breeze when she had awoken to her own sense of self and had told them to go to hell and in that declaration had ended most of her usefulness to a government who didn't care whether she lived or died so long as she went on missions and achieved results.

He had used all his power and influence built up over the years of self-deprecation to have her life spared, to have her on immediate re-call should the need arise and thus grant her a measure of isolation from those who would just as soon erase her as use her and rid their consciousness of any connection to a project that should have never existed in the first place.

And now she was back again, dragged into a world she no longer wanted, working for people she hated and who despised her despite her usefulness in such occasions. Cav could see, with his years of experience like his Buddha belly attached, nothing but trouble brewing in this puzzle.

She stirred and he turned to leave, feeling unreasonably guilty for having stared at her for so long. Her soft voice made him stop, that voice that had at times strained his heart to such an extent. "You really need to find a hobby or something, Cav, because staring at me is not really your best option." She eyed him as if she knew exactly what he had been thinking, had been recollecting in a parody of selfish recriminations. "What time is it anyway?"

"O six hundred. You need the rest."

She leaned back and yawned with a stretch making her firm, rounded breasts press against the black shirt, the bralessness obvious. He averted his eyes and looked at the wall, the floor, the ragged clouds passing by the window in wisps of darkness; anywhere but at her. He had already been accused of leering at her earlier and didn't want to re-visit that false perception any time soon. That she was like a daughter to him made any suggestions otherwise ludicrous.

She eyed him a moment, saw the look of avoidance and smiled faintly. She knew how Cav felt about her, but he was sometimes a little too open with his praise for her anatomy and although she was fully aware that as a geneticist he was far more interested in her molecular structure, his eyes still sometimes gave her a wrong feeling inside.

She relaxed, leaned back again and stifled another yawn. She was unaccustomed to staying awake for such extended periods of time. Where once it had been common place for her to stay alert up to fifty hours without a hint of a problem, her retirement and easy life had taken its toll on her abilities and she saw it as a problem needing to be dealt with soon, else this might just turn into the shortest mission she ever started. "Next time, don't just stand there and stare at me, Cav. I don't appreciate it. No woman does."

"Find anything useful?" he asked as he looked back at her stoically. Any answer to her rebuff would only cause more grief, regardless what he said, so silence was always the best option at this juncture.

"Maybe." She brushed the keypad with a hand and the screen came alive with the data she had been pouring over when she had fallen asleep. She acknowledged his silence as a tactic 'yes' to her request and left the issue laying. "It's hard to tell." She turned the screen so that Cav could see it, then stood and stretched her legs, rubbing her forearm and noting that the room was cooler than usual.

Cav looked at the lines of data that seemed to have no connection whatsoever, the random associations appearing as just that: random. But then, he was not the expert at such things. That was her specialty.

She spoke as she walked around the room, hands now crossed under her breasts. "It appears that Kido and Alex attended one lecture together at the conference they attended, entitled Higher Reasoning in Artificial Intelligence."

Cav nodded his head in assent. He knew that much already.

"They didn't sit together and probably didn't even know that the other was there, so I don't think that the conference is a place to look, or the other participants or the keynote speaker. However, they did meet for lunch, on the second day of the conference. They talked for about forty minutes, from what I can gather, and then went their separate ways. What they talked about, I don't have a clue. How they knew to meet there, at that conference and at that time, I also don't know. There's no trace whatsoever of any contact before or after the conference, so perhaps they just caught each other's eyes across a room or some one else, another player of whom we have no clue, introduced them."

"They may not have talked about anything at all when they met at the conference," Cav interjected, wrinkles appearing like fine lines above his eyes as he looked at the data and found nothing that seemed to be anything worth pursuing.

"Well, I have to assume that since they didn't know each other before the conference and didn't have all that much in common, that they must have talked about something other than the weather and the state of the economy. Why else even meet?"

"Maybe they were attracted to each other?" he offered.

"I don't think so. I mean, I suppose it's possible, but not very likely. They're too different and Kido had a steady boyfriend for the last five years. It's just not likely to me."

"So in your world people don't cheat on each other, or is it that your son doesn't cheat?"

Her eyes flicked to him menacingly. "Don't go there, Cav. This is professional and whether he's my son or not has nothing to do with it. And yes, people cheat all the time in my world, as you put it, but not like this. If they had really been interested, they could have easily gone up to either's hotel room and gotten their jollies that way. But this, this just doesn't feel or smell like a sexual encounter. Besides, why not at least send a few e-mails afterward? Why not at least acknowledge that they had met and follow up on whatever they were talking about? We're missing something here."

"It'd be nice to know what they talked about," he said as he stopped looking at the screen, now certain as to why she had fallen asleep going over this crap. It was boring. He was getting a headache just looking at it this short time.

"Yes, it would, and I think that's where I need to start. There's something here and I think that if I can dig it out, then it'll give me a direction for the next stage. As a matter of fact, I've the unpleasant feeling that I'm going to have to go to all the places of employment of all five victims and talk to the people who knew them the best. I need to get some sort of idea what they were all doing that would mark them as targets in these elaborate staged-deaths. If there's a clue anywhere, it'll be there."

"Isn't that all in the files, the projects they were working on I mean? That has to be info my people dug up shortly after each death."

"I don't mean what they were working on for the company," she said dryly, almost patronizingly. "That's all rather mundane and useless. Nothing important there whatsoever. I'm talking about what they were working on in their spare time, on the sly, the pet projects they took home and planned to use to rise up the corporate ladder. That's where the secrets are most likely to lie, the shadows in the closet that people like these five always seem to have trailing them."

"Sounds good. What cover have you figured on using? I can't imagine going as CIA. Like you said, that would raise too many red flags. It'll have to be something more subtle, more commonplace." He frowned. "What about spouses and kids? Going to talk to them also?"

"It'd be one of the best places to start. The spouse is usually the person who knows the victim the best, or is the one who'll confirm that the victim was living a dual life, her ignorance of his life outside the home one of those clues I like to look for. Having caught many a double agent that way. One spouse had no idea what their significant other was doing on the side, didn't really know the spouse's job, or knew the people he normally associated with. As for the cover, I was thinking more along the lines of a journalist. Not many people can resist a story that has them in it or that plans to uncover something of which they're a part. Company loyalty isn't as strong as most corporate offices would like to believe."

"Story line?"

"Tragic, random acts happening to plain folk, maybe even something about the state of the industry or some such thing. Exposés always seem to get good receptions. I'm not really sure yet. I need to make these people confide in me, open up and spill the dirt."

He pursed his lips. She seemed to have a slightly different opinion of the reaction that reporters generally received at big corporate monopolies like the ones he knew. But then, she had been his best agent at one time and she had never failed him. He was just worried that she had been out of action for too long and was taking unnecessary risks she normally would not take.

Being a journalist, to his way of thinking, was one of those risks.

"I'll have clearance control make certain that you end up on the payroll of whatever media organization you finally chose. I have the bad feeling that any poking around into the deaths of these people, this late after their deaths, will cause certain people to take notice and certain checks to be made into your cover. We'll need to make certain that you're covered thoroughly. As for *Galileo Prime* and *Stargazer I,* I think it best if you go as an insurance inspector looking into the accident, a back-claim of some sort perhaps, maybe even death benefits for the relatives. That should raise the least eyebrows seeing that it seems to happen constantly these days. A newscast doesn't seem to go by without a story about some insurance company trying to cheat some grieving spouse out of their departed's life insurance."

79

"Sounds good. I've used that one before myself. Listen, I'm starved. I'm going to go downstairs for a bite."

"I'll escort you," he said, rubbing his extended belly caressingly. "It takes a lot of work to keep up this fine physique."

She looked at his belly as they exited the room. "Looks to me as if you already have most everything in there. Why the hell did you let yourself waste away like this? This isn't the man I remember. I assume he's still in there somewhere, lost in all that flubber."

They walked down the corridor to the elevator. "It wasn't easy, let me tell you," he intoned with a fake, serious took, patting his hard bulge of a stomach once again. "It takes a lot of effort to look this good."

They sat in the corner of the small cafeteria provided for the exclusive use of those working on the more sensitive concepts and designs. The room was habitually scanned for listening devices and the walls were made of a sound absorbing material making it almost impossible to hear the conversation of the table next to you, even if you were inclined to eavesdrop. At this time in the morning it was more or less empty, the few tables occupied on the other side of the room by scientists and workers huddled together whispering quietly over Danish and coffee or sitting alone, staring off into space blankly as they sipped their orange juice and chewed over last night's failures.

The majority of the workers had already arrived and eaten their breakfast an hour earlier. The night shift had already left for their mundane and dismal homes in the rain-drenched city below, to sleep the day away and then begin life anew with the coming of the night and the dawning of a new work period.

Alexis drank the last of her orange juice, small-scattered syrup-covered remnants all that remained of the pecan pancakes she had devoured in her hunger. Cav was still busy on his double order of ham and cheese omelet with sausages, grilled hash-browns, a stack of pancakes, a bagel with cream-cheese and a bowl of grits. She watched him gobble his food down with a relish she found so typical of those who enjoyed their food so much that it showed in their physique, a smile creeping into the corner of her mouth and reflected in her eyes.

"I can still remember when you used to be a vegetarian and you'd criticize people who ate what you're devouring at the moment," she commented as she pushed her plate away and leaned on the table with both elbows.

"That was during my psychotic stage," he said out of the corner of his mouth as he ingested a large hunk of pork sausage, not deeming it necessary to stop eating just to answer her observation. "I'm cured of that now, but it certainly was a test of my will power."

She raised an eyebrow, then leaned back so as stay out of reach of his fork in case he decided that the food on the table wasn't enough.

He finally finished, wiping his mouth with an already dirty napkin and looking up at her bemused smile. "Any connections between the others?" he asked as he reached for his coffee and took a large gulp.

"Well, it's certainly an interesting collection of people. None of them are really tops in their fields or well known for anything recent, or even well known. The neuro-surgeon Dr. Pratali is the most difficult. The others I can almost see working together on something because they all seem connected in some remote way to computers. But this doctor is completely out in left field."

"How do you tie the geneticist in with the others? He doesn't seem to fit in either."

"Well, I actually thought that at first also, but that conference that Kido and Alex attended ties her in somehow. If you think about it, that conference and that particular seminar don't really fit either of their profiles. As for Dr. Dumvo, his work can easily fall into what Alex was reportedly working on without that much of a stretch. I've reading up a lot on nano-technology and its recent applications to industry and every day life. Ever since the break through of Vasilieva and Berkinshire, that field has just exploded with potential. Since it's so new, I can easily see a connection there that I'm not aware of the moment."

Cav's beeper went off to a melody of rather comic proportions. He listened a moment in his earpiece, nodded at the information. He finished his coffee and the last spoonful of grits, which had been staring at him wanting to be eaten for the last few minutes, then rose. "Your documentation's ready, as well as your weapons. A personal hov is standing by, untraceable to this agency."

She rose with him. "You sure you don't want to get something to go? I can't even begin to imagine that that was enough to keep you going more than a few minutes."

– The term hov had come into popular usage thirty years ago with the advent of the first successful hovercraft for personal use. They are now everywhere, replacing the ground-based car with its pollution spewing internal combustion engine running off of petroleum as easily as the automobile replaced the replaced the horse-draw buggy at the beginning of the twentieth century.

"Ha, ha," he muffled at her in a mocking tone, unable suppress the smile that came to his lips. "When did you become such a comedian?"

"You should know. You're the one who put it in my genes...."

As for the fool, he hears not, he can do nothing.
He lives on that of which one dies;
his food is untruth.
— *Ancient Chinese Proverb*

9

10 August 2085, 0900 hrs.
Boston, USA

Alexis stepped out of her silver Mercedes-1450LS hov at the entrance to the branch office of Surya industries, the multi-conglomerate computer company that had arisen out of the Indian sub-continent after the break up of the Microsoft monopoly in the early part of the century. That slow and agonizing spin down of that once all-powerful monopoly had spawned off, in record time, smaller, viciously competitive companies in the wake of its demise like feeding piranha. This was where her late son had been employed, where his office had been a little over five months ago. It had been where his life was, a life she had never known and a life that had, somehow, led to his death.

She was now sporting a mane of luxurious red hair flowing down to her shoulder blades in cascades of liquid fire, the bright green of her now emerald eyes flaring from beneath her small, fashionable sunglasses as she looked out from under them at the men who stood gawking at her from the entrance as if she were some Indian goddess come to claim their libidos. The lavender silk blouse she had selected so carefully didn't flaunt her bralessness, merely suggested it. She wore no perfume or jewelry, just a thin golden coin glittering in the morning sun shining down between the skyscrappers of man's vanity in shafts of amber glory

Her short, pleated golden-colored skirt accentuated her curves as she walked, her long tan legs strong and firm, her lack of pantyhose like a magnet to the eyes of those who would undress her in an instant. She carried only a small, white purse containing her recorder and pocket computer, more than enough to conduct any interview. It also contained a system to download any computer file off of any computer to which she got near, palm-sized for easy concealment and use. She also carried a small handgun, made of the most advanced polymer plastics and guaranteed to defeat any metallic scanning system. It held more than enough of a punch to take down a man at a hundred meters; make that same man unrecognizable by his kin at point-blank. She could not foresee any possible use for the weapon here and that was the primary reason she had brought it along: the unforeseen.

She walked right passed the ogling men standing by the entrance to Surya Industries, their eyes plastered all over her body like leeches. She stopped, pulled out a small piece of paper from her purse as if she were checking for the final time the address and at the same time planted a suggestion into the men's mind that they were actually homosexual and found each other rather attractive.

She looked at them from behind the anonymity of her dark sunglasses, saw the confused looks on their faces as their eyes moved from her body to each other's buttocks, then pushed the doors open and walked in.

The lobby was a brilliantly designed, multi-functional edifice combining modern art with the flair of old-Europe, designed by the famous Jyotikavi Gibson, whose architectural masterpieces graced several of the major cities of the world. That he had been convinced to design this corporate office spoke volumes for the influence of Surya Industries.

Long green tentacles of vibrant and healthy plants hung down from the multiple open terraces above, the center of the building opening up into a skylight designed to make it look as if the building was open right to the upper sky, allowing a wide-open feeling to permeate the lobby like a breath of fresh air. The rich carpet on which she strode beautifully matched the slender Doric columns and arches speaking of a refinement beyond the scope of the company.

She was surprised to find a weapon detector at the main entrance, new looking and not quite broke-in. It had not been included in the intelligence brief and it bode ill for the further success of this mission. She didn't like sloppy intelligence work. She had, in the past, never trusted the pre-mission work to anyone but herself. It was obvious that she was going to have to revert back to that true and tried practice. Nasty surprises like this were irritating.

She waited in the short line for the detector, the grumbling of those around her convincing her that this machine was not more a day old, if not new today. She stepped up to the first guard, her face set in a mask of seriousness and insolence at having to suffer the indignity of waiting and handed him her purse, giving a look of derision as he stared blatantly at her chest and legs. As he searched her purse thoroughly, she reached out with her mind, found the main processor for the detector and gave it a slight overload. There was a shower of sparks from behind the desk where the guards were stationed and they jumped out from behind, looking at the malfunctioning machine as if it might just get up and attack them. There were muffled giggles and a few curses at the delay and Alexis used the confusion to slip passed the checkpoint unseen, calmly making her way to the main hospitality desk and the sign-in log.

"I was almost killed by that damn thing," she accused in an overbearing tone, articulating her words with particular deliberation. "The management will be hearing about this, you can count on that."

The guard, a large, brute of a man who looked like he shaved with a blow-torch, looked right through Alexis as he spoke in a brusque, bass of a voice. "Name and purpose of visit."

She eyed him a moment. This one was not about to be distracted by sparks or malfunctioning hardware, nor probably if she were to strip naked in front of him and dance. This one was all business. "Katrina Templar. Journalist for the New York Times. I'm expected."

He took her ID card without once looking at her and ran it over the scanner, then indicated toward the palm reader with a bored detachment, taking a brief glance at her to make certain that she looked like the picture. She placed her hand on the reader and then stuck her eye over the retinal scan clumsily as if she had never experienced such a thing before. She was beginning to question such intense security for a computer company.

Industrial espionage had been rampant the last decade, especially in the higher technology fields, but that still didn't justify the heightened security, so out of place in the well-apportioned lobby. It was far too much of a coincidence that all this came about the week she came here to check out on her son's life.

It gave her one of those foreboding feelings she hated so much.

She stepped back from the security devices and waited impatiently as the guard ran his checks. "If you don't hurry, I'm going to be late and I'm never late," she spit out with snake's venom.

Those appeared to be the words needed to make the guard finally look at her face, his smile cold, emotionless. He handed her ID back to her. "Sorry for the delay, Mrs. Templar," he said with a sugary sweet voice, which didn't match his face. "If you go to the third elevator on your right, it'll take you directly to the fifty-first floor. Enjoy your stay."

She sneered at him rudely. "That's *Miss* Templar, thank you very much," she said with annoyance as she snatched her ID back and turned her back to the man.

The elevator door opened on the fifty-first floor to reveal a scene looking like any other large corporate vista, the numerous worker drone cubicles joined together in a system of mazes and corridors defying description, almost like an ant colony on a mega scale in its simplistic complexity. She could only imagine that the ants actually got more work done with less stress.

She was met by a short, older man with a lion's mane of gray hair, a high forehead, deep wrinkles speaking of long hours staring at a computer screen in his youth and a nose that seemed misplaced between his eyes as if he had found it in the trash. His eyes lit up when he saw her emerge from the elevator and he shook her hand in greeting far too feverishly.

She pulled her sunglasses off with practiced ease and looked at the man, afraid that he might never give her hand back now that he had a hold of it. Inside, she wanted to crack up laughing at his over-friendliness and obvious need for a social life with females. It was also apparent that reporters from the *New York Times* didn't make it to his department with much frequency and he was eager to make a good first impression with the hopes that perhaps more reporters who looked like Alexis would grace his floor with their presence. This poor man was about to make a fool out of himself in front of all his employees and he didn't even know it. He probably had the fat wife at home who ran his entire life for him right down to the underwear he had on and the times he was allowed to go to the bathroom at night.

"So very glad to meet you, Mrs. Templar," he drooled with a saccharine voice. He moved his hand with subtle dexterity around her waist to guide her forward through the rat-maze of cubicles. "I hope that we can make this a pleasant visit for you."

"First of all, it's *Miss* Templar and secondly, you can start making this a pleasant visit by removing your sweaty hand from around my waist. This is a Sergio De Gruni and it doesn't take well to perspiration from old men."

He removed his hand at once and smiled that awkward, unnatural smile

86

men affected when they realize that they were making fools of themselves but were not quite sure how. Alexis opened her purse, dropped her sunglasses in and then flipped her hair breathlessly as she scanned the floor and kept her eyes off of him.

"I really don't have much time for this, so if you'll just please direct me to where Mr...." She frowned, gave a sigh of disgust, then looked back into her purse to remove a small computer pad and stabbed at a few keys. "Dr. Alexander Hart worked and I'll start there."

His smile stayed plastered onto his face as if it had frozen there until the words she had spoken and their implications sank into his Cro-Magnum brain. His smile finally faded like a rainy sunset as it dawned on him that this woman didn't want to have anything to do with him ... and he had struck out once again. He had probably tried this same approach with every attractive female on this floor and Alexis would be surprised if any of them had fallen for it.

"Of course, of course. Yes ... I understand completely ...." he spilled out with red splotching his face and massive drops of sweat escaping from his shiny forehead. "It's this way." He walked away from her with his head slightly bend down as if he didn't want anyone to see him at this particular moment. He left her alone after he showed her where Alex had once worked, her dismissal with a distracted wave of her hand like a mortal blow to his male ego.

There were four individuals who had easy access to the cubicle wherein Alex had worked. She would begin with them. She stepped up to the first cubicle and found a bird-like man with a hunched back and nervous movements speaking volumes into his computer interface at a speed that she was certain made only every fifth word register on the document he was writing. He nearly jumped off his chair when she spoke. He turned to stare right at her breasts, skipping the first look at her face that most civilized people try to accomplish.

When he finally did look up at her face, he had one of those stupid, happy grins attached making him look moronic to the extreme.

"You done?" she asked with hands on hips.

"Huh?" he queried in a squeaky little voice she had half-expected to come from his tiny mouth.

"If you've done undressing me mentally, I'd like to ask you a few questions," she clarified for him with an air of impatience and insolence.

His eyes widened at the accusation – and at the fact that he had been caught red-handed – and his cheeks turned bright red as he turned his face away from her and giggled like an adolescent.

She shook her head and sighed. How could she have possibly forgotten how difficult it was to deal with most people? It had been one of the primary reasons for her moving to such an isolated spot in Alaska. People today were morons, plain and simple. The men had only sex on their minds, the women only fashion and neither sex had a clue what they looked like from the outside.

A mellifluous voice saved her from having to slap this immature geek around a little. "You'll have to excuse Clovis here. He doesn't get out much."

Clovis? Who the hell would torture their son by naming him Clovis? "I can see why," she commented as she turned to take in this new arrival to her growing party of morons.

Clovis' savior was a young, dark-haired woman in her late twenties with melting bedroom eyes shadowed by an over abundance of make-up and long, tentacle-like lashes looking completely out of place among the rat-maze. She was almost as tall as Alexis, buxom – her loose shirt revealing far more cleavage than Alexis thought prudent for an office environment, the black bra obvious through the translucent shirt – with tight slacks conforming to a not-very-skinny lower body, bulges abounding where the fat had been compressed to fit like undulating waves at the beach.

Alexis never understood those women who insisted on wearing clothes that didn't fit them, making them look far worse than if they had just wore a size larger and not attempted to look like a super-model on parade. It was a virus affecting society that she didn't miss one bit while living in her cabin these last fifteen years. If you wanted to look skinny, then watch what you ate. Wearing clothes two sizes too small was not the answer to any problem.

The woman stuck her hand out toward Alexis. "Hi. I'm Valerie. Valerie Yeats." She had one of those faces that always seemed happy and a smile that was contagious if not permanent. "I heard that a reporter from the Times was coming here to interview a couple of us, but I didn't believe the rumors. People are always making up stories around here just to see how far they can spread them." Her voice rose and fell with the words like a song and Alexis half expected a giggle to come out of that large mouth at the end of every sentence.

Fortunately for Alexis, that didn't occur.

"This is Clovis Barks," she said in way of introduction as she pointed toward the bird-like man who was still giggling. "Funny name, huh?"

Alexis pulled her hand away from Valerie before the woman made it a permanent attachment.

"He's been here at this company a long time. Knows everyone. And everyone. Came over originally from India in the first wave of corporate expansion of Surya Industries. He's one of those genius types that never gets the recognition he deserves because he's shy and not very aggressive, but once you get to know him he's an alright sort of guy. Very polite and gentlemanly, if you know what I mean." She patted Alexis on the forearm as if they had known each other for years.

Alexis was unsure if the woman had even taken a breath during that exposition and was waiting for her to fall over from lack of oxygen. But she nodded nonetheless as if all this superfluous information was of vital importance to her life. "I'm Katrina Templar. And yes, I'm from the Times, here to do a story on Dr. Alexander Hart and his untimely death. Did either of you know him at all? I was told that he used to work here in this cubicle." She was having trouble seeing a son of hers working like a bee drone at a job that was senseless and getting him nowhere. What type of parents would allow him to waste his life like that?

She mentally chastised herself.

She needed to remember that he was not her son in the true sense of the word. Sure he was her biological off-spring but the connection stopped there and whatever it was that his real parents did or didn't do for him was no longer her concern, if it ever was and she needed to concentrate on what she was doing before she mis-spoke and blew her cover wide open. She was certain that there were cameras everywhere filming everything with men in dark glasses watching to make certain that she was whom she said she was.

Clovis stopped giggling long enough to speak a few words. "Katrina's a pretty name, Mrs. Templar."

"It's Miss ... never mind," Alexis aborted as she gave this social misfit one of her rare, broad smiles and the poor man appeared to have a small coronary where he sat. "Did either of you know Dr. Hart?"

"Alex? Oh sure we knew him. He was a great guy. Real cute too, if you know what I mean," Valerie said with an over-exaggerated wink and another pat on the arm that was becoming very annoying. Alexis might have to break that arm off before the interview was over. "He was always so nice to everyone. It was really terrible what happened to him over there in Greece. He was so looking forward to that trip and then he drowns. Isn't that just the shits?"

"It was Egypt," Alexis clarified, though she was not sure why she even bothered.

Valerie gave her a quizzical look. "There's a difference?"

"I think he was murdered," Clovis blurted out like a sudden bark of a dog.

Alexis looked at him with her with penetrating eyes, thankful for not having to answer Valerie's geography conundrum. She reached into her purse and pulled out her pocket computer, setting it for record. "Why would you say something like that, Clovis? Is it okay if I call you Clovis?"

"You can call me whatever you want, Mrs. Templar," he responded with another round of giggles and a fresh paint of red on his face.

"Good. Now, why would you say that Dr. Hart was murdered? That's a pretty strong accusation." She had to remind herself to stay in character. A reporter would jump all over his admission while Alexis herself wanted to drag him into a back room and drain his brain of everything he knew.

"Because he was always working in the restricted area at nights and right before he left on his trip to *Egypt*" – he looked over at Valerie as if amazed that she could find the bathroom with her great sense of geography – "he told me confidentially that he was onto something huge. I mean really big,"

Alexis wondered how many other people her son told the same thing. He didn't seem all that concerned with the confidentially of this big project if he told this Clovis. Perhaps he was one of those people who were more concerned with letting people know that he had a secret than with actually keeping it a secret. But the words, which Clovis had just spoken, told her more than the hours she had spend poring over the data Cav had at his disposal. There was something here after all. "What restricted area?" she asked softly.

Valerie chimed in quickly, as if Clovis had perhaps let loose a company secret that might get them all fired ... or worse. "It's not really a *restricted* area. At least it wasn't for Alex. I mean, it is restricted in the sense of the word but Alex had access to it and so to him it really wasn't all that restricted, if it could be called restricted to him at all." Valerie seemed confused for a moment with her own words. Then she looked back at Alexis and smiled, as if suddenly remembering that she had been talking. "Alex was promoted to that area about seven months or so before his death. It's up on the seventieth floor. Well, actually, he worked here and there, so I guess it really wasn't all that much of a promotion." She looked around now to see if anyone else was listening, then continued as she leaned slightly forward and lowered her voice. "Since he had access, he went there a lot at night, during off hours, logging over-time I suppose." She leaned even closer and Clovis did the same to hear what was being said. "He used to work on his own projects ... You know, things that the company would frown on if they were discovered, things that they weren't paying him for."

Alexis nodded as if she understood perfectly. However, she found it extremely hard to believe that a company as security conscious as Surya Industries would allow an employee, any employee to use their equipment for personal projects. The truth about Alex was probably more along the lines of extra work to get a project running he had been assigned and which was proving far more difficult to finish than anticipated. If he truly had been promoted, she doubted that her son would be foolish enough to jeopardize it by doing something against company policy right away.

Anyway, even if Alex was using the company computers for his own work, it would certainly be a reason for his dismissal but not his murder. No one was that competitive.

She felt his presence behind her long before she smelled his sick, cloying and over-powering cologne that should have never been sold to humans. She probed the mind and found that it was, not surprisingly, a male in his late forties, eyeing her ass and imagining it bumping before him as he had her bent over a sofa in the back office. She registered that his minuscule mind held very little besides his pornographic fantasy.

She turned to face him and he brought his eyes up slowly from his perusal of her ass, not in the least bit ashamed, it seemed, that he was undressing her in such a blatant fashion.

"Vell, vell ," he said in a little voice holding more connotations than a dictionary. "I didn't know that they made reporters who looked like thiz. Zamachetelny." His Russian accent was thick and obnoxious, almost as cloying as his cologne.

She appraised him a moment, smiling as if he actually had a chance of getting her into bed. "And I didn't know that they had assholes who could talk. Amazing what technology can do these days, isn't it?"

Clovis guffawed loudly and several heads peeked out of cubicles to see what the commotion was.

The Russian seemed completely non-pulsed by the comment, probably because he didn't understand it fully. "Feisty. I like that. Bez perevoda." He moved closer, a near impossibility as he was already standing so close to her, his presence like a wet, woolen blanket.

Alexis backed up a step and gave him her best vicious stare. She had dealt with these men before and knew that they thrived on fear and at the moment, she feared that he meant to kiss her. Nausea coiled in her stomach. "Back off, big boy, before I have to hurt you."

Valerie stepped between them and took hold of the Russian's arm, pushing him away slightly in a subtle way that Alexis found impressive. She might not know the difference between Greece and Egypt, but she certainly knew her way around men. "This piece of male chauvinism is Vladimir Puskin. He knew Alex also, though Alex didn't really want to know him." She smiled up at him.

Vladimir looked down at Valerie appreciatively, his eyes taking in her open shirt vulgarly as he smiled at her and began to chew what Alexis took to be gum, his mouth working like a cow on steroids. "That be not fair, Val. Alex and me make big plans, go many places where women like to fuck." He pronounced the word as if his mouth were doing the deed right there and then, drawn out and grotesque in its imagery. "Women like reporter here, but not so cold, da?" His Russian accent had gotten stronger and made his speech almost comical. He hugged Valerie to him and managed to fondle a breast on the sly. "Perhaps cold reporter be willing to come tonight to club where women want to fuck, da? Ve have good time, you see."

Alexis could tell that he was undressing her again and his surface thoughts began to give her a headache, the disgusting images he was percolating through that pea-sized bundle of nerve fibers coming close to making her physically ill. Where did they raise these people? "Nyet," she answered smoothly, switching into Russian with such ease that it took Vladimir off guard. "You are by far too small a man to please me."

His face fell a moment, then he squeezed Valerie to his side even tighter, perhaps trying to make up for his failure with a free fondle of Valerie's body. "You interest me, pretty woman," he dragged out with his smile not losing one decibel of clarity.

Alexis turned back toward Clovis, who was following all that was said with a wide grin of understanding, his eyes telling Alexis that he agreed with her assessment of Vladimir completely. "So you happen to know what Alex was working on in the restricted areas that was so confidential."

Clovis made to answer but Vladimir cut him off with such practiced ease that she could tell he made a habit of it. "The funny little man knows nothing. Alex was company man, worked hard for company. Nothing more." He had let go of Valerie and was standing with feet apart, staring at Alexis with such blatant sexual connotations that Alexis wished the man would just go away.

But she did notice that the tone of his voice changed slightly when he spoke of Alex and the restricted areas, a subtle change to be sure but a change that told her that he was hiding something he thought important. She reached out with her mind and found the floor manager who had greeted her at the elevator and planted within his mind the idea that he needed to see Vladimir immediately.

92

It was not but a few seconds before the floor manager's voice came over the intercom system, demanding that Vladimir come to his office forthwith. The Russian made to take her hand and kiss it but she reached into her purse as he leaned forward, taking away the opportunity. He bowed instead with his greasy smile dripping pheromones all over the carpet, then gave Valerie a peck on the cheek and squeeze of ass eliciting a tiny squeak from her and left the area. "I vill be back to conversate, Miss Templar."

"Let's hope not," she whispered under her breath as he walked away.

Both Valerie and Clovis heard her and stifled laughs until he disappeared around the nearest corner.

"He can be too much sometimes," Valerie commented as she straightened her shirt a little, giving Alexis a half-smile that told her she also hated the man's presence. "But what are you going to do? He's part of the team and I have ... I mean we have to get along with him regardless how obnoxious he is."

"You could always kick him real hard in the balls. Maybe he'd get the message that way if no isn't enough for him," Alexis offered as she tried to clear her mind of Vladimir's presence.

Clovis laughed again, tears starting to come out of his eyes and snot out of his nose. "I like you. You're funny."

She gave the short man a half-smile and his whole face lit up. "I can't see how he doesn't fall in love with himself."

"I think he did that already and thus doesn't understand why the girls around here don't do the same thing," Valerie said with a glint in her eyes.

"Was Dr. Hart really working on something personal at night?" Alexis needed to get this conversation back on track before the higher up corporate types noticed her spending all this time down here and took umbrage.

Clovis and Valerie looked at her a moment as if hesitating at what to tell her, then Valerie indicated with a tip of her head to the ceiling. Alexis didn't have to look to understand the implications. The room was monitored and they had probably told her too much already. She wondered what it must be like to work for such a company that didn't even trust its own employees. "I understand. Is there somewhere more private where we could talk? Perhaps lunch? I'll pay."

Alexis was a little confused when Clovis went back to his computer and began to type away frantically, shoulders hunched and face absorbed in whatever it was before him. Valerie looked down at the floor as if pondering the question and not sure how to answer.

Then Alexis realized that there was yet another presence behind her, a presence that had snuck up on her while she was clearing her mind of Vladimir's filth. It was powerful, far more in control of its surface thoughts than the Russian had been. She turned to find a tall, dark-skinned man at the corner of the corridor dressed in an expensive suit and tie, face chiseled with one of those aristocratic airs speaking of a superiority which he didn't possess but which he tried to project to those around him forcefully. He had a blinding, bone-melting smile that seemed to be lit from within and a charm around him Alexis found quite disturbing. *Of course he's charming*, she thought to herself as he made his way toward her, swaggering with supreme confidence in his virility. *He probably practices in front of his mirror.*

His voice was a husky rumble as he addressed her. "Miss Templar, I presume? Perhaps I can be of more help than these two. They should really be getting back to work now. They've wasted enough of your precious time, haven't they?" The words had barely left his mouth when Valerie disappeared around a wall and Clovis cowered down even more before his interface.

Alexis arched an eyebrow. "And you would be?" This man had an unquestioned and unchallengeable power here and it was as she had feared. She had spent too much time talking here in the office and those who considered themselves more important had taken notice. For all intents and purposes, her information gathering here at Surya Industries was at an end.

He stepped forward and offered his large hand, his eyes never once leaving hers. He didn't check out her body, didn't mentally undress her as most men did. This one was smooth and knew what he was doing. He had been sent to get her away from Valerie and Clovis and what they might inadvertently let slip. This one was more than confident in his power here and his ability with women to have to ogle her. He probably already knew what she looked like naked and found it boring.

She probed casually with her mind and found a strong, powerful image of a man who knew exactly what he wanted and how he was going to get it and she was not a part of that overall plan. At the moment, he wanted Alexis in his office and away from those who might tell her something she had no need of knowing.

"Avery Spielman. Executive vice-president in charge of system analysis, at your service. We here are Surya Industries are always happy to cooperate with the press."

By cooperate, he probably meant showing her to the front door. She didn't bother to take his proffered hand or to acknowledge his title and position and she noticed a slight twitch in his blinding smile, but no other obvious sign marred his chiseled face and hawk-like eyes, the type to see everything at once. "I was doing just fine with the two employees I was talking to," she said with scorn. "I don't need to hear the company line from you. I was guaranteed free access to any employee I wanted to interview and this does not constitute free access to me."

"Let me take you up to my office and I'll be more than happy to answer any questions you might have about our operations here."

"And Dr. Hart? Will you answer my questions about him also?"

"Of course." He indicated for her to walk toward the elevators. "We have nothing to hide here."

Translation: we don't talk about Dr. Hart or anything he was working on, she thought to herself as she stood her ground, as any good reporter would, and looked at him with impatience and impudence. "What goes on in the restricted areas that Dr. Hart worked in?"

His dark eyes looked foreboding under his bald-head. He looked at her a moment without answering, as if trying to decide whether it was Clovis or Valerie who had opened their big mouths and thus which one he should fire. "We have many restricted areas, Miss. Templar. You'll need to be a little more specific with your questions. And even then, they *are* restricted areas and I'm not really sure how much I can tell you that you don't already know."

"Did Dr. Hart work in one of these many restricted areas?" She held her recorder up a little as if to indicate that she was recording all this and might want to be more forthcoming.

"Yes, he did. Please?" He indicated again with his arm for her to move toward the elevators. "Let's go up to my office where we can sit down and have a nice, civilized conversation."

"This corridor is just fine, thank you."

Clovis stood up with a start and ran down the corridor toward the restrooms, his face screwed up as if he were going to puke at any second and hoping that he made it to the toilet before then. He had probably never heard anyone talk to Mr. Avery Spielman like that before and didn't want to be around when the shit hit the fan.

"I'm afraid that I must insist, Miss Templar." There was now an undercurrent in his voice setting off alarms in Alexis' mind. She eyed him darkly a moment as she probed his mind a little deeper, not sensing any form of mental powers to counter her own. She did find that he was becoming rather disturbed at her stubbornness and arrogance toward him and was not used to people openly defying him like this, in view of all his little worker drones.

And there was also a note of panic within him, perhaps even of confusion as to why this reporter, at this time, was poking around for answers about a man who had died months ago. It made him inwardly nervous. Of course, she found within his surface thoughts anything she might want to know about the restricted areas wherein Alex had worked. As with most humans, the simple act of expressing the existence of something caused the mind to bring involuntarily forward information on that subject for ready access in a subconscious summoning. There was nothing new or interesting there that caught her attention. It was all rather mundane. Whatever it was that her son was doing had nothing to do with the company, that was for certain.

"In that case," she said as she put her pocket computer back into her purse. "I guess I'd better go with you."

Avery's office was large. It was not as large as Cav's, but large enough to give the impression that it was an office of command, the modern art adorning the walls and pillars in the corners striking in their ugliness. The expansive, ceiling-tall windows over-looked downtown Boston with a commanding view, the myriad of hovercraft passing by on their way to somewhere unimportant like a busy hive of bees.

He indicated for her to sit down in one of the over-comfortable chairs as he moved to the bar. They always seemed to have a bar. Whether they drank or not, the high-rollers always needed to have that status symbol in their office as if it meant something to those who dreamt of being here one day. Avery, however, did appear to drink and poured himself a scotch on the rocks.

"My I offer you a drink, Miss Templar?"

"This isn't a social meeting, Mr. Spielman. Now about Dr. Hart and those restricted areas ...?" She didn't take the pre-offered seat, preferring to stand in situations like this if the need to react quickly became necessary. She pulled her pocket computer back out and looked at him insolently.

He finished fixing his drink and put the bottle back to the clink of expensive glass, then walked back slowly and deliberately to his over-large desk where he stood, looking out the expansive window with his back to her. "I find it strange that a reporter for the *New York Times* would be so interested in a nobody like Dr. Hart, over two months after he dies of a tragic accident in Egypt on a non-company related vacation." Now he turned to look at her as he sat down, unbuttoning his jacket and placing his glass on the shiny desk, which was unusually empty of anything that even looked remotely business related.

In fact, she noted with amusement, the desk was practically empty.

"Perhaps you could enlighten me as to why that is. And you can put that computer away, my dear. This room is shielded and emits blocking signals that'll make any recording you make nothing but gibberish." His voice had the tone of quiet authority. This was no vice-president in charge of system analysis. This was the company's resident enforcer.

She looked at him from under her eyebrows for a moment, then put the computer back in her purse, a facetious smile playing across her lips. "I don't think it would go over too well with your bosses if they discovered that you hampered me in my investigation, or with the public for that matter if I print that one of the biggest companies in the world believes themselves above the inquiries of the free press."

"Is that a threat?" he asked as he lifted his glass to his lips and sipped.

"Not in the least bit. It's a simple statement of fact. Now, the question that I'm asking is a rather simple one: was Dr. Hart working in one of the restricted areas and did it have anything to do with his suspicious death?" She could care less anymore about the restricted areas or what this man had to tell her about them but she had to put up a good front before she left. There was something more here than Surya's insistent need to protect its patent rights or it industrial secrets.

"Because it certainly sounded like a threat to me and I for one don't like to be threatened by piss-ant reporters who think that they can just demand answers from anyone." He was now scrutinizing her with narrowed eyes. Then with a suddenness that almost made Alexis assume a defensive stance, he rose and buttoned his jacket. "This interview is over. Good day."

She was slightly shocked at the rather abrupt end to their conversation, though it was hardly unexpected. She raised an eyebrow as he walked to the door and opened it for her. He was apparently done talking and would say no more. She raised her chin up slightly and walked out, talking over her shoulder as she did so. "My editors will be in contact with your bosses about this rudeness, Mr. Spielman, you can count on that." She stopped at the threshold of the door. "You'll be hearing from us."

"Of that I have no doubt." He closed the door and it actually bumped her forward as it hit her rear with a thud of finality. She turned to look at the door, pretended to mess in her purse for something, smiling at the secretary as she did so. She checked to make certain that her little device for emptying the contents of any computer had been turned on – it was. Blocking emitters her ass – then probed back into the closed room to find out what it was that Mr. Spielman would do now, whom he would call.

But there was nothing worthwhile for her catch.

He had, apparently, completely pushed her out of his mind and was now thinking of concepts and meetings he had on his schedule today. She found this a little disconcerting. He either was aware of her mental abilities and was waiting patiently until she left before reporting or he actually was that anal-retinal when it came to his job. Either way it made for a scary individual.

This was, apparently, not going to be easy.

A smile attached itself to her face as the elevator took her rapidly down to the ground floor. She stepped out into the bright light that was the street and placed her sunglasses over her eyes. She looked around and saw that there where not any bruisers waiting for her here, waiting to rough her up so that she got the message to not look any further into Alex Hart's death, at least not any who wanted to make themselves known.

Trees and grass had replaced the ugly main streets, which had marred most American cities over the past two centuries, the introduction of the hov and the abandonment of the internal combustion automobiles making such streets superfluous. Benches and street vendors now replaced the pollution belching cars and their petroleum dependence, making not only the air cleaner but the general feel of the city far more relaxed.

She took a deep breath, then looked back up at the building from which she had just exited as it rose like a giant finger making a vulgar gesture to the heavens, its sail-boom construction making it look almost artistic. She frowned. Unless she could find more information in the computer files she had managed to copy from Clovis' and Spielman's interfaces, this had been a waste of time and it didn't bode well for her future interactions with those who had once known the deceased.

A hand touched her arm lightly and she turned briskly to see what it was, the distraction of the grass and trees and sunlight causing her to miss the person's approach. Clovis stood next to her, a light windbreaker with the hood up covering his head so that only she could see that it was he. He looked nervous, even frightened, his large intelligent eyes pleading at her like a lost puppy's.

"They all think that I don't know what goes on around here, that I'm out of touch with what others say and do," he said in hurried phrases, his eyes darting around like excited fish. "But I know what's up. Alex told me."

The valet brought her Mercedes around as Clovis finished talking and she indicated for him to get in as she moved over to the driver's side and sped away.

"I need to be back soon else they'll notice that I'm no longer in the bathroom and come looking for me. They have a very strict rule about breaks and accountability during working hours," he informed her as he keenly inspected the interior of the Mercedes, speaking with repressed emotions.

She figured that they already knew that he had left the building but figured that telling him that would only make him more nervous and perhaps shut him up entirely. "How long do we have before they notice?"

"I'd say about fifteen minutes. I bypassed the main cameras in the stairwell and went out the back service entrance carrying a box like I was a loader. Nice hov. Is this the newer version or last year's?"

She raised an eyebrow slightly. This Clovis was more on the ball than she gave him credit. "Why do you think that Dr. Hart was murdered?"

He didn't seem to care that she had ignored his question about the hov, or perhaps he was so used to it that it no longer affected him. "Alex used to confide in me. I think he took pity on me because people like Vladimir always picked on me and made working here a living nightmare sometimes. You know, the guy who doesn't fit in, who the girls are always laughing about behind his back." A tight smile crossed her lips. "Anyway, Alex was a real good guy. Classy, not like Vladimir described at all. He used to tell me how he would get out of going to the strip bars and sexual entertainment districts with the oaf and we'd get a chuckle out of it. We used to talk about baseball and stuff. Even went to a few games. The Sox are doing pretty good this year. May even win the pennant for the first time since '04."

She parked the Mercedes in the middle of a park under a stand of old elms several kilometers away from Surya Industries and turned to look at him. The last thing she needed was to hear this person's life story. "Alex, Clovis. What was he working on that no one wants to talk about?"

"I know about Kido," he said almost apologetically, looking down at his hands and then back up at her face and smiling halfheartedly.

"What about her?"

"She and Alex had an idea, an idea that came from that Dr. Godonov on *Galileo Prime*. He wouldn't't' tell me what it was but he said that it was big. I mean, really big, like world changing big."

"Did it have anything to do with the restricted areas?"

He shrugged. "Not really. I mean, I don't think so. I don't see how he could use them for anything but research for Surya. They aren't like normal computers. Not these. And anyway, there isn't too much special that goes on at this branch office, so they don't have the real good machines here."

"How do you know that nothing special goes on here?"

He looked at her, his wide, beaming smile indicating the pride he felt in the knowledge he was about to impart. "I broke into the security system a few days after I was assigned to this office. I know all the projects that're currently being worked on here. And let me tell you, there isn't anything special here."

She looked at him with a higher level of respect. She knew from experience that what he was relating to her was not the easiest thing to do. Breaking in was simply enough. It was the part about not getting caught that was the catchall. Almost any third-rate hack could break into such a system. It was only the extremely talented ones who managed to escape detection, especially for as long as Clovis had been doing it. "So then what was Dr. Hart doing in the restricted areas at night? I find it hard to believe that he had that much extra work to do."

A dog barking close by made him jump, looking out the tinted windows for the man he was certain would bring his life to an end. It took several minutes before he was calmed down enough to continue, wiping sweat from his brow and looking at her with a smile of guilty obsession. "Sorry."

"I understand. You're playing with fire breaking into Surya's secure areas like that."

He shrugged again. "It's not that bad, really. They think they've got such a good system that they don't even bother to look for certain anomalies."

"And you're the anomaly?"

His face lost a little of the paleness it had acquired and he looked down at his hands again shyly. "He was using one of the larger machines to run simulations. Strictly off disc, or downloaded from an exterior source with a secure web-clip attached to prevent back-logging. He was good, I'll give him that much. Almost as good as I am. He never left a trace, even one that I could find and that's damn good." His face lit up as his eyes moved off her and stared blankly out the hov window. He laughed slightly, then looked back at her. "He even had a program to erase the master bus that logs all the e-mails coming and going from Surya so that there was never a trace of any of the communications between him and Kido and Godonov." He paused a moment as if reflecting back on a joyous memory. "And there was another person, though they used an alias and a series of multiple line-links so that no one could ever trace the line back to them. That was something else."

Now she was getting somewhere. Clovis had given her the link between Alex, Kido and Godonov and most likely one of the others. Now if she could just figure out what they were working on that would cause them to all be killed. "Simulations of what, Clovis?"

"That I really don't know. He never told me and I could never find any trace of the programs after he ran them." He looked at her again with those intense, intelligent eyes. "I have something for you." He reached down the

100

front of his pants and for a bad moment, Alexis thought that he was going to expose himself and ask for some kind of sexual favor for the information he had given her.

If this had all been a charade to satisfy the man's erotic lust, she was going to have to hurt him badly. She turned her head away from him and acted as disgusted as her character would, putting a hand over her eyes as if to shield them from nature's own creation. She probed his mind and found that sexual thoughts were the furthest thing from Clovis' mind, found, in fact, that the man was simultaneously working out several work-related problems while also holding this discussion with her. She was impressed yet again.

When he saw that she had turned her head away from him, he turned a bright crimson, looking down at his pulled-forward pants, the black, crinkly pubic hairs looking out hesitantly and realizing what he had just done. He finished pulling the disc out of his underwear. "I'm so sorry. I didn't think about that, it's just that ... er ... well, it's easiest to hide such things there because there aren't too many security guards willing to pat down a guy there, if you know what I mean. Really, Mrs. Templar, I didn't mean anything by it. Honest."

She turned back to look at him, at the disc he held tentatively in his hand and thought about where it had recently been and if she really wanted to touch it.

He noticed and wiped the disc thoroughly on his shirt, then offered it to her again. " Alex gave this to me before he left on his trip to Egypt. It's his journal and other related items. He told me that if anything should happen to him, I was to give it to someone who would know what to do with it ... and ...er.... um ...I think that's you, Mrs. Templar."

She took it, inwardly ecstatic that she finally had a hold of someone's journal, a record of what they had been working on and perhaps the clue that would break this conundrum wide open. "Do you know where the simulations might be?" It was a long shot but worth asking.

"No. He never told me where they were or even about them. I figured that out on my own. Here." He pushed it toward her again. She took the CD and put it into her purse quickly in case he changed his mind.

"But if it helps, Kido was also working on the same simulations, so it's possible that she might have a copy somewhere."

She patted his hand tenderly and he blushed. "Thank you, Clovis. I'll take good care of this and make sure that the public finds out about what a good person Alex was." She turned the ignition and lifted up off the ground, merging back into the traffic lanes above. "Why are you doing this? I mean, besides the fact that Alex asked you to do this. You're risking a lot doing this."

He shrugged again as she watched the landscape flash by outside. "I think Surya Industries had something to do with Alex's death. It was no accident. He was a good swimmer and had a life-vest on." He looked over at her. "I want the people who did this to pay and I think that there are clues in that journal that'll help you find them."

She nodded her head. This Clovis was a rare one indeed in these times of selfishness and uncaring. For him to put his life on the line for a man who wasn't even his friend spoke a lot about Clovis' character ... and Alex's.

"Could you please set me down a little bit away from the main entrance. I need to try to sneak back in with the workers in the back. I don't want anyone to know that I was talking to you," he said with a little more confidence than he had displayed before.

I think it's a little too late for that Clovis, she thought to herself as she set the Mercedes down a good half-kilometer from Surya Industries. She had the particular feeling that this man's life was about to be over. Companies like Surya rarely liked to have their employees running around talking to reporters, much less breaking into their secure files.

Clovis opened the door, then closed it again and looked at her. "Thank you for believing me and not treating me like I have the plague or something."

"You take care of yourself, Clovis. I'll check back in a week or so and let you know if I've found anything."

He opened the door again and climbed out. "I don't think that would be a good idea. I'll just look for it in the paper."

Alexis leaned over as he started to close the door and blocked it from closing. "Did you read any of this, Clovis?"

He pulled his hood back over his head to obscure his face. "No, but I'm pretty sure I know what's on it. At least I think I do."

"Do yourself a favor, Clovis, and forget that you ever saw this CD, or me. You never saw it and Alex never gave it to you. Okay? It's for your own protection. When this story breaks, the company big-wigs are going to come down hard on everyone in Alex's old department and it'd be better if they had no reason to suspect you."

He smiled again, then turned and walked away, melting back into the crowd on the walkways, which wound their way like a living river toward Surya Industries, becoming yet another faceless drone in the ocean that was corporate America. She watched him a moment, then pulled the CD back out of her purse and looked at it.

She was not going to get excited over the contents until she had a chance to look at them critically, but she was certain of one thing now: Japan was going to be her next stop.

Wisdom for a man's self is the wisdom of rats,
that will be sure to leave a house somewhat before it falls.
— *Francis Bacon*

10

10 August 2085, 1203 hrs

She sat in front of the small, corner deli, half of a large pastrami and rye with extra mustard sitting on her plate, the pickle already eaten, the diet drink fizzling in the cup as the afternoon sun passed the zenith, heating up the slight breeze barely moving the awning over her head. She was watching the people as they walked passed along the avenue or lounged on the grassy lanes, eating, playing, sun-bathing, sleeping on their lunch breaks like they did every day, their lives a routine of repeated acts making time pass by in their cursory lives from one season to the next in a pageant of somber and joyous procession.

She had once enjoyed people-watching, seeing what people did, how they acted, what they wore that made them think they were special or sexy or comfortable while all the time simply conforming to trends set into place by large corporate bosses sitting in board rooms and deciding what the next fashion statement should be.

But now it was more of a torture to watch these people parade around as if nothing in the world was amiss, as if their lives were not touched by the actions of some spoiled dictator halfway around the world.

They were all delusional.

And she hated them for it.

She hated the new laws against immigration and the new laws concerning the new laws and all those people who spend billions to get elected so that they could ignore the people who voted for them in the first place. And she hated the new age-prolonging techniques and the subsequent laws and problems that can of worms produced. With the advent of the newer age-prolonging medicines and genetic treatments, most people now lived to the ripe old age of one-hundred-twenty to one-hundred-thirty, one of the better improvements of the human condition over the past thousand years or so.

But it had also created problems, as any improvements in the quality of life were wont to do. With people living longer, it soon became apparent to most every one that the birth rate would have to slow if not reverse itself before the planet was completely over-crowded.

The O'Neill Colonies relieved the strain somewhat, as did the advent of the Mars Colony, but with only a maximum capacity of 20,000 souls for the Colonies and a mean time of ten years for the construction of each O'Neill Colony, as well as the exorbitant cost of sending colonists to *Galileo Prime* on Mars, the immediate solution was not forthcoming. It had caused, in fact, at least one American President from being re-elected and a few other leaders getting assassinated.

As such, the major industrial countries had instituted strict birth controls among their population over fifty years ago and had made the large family a relic of the past. Each family was now only allowed to have two children, after which both parents were sterilized to insure that no more children were born from that pair. Needless to say, these laws had caused a virtual riot among most populations and Alexis remembered the early wars that had broken out in many countries over the complete control that the governments were attempting to place on such a fundamental human function as reproduction.

But the process had eventually taken hold and was beginning to see the first real positive results. Populations in those countries that had successfully established these laws were beginning to stabilize and the cries of outrage were beginning to become topics for the history videos. Of course, the countries that deemed themselves above such demeaning laws were creating problems of their own and would have to be dealt with sooner or later, the sanctions being leveled against them by those countries who had accepted the new laws slowly but surely having the desired affect.

Alexis was always fascinated by how easily certain countries could control others when the correct leverage was applied, especially when that leverage involved clandestine military operations and illegal assassinations, a subject she knew of from first hand experience.

Longer life spans, however, also had the unintended effect that the retirement laws as well as the entire concept of old age had to be redefined. That had created a whole new set of problems. The revolution in age-control had only come about a little over forty years ago and the population was just now starting to see the inherent problems it caused. With people staying in their jobs far into their nineties and now even a few into their hundreds with no impairments or mental degradation, the job market was beginning to react. Many people had already foreseen that this would eventually cause large unemployment problems among the younger generations as the jobs that generally opened up due to retirement or death would now remain filled for another forty to fifty years.

It was a headache most politicians made grand speeches concerning but which they never actually made any plans to correct. It made her sick. People were not meant to live forever. They were enough of a headache to the others when they lived to be ninety. Now they were just a nuisance. And here she was in the midst of them, stuck like some stranded alien in a society she detested, wondering when some nutcase was going to nuke the whole lot of them back to the stone-age and a far better way of life.

Finishing off the last half of her juicy, greasy pastrami sandwich that melted in her mouth like any good pastrami sandwich was supposed to, she wiped her hands clean and placed the visual interface before her right eye again, hooking it over her ear. The device was basically a miniaturized version of a heads up display the military had been using since the late twentieth century, attached to the computer in her purse via hard wire, thus severely limiting the possibility of anyone picking up the transmission and tapping into her database. It gave her the illusion of a full screen, which she could manipulate with vocal commands. It had all the features of a regular computer system without all the encumbrances. She leaned back and brought the files on the CD back up to take another look at them as the sun warmed the air around her in a typical Boston humid swelter, the slack breeze providing little succor.

The CD had been, essentially, a journal of Alex's work over the past year, including brief yet telling snaps of his personal life, which told her more about her deceased son than the contents of the technical aspects of the journal ever could. She had learned, for instance, that her son had a girlfriend, a little fact that the intelligence corps working for Cav had either managed to leave out of the report or not been able to discover.

It was this girlfriend who was now holding Alexis' attention, the more she read, the fuller a picture she was developing; and it was not a picture she wanted to see. It was not all that informative in some aspects, but it did give

106

her new clues and a glimpse of a life that her son wanted hidden and within that, she had learned over her many years working, were more clues than anything else she might come across.

Secret women always provided tantalizing clues.

Her name had been Marie. No last name had ever been given and she had appeared in his life shortly after he had been assigned to the restricted areas at Surya Industries. That simple fact raised a flag in Alexis' mind immediately and she had assumed at first that Surya Industries had attached this woman to her son to make certain that he was not abusing his privileges, becoming cozy with him at night and hopefully learning of his improprieties with the company equipment.

The relationship had started slowly but then had, in a matter of weeks, escalated into a full-fledged passionate romance with many hours of sexual activity that her son had succinctly placed in the journal with a few well-placed words such as, *she was unbelievable again. I've never had that many orgasms in one session in my life and she has the energy to go all night long if I let her.*

A small voice in the back of Alexis' mind had continued to complain that she should feel embarrassed at reading these very personal entrees of her son's, but she didn't have time for such trivial, emotional responses. She should have probably been disturbed by the lack of emotion but it was a problem for later, when she was done with this mess of Cav's. Then, and only then, could she perhaps sort out the messes that were her own emotions and figure out what had happened to them over the years.

Marie had, interestingly enough, gone with Alex on the trip to Egypt and then disappeared right after he drowned and she had not been heard of since. It was possible that the woman was so thunderstruck by the sudden loss of her lover that she had gone insane with grief and was wandering some back alley in Tangiers, but Alexis somehow found that solution hard to believe.

Upon running a web-wide check for her, Alexis had not been surprised to find that the woman didn't exist. Neither her image nor her name nor her family existed in any of the data-bases accessible, which meant that she was a deep-deep undercover agent for an organization like Cav's, for it was only those types of people who never seemed to ever show up on any data-bases. Alexis was certain that her own name and image had been completely removed after she had retired, if not earlier. All that ever appeared were fake aliases, cover names, images used to convince others that she existed as someone else and that was what this Marie had going.

107

There was no longer anything in the databases because the databases had been swept clean of her presence, to make it appear that she had never existed in the first place. It stunk of undercover and it stunk of government involvement but it didn't stink of Surya Industries and that threw an entire new player into the mix, for if it was not Surya who was keeping tabs on her son, then who the hell was it? And why? Why keep track of such a low level employee when it was obvious to anyone paying attention that Clovis had far more to offer than Alex ever did.

Were they connected to the people who had broken into her cabin? Most likely. And it even confirmed Alexis' earlier epiphany that they had not been there for her but for something she had in her possession.

They had wanted the other names.

The remainder of the CD contained notes, techniques, trouble-shooting solutions and problems, as well as a vast amount of e-mail correspondence between Alex, Kido, Godonov, and to Alexis' mild surprise, Dumvo on the O'Neill Colony. That had been the other party to which Clovis had referred and it brought many pieces together. This was the first real, tangible link between Dumvo and the others. They had apparently communicated for almost a year without a trace of the e-mails anywhere. It was, she had to admit, a brilliant system.

A feeling of pride swelled for a brief moment in her chest, only to be immediately snuffed out as she took a sip of her now warm soda. Alex had been aware of both Kido's and Dumvo's deaths and that would explain why Alex gave the CD to Clovis. Her son had been smart enough to realize that there was someone after them, that the deaths could not be mere coincidences and this had been his safety net just in case.

Unfortunately for Dr. Alex Hart, he had not realized that the people with whom he was involved, who had killed the others, had planned all this very, very thoroughly and had not taken into account that Alex would give anything of value to another. Or they just didn't care whether he did or not.   Perhaps they didn't think that the project he had been working on could be resurrected by anyone with the main contributors out of the picture.

They were probably correct.

The plethora of e-mails between the parties, unfortunately, were rather cryptic and short, written in a type of code that, it could be assumed, only the four of them knew. With all of them dead, the secret most likely died with them, for such codes, without any basis for what the communiqués had been about, was impossible to crack. The e-mails also explained how Kido and Alex had known to meet at that conference and it was there that they had discussed in more detail, away from prying eyes and ears, their secret project. It also meant that there was nothing she could glean from the e-mails.

On the bright side, most of the technical schematics and entries dealt with a new type of expandable and flexible memory system using a type of holography to store the data arrangement, a system Alexis didn't even pretend to understand. It was, apparently, what her son had been working on at night with his simulations. He had been using the large capacity of the machines to run his holography memory and find the bugs that always hide within the code.

Other than that, there was really not much to help her, though it was certainly more than she had before she ran into Clovis. And it was a place to start, which was what she had been hoping to find.

She saw them as she was finishing her drink, strolling along the lane, his head down deep in concentration, hands in his pockets, Valerie beside him jabbering away. She had obviously managed to get Clovis away from his computer interface long enough to have lunch with her and it seemed that the man was not enjoying his time in the fresh air.

Alexis was rather pleased when she noticed that they were headed for the deli on whose patio she was sitting. Now she could speak to them, without the prying eyes of the company watching and with the new information from the CD. Perhaps she could get a little more meat onto the bones of the facts she had so for discovered. Clovis was certain to know about holographic memory and its applications. She quickly put her interface away and made ready to act surprised to see them when she first felt it. It was that same feeling of wrongness she had felt that night in cabin and she immediately came alert.

They were here.

She probed with her mind into the surrounding area and found them standing off on the other side of the lane that had once been a street, their shadowy existence blurring into the landscape around them. She opened her eyes and was not surprised to see that she could not see them with her naked eyes. The waves of wrongness were flowing from them like sound waves, almost visible when she concentrated on them and saw them again with her mind's eye. It was as if the very air around them was rebelling against their presence, the dimensions around them buzzing like static electricity, sizzling in its intensity, potent in its juxtaposition. If only she could figure out why they had such a feeling of wrongness, as if they didn't belong, perhaps then she could understand more about from where they came but she didn't even understand the feeling of wrongness.

Both of them were intently watching, under their black sunglasses, Valerie and Clovis saunter down the breezeway. Alexis sensed weapons. She sensed violence in their stance, in their thoughts and quickly figured out that these two assassins intended to liquidate Valerie and Clovis, the last link to Alex and his idea, whatever it might be.

Valerie and Clovis moved closer to the deli, her shrill voice now reaching Alexis as she babbled on about things to which Clovis seemed impervious. The two assassins moved forward also, as if timing the attack precisely to coincide with the pairs' arrival at the deli. Alexis reached into her bag and placed her hand around the grip of the gun, though she had the odd feeling that as before, her weapon would be useless against them. She was also aware that she could not just whip it out and challenge the two assassins whom, she was certain, only she could see.

That would certainly blow her cover both to Valerie and Clovis and to whomever might be watching her from Surya or from wherever. Besides, brandishing her weapon when there appeared to be no threat to the people sitting around her would certainly produce the wrong reaction. She was lucky in one respect, however. The assassins appeared to be concentrating so hard on the targets that they had not yet noticed her sitting here, for she was certain that they came from the same bosses who had sent the team to her cabin. Why should they be expecting her here anyway? It was not as if she ever ate here before.

She would have to do this some other way, some way that would not reveal her presence, that would not indicate in any way that she had done anything or taken part.

Then Valerie recognized Alexis and waved, making Clovis look up to see what could have possibly happened to make Valerie stop talking. There must have been something that tipped him off because he stopped in mid-stride and stared right at the two assassins as if he could see them.

They pulled out two large shotgun-looking weapons from under their long coats and cocked them in that recognizable sound actually echoing among the trees in an odd, almost surrealistic, undulating sound, causing a flock of birds to rise up into the air, their loud and squawky protests covering for a moment the sounds of life in the park. Time slowed to that frame-by-frame lethargy that always seemed to accompany such events, as if the very time-space corridor around the deli had been slowed to allow full recognition of the imminent death of so many innocents.

Alexis had a moment of confusion as she tried to figure out how these two were going to hurt anyone when only she could see them. Were they actually corporeal? Did they even exist at all or was she somehow imagining all this?

She didn't have much time to clarify her confusion.

The assassins began to fire into the crowd of customers. People and blood began to fly freely as the projectiles found their random marks and laid customers and by-standers to the floor in grotesque caricatures of death. The large window to the deli shattered with the impact of thousands of little pellets and blood splattered across the stone floor of the patio as a head exploded from the impact of what Alexis surmised were depleted uranium explosive rounds.

These assassins had come here to make certain that they finish their assignment this time. Their weaponry was state of the art and deadly. They continued to move forward as they pumped round after round into the storefront and the customers who ran and fell and sprawled and prayed and died in the killing zone that the deli had become. With no obvious cause for the deadly carnage, the people in the area had resorted to panic and rather than falling to the ground and remaining motionless, where the projectiles would have cleanly missed them, they ran around without direction, running generally right into the field of fire and ending up splattered over the grass or concrete in crimson stains.

Alexis had learned a long time ago that panic was a far more potent killer than bullets. It was fine to be afraid. Fright produced the required adrenaline and endorphins the body needed to react properly, but panic seized the heart and the mind and in the end killed more people who didn't need to die than fright ever did. With that in mind, as well as the fact that she had been in worse fire-fights than this, she stayed seated, aware that the spread of the projectiles was slightly above her and off to the side where Valerie and Clovis had been standing. She waited calmly until the first assassin cleared the ornamental railing separating the patio section from the rest of the walkway.

She saw then that one of the assassins had noticed her nonchalant attitude and as he neared her position, turned the barrel of his weapon toward the ravishing red-head who sat rooted to her chair, lazily sipping on her now empty drink as the carnage rained down around her.

Their eyes met suddenly like an electric spark and he realized with a visible start that she could see him. There was a sudden recognition. She could tell from his reaction that he thought a mistake had been made, that she was not supposed to be here and that he had just reached the end of his life.

Alexis gave him an inexorable, scornful smile and squeezed the trigger of her own weapon. It discharged through the end of her purse and laid the assassin down heavily onto the grass, his weapon flying free and landing several meters away with a muffled thud, the actuator clearly audible as it cooled down with the loss of the pressure on the safety stock. There was a sudden discard from the assassin, an electric spark flaring a brief moment, covering the man in what appeared to be an envelope of fire and sparks for a handful of seconds. His body twitched and jerked with the intense energy that engulfed him.

Then he became visible to the gasp of those laying or standing around him, his lifeless body laying there with eyes wide open staring at the cloud-less sky above. People ran from the body or stood stock-still looking on as if this were something really interesting.

Alexis raised an eyebrow, then looked down at her weapon. That should not have happened. Her weapon was not a stun gun and had no energy except for the momentum of the projectile. And she certainly didn't remember Cav every saying anything about the ability to turn invisible men visible. Besides, if she couldn't see them then how in the world was her weapon able to hurt them? *What the hell was going on here?*

She turned her attention to the other assassin, who, in his desire to create as much havoc as possible, had not noticed the demise of his companion. She waited a moment until he cleared one of the table umbrellas, coming toward her direction with the obvious intent of killing yet more people to cover up the real target of the assassination. His eyes fell on her as she looked dead at him and fired. The impact sent him careening into the last intact window of the deli, his weapon firing uselessly into the air. He was dead before he landed, the same reaction occurring to his body as a stench of cloudy effusion rose from his now visible body.

Alexis became aware of the screams around her and frowned. People could be so annoying. It had taken all of perhaps ten seconds from start to finish and the horrendous cacophony that had accompanied the carnage was now replaced with the sobs for the dead and dying, the scared and confused, and most importantly the urgent wails of the heavily armored police hovs speeding toward the scene. Alexis was well aware that she needed to be gone before the police arrived and starting asking questions.

She was certain that no one had noticed her part in the shoot-out. She stood up amidst the shattered glass and blood and deli meats strewn about only to find Valerie kneeling over a prone and lifeless body, the large, bloody hole in its chest more than enough prove that Clovis had been killed.

She found herself looking at his face as she hurriedly walked passed, his eyes staring up with a startled look of what she took to be curiosity, Valerie's sobbing like a morose dirge for a man she probably didn't even like. Within moments she was inside her Mercedes, speeding away from the scene as the police arrived to sort out the mess. She punched in one of her many of her personal communication codes into the rental car's comm system and composed a simple message. Cav would be reading it within the hour.

No luck on the Christmas shopping, but I did find some interesting items for your birthday. By the way, if you're ever here in Boston, you should visit the Metro Art Museum and take a look at the new exhibit by Berronitti. It's really quite fascinating. It opens at 0900. Love always.

It is to him who masters our minds by force of truth;
and not to those who enslave them by violence;
that we owe our reverence
— *Voltaire*

11

11 August 2085, 0903 hrs

She sat on the cool marble bench staring at the rather obscure painting on the wall, its vivid colors and oblique lines supposedly representing something profound. She didn't really see it. To her it didn't exist but was rather just an object in the general direction in which she looking, deep in thought as she waited for her initial contact. She spent a sleepless night in the hotel room. It was not like her have insomnia and it frustrated her. So rather than be bored staring at the walls or watching what they tried to call news on the television, she had spent much of the night changing her looks. She now had raven-black hair falling to her shoulders in waves of undulating curls, fanning out around her face, punctuated now with indistinct gray eyes, pale lipstick accentuating her compressed smile, and large sunglasses, which she kept on even in the dimness of the museum.

Her breasts had grown also, the insertion of pads making her several sizes larger than nature had made her. She wore a pair of loose slacks and blouse and looked like any other patron at the art center. The change had not taken nearly as much time as she would have liked, her proficiency at altering her appearance far greater than she remembered.

That left her with but a few options and so she had spent the rest of the evening going over and over her son's journal for anything that she might have missed. Finding nothing there, she had hacked into the Internet and learning all she could about holography and its applications to computer memory. It had not been a very fruitful search.

Several attempts at a working holographic memory system had been tried at the end of the last century and the beginning of this one in order to create

114

virtual memory systems, but nothing had come of it. The systems, hardware, and complexity of code required were so enormous that the projects usually stalled after only a few mediocre starts. Her son, apparently, had found a way around all that, or so she gathered from the journal. Whether or not he had succeeded in generating a working model she could not tell. Her son was rather vague in his conclusions and whether he had been that way on purpose or was just sloppy with his lab work, she could not tell either.

She knew that there was something here, screaming at her from the pages of his journal and she was deaf to it and it made her angry as well as happy. There was an enjoyment to the hunt that made her feel alive, gave her a tingling in the back of her mind not unlike sex.

Unfortunately, she had also found that whenever she closed her eyes, the image of Clovis' serene face staring up into the deep blue sky with those exanimate eyes, haunted her. She had never, in all the years she had been an active agent, had this problem. Never had she seen the faces of those innocents killed around her, due to her, by her. Never.

And yet, this one face continued to haunt her for reasons she could not fathom in the least. It was perplexing. It was annoying.

It made her wonder what was so special about this one individual that made her mind grab onto his image so strongly and throw it back at her conscious mind over and over again. Did it have a meaning associated to it? Was there something there that she had missed, something about the man that her subconscious had picked up on and was trying in its own way to tell her? She didn't know and that made her very annoyed.

The idea that perhaps she had developed a conscience along the way had been briefly brought forward and just as quickly dismissed as ludicrous. A conscience in her line of work was a liability, a threat to her well being that she needed to erase immediately.

She had not even known the man for all of ten minutes, so why in the world would she all of a sudden feel guilty about his death. And yet, here he was in her dreams, haunting her sleep with his dead face, speaking to her in a language that she didn't, or perhaps couldn't understand and causing her no end of torment and frustration that, before this night, she had never experienced.

And now it was the next morning and here she was sitting, waiting and still his face came to her, his open chest with the blood and the splintered bones and the gore splattered over the bright sidewalk like one of the odd paintings staring back at her from the wall and speaking volumes she also didn't understand. She would have to shake this apparition from her mind and get on with the job at hand, because this mission was starting to boil over right before her eyes and she had the odd feeling that Clovis was not going to be the last person burnt.

There were several people already in the museum at this early hour, but none of them seemed to have made it over to the exhibit where she sat, or perhaps found other paintings more interesting than the jumble of colors she stared at.

Around nine-thirty, however, one lone woman did slowly wander over to the bench where Alexis sat. She was short but pert, attractive in that cute sort of way that make men look, but not too intently. She sat on the bench to rest, looked over at Alexis and flashed her a tight, friendly smile, then focused back up at the painting.

"I never understand these paintings," she said in her lilting soprano, the French accent weak but noticeable. "I don't see anything artistic about them."

Alexis focused her eyes on the painting as if interested. "I agree. And the money they get for them is obscene."

The lady continued to stare at the painting for a few minutes, then made a move to stand. "Do you know how much it would cost to take a taxi to the nearest airport remote terminal? I'm trying to decide whether it's cheaper to take the bus."

"I don't know," Alexis answered. "I use the credit system for mass transportation so I don't really pay much attention to the fares."

"Thanks anyway." She stood and walked slowly away, placing the disc-based automatic museum guide in her ear and continuing with the self-guided tour.

Alexis waited a few more minutes, then stood and left the museum. She hailed a taxi and a hov came down immediately to the steps. She got in and it took off into the air lanes in a rush. She leaned back on the rather hard seat and smirked at the general dilapidated condition of the passenger area. "You could have at least requisitioned one that was a little nicer," she said to the driver.

Cav looked up into the mirror at her. "I didn't exactly have much time." He was silent for a few moments while he negotiated the traffic, making for the express lanes that were higher up. "I saw on the news last night that the Army for the Liberation of Humans from Machines attacked a deli in the downtown district. They killed quite a few people before they themselves were gunned down by the police. Messy affair." He looked up in to the mirror again at her face staring back at him, her lips compressed. He saw that she had not slept last night, saw a strain in her eyes letting him know that she was in her element. "It looked a little like your handy work."

"They weren't after me," she said quietly, the image replaying in her mind, trying to find the exact moment Clovis had been hit and suddenly realizing for the first time that neither of the two assassins whom she had liquidated ever had the chance to blast Clovis in the chest. He had received a full charge and neither of the assassins ever got that close.

She leaned back. "Son of a bitch. I'm missing too much. Shit."

"Oh? Like what? Seems to me that you did a pretty good job of it. What did you miss?"

"There was another one, another assassin who must have been off at a distance," she said with an irritation at her lack of scrutiny of the attack. "He's the one who blasted Clovis, which was the entire point of the attack. The other two were just diversion. And since I never saw him, he must have seen me and how I killed his two companions. Damn-it all to hell!" She slammed her fist into the seat cushion and was a little surprised to see stuffing come flying out.

"You were kind of busy to have noticed something like that, Alexis," he responded in an attempt placate her despite the fact that he knew that she was right. She should have sensed the third assassin, if a third assassin even existed. She was damn lucky that the third one had not seen fit to finish her off. And that brought up a problem all of its own. Why had he not finished her off? What game were these assassins playing? If they were from the same place as those in the cabin, why would they not attempt to finish off Alexis at this perfect opportunity? "So they weren't after you, then? That's interesting," he mused for something to say as he settled into the express lane and caught up to the traffic that zoomed along.

"No, they weren't. They didn't realize I was there until I hit the first one. You'll need to get those bodies from the police before they disappear like the others and it hits the press. They were the same as the ones that attacked me at the cabin. I'm positive of it."

"Way ahead of you, Locke. And you're right, they are the same. By the way, what the hell did you hit them with? You fried them something good. Is it a weapon you got from me, cause I need one of those for myself."

"That's another thing." She leaned forward, putting her arms on the divider between the passenger and the driver. She threw her Glock onto the seat next to him. "I used that. Regulation ten millimeter. I don't have a clue what the hell happened. They reacted like they had some type of shield on and getting hit disrupted it or short-circuited it or something. It was the strangest thing I've seen in a long time." She leaned back again, looking out the window at the skyline passing by rapidly.

He reached over and picked up the gun, looked at it as he negotiated his way through traffic, then placed it under his own seat. "I'll have the boys look at it. There's another one in the side compartment back there. So what were they after this Clovis guy for? Do you think that he was the next on the list? This attack doesn't seem like it fits in with the others. Far too violent and public."

She reached into her shirt and pulled the CD out of her bra. "This is the reason, I would think," she said as she handed it forward and he grabbed it with his right hand. "It's Dr. Hart's journal for the last year."

"Really?" he said as he looked at it, then placed it in his shirt pocket. "How did he get it?"

"Hart gave it to him before he left for Egypt. He had the feeling that something might happen on his little vacation. He was in contact not only with Kido but also Godonov *and* Dumvo, so he knew that two of them had been killed already before he went on his vacation."

Cav changed directions and pulled into another express lane, following the flow of traffic converging on the main airport terminal. "How in the world did he do that? We didn't detect any communication between them whatsoever."

"It's all on the CD. And I don't think that Clovis was one of the pre-planned targets. This was much too abrupt and messy, like you said. I think I might have had something to do with it. It's too much of a coincidence that he gets hit right after giving me the CD."

She looked down at her hands a moment, shook her head at the improbability of it all. There was no way that she missed a third assassin. With the distortion that the other two projected, the wrongness she felt made it a virtual impossibility that she would have missed one of them.

Unless he was so far away that he was out of her range.

But than that didn't make any sense either because the weapon that had shattered Clovis' body had been fired at close range, almost point blank from the powder burns she had briefly seen as she walked pass his dead body.

No, if there had been a third assassin he had to have been right there with the others, walked right up to Clovis and killed him, leaving Valerie alive ....

That didn't make any sense either.

Why leave a witness alive who could identify him? These assassins were not that sloppy. Or, perhaps, as was the case with the three in her cabin, they just didn't care who saw them or who knew that they had killed.

Then, of course, this ruminating brought up the point of why they failed to

118

kill him before he gave her the CD, if they even knew about the it. Why allow that piece of vital information into her hands if they were willing to kill to silence Clovis? Did he know even more than he had told her, perhaps wanting to see if she did indeed publish what he had given her before divulging the rest? She took a deep breath, closed her eyes – to the annoying image of Clovis lying dead imprinted on her irises – and then tore her wig off and threw it on the seat in frustration.

"You still with me back there?" Cav asked as he looked into the vid-mirror briefly.

"It just doesn't add up, that's all. This whole thing seems to get more and more twisted the further I dig and I have the feeling that more people like Clovis are going to get killed before its over, if it ever ends." She looked up at him. "If Claudine is involved in this, then that bitch has more power than you'll ever have and I can expect even warmer receptions the next few places I visit, because they have to know that I was here, that Clovis gave me the CD, that he talked me and not to Katrina Templar of the New York Times."

"Not necessarily. This hit could have been in the works for months, years even. Maybe it had nothing whatsoever to do with the CD. Maybe this Clovis guy was mixed up with something else ---"

"No Cav. It had to do with that CD and with Alex and what he was doing. I'll bet my life on it."

"You almost did today. Do you have any idea what Hart and the others were working on?"

"No, not really." She stared back out the window and saw the airport far ahead, the planes circling and landing and taking off in some parody of normalcy that she didn't feel. "I have a few clues but nothing real tangible. What do you know about holographic memory?"

Cav lost altitude and entered into the slower, main fly-lanes leading back around the city in a lazy circle, away from the airport. "Not a whole lot. It's one of those pipe dreams the computer nerds are always trying to come up with, but so far, no one's succeeded in even coming close. Why? Is that what Hart was working on?"

"What use would it be if it did become practical?" she asked, ignoring his question.

"Fifty years ago it would have had incredible applications, but with the advent of the new quantum computer storage systems and the nano-technology that's leaked over into memory applications, I can't really see any use for it except as a research tool."

119

"How so?" she pushed.

"Well, it's basically the same system that it's believed the human mind stores data with and if we had a working model then we could use it to study the brain more thoroughly and perhaps understand it better. Other than that, I can't really see any other applications for it. It can't improve on the current memory storage systems we have in place, or at least I don't think so, not unless they really improve it beyond what they've been working on."

Alexis stared out again at the passing hovs and the scenery blurring by below, the lush green of the Boston suburbs cool in their pre-planned environs.

"Alexis, you okay?" Cav asked as he eased the taxi into another lane.

"Yeah, just thinking...." She was beginning to see the misty tendrils of a connection she was not certain were there, yet, sweeping over her mind like gossamer ripples of spider webs running off into the darkness, their connection points vague, even unknown. There was no getting around it. She would have to dig deeper.

"Where are you off to next? I have tickets to various destinations as well as new identities. Your choice."

They always thought that. It was her choice. What an asinine statement to make. There were no more choices that she could make. As with most of her missions, the mission parameters decided everything in advance, made the choices pre-determined and thus made anything that she might think was her choice a pure fantasy.

Choice was a figment of the imagination, a word used to comfort those who were naive enough to think that humanity had a free will in what they did. "I was going to go to Japan, to talk to some of the people who knew Kido. Clovis mentioned something about Kido having more information on the project that Hart was working on. But I think that I may wait on that one. Without the link to the others, the info that Kido might have had won't be worth much."

"*Galileo Prime* then?"

"No. I'm thinking that I need to find out more concerning the three that didn't have anything to do with computers, especially Dumvo and Pratali. I need to find the connection between them and Hart. Sure Hart and Kido might have been communicating with him, but why? What did he have that they might have needed, because he was an integral part of this project. If I find that out, I might be able to crack this one open a little more." She leaned forward again hit him hard in the shoulder. "And you need to find out who the hell these assassins are, because I have a gut-wrenching feeling that they'll be looking out for me now that I've made myself a nuisance, regardless where I go."

"Then is it *Stargazer I* or India?" Cav inquired, wondering where her mind was leading her, what obscure connections she was forming.

"I think that the O' Neill Colony would be the best place to look and it'll get me off the planet for a few weeks and maybe confuse our assassins a little." She didn't really believe that anything she did would confuse these assassins in the least. Although she had been one step ahead of them with Clovis and the CD, she didn't think that that would last.

She was certain that whomever was controlling these things -- for she was beginning to believe that they were more machine then human – was not about to let anyone like Alexis unravel all their well-laid plans and expose the entire scheme. It was certain that they would be awaiting for her in all the places she could possibly go. The one advantage she had was that she could get a rapid transport to *Stargazer I* right now and thus arrive on the Colony with a slight edge and some free time to poke around before the assassins showed up.

But then, they might just be there already. It was altogether possible that they had all the places she might go staked out, waiting for her arrival. It was a distinct possibility she could not ignore and she would have to be ready for them. With the sophistication they possessed, they would eventually figure out a way to deal with her much more effectively than they had been. She was not looking forward to that. She had the advantage at the moment and losing it meant losing any chance she might have at solving this conundrum.

"Then *Stargazer I* it is. You'll be going as an insurance investigator. Shannon Baker." He threw a set of ID cards back at her, the equipment to cover her own fingerprints with new ones, and contact lenses that would allow her to pass any retinal scans. "You'll have to change your appearance. There's some clothes and other essentials under the seat, as well as some info to read up on concerning the insurance company and the state of the business at the moment." He looked at the small clock set in the dashboard as the collision warning chimed politely and he swerved nonchalantly to avoid the passing truck maneuvering out into the wrong lane. "We're in luck. A transport leaves in a little over an hour for the main transition point. You're booked on it, as well as the connecting fast shuttle to the Colony. You should arrive in a little over thirty hours from now."

She opened the half of the back seat on which she was not sitting and pulled out the charming gray business-suit in with a pleated skirt that looked rather short.

"You need to very careful up there, Alexis," he said with a new and different tone, a drift of emotions flowing just under the surface. "The Colonies have their own set of rules and procedures and don't like it one bit when Earthers try to interfere with their lives."

"Earthers?" she asked as she unbuttoned her blouse and took it off.

Cav took one look, caught her hard eyes staring back at him and adjusted his rearward vid-mirror so that she would not think he was leering at her. He had seen her naked more times than he could count and didn't need to ogle her now.

"They call us Earthers?" she followed up as she pulled her pants off to change into the business suit. She had never considered that other humans would give those who still lived on the Earth a pejorative nickname. It seemed odd, somehow surrealistic in a way.

"The people in the Colonies are rather an independent minded lot. There've even been rumors that once they get five Colonies on-line, which should occur some time in the next seven years, they're going to petition for separation from their respective governments and declare themselves as their own country. As such, they frown very much on people like you going up and poking around. They see it as Earther interference or even as Earthers finding reasons why they shouldn't break away from the planetary governments."

"What's new? Everywhere I go people don't seem to like me poking around. And I have such a pleasant personality." she said curtly as she slipped on the skirt, finding that it was rather short on her. "And did you forget my size or something? This seems a tad bit short for an insurance agent."

"It's the new style among the more successful professional business women. You've got the body for it, so stop complaining. As I was saying, you need to be very, very careful about how you act up there. You'll be on your own. I can't very well help you that far away and communications planet-side are carefully monitored. Very carefully monitored. You need to be especially careful of their police force. It's small, but highly fanatic, if one can call it that.

"And they're very efficient. They've lost face with the death of Dr. Dumvo and aren't going to like you dragging it up again. It's the first intentional death that they've ever had and they're trying their damnedest to cover it up. Last thing they need is a panicky populace and a reason for the Earthers to deny them independence."

She pulled the jacket on and noticed that with the pads in her bra, her chest stood out more than the suit was designed to hold, making her look more like a sexual entertainment employee than an insurance agent. She frowned, then pulled the breast enhancements out, selecting a smaller size and trying them on. They were a little better, but she was beginning to see that the suit was cut to emphasize her breasts, so she stopped fidgeting with it. "Are they that self-sufficient that they can be independent?" she asked as she started work on the finger print alterations, trying to find a sitting position that didn't expose her underpants. If this was the new style for upward professional women, she wondered what they were striving upward toward? How did anyone walk in this get-up with any resemblance of professionalism.

"Completely, as of last year. They mine asteroids for all the essentials that they need in terms of water, minerals and oxygen; constant exposure to the sun gives them plenty of electricity and they grow more than enough food for themselves. So be very careful, okay?"

She looked up at him as he turned off into the airport terminal, wondering what was up with all the dire warnings. The man had never acted like this before. If she didn't know better, she would have the suspicion that he knew something he was not telling her. "Why Cav... I didn't know you cared so much," she said with mock sweetness of Southern drawl instead of the biting retort she wanted to employ.

"I don't, actually. It's just that I'm the one who'll have to clean up the mess if you blow it and I really don't feel like having to do that."

"How sweet."

The taxi pulled into the front of the main terminal of the space transition transport just as Alexis popped the contact lenses in, making her eyes an intense, dark blue, and pulled the pale blonde wig on with the pony tail tied up in the back with the pretty red bow and tassels coming down.

"I changed the taxi's ID transmitter three times as we drove and my men report that no one followed us so you're safe to depart." He turned around and gave her one last look. "I'll be expecting you back within a week, if not sooner. Otherwise I'm sending in the marines." He saw that look on her face that spoke of telling him to kiss her ass. "I'm serious. I'll storm that Colony if I don't hear from you."

She pursed her lips at him, winked, then stepped out of the taxi, pulling her luggage with her and handing him her monetary card.

With his best Boston accent, Cav took the card and spoke. "Have nice trip, Mrs. Baker. It was a pleasure."

She smiled at him as she took the card back. "Thanks."

* * * *

123

Claudine Maxwell stared out the window of her far too small office, the rain pelting the glass with an intensity uncommon for this time of year. But then, the last twenty years had seen a change in the weather patterns on Earth that the scientists had been unable to explain successfully. She remembered reading somewhere that the same thing had happened back at the turn of the century, causing large-scale problems around the globe and the introduction of the Global Weather Control Committee to understand better the intricacies of the fluid dynamics running the atmosphere.

The committee had not, as she was witnessing now outside her window, been able to produce any tangible results concerning weather control or even forecasting and as if to vouch for that, they were now right back in another series of weather phenomena defying explanation. It was almost, she sometimes mused, as if the Earth was giving subtle hints for Humans to find another place to call home if they were not going to take care of this one.

Although the slash-and-burn farming techniques of the South American and Asian countries had been banned and strictly monitored and the rain forests had been slowly growing back due to heavy popular pressure on the respective countries to curb their population explosions, the world still held plenty of areas that Humans could manage much better and plenty of animals still on the endangered species list.

She smirked at the window as if the weather were its fault somehow. Endangered animals. The only endangered animal on Claudine's mind these days was Alexis Locke. Claudine had never wanted to get involved with her in the first place. In fact, until that day those two people came to her – two people who had approached her from out of the blue, literally, and snared her in their web of their deceit – Claudine was not even aware that there was someone named Alexis Locke.

Of course, she knew about the projects on which Cav had been slaving for most of his life and knew about the production of proto-types and the problems that had come of that, but she had no idea of any specifics or of a successful proto-type named Alexis Locke. That was, until she had been approached by the male and the female, who had dragged her unwillingly into their obscure plans. The male and female pair who, to her mind, had seemed wrong to Claudine, as if they didn't belong to the air around them, as if it somehow was revolting against their very presence. And completely apart from that, there was something about them, the more she thought about it, that just didn't sit right with her and she was very good at reading people. It was what her job was all about.

She was not sure if it was the absolutely perfect faces and bodies they

124

flaunted, almost as if they were carefully carved out of marble and brought to life like Pygmalion and Galatea. She was not sure if it was the way they moved and the way they talked, so assured and exquisite, so confident yet fragile; or if it was just something she sensed about them, an aura thasetting off warning bells for unknown reasons that even now she could not put her finger on successfully.

Yet come they had, and laid on her desk a story so extraordinary that she had no choice but to believe it. It was almost as if the shear audacity of the tale, the complete inconceivably of it made it credible.   It had not taken much to bring her in, to involve her with their plot, to convince her that she was an important person – she was well aware of that little fact – and thus was needed to make certain that all went as it was supposed to.

As such, she did her part, the one part that they had asked of her: make certain that the agent working for Dr. Vincent Cavalier's organization known as Alexis Locke was assigned to the case. That she had done, her firm grasp on Cav's male libido assuring that she would get him to do what she wanted. The affair with the man those not near enough years ago had seemed at first like a great politic mistake, but she was beginning to think that perhaps, just perhaps, it had been one of the few bright spots of that time in her life. His usefulness to her now like an aged bonus for the horrendous sex she had to endure at his clumsy hands.

And then a light had slowly lit in the back of her mind, like a candle illuminating a dusty and forgotten treasure map and she started to realize that perhaps this was the opportunity for which she had been waiting. The opportunity that would open the window for her ascendancy to the top position she so craved, she could taste like the fine champagne she now sipped on delicately: the presidency.

If a stupid bimbo like Heather O'Rourke could win the highest office in the land, then why not Claudine, who was so much smarter and craftier politically, who knew what things to change and how to change them?   And so she began to congeal her own plans, to use the data the female and the male had given her to her own advantage and start making her own plans for her own benefit.

There had been a little man named Huang who had approached her a few years ago about her possible ascendancy to the presidency and how he was willing to finance her campaign if she were just willing to listen to what he had to say. His words had made an impact, that was certain. It had started her on her present course, his discreet money allowing her to take the slut prom-queen to the highest seat in the land as the first step to her own power-grab.

And now she had the final piece to the puzzle, the final way to make certain that she won the next election and then tell that little Chinaman that he could go to hell.

Yes, she would have to be careful but she could use this to her own advantage. So what if innocent people died in the process? So what if she had to abuse the very powers she had been sworn to protect? To gain the presidency was worth it. To gain the power that came with it and with the knowledge that she had gained, could gain, from her two visitors, was worth a million innocent people dying. Look at the nuclear wars that had killed in the millions in Pakistan and India. They had achieved their ends, that was certain. No one would disagree on that point.

Claudine Maxwell was not about to let something as simple as killing stand in her way.

No, Claudine Maxwell was headed for the top and when one went there, the path was unimportant. The goal was all that counted.

She watched the rain pounding on the window, the black, boiling clouds ripping apart from the very winds controlling them, unleashing their load of water in inundations threatening to flood vast areas of the city. She smiled, deviously. So too would she sweep away the clutter of the government that made her country so weak and ineffective these last few decades and turn the United States once again into the premier power in the world, controlling opinion and direction on both the planet and out in the colonies.

It was there that she would need to start: the Colonies. She was certain that they would become the hub of political power sooner than anyone realized. The Colonies needed to be reigned in and Dumvo's death, though certainly tragic for someone, had been a wonderfully unforeseen start to that process.

Her comm-system beeped and she placed her finger on the security pad that scanned her fingerprint. The message flashed by quicker than most humans could read, but she had gotten the gist of it. Alexis Locke was heading for *Stargazer I*. Perfect.

She keyed in a reply and then leaned back, imagining herself in the Oval Office and controlling the world. A malevolent look crossed her face and she smiled deeply, her face taking on a demeanor totally different from the one she presented to the world or even to her friends.

President Claudine Maxwell.

It had such a nice ring to it when she said it and so she repeated it several times as she finished her champagne.

Although they started small, the O'Neill Colonies were like the American British colonies of the Eighteenth Century, a haven for those who wished to live their lives without the constant over-lordship of the government. And like those British Colonies, the O'Neill Colonies eventually found that they no longer needed the support of the masters. And then they realized that they had become the masters before the old order even knew what had happened.

--- Excerpts from:
Commentaries from the
Journal of Meagan Locke

12

12 August 2085, 1730 hrs local time
O'Neill Colony *Stargazer I*

   The rapid transport slowly and gracefully eased itself into the docking port. There was a slight bump felt by the passengers, hardly noticeable and accompanied by a muffled thud, followed in rapid succession by a loud series of quick knocks as the locking mechanism engaged and secured the bulky transport to the Colony. The fasten seat-belt lights blinked out with a chime and the flight attendants began to get the exit port ready for disembarkation.
   The transports to the O'Neill Colonies were well maintained and nicely appointed, the large, roomy seats allowing one to relax and sleep during the thirty hour flight from the orbital transient station above the Earth to the three Colonies currently up and running, as well as the three Colonies still under

construction.

Tourism to the Colonies was minimal, the rapid transports made their way to *Stargazer I* once a month mostly for those residents of the Colony who still needed to do business planet-side, and even that was quickly becoming a minority as the self-sufficiency of the Colonies made such trips superfluous. It had even been suggested that the current service to *Stargazer I,* which had become fully operational two years ago, would be reduced to twice a year to diminish the amount of outside contact.

It was an idea that had the backing of most of those living on the Colony.

Many Earthers saw this as a blatant attempt by the Colonies to become elite isolationists, a concept not that far off the mark. The shuttle service was just one of many ongoing disputes between the Colony Administration and Earth and had finally resulted in the beginning stages of implementation of legislation to bind the Colonies closer to the home planet so that control could be maintained by Earth. Those in power on Earth could easily see the long-term benefits of the Colonies and their ability to easily and quickly mine the asteroid field for most any element known.

The possible loss of that control, of having the O'Neill Colonies have a virtual monopoly on the next source of almost endless supplies, was a concept that didn't sit well with those who thought they should hold that control for the Earth's benefit ... and their bank accounts benefit.

The opposite was happening aboard the Colonies and the rumors of secession from Earth that had been bantered around for the last few months were based very much in fact. As such, tensions between the original designers and backers of the Colonies – who still had major assets on Earth as well as lives they didn't want to throw away – and those pioneers who had moved into the Colonies and now called them home, was increasing daily. The Earthers were looking for any and all reasons to prove that the established ruling body of the Colonies was incapable of maintaining control and thus hopefully opening a window for those on the Earth to seize control.

The tragic accident that killed Dr. Dumvo was just such an incident. To have it turn into a murder investigation was out of the question for the local authorities. Crime was not a factor on the Colonies. With such a small community and no where to run, crime of any sort was the last thing the locals wanted or needed and thus it was, for the most part, nonexistent. Doors were left unlocked, people could walk the paths and through the parks at any time of the day or night without having to worry about getting attacked in any way. Theft was unheard of.

The biggest problem with which the Colonies had to deal was a pressure leak in the cylindrical structure that was their home, which could cause a cataclysmic failure of the structural integrity of the system and be a disaster beyond compare. The specter of the vacuum of space lay just outside the thin-sheeted triple walls of the structure, constantly waiting for that one opportunity to reach in and wreck havoc on the fragile humans within.

That was until Dr. Dumvo and the explosion.

The local authorities had quickly ruled it a tragic accident under investigation and the cause of the explosion rectified as quickly as possible so that a repeat would not occur. When it was learned that certain anomalies in the explosion itself and the circumstances of the death of Dr. Dumvo pointed toward a pre-meditated plan and not an accident, the authorities on Earth quickly jumped on the chance to prove the incompetence of the locals and to bring in Earth-based rule.

This had produced numerous clashes, both physical and verbal, when detectives from Earth had arrived to take over the case. Those detectives, made very unwelcome on the Colony, had been forced to leave shortly after they arrived, coming, not surprisingly enough, to the same conclusion as the locals: Dumvo's death was a tragic accident. The facts to the contrary were simply ignored, deposited far in the back of some police office files and forgotten.

The case was then closed on both sides, though doubts still lingered throughout the Earth detective community and even on the Colony itself. No one on the Colony talked about the death anymore. It had become a taboo subject better left alone. For the sake of the Colony, most people agreed that should anyone arrive asking questions, no answers should be forthcoming and those inquiring would be escorted as quickly as possible off the Colony.

This was the hostile atmosphere that Alexis, now masquerading as Shannon Baker, insurance investigator, found herself when she stepped off the transport and onto the Colony. She had been expecting far worse. She was well acquainted with what it was like to want to be left alone.

Waiting for her was a tall, burly man with an aquiline nose, prominent jaw, handsome, insolent eyes holding a depth Alexis found sinister, a deeply lined face and close-cropped hair above an austere and penetrating expression, which placed him as a military retiree almost as if it were printed on his forehead in big, bold letters. His name tag told her more than did his plain uniform, the words K. A. Viktorovna stenciled neatly across his broad chest.

Alexis was not surprised to see him here, waiting for her. She pulled up to her mind's eye his history, which she had read on the trip up here: he was the head of the security division for *Stargazer I* and was not a man she wanted to antagonize. But then, that had never stopped her before.

He was said to be kind and affable to the Colonists who stayed within the established boundaries and didn't break the rules, but brutal when necessary, clamping down with an iron grip on those who crossed him or broke the rules. During his reign as, basically, the most powerful man on the Colony, he had deported in excess of three thousand people for a variety of offenses deemed inappropriate to the welfare of the Colony, sending them back to Earth with the designation that they would never be allowed to live, work, or travel to any of the Colonies ever again. His was a wide ranging power but one he wielded with fairness, or so those who had not been affected by him directly swore to and those in control of the Colony hoped for.

He stood before her now with a composed and particularly amiable smile and a deferential but dignified politeness, which she took to be his first assault upon her in what was certain to be a non-agreeable relationship. She spoke first, not wanting to let him dominate from the beginning. She had dealt with more than her fair share of these men and knew that the one thing they hated more than people who didn't conform were women who thought themselves superior.

She smiled at him. "Captain Kiril Andrevevich Viktorovna, I presume. Nice to make your acquaintance," she said with a sweet, affable voice, the difficult Russian name rolling off her tongue with ease as she extended her hand out to him.

He looked down at her hand a moment, then back up into her eyes with an abject, intimidating air, glaring at her from under his bushy eyebrows, his voice stern and vibrant. "Don't get too comfortable here, Mrs. Baker. You *will* be returning as soon as this transport has been through maintenance and re-fueled. We don't need your kind here on *Stargazer I* and I don't intend to allow you to stir up problems that don't exist." He ignored her hand.
It was the first salvo of the attack.

She let her hand drop back to her side as she stood with her short skirt and tight suit, one bag slung over her shoulder and another in her left hand. At least there was one thing conforming to her expectations. "I just need to ascertain a few..."

"As I said, don't get too comfortable. You can wait in the VIP lounge if you like." His eyes, those rock-hard brown orbs locking on her like a hawk onto its prey, drifted down her front slowly and methodically, appreciating the lines and curves making up this newest attempt to discredit the Colonies.

It only took a few seconds but it made Alexis feel very dirty and she suppressed a shudder running down her spine, perhaps from the chill air that was part of the air lock, perhaps from the new environment, perhaps from the lascivious thoughts tumbling into her mind from him like an avalanche of rocks. Such things had never bothered her before, but when this man did it, when he fantasized about her body and his together, it brought a shudder to her mind unfamiliar and bothersome.

She wondered a moment if he had his own set of mental powers.

He didn't even bother to lift his eyes back to her face as he turned and purposely strode away, his authority complete, his will having been imposed. She watched him leave, anger seething inside her for a brief moment, then subsiding. Another clear reminder of why she had lived in the remoteness of Alaska for the past fifteen years.

Several other passengers had been passing by as they emerged from the transport where she was standing in the middle of the ramp, and as she watched the haughty and sanguine security chief walk away, thoughts of what she would like to do to him cascading behind her forehead, a voice spoke to her that was cheerful and bright, a refreshing change after Viktorovna.

She turned with a facetious smile on her face to find a man who stood at her height with wild, wavy brown hair and a radiant serenity that seemed almost comforting with his large, kind, intelligent eyes. He had fine lines along his nose and mouth as if he had smiled too much in his lifetime and a look about him of calm detachment.

"Don't pay him much never mind," he said, referring, she assumed, to the security captain. "He's gruff and comes across mean, but he's really a good person to have around. He's kept this Colony crime free for all the time that it's been up and running." He looked into her eyes with nothing but friendship. Then, realizing that he had forgotten the most important part, stuck out his hand to introduce himself. "I'm sorry. Quite rude of me to just interfere like that without an introduction. I'm Hugh Crow. Welcome to our little bit of heaven, slightly closer than Earth ever came."

She brushed a loose strand of hair out of her face and shook his hand hesitantly. The last thing she needed was some hard-up executive trying to pick-up on her. "Shannon Baker. Does he introduce himself to all the new arrivals like that?" she asked, indicating with a tilt of her head the security chief.

"Kiril? No, that was pretty special. You should feel honored. The last time he came down to the disembarkation docks and talked to someone personally was when the detectives from Earth came up here back in June.

Other than that, he lets his subordinates watch the new arrivals." He motioned for her to move down the ramp, his hover-bags following along behind him obediently. "You'll be going to the new arrival orientation and inspection area first, before you ever see the Colony itself. It's this way."

"You mean this isn't the Colony?" she asked, acting as innocent and naive as Shannon Baker would. Maybe she could make a connection here that just might allow her to slip past the invincible Viktorovna. This Hugh Crow might prove valuable after all.

"This?" he said with a slight laugh lighting up his face and sparkling green eyes. "This is just the docking ports. You'll know when you get to the actual Colony. It's beautiful." He spoke with such ardor and feeling that Alexis was beginning to want to see the actual Colony, if for no other reason than to see what could possibly make this good-natured man so radiant. She had read the technical manuals on the Colonies, but they hardly expressed any feeling of the true impact she expected to get upon seeing the interior of the living areas.

He led her to a large holding area with several doors along the walls and large tables in the middle with a variable array of scanning and medical equipment. This must be the inspection area. Everything entering the Colony, before it ever came into contact with the actual air of the main Colony itself, was tested and scanned, prodded and probed, to make certain that, first of all, no infectious diseases found their way into the environment, and secondly that no weapons made it in. Except for the few weapons the security force had locked away, all the Colonies were weapon-free zones and they intended to keep it that way.

If she had not been on an assignment, she would be duly impressed with the way these people had organized and administrated the Colony. She doubted that she could even name one area on Earth, apart from militarily controlled compounds, which were weapon-free. "I don't think that your esteemed Viktorovna will let me even go through this process," she said as she watched it all unfold around her.

Strip searches seemed to be mandatory, thus the small side rooms for privacy, and Alexis was beginning to think that there was a good reason Cav had warned her more sternly than he usually did. They didn't fool around here. It was professional and efficient. "He seemed quite set on not letting me in."

"Yes, I overheard that. I wasn't eavesdropping, though. It's just that with Kiril's voice it's kind of hard to not listen in sometimes." He looked around at the guards who stood about, all of them more or less busy with the disembarked passengers. "I think I can get you in. What's your business here?"

Alexis became weary. Although she had thought that she could use him to help her get past Kiril and into the Colony, the last thing she needed was to get associated with a smuggler, which she was beginning to believe this man was if he had any notion of getting her past security. She found nothing of a sinister nature in his surface thoughts and he certainly was not carrying enough luggage to suggest that he was doing anything vastly illegal.

Her gut told her to trust him, for now, and she smiled at him. "I'm an investigator for the insurance company that handles the Colonies."

He nodded his head with a knowing look in his eyes. "Ah, yes. I saw that memo when I was planet-side. Of course. Shannon Baker. When you said your name, it should have clicked. Here to look into the claim of damages and survivor benefits for the death of Dr. Dumvo... I thought that was all taken care of."

She noticed the slight change in his demeanor at the mention of her occupation and realized that this man was not just some Colonist and the idea that he was a smuggler began to drift further way from the realm of possibilities. That he had seen a memo with her name on it spoke of someone connected. "I'm sorry, but I didn't quite catch what you said you did here," she said with a broad, unnatural smile she had seen the fashion models and those who thought themselves beautiful affected when they wanted something out of men

"That's probably because I didn't say."

The line moved closer to the front of the queue. She looked over at him with a look of frustration.

The guard looked up, a glint of recognition sparkling in his eyes as he spoke to Hugh. "Mr. Crow. Good to see that you made it back safe from planet-side. Did you have a good trip? Just step this way and we'll get you through as quick as possible."

Hugh motioned for Alexis to go where the guard was indicating and she tentatively stepped over to a clear table with no one in line, a lone guard standing sentry.

"Do you know this lady, Mr. Crow?" the guard asked in a southern drawl that seemed lazy and doleful. "Cause I've strict orders not to let her into the main Colony area."

Hugh looked at the guard a moment as he placed his smaller hand-carried bag on the table and the hover-bags floated to the designated inspection area. "Yes, I do know her. We're old friends."

Alexis looked at him a moment with pursed lips, then decided to let it flow. His surface thoughts revealing no hidden thoughts of danger against her and despite his reluctance to tell her his occupation and his obvious connections, she needed to get a look at Dumvo's lab and talk to his assistants and she could not do that all too well sitting back on the transport as Kiril wanted. She tried to remember the name Hugh Crow from the data Cav had given her regarding the Colony and drew a blank.

She had not run across that name anywhere in the list of officials, but he was certainly someone who held a hidden power here. "I'll take responsibility for her, Jack," Hugh said with a familiarity that spoke of a long-term relationship to the Colony. "If you get any flak from Kiril, just direct him my way."

"I'm not so sure, sir. I'd rather not," the guard said, the fear of his boss seeming to out-weigh any pull Hugh might have.

Hugh beamed a smile at the guard and patted him on the shoulder, then leaned in and whispered into his ear. "She promised to sleep with me if I got her into the Colony, so don't ruin this for me."

Alexis, of course, heard it quite clearer, her superior auditory senses capable of such simple feats. She could barely keep a smile from shooting across her face and revealing that she had heard. This Hugh Crow was certainly quick on his feet.

The guard smiled widely and nodded his head. Sex seemed to out weigh any compromise of the security chief's orders. "Of course, Mr. Crow. We'll process you through right away. I'll need to see your bag, Miss."

Alexis gave the guard a half-smile and lifted her two bags onto the scanner table. She didn't think that he would look too kindly on the weapons she had stored in the secret compartment in the bottom of her bag. She gave him her best, crooked smile and tilted her head slightly as he looked at her and smiled back, that shy, knowing look glazing his eyes a moment as he imagined being able to sleep with this young woman tonight also. She caught the surface thoughts and slightly prodded them a little as the guard turned and began to blush furiously.

"She's cleared, Mr. Crow," he stammered, unable to look into her eyes again as various thoughts danced in his head and blood flow began to increase to certain areas of his body. "You two can step over to the next station."

Hugh smiled and nodded his head as he thanked the guard, then moved over to a table by one of the dressing room doors. "This next part is the worst," he said in apology. "It's sort of humiliating, but it's necessary for the safety of the Colony. Any type of disease that we may have picked up planet-side would run through this place like a plague and wipe us out in no time. Plus, we've already found several people who found it necessary to try to sneak in contraband in places that only a strip search can detect." He gave her a knowing smile.

"What's wrong with the standard medical scanners?" Alexis asked as she set her bags down and waited for the female guard to open the dressing room door for her. A strip search would certainly reveal the padding in her bra. That would be a rather embarrassing event, but there was no way around it. She could always plant an image in the guard's mind that the pads were not there, but then the cameras she was certain would be there would pick it up and explanations of such things always became more complicated than they needed to be. There was no way around the imminent discovery and she just hoped that the guard would have pity on her, understanding the reason that someone would want to increase their breast size in such a way. The things she had to do jus to survive.

"Nothing's wrong with the medical scanners, but they can be defeated," Hugh responded as the guard opened his door for him. "This way can't, not at least for the obvious things. We scan everyone also, but you've nothing to worry about." He stepped in and the door shut.

Alexis' door opened and the burly female guard, who looked more like a man in women's clothing than a woman, indicated for Alexis to step in and take all her clothes off, bend over and cough. She didn't look like the type of woman who would understand anything about padded bras, her own immense set of mammary glands making that obvious.

And to think that I could be home right now enjoying a beautiful evening with my dogs and the wildness of Alaska, she thought as the door closed and she began to undress.

*   *   *

Kiril Andrevevich Viktorovna watched the monitor with keen appeal as the woman who called herself Shannon Baker undressed. He could not believe the body that this one had, her perfect lines and curves almost appearing sculptured in their flawlessness. Women this perfect didn't appear very often on *Stargazer I* , the women he usually saw the more hardened adventuresome types who couldn't find a life on Earth and came here for who the hell knew what reason, their bodies more along the lines of barlap sacks.

Thus, he made certain he was taping the scene before him for later use.

He taped all dressing rooms on the off chance that he might catch something that the guards conducting the strip search might miss ... and of course for the reason that he was staring at the screen now. What was the point of having all this power and authority if one couldn't enjoy it at times like these?

When she took off her bra and revealed that she padded herself, he was slightly disappointed. He liked his women to have large, soft breasts, to which one could grab onto and hold. Small breasts seemed to Kiril to be a waste, especially on one with a body like this one. What was the point of having an ass that fine and not getting breast implants to complement it? But that was a minor point,

"Is she the one?" he asked in his thick voice to the woman who stood behind him, watching the monitor intently with a look less malicious then it was curious. She was dressed all in black. The color fit her well. She was tall, as tall as Alexis and had a look about her that spoke of wrongness. But it was not wrongness with her character or her morals ... or even her mission. It was as if she didn't belong to the air in which she stood, as if the air was rebelling against her and creating a barrier seething with unbridled ebullience like a sheath over her. When she came close to Kiril, he could feel the wrongness on his arms, his short hairs raised up as if a static charge was attracting them. His stomach would boil also, like it did sometimes when he left the rotating cylinder of the main Colony and made his way through the null-gravity of space.

And the worse thing was that he could not read her mind, not even the surface thoughts. It was just like that Shannon Baker woman or whatever her name was. He had been unable to probe her surface thoughts either, a disturbing if not frustrating setback to discovering if she was sent from the United States government to spy on him. All he got out of Shannon Baker was a headache and that had never happened before.

But this one who stood behind him now was different again. It was as if her mind was not even there, as if he were looking into an empty space filled with a nothingness as blank as the empty space around the Colony. In fact, he almost felt as if his own mind was being sucked into this one's when he probed her, as if a vacuum had been created inside this female.

It bothered Kiril, but then there were many things that bothered Kiril these days and in this particular case, he didn't have much choice in the matter. This one had been forced on him by the owners and so he would cooperate, for the owners signed his paychecks and that was one of the better benefits of this job. Anyway, this tall female was extremely attractive and perhaps he could work his charm on her, and if not then maybe his strength. Kiril was

136

not beneath using his physical capacity to get what he wanted.

"Yes, she's the one," the women in black answered with a quiet voice that seemed like a mere whisper but carried through the room easily. "Look how perfect she is. I never saw her like this when she was young." She was silent for a while as Kiril leered at the naked Alexis as she was searched.

He made strange noises as she bent over and coughed, the camera strategically positioned so that a full view was always possible. He re-adjusted himself in the seat. Damn tight pants.

The woman looked down at him with disgust. "She's not to be touched by you or your people until I say so, is that understood?" she said in a firm tone telling him that she meant it. "She'll be taken care of if that becomes necessary. I promise you that I'll make your death long and painful if you disregard me in this." She never once bothered to look at Kiril.

He nodded his head slowly, not really listening to what the bitch had to say. He might have let them into his security offices and given them access to all his files, but he was damned if he was going to actually take orders from her. Kiril Andrevevich didn't take orders from females.

Besides, he was far more interested in how he was going to have fun with Shannon Baker while she visited his Colony. Yes, so much fun.

*The inherent wickedness of theft does not disappear
because it is achieved by democratic processes. Two wolves
and a sheep voting on what to have for dinner may be called
democracy; but it is not justice.*
                    — President Heather O'Rourke
                    Commentaries from the Rose Garden

13

Alexis stepped out of the dressing room with a curt expression on her face, the humiliation of having to strip for a total stranger only off-set by the fact that the total stranger seemed more humiliated than Alexis did. Her sleek, firm body apparently caused some discomfort to the larger boned guard, who continued to click her tongue as she examined Alexis, mumbling under her breath that Alexis should be eating more and not starving herself just to look like a toothpick.

"Did I pass?" Alexis asked the burly female who had searched her and ran the medical scanners over her body with professional detachment.

The guard looked at Alexis with a vicious stare, as if Alexis had insulted her somehow without even meaning to, then in a high, shrill voice that didn't fit the large body whatsoever, the guard told her that she was the healthiest person she had ever seen pass through the inspection station, and to have a nice visit.

Alexis seemed to think that the guard didn't quite mean it.

Hugh was waiting for her with a smile, no doubt, she thought, because he had been watching her on the small, hidden camera Alexis could feel was filming her in the dressing room. They had certainly hid it well and she was certain that Viktorovna was the mastermind behind that little improvement.

"So now what?" she asked as she picked up her bags. "Psychological tests? IQ tests? Manual dexterity perhaps?"

"No, that's about it for the inspections." He appeared not to have caught on to her sarcasm. "Next would be an orientation session to acquaint you with the peculiar precautions and rules we have up here on the Colonies, such as alarms and where to go if one sounds and what you can and can't do and so on." He looked her over a moment as his hover luggage pulled up behind him, almost as if he were checking her out but his eyes held no lascivious intent. "But I think we can skip that with you. I can explain the highlights and you seem more than intelligent enough to be able to figure out the rest. Most of it's common sense, like don't break out any main support walls and don't open any air-locks that lead out to space. That sort of thing." He smiled brightly.

"Sounds good to me," she said as she followed Hugh out of the inspection area and through a series of air locks and de-contamination rooms. Alexis was starting to believe that Hugh Crow was even more important than she had at first thought and perhaps he could even enlighten her on some of the questions she had still lingering like a bad after-shave. The man was obviously attracted to her and it was a good bet that with a little persuasion she could get him to tell her quite a lot, or at least point her in the right direction. She was well aware that he had tried not to check out her body but, like with most men, the temptation had been too great and his surface thoughts seemed to be focused on her legs and short skirt much more than on any orientation.

The fact that he had not mentioned his occupation for the Colony, even though Alexis had asked twice, grated on her nerves and made her slightly wary. People like Hugh Crow never did anything without a reason. They chose their words carefully and deliberately and even though they might appear to have let something slip or seemed slow, they were well aware of exactly what they said and what it implied. When people like Hugh Crow wanted something, they almost always got it. He might just be the best place to start here on the Colony.

"So where do they have you staying?" he inquired as they stepped out of the last air-lock and onto a balcony with a guard rail over-looking the entire main Colony length-wise down the center of the cylinder, the fresh, clean, cool air embracing her face and cheeks and invigorating her after the stale air of the transport and the inspection area.

She had heard all the tales and rumors concerning the O'Neill Colonies, had even downloaded all the technical manuals and schematics and memorized them. She was well aware that the engineering of the Colonies was a feat in itself and that those who had come up here, without exception, had praised the construction and the livability as beyond compare, but she was never one to believe such things. Alexis had always been one to shun other's descriptions of places, preferring to see them herself and have an open mind about it all.

With the Colonies, the descriptions that she had read had been extraordinary, vivid and filled with a wonder she thought just the ramblings of the overwhelmed journalists who had never really experienced anything real in their lives anyway and who had been paid by the Colonies to make the Colonies look good to the Earthers. But when she stepped onto that balcony and beheld for the first time the unparalleled view, she found that even the vivid descriptions didn't do it justice. She was, for one of the few and rare times in her life, overwhelmed by what was displayed before her and it caused her to miss the question posed by Hugh.

It was over a hundred years ago that the Princeton particle physicist Gerard O' Neill had first proposed the possibility of building colonies in space that could house Humans in an Earth-like environment and ease the problems of over-crowding on the planet. The Colonies would be situated at the Lagrangian points between the Earth and the Moon, where the gravitational pull between the two massive bodies balanced out and any object thus placed would not need to constantly correct their position due to gravitational affects. O'Neill had originally chosen the Lagrangian point L5 as the most promising for a colony and that was where *Stargazer I* now serenely floated in the boundlessness of space.

As with most ideas that were ahead of their time, O'Neill's had been scoffed at and billed as impractical by the supposed experts in the field, who, it generally turned out, tended to not be experts in much of anything but nay-saying. However, with the staggering growth of the planet's population after the turn of the Twenty-first Century and the slow progress with the drastic population control methods being introduced as well as the expanded life-expectancy, it was quickly realized that something would have to be done to ease the over-crowding problems that would eventually turn the Earth into one big city and eat away its limited resources before this new century was over, plunging humans into a crisis greater than any they had ever faced before.

The small scientific colony on the Moon was impractical for any type of large scale colonization and the colony an Mars, christened *Galileo Prime* and only completed twenty years ago, was too far away for any practical usage. The terra forming that was just in its infancy on Mars could transform the small planet into a human-friendly place, but that was decades if not centuries away and such time was not envisioned for the survivability of the

140

Earth as a viable home.

As such, the concept for the O'Neill Colonies had been revisited by a group of investors with the capital and power to see their plans through. *Stargazer I* had been the result. Taking nothing from the Earth except for during the initial construction period, and providing permanent living space for up to 50,000 souls, the construction of *Stargazer I* heralded the beginning of a marathon construction project which, at the moment, had three more Colonies near total self-sufficiency and three more under construction with an unlimited number of follow-up Colonies already slated to be built. The asteroid belt had more than enough materials to supply an unlimited amount of colonies.

Unbeknownst to most Earthers, the construction of *Stargazer I* was the harbinger of a new order that would shift the balance of power and begin the first major step of the human colonization of space. But that was still in the future, a future that seemed rather far off at the moment.

The main area of the Colony she was now gazing over was basically a large, elongated cylinder rotating about a fixed central spoke for the simulation of gravity – about four-fifths that of Earth – and housed the living and working spaces of the inhabitants. Huge solar panels constantly facing the sun provided more than enough power. A latticework of transparent aluminum plates and trans-aluminum girders composed the upper half of the cylinder allowing an unparalleled view of space.

The velvety blackness with its patchwork of stars, nebulae and galaxies greeted the senses with an over-abundance of visual delights that was only obscured by the passage of the bright blue and white globe spinning into view with a regularity one could set a watch by. The lustrous illumination of the sun in the distance shining like a lone beacon in the night for all the lost souls and wayward lovers who sat in the lush gardens and parks and looked out on the theater of God's own handiwork, was resplendent in its subtle hues.

It was larger then she had expected.

Though she knew the exact dimensions, the numbers somehow didn't relate to the shear immensity now laid out before her. The main living area ran for ten kilometers and was filled with beautiful, charming, old-European houses clustering together in a random layout, grabbing and holding the eye with a grandeur belying the intricate, detailed plan actually in place, the verdant green of the parks and gardens interspersing in a medley of function and artistic flair. Tall trees towered above the landscape like pillars holding up the sky while a long, narrow lake ran the length of half the ten kilometer

141

expanse, the triangular sails of the numerous boats plying its waters looking like toys in the distance.   A rising set of steps and small hills, covered with an abundance of pines, firs, alders and lusty green aspens sat in the crystal clear distance, as if set there with a precision looking almost natural. There were no roads, only walkways. There were no hovs only bicycles, and an efficient mass transportation system bringing the inhabitants to and from work, to and from home with the precision of a model railroad.

The living areas were not, as one would expect, confined only to the lower portion of the cylinder. They rose up at least half-way up the sides so that at any time the occupants had the uncanny and unnatural feeling of having trees, houses and people almost above them, hanging onto the side of the cylinder and not falling. For those who lived there it was but a part of the landscape, accepted as natural and not seen anymore. To a visitor it was one of the oddest experiences, as Alexis could attest. Although from a physics standpoint she was well aware how it was possible for the landscape, buildings and people to remain where they were, she continued to wait for them to fall, for the water to spill out.

It made her smile, for the designers had the touch of genius that seemed rare in these days of tall mega-structures without purpose or form. But this place, this place was a mélange of function and livability, of form and design, a veritable oasis in the desert that was space and it impressed Alexis more than anything had impressed her in a long, long time. It was not often that she as able to stop during one of her assignments and actually enjoy the landscape in which she found herself.

She had been to almost every corner of the world and yet she had no photos, no real memories of what any of it looked like, the buildings, castles and monuments lost in a whirl of activity and death which seemed to have followed her like an avenger shadow. That she was able to see this place for what it was, was able to soak in the surroundings and have time to be impressed struck a cord in her lessening her smile and making her self-conscious of the fact that she should be concentrating on her mission and not the scenery.

Hugh beamed a self-conscious smile as he watched her reaction and waited for her to come back to him. It was more or less the same with every one who saw the Colony for the first time and almost all of the adherents to the benefits of living in the Colonies were created at this balcony, which had been set in this precise location for that very reason.

Alexis pursed her lips, realized that she had to stay in character and continue to be impressed and turned to look at Hugh. "This is the Colony," she breathed as she looked back at the expanse before her, leaning on the railing and absorbing the view in all its glory.

"This is the Colony," he replied casually, watching her back, her ass, and the tight skirt fitting to perfection and giving her a definition most women would kill to have. "Like I said, you'd know it when you saw it".

"Do they all look like this?"

"For the most part, but each Colony has its own say as to how the interior looks, how much water, forest, mountains or plains. They each have their own personal touch."

"It's fantastic. It's really beyond words," she said as she regained her composure and looked at him with her crooked smile. "No wonder people want to leave the Earth forever and move here. Where are the food growing regions? I know that you don't transport it up from Earth."

"That's in the Ag-Complex beyond the far wall. We produce enough food, through genetically engineered products, to have a surplus that we actually ship to the other Colonies still getting started. We never have to worry about food here." Hugh guided her to the elevators leading to the ground level. "Within the next three decades we expect to have twenty to thirty Colonies built, each totally self-sufficient. There's more raw material and resources in the asteroid belt then we could ever find on Earth and the mining companies are growing rapidly, increasing their efficiency at extraction with each passing day. I wouldn't be surprised if the Colonies began to exert political influence in the near future, because this is where the future lies."

She looked at him, the radiance on his face and the conviction in his voice telling her that Hugh Crow was completely convinced in what he was doing. She had her doubts about his last statement, but one never knew with the way politics ran nowadays. Twenty such colonies at 50,000 each came out to one million people. If they all stood together during elections, they could conceivably make a large impact. She began to understand more why those on the Earth wanted to maintain control so fervently. To have that many people completely independent and self-sufficient would make any politician nervous.

The elevator stopped and they stepped out to the sound of birds and children and life.

"You never did tell me where they have you staying," Hugh asked as they stood by a stop for the light-rail. "It's not like we have hotels or anything like that, at least not yet. They did give you a place to stay, didn't they?" He asked with a slight alarm in his voice, looking at her with consternation.

"Yes, they did. Someone named Grace Ackland is what I was told."

"Grace?" Hugh said as if the name was a curse. "You don't want to stay with Grace. That's where they put people they don't want to stay long. You wouldn't get along with Grace, I can guarantee you that."

Alexis saw the invitation coming from a kilometer away. He had been hitting on her since he had first spoken, even if it was subtle and well-played and she was not at all surprised that he discouraging her from staying with Grace Ackland. The thoughts floating about his mind like ping-pong balls were more than obvious enough in their connotations that she could fill out the picture reasonably well enough.

"Why don't you stay with me while you're here, Ms. Baker. I've got more than enough room," he asked with such ease and self-assurance that she had to compliment him on his technique.

The light-rail came to the station and people began to move about as the doors opened to disgorge the occupants.

"Thank you very much for the offer," she said in a light voice, trying to play hard-to-get while not turning him off completely. He still had usefulness to him that she could exploit. It was not like he was all that bad looking. "But I don't think that would be appropriate. We just met."

He smiled at her as he guided her into the light-rail and motioned for her to sit. "My wife loves to entertain visitors and I think that you two would get along quite well."

She blushed, a response she didn't have to fake. There had been nothing in his surface thoughts about a wife. Nothing. Coupled with no ring on his finger, she had taken that as proof that he was not married. That was rather embarrassing. She was beginning to assume facts not in evidence and that was a bad sign. If she wanted to stay alive past the night, she was going to have to pay much more attention and stop daydreaming and being impressed.

This was not a vacation.

This was deadly serious.

"In that case, I'd be delighted. Thank you very much for the offer and I apologize for the assumption..."

He cut her off with a wave of his hand indicating that he had taken no offense. "Perhaps I can even help you with your investigation, or at least introduce you to the people who might know something." He looked down at his ring-less hand. "And I left my ring behind when I went planet-side, in case you were wondering."

"I was, actually, and I really do appreciate the invitation to stay with you and your wife. Staying with people can be trying sometimes. By the way, you still

144

haven't told me who you are around here and I'm fairly well versed with the names of all the important people on this Colony and I don't remember seeing your name on any of the lists," she said innocently as she watched the landscape pass by and had to remind herself that she was inside a large cylinder in the coldness of space and not on Earth. This was one of those places where one had to constantly remember that all that stood between you and death was the common sense of those around you and the thin trans-aluminum bulkheads.

He smiled at her as the light-rail worked its way around the long lake, complete with waves and sandy beaches holding small groups of bathers in various states of undress, some even totally naked. It was apparent to Alexis that the inhabitants of *Stargazer I* had a rather liberal idea of a dress code.

"Perhaps that's because I'm one of those rare individuals," he said with a diligent and modest air, "who are powerful enough to be able to keep our names off such lists."

*   *   *

Alexis stood before the laboratory once housing the offices of Dr. Mbombo Dumvo. There was no sign of the explosion that had gutted the labs back in May. The authorities had quickly repaired the damage and had the lab up and running again within weeks. The sooner people forgot about the good doctor and his death, the better.

Hugh had given her a list of names of people to whom she could speak and who might have some knowledge of the explosion. She was not surprised that it matched her own list from Cav fairly well, except for one name she noted was missing from Hugh's list but was near the top of her list. Such obvious signs were always a good place to start and so it was that she was looking for a one Dr. Tsi Shu. She had been Dr. Dumvo's primary lab assistant and one of the people whom Alexis was certain would have information that would be useful, if any such information even existed.

Alexis was convinced, from what she had seen so far and from the people that she had met, that getting information out of anyone on this colony was going to be harder than pulling teeth out of a mother grizzly bear. They had been warned, she was convinced, to avoid answering any questions related to the doctor's death or the explosion.

And it was very telling that Dr. Shu had not been on Hugh's list. Hugh would have certainly known that Shu would know more than anyone else about Dr. Dumvo's work and his death and the very fact that her name had been left off had told her much. Hugh was not all that eager to help her despite his outward friendliness and willingness. It would have been nice to be able to contact Cav and ask him about this Hugh Crow, but she had noticed Kiril keeping a sharp watch on her and was certain that any transmission planet-side would be monitored, analyzed and dissected instantly. Any mention of Hugh's name and red flags would start rising for the man almost instantly.

No, contacting Cav was out of the question. She was on her own this time ... and that was the way she liked it anyway. She set her face into the friendly pose that was Shannon Baker and walked into the lab. There were several people wandering around, holding pocket computers, scanners or various small experiments with which they all appeared to be extremely involved. Alexis spotted Dr. Shu quickly, her resolute, impassive oriental face standing out among the other Caucasians.

She walked up to her and spoke, her accent perfect. "Neh hoh mah?"

Dr. Shu looked up at the sound of her native Cantonese tongue, her black, short-cut hair and attractive dark eyes with that distinctive Chinese look placing her in her late eighties, perhaps even older, the age-lines that one would expect not to appear until one-hundred-and-ten or later prominent on her face.

"Ho-ho," she said in response, finding it odd that this obvious quai-loh was speaking her language extremely well. When she had first heard it, Shu had thought that another Chinese assistant had been hired. But this one was not Chinese. She had the look of trouble about her.

"Dr. Shu?" Alexis asked, though she knew exactly that this was Shu. She had memorized the doctor's dossier.

"Yes, I am Dr. Shu. What can I do far you?" She seemed perturbed that she had been interrupted and her tone indicated that she didn't want to have to talk to Alexis for very long, if at all.

"I'm Shannon Baker and I work for..."

"Yes, I know. who you are," Shu interrupted irritably, standing up from her workbench housing several computer monitors as well as special graphic interfaces. She walked over to another station and Alexis followed. "There's nothing here for you to find. It was all discussed already. The case has been closed, was an accident." Her succinct, edgy remarks told Alexis that all had not been discussed and that there was much to learn here, although perhaps not from Dr. Shu.

"I see. Well, then perhaps you won't mind answering a few questions for me that I have concerning the death of Dr. Dumvo. We've been recently lead to believe that perhaps the death wasn't as accidental as it had been thought and the survivor benefits for the spouse and the compensation for the Colony for damages can't be released until we have a firm grasp on the facts."

Dr. Shu stopped her work and looked at Alexis, her eyes intense and, Alexis could see, frightened. She probed and found that, indeed, Dr. Shu was very much afraid, thoughts of Dr. Dumvo, his work, and most interestingly, Hugh Crow foremost in her mind. And it was not a very flattering image of Mr. Crow dancing in the vivid black of Dr. Shu's surface thoughts.

Shu looked away quickly, as if aware that Alexis was reading her thoughts, and walked back over to her workbench. Alexis noticed that the other workers seemed to be stiff and edgy, as if they were listening to the conversation and were afraid that Viktorovna would walk in at any second and deport the lot of them for cooperating.

Alexis felt that Shu wanted to talk but was deathly afraid to, at least here in the lab. She spoke again, this time in a whisper. "Yin ksiao shih ta." *We lose much because of a small thing.*

Shu looked up at Alexis with rapt attention and responded back in Cantonese, just as quietly. "Yes, yes we do. You must not press me on this. I know nothing."

Alexis replied in English, hoping to draw the reluctant woman out. "Then why are you so afraid? Listen, Dr. Dumvo had an extensive insurance policy that gives his spouse and kids more money than they'll know what to do with. I could really care less about the company that runs the Colony and their money for the damages, but Dumvo's family deserves something for their loss. I know that it can't make up for his death, but at least they won't have to worry about their finances. That's all I'm trying to do here. If I can just convince my company that there was no hanky-panky here, then I can clear this policy and get them their money. I'm sure that you can understand that."

Shu looked away and was quiet, pretending to stare at her screens and absorbed in her work, but Alexis could tell that she was getting through to the woman, that her thoughts were beginning to form around bits and pieces of data about Dumvo invaluable to Alexis. If she could just reach in and drag them out of the woman's head, she would. But unfortunately, her ability didn't work like that. Anything that was suppressed or buried deeply, as was certainly the case with Shu and Dumvo, Alexis was unable to extract. Only surface thoughts were accessible. It normally gave her the advantage she needed. This was, unfortunately, not one of those times.

Shu finally turned her chair around and looked up at Alexis. "Chi pao pu chu huo," she said quietly, almost as a whisper of wind, the words pronounced delicately and distinctly, as if wanting to make sure that Alexis understood but no one else overheard.

Alexis translated with ease. *Paper cannot wrap up fire.* It was an old saying, an idiom difficult to translate if one didn't understand the hidden meaning, as was the case with most idioms. *A secret cannot be kept forever.*

"Do you want to go somewhere more private?" Alexis whispered in English, aware that the lab was most likely bugged. Perhaps everything in this Colony was bugged.

Shu switched to Mandarin and spoke harshly, her eyes flaring at the proposition spoken in plain English and out in the open. "An jing yi xia!" She was telling Alexis to watch her mouth, that there were ears and eyes everywhere. Still in Mandarin, Shu continued. "Meet me at the Gerard Memorial park, third bench from the large acacia tree in the middle. Half hour."

Alexis nodded her head. "Doh Jeh."

"Don't thank me yet, Ms. Baker. You haven't heard what it is that I have to tell you."

Alexis spent the next thirty minutes wandering around the park Dr. Shu had specified for the meeting, enjoying the pleasant temperature and peaceful feeling she seemed to get from this Colony, almost as if every day were an idyllic cool summer day in the mountains. It almost reminded her of her mountain home, of the peacefulness that seemed to seep from the trees and grass like dew. But it was also a feeling speaking to her of something wrong.

No place was this peaceful and pleasant without a price to be paid. Her own cabin in Alaska had taught her that. The lack of any companionship and the time to reflect on her own soul and its journey was more than enough of a drawback to make it suspect. And this place, out here in the void of space with its perfect climate and perfect people spoke to Alexis' soul like a knife to her heart. There was a danger here that was almost tangible.

She thought about all the information she had on Dr. Dumvo and his death, the terrible plasma fire engulfing his lab and incinerated him till all that was left were but trace elements of his existence. Her eyes narrowed as she realized that they had, actually, never found a body. All they had found were ashes mingled in with the remains of the lab structure and a missing scientist. It was a foregone conclusion that Dumvo had been the one to die, but perhaps that was wrong also. Although DNA analysis had confirmed that the partial remains were Dumvo's, perhaps too many assumptions were being made about each of these deaths. Her own son Alex had been chewed up so much that it was a miracle anyone was able to identify him. Pratali's body was badly smashed against rocks, his head shattered and unidentifiable. Godonov had also been burned beyond recognition and Kido was shot so many times in the face that it had been a mess of blood and brains and not much else.

Perhaps that was where the connection lay. Perhaps the connection that Cav was trying so hard to make was that all the bodies had been beyond simple identification and if someone wanted all these people to disappear, what better way to do it. She had more than enough experience in such things herself to dismiss them as inconsequential. If someone had kidnapped all of them, or better yet, if they had all decided to disappear and work on their discovery in solitude, what happened to each of them would be the perfect set-up to vanish from circulation. It was a sobering thought.

Dr. Shu was punctual, as Alexis had expected, and sat down next to her on the bench, looking around her as if she had been followed. Alexis probed out with her mind to see if indeed she had been followed and found nothing but the simple folk enjoying the day in the park. But she kept up a continual survey anyway, just in case. Something didn't feel right about this whole situation and the way that Dr. Shu perceived of Hugh Crow in her surface thoughts was disturbing.

"We must keep our voices down," Shu said in Cantonese, her voice clouded with a tangible fear.

"I understand that the explosion that killed Dr. Dumvo didn't originate in his lab," Alexis started with, not wanting to jump right into the only question with which she was really concerned, namely what Dumvo was working on the side.

"Yes, that is correct. The explosion occurred in the lab next door, that shares a common wall. They were working on a new plasma containment system and they had a catastrophic failure that devastated the entire lab complex."

"But only Dr. Dumvo was killed."

"No, there were three workers also killed. Two in the plasma lab and one with Dr. Dumvo."

Alexis was intrigued. None of that had been in the reports Cav's people had compiled and it was not like Cav to leave out such important facts. Could it be that there were facts left out of her son's death also? And if that were the case, then who was holding them back? Who didn't want her to solve this little riddle?

"This may sound callous, but why weren't you killed? Weren't you his primary assistant?"

Shu looked out over the small pond sitting before them, the ducks gently glided on the water looking serene and happy. "The explosion happened at night. I don't work at night." She looked up at Alexis. "Neither did Dr. Dumvo."

Now that was something certainly bot in the report, Alexis thought as she tried to understand what Shu was saying. Why would he choose that night of all nights to go to the lab then? That had to be the worst luck imaginable. "Then why was he there?"

Shu shrugged her shoulders. "This I don't know." She peered deep into Alexis' eyes a moment, then looked back at the ducks floating nearby, almost as if trying to gauge the depth of Alexis' sincerity. "How much do you know about nano-technology?"

That was an odd question. "I know the basics, but that's about it." Alexis had to lean forward to hear the barely audible whisper Shu was using, almost like a breath of wind rather than a voice. This woman was terrified of something, that was certain.

"Back at the end of the last century when the applications and know-how necessary to create nano-technology was first realized, it was thought that the field would produce some of the most radical changes in human evolution and knowledge ever imagined. The main applications that were foreseen were all in terms of medical aspects, but it was soon discovered that although the nano-probes could be readily manufactured, the process of placing the proper instructions in them, of giving them enough memory to function properly on their own, and the ultimate rejection by the body of their presence made the effort not worth the money or time.

"Dr. Dumvo was not a great scientist. But he was a good one, who was neat and orderly and had a penchant for working hard and discovering ideas more by accident than by design. As such, his work here on *Stargazer I* was never all that important." She turned now to look at Alexis again, her eyes intense, her voice like gossamer threads. "But it was what he was working on apart from the main research grants, where he found his greatest discovery and secret. Mbombo had found a way, completely by accident, to create a system that mimicked the human mind, a nano-tech aggregate that when working together could produce the same patterns as those found in a human mind. By itself, it's nothing special. It really has no functional application apart from the shear interest of it, but it was a breakthrough nonetheless. He was just starting to work on a system for the aggregate to reproduce itself when he was killed."

Alexis was confused. She had expected to find out about some revolutionary break-through in medical sciences involving nano-probes and their application to human physiology. But this... It was almost as meaningless as her son's work on holographic memory, another concept that was interesting in its own right but which really held no applications to anything else since the technology of the time had already found better ways of doing the same things. And now this...

She was beginning to think that perhaps there wasn't a pattern to these killings at all in terms of their occupations. If it was not for the suspicious circumstances surrounding each death and the fact that a majority of the participants had been in communication shortly before their deaths, Alexis would think, as she had upon first seeing this mess, that there was really nothing here at all.

Her idle thought of earlier about the five dead scientists not really being dead rose again to the surface of her thoughts. "That's it?" she asked a little incredulously.

Dr. Shu turned to look at her again and narrowed her eyes. "But you don't understand," she said in English, lapsing into that language without being aware. "He would never have even been working on it if that nice young man from Earth had not spoken to him about an idea that he had. He was doing this for someone else, and that someone else has died also, just a day before Dr. Dumvo was killed. Do you not see? There was something here, something Mbombo either didn't see or didn't share with me that was of immense importance. Why else murder the man?"

Just like Clovis, Shu had used the term murder with deliberation. Was it possible that Dr. Shu was to be the next one murdered by the mysterious assassins? And if she was, should Alexis tell her and blow her cover? Should she do something to prevent it from occurring or just ignore it and hope that she was long gone from this Colony when the assassination took place?

"What nice young man, Dr. Shu?" Alexis prodded, aware that Shu was talking about Alex. Her bout of conscience would have to wait.

"Why, the one who sent all those e-mails using that program that erased all evidence of their existence. Alex Hart I believe his name was. Yes, Dr. Alexander Hart. Dr. Dumvo liked him very much."

There's the connection again, right back to my son, "So you're saying that if was Dr. Hart who asked Dr. Dumvo to work on this project?"

"Yes," Shu said as if such a question were self-evident. "But not specifically, mind you. Dr. Dumvo had already been working along these lines. The conversations with Dr. Hart just kind of gave him an impetus and a different direction to try. It wasn't like they had a real collaboration or anything, at least not that Mbombo told me about."

Although interesting, there really was not anything new here for Alexis to use. There was nothing here accounting for their deaths or for the fear Shu was experiencing and the cloak and dagger bit on which she had insisted on by meeting in the park.

Alexis frowned slightly, wondering who she was going to visit next when Shu spoke again, still quietly, the quacking of the ducks almost overwhelming her voice. "But the most unusual thing was what Mbombo told me the day before he was killed. I asked him where he was getting all the funds from to do this extra work, because he was using much equipment and consumables and I knew that on his salary he couldn't afford all of it. It was impossible. That's when he told that it was Mr. Crow who had approached him shortly after the first communication with Dr. Hart and offered to fund the entire project, so long as he kept it quiet that he was involved."

Alexis was not surprised. Stunned would have been a far better description. Hugh knew about what Dumvo was doing. Was he the one who had him killed? She could easily see the man having that much power up here, but the question was still why? Why in the world kill the man over a discovery that didn't hold any promise? There had to be something else. And if Hugh was involved, why was he still alive? He would be the only one out of the group to have survived the assassins and oddest of all, he didn't even seem concerned about it. His business partner was killed along with all his friends and Hugh was acting as if it meant nothing to him. In Alexis' world, that could only mean that Hugh Crow knew of the assassinations beforehand and was thus a part of them.

"Now you understand my reluctance, yes?" Shu said as she stood and made to go. "I have already said too much. Hugh Crow is a powerful man and I don't want to end up like Dr. Dumvo. I must go now. I am sorry if the information I gave you was not what you were looking for."

"Can you tell me what it is that Hugh Crow does here?" Alexis asked in exasperation. She hated being in the dark about anything and this was a major piece. Cav should have known about Crow, should have had all the dirt on the man and certainly should have known that he was involved in all this. And here she was sleeping in the man's house, as his guest.

Shu bowed to Alexis and then scampered off without answering or even acknowledging the question still hanging in the air like stale air. It was then that Alexis felt it again, her sub-conscious alerting her to the presence of one who didn't belong, the same blurred, wrongness she felt twice before. But this time there was no malevolence to it, no feeling of danger or weapons or attack as there had been with the others. This was more of a sensation of watching, listening, reaching out with the mind to try to find the gist of the discussion between Shannon Baker and Dr. Tsi Shu.

And there was something else. There was a pathos of commiseration in this one, for it was only one person she sensed and not a group, a feeling that in some odd way Alexis and the watcher were connected. It was not just because they could probably sense each other mentally, each aware of the others probes, but rather something more. It was something more along the lines of..... She could not place it.

But it was there, tangible and vibrant and real, as real as the ducks swimming in the pond or the trees providing the shade around her. And it bothered her as much as it intrigued her. This was something new, something different from anything she had ever felt before... except for one time. There was one time in her life she had felt a connection that was anything akin to this.

She almost bolted from the bench with the conclusion she reached, a conclusion that was an impossibility. She looked around as non-chalantly as she could but saw no one within her immediate sight who looked out of place, who looked wrong as the others had. If her feeling was correct, then this mission had just taken on a whole new meaning and she would have to get in contact, personal contact, with Cav as quickly as possible before she went any further. This even put Hugh Crow's involvement on the backburner. This changed everything.

And it put her life in danger aboard *Stargazer I* far more than she had thought possible.

Man may wish for concord, but nature knows
better what is good for the species.
Nature wants discord.

14

13 August 2085, 0230 hrs

Alexis lay in the comfortably small bed of the Crow's guest room, wearing the silken pajamas Cav had thoughtfully packed for her. She was surprised that Cav had not included a revealing teddy or other alluring nightwear in which she could strut around as she stared at the ceiling of the moderate-sized but lavishing decorated house. The man seemed to have become more or a admirer than a father-figure and she had to laugh about his presumptions. Like she would sleep with someone like him. Hardly.

The Colony had devised a simple yet ingenious system for creating the illusion of night-time within the main Colony, moving the solar panels to block the light from the sun and basically casting a shadow over the Colony simulating a darkness caming straight from space itself. Unfortunately, it also blocked out any star field one would normally see, but then as she had said often before, there was always a price to pay for utopia.

Her price was not being able to sleep again.

She was having trouble figuring out what her reward was at the end of the day. For Alexis, rewards were dreams and dreams were myths created for other people who actually had life to live that didn't include having their every move planned, their birth controlled, their mind implanted with such a wealth of shit that she sometimes wondered how she had ever managed to not suffocate on her self-righteousness.

At least this time her insomnia had nothing to do with Clovis. His memory seemed to have finally sunk to that deep, dark hole that all the other deaths for which she had been responsible sank in her bottomless mind, that hole of conscience acting like a deep well, the rope for which is not long enough to reach and thus the water sits stagnant and tranquil, unperturbed by the world outside.

It was the same place she assumed all her emotions sank, refusing to see the light of day and denying her even the merest normalcy those she pitied for their over-abundance of emotions found so endearing. She was well aware that she was not normal by any competent definition. She had stopped trying to be normal at the age of ten when Cav had used her for her first assignment. She had stopped trying many things that day, which an ordinary ten year old would find enlightening.

Perhaps that was the day she had first died.

No, Clovis was not the issue tonight, though perhaps he should have been. Tonight her thoughts were fastened firmly on the revelation she had received from the shadow person whom she had seen in her mind, the revelation she knew could not be true but which she could not explain in any other way. There had been a connection there of a mother to a child like a fine gossamer thread a spider might weave on a warm spring day, drifting in the wind, just waiting for a passerby to snag and pull away into oblivion. It was a connection stronger than life and she was now beginning to believe that it was haunting her from beyond the grave in a nemesis of guilt. Because if it was not from beyond the grave, if it was not a mental projection of a lost and suppressed guilt languishing in her deep well of a mind, then it meant only one of two things: either Alexander Hart was not dead or Alexis had another child in the world who was following her, playing with her mind like a cat with a mouse till, in the end, all that was left was a shell of a body that was lifeless.

And Alexis was certain that whatever it was, whomever it was, had to do with this mission, with this seemingly disconnected series of events and data screaming at her for resolution. But more than that, more than the tenuous connections she was formulating between all these dead people, it begged the question of how she could have had another child without her knowledge.

Did Alex have a twin? That was a remote possibility but one she found hard to swallow. She would have known about a twin. She had been awake during the delivery – another moment through which she would have rather slept than bear the guilt of loss. There had to be another explanation, an explanation she was beginning to think led back to Cav.

She laughed a moment.

Everything she was seemed to lead back to Cav, as if he had been her mother in some demented way almost fitting into her life too easily.

She rolled over onto her side, stuffing the pillow under her head in brutal stabs. There was a large plate-glass window comprising one of the walls and it opened out onto a partially obstructed view of the Colony, the dimmed lights of the walkways spilling their subtle yet delicate light onto the sheets covering her like a shroud, casting their luminous shadows in soft, ethereal grays upon her mind.

There was a quiet seeping through the threshold of the windows, under the doors of the house, through the very walls surrounding her like a tomb in the darkness that seemed surreal in its intensity, lapping against the walls in ripples of solitude and tranquility, speaking volumes from the darkness outside.

Alexis had always admired the night with its hidden world emerging with the setting of the sun and the cooling of the land as if it, too, deemed it necessary to sleep in a slumber of nocturnal bliss opening the world to a peace cloaked in darkness abundant with life. It was the night that allowed her to see into the infinity that was the Universe, to see beyond the limited shell of the atmosphere humans had called home for so long. It allowed her to gaze out onto a time-machine of stars winking and twinkling and radiating like miniature candles from afar, their desolate lives forever intertwined with each other through invisible threads of gravity, whose embracing power stretched to the very beginning of life and laid out the fabric humans so blithely called time.

The night held a mystic for her that was priceless and beyond words, that gave to her a comfort, an appeasement, a justification sweeping in from the dying day like an off-shore breeze and blowing the brumes veils of urbane compaction into tattered wisps of starlit abatement easing the mind as much as the soul in its fragmentary nebulosity. It was a time of reflection, of quiet where many of her best ideas had flourished under an expanse of Alaskan sky that seemed to stretch to heaven and back in a kaleidoscope of colors, allowing the stars their full glory, her mind its full range.

Of course, the night was also when she would do some of her best work, the sneaking and prying and stealing that had been so much a part of her life, ingrained in her like her very genetic code, a part of her she could not, even if she had wanted, remove and shake off like an old jacket passed its usefulness and no longer needed.

She was a bringer of death.

There was no getting around that and like those things who had died when she was ten, so too had any resemblance of guilt over what she did, who she was, why she existed at all died that day. For night was also a time of death, the proverbial period of evil lurking in the very shadows of the day lingering in the dusk and giving to the penumbra silhouette of man his concept of self, the monsters of the subconscious allowed to roam freely, their cages of the mind unlocked. Night was darkness and darkness was shadows and shadows were hiding places for that which we, as a species, know exists within our selves but which we deny with a vigor that goes beyond mere denial and eats away at our souls like a cancer, giving it the dark wings of flight where evil lurks and rides in its passage across the moonless phantom of our anima.

It was here, in the night, that life was at its most precious, that humans had, since their first primitive step onto the stage of life, been afraid due to their lack of defense to the mysteries lurking within the dark embrace of eternal mysticism. And it was here, in the dark of the Colony, in the house of a man whom she now knew to be deeply involved in all that she was finding, that she found herself listening to the silence permeating the air like a fog, laying in her silken pajamas feeling so delicate and sinful against her body in such stark contrast to the abrasion she felt in the air.

Crow had never been mentioned anywhere in Alex's journal entries. Not even as a shadowy non-entity. There was nothing to lead her to believe that her son had any contact with Hugh Crow and yet, his willingness to front the money for Dumvo's experiments, approaching the good doctor without ever having been asked and knowing what the project entailed spoke of a knowledge that had to have included Alex. Had to. There was no way that this project, which seemed at the present moment to have been the brain-child of her son and Kido Nakamura, could have involved a man like High Crow without the principle players knowing of it.

There had to be something she was missing. There was a clue here staring her in the face that she couldn't see, or perhaps didn't want to see for the connotations it would surely imply.

And that intrigued her more than anything else.

She felt him coming to the front door, his heavy, musky, masculine mental projection like a hammer to her mind. He opened the unlocked door and worked his way quietly through the house to Alexis' room, his thoughts a rushing trainload of sexual tension whose outlet she knew all too well. He knew the house, knew the layout, knew where she was as if he had done this a hundred times before and now it was by rote.

She readied herself for the assault, stretching one long leg out of the sheets so that its bareness lay like enticing bait, the smooth curves of her partially exposed buttocks sure to gain the attention of the intruder. She also knew this game by rote, having played it to its deadly conclusion more than one time.

The door opened on silent hinges and she closed her eyes in a feint of sleep, ready to explode at him the moment he touched her. Kiril Andrevevich Viktorovna had a lascivious smile that would have appalled the most hardened sexual entertainment employee, his gaze fastening tightly on her exposed body as if it were his to do with as he pleased. And as far as he was concerned, it was.

She could tell that this was not the first time that this man had done this, had violated a woman on the Colony with his absolute power and then covered it up with his corruption. She was beginning to see more of the price to be paid for the varnish of serenity glazing over the Colony like a sugarcoated bitter pill, a glazing hiding a world of powerful forces with baneful intent.

She wondered if Hugh Crow knew Kiril did this, that he was here now at her bedside, in his house, ready to have his way with Shannon Baker and then deport her, or even eliminate her, with the ease of a spoken word. She almost laughed again. Of course Hugh Crow knew. Despite his open hospitality, Mr. Crow wanted Insurance Investigator Shannon Baker out of his hair as badly as the others did. Unfortunately for Kiril Andrevevich Viktorovna, it was not Shannon Baker in the bed.

He laid his big, fleshy, sweaty hand on her lower leg and slowly, gently began to move it up to her firm, tan thigh -- his pants tightening under the constrictions of his lust -- then higher to that luscious, wet place holding the pleasures of a thousand worlds.

With a quickness stunning him into in-action she spun up and around and grabbed his wrist in a vise-like grip, her eyes burning at him in the semi-darkness like fanned coals. "You picked the wrong girl to rape," she hissed in a controlled spray of rage.

He flushed apoplectically, his smile forced yet devious. "I like it when it gets rough, slut," he ejaculated sardonically at her as he struggled to free his hand and, finding her grip far stronger than he had ever imagined, brought his other hand around to strike her a forceful blow across the face and teach her what power was and where women belonged.

Alexis knew at that moment that the only thing that would stop this man was his death, his rapid death. If nothing else, she needed to stop him from doing to anyone else and perhaps atone for all the girls who had cowered under his male-driven lust. She moved with the rapidity of a cat on the attack, her hand a blur of motion. She opted for a throat blow. It was the easiest and least messy option and would eliminate any screams he might emit. In an instant she punctured the trachea by splintering the delicate bones beneath the jaw. His death came quickly, a gurgling sound escaping from his mouth as his eyes lost their spark in a dull fading of life heralding his swift end.

She allowed his body to slump to the floor unceremoniously as she wiped her hand on the sheets to get rid of the greasy slime of his sweat. It was then she sensed the others, those that had been waiting for Kiril to finish so that they too could have their turn, his vaunted security force that every one publicly admired and privately dreaded. And she also felt her again, that presence she felt in the park after talking to Dr. Shu, that presence that had caused her such consternation, like a shade in the background, watching, waiting, knowing.

This time she was not alone, for there were four other blurred images standing around her, the space they occupied distorted as if time itself stood still within it.

Time itself...

The thought perked something in her mind but she didn't have the luxury to follow it up. She would have to leave and do it quickly and quietly. It no longer mattered that she was Shannon Baker or Alexis Locke. All that would matter to those in power here on the Colony was that she had killed Kiril. No one would believe that he had tried to rape her, of that she was certain. Breaking cover was no longer a concern.

Living was.

She ripped open her luggage and pulled out the two weapons Cav had hidden and that the ignorant security guard who was too busy staring at her breasts had missed. One she belted around her silken pajamas as she haphazardly pulled on a pair of tight jeans. The other she held in her hand at the ready. She grabbed the computer scanner, the explosives – that Cav had also been kind enough to hide in her hair conditioner – and her pocket computer, stuffed them into her smaller bag and opened the side window in the bathroom. She suffused the minds of the security force with an image of her and Kiril in the bedroom having riotous sex, then crawled out and melted into the subtle shadows falling in shafts among the tall trees and shrubbery.

Unfortunately, she could sense that that the woman and her four companions were not fooled by the ruse easily placating the guards. If they chose to aid in the chase, Alexis was in for a difficult next few hours.

Having memorized the layout of the main colony area on the trip up to

Stargazer I, she quickly decided on a course and made for the secondary docking port attached to the Ag-Section. She had missed by several hours the return trip of the rapid transport that the now dead Kiril had wanted her to take, so she would need to devise another plan of getting off as quickly as possible. There was no way she could stay here. Shannon Baker was now a liability and she had learnt over the decades that liabilities generally ended up dead.

She also needed to urgently speak to Cav. He needed to know, if he didn't already, that there were more people involved with whatever the five dead scientists had been working on and they were still alive and kicking. What she really needed to do was kick Cav in the balls and demand that he tell her all that he had left out of the reports, of the pre-mission briefings because she was now dead certain that there was a whole hell of a lot more to this than just five dead people. But first, she needed to ditch the woman and her four companions before they decided that it was time for Alexis Locke to disappear. She was well aware that it was not going to be easy. But then when was it ever easy?

Although the Colony had an overabundance of escape pods should the unthinkable occur and a mass evacuation be necessary, they could only be activated if a Colony-wide emergency was declared and although that was not a bad idea at the moment, the only way to create such an emergency was to either break into the main control center or actually cause an emergency. Neither prospect attracted her much.

She noticed that the light-rail didn't run at night, making her trek to the Ag-Section that much harder. It was a good four kilometers from her current position. It was not that far of a hike under normal circumstances but with her little entourage in tow, it might be the longest four klicks she had ever run. She made it to the airlock in a little under eight minutes, sweat glistening on her forehead and making her silken pajama top cling to her bare breasts with a rather erotic sensation as her nipples rubbed against the satiny material. She stared at the lock mechanism keeping the air-tight hatch locked and knew instinctively that there had to be another way, a way that would allow greater access for all the workers toiling daily in the hydroponics sections of the Colony.

She thought back to the schematics of the Colony, brought up the plans in her head, found the entrance for which she was looking and made toward it to her left. It was not long after that that she felt their presence, a phalanx of Colony police making their way toward her. No, not toward her but toward the entrance to the Ag-Section, their thoughts betraying the fact that they were indeed after her but had no clue as to where she was at the moment. They were just blocking off the more obvious escape routes.

She waited and watched from behind a full, leafy bush as the police opened the large, hanger bay-type doors separating the main Colony from the Ag-section and went in, leaving two guards behind to watch over the entrance. She quickly figured out that unless she wanted to create a mass hysteria among the police force and put the name of Shannon Baker on the ten most wanted list, she was going to have to find another way to get to the escape pods. There was no way she would be able to take out all the guards blocking the entrance without attracting the attention of more of them. It was also obvious that now, with the likely discovery of Kiril's body, she would not be able to just waltz onto the transport and leave.

There was a stabbing pain in her chest for a moment, then the report of a weapon, the high-pitched whine and thwack of a silencer audible to her superior hearing. She was knocked over by the impact, the momentum of the ultra high-velocity projectile transferring itself to her body in an instant of searing, white-hot pain, the unexpected shock taking her completely by surprise. She instantaneously isolated the affected area with her mind, cutting off the flow of electrical impulses telling her mind that she was in pain. Next, she began the process of healing, setting her own body to work to regenerate itself from the damage the bullet had created on its trajectory through her body.

Fortunately for her it had missed any vital organs, only shredding the skin and tissue above her left breast and chipping her clavicle, tearing apart blood vessels in its pernicious path and shattering muscle as it exited her back in a spread of crimson blood.

"Shit!" she exclaimed out loud, the pain having subsided and the gushing blood ebbing to a trickle and then stopping altogether. "Those fuckers shot me. What the hell?" She crawled away from the area in which she had been hiding, trying to ascertain exactly who it was that had fired on her and where they were located. She found them quickly enough, the stampeding beat of multiple-booted feet coming to her quickly a hundred meters across the grassy knoll situated between her and the first house.

She made her way back toward the lake, remembering that there was an emergency escape station on the other side of the library structure butting up against the shore on the far side. That would have to be her next attempt.

An alarm began to wail, a whining, lonesome, annoying noise grating against her nerves for the thirty seconds it sounded. It was followed by an announcement for the residents of the Colony to stay in their houses as there was a fugitive on the loose and the police would be capturing her shortly. She was considered armed and dangerous and no one should attempt to apprehend her for any reason.

Alexis came to the rather sudden but not unsurprising opinion that this was getting more serious much quicker than she had anticipated and she would need to do something soon or else end up a trophy on the wall of the local authorities.

There was fusillade of shooting at her as she dove for cover behind a mound of grass, a bullet nipping her lower leg. She quickly set her body to work on that wound. It was a bad place to be wounded for someone who needed to move quickly, but then was not this par for the course? She could easily remember a dozen times when she had been shot or stabbed and none of them helped her mood at the present moment.

She sensed about with her mind and found that the police had anticipated her move and blocked her off from her intended escape route. This was something about which Cav had been correct: the police force was fanatic and efficient, especially with the death of their revered leader inspiring them. She looked down at the blood-encrusted jeans now plastered to her lower leg with a congealed mass of plasma. This was not working according to plan. She drew her weapon free from its holster and pulled out some of the explosives she had brought along. She was hesitant about using explosives on what amounted to a space station, not sure what a series of explosions would do to the Colony, but hoped that the million or so metric tons of dirt comprising the ground would absorb the majority of the blast. The last thing she wanted was to puncture the outer skin of the Colony and create a catastrophe.

Well, maybe it was not the last thing she wanted. Setting the micro-timer for five seconds, she heaved the small ball of high-density plastic explosives and then ran in a low crouch as best she could with her wounded leg. The explosion rocked the ground beneath her with a force far in excess of that which she expected and it spilled her to the grass in a tumble. She stood back up, the soreness in her chest and leg beginning to make it through the mental block she had placed, and continued to move, getting another ball of the putty-like explosive ready.

She should not be feeling any pain, her advanced pain-blocking techniques capable of easily handling the wounds she had sustained. She had worse. There was that time in Istanbul when that stupid hawker had ... She dropped the image from her mind and concentrated. Something else was interfering with the process. Perhaps even *someone* else was interfering as she sensed the shadow woman hovering close-by, watching and waiting, for what Alexis had no idea. It was almost as if she were testing Alexis, or perhaps even waiting until the police force had wounded Alexis enough so that she would not be such a threat, only to sweep in and take Alexis out herself.

She took a quick look back and saw a blackish cloud with tints of orange highlights rising into the air, its presence in the darkness of the Colony night foreboding. She looked down at the wad of explosives in her hand and wondered how it could have created such a large explosion. What had Cav given her? It certainly was not the normal explosive material with which she was familiar. There was no way that such a small ball of it would produce an explosion that large. Maybe she had been out of the action for too long. Maybe what she held in her hand was now the standard issue explosives all agents received. She felt a laugh escape through her clenched teeth. What other agents? She was all that Cav had.

Three police stepped out from behind a grouping of low trees directly before her. She didn't think, just reacted. In an instant she fired three, precise rounds echoing through the air like a beacon, the harsh sound of the rapid-fire, high-velocity hand gun more or less lost in the cacophony that was the explosion she had created. The three guards fell with small, bloody holes in their foreheads and the back of their skulls blasted out in a crater of scrambled gray matter and bone fragments.

She continued to move, knowing that stopping would be her end. She could sense the presence of the guards moving in behind her, of the guards moving to block her path toward the lake ahead of her. They knew her moves, her path.

Of course! She chided herself as she began to think of a new plan. They probably have sophisticated monitoring systems in place throughout the Colony to keep an eye on everything, if not for security reasons then for engineering reasons. *They can easily track me, especially if I continue to make big explosions and fire off weapons. Why am I being so sloppy? Think Alexis, think! This is your life your playing with here and at the moment it's not going all that well, in case you had not noticed.*

She found herself moving back toward the Ag-Section hanger bay doors and found, to her surprise, that there were now only two people guarding the large entrance.

A trap.

They were herding her toward the Ag-Section. But why? She had no choice. She could feel them coming up behind her, closing the noose. She took aim and laid out the two guards standing by the entrance with clean shots, then sprinted through the large hanger-like entrance and into the Ag-Section...

... and bright sunlight, the long rows of assorted grains, corns and vegetables stretching off into the far distance. It was obvious to her that this part of the Colony was not subject to the shadow cast by the solar panels and thus in perpetual sunlight to facilitate twenty-four hour growing. She remembered reading something about that and finding it interesting. Now it was just annoying. Shielding her eyes with a hand from the harshness of the bright light, she took her bearings and made toward the nearest escape pod station, then stopped. That was what they would be expecting. She would have to start thinking differently or else they would certainly corner her like a rabid animal and treat her just as badly.

She didn't have much time to think.

A series of plasma blasts rocked the ground around her as guards came pouring in from the main Colony and from the far side of the cornstalks, closing in on her with newer, more powerful weapons and the intention of not capturing her alive. She had killed too many now for them to even begin to think about having mercy.

Although panic, the silent killer of people in her position, was not setting in, she was beginning to get a little nervous. She was getting too old for all this crap.

A plasma blast grazed her right leg and it took all of her will power to not scream out in agony and fall over. "Son-of-a-bitch!" she exclaimed as she again isolated the blistered burn, the blackened skin and oozing, bubbly flesh transmitting that sickly-sweet malodor so common to burnt, human flesh. It was not a large wound, but it was big enough; big enough to cause her major problems.

She thought a moment, sensed where and how the guards were moving, then made her break for the Colony maintenance center off to her left, one of the few places free of converging guards. A plan was forming in her mind that was risky but might just be the only way out of this mess. She sprinted over to the maintenance center and through the open door, closing and sealing it behind her. Working her way toward the area where those personnel who worked on the outer structures of the Colony, in the vacuum of space, had their equipment, she found what she was looking for.

Five of the massive, advanced Human Enhancing Equipment, or HEEs, stood in their power-restoration cubicles recharging. Three were still in the process of renewing their energy supplies. The other two showed green lights across the boards, indicating that they were ready to be used. The

HEEs were made out of high-impact poly-duranium metallic compounds giving a dull, metallic silver sheen to them and an indestructibility making them very safe and stable platforms for the work for which they were intended.

They were anatomically correct with two tremendous, jointed arms and two equally enormous legs allowing the user, who stood in a transparent-aluminum bubble atop the device, unlimited visual access. The HEEs were controlled through an advanced system of virtual reality controls. Simply moving the arms or legs of the operator created the identical movement for the HEE, from walking to climbing to manipulating the powerful hands to turn in a bolt or easily lift objects with masses of several metric tons.

They had been a godsend to the Colonies. Much of the necessary work on the solar panels, the lattice-work repair of girders and transparent panels, even the construction of the Colony itself had been made possible by their advent. They contained a simple yet effective life-support system allowing the user not to have to wear any type of bulky pressure suit as they sat comfortably within the heated dome. And they were tough, capable of surviving repeated micro-meteor strikes and even larger impacts on their hardened bodies without so much as a scratch.

She hit the activation switch on the closest powered-up HEE, threw her remaining equipment into the storage bin on its side, then climbed up the three meters to the access portal t slowly yawning open for her. She had read about these devices several years ago and had memorized the schematics and the operating instructions, but that was not the same as actual experience. As she settled into the operator's seat, placing the communications gear on and strapping herself in, she had the uncanny feeling that this was going to a rough ride. She began flipping switches both manually and mentally, bringing up the command sequences that would allow her to move and ordering the inner airlocks to open so that she could get out.

With the clearing of the initial start-up routines and the self-test, she was given a green board and took her first tentative step out of the re-charging station. It was almost her last. She stepped much too short and quickly had to thrust her arms out and heavily plant her other foot to keep from toppling over onto her face. She shook her head in self-disappointment. She was going to have to be more careful about this.

Why are you going through all this trouble? A voice chimed in her head, a voice not her own but sounding familiar somehow, intruding into her inner sanctuary and giving her pause for a moment. She had never been communicated with like this before, not when she had her defenses up and it was disturbing that this person had been able to break through.

They'll never let you out and if they do, they'll let you stay out there until your use up your life-support and then they'll go out and pick up your life-less body. Just give up and I'll make certain that you're not harmed

Alexis began to walk the HEE awkwardly toward the open inner airlock, the bright, revolving blue lights of the air-lock warning system giving the room an air of the surreal.

She answered the voice back, knowing somehow that it was coming from the shadow woman, the distortion of the words almost as if they were out of phase with her own mind, a distortion within them that spoke of a phase shift. *Fuck you. Those clowns with the plasma rifles don't give a damn about your concerns. They're going to fry me for the death of their beloved, sick boss and there's nothing that you can do about it, so I'd rather pick my own method of death.*

She finally made it into the air lock and ordered the doors to close, her walking becoming smoother with each step as she became used to the device and its control systems. A plasma blast scorched the outer hull of the HEE, but except for the burnt paint, left it undamaged. She looked into her rear-view projectors and saw that the guards were setting up a heavy plasma rifle that would surely penetrate the thick armor of the HEE after a few well-placed shots.

She would have to work quickly.

She noticed that the inner doors would not close. The guards were sending in conflicting orders to the main air-lock computer and it was uncertain what was wanted. With the inner doors still open, the outer doors leading to the cold of space would never open. Not unless, that was, she could convince the computer that the inner doors were closed. She accessed the main computer through the HEE and began to hack in, working calmly and efficiently against the guards who were trying to keep her from getting out, trying to kill her.

You're being foolish, the voice scolded her. This is unnecessary. *There's no reason for you to have to die.*

Tell that to the boys with the heavy plasma rifle, idiot, she responded with a hint of annoyance. This woman, whomever she was, was becoming old very quickly. *I don't think that they feel the same way.* She worked rapidly through the inner-locks and the safety protocols, trying to fool the main computer into thinking that the inner air lock was closed so that the outer doors would open.

166

You won't be successful, the voice said, still in that same collected, matter-of-fact tone she had been using all along, as if somehow she knew that taking a harsher tone would be useless. *This is a dead end.*

Dead end this bitch, Alexis exclaimed as the activation of the rotating red lights above her heralded the opening of the outer air-lock doors and her success. As the pressure seal was broken and the doors slowly opened, the pressure differential between the interior of the Colony and space made itself known in a rush of outward air, taking with it everything not bolted down, and some things that were. She looked into the rear-view projectors and saw the terror on the faces of the guards as the worse possible scenario was becoming reality.

With the inner doors wide open, the Ag-Section of the Colony was now exposed to the rapacious appetite of nearly pressure-less space. Bodies began to fly past Alexis -- safe in her HEE, its mass more than enough to off-set the brutal wind -- as they were pulled out of the Colony. She watched as they writhed and jerked in unimaginable agony and then exploded in a silent flash of crimson gore congealing into tiny, floating, sparkling spheres as their flesh was unable to support the pressure gradient and detonated. Disregarding this gruesome scene, Alexis walked out through the airlock doors and began to make her way along the main access gantry toward the nearest escape pod station.

Inside the Colony, it was a different story.

Terrifying alarms began to wail in abject consternation, their shrill, piercing tones waking up the inhabitants of *Stargazer I* to the horror that was never supposed to happen. The hanger-like doors separating the Ag-Section from the main Colony slammed home with a ringing finality. The lattice-work of girders and transparent aluminum panels that were supported as much by the pressure in the Colony as by their own integral design, began to shiver and buckle as the pressure dropped with a rapidity that didn't seem possible for the small opening of the outer lock, the howling of the wind created like a tornado, rumbling through the fields of wheat and barley and corn, the cattle and pigs and other assorted animals sensing the change and becoming nervous, stampeding away from the danger.

Emergency safety procedures were immediately instituted and heavy airlocks began to shut throughout the complex, sealing off areas from the escaping gases and isolating the maintenance section.

Those guards unfortunate enough to be trapped inside, at least twenty of them, didn't have a chance. As the pressure dropped and dropped with the escape of the vital life-support gases, those who had been able to grab onto something to arrest their flight quickly lost consciousness and were pulled out anyway to die a horrible, bloody death leaving grisly remnants of their battered bodies floating around the Colony like some macabre set of orbiting, bejeweled moons.

And Alexis felt nothing.

Although she had never intended to cause so much death and destruction as was apparent, she felt nothing toward those who were dead, were dying or were about to die. Life was harsh and those on the security detail – an awful lot of them for a Colony supposedly so crime free – had signed up for adventure and here it was. Besides, they worked for Kiril and Kiril was a bastard. There was no reason to feel sorry for any of them

But it seemed to her, as she made her way along the main service gantry, that wherever she ended up, death and destruction followed in a sanguinary trail of mayhem. She had fleeting thought of why that might be but passed it over as more pressing matters took her attention. Her chest was stinging from the hole in it, her body working over-time to repair the damage she had sustained and her leg was pounding away at her senses like a hammer and anvil.

She had never before thought about dying, death having been an integral part of her life for so long that death was nothing but another word to describe what life was. And now was not much different, although she was beginning to have thoughts of all the things she would miss. But more than that, she was irritated to no end that her body was refusing to cooperate and heal itself properly. Where the hell were all these damnable useless thoughts coming?

"Mrs. Baker. You need to return to the nearest airlock and turn yourself in," Hugh Crow's voice blared through her earpiece. "I know who you are."

Alexis was tempted to rip the communications set off her head so that she wouldn't have to listen to his voice, a voice she now associated with Kiril and all the corruption that must be taking place in this far-from-utopian Colony.

"I know that you can hear me and I know that your name is not Shannon Baker."

What was he implying? Only Cav knew what her real name was and if this Hugh Crow knew it also, then she was definitely going to wrap Cav's balls around his neck. "You've got the wrong person, Hugh," she said back with a hint of panic in her voice, as Shannon Baker would be experiencing at the moment.

"Do I really? I was warned about your arrival. Why the hell do you think I was able to get your through the inspection and past Kiril? You know, you

168

didn't need to kill him. That was stupid."

"Fuck you, Hugh. He wasn't trying to rape you, now was he?" She saw up ahead the first of the escape pod stations. She also saw a sight making her heart skip a beat. There was another HEE making its way toward her from the far side of the escape pod station.

"Come on in and we can talk about it. I had no idea what Kiril was doing. He has access to all the buildings and houses here. This wasn't suppose to happen this way," Hugh pleaded with her in false sincerity that was so obvious to Alexis it almost made her want to puke.

She ripped the communications set off her head and started to walk faster to the station but she could tell that there was no way she would beat the other HEE. She wondered who had been adroit enough to don another HEE and figure out where she was headed. She didn't have to wonder long.

You're making a big mistake, Alexis.

She almost stopped. The use of her name was a shock. Who was this person who could so easily penetrate her mental shields and who knew her real name? She had a very bad feeling starting to boil in her stomach that she had been set up, that this whole trip had been one big trap. Could Cav be capable of that? *Yeah, Cav was more than capable of something like this, but he was not behind this. It was that bitch Claudine Maxwell. She was the only other person with the access, the power, and the balls to have done something this asinine.*

I don't want to hurt you, but you're making it harder and harder for me to justify not killing you, the voice implored.

Alexis and the other HEE stopped when they were within four meters, staring each other down as Alexis saw that her adversary was the woman she had felt all along. She had dirty blonde hair tied up in a ponytail, fine facial features speaking of a beauty rivaling Alexis' with full red lips and a body looking strong and firm, hard and powerful. There was something familiar about it, but Alexis didn't have the inclination to figure it out at the moment.

Alexis squinted, finding it hard to concentrate on the face as it appeared to shimmer, fluctuate as if it were there one second then gone the next, like a malfunctioning holo-vid. *Who are you?* she asked as they faced off. It really was not the question she wanted to ask, but it was the first one that popped into her mind and consequently to her lips.

Someone who wants to help you.

Alexis narrowed her eyes and studied the adversary in front of her closely. She tried a mind probe and found, to her dismay, that there was nothing

169

there. Not that her mind was empty. She certainly knew better than that. It was more as if the person herself was not there, as if what she was seeing before her was indeed but a reflection of a physical body that wasn't present.

A wave of distortion seemed to cross her face for a fraction of a second, like a weak-signal on a holo-vision screen. Alexis would have said that it was a hologram, a projection of something somewhere else if it wasn't for the physical bearing, the physical impression she could feel with her mind in the other HEE, a feeling of a person who was there but not there, as if lost somehow in a transitional state that was not a natural part of this Universe.

It was the same phenomena as the attackers at the cabin, the assassins at the deli, the watchers in the park. It was beginning to frustrate her, a feeling she hated. Frustration was an emotion and right now she didn't need any emotions clouding her senses.   What were these people? Who were they? She doubted very much that they had any connection whatsoever with the military, at least not any human military force and the thought that they might be extra-terrestrials put a lump in her throat she didn't need nor want at the moment.   She didn't believe in little green men from other planets traveling to Earth to explore the irresistible human race.

If there was intelligence in the universe other than humans, they would be more than smart enough not to engage in any experiments of contact with a species as hostile and ignorant as humanity, of that she was certain. But the possibility was there for her to explore. Were the five assassinated people about to discover some secret to which another civilization didn't want Humans to have access? Was Hugh Crow one of them?

A corner of her mouth rose up slightly as the idea was discarded out of hand. Alexis had the feeling that whatever this was, it had a very down-to-Earth, human side to it, having had that all too familiar stench of human power and corruption.

A powerful blast shook the gantry on which she was standing, transferring to the massive HEE with a shudder and shaking her with a vengeance in her seat. The gantry began to buckle under the strain. She looked at her rear-view projectors and was dismayed to see a large cloud of debris, dirt, trees, bodies and equipment, all tinged with an orange-reddish cast blowing out like a slow motion cloud into space.

The rapid decompression of the airlock staging area had caused an explosive reaction ripping open a portion of the side of the Ag-Section, exposing even more of the Colony to the merciless appetite of space. A catastrophic progressive explosive de-compression was starting and Alexis was uncertain if it could be stopped.

The onboard computer spoke up in one of those calm and detached voices that usually had the opposite effect on people, creating a panic in them at the temerity of the computer in telling them in that calm voice that they were all about to die. "Emergency status Alpha One has been reached. All personnel will need to make their way to the nearest non-effected airlock and prepare for evacuation."

A map flashed onto one of the many screens before her as well as onto the HUD covering one of her eyes, out-lining the quickest and safest way to the nearest escape pod station. There was another explosion and the whole Colony seemed to shudder, as if it knew that it had been mortally wounded. The gantry gave way under the two immovable legs of the HEE and both Alexis and her foe were suspended in the null-gravity of space as the side of the Colony to which the gantry had been attached splintered away in a silent, grinding turmoil.

A flash out of the corner of Alexis' eye caught her attention and she was just in time to see the other HEE come flying at her intentionally. They collided in a fury of metal on metal. Alexis was sent tumbling away from the escape pod station by the momentum of the impact. She reached out and grabbed, trying to get a hold of anything solid to arrest her motion. Then she remember that the HEEs had propulsion units on them, which of course was how her opponent had managed to get one up on her and slam into her like that. As Alexis activated the reaction-control thrusters and stabilized her tumble, she suddenly realized that she should have sensed the attack that just hit her.

Her opponent had covered it, hidden it mentally from her and that in itself was a problem Alexis didn't expect to ever face. First, her opponent had been able to break through Alexis' mental defenses and now she was blocking her own thoughts and attacking from a blind position. If it were not for this woman trying to kill her, Alexis would actually be very interested in talking to her.

Was this another of Cav's creations? A later version of herself? Was that why she looked so familiar?

Alexis was hit again hard, from the blind side and she slammed her head against the dome, sending searing lances of pain through her skull, her sight blanking out for several moments. She would have to put a stop to this. Clearing her head, she stabilized her tumble again and flew off to the other side of the Colony, which was shaking and shuddering under the explosions that were the precursor to the complete de-stabilization of the structure and a cataclysmic event.

Reaching out with her mind, she found her adversary charging around after her, trying to cut her off. An escape pod station came into view and Alexis headed toward it, hoping to reach the airlock and get inside before the other HEE made it around to this side.

Other escape pods were starting to explode off from the Colony and careen back toward Earth in slow, low-burn orbital flights that would take them to a safe landing on the solid ground of pre-determined landing areas.

Alexis saw none of it.

This was now her only chance.

She reached the airlock and opened the outer doors. As she stepped the HEE in she was hit from behind again, the impact slamming both of them into the inner doors with such force that they buckled and bent to the sound of alarms. Warnings began to blare in Alexis' ears as her HEE, not meant to take this much punishment, was starting to come apart, sparks erupting from various instruments and broken relays before her.

She swung with all her might and slammed hard into the dome of the other HEE, knocking it back against the far wall where it fell to the floor, a hairline crack forming along the center of the plexis-glass. Alexis scrambled up and tried to open the inner doors, but the HEEs impact into them had caused too much damage and they were jammed. There was a muffled explosion and the floor under her shifted and groaned. More escape pods erupted off in shards of insulation and pressure seals.

Alexis didn't see much hope for getting passed the jammed doors and started to leave. Something grabbed her from behind. She twisted and kicked up, cracking the dome even further. Her adversary released her grip as she noted that she was in peril and needed to look after-herself before her HEE ruptured open. As Alexis was about to step out of the airlock and make her way to a new one, finally able to move without the annoyance of getting hit constantly, an explosion behind her grabbed hold of the HEE and lifted it out among the debris that was the Colony, slamming Alexis' head hard back against the seat and knocking her out cold.

But before blackness fell over her eyes and her mind in a soothing sheet of oblivion, a voice penetrated her mind, soft and easy, reaching her across space in a last gesture of defiance.

We shall meet again, Alexis Locke.

Truth generally lies in the coordination
of antagonistic opinions.
— Spencer

15

15 August 2085, 0730 hrs
Washington, D.C.

The summer lay heavy on the city, as heavy as the corruption permeating the rarefied air of this district without a soul since its first brick was laid. The stifling humidity was like a cloying blanket, sucking the very vitality out of those mortals brave enough to go outside and those unfortunates without the capability to have air conditioning, reducing to a minimum all non-essential movement and non-essential life.

It was one of those summers when people wondered why they even bothered to live in a city at all. The heat sapped all strength, leaving one with the desire to neither move nor lay still, a wetness covering the soul as much as the skin with even the slightest movement. Even the trees hung down with trepidation in their leaves, limp and broken, waiting for the coolness of the night that never came and draining all their color until all that was left was a dull, vibrant-less green, looking more like a washed out sock than a living organism.

It was a heat that baked the brain.

Inside the White House, with its corridors oozing a power almost tangible, the elite of the puissance went about their daily lives in the oblivion of air-conditioning, unaware of the millions their petty decision affected, of the singular lives destroyed by the isolation of the decision-makers. Like the heat, the policies of those who walked these halls were unmoved by the plight of those affected, continuing in torrid waves of apathy.

In the Oval Office, the nucleus of this power that corrupts by its very presence, President Heather O' Rourke was in one of her very rare moods, a mood giving those who thought so little of her a tiny glimpse of the leader she could be, she would be were she allowed out from under the heavy hand of those who wanted her position and power and knew that the only way to get it was to control her completely.

"What the hell were you thinking?!" she screamed with a lethal vehemence. "Do you have any idea what the ramifications of this are going to be? *Do you*?! Who the *hell* authorized you to destroy half of Stargazer I, because I sure as God-damned hell DIDN'T DO IT!!" Her face was two shades beyond red, the veins on her petite neck standing out like jackhammers.

Cav sat in a plush chair, his corpulent body hanging down in the heat like wet rags, his forehead soaked in a sweat running down the side of his face in streaks of glistening indolence. He projected an affectation of deep thought with a querulous contempt hiding just beneath the surface. His hair stuck up in quaint little tufts, as if he had not deemed it necessary to comb it, or had been summoned so quickly that he had not the time for such trivial matters. He was trying to look chided, mollified, even terrified at the tantrum the President was directing toward him, at her very well taken points concerning the debacle on the O' Neill Colony, but she was becoming tedious and Cav had much better things to do at the moment then listen to this chattel.

But whenever he tried to get a word in edge-wise, to explain a particular point or defend himself and his agents from her misplaced wrath, Mrs. O' Rourke would cut him off with a renewed attack, which he was obliged to listen to with a blithe expression on his face, wanting to look at his watch but not daring. She was in her second half-hour, going on and on about the repercussions and the dangers and the political fallout and yada, yada, yada.

She turned away from him and stared out the curtained windows, past the Secret Service men standing guard outside, holding a glass of scotch, neat, in her shaking hand, the other hand firmly and irretrievably planted on her hip. "We *already* have a bad relationship with the governing council of the Colonies and their misplaced beliefs that we're trying to take over control and bind them to the Earth and now this. Is this how your best works?" She turned to look at him as she drank robustly of the alcohol. "Because if it is, then you'd better start looking for a new line of work. This is absolutely unacceptable. UNACCEPTABLE! Do you hear me?"

Scotch splashed out of her beveled glass as she railed at him without remorse. "What was she thinking? Can you at least answer me that? What the *hell* was she thinking to kill the chief of police, go on a shooting and bombing spree through the main Colony and then, as if that wasn't enough to piss off everyone and their uncle, jam the inner air lock and open the outer doors so that there's an explosive decompression that wipes out the majority of the food producing capability of the Colony?!" She looked at him as if waiting for an answer she didn't want to hear or believe anyway, then went back to her pacing before the curtained windows looking out onto the stifling heat of the morning air, a haze obscuring most everything beyond a kilometer or so.

She went to drink but found, to her dismay, her glass now empty, most of the contents absorbed into the plush carpet and the presidential seal. She went to fill it back up again, saw the quaint if not amused expression on Cav's face and set the glass down on her desk instead, pushing strands of hair out of her eyes and taking a long, hard breath sounding more like a sigh than an inhalation. "I'm just glad, *damn* glad that they'll never know that she wasn't who she claimed to be, that she was just this insurance investigator who went space mad or whatever it is they call it, that she was killed and her body never recovered and *no one* will ever find out that she was part of this administration and sent by this government to a Colony to..." her voice broke off as if the thought was too terrible for her to utter, her hand going up to her forehead as if a headache were forming, then down to her mouth, which she wiped as she eyed Cav out of the corner of her eyes.

She tried to speak, to put voice to her thoughts but found her words far too impolite even for this fat lard of a man and bit back her more caustic comments as she put hands to hips again, her nostrils flaring with each intake of breath.

She fixed her feverishly glittering eyes on Cav and saw, for the first time, that the man, though feinting to be humbled, was in fact bored with the whole routine and this made her even madder. "Am I boring you, Dr. Cavalier? Does it bore you when the President of your country catches you in a blunder that you fail to take responsibility for? Because if I'm boring you, then you can just go to hell, Sir, and so too can your whole organization, because I'm not going to just stand by and let this go unpunished! Believe me, I'm not. You can bet on that!" She stood with arms akimbo, staring at him and waiting for a reply, waiting for an excuse so that she could pounce on him again and vent her anger at someone other than her staff for what might just cost her the election.

Cav frowned, a deep frown showing his vexation with the whole matter. The only reason he came to her at all was to keep the Secret Service idiots from trying to strong-arm their way into his office when he refused the first three summonses to the White House. The last thing he needed was for there to be a bevy of dead Secret Service agents laying about the lobby of his building.

And now he was beginning to think that perhaps that would have been a far more acceptable option compared to what he was enduring at the present moment. People like Heather O'Rourke allowed him to partially understand why Alexis hated people so much and wanted to live so isolated in Alaska. He didn't blame her at all at moments like this. "First of all, Mrs. President," Cav said in his slow, firm voice making her shrill pitch seem out of place in the finely appointed office. "I'm certain that my agent didn't intentionally sabotage Stargazer I or ever intended to. I know for a fact that she did what was necessary to save her own life and accomplish the mission. If – "

"IF?" she interjected with a spray of outrage that smelled like scotch. "IF WHAT?! There is no if here. Whether she intended to blow the place up or not really doesn't matter, now does it? If someone were to assassinate me and then said that they never meant to and that it was just an accident that occurred during the process of an unrelated assassination and so fucking sorry about it, they would still be tried and convicted for the assassination! There are no ifs' here, there's only the simple fact that your rogue agent made a mess of things that now I have to clean up!" She sat heavily in her chair and continued to stare at him, waiting for him to dare challenge her, to say anything that she could use against him.

Cav refused to rise to the bait. He was through explaining. He had been forced to activate Alexis against his better judgment and now that it had blown up in their faces, she was the one being blamed for it all. To hell with them, then. Besides, he was not the type of man who people scolded, had never been and was not about to have it done to him by some prom-queen president who didn't have all the facts and who was not even born when Cav was starting to formulate his theories on genetic manipulation.

He could sense Claudine's hand in this, could almost taste it in the air, her heavy-handed back-stabbing iniquity wafting off Heather like a bad perfume and it rankled him to the extreme. He had already read a detailed description of the entire incident on the Colony from the back-up agent who worked on the Colony and had been tasked to monitor things and he saw nothing in it that Alexis did wrong. Nothing that she did for any other reason than to save her life. There was no way that he was about to blame her for that.

She did what she had been trained to do and he could ask no more of her, regardless of the situation. The only good thing that had come out of this futile, one-sided discussion with the president was that prom-queen Heather believed Alexis dead, killed in the explosions that rocked the Colony and destroyed the Ag-Section in its totality, severely weakening the remainder of the structure. It meant that everyone thought Alexis dead.

It was the only good thing to have come out of this absolute cluster-fuck. A smile crossed his portly face for a fleeting moment.

"Do you find something humorous in all this?" the President flared, completely galled by the fact that this fat, little man who disgusted her so with his plump white hands and his Buddha belly and those intense, intelligent eyes that didn't belong to the body would have the chutzpah to dare find anything funny in all this. "I find nothing humorous in any of this! Get the hell out of my office you fat fuck!!"

Cav sighed dolorously and rose, eyed her a moment, then turned to leave. *Fat fuck? Such vulgar language from the leader of the most powerful country in the world,* he thought as he made his way to the door. *It was no wonder that most people hated America.* At least he wouldn't have to listen to her high, whining voice anymore. Or so he thought.

She apparently was quite done yet. "And you can expect to find that the power that you've been so used to wielding in that little world of yours will soon be severely curtailed," she spit at him as she rose, hands on desk, elbows locked, face once again that red heralding a heart-ache a few years down the road. "I'll see to that personally!" she sang out in a final, defiant act, her rage not nearly spent.

Cav stopped at the door, turned to look at her as he grabbed the knob, and pushed the door open. "Don't threaten me, Madam President," he rapped out coldly, his words quiet yet with a staccato beat emphasizing his displeasure. Who did she think she was, anyway? "This isn't my country and you're not my president, so your opinions are about as practical to me as a homeless person's asshole." His eyes stabbed her like icicles. "And they smell just about as bad." He nodded his head imperceptively. "Have a good day."

He closed the door and was not surprised to find Claudine Maxwell waiting, seated in a small chair across the hall, her legs crossed, her skirt tight and revealing, her custom-fit suit pert yet professional. She looked up at him from the pocket computer she had been studying, acting as if she was surprised to see him there, then gave him an inquiring look.

"That was a little rough, wasn't it?" she said as she put her computer away and stood, smoothing her skirt and pensively sighing. "I'm sorry to hear about Alexis."

Cav looked at Claudine so hard that she took both a physical and a mental step back from him, her face falling for a brief moment of doubt, then regaining its composure to its usual self-assured yet courteous bearing.

"Don't think for a second that I don't know what you did, Claudine," he spit out in rapid, quiet, abrasive words leaving echoes on her conscience for several minutes. "We're even now. All bets are off. You've just turned me into your worst enemy and believe me, that was the last thing that you wanted."

She gave him a caustic smile, as if the words had been but small talk about the weather, then walked past him into the Oval Office and shut the door, softly. Cav stormed off, his blood pressure turning his face a beet red that would have drawn him attention if it was not for the fire in his eyes burning holes in all they crossed and turning away even the most ardent answer-seekers.

*　　*　　*

She dreamt.

She dreamt of Clovis and Alexander and Cav, of the explosions on *Stargazer I*, of the battle with the HEEs, of her dogs and her cabin.

Her cabin.

She could taste the cool crisp air of August, taste the stream winding its way behind her home with the way the wind made the water ripple and change color with the shafts of early morning sun beating through leafy, glittering aspens and pungent pines and dappled dancing patterns of demure light on the ever-changing waters flowing passed her cabin, always new, always revitalizing its appearance.

But mostly she dreamt of her life, that momentous reflection a human is lucky to get once in a lifetime if at all. It grabs hold of one's soul and lifts it from the rottenness of its mortal existence, slamming the past into one's mind with a discommode that's a culmination of man's feeble attempt at understanding. She saw to her horror what she was, what she had become, what they had made of her in their lab underground, hidden from the prying eyes of those who would have said, *no, this is wrong.*

Her sixty-five years passed by in such a rush she was pressed to find one bright spot of hope or caring or compassion that would reach out and say, *yes, this is where you made a difference, where your spirit soared and freed itself from the confines of the body and for one, effulgent, fleeting moment, you became human.*

But it was not to be.

178

Nothing in the whole span of turgid years passing by in sycophantic delusion allowed her to see any speck of hope for what she could become. Nothing came of what she had thought she had found in the cabin by the stream, in the meadow butting up against the snow-capped mountains, in a land where time stood still and allowed a person's spirit to commune with nature and free itself from the shackles of humanity and soar like an eagle.

Nothing.

It was as if she had lived someone else's life, a life filled with hatred and killing and greed and beliefs not her own. They screamed out at her now with a passion tshe only wished she could actually feel. It was a life of singular purpose, lived with an abandon leaving her now wondering how she had ever survived it.

And in this self-reflection, when the fountainhead of her soul poured out into the wishing well of life its contents, swirling and undulating in contradicting lessons of morality, she saw for the first time the barricade that was her life, the emptiness that was her soul, the shallowness of a psyche that was not even her own.

And still her dreams continued, pouring out the vile contents of her subconscious in a vision of reverent revulsion battering at her ego like a ram, wanting to break down the walls she had erected and in that destruction, create a new life. It was almost as if she could sense something in her that was not human, that was struggling to release itself from her human body and in that release explain all that she had been lacking and in that release bring her true essence forward. But it was not to be.

She thought of her son, a son she had in a fit of demented defiance with a man she didn't even love. Love was not something for which she was slated, that she was allowed, that the gods on high kept from her as if it were a forbidden emotion given to those who knew not how to use it. She had lusted after Alex's father, like a dog lusts after a juicy bone and perhaps in some small way had loved him after all. But it was by no means that love that speaks of candle-lit dinners and holding hands, walks on the beach and tender nights in satin sheets, that cuddles the mind as much as the body till all that is left is a unique, unambiguous feeling of unimagined stasis where two are one and all thoughts flow toward that harmonious juncture that humans define as love.

That type of love Alexis had never tasted, had no concept, had no knowledge. It was beyond her and she didn't know why. With the father of her son, a son she had not even seen much less held, taken away from her the instant that he was born. It had not been love, of that she was certain.

179

She may have been convinced at the time that it was love, but in all reality, it had been a mistake, a mistake made in the heat of a forbidden passion. It was a mistake that had cost Alex's father his life, his car accident fixed and caused by the same people who directed her motions like a marionette.

And yet, here she was reliving in her mind a life she could have had, that could have easily been hers, teasing her with the knowledge that she didn't live it.

And not one tear fell.

Not one iota of emotion passed her mind, an empty vacuum where nothing but the coldness of space exists in a state of perpetual nothingness, the fleeting passage of a distant ardor lost in the sinkhole that was her life. For what was life? Is it a mist that appears for a little while and then vanishes, never again to grace this world? Was that what all this was that she was seeing and feeling and experiencing in her dreams torturing her in their reality and veracity until all that was left was a vapor of a passion that never was there to begin with? Would her life have been different had she made different choices or was all life fixed, destined to pan out in an unfolding drama that had already been written?

Were there signposts along the way she had missed, beacons that had called to her that she had ignored? Or did life have only one path, one way and one goal and whether one wanted that path or not was pointless to that planned it and executed it in a welter of punishing steps? Was it all pointless?

And then, as if those dreams and life-revealing seconds were not enough, she dreamt of her. Of that face flashing before her like a phantom. It was a vortex of thought and feelings and conflicting emotions screaming for her to understand but which she could not descry in an upwelling of pent passionate purpose beyond any mortal who denied herself the simple joy of love. The face of that person in the other HEE flashed before her with matching eyes, matching hair and a mind still linked with Alexis' in a communion spanning time itself. It was that communion, a connection that had been established and had blotted out everything else and spread a blank sheet over her thoughts, absorbing all it touched and muting it in diffuse images of lost time.

That woman who had been in the other HEE, who had touched Alexis somehow was all that now remained in her mind, a solitary, encompassing turmoil of heat and passion and emotion starting to form an outcry in her soul, an outcry that slowly and irrevocably worked its way up to her mouth as unknown images of bird-like creatures flashed before her mind's eye in telling tantrums of tortured questions.

A dim light started to glow in her vision and cast all else in a shadow of dismal failure and forfeited futures imprisoned in the deep darkness that was her life. Then the images and the light both exploded in a spectacle of brilliance and she rose from out of her slumber and awoke to her old life that was now so much improvident appurtenances...

She bolted upright up into a sitting position, her face a mask of terror, her scream caught in her mouth as if afraid to come out, leaving a bad taste like death. She didn't know whether she had dreamt the scream or whether she had actually vocalized it, her mind still lost in that transition period between the dream world and reality -- as if one could actually tell which is which. Echoes of her dreams and her scream bounced around her head as she focused her eyes and tried to figure out what had happened and, more importantly, where she was.

"God, I built you well."

She focused her eyes, the haziness clearing to a crystal clarity as she followed the voice to find Cav seated in a chair in the corner, his unkempt appearance and scruffy un-shaven face so out of place with the man that she once knew.

Her head still throbbed, her eyes felt as if someone had a candle lit behind them, her mouth had not tasted this foul since that mouthful of swamp muck so many years ago.

"It's nice to see you too, Cav," she answered back caustically, looking around the small room in which she found herself, that familiar smell of a hospital hanging in the air like a specter. "How long have you been sitting there? You look like shit."

"Thank you for the inspiring words." They stared at each other for a few pregnant seconds. "Long enough," he answered, the fatigue in his voice apparent. He leaned forward and a small smile touched his face. He had in fact been waiting two days, two days wherein he had watched and waited for her body to repair itself, to heal the physical wounds so prevalent when he had first seen her. Now she was totally healed, no marks whatsoever on her leg from the plasma burn or from the two gunshot wounds she had sustained. Also gone was her concussion and she was, for the most part, whole.

But Cav could see that although the physical wounds had been healed, there were deeper, more penetrating emotional wounds seething beneath that beautiful head of hers, eating away at her from the inside. These, he knew, she could not heal, her systems, though balanced and perfect in most every way, unable to handle the turmoil of feelings he could see were just about ready to breach and tear her apart.

"So what the hell happened up there?" he asked, though he already knew all the details. He wanted to hear her side, hear from her what had happened and why. He needed to know what had gone, in essence, wrong. Regardless of her time spent in Alaska, she was still better than any agent he ever knew or ever would know. Her version of events he would believe above any others.

She pulled the sheets off herself and swung her legs over the side of the bed to plant her feet firmly on the ground. She was dressed, she was glad to find, in a soft and silky satin pajama top and bottom rustling delicately as she stood on firm legs, the pliable, thick carpet feeling good between her toes. "Do you have some clothes for me, Cav?" she asked in answer to his question.

He pointed to the small closet. "In a hurry?" He paused a moment as he watched her open the closet door and pull out the set of clothes hanging there. "So what happened up there?" he asked again, knowing full well that she had heard the first question and ignored him. He was used to her little idiosyncrasies. She was telling him, in her own way, that she was not yet ready to answer that particular question.

She laid the clothes on the bed and stared at them a moment as if she had never seen anything like them before, then looked over at him, her eyes narrow and distant, yet somehow acute in their intensity as they stared at him. "Where's my home, Cav?"

The question took him by surprise. His brow furrowed, deep wrinkles setting in as he screwed up his face and gave her an inquiring look. "What...?"

"My home, Cav," she repeated, sitting on the edge of the bed with a tenderness and childlike innocence he had not seen in her since he didn't know when.

"Alaska, of course," he answered, his tone more in the form of a question than a statement. He was beginning to worry that perhaps there had been more damage to her brain than he had suspected. If he had not looked at the scans himself, he would have her re-examined immediately. Was it possible that the other agent had not told him everything that had transpired?

She looked up at him. A dimple creased the skin next to her mouth, a sign of slight amusement. "No Cav. That's not what I mean. You have a home, a place you grew up, a family that cared for you, friends, school, memories. At least I assume you do. I suppose that you could have come from some test tube also, but I doubt that. Who would want to produce a specimen like you?" She hesitated, made to say something else, then looked down at her hands as if they somehow held the answers for which she was searching.

When she spoke again, he could tell that she was deeply troubled by something, that some event experienced on *Stargazer I*, or perhaps even while her body healed itself, had placed her in this desultory mood. She looked up at him again, her blue-green freckled eyes radiating an intensity that seemed to bore into his very soul, lay bare all his secrets before her and expose them to the scathing lash of her whip-like intellect. "A home, Cav," she repeated, demanding an answer to a question Cav didn't understand. "A place that I belong; where is my family?"

Like the searching beam of a lighthouse cutting through the fog in a concentrated shaft of light, Cav discerned her intent. "You know the answer to that, Alexis," he replied quietly, uncomfortable now with where the discussion was going.

"Do I? I don't think I do. I know your answer to that question, but is that the correct one? Is it the only one?"

He leaned back again and closed his eyes. "I don't know what else to tell you, then," he said pensively.

"I want a home, Cav. I'm tired." Her voice trailed off as she stood again and pulled her top off without a second thought to Cav sitting right before her, her firm, round breasts laying exquisitely against her body, the high-riding nipples hard and erect in the chill of the room.

Cav turned his head to the side, embarrassed once again at her immodesty. He didn't remember her like this before. She was, if anything, very modest in her sexuality around him. Now she seemed to be flaunting it as if in punishment for an offense he didn't know he had committed. He spoke to alleviate his embarrassment as he heard her take off her pants and change into the regular clothes, the very charge in the air from her nakedness, tangible.

He was not sure why he should even be embarrassed.

He knew her body like the back of his hand in both the clinical and sexual sense and yet now, here, he felt embarrassed, as if her questions had somehow changed everything.

He stared hard at the wall. "Why this sudden urge for a home, Alexis? I don't understand what you're asking."

"You can turn around now," she said with that old, coy, Alexis tone. "I'm done."

Cav turned his head back. "You're home is wherever you settle, Alexis. Your home is Alaska, the cabin, your two dogs. I don't know what else there is." The very thought made him involuntarily examine his own life, his own concept of what made a home a home and whether he, like Alexis, was homeless, wandering, lost forever in a sea of work and assignments and missions making a home an impossible goal to obtain.

Was this what his work had created?

Was it what afflicted all those whose work came before their lives?

She looked at him from under her eyebrows as she finished buckling the belt on her pants. "Did I have another child, Cav?"

Her question was so unexpected, so off the track from what she had just been talking about that he stammered for a moment, his eyes wide, mouth opening slightly as if to speak. "N-no. Of course not." He regained his composure, but his mind was reeling with why she would ask such a question. What was she driving at now? "How can you not know whether you had another child? That's an absurd question."

"Is it?" she queried, standing before him with that cock-sure look of confidence severely weakened by the glow of confusion in her eyes. "I'm sure that there are things about me that you've never told me, never intend to tell me."

"What's going on, Alexis? This isn't like you, not at all. I think that maybe we need to do some more tests before I release you. There may have been more damage to your systems than I had anticipated."

She laughed.

It was almost demented.

She stood before him in all her glory, her comfortable fitting jeans and loose, white shirt highlighting her precious looks and no nonsense smile. "I'm fine, Cav. You needn't worry about that. It was just a question, that's all. I accept your answer ... for now."

She started for the door but Cav stood and intercepted her.

"Like hell that's good enough for now. That's not the answer the Alexis I know would ever give. What's wrong? Tell me? What the hell happened up there?"

She stared at him a moment as if deciding whether to push him out of the way so that she could exit, or just sit back down and tell him everything. She settled for an option halfway between. She stepped close to him, his breath like a stagnant pool of crap. "I was set up, that's what happened. Who the hell is Hugh Crow, Cav? Is he one of yours?"

Cav was astonished at the mention of the name. He had forgotten how insightful she really was. She had picked up on that one quickly. "Crow is my main agent for the O'Neill Colonies. His cover is as a consultant and he's worked his way into the highest levels of the administration. Why would you ask about him?"

She realized that Cav was completely ignorant of the fact that his own agents were working against him. "He's turned, Cav. He's the one who ambushed me." She pointed to her breast, where the wound had once been but where now only smooth, tanned skin remained. "Did you notice anything unusual about that impact site, Cav?"

He ran his hand over his mouth, beginning to see something in what she was saying. "Yes, as a matter of fact I did. I can't determine what made it. It doesn't match any of the known weapons in our database."

She pushed past him and opened the door, stepping out into the deserted corridor. "It was silenced, Cav. That one didn't come from the Colony guards. That one was meant to kill me and it came from somewhere else. I'll let you guess from where."

With brow furrowed in concentration, he followed her as she strode purposefully down the dimly lit corridor. She could tell that she was underground, the weight of the Earth above her palatable to her senses. She knew this place, her birthplace, as if it had a connection to her that went beyond the physical, a baleful impression anchoring her soul to the rocks of her own, restless past.

"And you think Crow did it? That's ridiculous," Cav finally burst out with an undertone of near belief.

She stopped and spun around, forcing him to brake hard to keep from running into her. "Then you explain it, Cav. Explain to me why your Mr. Crow had me stay in his house to make it easier for that bastard Kiril to rape me, for his little security force to gang-bang me all night long. Explain to me where he was when that was happening." Her nostrils flared with her anger. "And explain to me why he blew my cover, over a channel that's monitored and where many people heard it, where it was most likely recorded. EXPLAIN THAT TO ME, CAV!" Her voice had risen steadily as she spoke so that by the time that the last word came out, she was almost screaming,

Cav's inability to give her any comfort, to answer such a simple question as where her home was, eliciting something within her that was primal and ferocious, like a wounded, cornered animal.

He was all she had at the moment, so he received the brunt of her tongue lashing, the full force of all the doubts and failures and questions that had arisen in her mind from the depths of her inner-self breaking the surface with a splash of vengeful fury.

He was as surprised by her tone as he was by what she said. He had

185

certainly been yelled at by her before, that was nothing new. But not like this. Not with such accusations and not with such full fury. "I'll look into it, Alexis." He could not think of anything else to say. "I find it hard to believe, but I'll look into it. Fortunately, there's no surviving record of any communications between you and anyone else while you were in the HEE. They were all destroyed. And I'm sorry about Kiril and all, but at least you made sure that he won't be doing it to any more women." He was well aware that his answer was completely inadequate but he had no more to give, to say. Her accusations flayed him to the bone.

If Crow had truly turned, then who was to say how many others had been compromised. What was even more important was who was it that was turning his agents if they were indeed being turned. And who even knew that they existed in the first place? The short list of those who worked for him was locked away in his mind and his mind only.

One name came to his mind as if by magic, as if it had been waiting for just such a moment to make itself known: Claudine Maxwell. If anyone could know, she would be the one and yet, he was certain that she had neither the intelligence nor the resources to ascertain that information. But if not her, then who? Sure, Claudine was a convenient name to accuse, but did she really have it in her to tap into his mind and extract those names?

Alexis studied him a moment, wondering if he really was as ignorant of Crow's duplicity as he claimed, as he looked. Did it really matter? She turned and started walking again. She was becoming as uncertain of his duplicity as she was of her own sanity.

"Wait a minute, Alexis. Where are you going in such a hurry?"

"How did I get here, Cav?" she asked over her shoulder.

He assumed that she meant from the Colony to Earth and answered using that assumption. "You were picked up by one of the rescue vessels sent to help from the other Colonies. Hugh Crow made sure that it appeared that you were dead and brought you to me. If he truly wanted you dead, he could have killed you then and no one would have been the wiser. Your assumption is lacking, Alexis. Why do you ask, anyway?"

She stopped and turned around, forcing him once again to pull up short to avoid running into her. "So Crow knows that I'm alive?"

"Yes, but besides me, he's the only one. I'm telling you, he's not the one. He hasn't turned else why save you and make sure that you made it to me?" He reached out to touch her shoulder, saw that it would be a horrendous idea and dropped his hand to his side in frustration. "Listen, you've got a great chance here to move about unseen, without a trail of any sort. Even the president thinks that you're dead. We need to move on this now, solve it while we have the chance."

"You can bet that our assassin friends aren't so easily fooled," she spewed out with sarcasm. "Not in the least bit, I'll guarantee you that."

She took off again down the corridor and he sprinted to get in front of her and stop her, this fast pace a little too much for his body to maintain. "Would you just wait a minute! Tell me what the hell's wrong? This isn't just about you not having a home or parents or any of that bullshit. There's something else here, something that happened up there that you aren't telling me, that Crow didn't see or doesn't know about and wasn't in the report. He's not the enemy, Alexis. You've got to believe me on this. He's as much your enemy as I am."

She stopped when he stepped before her but refused to look at him.

"What the hell is bothering you? This isn't the Alexis I know."

Now she did look at him, her eyes glittering with passionate severity as she spoke rapidly, harshly. "The Alexis you know, the one you built like a piece of machinery is dead, Cav. Gone. She no longer exists. She died a long time ago when I gave up on this life, when I became aware that I wasn't just some mindless droid who did your bidding."

"That's not fair, Alexis. You were never a mindless droid to me and I never treated you that way. You've always been my most valuable asset and – "

"That's just the point, damn you!" she cried at him. "I'm not an asset, Cav. I'm a person! A flesh and blood person, despite the fact that I was created. Perhaps even because of it...." Her voice trailed off, the hurt in her eyes the most emotion he had ever seen her display. "I'm tired of it Cav. Sick and tired of it all. I used to be able to kill people who got in my way without blinking an eye. But now, now they stay with me, they haunt me Cav and if that wasn't enough, there's a group out there that's..." She took a deep breath, looked up at the overhead and stood arms akimbo, her mind rebelling against the words released, the emotions derived from decades of uncaring. "I don't know what... but they're trying to kill me with advanced weapons and systems and mind-control that I've never seen before.   And they aren't even really there or here or whatever the hell it is. It's like they don't belong, like they're ...like they're from somewhere else."

"Whoa, whoa, slow down," Cav said as the barrage of information came at him in a spray of wrathful rage. "What the hell are you talking about? Are you referring to the assassins who attacked you at the cabin and that killed that computer nerd?"

She stiffened and Cav thought for sure that she was going to strike him a blow that would end his life there and then. "His name was Clovis," she said slowly and distinctly, enunciating each word clearly so that there would be no misunderstanding. "He wasn't a nameless victim, just like the others weren't nameless victims. He was a *person*, Cav, with a past and a future and a life, just like all those others who I killed on the Colony or who died due to the explosions." She looked at him with an uneasiness feral in its conviction, giving him a shiver up his spine and setting alarms off in his head that were more medical than emotional, more clinical than impulsive.

She jabbed a finger into his fleshy chest. "I'm going to figure this one out, Cav, don't worry about that. I'm going to find the people who murdered my son and all those others." With each sentence, she jabbed him hard, the pain almost like a penance to his soul. "And when I do, I'm going to kill every last one of them." Her last jab was particularly hard, as if subtlety telling Cav that she suspected him in some form of embroilment in regards to the murders.

Their eyes remained locked and Cav knew that there was more coming, one last, final statement she had to make to clear her of the heavy burden somehow landed on her shoulders between Boston and *Stargazer I*. "And then that's it. You hear me, Cav? I want out completely. I want my name stricken from any and every list, I want my death publicly announced and I want you to forget that you ever knew me. And if you come looking for me, I'll kill you like any other scurvy dog. Is that clear? Do you understand what it is that I'm telling you? I want to be completely severed from anything to do with you or your agency or any government. I don't want your fucking money or your fucking cabins or anything from you! I can certainly make it on my own, with my own identity, that only I know about! It's over Cav. Over." She turned on her heel and walked down to the end of the corridor, opening the door hard and slamming it behind her.

"Shit," Cav said as he began to follow slowly, hesitantly. He had suspected for some time that this day was coming. He just didn't expect it this soon.

Each moment is not only something new but
something unforeseeable.
— Bergson

16

6 August 2085, 0800 hrs
City of Heihe,
Greater East Asian Co-Prosperity Sphere

The Heilong Jiang, or Black Dragon River, lazily runs along in murky blackness down the middle of the bustling Chinese city of Heihe, its white-tiled skyscrapers and towers of steel and glass stretching along both banks in an intermix of modern and classic design, the hotels, casinos and trade centers clustering along the course like perched water beetles.

The river itself rises in the Highlands of China and begins a long, sinuous path through the once endless Birch forests and taiga, finally bubbling its way in murky and muddy fatigue into the Sea of Okhotsk by the grim looking city of Nikolayevsk. It is the eighth largest river in the world and little known outside the two countries housing its banks. Frozen for six months out of the year, it surges lustily eastward, depositing more than 25 million tons of silt into the North Pacific annually. The Irish-green plush flood plains near the Tatar Straits are known for their untouched beauty, the crystal cobalt blue river passing through in torrents of time and change as nature ignores the few humans who have dared challenge her.

There once was an extraordinary variety of wildlife along the banks: sable, roe deer, reindeer, boar, brown bear, moose, and snow sheep. But now they are few and far between, the extinct Amur Leopard and Panthera Tigris Altaica, better known as the Siberian Tiger, a stark reminder of the depredations of man upon the Earth.

The river had not always been called the Black Dragon on both banks.

It had once been called the Amur on the Siberian side until, in 1689, the Treaty of Nerchinsk, signed with Jesuit Priests as translators, had given both banks to the Chinese. The Tsar, however, had found that particular treaty not important enough to obey and thus a hive of dirty and grim Russian cities and towns had sprouted up overnight and the river became a border between two large and antagonistic countries.

As is the nature of these things, Heihe had not always been Heihe.

There had once been a sprawling recreation center for the more affluent of the Russian and Old-Soviet Regime officials that had gone by the name of Blagoveshchensk and had, for a time, been all there was at this particular site, the infant village of Heihe on the Chinese side not even a cleared patch in the forest. But the Russian-Chinese War of 2025 had changed all that. Tired of the constant bickering and squabbling over who was allowed to dam the river and build the cities and control the trade, both sides had finally resorted to open conflict that was both brief and vicious. The Chinese had won easily and before nuclear weapons were involved, a peace treaty was negotiated and the Amur River became, officially, the Black Dragon River with full Chinese control of both banks with over four hundred kilometers of former Russian land along the entire length of the river bordering both countries as a conciliation prize.

With this treaty had come a massive influx of Chinese to settle the land and make its possession unequivocal and the beautiful green sea of the Far Eastern forest with its virgin tracts of larch, pine, hemlock, spruce and birch had been devastated, cut down for the valuable lumber the Chinese had been craving for centuries, and for the open space for the crops and the people. And so too had gone the pristine caliber of this part of the world, this last piece of untouched ancient forest along the river.

Not even the existence of the Nanai, Ulchi and the Evenk tribes with their primitive living and their Shamans, travelers of the spirit world and healers of the sick, had stopped the Chinese from tearing down the forests to make room for their ever-growing population. Although vast tracts still stretched in a dark green carpet to the broad, blue expanse of the distant hills, the character of the land was changed and despite recent efforts to preserve this last piece of wilderness, its future was doubtful.

This area was a perfect example of humanity's inability to keep even a small part of the Earth untouched. For every activist willing to give up their lives for the preservation of what once was, there were five developers who only saw money in the vast tracts of open land and un-cut lumber. It was a fight not about winning but more about inevitable defeat.

It was here, on the outskirts of Heihe that melted into the tufts of lone stands of pines and birch that Alexis found herself deposited ungraciously by the hover bus with a mixture of contempt and hatred from the driver and the passengers for the quai-loh who dared to intrude on their land. She was looking for an associate of Kido Nakamura. When Alexis had been first told that Aobe Fujita had left the small software firm for which Nakamura had worked soon after her death and been moved to this metropolis on the Black Dragon, she had been extremely doubtful that he would provide any help even if he lived in this remote outpost of civilization. She had figured that the other workers in the software firm had been told to tell this lie, hiding the true destination of the elusive Aobe.

But Alexis had quickly ascertained that the man had indeed moved to the predominately Chinese city, hired by a prestigious software company whose headquarters happened to be in Heihe. His official title was as a consultant. Alexis figured that he was now nothing more than an embarrassment, a problem to be hidden.

And so it was that she now stood in the lush, green meadow where large honeybees buzzed in the wildflowers giving the landscape a splash of brilliant color in the chill air working its way down from the Arctic.

She frowned, pulled her pocket computer out of her bag and looked at the address again. Gazing around at the open expanse before her disappearing into a stand of larch and birch, she realized that there were no addresses here, no numbers posted. All that was here was a small, tidy, misplaced Japanese house sitting to her left, a large garden in the back with chicken wire and posts and what appeared to be a bumper crop of assorted vegetables and fruits.

Behind her, the skyline of Heihe rose out of the green meadow like a spore, the numerous houses nestling against its immensity and constituting this suburb, appearing to peter out with Fujita's small house. Soft, distant sounds drifted on the slight breeze stirring the short grass, sounds of the city and the numerous hovs buzzing around the tall buildings almost as delicately as the bees buzzing around the flowers.

She shook her head and began to walk over to the house, her tailored business suit of dark green and yellow design and her high-heels not at all conducive to the terrain she was having to negotiate. Her auburn hair had a reddish glint to it and was combed strikingly back from her face and fell gracefully to her shoulders, where it flared back against the dark green of the jacket. Her face was not her own but rather a poly-mask, a synthetic compound forming to her features and giving her a completely new identity, her sparkling bright blue eyes standing out against the non-descript nature of the new face like diamonds.

She noticed motion in the garden and found, to her surprise, a beautiful Japanese Sekitee tucked into the corner of the lot and an older man working diligently with a rake. He had thin, bony legs attached to a frail looking body that worked the rake with a gusto seemingly misplaced. His large, sleepy, expressionless eyes and sallow, wrinkled face told Alexis that this man was most likely near eighty if not older and was one of the first of the batch of age-extended people that the early attempts had produced, before they had been able to greatly decrease the visible effects of aging.

But as she watched him work, oblivious to her presence and anything else that didn't have to do with the garden, she noticed the liver spots on his wrinkled and bony hands, the graying hair barely there and the bend posture of his body and knew immediately that this man had not partaken in the new gene therapies and aging drugs that had been available. Aobe Fujita had aged naturally and had lived his years as humans once had, without the aid of the new, miracle medicines. What she was seeing was the age that Mr. Fujita had become by just living and she already found herself liking him.

She watched him for quite some time without saying a word or announcing her presence, content to just observe him rake his patterns in the fine-grained white sand, the peacefulness of the action somehow lost in the clutter that was the world.

"Have you come to watch me rake sand, young lady, or are you here for something of less importance?" he finally asked without looking up, his voice vibrant and strong. He spoke in Japanese, with that lilting, flowing quality that English could never come close to matching.

"Ohio Gozaimasu," she answered back, greeting him for the morning.

His raking continued as he answered, his voice taking on little to no inflection. "Hai, hai, dozo. Ah, nihongo wa jotzu desu." *Yes, oh you speak Japanese very well*.

"Lye, sukoshi, gomen nasai," she answered back, explaining that she only spoke a little. "Doko ni Fujita Aobe-san desu ka?" The words flowed off her tongue like water and Fujita smiled to himself at the modesty of the young lady who spoke his language so beautifully.

"I am Aobe Fujita," he said guardedly, moving to a different part of garden and making patterns in the sand there. "And who would you be? I don't get many visitors and certainly not attractive young ladies."

192

"I'm Jill Rousseau. I'm a journalist working on an article on the rise of violence in Japanese society and the impact on the victims."

He stopped raking and looked up at her, his deep-set eyes narrowing as he studied her for several seconds with a discernment that was disquieting. "Then I must apologize for your journey out to see me, for I have never been involved in any violent crimes either here or when I lived in Japan."

She gave him a coquettish smile as she answered. "You're correct, but you did know someone who was killed in a violent crime and that makes you a victim and a perfect person to interview, if you don't mind."

He continued to look at her for what seemed like an eternity, then lifted his rake off the ground and carried it over to one of the posts supporting the roof over the patio. He grabbed a rag and wiped his already clean hands on it, then turned to look at her again. "You speak of Nakamura Kido-san."

"Yes. I'm led to understand that you two worked together quite extensively in Osaka."

He gave her a shrewd look for a moment, then put the rag away carefully. "Do you speak Mandarin?"

She found that an odd question. She had already probed his mind and found that while he was raking, his thoughts centered almost exclusively on the patterns he was making and their aesthetic, pleasing qualities. Now his mind was a morass of conflicting thoughts that seemed to have no direction or drift and seemed to wander around aimlessly, though they mostly hovered in the vicinity of Kido, her face and their time together coming to her with the one, strong notion of master and pupil prevalent.

Alexis also noticed a darker, deeper feeling fading in and out in shades of fright, a feeling coming from Kido's death and Alexis' presence, almost as if he had been expecting her to come, dreading the arrival of one such as her. "Yes, I do, as a matter of fact. Cantonese also." she answered back with as innocent a look on her face as she could muster.

"Then perhaps it would be better if we were to go to the city and find a local restaurant to talk in. It will be my treat, please." He appeared to already know her answer, for he bowed to her and then walked inside, to come out after a few moments, his gardening clothes discarded for more appropriate restaurant attire.

As she waited the brief few minutes that it took him to dress, she thought about the odd request that he had made to not talk at his home. It was possible that he thought it safer to talk in a more public area or perhaps even more proper, the prospect of having a younger lady in his home alone not sitting well with him and his obvious ancient Japanese customs. Either way, she found it odd and decided to pay even closer attention to her surroundings as she conducted this interview, aware that so far she had been set-up at almost every place she had gone. This might prove to be no different.

The restaurant on which he finally settled was in the outskirts of the downtown area and was apparently one to which he had never been. Alexis was amused to find that although hovs plied the skies above in numbers too numerous to count, there were still hundreds if not thousands of Chinese riding their bicycles along the tree-lined paths meandering through the district, a tradition still strong.

It was a bizarre mixture of comely peasants with their tattered clothes and thread-bare knapsacks and businessmen and women with their expensive, custom-tailored suits who rode their bikes in a mélange of drab grays and blacks, the occasional colorful dress or tourist shirt standing out with striking clarity.

Alexis and Aobe sat on the outside patio of the small restaurant, the hustle of the morning crowd gone, but more than enough lingerers hanging around to make it possible to hold a conversation that would be drowned by the ambient noise.

The waiter came up and Alexis spoke, knowing full well the customs of the land and the aversion to small talk. "Ni zao," she said with a smile that seemed to bounce off the apathetic waiter and fall to the floor with an unceremonious clang.

The waiter turned to Fujita and gave him a look of utter contempt for both the quai-loh woman and Fujita's Japanese ancestry.

"Wo yao liang ke cha," Fujita said through compressed lips, ordering two teas for Alexis and himself. When neither of them said anything else, the waiter frowned, gave a huff, then walked away.

Fujita smiled an apologetic smile to her and shrugged his shoulders as he spoke to her in hushed tones of Mandarin. "I am sorry for the inconvenience, but it is better this way. The animosity between our two peoples is still strong," he explained as they waited for the tea Alexis knew would be a long time coming. "To him, and to most of the lower class citizens here in the country, I am lang syin, gou fei: wolf's heart, dog's lungs. It is what Japanese men are still called by the Chinese. It is a reference to the numerous wars that have erupted between our two cultures over the thousands of years and I doubt that it will ever go away."

"So if that's the way they feel about you, why did you move here in the first place?" she asked, aware of his reasons but needing to act dumb to stay in character.

194

He shrugged his shoulders again as he looked out over the throng of people who rode past. "I was offered a job and benefits that I could not refuse. It is now a younger man's game. I was once the best at what I did, probably still am in some ways, but I am an old man with little of my life left to me. I didn't opt to partake in the aging-drugs that have made life too long. As such, I must make do with what has been handed to me. I don't mind."

Alexis gave him a tight smile. "And why did you want to come here to talk instead of at your house where the service, I am certain, is much better?"

"That is a more difficult question to answer, but one that perhaps you don't need to know. It is for the best that you are not seen at my house. There are certain..." he paused a moment as he looked around, as if expecting to see someone hovering near them but finding nothing. "...people who have been asking odd questions of me and Kido, when she still lived. You are simply the latest, though I don't believe that you and they have any connection. They were not quite as pleasant about it as you have been and I didn't like their looks. I thought that perhaps in this way I could avoid them and save you the trouble of dealing with them afterward."

Alexis understood perfectly and immediately probed the surrounding area for any signs of people who didn't belong. She found nothing at the moment but that had been the case before and she was not lulled into any sort of complacency.

The waiter returned with a tray, two cups and an ornate, cheap imitation teapot. He slammed them on the table and then locked eyes with Alexis for a moment, a moment in which she looked back and probed, finding something that she didn't like at all.

She narrowed her eyes a moment, probed deeper, then spoke. "Qing jie shu," she said rapidly, asking for the check and staring him coldly back.

He looked affronted as he straightened up, his eyes flaring then constricting. He reached into the front pocket of his apron and began to pull something out.

Alexis responded instantly.

With her cat-like reflexes she rose up and belted him hard in the face. He flew back, tripped over a chair and fell heavy to the patio floor, the weapon he had in his apron flying out and landing in the soup bowl of a nearby customer, cracking it apart and saturating the startled woman with noodles.

There were looks of shock, astonishment and fear as Alexis grabbed Fujita's hand and pulled him out into the street, trying to get as far away from the restaurant as possible. He said nothing as she pulled him along, still shocked that the waiter had hated him enough to try to shoot him.

Alexis made her way to a corner and hailed a hov taxi. When one zoomed down to pick them up, she shoved Aobe inside, slammed the door and ordered the driver to the airport. It had been an instinctual impulse. The moment Alexis had asked for the check, she had sensed the presence of the shadow people in the background, had felt them in all their distorted imagery coming through the back of the restaurant toward them, their blank minds like a void in the torrent of thoughts cascading around her from the ordinary people leading their ordinary lives.

Their emptiness had keyed her in more than anything else, the presence of a body without the accompanying endowment of mind, a cue for her to analyze her surroundings more intently and in that analysis, found the gun in the mind of the waiter as he reached for it in his apron pocket. It had been pure, damn luck. She was not really concentrating on the waiter despite the fact that she should have been and only the sudden appearance of those who were quickly becoming her prime nemesis had alerted her to the imminent danger right before her.

How they found her, tracked her to this obscure place was beginning to really grate on her nerves. She refused to believe that they were waiting at every conceivable place where she could visit, that they could see through her disguise, that they were stalking this frail, little old man for the off chance that she would show up at his doorstep. And to make matters worse, she was not even at his doorstep and she didn't even look like herself.

They had been at a restaurant that Fujita had stated he had never visited. The thought had crossed her mind that Fujita had set her up, had purposefully led her to this place, but she found nothing to indicate that in his thoughts and could tell, just from the short time she had spoken to him, that he would refuse to do such a thing if he had been asked.

It was altogether possible that the shadow people were able to read her thoughts, were able to tap into her mental image and find her in that way, making any disguise she chose to wear irrelevant. The more she thought about that possibility, the more she started to believe it was the prime possibility, for that woman in the other HEE, the one who had looked so much like her had been able to not only shield her mind from Alexis but project forcefully into Alexis' mind. This was becoming more than annoying. It was becoming problematic.

She would have to get this man away from here, away from those who would have him dead. She didn't want him to end up like Clovis. That was the last thing she needed: another face haunting her in her dreams.

She spoke to Fujita in Japanese, rapidly, knowing that the driver would not understand a word. "Why would someone want to kill you, Fujita-san?"

"Perhaps they are the same people who killed Kido. I don't know." He seemed sincere enough and certainly frightened, his hands trembling as they sat in his lap. He looked at her and she knew at that moment that Fujita had more to tell, that he also knew that Kido's death was no accident. "What she was working on, with that Dr. Hart, it was a bad thing. It would only lead to trouble. I warned her of this numerous times but she only saw the good in it. She only saw the good in all that she did and observed. She was that way."

"What was it that they were working on?"

"You are not a journalist, are you?" he asked with a perception that matched his years.

"We'll be at the airport soon, Fujita-san," she said calmly, knowing that she was running out of time. "Can you tell me what Kido was working on? It's very important."

"Why must I leave? I had nothing to do with what Kido and Hart were doing. I tried to dissuade them. I don't want to leave my garden and my home. Why must I leave?"

"Because you know too much, or at least someone thinks that you do and at the moment that's a serious problem. You'll be taken care of, Fujita-san. I promise. Now what was it that Kido was working on?"

He sighed, not understanding why his life had been suddenly turned upside down. And the day had started so well for him, until this white-eye showed up. He smelled trouble on her the moment he saw her step off the hov-bus but did as he always did and was nice to the pretty lady. One day he would learn. He puckered his lips and looked out the window at the passing traffic. "Kido was developing a transfer protocol for computers, a very advanced and complicated transfer protocol."

"For what purpose?"

"To use with the hardware that Dr. Hart was developing, of course," he said with a slight hint of frustration at her obtuseness. "And also with that nice man who visited once but used a different name than the one that Kido called him by. What was that name...?" he contemplated as he screwed up his face in an attempt to retrieve the name from his memory.

Alexis was beginning to notice the increase in traffic around them and realized that they were getting near the main airport complex. She had still not figured out how she was going to get Fujita out of the country in such a hurry, but there were always ways to do these things. Although she was technically a rogue agent, without the benefits of the company, she still had Cav on her side and he would bend over backwards to help her. He might be

197

the world's biggest ass-hole some times, but he would stop at nothing to assist her. She knew that for a fact.

Fujita's face lit up as the name came to him and he turned to look at her. "He called himself Georg Holstein but Kido called him Ian, Ian Montana."

Alexis' heart almost stopped at the name and she snapped her head to look at the old man in a mixture of hostility, passion, and disbelief. "Did you say Ian Montana?" she asked slowly, her mind reeling with the cover name she had not heard in God knew how many years, a face rushing to her as if they had just parted yesterday, his touch on her palpable and real.

"Yes, yes, that was his name. It was apparently his idea, this whole plan that they were working on, from what I understand. Though he didn't seem intelligent enough to have come up with such a plan if you ask my opinion."

Alexis could not believe it, refused to believe it. It had to be a coincidence. There were probably many people with that name in the world. *Sure, Alexis. just like there're lots of people with the name Alexis Locke running around. It's him, you damn fool. And if it's him, then that means they know all about you because Ian knows all about you.*

There was a blinding light, a wave of heat and sound rocking the taxi and filling the passenger compartment with acrid smoke burning the lungs and searing the eyes. The taxi began to descend rapidly, out of control. A long stream of dark, dense, caustic smoke lanced out from behind like a tail, marking their drop to the hard ground like a beacon.

She recovered quickly, willing herself to ignore the smoke bellowing in the taxi and filling it quickly, ignore the fire raging in the driver's compartment, his burnt, blackened, flaming body slumped against the controls in a grotesque parody of sleep. She turned to Fujita, aware that she would only have one chance to get out of the crashing vehicle alive and save the man at the same time. She still needed to get more out of him, for she could tell that he had more to give and she needed to know how Ian was involved, what part he played.

She leaned over through the blinding smoke to comfort Fujita and touched slick, wet, hot blood covering his chest in a spreading circular pattern. She was aghast. He had been shot clean through the heart, the hole in the shattered spider-web pattern of the window behind him indicative of where the bullet had come entered. He was definitely dead, his eyes wide open from the instant shock that had laid waste his heart and left nothing behind but a twitching mass of muscle.

This had been well planned, the missile slamming into the taxi a final nail in the coffin to burn the bodies beyond recognition and cover up the murder.

She sensed the work of the assassins that had been following her since the cabin in this. It had to be.

"Shit," she cursed to herself as she kicked her door open and watched as the ground came up in a dizzying spiral descent that had but one outcome. She calculated quickly, instantly, measured the distance, then leapt with all her might toward the passing hov zooming by down below, knowing that she would land on the roof with a harsh, bone-jarring impact. The only doubt she had was whether she would be able to hold on or not after she landed.

She flew through the air like a bird and landed with a thud on the roof of the hov unfortunate enough to be passing nearby, unaware of the falling taxi descending behind it in a blaze of seat cushions and flesh. Her impact dented the roof and jarred her to a stupor, the bowl-like indentation she had created keeping her from falling off as she regained her wits. The startled driver of the hov, unaccustomed to objects falling onto his roof with such an impact, chattered away in fear and excitement as the flaming taxi passed before him and he pealed off to the nearest landing site, cursing at his bad joss.

Alexis was able to regain enough sense to jump off the hov right before it landed and snake off into the nearby bushes so that the driver of the vehicle, when he came to find the source of the deep dent in his roof, never saw her at all and ranted and raved, jumping up and down in that excited way people have as he cursed his life and his wife and his car and anything else that caught his fancy at that moment.

She lay in the bushes, breathing deeply and evenly, performing a self-diagnosis to determine how badly she had injured herself. She had knocked the wind out of herself, that was certain, but she found no other serious injuries besides a few bumps and bruises and after making certain that the frantic driver of the dented hov was busy describing his bad joss to a policeman, she slipped out of the bushes and merged into the mainstream of the crowd gathering around the wreckage of the crashed and burning taxi in which she had so recently been riding.

After watching for a few minutes to see if she could spot the assassins, she slipped off and made her way back to the nearest Internet center to place a call and get out of the country. Although Fujita had not given her the amount of information she had hoped, he had given her a name, a name that she was slowly beginning to realize was most definitely connected with this whole, crazy game.

It only made sense.

And the fact that he had used an alias told her much also, more than she wanted to know. By using the name Georg Holstein, Ian Montana had thrown the assassins off and had survived their deadly stratagem. Either that or Ian was mixed up in the assassinations, perhaps having gotten out of these people the information he needed and finding them then superfluous to his plans.

But if it was the man whom she knew as Ian Montana – another alias she had discovered shortly after she lost contact with him -- she had no problem believing that he would have the balls to implement such a plan right under Cav's nose. And that thought brought up another, far more disturbing thought. For Ian Montana had been one of Alexis' few former romantic interests and one of the few men whom Cav had despised for it. Ian had also been one of Cav's better agents, a normal agent not imbued with genetic talents surpassing normal human abilities.

And Ian Montana was supposed to be dead.

History is the art of choosing, from among many lies,
the one which most resembles the truth.
-- Croce

17

17 August 2085, 1145 hrs
Dr. Cavalier's office

  Cav sat in his large, plush chair, leaning back and rocking slightly, a nervous habit he had since he was young. His hands were clasped together under his chin and the ascetic look on his face was both pensive and somber. The lights, as always, were dimmed, the little cones of illumination they projected barely reaching beyond the boundary of their dark-colored shades. This dearth of light cast melancholy shadows across the furniture and the paintings of Rembrandt and Raphael, Jan van Eyck and Renoir, their own little lights casting the canvases in a dull brilliance, placing them in little worlds all their own along the walls.
  The heavy curtains covering the tall windows blocked out the glaring light of the noonday sun and the humid heat rising from the fetid, stagnant water that was the city. The rains had finally stopped, the tattered and torn metallic blue clouds flirting over the deep azure sky only echoes of the brooding thunderheads that had inundated the land for days. Hundreds of thousands were homeless, food and clean water scarce. The bodies of those who had died in the torrential downpours and the massive flooding were now coming to the surface in a morbid ballet, popping up at random intervals and spinning and bobbing among the rows of houses and offices and stores now so much water-logged refuse.
  But none of this bothered Cav.

His thoughts didn't even touch on the plight of those less fortunate than him, on the millions without power, of the city that the land was trying its hardest to reclaim lying flooded at the base of the massive tower in which he sat, immune from nature's wrath. He was not even interested in the assortment of foods sitting idle and untouched on the side table; mushrooms, rye cakes made with buttermilk, honey in the comb, nuts, chocolate confections, herb brandy and cherry brandy. They were his favorite snacks, brought in several hours earlier per his request and yet even they didn't intrude on his thoughts, all but forgotten as they sat alone on the table.

He stared into the darker corners, his deep-set eyes narrow and hard, yet unfocused, his thoughts concentrated on one idea and one idea only, working through the numerous perturbations this one idea could take in the future.

He had heard from Alexis through the dummy account in Hawaii. Although not quite clear on what had happened to her contact, Aobe Fujita, his fate was not all that important anyway. What had him in such a pensive mood was the name that she sent to him, requesting status and residence.

Ian Montana.

It was a name Cav thought he would never hear again, that he had hoped and prayed he would never have to deal with. Of all the lovers Alexis had in her torrid past, all the sexual exploits she fell into after her awakening and her defiant rebellion against her role and her design, the affair with Ian Montana had by far held the most promise for destruction and scandal.

For it was Ian Montana with whom Alexis had come the closest to failing in love, though she never saw it coming nor knew it had happened till it was too late. Cav had seen it from the very beginning.

The affaire d'amour with the father of her now dead son had been bad enough, his death in that car accident an unfortunate necessity Cav himself had ordered. But the liaison with Ian, though never producing any offspring, was worse. Cav knew it the moment he saw them together, the moment he saw the look on her face and the way she responded when around him. Cav had needed to work hard to break that one up. The last thing he had needed at that time was for Alexis' concentration to be on Ian rather than the missions, a possible deadly distraction.

It worked fine in the movies and the novels springing up like mushrooms from the plethora of home computers, but in the real world, in Cav's world, such affairs and distractions led to one thing and one thing only: death. And that he could not allow. Alexis was his pride and joy, the apex of his work and research. And to allow her to throw her life away for a fleeting happiness that she might never truly obtain was not the life he had chosen for her, would allow for her. Alexis was his to control and any thoughts of love or infatuation for another, especially that other, were paths down the wrong road. Or so he used to think.

Now he saw the affair as a warning he should have caught, saw it as the first step toward her own awakening, which led inevitably to her quitting and moving to Alaska. It was very possible, with the commodity of hindsight, to even say that Ian's leaving led directly to Alexis' breakdown and her resignation. Was he then responsible for it all?

Most likely.

He seemed to be responsible for most of the bad aspects of her life, so why not this one also. But even that didn't bother him all that much. He had long ago come to the conclusion that it had happened and would have happened anyway and so why chastise himself over it constantly. What did bother him was why now, of all times, would Alexis want to know where Ian was, even think that he was alive?

Did her odd behavior when she awoke from her recovery so recently have anything to do with Ian? He doubted it, since she had only now mentioned Ian to Cav. But it certainly would explain her behavior. Her sentiments on home and family and wanting to sever all relationships with him and his agency had seemed misplaced and out of character at first, but now with the name Ian Montana in the picture, it was a different story. It was beginning to make sense to him.

When she had left the last time, she had still wanted to stay in contact, still understood that she could, if the situation warranted it, be recalled and placed back on active status. Her most recent tantrum had put an end to all that, had set the ground rules without question and made it crystal clear that Alexis Locke no longer wanted to be Alexis Locke.

She seemed to fail to understand that such a request was an impossibility. But that was neither here nor there at the moment. All he needed was for her to keep focused just a little while longer, just long enough to crack this mystery and discover what was behind this bizarre and complicated scheme that had a group of shadowy assassins killing off people who seemed to have no bearing on anything important. When she was done with this, it might be possible for him to grant a limited part of her request. She was, as far as Claudine and the president were concerned, already dead so that avenue was already closed.

But why Ian ...?

And why now?

A former CIA agent and consultant who had left the government and the Company disillusioned with his work and his life, Ian had been one of the few outside, non-genetically engineered people whom Cav had hired, had recruited into his clandestine organization to work behind the scenes. He came with impeccable credentials and background, despite the smear campaign the CIA had launched to discredit him after his less than complimentary departure from their clutches. Ian had proven to be a valuable asset, especially in the research department, where his skills pulled Cav out of several messes.

It had, as was more often than not the case, been a chance encounter that had thrown Alexis and Ian together. Occurring right in the very office in which Cav now sat. Cav had no one to blame but himself. He had summoned Ian for a detailed report on something he could not even remember and Alexis had come storming in after a particularly dangerous assignment, as she was wont to do back then. Cav had seen from the first frosty eye contact between the two that there was going to be trouble.

It had taken all of two weeks for Cav to learn that Alexis and Ian had been seen at lunch together, then at dinner. It was not long after that Ian and Alexis became sexually involved, a steamy passion seeming to rise from the very forbidden self-imposed ardor Alexis had exiled herself to after the birth of her son and the death of the father.

It was at that point that Cav had taken action and had sent Ian to another branch office on the other side of the world, telling Alexis that he had died, telling Ian that Alexis no longer wanted to see him, that it was her request that he be sent away and for Ian to never make contact again with her on threat of his life. Cav then made damn certain that neither of them ever knew different.

The death of Alexis' son's father had not hit Alexis nearly as hard as had Ian's supposed death. She had been morose for several months after she had been informed about it and after her period of mourning, she had begun to think that there was more to all these deaths of her lovers than Cav was admitting. She first began to suspect the accident that took the life of her other amorous relation and one thing led to another until Alexis ended up in Alaska, retired and damned if she was going to do anything for Cav ever again.

It had been a time of great upheaval at the agency and in Cav's life. Now with the re-emergence of the name Ian Montana coming from the mouth of Alexis, all those emotions and troubles and sentiments had come crashing to the surface like a pounding surf, smashing his fragile beach with their relentless battering till all that was left was his unfocused gaze at the wall and his food laying uneaten on the table.

He stirred slightly, then spoke, his voice soft yet rich, filled with a harshness both subtle and tired. "Computer. I need a transport to Kazakhstan and a Rapid Response Team immediately."

There was a slight beep as acknowledgment, a pause and a reply. "Transport fueling will be complete in five minutes. The Rapid Response Team has been notified and will be waiting."

Cav smirked, his face taking on a hardened look as he heaved his bulk out of the chair. In whatever aspect Ian Montana was involved, Cav was not about to let him interfere with the resolution of this mission. When Alexis had asked for the last known residence, he had accessed his database to find where exactly he had sent the man and a small tidbit of information had come up on Cav's screen he now found quite interesting, that he had not shared with Alexis. It had to do with a certain woman whom Mr. Montana had been in communication with recently, a certain woman whose presence Cav was not about to tolerate around all his former agents.

He had to get to Ian before Alexis, or at least shortly there after, before she could re-kindle that relationship and find out the true reasons that Mr. Montana had been exiled from the main office and eventually from the agency itself, the true reasons Cav had to lie to her and make his death convincing, funeral and all. He was not about to let his life disintegrate now, not after all that he had done, suffered, sacrificed.

If he didn't know better, he would almost believe that Claudine had set this all up to destroy Cav and Alexis. She was certainly more than enough of a bitch to do it without batting an eye.

Cav looked at the food on the table and in a moment of pure rage brought on by the connections he was beginning to see in this mess that had been dropped in his lap, swept the table top clear of all the food, sending it sprawling across the office in a shower of bowls and nuts and mushrooms. The two brandy bottles tumbled hard across the plush carpet, coming to a firm stop, the contents running out in a splash of sweet smelling liqueur soaking into the fibers and filling the room with their delectable aroma.

*　　*　　*

1

7 August 2085, 1204 hrs
Kazakhstan

The heavy Boeing 800 Star-lifter settled onto the tarmac of Nazarbayev International Airport in the Kazakhstan capital of Aqmola with slight bump and puff of white smoke from the tires firmly gripping the runway as it applied its reverse thrusters and began the long deceleration to mark the end of its trip from Tokyo. The advent of the ballistic airliners lifting off like normal planes but then ascending nearly vertical, pulsing out of the atmosphere and in low orbit bringing them halfway across the globe in a little under four hours, had made air travel much more efficient and timely, bringing the world that much closer together.

The city if Aqmola, which means white grave in Kazak, was turned into the new capital of the Republic of Kazakhstan (Qazaqstan Respublikasï) in 2001. It sat at the junction of the Trans-Kazakhstan and South-Siberian railways and the flowing course of the Esii -- or Ishim, depending on what side if the river one lived -- river which, along with the mighty Irtysh and Tobol, flowed north through most of Russia, emptying out into the Arctic Sea in a rush of white, half-frozen water. The land around the capital consisted of gently sloping and undulating hills and plateaus and was dotted by depressions made by salt lakes long since evaporated, all of which had been converted into rich farming and pasture land. The fertile soil of the northern highlands erupted yearly in a bounty of food to complement the abundant mineral resources the area enjoyed and brought a measure of prosperity to this land that had for so long known nothing but the iron hand of conquerors.

Alexis, after barely making it out of the Heihe airport on a scheduled flight to Beijing, worked her way over to Tokyo under a different name and disguise and then booked a flight for herself to Aqmola using the emergency debit card she always carried with her under the name of Natasha Baklanova. With Ian's name popping back into the equation, she was beginning to suspect that trusting Cav and his people to arrange her movements might not be that wise of a decision. She was becoming more and more of an independent, a turn of events about which was not too happy, especially with the current problems she was having.

As much as she hated to admit it, she needed Cav and his retinue of researchers and weapons experts, especially with a group of assassins after her whom she was beginning to believe more and more were not from around locally. In fact, as Alexis had sat on the plane trying to catch up on her sleep, she had begun to evaluate the trend of events that had been playing out around her and she had came to a startling conclusion that she didn't want to believe. She had thought up ways to test her theory, but after much deliberation, had come to the conclusion that there was no way to truly test it.

As such, her best option was just to go along and see what happened, reacting as circumstances dictated and hoping for the best. It was not a plan conducive to survival. Her thoughts, unfortunately, continued to focus back on the man she was going to Kazakhstan to meet, a man who she had thought had dead on a mission those many years ago.

The mere name brought up a fresh spate of emotions she had thought she was over, buried deep and discarded for wont of a better solution. But when Fujita had mentioned his name, that name that for so long had brought nothing but pleasure to her mind, Alexis realized in a flash of unwinding memories that seemed as fresh as the day they had been made that she had not forgotten them at all, was not over the hurt and the betrayal and the loss of faith she had experienced because of Ian Montana.

The emotions she was feeling deep inside, that churned and boiled in her innards like a morass of maggots, were not pleasant ones. They were emotions of anger and hatred, a brooding indifference wanting to know why and how. If he was not dead, why had he not contacted her? With all the resources available, why had he not at least attempted to send her a singular message stating that he was alive and well.

Of course, there was always the possibility that his life had been in jeopardy and any contact with those he had once been close to would blow his new cover. But with the way they had felt about each other, he should have found a way, after all these years, to contact her, at least to let her know that he was alive. It would have been the compassionate thing to do.

So as she sat in the business class of the Boeing 800 and felt the absence of gravity on the apex of the ballistic track, she realized with a finality hitting her as substantial as a punch to the stomach that these thoughts were thoughts that killed. She would need to purge herself of all of it if she expected to survive long after touch-down. With the assassins on her trail, shooting missiles at her taxis and killing all the people she happened to talk to – she had half expected the star-liner she now rode to come crashing out of the sky in flames – Alexis knew that she would need all her resources and all her concentration to stay alive, to stay alive long enough to solve this riddle and make those responsible pay. Even if one of those responsible turned out to be Cav.

She involuntarily flashed back to her hasty and impromptu departure from

China. She had barely made it to the Heihe airport when heavily armed police units showed up and literally closed the place down, looking for a suspected terrorist who, amazingly enough, fit the description of Jill Rousseau quite well. With this in mind, she had hurriedly slipped into a restroom and ditched the disguise, reverting to her own face and hair and changing to a gray halter tap and tight jeans, a combination as far removed from what she had worn as Jill Rousseau as she could get.

Then she had made her way as loudly and garishly as possible to her gate, knowing that the more noise she made the less likely the police would be interested in her, brushing her off as just another rude, noisy American tourist and wanting as little to do with her as possible. It had been easy after that to slip past the security checkpoints and board her plane.

It led her to this moment in time now as she stood in the main lobby of Aqmola's Nazarbayev airport dressed in jeans and a white T-shirt, a brown leather bag she had purchased in Tokyo during the lay-over slung over her shoulder, her short hair a vibrant bleach blonde with glaring brown roots, eyes a cerulean blue, face that of an older woman with deep lines etched around her eyes and full red lips. This was the last instant disguise she had left on her person and she was already beginning to wonder how she was going to slip out of this town if events turned on her here also. She could not remember a time during any other mission when she had been forced to change appearances so often.

She walked with a restrained swagger and a diligent, modest air about her as she made her way through the terminal. She was here to find and talk to Ian Montana, the man that she had banished to the far, far reaches of her mind long ago after his death. But now, with his name the last words on the lips of the dead Aobe Fujita, Montana's memories had exploded in her mind like a grenade, the shrapnel opening scars she had thought were healed long ago.

She shook her head to get the images of the man out, to purge her mind of all but the essentials. Despite how she felt, wondering what she was going to say when she confronted him after almost twenty years, she knew that she had to push him back once again to the far reaches, to stay there until she was ready to bring his memory forward and confront not only him but her own, lost emotions. But Ian continued to intrude, almost mockingly.

She watched the procession of people milling about the lobby, some dressed in modern, conventional clothing and others in the more traditional dress and headscarves. She could tell from this differentiation exactly from where each person originated, whether from the urban areas or the small farming villages dotting the countryside. The Slavs, Belorusians and Ukrainians were prone to living in the cities and the more native Kazaks confined themselves more to the country, their reverence for the old-life still strong.

In the last few decades, this area had grown at a tremendous rate, the industrial riches of the ground finally exploited in the western way, the large influx of Oriental and American companies bringing in their offices and their culture in bulk. As such, Aqmola, as the capital and the one city with a large enough airport and rail centers for convenience, had become the apex of a resurgent high-tech industrial complex. The result had been the emergence of one of the leading centers of research for the major bio-tech firms, the cheap land and cheaper labor much more conducive to operating costs than the labor union saddled America or the high tax-based Europe.

It was here that Ian Montana was employed, working for one of the many nameless firms specializing in the development of ideas and equipment that were changing the way the world functioned every year. She hefted the bag onto her shoulder better and started to make her way toward the large glass entrance where the bright light of the August afternoon greeted her. The temperature outside was comfortable, in the upper sixties with a slight breeze moving in fits and starts, barely waving the flags hanging like limp rags on their impotent poles.

There was a profusion of taxis waiting for fares and she stepped up to the nearest one, addressing the indolent looking driver who relaxed back on the side of his taxi with a smoldering, putrid stub of a cigar stuck in his mouth, his eyes undressing her slowly and methodically. It was obvious that the ban on tobacco was not as stringently enforced here as it was in the other developed countries.

"Marhaba, Allah u bi ma'akum."

The taxi driver's eyes popped back up to her face and he stood up straight, taking his cigar out of his mouth and holding it down in-between his short, fat little fingers. "And may Allah be with you also. Where can I take you today?"

She didn't bother to smile but just looked at the door as if waiting for it to open itself. He narrowed his eyes a moment, then stuck the cigar back in his mouth and opened the door. She climbed in and settled herself, then told the driver to take her to Bashar Biotech. He grinned at her through the mirror as the taxi took off into the air with a jerk.

"Do you have a hotel to stay in already?" the driver asked with his sing-song accent and happy-go-lucky tone telling Alexis that the man would be more than happy to recommend a hotel where he could better have his way with her.

"I'm fine, thank you."

The driver continued to jabber away as he drove her through the city and toward the main industrial park where the large corporate headquarters of Bashar were located. She ignored him completely, watching the new construction and the old city center fly past the window, wondering if they were out there, waiting for her. The shadow people had been on her tail every step of the way. It would be foolish to assume that they would not be here also.

After an interminable drive through which the cabby never shut-up once, they reached her destination and she gladly stepped out of the taxi. When he handed her money card back, he slipped her a small piece of paper she was certain was a phone number or house address or some such nonsense, his greasy smile telling her that he thought his chances good at bedding her.

She didn't acknowledge him or the note and, turning her back to him, walked toward the main entrance of the building to his whistles and cat-calls. She noticed the myriad of video cameras and security systems keeping the main entrance, the walkway, and the lobby under constant, tight surveillance. She walked purposefully to the main reception counter where an attractive, young female sat, her low-cut shirt over-exposing the voluptuous curves of her genetically modified breasts. Alexis was certain that if the lady were to bend over she would give the male visitors to the firm a view they would not soon forget. Although she could not see it, Alexis was certain that the receptionist was wearing a tight mini skirt of some type.

Alexis had dealt with this type of woman before. They existed all over the world. Young, attractive and not very bright, they gravitated toward the jobs that required little thought, the chance to dress up sexy and the possibility they would attract the eye of some young upward mobile executive and sleep their way into money. They were the girls who usually ended up with the Jaguar and the million-dollar home after the divorce.

Alexis was ignored by the receptionist as she talked away into her computer mike and answered phones and generally sat there trying to look busy. Alexis cleared her throat contemptuously, standing before the counter with arms crossed and head slightly tilted to the side. The receptionist looked up with puckered lips and narrowed eyes, as if Alexis had interrupted something extremely important.

"Ayna ana 'athara Ian Montana?" Alexis asked in Arabic, her face a mask of suppressed rage at the indolence.

The receptionist looked at her a moment, eyeing her figure and her facial features with a practiced eye. She had noticed Alexis walking down the walkway earlier, had seen the strong stride and the swing of the hips and, as vain women are prone to do when they come across another woman who they believe looks better then they do, felt a wave of contempt swell in her. How dare she look better, at an older age, than the receptionist did. As was also the usual case, the receptionist began to find all the flaws, real or imagined, that she could on this new threat to convince herself that she was indeed the better looking of the two.

After taking a quick, close-up view of the enemy, a smile touched the corners of the receptionist's mouth and she looked back at her computer screen and spoke into it in a dialect with which Alexis was not familiar. She was about to ask again when the receptionist spoke without even looking up. "He's not in at the moment."

When there was no more information forthcoming, Alexis spoke again. "Can you kindly tell me when he'll be back in?"

"Hard to say. He keeps his own hours, if you know what I mean."

Alexis raised an eyebrow. "Can I wait in his office?"

Now the receptionist looked up at Alexis with a penetrating stare and Alexis could not help but get the feeling that the receptionist thought Alexis the dumbest person in the world, her contempt reaching out in palatable waves of mental anguish. "Of course not. Who do you think you are? Perhaps you had better leave now. I'm extremely busy."

"I noticed that," Alexis replied sarcastically. "Can you gave Mr. Montana a message, or would that be too much for you to handle?"

The receptionist looked up again at Alexis. "Don't get smart with me, ma'am."

"I wouldn't dream of it," Alexis replied bitterly, reaching into the woman's mind and placing within it a recurring thought that she was too fat and needed to go on a diet. "Please tell him that Brenda de Vere was here to see him. Think you can handle that?" To make certain, Alexis placed the thought foremost in the woman's mind and forced her to move her hands and type it into the main message center. When Ian heard that name, if he still remembered, he would know that it was Alexis who had come calling.

When Alexis was certain that the receptionist had finished typing in the message and sent it, she turned and, smelling the aroma of freshly cooked food coming from the other side of the lobby, started to walk that way.

The receptionist, looking down at her flat stomach with a frown and noticing that she was starting to gain weight, looked after Alexis. "You can't go there," she lacklusterly called, noticing that her arms were starting to get flabby also and then took her lunch and tossed it into the trash with a longing last look.

Alexis ignored the voice and made her way toward the large cafeteria that was part of the circular ground floor, a pair of ornate glass, double doors separating the lobby from the eating area. She walked in as if she belonged, her stomach growling from the smell of the food drifting on the air, the strange, indigenous cuisine different to her palette, the rich fragrance of spices and blends enticing her to partake.

And she did.

She also noticed that those taking care of the security here at Bashar Bio-tech didn't see the cafeteria as a high security risk area, for there were no cameras here she could see, no obvious systems like there had been in the lobby and so she decided that it would be relatively safe to relax and eat something. After loading a tray up with a variety of new dishes and a few she recognized as typical American edibles, she found an empty table near a gaggle of women who appeared to be employees, perhaps even secretaries, the ones who actually knew what was going on in the workplace. They were talking away in what appeared to be contented tones, discussing affairs that had little to do with business.

A waiter came by to take her drink order. "Ana mathilu ba'adu ma'a," Alexis droned out and the waiter smiled and brought back the water she had ordered. She quietly ate her food, enjoying the new sensations presented and listening to every word the women at the next table spoke. It was amazing what one could pick up from a secretary if one only listened.

After several minutes, she hit the jackpot.

There was to be a big company dance tonight, a formal affair for the CEO who was coming in from Japan and all the employees were expected to attend, as a sign of solidarity. The women seemed quite excited about the soiree and Alexis was able to pick up exactly where it was to be held and how it was by invitation only since several non-employee VIPs where also expected to attend and the company didn't want just anyone showing up for security reasons.

One of the ladies, the youngest of the group with delicate facial features topped with puffy brown hair and a body that had seen a few too many jelly donuts, pulled out of her purse an embossed invitation card. It was obvious that this was the first such event this young woman had been to and she proudly showed off her invitation to the others, who smiled pleasantly at her excitement. After making certain that they all saw that she had also received permission to go to the dance, a fact that didn't seem all that interesting to the others since all the employees received the same invitation, the young lady put the card back in her purse.

Alexis smiled also.

This was too easy.

She wiped her mouth, stood, lifted her tray up, grabbed her bag and walked around the table with the chattering women, specifically to the side where the young employee sat. Timing it just right, Alexis tripped and spilled the entire contents of her tray on the lady, the tray clattering down and striking her in the chest, Alexis ending up on the floor next to the purse.

"I'm so sorry, oh my gosh, I can't believe I did that, I'm so sorry..." Alexis profusely apologized to the lady who was now completely covered in French fries, salad and various other delectable dishes that when mixed together made an awful mess on the beautiful cotton summer dress with the floral pattern.

The other women all stood, some of them going to help their friend, others kneeling down to help Alexis who had done such a good job of convincing everyone that the fall was real that they were actually concerned about her. Other employees from other tables came over to help or to watch and snicker or ohh and ahh at the ruined dress and the grease in the hair and gravy on her cheeks.

Alexis was helped up with many apologies rolling off her lips as well as offers to pay for the ruined dress. Several waiters came over to begin cleaning up and in the general confusion that prevailed, Alexis was able to slip away unnoticed, her new invitation tucked securely in her bra.

There was just one more small thing to take care of before she could show up at the dance and hopefully meet Ian. She walked quickly over to the small park the company had built for breaks, overlooking the hov parking area and waited. She didn't have to wait long. The young woman, her dress completely ruined and unwearable, came storming out of the entrance to the building, tears streaming down her face, her purse clutched tightly in her hand as she ran to the parking area and jumped into her personal hov.

Alexis already had her pocket computer out with the signal interceptor attachment and as the hov pulled out of the lot and headed for the main thoroughfare, Alexis quickly scanned the vehicle, pulling out of the non-encoded navigation system – for who would encode such a thing? – the address where the young lady was heading. After waiting a few more minutes, Alexis used her computer to hail a taxi and gave the driver the address.

She arrived shortly after the young lady. The woman lived in a high-rise apartment that had a brand new look to it that buildings get, the gleaming metal and glass and stone structure rising into the air with its sail-boom design like a needle. The finely manicured grounds around the ample park at its base indicative of a wealthy clientele. The profusion of stores running from the complex like roots on an old, gnarled tree, busy with the day's business.

Alexis walked over to the main directory and found that, not surprisingly, it had a security lock on it that didn't allow just anyone to walk up and discover who lived here. She pulled a small device from her purse that looked like a compact, attached it to the computer touch-plate and activated it. Within seconds the security system was bypassed and Alexis had found the apartment number of the young lady, whose name she pulled off the invitation.

She stepped out of the elevator on the ninetieth floor and, after checking to make certain that the corridor was empty, stayed in the elevator as she looked over at the security panel on the wall and frowned. This complex had ccnstant surveillance, she was certain, and probably one of those new holographic valet centers on each floor helping with the mundane daily questions and concerns the tenants had. She sighed, then pulled out the same device she had used on the panel below and pointed it toward the panel across the corridor. It only took a few moments to insert a virus into the system that quickly disabled the entire security system on this floor and that would look, to the self-diagnostic systems in operation, as if the program had suffered a power surge and temporary malfunction.

She would have to work quickly. The diagnostics in this center appeared quite advanced and she didn't want to be caught by the system while still on the floor. She walked quickly and confidently to the door belonging to her target. With the security system down, the door opened easily – one of the many flaws with the new hands-off non-human total security systems that all the new buildings were installing – and stepped in to the sound of cursing intermixed with tearful sobs.

If this were twenty years earlier, this poor young woman would be as good as dead.

But Alexis could not, would not kill her. There was no reason to kill her. She had done nothing wrong except flash her invitation when Alexis happened to be around and for that, Alexis was not ready to kill. Too many innocent people had already died and killing this one would make her no better than the shadow people following her.

Although she didn't know it at the time, it would prove to be a mistake. There were reasons she had been trained as she had by Cav and those reasons didn't become invalid with the passing of time. It was an inevitable bet that anyone not killed outright always managed to spoil the best-laid plans.

But to Alexis none of those thoughts mattered.

There would be no more unnecessary killing.

Not after *Stargazer I.*

The young lady stepped out of her bedroom wearing only panties. Their eyes locked and before she could get her scream out Alexis advanced on her and rendered her unconscious. Her eyes rolled into the back of her head and she fell down listlessly, the jellyrolls of her body flapping to the carpet. Alexis dragged her back into the bedroom with an effort and tied her firmly to the bed, inserting a cloth in her mouth for good measure, then placing in her mind the image of a man who had attacked her – Alexis' first taxi driver – to make certain that she was not connected in anyway to the scene.

The entire event took less then five minutes and soon Alexis was back on the ground and in a taxi making her way to the center of the fashion district to pick out the proper attire for the night's soiree.

As fire is obscured by smoke,
and as a mirror by dust,
as an embryo is enveloped by its covering,
so is wisdom obscured by passion.
--- Bhagavad-Gita

18

17 August 2085, 2230 hrs
Grand Kazak Convention Center

The ballroom reserved for the special dance of Bashar Biotech was elegant in its adornments, revisiting an older time when the great Tsars of Russia had entertained in the grand style that can only survive under autocratic monarchs. Expensive hovs pulled up to the entrance in a cavalcade of glittering dresses and black ties, of slits showing off legs and décolletage dipping low to reveal the curves of those who sought such exposure.
This collage of colors and styles, of expensive hovs and limousines, of valets and servants and tuxedos manifestly emphasized the gap that still existed between the haves and the have-nots. The small, shoddy houses huddling on the rich soil of the farms but a few kilometers from the luxury of the ballroom were a stark reminder of the poverty still holding this region in its grip despite the plethora of natural resources the land gave up to the few elites reaping the rewards. It was a state of affairs of which Alexis was well aware. She could see in the eyes of the porters and the valets who watched the glittering procession of the rich advance into the convention center with looks of smug disdain, also seeing the disparity and mocking it with hidden sarcasm. One could have easily placed this soiree in the heart of New York or St. Petersburg, Kyoto or Paris, the differences minimal, the wealth the

same, the opulent eyes of those involved no different despite the fact that it was taking place in the heart of a land that had, at the turn of the century, been non-existent to most of the world.

Wealth had a way of insinuating itself into every society that allowed it in. It had a way of creeping into the farthest nooks and crannies, working its way into the very fabric of the culture, and then, when it had assured that its place was secure, exploding into the mainstream and corrupting all it fell upon in a shower of corpulent licentiousness. It had happened here in this land that once had been home to nomads and simple farmers.

It would, eventually, happen everywhere and it made Alexis sick to think that these people who paraded themselves before this temple of prosperity, wearing their idols of Rolex and Yves St. Laurent on their waists and their wrists, looking like they were important and special because the fountain of wealth just happened to shower them with its favors, were the same as the humble farmer sitting in his unassuming abode with his mud-encrusted puntees. That the low wattage light flickering and dim and casting their shadows into the clean corners of the simple houses fell upon the same species who walked through the entrance with the blazing, fluorescent lights and flashing strobes of the convention center was somehow lost to the vagaries of vanity.

They say that success comes with a price.

For Alexis, she would rather say that wealth came with a curse: a curse that took for granted all that one had been given in a chance moment in a life that was nothing more than a mirage.

But who was she to criticize? She had been to more than her fair share of such parties in her life-time, dressed up opulently as they did and flaunted her looks just like the want-to-be models who strutted along the walkway to the large marble steps of the convention center with their hips waggling and their chests pressed out and their looks of utter disdain for anything that didn't cost a million.

But whereas all the other times she had been simply doing a job, dressing up for Cav and doing his dirty work which, when she thought back upon all of it, amounted to no more than a pile of dog shit, now she had a purpose that was her own. She was going to find the people who murdered her son and Clovis and Fujita. And she was getting a step closer this night, at this party when she found Ian and discovered just what the hell he was playing at pretending to be dead.

She arrived in the hotel-provided limo and stepped out into the ring of indulgence wearing a full-length jacket and a scarf around her head. Until

217

she was safely inside, safely past the press loitering around the entrance to watch the cortege and take photos of those they thought famous or important, she didn't want to cause a scene or have anyone take notice. Although a few heads were turned toward the hastily moving lady all bundled up, her lack of exposed skin in this zoo of tanned cellulite made them dismiss her quickly.

She had spent the time between tying up the young lady whose invitation she stole and this moment working on her dress selection, buying a flowing blonde wig braided tight behind her in a long tail and trying to find a way to make a new invitation that had her name on it.

She quickly discovered that the invitations were rather copy-proof. They were not even paper as she had at first suspected. Instead, they were made of the latest in the line of nano-tech electron sheets on which all the new books printed since 2015 had been made, if one could even call it printing.

The paper-like substance was actually a thin recorder sheet allowing one to display anything on its surface. A computer chip, using the latest in nano-technology, held the entire volume of the book in its memory and a simple touch of the finger changed the formatting of the electrons on the page so that new words appeared when one wanted to turn the page.

This technology had vastly decreased the amount of room one needed for book storage, for an entire thousand-page book could be kept on the simple, thin sheet. It was even flexible and easy to carry around. The old system of requiring huge buildings to house the reams upon reams of books were now as much a relic of the past as were paperbacks, libraries reduced to small storage facilities requiring very little room to store the assortment of recorder sheets, the main memory of the billion volumes of books taken off the Internet.

When one wanted to read another book, all that was needed was for the memory chip to be reprogrammed, a procedure taking but a few microseconds and the user walked out of the library with a brand new book. The invitation was just such a recorder sheet with one, minor exception: the invitations were encoded and encrypted, making it difficult if not impossible to change the name. Whereas the books were programmed to be changed at any library or bookstore, these invitations were designed to remain as they were to prevent anyone from doing what Alexis was about to do.

After several failed attempts with her pocket computer and attached scanner, she successfully broke into the chip just as the limo was pulling up to the convention center. She changed the name to Brenda de Vere and changed the corresponding genetic information and retinal scans to match her own. Her biggest problem now would be to add her name to the list she was certain would be cross-referenced at the entrance.

She programmed the necessary info into her hand-held scanner, the one she could just touch to a computer and extract all the contents of its memory in a matter of micro-seconds, and tried to think of a way to get close enough to the registration computer to allow her to download the virus she had programmed, which would add her name to the master list.

She followed the entourage of unknown, nameless people into the reception center where each invitation was carefully checked against the master list and then each guest's identity verified. As Alexis watched, she was happy to see that the young lady who was checking all the invitations on the master list was using a pocket computer not unlike her own and was standing close enough to the receiving line that Alexis would be able to contrive something convincing to be able to touch the master list with her own computer.

As she neared the young lady, she used the old reliable stumble and fall forward. A look of shear horror crossed the receptionist's face at the mere thought that someone would be clumsy enough to fall on her. Alexis reached out to catch herself, looking as shocked as she could and was able to just reach the hand holding the master list. She grabbed it as several men standing around attempted to catch her, each one wanting to be able to touch the lovely woman who was falling and perhaps get a name or a dance later for their effort.

Alexis nimbly and discreetly touched her scanner to the master list for the brief amount of time needed, then turned red with embarrassment, a pinkish color filling out her cheeks and flushing them, making her look even more attractive to those standing around. She was offered the arm of numerous suitors who had come alone to the soiree and, graciously declining all of them, straightened her jacket out, smiled at the young lady with the master list as she apologized, then handed her the invitation and was duly checked off as an official invitee.

Once inside, Alexis noted that she didn't need to worry about standing out in the crowd much. The amount of bare flesh visible on the ladies in attendance made her dress feel conservative, if not downright old-fashioned. Scattered about the large expanse of the dance hall, which had numerous tables and chairs arranged along the side and a live big band at the far end, were a variety of the newest line of dresses coming off the runways in Paris and Tokyo.

The trend in the last decade had reverted back to the revealing half-dresses that had been all the rage in the 2020's and then again in the 2050's and 60's. The most popular pattern was the `flower petal,' which consisted of nothing more than a few well-placed fabric flower petals – sometimes even real flowers for the more extravagant versions – on a see-through dress that was skin-tight nylon and barely detectable even to those standing right next to the wearer. The flowers varied from roses to orchids to simple violet petals and if the woman who wore the dress – if one could call it that – had a halfway athletic figure, the effect was highly invigorating to the men who stood around in awe.

Other dress patterns were typical styles with the exception of the other latest craze sweeping the fashion industry, another throw back from the 40's. These had a hole cut in them where a breast would hang, allowing it to be exposed in all its firm and round glory, the morals of such wanton displays of the body having relaxed greatly over the years. Sometimes it was the left breast and sometimes the right one, but never both. Which breast the lady choose to reveal supposedly implied something about her availability or some such thing, but Alexis had neither the inclination nor the desire to learn what it all meant.

She would have to be really desperate to wear anything that tawdry.

Of course, there were always the traditional dresses that never went out of style, which those who didn't want to expose their bodies to public display or had the bodies necessary for the flower petal designs wore at such events throughout the ages.

Such a simple dress Alexis wore.

She took off her dinner jacket and handed it to the coat check droid, then made her way into the main ballroom. Her dress was a blush-rose in color and was strap-less, the cut along her breast-line oblique so that the curves on the left were more exposed than the right, the dark shadow of the left aureole almost visible under the dresses lace edge. A gold and emerald choker provided the only coverage for the otherwise bare skin extending from chin to cleavage.

The dress extended just above the knees in front and the ankles in the rear, tapered in graceful folds toward the back where a gold and emerald anklet graced her left ankle and a high slit allowed the firm, long line of her tanned leg to be seen within a few centimeters of her hip. The dress was not too tight but flowing with an elegance suggesting her body shape rather than forcefully exposing it. The back had a small band clasped together running along the line of the shoulder blades on the right and down under her left armpit. The remainder of her back was exposed down to the low-cut just below the small of her back so that when she walked the firm roundness of her buttocks moved under the fabric in arousing and sensual grace.

High heels and a corsage of miniature roses and baby's breath intricately woven into her hair, topped off the ensemble and several heads turned as she walked down the arching steps and onto the ballroom floor. Since no one knew her, they all assumed that she was someone special, perhaps even a mistress of the CEO, the rumors and innuendoes flying fast and furious. She ignored the stares and the gawks following her, the side-glances and mumbled comments and observations floating on the air like a fine mist bouncing off her indifference as she scanned the crowd diligently.

She could almost feel his presence, sense him somehow in the room, the music of the band sweeping across the dance floor in palpable waves of energy that seemed to make those on the dance floor sway and gyrate unnaturally. To look more natural, she lifted a champagne glass off of the tray of a passing waiter droid and began to mingle slowly, always looking for him, smiling politely at those who tried to make conversation but staying unattached. She never drank any of the champagne, never having acquired the taste of the bubbly concoction that everyone else seemed to find so refreshing. To her it tasted like bitter sock-water.

After several chance encounters with the curious and the lustful, which she aborted early on the pretext that she had seen a long-lost friend on the other side of the room, she finally spotted him.

And he was indeed alive.

He stood in his white tux jacket with black pants and bow tie, a bevy of gorgeous women adorning his arms and his eyes with looks of hopefulness and anticipation, of adoration and desire. He was tall and had a coyness and reticence of manner seemingly out of place with his looks and the women hovering about him like flies to fresh meat. He had an aquiline nose reminding Alexis of a Roman patrician of old; large, kind, intelligent eyes of a striking light gray with green flecks deep-set that could quickly become somnolent and lusterless when he was bored. His light brownish hair was tied up in a low ponytail resting on his broad shoulders. He had a prominent jaw with a half-day's beard growth giving him an outdoorsy, scruffy appearance, a look which Alexis had always found attractive.

He stood casually with a jaunty stance screeaming success, yet had an unassuming air about him that seemed simple and innocent, demure and controlled. He would have fit into any boardroom, any major corporation or just as easily on a raft on the Yukon, a tour guide in the Alps, a man who had the world by the tail and knew it.

He could have come from any of the Scandinavian countries or Europe, but the flair of his long face gave him a marked preference that said Australian. He had a thick neck opening onto a medium-sized chest and trim body that Alexis knew, from personal experience, to be powerful and hard.

He looked as if he had not aged at all, appearing just as she remembered him with the exception of the tinted gray at his temples giving him that distinguished look. She had thought she had successfully purged all her feelings for the man, burned and buried them deep within her mind those twenty years ago, but upon seeing him it all came flooding back, like a dam in her mind had broke, ruptured with a ferocity sweeping her away to their brief time together in swift, flowing images churning and bubbling in tiny whirlpools and eddies, stripping the past clean in a cascade of boiling emotions.

Someone bumped her arm and she came out of the trance with a start, her mental defenses springing up like a cage. She unconsciously flashed the man who had unintentionally brushed up against her such a look of cold hard animosity that he dropped his drink and slinked away as rapidly as his little legs could carry him.

She frowned and shook her head slowly, aware that the trance into which she had just fallen was the worst possible thing that she could do while here, in this place; in this danger. She compressed her lips into a tight smile, then stared at Ian from across the dance floor, watching him move about with his horde of want-to-be concubines, the sagacious smile plastered to his face with such ease to be an affront to the men who stood about jealous of his attractive powers.

She watched him for several minutes, observing. She even reached out with her mind and tapped into the surface thoughts of the man who had abandoned her, wanting to find something into which she could latch and with it, hate him. But she could find nothing. His thoughts, while jumbled with prurient desires for the women who hovered around him like bees to pollen, seemed to focus primarily on a particular project in which he was involved and the trouble his team was having.

She smiled at this.

It was all too typical for him to be standing in a throng of women who would give their souls to bed him and his thoughts would be primarily on his work. She took a deep breath and realized with a suddenness that the man she had loved, the only man she could honestly say she had ever loved, was still alive, still functioning and apparently not at all concerned with her feelings or what he had done to her, how his leaving had devastated her more than she would ever admit to anyone, especially not to herself.

She reached out and placed various notions in the minds of the women who surrounded him and within a matter of minutes they all abandoned their object of lust and found new attachments. Ian looked about him with a good-natured complacency at the turn of events, sipping at his drink with a detachment that seemed natural. Then his eyes narrowed. His face screwed up slightly and he began to scan the room slowly, methodically.

She stepped up behind him, a serene, coquettishly crooked smile on her face. She had, after Cav had told her of his death, dreamt about meeting him suddenly, finding him alive and all that she would say to him at that moment of discovery and yet, now that it was actually happening, she was at a complete loss for the words she really wanted to speak. What she really wanted to do was hit him hard in the face, but she figured that this was not the correct occasion for such a re-introduction.

"It's been a long time, Ian," she said, her voice carrying through the multitude of noise sweeping over the dance floor like breaking waves. He turned casually, champagne glass to his lips.

When their eyes met there was a moment of regret, a glittering of terror, then a submission to fate panning out in a relaxed posture as he lowered his glass from his mouth and spoke. "You know, I'm not sure why, but I had a feeling that it was your doing when the Sheila's all left me like that." His voice was rich and flowed like a bubbling brook, a melodious mixture of accent that marked him from Australia as if a sign had been painted on his forehead. "I could almost feel you in my mind like I used to be able to. I never liked that feeling." He stared at her a moment, his eyes drinking in her ravishing figure under the exquisite dress as if she were a fine liqueur to be savored slowly and easily. "You're looking as good as ever, Alexis," he finally said, forced to take another drink due to the parchness of his mouth at the sight of her.

"Don't be too pleased to see me, Ian," she said coldly, the ice coming off her voice melting as it encountered the heat from his eyes. "This isn't social."

He lifted an eyebrow. "Was it ever?"

The question took her by surprise, slammed into her heart with the force of a bullet, searing her as badly as a plasma burn. *What did he mean by that? How could our relationship, the relationship that we had that was hotter than anything she had ever imagined, not have affected him as it did her? How could it have been anything but social?* She scanned him but found that he had blocked her out, closed his thoughts to her as firmly as if he had erected a wall, something that she had, regrettably, taught him.

She was about to launch into him about why he had not attempted to contact her, lambaste him for the lost and wasted years and ask him straight out – to hell with the mission – why he had just left her like that when they had been so in love, when there was a commotion at the entrance. Alexis had a sudden feeling of danger, a premonition of flight. She looked toward the top of the arching stairway leading onto the expanse of the dance floor and saw a throng of police standing behind what she could only assume was a high-ranking detective talking to the young lady with the master guest list.

Ian chuckled slightly, the remembrances of his former life coming to him in humorous irony. "Let me guess? They're here for you."

She smirked. "Let's move a little closer to the band." She grabbed his elbow and led him toward the crowd gathered by the band, smiling at those who looked at the cute couple they made. Her inquisition of Ian regarding the sudden end of their relationship would have to be put on hold. "Do you know the layout of this building fairly well?" she asked, standing where she could watch the antics of the police without being seen herself.

He smiled, a broad retrospective lilt covering his face like a moss-covered building. "Don't tell me that the great Alexis Locke didn't bother to memorize the layout of the building that she now finds herself trapped in. I find that hard to believe."

"Bite me, Ian," she said through clenched teeth, watching as the police began to fan out across the floor, looking at each of the women closely yet politely. She reached out to touch the mind of the detective in charge but was unable to filter out the multitude of thoughts flooding the room like a noxious gas. Whispers began to ripple through those gathered, sweeping through the crowd like a surge.

Colleen Trianfilidis had been raped and murdered in her apartment, the whispers pronounced with undulating emotions of revulsion, terror and disregard. *The suspects were reported here at the dance.*

Alexis narrowed her eyes with suspicion and incomprehension. Colleen had been the young lady whose invitation Alexis had stolen, whom she had tied up and left very much alive. Her premonition of flight was starting to become a burning sensation. "We need to leave, now," she breathed to Ian, conveying a sense of imminent danger to him that he had not felt in years. "Is there a backdoor near the stage?

He thought for a moment. He had been in this ballroom several times in the past but had never really bothered to check out all the exits. He had, of course, made a cursory survey of the more available exits in case of the necessity of a quick exit – an unconscious act drilled into him through the CIA -- but at the moment, he could not come up with a single answer for her.

That his thoughts were completely jumbled over the appearance of his former lover had much to do with it. He had never expected to see Alexis Locke ever again, Cav made that more than clear when Ian had been forced out of the home office and exiled to hell's backyard.

A new whisper made the rounds and now people began to look at Ian with that look of trepidation and suspicion preceding an accusation. *Ian Montana was one of the suspects. He had been caught on tape entering the young lady's apartment.*

His DNA had been found on her, in her.

Alexis grabbed Ian's arm more forcefully. "An exit, Ian. Now!"

Ian, completely caught off guard by the rumors circulating, of the implications floating around, was having a difficult time understanding what was happening. He had known Colleen. Had in fact dated her several times, slept with her just recently, not more than a few weeks ago. And now she was dead? Raped and murdered? Beaten to death if the rumors were to be believed. And most distressing of all was that Ian was being blamed. He had been seen there, a place that he had not gone to in weeks.

Faces were turned toward him in horror and revulsion, in disbelief. Fingers were being pointed. The police were moving closer and closer, like a mudslide working its way down the side of a weakened slope and crushing all in its path. But he could not move, could not believe that what was being said was real. That he was being accused of raping someone and then killing her brutally was so beyond any reasonable logic that he was having trouble processing it.

He felt Alexis tugging on his arm, heard her pleas in his ear but none of it registered. He was frozen, locked in place by the thought that people could believe something so hideous about him. That the very people he had just been laughing and drinking and dancing with were now ready to believe the worst of him, ready to betray him to the authorities in a flash of abhorrent dismay was beyond immediate comprehension. He had thought he had left all this when he had resigned from Cav's service.

His life had been so good here in Aqmola since that time, a place where he could start all over without anyone knowing who or what he was. He had been happy, working in a field that he may not have enjoyed completely but at which he was competent and interested. He had managed to completely forget about his former life, his work with the CIA, his killings and intrigue and mostly Alexis and Cav and all that those two personalities implied.

Alexis: she had been the one woman he had, for what turned out to be a fleeting moment, thought he could truly love and live with forever and who had then turned into his worst nightmare, his worst experience ever. And now here she was again, the very scourge of his life, his heart, his capability to make lasting relationships. That she had come back into his life so brutally, followed like a wake by an accusation of rape and murder made his head spin.

"Damn you, Ian!" Alexis screamed into his ear, trying to force the one thought of flee into his mind.

Finally, with a single phrase spoken by one of the many women who had formerly been attached to Ian's arm like a gadfly, her finger pointing at him like an inquisitor from hell, Ian was catapulted out of his inaction, launched into a nightmare world his former lover Alexis Locke had brought with her as tangibly as her sumptuous aroma and hardened nipples.

"That's him there! That's Ian Montana!"

The police seemed to react as if they were all part of the same mechanism, turning their heads in unison like one, big automated machine. There was a moment of hesitation, a moment of suspended time where the air in the room seemed to condense into an icy blast, as if the police were uncertain whether Ian would explode in wanton brutality or surrender peacefully. Then it was passed and the single-minded force began to close in, all thoughts of peaceful surrender gone.

"Sadda! Makana ala yaddik!" the detective shouted across the dance floor as he drew his weapon.

The crowd scattered as if they were a thousand ball bearings dropped on the floor, moving in random patterns like a huge, living, multi-headed creature to the accompaniment of screams and curses.

Ian turned to look at Alexis, saw the calm detachment in her eyes he had always admired, then bolted off toward the left of the stage and for the door he knew was back there, ignoring the order to stop. There was a rapid shower of weapons fire. Pieces of glass, plants, chipped tiles and wood from the stage erupted around them as they ducked behind the heavy curtain separating the main dance floor from the musician's electronics.

Screams burst forth from the patrons as the police rushed to apprehend the fugitives, ignorant of where the bullets impacted. Ian and Alexis reached the door and went through, closing it hard behind them.

"What the fuck did you do now?!" he yelled at her with a vehemence born from terror and frustration.

She ignored him as they rushed down the empty corridor, searching ahead mentally for any ambush the police may have set for them. "What's the quickest way out of this place?" she asked him with tight control, pulling her high heels off and flinging them away.

"Do you have a weapon?" he asked as they turned a corner and startled a pair of workers lazily pushing a laundry cart along.

They looked up just as she tore, to their utter amazement, the bottom half of her dress off and shoved it into the laundry cart. Now she could run easier, the fact that only her panties were keeping her modesty intact not important at the moment.

"Does it look like I have a weapon on me?" she answered back caustically as they continued down the corridor, the sounds of pursuit heavy behind them.

"Who the hell are you?" Ian interrogated with suspicion. "You look and smell and feel like Alexis Locke, but the Alexis I knew would never have let herself get caught in something this ridiculous without a weapon .... though those certainly are her legs."

She gave him an inflexible look of repressed shrewdness. "This isn't the time or place for a reunion, Ian, though I certainly have a few choice words for you when we get out of this mess. But in case you haven't noticed, we're in a bit deep here."

"No shit? I hadn't noticed at all. I always thought that tearing off your dress and running from the police who want to shoot first and ask questions later was a normal part of these types of dances. Kind of like the mamba."

They came to a large door with an attached alarm and an exit sign. Alexis skidded to a stop and kicked the door open with all her might, flinging it wide and slamming it against the stop with an ear-splitting crash, bending the upper hinges. The fire alarm began to wail in supplicating whines of panic.

Ian moved to go out the door in a rush and was pulled back so forcefully by Alexis that he almost fell over.

"What the ...?" he said as she dragged him along the corridor away from the door, his arms out-stretched toward the exit that led to apparent freedom.

"You've been out of the game for too long, Ian," she criticized as they turned another corridor. "We go out that way and we won't get a hundred meters. That was a ruse."

He looked at her a moment, scowled, then had to reluctantly agree that she was right, both with the mirage of an exit and his having been out of the game too long. Intrigue, espionage and running for one's life had been the purview of his former life, a life he had buried long ago.

"We need to find some way out of this building that the police haven't thought of already. Something that they've over-looked," she stated in simple terms as they came to a dead-end and had to backtrack, the sound of heavy boots echoing down the passageways.

"You're not going to get too far on the outside dressed like that, that's for sure," he said in reference to her black panties and garter-belt, which he eyed with an appreciative glare. Gun-toting thugs might be chasing him, but there was always time to enjoy the scenery. He had almost forgotten how irresistible she was.

"Let me concentrate on how I look, Ian. You concentrate on getting us out of here and quickly, cause we're running out of places to run," she said with a dynamic conviction, beginning to feel the noose tightening around them.

He nodded his head, beginning to realize that this was serious. "The sewer."

"Show me."

They changed positions and he lead through several smaller corridors and rooms. "If we can get to the main pumping station for the convention center, then it should be a simple matter of lowering ourselves into the main feed lines and working away from the building."

She nodded her head in agreement. It was an escape route the local constables would not even begin to consider, though her shadow friends might just be waiting for her. Fortunately, so far, she had yet to feel their presence. She was certain it was but a matter of time.

They turned a corner and found three guards turning the far corner ten meters away. The guards were more startled than Alexis and Ian but they quickly recovered and let loose with a spray of bullets.

Alexis reacted instantly, all her decades of training, all Cav's admonitions to work harder, to push herself further coming in handy. She put her hand out and shoved with her mind as hard as she could. Knowing that the projectiles were coming and having a narrow space with which to work, she could make a difference in this situation and the bullets were deflected from their deadly path and impacted into the wall in a shower of plaster and woodwork.

The guards looked at their weapons in wonder.

She sent a second wave at the guards themselves and they slammed into the wall behind them as if someone had physically picked them up and thrown them, slumping to the floor with dazed looks of utter confusion.

Ian puckered his lips a moment, then led Alexis past the downed police. This was more like the Alexis Locke he knew, though that piece with the bullets was something he had not seen before.

She picked up one of the weapons as they stepped over the dazed guards, then discarded it just as quickly as useless. The weapons were tagged for the guards DNA and thus would not work if anyone else held them. Another one of those stupid laws passed in the losing effort to control the proliferation of firearms. They turned a corner and the corridor came alive with a buzz, a bright, searing light lighting up the whole passageway and casting ominous shadows from the bluish light down the corridor they now traversed.

"They're using plasma rifles," Alexis said as if stating that it was going to rain today.

Ian looked back with disbelief, not imagining that such measures would be taken on two people that they just suspected of foul play. "What the hell did you do?" he inquired again, this time a little tamer after her recent exhibition.

"Now's not the time, Ian."

They found the main pumping station unguarded and as Ian worked on the door, Alexis made ready for the attack she was certain was about to descend upon them. A small object flew through the air, bounced once, twice, then rolled over to them with an innocence belying its gruesome intent.

She recognized it at once and slammed into Ian, throwing him into the still locked door with such an impact that the lock and the upper hinges sheared off and the door flew inward, taking them with it and hurling them hard to the floor. She grabbed him by the collar and threw him up against the wall supporting the door a fraction of a second before the thermite grenade exploded in a cataclysmic fireball engulfing the entire corridor.

A tongue of searing hot gases and plasma scorched through the broken door like a lance of death, melting fittings and hinges and plastic, the toxic foulness of the conflagration enveloping the room in a cloud of moribund. Holding her breath and placing her hand over Ian's mouth and nose, Alexis pulled the stunned and dazed man through the subsiding blast and over to the main access ladder to the lower levels of the convention center. The main circuit box for the pumping station was fused and welded shut by the blast, the stinking electrical smoke raising from it to the accompaniment of sparks, the other plastic parts and gauges and dials of the room smoldering from the intense heat melting them.

Only her ability to mentally deflect the blast from their small location where she huddled saved them from becoming crispy-critters. This was far more serious than anything else she had encountered before, with the possible exception of the episode on the O'Neill Colony and she wondered if the shadow people had decided that she was too much of a threat to keep alive. That they had opted to involve Ian told her much, for these people were, though it was difficult to believe at the moment, not after her but him, the death of that girl a sure sign that someone wanted Ian out of the picture, just like Clovis and Fujita. She wouldn't be surprised if Dr. Shu was already dead.

Ian regained his composure after she had dragged him down the first ladder sequence and he was able to move much better thereafter so that they reached the lowest level of the building within a matter of minutes. He had not had a thermite grenade thrown in his general direction in ... He had never had one thrown at him now that he thought about it and it bothered him to no end. These people were playing for keeps and he didn't even know why they hated him so much.

He directed her to a large watertight hatch and un-spun the locking wheel while she tried to get the security computer to release the main locks. "It's not going to work. Without the code, this thing' ll stay locked till doomsday," she grunted as she looked up for any other hatchways.

Ian frowned with the idea coming to mind, his old training starting to come back with a vengeance, then grabbed her elbow and led her to a small, perhaps half-a-meter wide hatchway that had no computer lack on it. He opened the locking wheel and pulled the hatch open to the putrid rankness of the cesspool.

She looked at him with almost a pleading look as he indicated for her to go ahead. "You've got to be kidding, right?" she said as she noticed that the ladder leading into the foul-smelling darkness was covered with a blackish, sleek mold looking almost alive.

"There's most likely a maintenance hatch that leads into the main drainage pipes and from there to the main city sewage system. We just have to find it down there," he said with less conviction then he felt.

"Most likely?" she answered back.

But with the noise of the approaching police making their way down the ladders to the lowest level and the memory of the thermite grenade fresh in her mind and her nose, she swung herself over the edge and descended through the tight hatch into the malodor making her stomach churn, the sleekness of the decomposed and rancid substance on the rungs making her hands and feet feel as if they were being eaten away.

Ian closed the hatch behind him, plunging the cesspool into a darkness filled with a repugnant effluvium. It took all of her mental powers to keep herself from throwing-up, to keep herself going through the waist-deep, thick sludge making it almost impossible to breath. She could feel creatures crawling over her legs in the muck, could almost sense the decayed and fetid matter composing the cesspool as if it were absorbing into her body.

She heard Ian retching behind her and felt sorry for him. If she didn't find the maintenance hatch soon, he would not hold out and would collapse into the shit that made up the cesspool, an event tantamount to death. She reached out with her mind and began to probe the walls, looking for any sign of an opening, anything that would lead out of this nightmare, her eyes useless in the pitch-blackness in which they found themselves.

She found the exit maintenance hatch with a sigh of relief and dragged Ian toward it, turning the main wheel and jabbing the unlock plungers. The hatch opened to a breath of air not much different from what they were breathing but which struck them as a wave of freshness. She pushed the thoroughly coated Ian through, then followed, landing with a thud on the floor of the larger circular tube that was a branch access to the main sewage system. A trench in the middle was filled with a foul smelling dark liquid but it was far better then the harshness of the cesspool-retaining chamber.

"Why in the world," Ian coughed out as he tried to regain his strength, his dry heaves racking his body with each occurrence, "have you decided to grace my life and ruin it for a second time? Once wasn't enough far you? You get bored?"

She looked at him as she stood and dragged him along the passageway toward the larger opening she knew was the main city sewer. *Ruined his life? In what kind of a fantasy was he living.* "Fuck off, Ian. I'm not in the mood."

I would warn you that I don't
attribute to nature either beauty
or deformity, order or confusion.
Only in relation to our imagination
can things be called beautiful or ugly,
order or confusion.
— Spinoza

19

The coolness of the night spread over the city like an umbrella, the scent of rain light and subtle on the air. Crickets sang their lonesome song of love to the darkness, a rising and falling melody echoing the busy, boisterous day. A drunk stumbled along the narrow sycamore-lined avenue, singing his heart out with a song to which he had long ago forgotten the words, his voice carrying into the desolate, expansive, empty walkways like a temptress of old, seducing sailors to their deaths on the jagged and unforgiving shoals.

He stumbled and weaved with a measured, hesitant beat that almost seemed choreographed, his disheveled clothes – consisting of an unbuttoned black tie, black designer pants and a tuxedo top – appearing as if they had been dragged through a mud puddle, his own vomit dribbled down the front in blobs of creamed color. He finished his song and took a long swig of the bottle of Jack Daniels.

After several prolonged moments with his head tilted far back and the bottle raised to the star-filled sky as if in prayer, he realized that there was no more liquor to be had and in a fit of commiseration flung the bottle to the cobblestones, where it shattered into a thousand pieces of glittering glass. He looked about him with a scornful smile, then launched into a new song sounding more or less like the first, strutting down the street like a majordomo.

When the manhole cover by the storm drain flew into the air a good four

232

meters and then crashed back down with a resounding clang setting the neighborhood dogs to barking, the drunk stopped in mid-stride, a word caught in his throat, his song lost as he squinted his eyes at the black hole now appearing in the middle of the avenue.

When the two figures began to climb out, one a male in tuxedo and the other a female dressed in nothing but what appeared to be the upper half of a once beautiful dress and a garter belt with black panties, both covered in what appeared to be and smelled like shit, he was quite confused. He pointed at them with a lone, wavering finger and spit out a crescendo of remarks in a slurred dialect almost mystic. Alexis looked at him a moment as he stood looking at her and eyeing her body with unrefined candor, his eyes focused solidly between her legs, his head tilted to the side, blinking with rapid stokes. She sent him a nudge and he fell over, toppling to his rump with a mixture of confusion and glee on his face. It didn't take long for him to slump over fast asleep, dreaming of beautiful women coming out of the ground for him in garter belts and panties.

Ian looked at the drunk only a moment, then over at Alexis. "So are you going to tell me now what the hell this is all about?" he spat out, nervously and irritably looking about him. "This isn't my life any more and I'd thank you not to ruin it a second time. And what the hell is with the telekinetic powers and throwing people around? When did you learn all that shit?"

She looked at him with feverish eyes, ignoring all of his remarks except the one that hit closest to home. "That's the second time that you've said that, Ian. What the hell are you talking about 'ruining your life?' You're the one who left, who abandoned me without a by-your-leave or good-bye or kiss my ass, so don't you *dare* lecture me about ruining lives, you son-of-a-bitch!" She grumbled to herself at losing control, at letting her emotions broach the surface.

She took a deep breath, which only managed to fill her nostrils with her own putrid stench. "We'd better get as far away from here as possible," she replied more evenly, looking around at the tree-lined lane in which they stood, looking as drunk as the man fast asleep on the pavement. "And we need to get a change of clothes while we're at it. We're both kind of ripe."

He leaned back slightly as he examined her lower half and gave her a half-cocked smile. "I don't know, I kind of like you in that get-up. There's something about it that screams refinement to me."

She started to walk away from him down the lane, ignoring the feelings beginning to resurface for this man, feelings she had told herself, promised herself she would not ever feel again. He looked after her a moment, then started to follow, not certain where she was planning on getting a new set of clothes or what she was planning on doing next. He didn't need this in his life again and yet, here he was following Alexis Locke as if she had tied a string to his genitals.

He did have, however, one detail to clear up before they walked much further. "I think you're slightly mistaken as to the nature of our separation. It was your good friend Cav who told me that you weren't interested in me whatsoever and were just using me to fulfill your sexual needs. He's the one who gave me a job over here in this part of the country so that I could forget about you, then cut me off from his agency like so much rotten fish. I never abandoned you, sweetheart. It was the other way around, so don't get all high and mighty with me about it all. This isn't my fault."

She stopped and spun around, shit flying from her hair in a spray of rankness that would have been humorous to anyone watching. "You've got to be the stupidest man alive if you truly believed that," she shot out at him. "What we had was special, at least for me it was, and I certainly wasn't using you as a .... a ...." She could not bring herself to say the words, her emotions once again flooding to the surface in an eruption she could not contain, perhaps even didn't want to contain.

Anger flared from her in waves of heat, but it was not anger directed at him. It was anger at herself for losing control, for letting the feelings she had been successful in hiding all these years come boiling to the surface in a turmoil of doubt and indecision. And it was anger at Cav for what he had done, first with the father of her now dead son and then with Ian. He had sent him away, told the man she loved that she was only using him for her own selfish pleasures. She had no idea that Cav was such a raving lunatic, because only a lunatic would do that to Alexis and not expect her to find out eventually.

"Sex-toy?" he offered to finish her thought, an impish smile touching his lips.

She didn't understand the feelings competing in her, driving her to rash, hasty actions and pronunciations that didn't come from Alexis. For over twenty years she had been able to control these feelings, had been able to place them in a holding bin deep in her mind and forget about them. And now, when she was faced again with the reason for the suppression of those feelings in the first place, they all came rushing out headlong in an uncontrollable rage she found frightening.

What was it about him that precipitated this reaction, which made her so unlike herself? Made her act like a damn fool.

"I LOVED YOU!" she screamed, causing even the crickets to stop in mid-song as if wanting to listen to the exchange between the bipeds that had now become interesting. "I loved you," she repeated softer, as if the declaration had taken all her strength to utter. "Damn you all to hell, Ian Montana," she finished quietly, as if all her strength had left and was laying on the unused street by her feet like so much discarded rubbish.

He looked at her and saw for the first time the lost, young girl she was underneath all the tough, gruff exterior she let few see passed. He saw the hurt and pain flashing across her eyes, the fragile shell cracking before his very eyes. He saw it all and understood a little better about that day long ago when Cav had first approached him. He stepped forward and touched her arm, gazing deep into her eyes.

There was a magic to the moment transcending both of them and took control, took over their movements, their thoughts, their emotions and brought them together for one, brief instant of time standing still around them.

At first, his lips gently brushed hers. It was a tentative, questing probe sending electric shocks through both of them in an explosion of sensuous passion. Then he deepened the kiss and her trance that the initial contact created dissolved in a swell of remembered joy and eagerness. Her body relaxed from the rigid stance it had taken of its own accord and she sighed as she opened her mouth and wrapped her arms around his neck.

The liquid stroke of his tongue against hers made her mind flash back to lost times of long ago when she had, for the first time in her life, been happy. He deepened the kiss and she met him willingly in an arousing dance of tongue on tongue, all the while caressing her neck with silky fingertips. She felt his hand begin to fondle her breast, making her nipples seem to swell and ache and her body respond to him like it had responded twenty years ago.

Then she awoke and remembered more.

She remembered the pain and the loss, but most of all she remembered the mission, her son's death, those who wanted her dead ... and she remembered, despite his admissions to the contrary, his leaving her and the hurt came back with a vengeance. She stopped abruptly, pulling away and leaving him deprived, every nerve ending afire with a passion he had forgotten he possessed.

A calenture of emotion crossed her eyes in a wink and she belted him hard in the stomach, causing him to double over in pain, the wind knocked out in a rush of burning excitement. She brushed her wet, slick hair back from her face, the acrid, putrid stench of the cesspool once again asserting itself to her nose as she stepped back and shook her head in utter disbelief. "Damn you all to hell, Ian."

He gasped for air, one knee on the ground in exasperation. "Christ, Alexis. I think you broke something."

She smirked as she began to walk away from him, re-building her walls in a frenzy of defensive fortifications. "You'll live," she offered with little conciliation, her rational mind back in firm control, the lingering taste and compassion of the kiss fading reluctantly.

"You certainly haven't changed," he said as he rose hesitantly, one hand holding his stomach as if it helped to relieve the pain. "How long has it been? Twenty years? It seems just like yesterday to me."

She continued to walk away from him, not certain at all where she was headed but just so long as it was away from him, the one man who had managed to break through her walls and touch her inside like no one else had ever done.

He was, in a word, dangerous.

He began to follow her, her taste strong and vital within his mouth and his groin; the emotions grabbing him so strongly those many years ago battering at his back door and wanting in. "Where are you going now?"

Alexis stopped and he thought for certain that he had reached her and she had changed her mind. But instead she kept her back to him as she titled her head as if ready to speak.

But he quickly realized that she was not listening to him at all, but rather to the distinctive hum of an approaching hov, the glow of searchlights over the tops of the houses several blocks away indicative of what was coming.

"We need to get out from the open," she said with her old, familiar Alexis voice, not bothering to look back at him. "Do you know this area at all?"

Ian looked around for the first time to get his bearings. The houses were middle-class abodes with well-kept lawns and fences, the few interspersed lights casting a dull luminescence over the area. He knew the area all too well.

"Yes. This way," he said as he started off across the small grass mound rising between the cobblestone walkways. "I have a lady-friend close by. She'll put us up for a while, but I don't really want to get her involved."

She followed him at a rapid clip as the police hovs came flying over the last row of houses and bore down on them in all their fury. She looked over her shoulder as the two hovs began to split up to corral them in and wondered how they had found them so quickly. There must have been thousands of possible access ports all over the city from where they could have emerged and yet here there were, closing in on them within a matter of minutes after their emergence from the sewer.

"How far is this *lady* friend?" She forced him to pick up the pace, emphasizing the words *lady friend* and placing an amorous connotation to it.

"Not far, maybe a few hundred meters." He didn't fail to notice her jealous reaction, but choose the wiser course and ignored the remark.

"We don't have a couple hundred meters, Ian." She calmed herself and brought her extensive mental capacity to bear on the problem at hand. The police had been able to follow them through the maze of corridors in the convention center, then through the warren of tunnels in the sewer to end up here, at this specific place. How?

No one was that good at guessing.

The answer came to her as one of the police Hovs roared up before them and fired a burst of cannon shot into the grass, ripping it up in a peal of thunder. She would have to act fast. Alexis grabbed Ian and pulled him under the eave of the nearest house. "Where is this friend of yours exactly, Ian? Which house?"

He pointed to the next one over. Lights were beginning to flicker on throughout the neighborhood as the report of the cannon echoed among the trees and into the empty night, shattering the peace that had laid here like a blanket.

"Sadda! Makana ala yaddik!" the amplified voice commanded them again, as if they would be more prone to listen to it now than in the convention center. "We will shoot to kill!"

Alexis shook her head, then bolted for the next house where Ian had indicated his lady-friend lived. Even though there was a barrage of cannon fire following them and slamming into the nearest houses in an explosion of wood, plaster, concrete, and screams, the thought that Ian would have lady friends like Alexis had gentleman friends seemed to rankle her to no end.

She had thought the man dead for twenty years and yet, now that she had found him alive and well, she was expecting, assuming that he would have never looked at another woman again after losing her. It was irrational to the extreme, but it continued to play in her mind as they burst through the door of the house next to the house Ian had pointed out.

"This is the wrong house!" he shouted at her as the owner of the infiltrated dwelling came out of the upper bedroom in open robes and sleepy eyes, a large club in his hand to deter the suspected criminals.

"I know," was all she said as she ignored the homeowner, who was now shouting at them in agitated Arabic, and made her way to the garage.

"What the hell are you doing, Alexis? This is mad. Those police hov's will blow us out of the sky in a heartbeat."

She kicked open the door leading to the garage in a spray of splinters, then rushed in and opened the driver's side door. "That's what I'm counting on." He watched closely as she sat halfway in the driver's seat and began to work on the on-board computer, voicing in commands rapidly. "Watch your back, Ian," she said casually.

He turned to find the homeowner rushing toward him with his club raised and his face more a mask of utter fright than anger. Ian didn't have to think. He reverted to his instincts, those that had been honed to a fine edge while he was an active member of the CIA and Cav's group, and struck. His foot kicked out in a blur and connected to the onrushing man's chest with a hollow thud felling the homeowner in a sprawling mess against the wall, legs and arms flapping about like a doll.

He turned back to see that Alexis had finished whatever she was doing and when she stepped back out of the hov instead of climbing completely in, he was more confused than ever.

"We're not going to take the Hov?" he asked as he narrowed his eyes and tried to think of what she was doing, what she was thinking. "No, we're not," she answered distractedly as she disappeared back into the house for moment. Ian leaned into the hov and stared at the navigation computer, shaking his head with mystification at the course she had plotted. It made no sense to him whatsoever.

There was another appeal for them to surrender from the gathering police outside, urging that innocent people were going to be hurt if they didn't leave the house with their hands up. Ian looked through the door leading into the house to see where Alexis had disappeared and saw instead an unkempt, rather ugly little woman and her two kids standing at the top of the stairs huddled together in abject terror.

He frowned, then caught hold of Alexis as she came back with a fine filleting knife in her hand and several other things that he could not make out. "I'll stop you if you're thinking of hurting those kids," he said in gallant tones sounding hollow even to him.

She grabbed his arm and led him back into the garage, closing the door behind her. "You should be worrying about yourself, Ian, and not the kids," she said as she sat him down by the workbench and laid his left arm on the table. "I figured out why they've been able to follow us all this time. I knew it couldn't be me, so it must be you." She put her back into his chest and leaned heavily on his upper forearm with her left arm, effectively pinning him down to the table. She placed the filleting knife down, opened up the bottle of

238

alcohol and poured some over his exposed forearm.

"What the hell are you doing?" he asked, unable to see around her back and beginning to get a bad feeling.

She deftly picked up the filleting knife. "You had a chip implanted in you, didn't you?" she asked as she probed with her mind under his skin for the telltale sign of the chip's beacon. She found it easily enough halfway up his forearm, embedded in the meaty part of the muscle.

"They made me when I left the agency. Why?" His eyes opened as the realization came to him. "Oh no! Not that. WAIT!"

She clamped down even tighter on his arm and then cut with the knife, precisely, accurately, quickly. He squirmed and fought her, bucking like a wild horse but her force kept him pinned firmly as she dug around for a moment, found the tiny chip and popped it out onto the floor.

"*Jesus Christ!* You've got to be the craziest bitch in the world! *You stupid fuck*!" he screamed as she poured some more alcohol on the open wound and then let him go, giving him a diffident look as she threw the knife onto the table and handed him a bandage.

"Stop crying, Ian. You've become such a baby." For some odd reason, that act had actually felt good for her, as if in response to him ripping her own heart out when he left due to Cav telling him she was just playing, not serious about the relationship What kind of a jackass would believe such a contrived piece of shit?

A man, of course.

"Close that up and get ready to leave."

He grabbed the bandage, looking at the small hole in his forearm, the pain from the incision shooting up his arm as if it was on fire. It felt like she had cut his whole damn arm off. "Let's see how you react if I were to cut your whole arm open!" he complained as he wrapped his arm and stood, the pain beginning to subside slowly in pulses.

She looked at him again with amusement, knowing full well that she would be able to control the pain and not wince one bit if he were to actually cut into her forearm. But then he really would not know anything about that. Although they had shared passionate sex together and a closeness transcending that experienced by most people, he had never really learned about all her abilities or her past in any detail. It was possible that had he known, he would have never left her as he did at the word of a fat idiot who was known to be protective of Alexis.

Perhaps it was time that he did know all about what she could do. Now, however, was certainly not the place for it.

There was a loud tearing sound from the back of the house, a roaring and rattling drowning out the terrified screams of the mother and her children.

"What ever happened to the patient police?" she asked sarcastically as she picked up Ian's bloody chip from the floor and threw it into the hov, then punched the activator and closed the door.

With a roar and a thunderous crash, the family hov slammed through the garage door in a shower of splinters and fragments as it tore into the night air. The police hovs gave immediate chase, falsely believing that Ian and Alexis were inside.

Ian watched with wide eyes, realizing that Alexis had given them enough time to make good their escape. She was good. He had forgotten that she was considered the best at what she did and at the moment was very thankful for that. But would it be enough?

She opened the door leading back to the house and marched forcefully upstairs with Ian following, hoping that he would not have to try to stop her from hurting the innocent family. He knew somewhere deep inside that she was not the type of person to do something that evil, it was just that he knew how it was when one was on an assignment gone bad and sometimes the innocence of those around you faded in direct proportion to the amount of danger facing you. That Alexis had killed in the past without regard to innocence or age also played a factor in his apprehension.

The mother and two children sank as far into the corner of the banister and the wall and the carpet as possible as Alexis jumped up the stairs, her stench from the encrusted shit on her and Ian filling the house with an odor that was nauseating. The mother began to plead for the life of her children in supplicating, pitiful wails but Alexis ignored her and went instead into the bedroom.

Ian stayed at the top of the stairs, trying to reassure the frantically paranoid mother and screaming, crying kids that they were going to be all right, wondering what in the world Alexis was up to now. She returned shortly with two sets of clothing and bounded down the stairs, dragging Ian with her.

"We need to leave now. They've probably shot the hov down and will soon discover that it's empty." She looked at him deeply, some of the emotion they had shared for that fleeting moment in the kiss glittering in her eyes in tiny specks of muted recognition. "I need you to think, Ian, to become that agent you once were and help me, because otherwise you're going to be a hindrance and you don't want to know what I do to hindrances."

He swallowed hard, the faint glittering that had been in her eyes vanishing in a flash of veteran impatience. He was well aware that Alexis almost always worked alone, and it was for a very good reason. Alexis was not beyond killing off her rare and far in-between partners when she felt that they were in her way. They left the house and made their way as far and as fast as they could in the darkness.

"Are you married, Ian?" she asked out of the blue as they crossed over grass and cobblestone and dirt in their frantic escape.

He hesitated a moment, wondered if she was just making small talk or if she had another motive behind her question. "I was," he said softly, the image of his lovely wife flashing before his mind's eye in crystal clarity.

"Divorced?"

"Widowed."

"I'm sorry to hear that," she said with a slight hint of actual sympathy that he caught and held on to, though he was uncertain whether she meant that she was sorry he was widowed or that he had been married.

They were quiet for the next ten minutes as they ran, his legs starting to get weak from the exertion. It had been a while since he had to flee from anyone. It reminded him in stark detail why he had been so happy to actually stop working for people like Cav. Then he understood where she was leading him and nodded his head, thinking out loud. "The river, you're headed for the river to use it as an escape."

"Yes. We can acquire a boat and make our way downstream several kilometers before daybreak. With your chip no longer leading them to our doorstep, we might just be able to get away."

The smell of the river reached them before its broad expanse greeted their eyes in the darkness, jumping out at them from behind a stand of birch. She looked up and down the bank, saw what she was looking for and headed for it.

"Not so fast, Alexis," Ian pleaded, his breath coming in ragged gasps, blood dripping down his arm from the incision she had made. "I'm not used to this anymore. It's been too long."

"I can see that," she said with a veiled threat.

He complained no more.

They reached a marina filled with boats in a shadowy pall from the four halogen lights standing along the edge of the fast flowing river. She made her way to the closest powerboat, a medium-sized hydrofoil looking fast. She threw the clothes she had gathered into the boat, then started to untie the mooring lines.

Ian jumped in and tried to start the engine, figuring that he had better do something constructive before she noticed that he was a hindrance. She undid the last line, jumped in and pushed him away from the controls. "We don't want to make noise, Ian. We can't risk the guard of the marina alerted to our acquisition of this boat until the morning, otherwise they'll be on us in a heartbeat. Think, Ian," she admonished him as the hydrofoil floated out into the current and slowly made its way away from the marina.

When they were a sufficient distance that the noise of the engines would not awaken anyone connected to the marina, she looked the controls over. They were simple enough. Operating the boat would be no problem. The problem was with the security system installed, which required a palm print for activation. She cursed the need for such things in the world, not failing to realize that the system was installed to prevent people just like her from doing what she was about to do. She studied the electronics for several minutes as Ian sat and regained his breath and re-wrapped his arm, the pain having now subsided to a dull throbbing that seemed determined to remind him that he had let her cut him.

She frowned as she debated about the best way to defeat the system and Ian watched her, saw the outline of her firm and hard body against the moonlight starting to make itself known as the white orb rose slowly and majestically above the horizon. She was even more beautiful than he remembered, even with the sheath of shit they both still had over them.

He thought back to something she had said and realized that he had been the stupidest man in the world for leaving her, for believing Cav and his jealous inclinations; for not staying in communication with her. But then, perhaps somewhere in his own sub-conscious he had wanted to leave her, to find a convenient way out of the relationship, a relationship that was far longer than any he had ever had previously. Cav had been so persuasive, so demanding in his insistence that Alexis Locke would never be able to love anyone, would only use him like a piece of bought equipment and then, when she became bored, toss him away, a hollow husk of emotions all that would be left of his soul.

It had been the convenient excuse for which he had been, perhaps, waiting. He had seen some of what Cav had described within her, had been aware that she could be very capable of such a deception and thus had believed Cav, taken the man's advice and left. He sighed mournfully, unable to take his eyes off of her as she stood over the control panel deep in thought. He had once been much more independent than that, much more capable of making rational decisions. He had moved on with his life, had loved again deeply and now here she was again, like some specter from the past come to haunt him for bad karma he had compiled.

And all the old feelings that had caused him to become so infatuated with her in the first place fell into place within his heart as if they had been but patiently waiting for her eventual return. What was it about her that turned his rational mind into jelly and his groin into rock-hard erection?

The engines came to life with a sudden roar and the control panel lit up in muted red. The hydrofoil lifted up off the water and careened down the middle of the river. Alexis set the autopilot, aware that most major navigable rivers now had the newest in global navigation systems, allowing one to plow down any waterway without ever having to steer. This river was, fortunately, one of those.

She turned to look at him, then at her watch, smearing the crud off of the crystal and noting the time. She pulled the remnants of her dress over her head and tossed it over the side into the now fast flowing river, her exposed breasts firm, her nipples erect and hard in the cool breeze flowing over her, her tanned curves accented by the soft moonlight as she bent over and began to remove her garter belt and panties. She took two items out of her garter belt before she removed it and stashed them subtly under a seat cushion nearby.

Ian leaned back and watched with unabashed voyeurism, the tightness in his pants telling him that she still aroused in him the passions that had first drawn them together. He was not proud of it, but it had been the physical attraction that had linked them together at the beginning and perhaps even through the whole affair, a shallow conceit to be certain but definitely a worthwhile one.

She looked at him a moment as she flung the last of the shit-covered clothes overboard, a long lingering moment as she stood before him stark naked, the moonlight casting shadows on her ravishing body subtle and illuminating. They titillated him like a cat's toy.

She smiled sardonically at him as he made to get up. She leaned forward, placing her hand against his shoulder and pushing him back down again, her closeness to him like an aphrodisiac to his libido despite the lingering aroma of shit. "Relax, Ian. I'm going to take a shower and wash this crap off of me. When I'm done, you can wash up." She stood back up and walked to the hatch that led down below. She stopped there and spoke again. "And don't get any ideas about coming down below and restarting that kiss. That's in the past and it's going to stay there." She turned her head back to look at him, to make sure that he understood. "It's over between us, Ian. You made sure of that twenty years ago. I've got more important things to be worried about and the last thing I need is for you to be in my head. We had our time and chance and we both blew it. It's over." She disappeared down the ladder.

Ian looked up into the tapestry of the stars exploding at him with their dazzling eternity and sighed again ... then smiled. In all the time that had passed between them, in all the lives they had lived, he could still see right through her at times and into her soul and knew that the connection they had once had was still strong, still playing at her heart strings as much as at her groin. He closed his eyes and enjoyed the cool wind blowing the stench of the shit away into the night.

*   *   *

Cav stood near the twisted, charred wreckage of the hov that had smashed into the ground shortly after it had lifted off, the smell of burnt interior hanging in the air like a fine mist. He watched the forensic teams search through it in detail. He already knew that Alexis was not in there. Not that the forensic team had said anything, he just knew, had an insight that she would never have been dumb enough to try to outrun the police hovs in something like this. This was a ruse and wherever Alexis was, she certainly was not in the twisted, smoldering wreckage.

He stood with his hands in the pockets of the dark brown overcoat he wore, watching silently the large, bulky police chief who was directing the investigation, aware that the man was convinced that his people had stopped the rapist and murderers who had been in the hov, the ID chip of the one called Ian Montana still sending a weak signal from within the charred remains.

It was not supposed to have happened this way.

Cav's Rapid Response Team had missed Ian at his apartment by mere minutes. The idea to frame him for the rape/murder of the young lady whom Alexis had mistakenly left alive had gone off flawlessly. The problem had occurred when Alexis had come into the scene and found Ian before the police had been able to pick him up at the dance. That had complicated things tremendously and had caused a cascade of problems which now stared at him from within the ruins of the hov.

The worse possible situation had come to pass.

Alexis and Ian were together, running, rogue, and most likely more determined than ever to find the cause of their flight. It was not the scenario for which Cav had planned. The reaction the police had taken in trying to apprehend Ian and the radical methods that they had employed were certainly not part of the plan. He was rather perturbed at the whole affair, as he was with this whole notion of taking Alexis out of retirement. It was all beginning to smell like shit.

He was already close to losing Alexis, having her slip from his grasp and turn into a true rogue agent. Now he was certain that this episode, unintentionally to be sure, had been the final event to throw her over the edge and turn her independent. Such a thought was so far from anything good that he balked at the very idea. To have someone like Alexis Locke running around making up her own missions and doing as she pleased was a disaster written in big, bold letters. It was, to say the least, an unfortunate state of affairs.

She would have to be dealt with, dealt with using extreme prejudice if her solo run lasted much longer. There was no other way out. Alexis was a one-woman army and to have her making up her own rules was one of Cav's numerous worse nightmares.

The police chief came up to Cav with a look of contempt and smug self-satisfaction for what he considered a job well done. He was a chain smoker, the ban on the use and sale of tobacco not a priority with the Kazakhstan government and especially not for the higher officials. He held his cigarette between his lean fingers as if it were a part of his body, bringing it to his mouth and inhaling the toxic smoke with a relish that seemed misplaced to Cav.

Why anyone would want to purposely inhale the cancerous fumes of those vile little moribund contrivances was beyond him. But the man seemed to think that it gave him class, style, a certain character that set him apart from the other less fortunates who didn't need nor dare insufflate their own demise. All it did was make him look foolish.

He spoke a rapid, crisp, toxic Arabic flying past his lips like the bluish venomous smoke of the cigarette. "We will find them, that you can be assured, and when we do, I will personally make sure that they pay in pain for the vile desecration of that innocent girl."

Cav looked at the man from beneath his bushy eyebrows with a loathing that was tangible, then looked away, disgusted with the mere sight of such a man in a position of power.

The police chief continued, unaware that he was skating on thin ice. "This is what happens when we allow such people into our country. I expect that you will be leaving soon. You presence here is not required."

Cav ignored him as he watched the forensic crew exit the wreckage and shake their heads, indicating that they had found nothing. He looked up into the sky where the blaring spotlights illuminating the crashed hov drowned out any chance at seeing the stars.

"This one female," the police chief said with a tone to his voice that set Cav's teeth on edge. "She was one of yours, no? Perhaps you should be more careful in selecting who you choose to allow into your organization. You damn Americans are so — "

He never finished his sentence as Cav grabbed the tall, muscular man by the testicles and squeezed with all his might. The police chief's eyes rolled back into his head and his face twisted into a grotesque parody of pain and ultimate discomfort as his knees buckled and he fell to the grass, trying in vain to pull Cav's hand away.

"Listen to me you piece of shit," Cav said slowly, caustically, choosing his fluent Arabic carefully, picking just the right words and making certain that the incapacitated man understood each and every one clearly. He took the cigarette that burned in the man's mouth, hanging on his lip as if attached, and put in out on the back of the police chief's left hand, burning the skin in a sizzle of sickening sweet smoke. "If you harm one hair on that woman's head, I'll tear you apart and eat you for breakfast. No one told you to go in shooting. No one."

He squeezed even harder, creating a pain that the police chief didn't think possible, forcing tears to well up in his eyes and his face to become even more contorted. "If it hadn't been for your incompetence, this would all be over by now." He squeezed one last time, felt something break, then let go as the man sagged to the grass emitting low, pitiful moans and sobs as he curled up into a ball.

Several officers came running up to see what had happened but stood some distance from the man who had laid their chief down.

Cav looked at the pathetic ball on the grass and spit on him. "And I'm not an American, you son-of-a-street-whore." He walked some distance away and let the other officers tend to their leader. He pulled out his encrypted cell-phone using its own, singular satellite and punched the speed dial. He listened to the connection tones and beeps, then the sleepy voice answering on the other end. "This is Cav. We have a problem."

L'amour est de tous les sentiment
Le plus égoiste, et, par conséquent,
Lorequ'il est blessé, le moins généreux.
--- Benjamin Constant

20

17 August 2085, 0105 hrs
Ishim River

   The sound of the shower woke up Ian with a start. The cool wind across his face and the throbbing in his arm told him immediately that it was not a dream, that what had happened this evening had been all too real. He stood and walked over to the control panel, then looked up at the onrushing river reflecting the silver glow of the moon like a serpent unwinding before him, the navigation system guiding them straight and true along the serpent's twisting spine. He looked back behind him and saw only the white phosphorous of the wake like a long tail magically set upon the waters, looked up and saw no police hovs giving chase.

   Satisfied that all was in order, he walked down the access ladder to the cabin below where the sound of the shower grew louder. He was drawn to the well-stocked bar and poured himself a tall shot of bourbon and downed it in a gulp burning its way into his stomach. Feeling much better for it, he poured another and plopped himself down on one of the plush chairs provided, staring through the open door into the bathroom and the glazed shower door where Alexis' blurred form could be seen under the stream of water.

   He watched unabashedly and waited for her to finish.

   It was not every day that one had such an opportunity and if she had not wanted him to watch, she would have closed the bathroom door.

Such were the thoughts of men.

   She opened the shower door and stepped out, water dripping off her sleek body as she grabbed a towel and began to dry herself, the eroticism of the moment more than Ian could stand as his groin tightened up and his pulse quickened.

When she had finished drying, she wrapped the towel around herself and looked up at him, directly into his eyes, letting him know that she had known he was there all along, watching. "Since when did you become a voyeur?" she asked in soft tones as she stepped out of the bathroom rubbing her hair dry with a smaller towel. She sniffed the air, then looked back at him and wrinkled her face up. "You smell like shit, boy. You'd better get in there."

He rose and began to undress, dropping the foul-smelling clothes on the floor. She watched with an unemotional face and when he stood before her naked, she knelt down, picked up the filthy clothes and walked out, completely ignoring his manhood and his physique. He frowned at the disappointment – she had not even raised an eyebrow or made a disparaging remark toward him – and stepped into the shower. Perhaps Cav had been right about her all along and she was just using him back then, the frigidity of her current state enough to make an Eskimo shiver.

Fifteen minutes later he emerged back on the deck, a towel wrapped around his head, the clothes Alexis had taken from the terrified mother a fit that was not quite right. Alexis sat in the stern of the hydrofoil wearing the colorful serape she had taken, its pattern of various random angles highlighting well her tanned skin and short blonde hair.

"So what now?" he asked as he sat beside her and offered her a glass of water. He was going to pour her a tumbler of scotch but then remembered that she was not known to drink, a trait he found odd and always a little disturbing in a female.

"We'll need to ditch the boat before sun-up and work our way to the nearest airport where we can hop a flight out," she answered as she took the glass and sipped at it. "We'll need a place to go where we can regroup and figure out our next step. Have any suggestions?" She had several already in mind but decided to let him make the choice. They would need a quiet place where she could regroup and leave him behind without worrying about his safety. The last thing she needed now was to have him tagging along.

He sat down next to her as he thought, the warmth of her body making him almost forget that twenty years had passed between them without a word. Although he had just been thinking that perhaps Cav had been right, another part of his mind chastised him for ever letting a body like hers go without a fight. He took another sip of his drink before he spoke. He was well aware that she had already chosen several places where they could both go, most likely to drop him off and leave him behind and she was only asking him to make him feel better, to make it appear that he had a say in the decision.

With Alexis Locke, one never had a say in the decision, regardless what she said or how she acted. Had he been around when Cav was coming up with the crazy idea to create her, he could have suggested a few improvements. "Sao Paulo. I have a few old friends there and a place I bought when still working for the CIA, just in case. That'll be the safest place. It's a large city where no one will notice two new people."

"Is the place secure?"

"No one knows I bought it and it's under a different name. It's as secure as it gets."

She nodded her head. It sounded like a good start. "How about getting us out of here?"

He was a bit taken aback by her quick and easy agreement to his suggestion. That had never happened, even when they were in the depth of their romantic affair. What was she driving at this time? "I assume that you can still fly most everything."

"Does a frog shit?"

He nodded his head as he sipped some more of the fiery liquid down his throat. They passed a slow moving barge going the other way that blared its deep, basso foghorn at them in annoyance for the wake that they created. "Then I think I have a way to get us to Baku. From there, we should be able to get a flight out. If we can make it to Atbasar before sunrise, then we can acquire a hov to Arqalyq, switch hovs and make it to Atyrau where we can catch a ferry across the Caspian to Baku. What are we going to do about money? I certainly don't have any on me anymore and I don't think it would be such a good idea to access my accounts at the moment and tip them off as to where we are. I don't even have an ID for that matter. What the hell are we going to do about that?"

She leaned her head back on one of the numerous soft cushions of the lounger seat and closed her eyes, trying to organize and contain all the thoughts pounding through her mind. She was silent for several minutes as she processed and arranged what it was that she needed to ascertain and what she was going to subsequently do with that information.

"Did you fall asleep on me?" he asked as he finished his drink and placed the glass down.

"No, just thinking." She produced a small money card from under the seat cushion, where she had placed it before, as well as an ID card identifying her as Natasha Baklanova, import dealer from Odessa. "This will access an unlimited monetary account in the Virgin Islands that not even Cav knows about. We should be able to get you a fake ID in a matter of minutes in any of the back streets around here with access to that kind of credit. Baku will do." She went quiet again.

He was not satisfied with her answer. Why was she being so damn cooperative? This was not the Alexis he knew and loved. This was some damn odd clone who didn't get the memo about the real Alexis Locke being stubborn and very uncooperative when it came to anything that was not her idea. He was about to voice his concerns, but when he went to speak, she turned to look at him with a flick of her hair and he lost his train of thought in her eyes.

"Speaking of Cav.... I think we have a problem." She caught his eyes a moment to make certain that he was aware that she was talking now and no dissension would be tolerated. "The young lady who was killed ... Colleen?"

He nodded his head.

"She's the one from whom I borrowed my invitation. I left her tied up in her apartment very much alive. You say you used to date her and you even screwed her?" She pursed her lips as she looked at him now, wondering why he moved on to such low standards after her.

He nodded again, unaware of her subtle dig at his taste. "But that was several weeks ago. We really hadn't seen each other since due to our conflicting schedules."

She rose and eyebrow and grunted softly. "That's what all you men say," she retorted with a derisive grin. "But that doesn't matter. Whomever killed her and set you up, and I'm fairly certain I know who did it, knew several key facts about you, like you were living in Aqmola; two, that you were dating her recently; and three, that I was coming here to see you. With all that put together, there's only one name that pops into my head: Cav."

She stared at him, so intense when she said it Ian sat up and looked at her with disbelief. She actually meant it. She was accusing the man she had always defended even with the most ludicrous actions. "You've got to be kidding. I can understand his jealousy in regards to you and me back then, interfering with your assignments and all that and not wanting me around to come between you two, but to frame me far rape and murder and then send the police after me with guns a blazing? That's even beyond him."

"I don't think so," she answered back with malice in her voice that told Ian more than the words. "He's the only one who knew that I was coming here to see you. The only one. That makes him the prime suspect." She looked at him again, caught him staring at her open robe and exposed breasts, smirked and closed her robe up again.

He chuckled at her modesty, another trait that was not Alexis. "That brings up another question then. Why are you here, Alexis Locke? Why have you come back into my life flaunting your gorgeous body before me and trailing behind you all sorts of shit that's forced us onto this hydrofoil fleeing for our lives? Why have you suddenly appeared back in my life? Wasn't one destruction enough for you?"

She stared at him a moment, then leaned forward. She also wanted answers to those questions but now was not the time. She was well aware that with all the others, her time with them was limited before they were killed off, usually right when they were about to tell her something important. She needed to pick Ian's brain now when she knew that they were relatively safe in the middle of the river. "What were you doing with Dr. Hart, Kido Nakamura, Dr. Godonov, and Dr. Dumvo?"

As the names rolled off her tongue, his eyes narrowed. He recognized three of them but not that last one and could not make any connection between them and Alexis or his life in Aqmola. Confusion crossed his face. "Don't try and change the subject on me. Why are you here?"

She clicked her tongue at his obtuseness. "Answer my questions and you just might find out."

He leaned back again, reached for his drink only to find it was empty. He started to rise for more but she laid a hand on his thigh and gripped it hard. "No more alcohol, Ian. Just answer the damn questions."

He looked at her hand, then into her eyes and saw that the old Alexis was definitely lurking in there somewhere. He sighed, as if he were about to relate classified information, then starting speaking, aware that she was onto something and afraid that he might be at the center of her target acquisition and that was the reason she had come here.

To kill him.

"I know Hart and Kido from several years back and Ykaterina only through e-mail. I don't know any Dr. Dumvo. What do they have to do with anything, or with me for that matter?"

"What were you doing with them?" she prompted again. "What project were you working on with them?"

He thought a moment, not believing that she could be referring to the idea he had broached with Hart and Kido separately, that they were working on as a hobby. "Nothing really. I mean, they hadn't even really gotten anywhere with it."

She looked hard at him, as if doubting his veracity. "Well Ian, it must have been something important because it got them all killed."

"That's impossible," he said flatly, convinced that he was right, that what she was saying was so far beyond the realm of reality that it was ludicrous to even think about it.

"It's the only thing that links them all together, Ian. Whatever it was that Hart and Kido were working on, that all the others seemed to be involved in, was what got them killed. There isn't anything else. Nothing." She leaned forward again. "What was it, Ian? I need to know."

He shook his head in bewilderment. "You don't understand, Alexis."

"Then explain it to me," she said, this time with a harsher tone.

He looked into her steel-cold eyes giving no hint of compromise and knew that she was deadly serious, that whatever she thought was going on she believed in firmly. "Is that what your mission's about? Their deaths? You think I had something to do with it?" He moved a few inches away from her, ready to jump overboard if it came to that. "Tell me the truth, Alexis. We were always good about that. Are you here to kill me? Is that your mission this time around?"

Had she not been so worried about the shadow people suddenly emerging from the frigid looking waters and capsizing their boat, she would have laughed at his morbid suggestion. "You always were too paranoid for your own good. Do you really think that if I'd been sent here to kill you that you'd still be alive?"

He had to concede that point.

"They were all murdered, Ian. And all made to look like accidents. This one came from the president herself and for her to involve herself in something that seems so trivial raises large, red flags for me. There's something here, I know it. Ever since I started on this mission, there's been a group that's been trying to kill me. That mess up on *Stargazer I*?"

"That was you?" he said, having seen the news bulletins describing the disaster that had struck the Colony.

"Whatever it was that they were working on for you, it got them killed and would have gotten you killed if I hadn't've shown up here when I did in Aqmola. What was it Ian?" She was becoming, much to her disapproval, frustrated with his lack of cooperation. It didn't occur to her that perhaps he was still in shell-shock from discovering that she was alive and never requested that he be sent away.

Ian still refused to believe that his idea had any relationship to the deaths, refused to believe it for the simple fact that he didn't want to be responsible for more deaths. His time with the CIA and Cav gave him enough of death guilt to last several lifetimes. To think that his simple idea, which he had thought would, in the end, save millions of lives had instead turned into a death-wish for those involved was a terrible burden.

He didn't want to believe it at all, but gave in to her demands and spoke up anyway, knowing that her patience was not infinite and that she was liable to become physically aggressive very soon. He took several deep breaths, then leaned back again and crossed his arms over his chest. "I had come up with an idea after watching some special on the holo-vid about the trouble they were having with the newer brain-surgery operations and the life prolonging techniques. Science has reached the point where almost all the major organs can be grown from DNA samples and then transplanted without the risk of rejection, allowing life to be prolonged even further. Everything, that is, except far the brain."

"But I read somewhere that they were coming close to recreating a brain from DNA samples," she interjected, drawn into the explanation he was providing, aware that her suspicions, the vague conclusions she had formulated were beginning to pan out with his answers.

"Yes, that's true, and it's very possible that the more secretive of the companies may have even succeeded in solving the problems, but its still only brain tissue. The major problem is that with a heart or a kidney or a lung there's no need to place into the structure the instructions on how the organ is to behave. It's encoded into the DNA and when a kidney is grown, it's ready to function without any more work.

"But not the brain. Sure it'll work just fine, but it'll be empty. Except for the basic, primal, life-support functions, there wouldn't be anything in the memory. If you were to transplant it to a human, he would be like a baby just out of the womb." He was becoming excited as he recanted his idea for her, his dreams of a way to help people rather than always find better ways to kill them rekindled. "What I thought of was a way to transfer the contents of a human brain into a computer, as a temporary storage facility, and then transfer it back to the new brain in totality so that when the patient awoke, he would be himself with all his memories and thoughts and personality intact. I thought it was a pretty good idea. I mentioned it to Alexander, whom I'd known for years, and he said that he knew some people that he could get together with and work on it in their spare time. It was just an idea. I'd supply the money and they'd come up with the product. That was it."

Alexis was shocked that Ian had known her son for what he described as a long time. Did he know that the man had been her son? Not likely. Alexander had not even known.

But it shocked her nonetheless.

Life was funny that way, the way it sometimes came full circle without one even realizing it, bringing together people from across the globe in chance encounters eventually working into relationships. Perhaps it had something to do with soul-mates finding one another, some cosmic game spreading them out over time and space and then watching as they were slowly, inexorably drawn together without even knowing that they were suppose to be together, like a glob of mercury been spread out on a table and then, when the table is titled, runs back together to make one, big glob again without any trace that it had been separated into many parts.

Those in the East had a name for it, the Hindus and Buddhists and Taoists who believed in the whole reincarnation bit and karma. They called it fate, soul binding, life. Perhaps that was what was happening here, what had happened with the friendship that evidently had sprung up between her former lover and her lost son and now led her to be here with Ian again, talking about it all on a hydrofoil speeding down a glittering black river.

"That's one hell of an idea, Ian," she stated. "I can now see why all the secrecy."

"That wasn't my idea. That was Hart's idea, all the secrecy. He seemed to think that it needed to be kept quiet until they had something substantial. Something about the bigger companies stealing our idea, as if they hadn't thought of it already. He was like that, kind of naive in some ways."

"He was obviously right," she said with a barely detectable sigh onto which Ian latched on easily.

He was not certain to what the sigh was in reference, or whether it was even in reference to anything, perhaps just an expression of fatigue. But the Alexis he remembered rarely farted without some meaning attached. "Did you know Hart?" he asked her, aware of the recognition manifesting itself in her whenever the name was spoken. "You're eyes tell me that you did.", He was also aware, for the first time, how much Hart had looked like Alexis, how much his nose and the setting of his eyes, his manners and his hair matched Alexis'. "You would have liked him, I think. Maybe a little young for you, but then I seem to remember that age wasn't all that much of a factor for you."

"No," she said simply, answering all his questions with that one word, telling him with her tone that she wanted to move on with the discussion. "How far had they gotten? And how can you say that it wasn't anything important?"

He raised an eyebrow as he spread his arms out. "Because they hadn't gotten anywhere before they all started to end up dead, that's why."

"And you didn't find that a little disturbing?" she questioned him with a mocking tone.

"Not at the time. Shit happens. They were all accidents."

"Then why the alias, Ian? Why not tell them your real name, or at least the name you usually go by."

He frowned as he rubbed his chin, the stubble beginning to itch a little. "Ah, yes. I had forgotten about that."

She could see that he was telling the truth, that he was not trying to intentionally deceive her.

"That's actually a simple one," he continued after a moment. "I didn't want my current employer to know what I was up to. They frown on extra-office work like that. I guess they're my *former* employer now, wouldn't you say?"

She frowned, then stood and began to pace the deck. "So you're saying that they hadn't gotten anywhere with it. That makes no sense then as to why they would be murdered for it. You must be leaving something out."

"That's what I'm trying to tell you, Alexis. Your theory doesn't make any sense. Why kill them for working on something that was getting nowhere? Kido was having major problems with her transfer protocol. Godonov was having problems finding the correct sequence of gene controls to find the memory algorithms in the brain. Hart was the only one who seemed to be getting anywhere with the physical hardware for the job, but even that was causing problems for him. As for these other two, Hart must have approached them for whatever purpose. What were their specialties, if you don't mind me asking?"

"Nano-technology and brain-surgery," she answered without hesitation.

He leaned back again, his eyes starting to get heavy from the lack of sleep and the wearing off of the adrenaline keeping him going so far. "Hmm. That would make sense. We would need both those fields." Perhaps Alex had gotten further than he reported. "But like I said, they had barely gotten started when they were all killed. It makes no sense that it was the cause of their deaths." He gave a big, gaping yawn.

"No, it doesn't..." she said as her voice trailed off and she stopped by the port railing, watching the darkened landscape pass by, the wind pushing her hair around her head. She stayed there for several minutes, thinking, trying to come up with some way to salvage her theories and ideas. The mind transfer concept had to be the key to this. If it wasn't, the murders might as well have been random events with no connection whatsoever and she refused to believe that. She compressed her lips together and shook her head. "What else could this technology, if it were successfully created, be used for?" she asked without turning around toward him.

There was no answer and she turned her head to see what Ian was doing, why he was ignoring her. With his head back against the soft cushion and the raising moonlight flush over his face, casting desultory shadows across him etching out in subtle hues the lines she had loved so much once upon a time, she could see that he had fallen asleep. His chest rose and fell in shallow, steady breaths and his mouth hung open in that embarrassing position all humans found themselves in at least once in their lives when they fall asleep all of a sudden, exhausted from some hard task.

She stared at him a while longer, far too many memories forcing their way to the surface and exploding like a breaching whale. She ran a hand over her mouth, then went down into the cabin to get a blanket to cover him. After she had tucked it in around him so that the wind would not carry it away, she went back to the control platform and sat down, staring at the ebony serpent reflecting the hovering moon in glistening twinkles of subdued white as it rushed beneath the hydrofoil.

She had thought that Ian's answers to her questions would have solved the problem for her, dropped the key to the riddle in her lap and allowed her to come to a solid conclusion. It was, unfortunately, not to be and she knew better than to have expected it. She had known from the very first moment that Cav had shown her the computer disc that this one was going to be difficult, was going to tax her to no end and perhaps even be the one assignment that would prove to be her undoing.

Cav.

That name was now a curse to her, a name to be placed on her enemy list and plotted against. She shook her head at the thoughts that funneled into her mind about the man who at one time she had seen and loved as a father figure. Everything pointed to his involvement with the debacle back at the dance. Everything. And what really bothered her the most, what grated on her nerves and flared inside her like a burning sun was that she could easily see him doing it. She could see his intimacy with the whole scheme as if he had explained it to her once. Why that was, she didn't know, but it made it even harder to acknowledge the fact that not only had he lied to her about Ian and the father of her son, but about this entire assignment and had, it was becoming clear, meant to kill her off from the beginning.

She had warned him that if she ever found out that he was involved, that he was going to pay with his life. That was one more little piece of the puzzle with which she was going to have to deal when this was over, a loose end that she would have to tidy up. Cav had to be dealt with. No one played her like this and got away with it. Not even him.

She shook her head again, wondering just how far Cav was involved, just how much he knew and how much he had to do with the assassins at the cabin, at the Colony. But it would all have to wait till later.

At the moment, she needed to resolve the problems with the project Ian had initiated with her son, which had unknowingly set him on his own path of destruction. She tried to recall all she knew about the life-prolonging drugs and procedures now in place, of the other applications that had spun off of each and of what other applications Ian's idea could have in the long run.

It was easy to see that with his memory transfer procedure successfully implemented, Ian's idea could revolutionize the interrogation business, if one could even call it a business. It would make the concealment of secrets superfluous, for all one had to do was capture a person with the knowledge one wanted, download his memory into a computer and pick through it with all the sophisticated search engines until the wanted information popped out. Then you could either dump all the memory and kill the person off or download it back into the brain and the person would know nothing of what had happened. Any and all governments would certainly kill to have that knowledge. But that was just the point. They would not have killed the creators of that project before the project even got off the ground. That would be completely counter-productive.

They would instead either let them successfully produce the necessary components and then take it from them or take them out of society and place them in a secret think-tank to produce the technology there, for them, without anyone else ever finding out. That was a real possibility that she had to seriously consider. Since several of the bodies were either burnt or eaten beyond recognition, it was not that far a leap to come to that conclusion. She already had the suspicion that her son was not dead, that Dumvo may not be dead. But then why pick out just a few members of the team to secret away and not all of them? Kido was obviously dead. Her body had been recovered from the botched robbery fairly intact. And Pratali's body, minus most of his face, was also recovered.

There were too many loose ends for her to come to a firm conclusion and the whole idea of a government being involved just didn't sit right with her. It was too simple and obvious. Most governments with the power to do this would be far subtler. And they certainly would not bring her out of retirement to solve the case and blow their whole scheme wide open.

Her gaze at the river become unfocused as she realized, for the first time, that that was exactly why they had pulled her out of retirement. It was all a ruse to kill her. The whole plan. They wanted her out of the way. Whomever was running this, and she had to believe that it had to be people with whom Cav had a close relationship, had to have known that Cav would have eventually called her in and they had simply moved one step ahead and called her in themselves, thus giving away her living place and allowing their assassins to strike first. With Alexis out of the way, the rest of the plan, whatever it might prove to be, could be executed without interruption.

Only problem was that Alexis had not been killed.

And this all gave raise to another point, which she didn't want to acknowledge or even contemplate at the moment: Cav was not involved, at least not in the initial stages. He had been used as badly as she had been used and he might just be dead by now, a liability not worth the risk of having around.

She smiled into the moon-glow.

These people ... no, she should be more precise. *Claudine* had chewed off far more than she could possibly handle and it was going to bite her in the ass as surely as the sun shined in the summer.

She leaned on the side railing.

The only way she was going to stop all this was to figure out what her son had been striving toward with Ian's idea. Whatever it was had to be huge, almost species changing huge if a government was willing to kill so many before the idea even became a reality. So for what else could Ian's idea be used? To what other applications could it be applied that would be so catastrophic, or perhaps so vital to a nation's security, to push such a sinister and complicated plan forward?

Another application came to her mind quickly enough.

One could clone an entire new body and then transfer a person's memory and experience to the clone when the original body began its inevitable decay. In this way, one could theoretically live forever, constantly changing bodies when needed but keeping the memories, thoughts and personalities through each change. That would be a major boon for whatever company developed the technology, allowing them an almost virtual monopoly on pseudo-immortality. It would make said company rich and powerful beyond their wildest dreams for they could charge whatever they wanted and be assured of an ever-increasing client base. And a mega multi-leveled corporation would be more than powerful enough to find out what her son was up to and in that instant decide that his death and the death of his co-workers was worth the risk for first shot at the most important human improvement to come along since the invention of the wheel.

She realized with a clarity that made her stomach lurch with its implications that the technology had already been discovered and the company or government that had achieved it didn't want anyone else to possess it, thus killing off anyone who even had the slightest inkling of stumbling onto it. That seemed more likely, but once again it begged the question of how they found out what Ian's people were working on when they had barely started the procedure in the first place, and why Cav had not heard anything about the project. If such a procedure truly did already exist to extend life virtually forever, then how was it that Cav and his insidious band of spies had not managed to get even the slightest whiff of its existence?

Or had they?

Did Cav already know and was playing both sides here? Did he reluctantly agree to re-activate Alexis only as a ruse, to throw off his own suspicion and thus use her for his own purpose of finding the company developing this technology and destroying it before it could bring its magic to market? This was not the movies and she was not James Bond, who was always left alive so that he could spoil the bad guy's plans even though the bad guy could have killed him off twenty times before the movie was half over.

No, she didn't believe that Cav had intentionally meant for her to be killed. But she did believe those who had told Cav to get her into the picture had meant for only one outcome of that request. Her termination. Either way, whether Cav had actually given the order to have her terminated or not was irrelevant. Someone had done it and Cav was not making an effort to stop them, making him just as accountable. But it still made no sense.

The possibilities that she was foreseeing were just too obvious. A military power could use the technology to create the perfect warrior and then copy his memory into a multitude of cyborg bodies and create an invincible army. It could be used to brainwash. One could easily adapt the technology to be able to insert particular ideas into one's mind, along with the necessary technical data to carry it out and create the perfect assassin.

It could be used to increase the learning of children without ever having them go to school. Just download into their memory all the pertinent facts and laws and information they needed and within a matter of minutes, fourteen years of schooling would be accomplished, creating brilliant ten-year olds as easy as baking cookies.

They were all far too obvious and there were far too many choices. Any third-rate CIA employee could have cracked this one given enough time and that would defeat the whole purpose of the assassinations. There was still a piece of the puzzle, a large piece, missing and although she was closer to finding it than when she had first received that message in her cabin, there was still too much data missing. Where was the key? She had thought that Ian held it, but he just presented her with more questions than answers.

There either had to be something she was missing or something onto which she had not yet stumbled, for that was what she felt like she was doing; stumbling. Worst of all, now she was stumbling on her own. She certainly could not trust Cav anymore or anyone associated with him and that limited her options tremendously. She would have to go this one alone, using all the traits Cav had genetically built into her and find the missing piece. It was there, she knew it was, there for the taking and she was becoming more and more convinced that the shadow people, the woman she had fought with in the HEEs, were involved, deeply involved.

She looked behind her and saw the first shimmer of the brightening horizon as the terminator line receded away from the sun and brought with it daylight. The sky was awaking to a subdued radiance of subtle reds and orange, streaks of golden hued rays warming the bottoms of the long line of puffy, metallic-blue clouds hanging low against the rolling plateaus leading to the Torghay Valley. Daylight was coming in slow, delicate, exquisite colors painting the darkness of the receding night with a surrealistic touch only the laws of physics could create; with a little help from God. Pinks and ambers exploded in a panoply of light as the first edge of the sun peeked over the horizon, greeting the new day, accompanied by a chorus of bird-song lending an air of illusion to the whole experience.

She walked back to Ian and shook him awake.

He came too with a start, his eyes hazed in that cloud that follows a deep sleep. His mind, coming up out of the fog of the dream he was having, trying to grasp onto the reality of the world around him and it took several moments before he was able to make any intelligent sounds. "Did you get any sleep?" he finally asked as she climbed back up to the control platform and slowed the boat down in preparation for their disembarkation.

"No," she answered as the whine of the engines subsided and the boat settled off its pylons and into the murky waters of the river that at this bend slowed and lazily worked its way west.

"Do you think that's wise?" he asked as he stood and stretched, the crick in his neck stabbing him with pain. He had not meant to fall asleep on this stupid cushioned bench when there were several perfectly good beds down below.

"I'll be fine, Ian," she said firmly, coldly. She came to the obvious conclusion that she needed to stay distant from him, see him as nothing but another agent, her partner and nothing more. Any romance they had was lost when he left her and she was not inclined to rekindle it at the present moment. "We need to get out here. See if you can gather some food up and anything else that you think necessary from down below. Then we'll set the autopilot back on and let the boat go till it ends up at the border, where the Russians will certainly stop it."

He nodded his head as the hydrofoil gently bumped the bank. He came back a few minutes later with two small carrying bags stuffed with provisions and clothes. They jumped off as the engines kicked in again and the nav-computer took the hydrofoil back up to speed and down the center of the river and out of sight around the far bend, its noise receding into the chorus of birds sitting high upon the birch trees lining the bank.

"How far are we from Atbasar?" he asked as he handed her one of the bags and they started through the thick brush that hugged the bank.

"About three kilometers or so. We'll need to acquire a hov as soon as possible and make it to the next stop before the authorities figure out what's happened." She looked at him as they marched through the tough country. "I did a little thinking last night and I've got a feeling that things are going to get a lot hotter for us real soon."

"Great, that's just what I wanted to hear." He trudged along behind her, his body used to parties and pretty women seeming to be rebel against any real exertion. "Can I ask you a question without you punching me again?"

She smiled, subtly. "I make no promises."

He frowned as he tripped on the exposed root of a gnarled tree and almost pitched headlong into the soft dirt. "Why did you ask about whether I was married if you didn't want to start our relationship over again? I mean, you've shown me you body now in various states of undress and teased me beyond belief and yet you say you don't want any type of relationship. Those things don't go together, you know. You were never a tease or a flirt, it was one of the things I always liked about you. But now..."

She looked back at him stumbling through the tickets, giving him her famous half-cocked smile putting dimples in her cheeks and melting his knees. "Don't flatter yourself, Ian. I was asking to find out whether you were leaving anyone behind, that's all. We don't have the time and I don't have the inclination to start in with you, or anyone, ever. You're just going to have to curb your lust while we're together. I'm sure you'll manage. You don't have any kids, do you?"

"No," he said as he walked up next to her, the thick bushes opening out onto the rolling, green plains of the plateau. "They were killed along with their mother in the first of the starlifter accidents."

She nodded her head as they came to a road in the early morning light and followed it toward the outskirts of the city rising before them with the glory of the sun reflecting on the tall glass buildings making up the small downtown section, causing it to look like Camelot rising out of the dawn mist. "Yeah, I remember that crash. That was like ten years ago, wasn't it? Sorry I brought it up, but I needed to know if our pursuers would have any way of forcing you to go back, you know, take it out on your family and all."

"No, nothing like that. And it's okay. I've gotten use to the pain and the emptiness. There were a few months afterward where I didn't see any point in going on, but I got over it. It's a part of life, I suppose. Death."

She didn't say anything in response to his statement. She didn't have anything to say about it. Death was such an integral part of her life that she had become immune to it. At least she had until Clovis, who still came to her late in the night and just stared at her, as if he were blaming her for his death, haunting her with his lost soul wandering between the worlds of the living. Death had been Alexis' constant companion for all the years she had worked for Cav and they had a good, working arrangement. She would provide death with the victims it craved and death would leave her alone, would stop those she had dispatched from haunting her dreams and her consciousness.

But it was becoming apparent to her that her bargain with death was over, that the fifteen years she had been out of the game, had not killed anything more consequential than a fish – which in itself, she supposed, was enough to damn her soul anyway – had voided her arrangement and let the floodgate open to the shadowy world of those who had once been. Clovis was only the first manifestation of that deluge she was certain was to follow. A deluge of which she would need to keep one step ahead until she had solved this riddle and found those responsible, because she knew that when the deluge hit, it would inundate her with such a passion and fury that she would most likely not survive.

The first house that they came to along the old and abandoned road they were following was a moderate-sized affair enclosed with a long, winding fence running off into the ground mist hugging the sloping hills. Several horses stood in the mist, grazing on the grass, looking up occasionally at the intruders. Alexis could discern movement in the main house, the owners starting their day early for the work that was certainly ahead of them.

A three-hov garage sat off to the side of the main house and that was where Alexis and Ian made for, finding within a short-range, economical city hov, a long-range travel hov, and, surprisingly, an old hydrogen-based car. It was one of the numerous Japanese models of the early century, a true antique and in good condition. While Ian checked it over, his love for the older wheeled vehicles over-coming any inhibition he felt at being in someone else's garage, Alexis went to the city hov.

When it had become apparent that the oil on which man depended to run his society would be used up by 2070 at the latest, the production of gasoline engines had slowed to almost a trickle and then eventually stopped, replaced by the far more efficient and cleaner hydrogen engines and then by the hov. As a consequence, any type of wheeled vehicle, especially from the earlier part of the century, or even from the last century, was an antique. There were not many left and only certain types of people still kept them around as links to the past.

Alexis was one of them and so was Ian.

It had been one of the few things they had in common.

The hov Alexis choose was unlocked, fortunately, and she reached under the main control panel and tore out the main connectors supplying power to the tracking computer. Then she pulled the computer itself out and tossed it in the corner of the garage.

"Come on, Ian. We don't have time to stop and smell the roses."

He looked up at her from under the hood of the car and frowned. This one was a classic. If he could, he would talk her into taking this one instead. "Why the short range hov? I doubt if it'll have enough power to get us to the next stop," he asked as he climbed in and she pulled out of the garage and away from the house to the west in a spray of hay and dirt.

"Because when this is reported stolen, those who are following us will find out and if we'd taken the long range hov than they would know that we were headed far away. This way, they can't be sure exactly what we're up to, whether, in fact, we even back-tracked and went back to Aqmola. We'll need all the advantages that we can get from now on."

He nodded his head as the ground rushed by beneath them, the low altitude at which they flew brushing the tops of the few trees gracing the open plains and farms. Alexis looked at the nav chart and set her course to the northwest, away from the city Ian had suggested and toward the further town of Lisakovsk on the Tobol. It was, technically, beyond the range of the hov in which they sat, but she had ways of squeezing out a few extra kilometers.

She had a bad feeling that Cav would be waiting for her at Arqalyq, the city Ian had suggested. She had a bad feeling about everything at the moment.

When the decision has finally come, after all the considerations
and debates, that the survival of the species as a whole is
dependant on the death of the individual, can that individual
be truly considered innocent? Is his death truly wrong
when the advancement of humanity is at stake?
Perhaps at this stage, the line between innocence and
guilt is no longer a viable principle.
--- Excerpt from
The Journal of Meagan Locke

21

18 August 2085, 1300 hrs
São Paulo, Brazil

The starliner cruised low over the Reservatório Edgard de Souza on its way to a landing at the Aeroporto Internacional de Viracopos in São Paulo, the soft, throbbing hum of its engines drowned out by the noise of the city below. The ever-growing maze of modern dura-aluminum and glass sail-boom designed skyscrapers rose out of the hills of the Serra do Mar like a cancer upon the land, the gleaming, black-reflecting edifices of man's vanity rising like overgrown weeds from the ragged hills. The city had, in recent decades, worked its way back toward the airport at Viracopos that had at one time been almost ninety-six kilometers from the city center but which now sat right at the suburbs, the rising oceans having swamped the low-laying coastal regions back in 2012 and 2013. The massive increase in population pushed the city further inland even as the waters rose ever higher, turning forests into malls and swamps into apartments.

The city center, still focused on the famous Triângulo – despite the fact that the old Edificio Itália had been torn down to make room for the more modern structures – was still a vibrant blend of finance and industry, driving the country of Brazil ever forward. The new city that had arisen as the population pushed ever inland had been laid out with a higher order of precision and city-planning, as opposed to the old city that still retained a colonial character with narrow streets – turned into walkways long ago – shabby buildings, and old churches and convents built along the Jesuit and Franciscan style. The newer sections were built around commercial centers and clusters of red-roofed quaint houses saddled around parks and lakes, all within walking distance of each other and planned with an eye toward community.

Ian's estate, which he had purchased through a dummy company using an alias and with no possible trace back to himself, sat all the way on the other side of the massive, sprawling mega-metropolis, butting up against the shore of the Reservatório Rio das Pedras, the forests of the Serra do Morrao rising up in majestic backdrop. With the movement of the city toward the northwest, Ian's estate had been left behind, straddled by residential districts enjoying the waters of the large reservoir and sloping hills and a measure of solitude from the fast life of the business district.

It was, for all intents and purposes, the perfect place for them to hide out, to get lost in the sprawling millions who braced this city with their miseries and corpulence.

Alexis and Ian's taxi settled down before the large ivy-covered wrought-iron gates brooding before the entryway to the twenty-acre estate like decayed teeth. The lines of birch and poplar, that now in the South American winter were barren, stood like skeletons of a vanquished army, their drooping branches and stark, straight lines lending an air of contriteness to the leaf-strewn grounds the massive gates guarded.

"Charming," Alexis said as Ian opened the door on his side to step out.

"I haven't been here in over thirty years. I guess the tenant landlord hasn't been keeping up with appearances. I was only going to use this for emergencies, and of course, when I retired. I think I'm going to have to fire someone."

As Ian spoke, a wave of energy passed over Alexis like a surge, shorting out her mind momentarily as if time had ceased moving for a moment. She blinked as she sat dazed, wondering what it had all been about.

It was then she felt them.

There were seven this time, seven human-sized distortions on the grounds, distortions completely out of place, as if time had been warped, malformed, bent in a cruel deformity of itself. They were scattered about the grounds as randomly as the leaves littering the over-grown grass, waiting.

She reached out with her mind, probing into the distortions and found the same blank, emptiness she had experienced before, the same nothingness of mind attached to the bodies screaming out at her in their unmistakable physical presence. She reached across the seat and out to where Ian stood and grabbed his arm hard, digging her nails into the skin and causing him to wince at the pain.

"What the hell are you doing now? That hurts, you know!" he complained as he tried to pry her death-grip loose.

But she was beyond hearing him, beyond knowing he even existed. All Alexis knew was that there was danger and she had to protect him. She concentrated and probed harder and further than she had ever done before, wanting to break through the barrier she knew existed, the barrier keeping her from seeing into the thoughts of those people who were so determined to kill her.

You are even more powerful than we were lead to believe.

With her eyes wide open, Alexi's whole body shuddered as if an electric shock had passed through her. The voice came across to her like a ripple in the air, subtle and soft, barely penetrating her mind in delicate wavelets of thought. She was here. The woman from the HEE.

Alexis stretched out her mind even further in an attempt to find her, to tap her mind and learn once and for all the cause of the distortions undulating and shimmering continually. In a flash of recognition opening her mind like a fan, she made a connection that was primal in its union. Images began to reel before her mind like holo-vid on fast forward, coruscating with an intensity sending another shudder through her body and making her clamp down even harder on Ian's arm, drawing blood as he frantically tried to disengage. The images were of people, places, events zooming by as if she had tapped into the main-core memory of a library computer, a history of the world impacting into her in wave after crashing wave of simulacrum making her reel from the passion they entailed.

She tried to concentrate on the images, tried to slow them down or understand them. She felt that the connection was tenuous yet unfaltering, that the other mind was trying desperately to uncouple. The images began to slow, to come to a focus she began to comprehend and in that comprehension saw that although she recognized the places, the people and events were completely unfamiliar, as if they were a re-written history of the past that should have been, a past from a different time and place.

Then she realized in a quiver of trepidation that the images she was seeing, she had tapped into in an unexpected conjunction of thought, were not images of the past but of the future. They were a record of the mind she had tapped, a record of a life lived not now or in the past, but in the future.

The images sped up again like a projector gone mad until there was nothing left but a blur of colors spinning and colliding like a psychotic kaleidoscope. And in that amalgam of images slamming into her mind like the pounding waves of surf, she saw a connection of which she was uncertain, a connection that for Alexis was as real as her fingers dug into Ian's flesh but which she didn't understand, which she could not believe.

In a flash of light the images vanished, the connection severed, the waves of energy collapsing into a sifting pattern of incoherent visualization trailing off like a mist in the rain.

She pulled Ian back into the taxi with such force that he flew in and slammed against the far door, the red half-moons on his forearm a testimony of her strong grip, blood dripping from the wounds.

"Hey lady!" the cabby screamed at her as he turned his head to look back into the passenger compartment, speaking in a thick, slurred accent obscuring most of his English in half-eaten bits. "VVha ya d'ing? Dis in't ya tay pen!"

"Drive!" she said through clenched teeth, feeling the seven assassins closing in on the cab now that they knew she was here.

An inimical smile lit the corners of the cabby's mouth. "Wy dit ya mak up ya mind!" But he didn't nothing to make the taxi move.

Ian, stunned and dazed from the impact into the door, sat up rubbing his arm, examining the blood imprints Alexis had made. "You're one crazy bitch, you know that? First you slice open my entire forearm and now this. What the..." his voice trailed off as a movement out Alexis' window caught his eye and he shifted focus to the grounds beyond the gates. He blinked once, then squinted his eyes and leaned a little closer. There were images moving toward them, images he saw but didn't see, formless shapes disturbing the leaves in whorls behind them, moving like a ripple in the bright afternoon air that was cold and crisp. He pointed. "What the hell is that?"

She turned to look, but already knew the answer, the mental projection of the assassins clear and crisp in her mind's eye. She flung open her door and jumped out, then pulled open the locked driver's side door in a screech of metal and breaking locks, grabbed a handful of shirt and chest hair and yanked the startled driver out onto the dirt. He fell against the weather-worn stone towers supporting the gates, stunned and dazed by the sudden exit.

Alexis jumped in and slammed the accelerator forward. The taxi jumped into the air and careened away from the estate as fast as the machine would go, throwing Ian back against the seat like a rock. There was a blast, two, three rocking the cab and sending showers of sparks at Alexis from the main instrument panel. The coil assembly of the main actuator melted under the intense heat of the penetrating plasma lances, melting in turn the main power conduits and effectively crippling the hov. She tried in vain to control the taxi but in a graceful arch, it slowly turned onto its top and began a plunge toward the ground, trailing behind it a greasy, grayish-black tendril of smoke looking like a kite's tail.

With a splash the taxi plunged nose first into the cold waters of the large lake sitting like a splayed finger in the rolling hills, sinking within a matter of moments, the slight breeze disrupting the long line of smoke pointing toward the impact site like a finger from heaven.

*   *   *

Tehran, Iran
18 August 2085, 1330 hrs local time

The Presidential starliner sat on the far corner of the taxiway at the Mehrabad Airport, ten kilometers west of central Tehran. It was surrounded by security forces in armored vehicles, the recent flurry of rebellion in the unstable area a just cause for the heavy protection. Although religion had certainly been a precursor for the majority of conflicts in this region in the past, a new source of tension had burst upon the scene and it, rather than whose god was better, was the driving force behind the violence and instability.

With the conversion of the majority of wheeled vehicles from gasoline to hydrogen burners, the worldwide demand for oil had dropped dramatically by 2050. Then hovs had come along and the demand for oil had plummeted. The oil-fields began to dry up and by 2078 the countries depending solely on the revenues produced from the sale of crude oil found themselves in the same state of affairs as before the oil had been discovered: with no secure source of income. The sudden lack of income and the unpreparedness of the governments to cope with this new state of affairs in any long-term plan had led to rebellion, starting in Saudi Arabia and spreading like an infection to the other former oil-producing countries till the entire region had become a war-zone. Without the importance of oil as a reason for interference, the United States and the European Union had decided to stay uninvolved, the problems of a region of the planet now no more than a hot, arid, useless desert – as it had always been – no longer a matter of national security, or importance.

The rebellions and coups and general slaughter had reached a crescendo by 2083 in a volley of small, dirty, nuclear weapons devastating Kuwait, Baghdad, and Riyadh. The aftermath was just now slowly petering out in a morass of hostile fractions vying for control of areas that were, for the most part, uninhabitable to man. The majority of those who still retained a measure of wealth and power had long since fled to greener pastures, leaving the large cities once teeming with vibrant life nothing more than hollow shells of empty buildings and shattered dreams, the sand beginning to reclaim what had once been its domain and would be again.

It was to this region of the globe that the President's starlifter had come, one of the last places anyone would look for it and certainly one of the last places any spies might be lurking about, the now darkened taxi-way far enough away from the terminals that no one could tell what was parked out here.

Claudine Maxwell sat in the large chair normally reserved for the President, glancing over the reports Cav had submitted to her on the botched job in Aqmola. She was dressed in a conservative black, pinstriped business suit with a skirt tailored to fit high on her thigh. With her legs crossed, the line of the skirt barely covered her black panties, exposing almost every centimeter of her long, sleek legs. She would not have worn such an outfit around the president, that was certain. Heather would be far too jealous to allow such skin to show in her presence. But the president was not here on this trip, had no knowledge of this trip and that was the way Claudine liked it. Besides, that letch Cav was coming to visit and this was the perfect presentation for that man. Let him ogle her legs and almost hidden panties and not think all that hard on what she was about to do and everyone would be happier.

The time for the coup – although she hated to use that word with its connotations of immoral power politics – was close at hand. The mess that was Alexis Locke as she rampaged throughout the world and the fiasco Cav was now creating with his own blundering was just the type of spark she would need to ignite the storm that would oust President prom-queen and install Claudine Maxwell to power.

Then she would begin the reconstruction that would herald the new world order and bring all those damn countries, like the puny powers of the Middle East now nothing more than squabbling nomadic tribes killing each other over water holes, into line. She would form the North American States, as she had promised her financial backers. It was an idea that had been bantered around for years and but for weak-willed politicians, would have already been accomplished. It would bring Canada, Mexico and the United States into one, big, overwhelming economic and military power, under one government – hers – and would begin the gradual change so desperately needed in the world.

She would have to curb the independence of the O' Neill Colonies. They might prove a thorn in her side in a few years. The virtual destruction of *Stargazer I* – she would have liked to have thanked Alexis personally for that one – was a wonderful start, but more was needed to get those damn independent-thinking colonies to follow her orders. Their resource rich mining operations and vast voter support would definitely be a vital necessity in the near future.

Now all that was missing was the proper time to strike at that bimbo Heather O'Rourke and finish what had been started with Claudine's nomination to Chief of Staff.

There was a knock on the door.

She called out for them to enter and the door was opened by one of the numerous Secret Service agents, allowing the short, corpulent body of Cav to waddle in, his face a mask of distress and discomfort.

She uncrossed her legs. "You look like you could use a drink, Cav," she said, motioning to the bar but not offering to get him one. "Make mine a double martini."

He walked around the large desk and right up next to her, the blackness under her mini-skirt as inviting a trap as a spider web to a fly. When he didn't move to get the drink, she laid the pocket computer down on the seat beside her, crossed her legs and spread her arms behind her back, emphasizing the line of her breasts, and relaxed with a sanguine smile on her face.

Sweat stood out on Cav's forehead and stained the fabric under his arms from the oppressive heat rising off the ground outside in visible shimmers. His loose cotton shirt and trousers allowed some measure of breathing space but his overworked system was straining under the tepidity nonetheless.

"Well okay then," Claudine said as she stared at him, trying to see through the fat layers sagging on him like rolls of dough, looking for the man she had once known, with whom she had once had glorious sex. "No drink then. What's this problem we have that forced me to drag myself halfway across the world to meet you here in the middle of a war-zone? And sit down. You're making me nervous hovering over me like this."

"Iran is the most stable of the regional powers," he said with quiet conviction, hating every minute he had to be in here with her, talking to her, looking at her ravishing legs and lines and mini-skirt and reliving the moments they had shared together over and over again in his mind as if they were all he ever knew. "No one will even notice this thing sitting here at the end of the runway."

"Enough of the chit-chat," she said with obvious tedium. "What's this problem?"

"Didn't you read the reports?"

"Yes, I read the reports. Do you think I'm some kind of idiot? Like perhaps the president? What the hell's the big deal? It appears to me that things are working out just fine, except for the minor fact that your little slut is still running around. I could have sworn you said that she was dead before, Cav. I don't like being lied to, fat boy. Not at all, and that was one hell of a lie, letting me believe that Alexis Locke was dead and then helping her to rape and murder some innocence teenager. But other than that...."

"She's not a slut and I know that because I see one sitting right here before me and she's nothing like you." Anger passed over his face in a wave distorting it momentarily. He ground his teeth together unconsciously. She had never come out and said it before, had never confirmed directly her obvious intent to have Alexis killed off. But this declaration was the closest yet. He narrowed his eyes and looked at her, at the corruption leaking from her as strongly as the expensive perfume hanging in the air like a miasma. "Killing her was never part of the plan, Claudine. Never," he voiced quietly, somehow unable to speak louder, something in the air causing him to be subdued, a voice shouting in his mind to get out, to get away, to distance himself as far as possible from this person and her plans.

Claudine uncrossed her legs and leaned forward, her face a mask of amazement at his naivete. "Get real, Cav. What the hell good is she to us sitting in a house somewhere living off the government? She's ours to do with as we please. We created her and we can kill her off. It's not as if she's a regular person. For God's sake, you can't be that attached to her. She hates your guts and if you're thinking that you'll ever get your dick in her, then you're more of a dreamer than I thought you were." She laughed a short, derisive laugh making him feel ten centimeters tall, then leaned back again, her skirt climbing all the way up her legs and exposing the tight mound under her panties. "You're such a fucking fool. Did you really think that we, the government, would let you keep her to yourself? Let you hide her away and allow you to have her as your play-toy?" She shook her head in wonder, laughing again, the merriment spreading on her face until her eyes danced with twinkling sparks.

He noticed that she equated herself with the government, as the government. She had said we as if the government structure revolved around her bidding and he started to see for the first time the lengths to which she was willing to go to wield that true power in name and principle. He knew she had crossed the edge, that the power had eaten into her soul like a cataract and altered her very personality, turning her into a dangerous and potentially explosive threat to Cav's world.

"I'll not have you talk about her like that, Claudine. She's as real as you are, perhaps even more human. And for your information, I paid the U.S. back what they lent me to start the project so she isn't yours to do with as you please." He noticed ire cloud her eyes at that remark and was somehow satisfied that he had caused her consternation. "You can't just control her like a pet or a droid. It doesn't work that way and if you're not careful, she'll figure it out and you'll be the next one on her list of people to eliminate."

She tilted her head to the side and looked at him with a state of suppressed vexation. "My, my. Aren't we the chivalrous one. Protecting the virtuous maiden and all that. Perhaps you already have had your pleasure with her and she's wrapped that little dick of yours around her finger." She scanned his body a moment with obvious revulsion. "Though, for the life of me I can't imagine what she would find in you, if she could find it at all under all that fat." She stood, leaned on the desk and looked him directly in the eyes. "And *don't* threaten me, Cav. It's not good for the heart." She tapped the end of his nose briefly, then walked passed him to the bar and fixed herself a straight vodka tonic.

Cav flushed with outrage. He wanted to throttle her there and then, but knew that her bodyguards would shoot him dead before he finished. Shame, really. He turned to face her, watched her down the drink as she eyed him intensely over the glass rim.

"So you still haven't told me what the hell the problem is, fat little man. Speak. I await your words with eager ears." She walked around him back to her seat, running her hand along the waddle of his neck, enjoying every minute of her ultimate power over this man who had once held the world in his hands and then let it slip through them.

Cav had enough.

He had been the consultant for numerous presidents for more than sixty years, longer than Claudine had been in politics, almost longer than she had been alive. He was not about to take this crap from her. He refused to take it from the president so he was sure as hell not about to take it from her Chief of Staff. "Never mind," he said with an air of cool contempt, turning toward the door and walking toward it. "I've plenty of other governments in my back pocket. I don't have to take any crap off of you."

He could feel the heat on the back of his neck from her eyes as she screamed at him in that shrill voice of a virago. "Don't you DARE walk out on me until I say you can go! I'm not some little office lackey who you can walk all over, Cav. I'm the FUCKING Chief-of-Staff and you'll treat me with the respect that I deserve!"

"I am, you stupid bitch," he said as he turned his head back to look at her. "I never signed on for all this. I brought my agent onto this assignment because you said that it was a directive from the president and of global urgency. Not once was it discussed that she would be killed, sacrificed for some amoral principle that you've latched onto. I'm going to get myself as far away from you and this mess as I can, because I don't want any part of it. I only called you to inform you that events had taken a turn that I hadn't expected.

But you, you've gone far beyond what's necessary and I'm breaking from it clean, here and now. When you fall, and you surely will, I don't want to have any connection to you whatsoever. It's finished. I told you outside the Oval office that it was over between us, that you made an enemy out of me and I should have stuck with that, but my damn, fucking sense of fair-play got the better of me and I thought, as if it would have ever happened, that you might be grateful for some inside information and the opportunity to fix a problem, but that's obviously not about to happen."

She looked at him with a hostility sweeping the room in palpable waves. He half expected her to throw her glass at him or call her gun-toting body-guards and have them shove him out of the plane at 93,000 feet.

But then a smiled crept onto her face, dallied there a moment as if testing the waters and vanished again into a tight-lipped scowl as her eyes cooled slightly and she turned away from him and headed back toward the bar. "Cav, Cav, Cav.... Did you truly believe that that ruse of an assignment was real? You did, didn't you? I can't believe that you'd think that the government would be interested in the meaningless death of a few people who aren't even citizens and who aren't important in the least way. You used to be a lot quicker than that, Cav. A lot quicker. I guess your body isn't all that old age has effected, huh?"

His look of confusion melted into fury as he figured out what she was saying

His expression told her all she needed to know. "I've got a much, much bigger agenda to push forward, Dr. Cavalier, than your stupid assignment and insignificant agent. She was a loose cannon and *needed to be silenced*, that was all. This just happened to be the easiest way of doing it without raising your suspicion. But then, that's a moot point now anyway. God, you've become so damn, fucking stupid if you thought that I was actually interested in prissy Alexis Locke solving any meaningless riddle for me. What a fucking joke."

Cav shook his head. He refused to believe what Claudine was telling him, that he had failed to see through it. For now that he knew, now that she was laying it all out before him, it appeared all so transparent. She was after Alexis all along, wanted her dead so that Alexis could not interfere with Claudine's plans. Why had he not seen it before now?

She downed the second vodka tonic straight, playing with the glass on the bar top, holding it up on the edge with the tip of a finger and rotating it slowly as she stared at it. "And if you've got any ideas floating around in that minuscule brain of yours about telling your precious little whore about all this, just remember that you're in as deep as I am, perhaps even deeper. There's no way out for you, Cav. If I go down, then so will you, I've made certain of that, just like I've made certain that ninety percent of the congress will go down, literally, if I fail. It's just a little insurance package my friends have created as a back-up. Do you have friends like that, Cav? Because you just might need them about now." She walked the glass to the edge of the bar and worked it back and forth, alternating between balance and imbalance.

"And if little Alexis finds out, then you'll be the first person to feel her wrath down your throat, dearest Cav, because you're the one who told me all sorts of wonderful little tidbits about her and, basically, what the best way to deal with her would be. As far as she's concerned, I'm certain, you're as involved as I am." She let the glass tip over the edge and it fell to the floor and shattered into a shower of pieces sparkling in the carpet like lost jewels. She looked up at him and smiled cynically. "Just a little food for thought, Cav. Now, if that's all, you may go." The dismissal was caustic in its delivery as she looked back down at the bar and decided on what her next drink would be.

Cav stood his ground, staring at her with narrowed eyes burning like flaming embers, his fists clenching and unclenching in spasmodic jerks of rage.

"Are you still here?" she said without looking up, examining a bottle of thirty-year old Cognac. "Perhaps you'd like to enjoy the hospitality of my Secret Service boys? I hear they have great personalities."

Cav closed his eyes a moment.

She was not leaving him any choice.

He grabbed the door knob and pulled, walking out of the office and then the plane with an inner rage he had not felt in years. And it was directed mostly at himself for his complacency in this scheme that he knew, just knew from the beginning would lead to a cluster fuck par excellence.

He could hear Claudine laughing through the closed door.

*   *   *

São Paulo, Brazil
18 August 2085, 1335 hrs

When the hov violently hit the water, Ian was thrown into the cushioned back of the separator wall and temporarily stunned. As the water started to lap at his body, pouring in from the shattered windshield and broken doors, he came to. It was pitch dark in the vehicle and the pressure he felt from the water was intense. He tried not to panic, but found it difficult, the coldness of the water on his body like a giant sponge sucking the life energy out of him. He could not even see his own hand before his face and so had no idea how he was going to find Alexis and pull her to safety.

As the water filled in over his head and he took what might just be his last breath of air, he realized that he had one chance to save his own life and trying to save Alexis would not be possible. As in most situations of this type, when the survival of the individual is threatened and the rescue of another, even if it were a loved one, would cause the death of both, the mind jumps into a self-preservation mode forestalling anything but the survival of the individual. All animals have this instinct for self-preservation and Ian was no different. Those hardy souls who try to tell others that they, in the same situation, would react differently, would try to save the loved one before ever thinking of themselves have obviously never been faced with the decision, for it is a foolish person indeed who can say with certainty what they would and would not do when faced with death.

One can only know when one is face-to-face with such a situation, when one is caught in the middle of such a decision and death is staring you smack-dab in the face, daring you to save the other and in the process seal the fate of both.

It might not be what we would want to do.

It might not be what we would like to do.

But it is part of the animalistic instincts still dwelling deep within our souls, still compeling us to look at attractive women, to eat when we're hungry, to empty our bowels when they become full. To think otherwise and condemn the person who saved themselves but not their spouse, who retreats into their own world when faced with such a decision and instinctively saves themselves, is senseless. One needs only look at all the mothers, whose bond with her children is supposedly the strongest around, who abandon their babies when faced with death, who flee from the new-born as if from a fire when the black cowl of death bends over them and gives them a choice.

Is it morally correct?

Is that the question that should even be asked?

It is a strong person who can truly say that he overcame this innate trait and went against the grain. It is also a rare person. Ian raged at himself for his selfishness, but as the pressure equalized between the outside and the inside of the hov, his instinct for survival took over and he kicked the door open and swam out and to the surface, his body complaining all the way, his lungs screaming for air, his mind retreating into that world of justification.

He rationalized his decision by assuming that Alexis would have already escaped, that she was far superior to him in this type of thing and that he had barely saved himself. She would certainly be waiting for him above, most likely even had a boat standing by to take them to safety. But when he was pulled out of the water and into the small fishing boat by the stunned people who had witnessed the crash and come over to lend what assistance they could, he found out that he was the only one to have come to the surface.

He cursed himself for his selfishness as he lay in the bottom of the boat panting for breath, then made certain that they knew that there was someone else down there who needed to be saved. He was informed that the rescue teams would not be on scene with the proper equipment for such a rescue for at least another twenty minutes.

He stared up into the blue sky and the high cirrus clouds running before the wind and cursed himself again. He had been weak-willed enough to lose her once before and now he had done it again.

*   *   *

Alexis tried to brace herself for the impact she saw coming but realized at the last minute that that would be the worst thing she could do and instead relaxed a fraction of a second before the hov struck the water. A tense reed was far more likely to be broken by the falling rock than a soft one. She felt the airbags inflate, felt the crushing force of her body against the control panel. She felt two ribs crack, the bruise to her kidney, the cut across her face from the glass, the fracture to her wrist. The next thing she felt was water, cold and deep covering her up in an inky blackness so very, very empty. She had a moment, a fraction of a second of panic when the thoughts flashed through her mind that this was the end and that she was utterly alone and she didn't want to die alone.

Then her training took over, instinctively calming her down and beginning the procedures that would allow her to survive until rescue came, the rescue she was hoping Ian would send. With her legs trapped under the crushed control panel and with the cold seeping the very life out of her, the air in her lungs already beginning to wear thin, she knew better than to sap the last of her strength to try to force her way out. Instead, she relaxed and fell into the ancient Hindu meditative trance that would allow her to survive, that would allow her to shunt, to turn off all the organs that at the moment were not necessary for survival and transfer all the blood and oxygen to the brain, to the nerve center of the body and in that way preserve the life she had. Her pulse fell to almost nothing and then stopped altogether. With no air for the blood to carry to the brain, the energy to pump it was not wasted on the heart.

With her eyes open she stared into the blackness of the water and the hov and began to transcend her body, to rise to a higher plane where she could hold herself intact while waiting for her salvation. She saw lights; subtle, subdued lights sparkling around her as if through a curtain. She saw people and faces, images and events. The memory she had touched for that brief instant outside Ian's estate when she connected to the shadow woman came back to her in a rush of images that this time she could poke through one at a time and study, examine, and learn.

And learn she did.

She saw the future and its implications, the plan and its designs, the overall picture and the smallest details and then she lost it all in a sweep of colors and madness washing into a nightmare existence hinging on the one thing no one had foreseen. She saw the darkness of the vision, the utter despair and confusion, the ruthless culling of the weak and the dark, bitter result of the power that had come of such a simple idea, an idea that had its roots in righteousness and virtue. It was a future screaming at her for revenge, that called out to her, *I am wrong, fix me!*

And then the past began to push in, to make itself known to her in ever increasing waves of regret and aggression just when she was about to see what it was that had caused the utter darkness that was the future, as if that particular vision was denied her. The future was now supplanted with the past, with the men she had known, with the few women with whom she had been intimate in the line of duty, perhaps even in the pursuit of pleasure. She saw her past for what it was and it gave her a thorough beating. It was remorseless in its persistence, domineering in its veracity, punishing in its exposure. Her life was a morass of splintered pleasures and vanquished dreams and it beat at her ego remorselessly until all that was left was a slab of quivering nothing, nothingness like what she found within the shadow people.

Then all went black again in a vacuum tugging at her soul as much as the rescuers tugged at her legs and she slipped into the long, dark tunnel of truth that precedes all of our deaths.

When Jotak Davidson compiled his master-piece involving
the theories of Special Relativity, The Pauli Exclusion Principle and the
Kondo Space-Time Non-Continuous Symmetry Axiom, it was
heralded as the final word in time travel physics and was thought to have put
to rest forever the fantasy that time travel was a reality.
But then one must only look back to the time when
Ptolemy stated unequivocally that the Earth was the center of the universe
and how that was assumed to be the final word in that field to understand
where Davidson's Theorem fits into the greater scheme of things.

--- Taken from the lecture notes of
Nobel Laureate Hachii Toyoda
2175 CE

22

18 August 2085, 1400 hrs
São Paulo, Brazil

"How long has she been under?"
"The witnesses say at least twenty minutes."
"We have no pulse or respiration. Begin CPR."
Ian watched from a few meters away, a blanket draped around his shoulders as the medics began the procedures to bring Alexis back to the living. He was shivering with the cold but he didn't notice. People were talking to him, but he didn't hear them. All he did was stare at her life-less body, wondering why he did nothing to save her. She was thoroughly soaked, almost blue, her shirt torn off to reveal her delicate breasts, the equipment of the medics attached to her like an anemic octopus from the deep.
"Let's get her transported to the hospital."

An ambulance hovered over the sight, its glaring lights flashing in useless revolution as her body was transferred carefully, quickly, efficiently. A hand touched Ian, guided him to the med-evac but he didn't sense any of it as being real. Although he had thought he had lost her twenty years ago, had gone through all the grief and anger and had come to a satisfactory if not completely pleasing compromise, to see her like this was as if he were reliving the whole episode all over again.

He could not afford to lose her again.

He knew that he would not survive this time.

Questions were asked. Statements were given.

"We'll continue to work on her all the way to the hospital, Sir," a medic told him in sympathetic tones, but Ian heard none of it. "But I've never seen someone recover from an immersion this long, at least not in waters that weren't freezing."

Ian stared listlessly at her. He felt the ambulance move, watched the medics working with the full range of equipment modern medicine had to offer to bring her back, but nothing seemed to be working. Her skin had taken on that dull, lusterless look of death. Her eyes stared vacantly, the delicate color of the iris muted.

His chin sank to his chest and he closed his eyes to the oblivion of it all.

*   *   *

She could hear voices.

She could feel the pressure on her chest, the electric shocks meant to get her heart started again, the medicine being pumped into her body.

She could feel movement   Before her were two choices, two options both of which were completely viable. One was freedom and light. The other was bondage and darkness. She knew what each choice entailed, knew where each would lead her, what each would mean in the end. But when it came down to it, when the issue was pressed, when the pressure on her chest and the thoughts in her mind and the respirator over her mouth and nose all screamed at her to come back, the choice she made would didn't depend on any of it.

Her choice – did she really have a choice or was that just another illusion of life, perpetuated by the gods of fate who toyed with free choice as if it were a marble, sometimes rolling to one side, sometimes to the other? – was dictated by what she had seen in that brief, infinite glimpse of the future still echoing in her mind like a cannon-shot.

280

She chose the darkness, not because of any moralistic reasons or because of Ian or Cav or Claudine. She chose it because it was all she could choose. It was a choice forced upon her by her own destiny, linked to her mortal body like a thin, thread-bare cord left to burn over the candle of human infallibility.

She chose the darkness because it was within the darkness she would be able to find the answers. She rose out of the murkiness of the light as if into that realm of dreams, which clouds the mind with its reason and illogic and leaves us wondering if the dream is reality and reality the dream.

Alexis Locke awoke with a gasp, a long drawing-in of breath that was the last instinctual instruction to the lungs before the mind shut them down. The medics standing around her ready to declare her dead were shocked and took a moment to understand what had happened before they began the procedures to stabilize her. The looks of utter amazement on their faces from her revival shot between their eyes like ricochets. This one would be remembered for a long time.

No one had ever spontaneously recovered from clinical death.

*　　*　　*

Ian sat in the waiting area, staring at his hands clasped before him. He had a recorder sheet lying idly on the seat beside him full of unanswered questions blinking annoyingly that the hospital administration was expecting him to complete sometime in the next century, if not sooner. But his mind was not focused on the questions of family medical history and most recent surgery that the recorder sheet impatiently waited for him to answer. He heard the voices of the doctors and nurses around him, at the nurses' station, walking by in close consultations, all speaking of the astonishing recovery of the drowning victim, of her healed bones and body, of her blood work showing a chemistry and profligacy of nano-bots startling even the most advanced of the medical teams.

They spoke of DNA that was not normal, showing signs of tampering, altering beyond the trifle affairs used to correct birth-defects or prolong life. But he registered none of it.

His mind was focused on the attack back at his estate, the images he had seen moments before Alexis had pulled the stunned driver out and driven the taxi away.   What they had been, what Alexis had seen or sensed that had caused her to launch the taxi into a suicidal move was beyond his comprehension. He had never seen anything like that before and now Alexis was dead and he didn't understand how it had all come to pass, how he had become involved when for so long he had been able to remain above it, pushing her hurtful memories into the far corners of his mind and leaving them there to decay under the weight of time.

None of it made any sense.

When the doctor approached him, spoke to him of his female friend's miraculous recovery, it took him several moments to understand that he was speaking of Alexis, that she was somehow alive and the remainder of the doctor's words were drowned out in the rush of blood to his mind.

Alexis, by all rights, should be dead.

Her sudden revival and apparently unaffected body – the doctors found signs of recently healed fractures in the wrist and the ribs and absolutely no other damage from the impact into the water and the control panel crushing her legs that would have instantly killed anyone else – had been the most recent in a series of episodes he had witnessed concerning Alexis and this, more than anything else, convinced him that she was not the same lady he had known.

Even though he didn't want it to be, she should be laying on that operating table stone-cold dead, not recovering with nair a scratch on her. She should not be able to push guards across a room or deflect bullets. This Alexis he was with now was a different person, a different entity forced on him by those who wanted him to go insane. Either that, or she had hidden from him an entirely different side of her life during those torrid months when their love had obscured most everything else.

And it scared him. It scared him like nothing else before had ever done. Before he had joined Cav and his organization, Ian had heard the rumors about Dr. Cavalier and his experiments, heard the stories – for that was all they were to Ian – of the demi-humans Cav had created who had subsequently gone insane in the face of their own mortality.   He had also heard that the entire project had been shut down after the last of the creations had killed several people in a rampage of genetic modification. Ian had never believed any of it, had dismissed the rumors as the ramblings of people with nothing better to do than find fault with others, the horror and abomination of such an act as creating humans to be used as military slaves was just not something Ian thought happened in the real world.

But now, here in this hospital, in that cold, dark lake in which Alexis should have drowned, Ian was beginning to see the faint glimmers of a reality he was not ready to share.

To discover that Alexis, a woman he had loved more than he thought it was possible to love, a woman with whom he had spent so many exquisite nights, was in fact one of Cav's demi-humans, created for one thing, one thing only and it didn't just turn Ian's stomach but his whole world upside-down. The mere idea that someone like her existed in the world was an abomination. To think that he had slept with her, had loved her as much as any man can love a woman and not known what she was sent shivers down his spine and images of mutant off-spring careening in his mind.

Maybe Cav was not trying to protect Alexis when he sent Ian away but rather was trying to protect Ian from Alexis' spawn-created insanity, which was certain to manifest itself one night while they had sex and he would find himself dead, mutilated like the others who had been, unfortunately, involved with the original project.

A shadow moved over him and hovered. He grabbed the recorder sheet and brought if to eye level as if he were busy answering the profusion of questions that seemed senseless and somehow ironic to him now. "Sorry," he said quietly, as if being scolded for spilling milk. "I'll start on it right away. I'm still a little shaken from the whole ordeal."

"There's no time for that," the familiar voice intoned as a hand took the recorder from him and threw it onto the chair next to him. He looked up and into the sparkling eyes of Alexis, now dressed in the uniform of a doctor, looking none the worse for wear after having been clinically dead.

He narrowed his eyes as his brow furrowed, causing the lines of his age to wrinkle like little dirt road runnels on his forehead. "What ...?"

She reached down, took hold of his hand and pulled him up none too gently. "We need to leave here now, Ian. They'll track us down soon." Alexis watched for the nurses who she had sent away on some non-existent task. She didn't want anyone to see her rapid exit. There was already too much to clean up after this debacle and she had little time for the niceties Cav and his men used to perform when she had been compromised in such a glaring manner.

She had managed to clean out the main computer of all memory pertaining to her admittance and her peculiar DNA, the nano-bots, the bones healing in less than thirty minutes. The last thing she needed was her face plastered all over local news with headlines screaming about genetic mutants and such. It was enough that her every move was known, followed, anticipated by the shadow people. She didn't need common, ordinary people also trying to track her down for a reward or just to see the freak mutant.

She was not even going to think about the governments that would send their best people to kidnap and study her like some lab-rat for the rest of her life in the hopes of cloning her or creating off-spring with Ivan the studly or whatever. She needed to distance herself and Ian from this hospital, this city and move on to the next stage of her investigation. She knew she was close and as was mostly the case, when she got close to the answers, all hell broke loose around her.

"Who? What are you talking about?" he stammered out in confused half-sentences as she lead him out of the hospital and toward the public transportation station squatting but a mere twenty meters from the entrance. "How did you get out of there? Where did you get that outfit?" He realized that his questions were inane and not even close to what he really wanted to ask her but it was all his mind could produce at the moment.

He pulled her up short as the mag-lev train came into the station, the wind created from its passing blowing Alexis' hair about her face and giving her a cuteness that almost made Ian forget all his earlier doubts. However, images of her killing some poor, innocent doctor to get his jacket began popping into his mind like mini operettas and he was brought back to his initial abhorrence at her existence. "How the hell did you survive that crash?! You were underwater without air for *almost thirty minutes*. No human can survive that, and I emphasize the word *human*. What the bloody hell are you?!" His agitation had brought his Australian accent out in full force, his face to a fevered pitch of crimson, his words and sentences jammed together in a prolixity of words.

"I'll explain it all later, but for now we need to get as much distance between us and this hospital as possible," she retorted in even tones as the mag-lev train came to a stop and the doors opened to disgorge an excess of faceless passengers who shoved and jostled past the two who stood so inconveniently in the way.

"No," Ian stated flatly, refusing to move into the train. "You'll explain it all *now* or else we part company here and now. I've had enough of this crazy bullshit!"

She looked at him with confusion, as if he had spoken some language she didn't understand. She had thought that if nothing else, Ian would be happy to see that she was alive, not pissed about it and ready to throw a temper tantrum.

The flux of people entering the train began and elbows and hips bumped into them without apology as the normal passenger traffic rushed to get into the ever-crowded train.

"Just get in the damn train, Ian. I'm not in the mood for this and you don't want me to embarrass you, do you?"

He stood his ground, refusing to move from his position. "You're not the person I once loved," he said in reply, staring at her hard, trying to force her to say the words that he didn't even want to hear, having it vocalized more of a horror than the mere thought of her inhumanity.

Her face changed for an instant, softened for the briefest moment, her eyes betraying the emotions boiling down deep inside. Her usually logical and stoic voice shouted at her to leave him here if that was what he wanted, but she was more than aware that doing that would seal his death as surely as if she were to pulled the trigger herself. She had lived all these years thinking he was dead and to be thrown back together with him in this rapidly changing and surreal situation was beginning to fray her nerves. Her eyes hardened again just as quickly as they had become soft and a bitterness entered her eyes like lances.

She shoved him into the train. "Just get the fuck in."

The doors closed and the mag-lev shot off toward its next stop forty miles down the line, its express schedule taking it clear around the city in a little under thirty minutes. Ian sat brooding dejectedly on one of the cushioned seats, not looking up at Alexis who stood above him as if protecting, constantly scanning the passing landscape flashing by in a blur of distraction. She had no idea for what she was looking but it was far better than looking at the face on Ian, who had become more of a stranger than most of those standing around her.

When they reached the next station in mere minutes, she grabbed him as if he were an unruly child and dragged him out to the off-hand looks and derisive comments of those around them. Her face was set hard, her thoughts running a gambit of emotions, feelings, decisions she was actually having trouble correlating. She flagged down a taxi and they climbed in, or rather, she shoved Ian in to the amusement of the cabby.

"You can drop me off at my estate, Alexis. I've had enough."

She probed the driver's mind a moment, discovered the languages he understood, then answered Ian in Arabic. "I can't do that."

He unconsciously switched to the same language. "Why the fuck not?! What's it matter to you? You don't need me, that's obvious."

She looked out the window as she answered, probed for the presence of the shadow people who she knew were out there, waiting for her no matter where she chose to appear. She continued to stare out the window as she answered his questions. "They weren't after me, Ian. They were after you."

"Who? You mean the people who tried to kill us, who shot our hov down? Why the hell would they want to kill *me* all of a sudden? You've gone crazy is what you've done. Bloody crazy," he answered in exasperation, not believing anything she had to say.

"Because it only makes sense," she said laconically, wanting to use harsher language but losing all ability to project it at him.

"Well that certainly explains it all," he said as he crossed his arms and hunkered down further into the seat. "I'm so *fucking* glad that you made it so obvious why they're after me and not you."

She turned to look at him, saw that something else besides his brush with death was bothering him and probed his mind, hoping that perhaps in his agitation he had forgotten to block her out. He had not. She had taught him too well.

"You're the last person connected with the project you gave to Hart and Kido. You're the last one with the knowledge to get it accomplished. Since all the others have now been eliminated, then it only stands to reason that you're next. That attack back there at your estate, as if I need to remind you, was designed to kill you, not me."

He finally turned to look at her. "But why? I still don't understand how a project that hadn't even gotten started is causing this much trouble. None of this makes any sense to me, least of all how the *hell* you managed to survive in that lake for so long. As far as I'm concerned, you're not human. You may look human, but you sure as hell aren't! No human could have survived that and because of that I don't want to be around you any longer." His face screwed up into a perplexity of disgust. "I can't believe that I fucked you, that I shared your fluids for Christ sake! When's it going to start affecting me, Alexis? When do I start turning into some monster, some abomination? AND THE WHY THE HELL DIDN'T YOU TELL ME?!"

Now she understood. He was not worried at all about the assassins out to kill him. All he was worried about was that his former companion was not human. A smile crossed her lips a moment as if testing the waters, then vanished just as quickly. "And you wonder why I didn't tell you? Let me assure you, Ian, I'm quite human. Made from the same basic DNA as you are. Nothing special there. You're over-reacting, as usual."

"*Bullshit!* And don't tell me that's it all just training either! Don't insult me like that! You're one of Cav's mutants is what you are!"

The driver looked back at his fare, wondering why the man was so angry and how he could yell at such a ravishing lady. He muttered to himself that she could do far better than this guy as he turned back around but continued to sneak glimpses through the mirror.

"Lower your voice, Ian. There's no need to get excited," she said quietly, calmly. She had never expected this strong a reaction, though perhaps on

286

some sub-conscious level she had and that was why she never bothered to tell him the truth.   But then, the truth was not all it was cracked up to be. "This isn't the place for this discussion. We need to be worrying more about those assassins rather than what I might or might not be."

"And that's another thing," he rasped out in a harsh whisper carrying as well as his yelling had. "How the *hell* did those people know that we would be coming to my estate? How did they know that I had an estate here in the first place? No one knew it. No ... one." He drew the last two words out and enunciated them clearly to get his point across. "That estate is under a completely different name that has no connection to me whatsoever, none. There's no way in hell that someone could have both figured out that the estate belonged to me and that we would go there. What's going on here, Alexis? This isn't just a simple assignment and a simple assassination. For once in your damn, mutant life, be honest with me."

She looked back out the window again, then ordered the driver to stop as they approached a large, rolling, green park filled with tall trees sitting like lined up soldiers awaiting orders. They climbed out and Alexis lead Ian to a flowing hillock of short-cut grass looking rather life-less, moving constantly as she spoke, awaiting the feeling she knew would come of the shadows, of another attempt.

"No, you're absolutely correct. This isn't just a simple assassination. Nor is it a simple assignment." She was quiet for a while as they aimlessly wandered the hillock and the small dales dotting the park.

"Who are they, Alexis? *Who are you*?" he asked in a far calmer voice as he pulled her to a stop, disengaged his hand from hers as if he might catch something from her and stood with arms crossed, defiantly, standing back away from her.

She rose an eyebrow, not certain which question to answer first, and in the back of her mind not giving a damn about any of it. She had lived long enough without his presence in her life and this was not what she needed now. Not even close. "Those are both difficult questions and I'm not certain how prepared you are to hear the answers. Or how willing you are to believe them. Perhaps that's more important."

"Stop stalling and just spit it out, damn it!" he swore at her, a feeling of some type of life-changing event about to take place strong in him. He had always thought that he was an open-minded and strong man, but this was beginning to test his beliefs. He never thought he would react like this, but then it's a rare person, he knew, who can predict his actual reaction to stressful times.

She cocked her head to the side, ran her tongue along her teeth and rubbed her forehead. "Okay. If that's how you want it," she spit out tersely, knowing that he was not going to believe a word she spoke, and no longer caring either way. "The people who tried to kill us just now, who have killed off all the others whom Alex and Kido were involved with, are from the future. I saw it, as clearly as I'm seeing you right here before me."

He looked at her a moment as if she had gone stark, raving mad. "You've got to be kidding, Alexis. Jeez, do you think that I was just born yesterday?" His face was a mask of outrage and defiance at the gullibility she assumed he had. "I'm well aware of the Davidson Time Exclusion Principle and the Jotak Continuum Theorem. Time travel is impossible, Alexis. Every first year physics student is taught that. How stupid do you think I am?" He walked away from her and stopped near a large, gnarled oak brooding like an aged sentinel over the open expanse leading down to a small pond.

"I'm aware of the problems, Ian," she said to his back as she watched his muscles flex with stress, the light breeze filling the air with the freshness of late winter ruffling his hair delicately. "And I can't explain how it's possible, but I know what I saw. And I really don't give a *fuck* whether you believe me or not. Your disbelief, I'm sorry to tell you, isn't going to make me change my mind."

He spun around to face her. "And what exactly did you see and where did you see it? In the delirium of your near-death state?" He laughed too loud and abruptly. "Do you really expect anyone to take something like that as the gospel truth?" He shook his head at the gall she was brazenly displaying before him. "And I have news for you: I don't give a fuck either anymore. I don't need you anymore in my life and I wish to hell that you'd never come back. Cav was right, you know. You're just a user, a player, chew 'em up and spit 'em out and that's all you're good for. A quick fuck and then g'day to ye, Sheila. Maybe Cav programmed that into you also."

She narrowed her mouth until it was nothing but a prim line of control, took a calming breath to make certain that she didn't strike out and kill him in her anger at his words. She was well aware that she deserved most of them and killing him for simply stating the truth was not her style. She would stick to the explanations and leave the personal quips unanswered. "I saw it when I touched the mind of the leader of the assassins. I experienced it, the future I mean, through her. And how those in the future managed to get around the laws that we take as solid fact, I don't know. People used to think that the sound barrier was an absolute. It's not like physics doesn't change, doesn't adapt, doesn't evolve as we learn more."

The look of ridicule on his face made him look distorted and old. "And did you perhaps think that maybe she *wanted* you to think that? That maybe she was trying *hide* the true purpose of her existence."

"Yes, Ian. I'm quite well versed in these things." She was not used to having her abilities questioned in such a way. She was quite aware that making people think one thing when you really meant something else was a common trick in the mental arena of the telepaths. "What I tapped into was the core memory of that person, that part of the mind one can't just alter to fit a purpose. It was real, Ian. As hard as if might be for you to believe, someone from the future is trying to kill the project *you* initiated and all those who know about its existence. There's no other explanation. You said it yourself. How the hell did they know that we would be here, at this time, in this place?"

"Good intelligence," he threw back at her without conviction.

"Good intelligence my ass. They know where I'm going and where we'll be because, for them, it's already happened, it's all the past," she said without really understanding it either. "All they need to do is look back into the past and see exactly where we'll be at any given time and adjust their attacks accordingly. It's not all that difficult to imagine."

He took a few strides toward her, aware that she was keeping her distance and her temper at bay and thankful for small miracles, for otherwise he would be dead several times over. He peered at her face, looking for something in her eyes telling him that she was teasing him, making it up as she went along. But there was nothing to indicate that brand of deception. She obviously believed all she was saying and it was disquieting to him. Very disquieting. "You actually saw that they were after me, specifically."

"No. Not specifically. But you're the only one left and every other person I've talked to about this has ended up dead, so it just figures."

They stared at each other for what seemed like an eternity, then she sighed, pursed her lips and looked down at her shoes for what reason she had no idea. It was just something to do. "We should continue to walk," she stated quieter. "We make too good of a target standing around like this."

He laughed. "What's it matter? If what you're saying is correct, then what the hell does it matter whether we stand here or walk over there or strip naked and run into the lake?" He gestured with his hands in a bird-like animated way. "If what you're saying is true, then these fantastic assassins from the future know all about us and it's just a matter of time before they find us again, so what possible good does it do to hide from them? Tell me that?"

She looked back at him with the full intent of shoving his teeth down his

289

throat. "Well it's pretty obvious that they aren't all that efficient at what they do, otherwise you'd be dead already, asshole," she shot at him as she grabbed his arm and tried to get him to move. "And they apparently aren't all that interested in killing me, just the people I talk to."

He pulled his arm loose as if she were contagious. "Don't touch me!" he said through clenched teeth. "Don't...."

She stepped back, aware that he had seen and heard too much. "I'm not any different than the person you knew before, Ian. It's still me. It's still the same Alexis with whom you used to laugh with and cry and have night-long marathon sex with! I'm not some kind of monster, Ian! Damn you! I thought that of all the people, you'd be the most understanding."

"And that's why you told me as soon as we started getting serious, right? Fuck off, Alexis. Just fuck off and leave me alone." He looked at her sideways, as if seeing her for the first time. "And there's no way that you can ever convince me that what you can do is normal."

"What the hell's normal? You? Kido or my son?"

"Your son?" he said with bafflement. "Since when do you have a son?" Now he knew for certain that she had gone insane. Alexis Locke was the last person to ever have children, he knew that for a fact.

She felt them at that moment, coming toward Ian from all directions and a feeling of inevitability came over her like a comfortable blanket.

He noticed the look on her face change to one of alarm and looked around at the calm winter day. "What? What's wrong now? And what son are you talking about?" But as soon as the words left his mouth he knew to what son she was referring, the likeness he had noticed the first time he had been introduced to Alexander Hart now coming back to him in waves of substantial anguish breaking on his mind like the crashing surf. Of course he was her son. How could he have not seen it before?

But Alexis had already forgotten all that had been said, all the arguments and the harsh words spoken as she felt the presence of the huge object coming down at them like a summer stormcloud laden with rain. She looked up as her mind caught the mental images of the assassins moving out of the grass and the trees toward the area where she stood and stopping, watched.

What caught her attention was the sight of the crashing industrial hov as it veered out from behind the stand of stark, bare aspens, trailing fire and smoke. It had such a speed to it that she could not react in time, could not move one way or the other, the distance between her and Ian too great, the crash path of the massive hov too wide to avoid getting hit.

She saw in an instant of time what was happening, as if it all froze just so that she could feel the full impact of what was about to transpire and have time to think about it, to contemplate her inaction and inability to react, to save herself or Ian from the fiery death about to rain down from the sky.

But her mind did react despite her body's utter reluctance, as if something in her mind snapped and engaged, something long forgotten and hidden, tucked away for an emergency, given to her, perhaps, for this particular moment in time. She reached out mentally, found the mind of the leader of the assassins in that distorted trap of air and gravity waves and tapped into it in an obtrusive intrusion boring into her like a drill, the target completely unable to stop what was happening. She saw the future again, but this time she saw something she didn't expect.

You have seen too much, Alexis, the voice said in that frozen time between seconds hanging in the air like a suspended raindrop, the reflections from a thousand worlds gleaming off its surface.

And you've gone too far, Alexis replied. *I could kill you right now if I so choose.*

Yes... You definitely could, the voice replied with that even-tempered tone conveying confidence and certitude. *But you won't.*

The flaming hov moved closer to the position Alexis and Ian occupied, ground zero for the massive impact that would occur. Ian was running, screaming for her to do the same as the shadow of the vehicle descended upon them ominously.

Your confidence is misplaced, Alexis responded as she began to notice doors to the voice's mind closing around her, leading her to a memory Alexis didn't want to see. *All I need do is —*

I'm well aware of your capabilities, Alexis Locke. I share many of them myself.. But now is not the place for a discussion on what you can or cannot do, or will or will not do to me.

Alexis was beginning to realize that she was going to die, as surely as the crippled hov was going to crash. And she was damned if she was going to leave this life without exacting some revenge for the death of her son. *Say good-bye to all you know, lady*, she projected across the void becoming apparent between them, separating them not only in space but also in time.

Then the memory to which Alexis had been lead burst forth like an exploding snowball, spreading its coldness through her sense. She was shown a vision, a birth, a mother, a time in the future between now and then congealing in her mind like a catalyst. She saw herself giving birth, the joy on her face and that of the unknown man who stood beside her reflected in the eyes of the baby infant girl.

I find it difficult to accept that you could kill your own daughter ... Mother. Sorry, but the fate of the future is more important than any individual life. It was not meant to end this way, but fate is a fickle bitch.

Alexis was thrown into a tumble of contradicting thoughts pounding her mind like a jackhammer, slamming into her in the space between the seconds sitting on the edge of eternity like a fine-balanced razor, ready to topple off into oblivion with the touch of a hand, the speaking of a wrong word, the chance encounter with a rogue gravity wave. She saw her past and her future merge together into the present and in that instant, that finite instant of eternity sealing her fate with the impact of the flaming industrial hov into the soft grass as it ploughed its way through the stand of trees and into the small pond in a shower of scalding water, turning Ian Montana into an elongated smear on the side of the gouged out dirt track, her world changed forever.

As time reasserted itself and began to flow at the rate Earthlings were accustomed and her crushing death from above was certain, Alexis mentally grasped onto whatever she could in the mind of the voice with which she had been engaging and saw her one life-line, the one string of knowledge in the infinite set constituting the human mind and held on for all she was worth, knowing this was her only chance.

She felt a distortion wave pass over her.

For the briefest moment he felt the heat of the impact sear across her back in fiery pain never known before for, then the coolness of emptiness bathed her back in a sea of eternity. She felt disembodied, the entire scene before her of the hov slamming into the ground but a few meters from Ian frozen for an instant, the images of a thousand alternate realities flowing around her like a crystal ball. It was as if she were trapped in one of the old toys holding an entire scene confined within its see-through container, the slightest twitch sending the fake snow swirling in a sensation of motion concealing the whole world outside the container till all that was left was white.

And in that moment, Alexis Locke saw the stream of time flowing, its ripples and eddies wherein whole civilizations were trapped, its shoals and backwaters, its rapids and rocks breaking the flow into numerous branches weaving and spinning their way through space in a complex dance of consummate creation. She saw it all flow back together, saw that it was complete in its totality, infinite in its size, eternal in its conception.

It was here that Alexis Locke saw the secret to who and what the voice was and how it had come here, to this time and place. And Alexis knew a split second before her physical death how she was going to survive.

*Who knows what lies in the future, what
discoveries await us tomorrow or perhaps
next year or one-hundred years in our future?
Who knows whether tomorrow will produce such
startling discoveries that will change the very
foundations of what we call civilization? Who knows
whether we will even have a tomorrow?
Maybe that's why they say that the future is but a
darkness hovering over our past.*
— Mahrisa Pasha

23

19 August 2250,
0735 hrs (Colony Time)
O'Neill Colony *Einstein XXI*

"How did this come to pass?" the man asked as he reclined in his soft chair. He sat before the large expanse that was the majesty of the Large Magellenic Cloud in all its radiant reds and subtle blues, like a giant dew-bespeckled spider web in the first morning light, the panoply of stars sitting in space like diamonds embedded in coal dust shining forth in time-compressed glory. In another forty minutes, the globe that was Earth, in all its brown and gray dullness, would come into view, filling half of the force-field protected opening with its putrid reminder of humanity's feral past. It would certainly spoil the view.

The room itself was an enigma, filled as it was with relics of the past, few outside of the archaeological community would even recognize. Several antique globes sat scattered about in apparent random chaos, but a closer look by a discerning eye would easily pick out the precise pattern present. A small side table held a personal computer from the late 20th century that still, amazingly enough, worked. Various antique weapons as far back as 2000 B.C.E. adorned the walls in clusters of organization defying logic, the bows and arrows of the American Plains Indians grouped with the plasma weapons of the early 21st century. The lights illuminating the wall displays cast their oblique shadows on the floor and the ceiling in abstract patterns of criss-crossed superposition, the main lights dimmed and muted so that the full grandeur of the star-field seen out of the force-field could be enjoyed.

The female to whom he had posed his loaded question stood on the far side of the large room, her hands firmly clasped against her side, her chin held high, her chest out, the tight suit of the Colony Time Guards emphasizing her strong feminine lines. She stood almost two meters tall and appeared strong, the firm, toned echelon of her body in stark contrast to the delicate beauty of her face, the sparkle of her greenish-blue eyes under the short-cropped mat of dirty-blonde hair giving her the adored appearance of one of the sexual entertainment employees who worked the pleasure houses on the Colonies.

Her resemblance to her infamous mother was striking if not slightly disconcerting. But there was a sternness behind it all, a countenance brooking no opposition. She didn't suffer fools lightly and didn't countenance failure. But, ironically enough, that was what she was facing at the moment: failure. And worst of all, it was a failure on her part, the worst of the worst as far as she was concerned. To fail at one's mission was akin to not going on the mission in the first place, putting in jeopardy others who would have to pick up the slack and possibly get killed doing what she was supposed to have accomplished.

That was why she was standing at ramrod attention before Skre Finehair Yellowleaf, the Commandant of the Colony Time Guards, his disapproval radiating from him in waves of unmistakable anger. As First Adjutant to the Commandant and the finest of the Corps, she had been placed in charge of the historic mission of which she had made, in essence, a complete mess. It had seemed at first such a simple assignment, but then she should have stood by her own ground-rules and known that when indexing into the past, there was no such thing as a simple, straight-forward assignment.

She would not protest if the Commandant relieved her on the spot for her complete incompetence at her assigned task.

When the female didn't respond to his question, Skre Finehair Yellowleaf steepled his hands before his chin and let out an audible, pensive sigh filling the room with its trepidation. "It's not like you to remain quiet when a direct question has been put to you, Colonel Locke. This is ... disturbing."

She cleared her throat quietly, not really sure what to say that would explain her failure. Sometimes, no explanation was the best.

Skre Yellowleaf seemed to think otherwise.

He turned his chair now so that he faced the middle-aged female whom he believed to be one of the best he had ever seen, the latent abilities she was just now beginning to use effectively a clear advantage in their line of work. Skre was one of those leaders who liked to lead by example. He liked to get to know his warriors, know their problems, their emotions, their joys so that he could better understand how best to utilize them. He had gone on more indexes that anyone else in his command and yet he still felt that tinge of trepidation before each one, experienced that feeling of dislocation ruining many a career.

And he knew what failure was.

What he had before him was certainly not what he would consider failure.

He had large, sleepy, expressionless eyes of an off-gray color gazing out from beneath his bushy white eyebrows and deeply lined face, wherein sat his snub-nose and fat, puffy lips. His face was lean in its vertical height but held a hint of pleasure in its depths making one believe that he would, at any moment, burst out into spontaneous, ringing, joyous laughter. All this was topped by a shining globe of bare skin that, by his own choice, would remain hairless. His body was worn like an old pair of leather moccasins that have just become comfortable, his long years of service having taken their toll in more ways than he could remember.

Since the Colonists refused to use the pseudo-immortality that had brought Earth to its present state of amoral decline and dictatorial stasis, Skre showed all of his one hundred and thirty years, the remaining fifty or so left him like a weight sitting heavy on his broad shoulders.

Locke, on the other hand, had her mother's capacity to never look her age, the time-indexes and her inbred genetic superiority allowing her to look not more than the short side of forty for all her one hundred and fifty years of life.

"You have nothing to say for yourself in this affair?" he asked again, glowering at her from under his lowering brow.

She didn't move a muscle from her solid stance as her eyes stared off into the empty space beyond the force-field, daring not to meet his eyes. "Sir, I have no explanation, Sir." Her voice was tranquil and discriminating yet with a hint of underlying power rocking the very walls of the room.

He rose an eyebrow at her all too official and military answer. "Is this so? So then is it your understanding that the current situation we find ourselves in is of your doing?" His voice, even though quiet now in that elderly kind of way, echoed about the room and her ears like a sonic boom.

She shifted slightly as her right eyebrow scarcely twitched up. "It was my responsibility, Sir," was all that passed her lips.

] A smile crept into the far right corner of his mouth, dallied there a moment, then left as he leaned his head back and closed his eyes. "So then it's your understanding that all the unforeseen circumstances that could have possibly arisen during this particular index would also have been your responsibility."

She was not sure at what he was driving. If he was trying to make her feel even worse for the catastrophic screw-up she had allowed to happen, then he was doing a fine job. Otherwise, she was at a loss to explain his words. "Sir, I was in command, Sir. The responsibility to determine all possible factors leading to failure should have been thoroughly investigated before any move into the stream was undertaken, Sir."

She continued to stare hard at the dazzling display of the universe, neither seeing nor recording any of it, her eyes not focusing on anything and yet everything at once. "It is the Senior Controller's job to make certain that all permutations of the time index are accounted for. In this, I was negligent. You'll have my resignation on your desk in an hour." She hated lying to him like this for an event she had wanted, if she were to be honest with herself, to happen just as it did.

He was quiet for a moment, but the lusterless expression of his eyes had changed slightly to show a sparkle of humor. "Is this so...? Is this so...?" he repeated almost to himself as much as to her.

They both were quiet, her staring off with that professional look of detachment and paranoia, him with a glint of humor and confidence.

When he spoke again, his words were harsh yet somehow easy, like a chair that makes one sit up straight but feels right. "Have you ever heard, Meagan, of such a phenomena occurring ever before?"

The use of her first name caused her eyes to shift from the emptiness to his face sitting before her from across the room in a miss-mash of shadows making it impossible to see whether he was smiling or frowning.

"No ... No, I can not say that I've ever heard of an entity from the past latching onto a member of the Colony Time Guards and pulling herself to the future, Sir. It is, I am certain, unheard of."

"Till now," he added to her last statement, as if teasing her with her failure in an open display of satire.

"Till now," she repeated as if chanting her own penitence.

"Then if this is an aberration, an anomaly that has never been observed

296

before, how is it that you can hold yourself responsible for not foreseeing it beforehand?"

She blinked, narrowed her eyes at him at his statement that seemed to fly in the face of what she expected him to say.

He continued. "Your logic in this regard is faulty and it is in this that I find fault. Not in what happened during the time index. Do you understand?"

Meagan puckered her lips slightly, trying in vain to see the expression on his face. "Yes, Commandant," she repeated rotely, though she still felt an overwhelming surge of guilt for having let it all happen as it had, for wanting it to happen.

"Good," he said with a resounding thump on the deck as he rose and began to pace, his hands clasped firmly behind his back, his fingers intertwined and grappling with on another as if on their own volition. "At ease, Meagan. At ease."

She relaxed, the stiffness to her spine loosening to a more natural stance that made her curves stand out in the tight jumpsuit.

"Now that we have that out of the way, we must decide what it is that we are to do with our newly acquired visitor. As we have just logically concluded, this is an unforeseen development."

"Yes, Sir." Had he just decided that she had done nothing wrong? She must have missed something in the conversation.

"Is she well, your mother?"

Meagan frowned at the use of that word, the look of perplexity and restlessness on her face making Skre smile.

"She does know that she's your mother, doesn't she?" he asked with a raised eyebrow as he stopped for a moment in his pacing.

"Yes Sir, she's aware that she's my mother, or will be my mother. And she is doing as well as can be expected given the circumstances, Sir."

"Good, good." He continued his pacing. "Have you any idea how she was able to come to our future? Any ideas at all? This could prove, perhaps, to be a significant problem for us. If the United Earth Forces catch wind of this, it could be a giant step backward."

Meagan barely shook her head. "I've been unable to come up with a viable path for her to have used. I believe that we greatly under-estimated her capabilities and tenacity, Sir." Could he tell that she was lying? Would it really matter if she told him that she wanted her mother to come here rather than die, that although it was a separate past, a distinct time-line, it was still her mother and despite all the faults, still her flesh and blood?

He smiled at her answer, large and bright, though it was lost in the shadows and hard for Meagan to tell. "Yes, yes, this is certainly true. You should feel a sense of pride in her accomplishments so far. It's a rare individual who can out-think both you and me."

"Yes Sir," she said more as an automatic response than anything else. Pride was not the foremost of the thoughts vying for prominence in her mind. Pride was certainly not a word she would use to describe her feelings toward the woman that was her mother, if one could even use the word beyond the biological connection.

"I would like you to speak with her, with the intention of discovering how it was possible for her to achieve what our esteemed scientists have been telling us over and over is a physical impossibility."

"But then until ten years ago, it was held as a firm scientific fact that time travel was a completely impossible occurrence, a fundamental violation of the laws of the Universe," she said without a hint of humor on her charming face. "I suppose that it's not all that inconceivable that what we have experienced here is a phenomena more common than we could ever dream of, Sir." Why she made this statement, she didn't know. She normally didn't speak this much in Yellowleaf's presence and she certainly never advanced opinions of her own.

"Very astute, Meagan. Very astute. This is a possibility." He now walked up to her and she finally caught a full look at his face as he emerged from out of the shadows. She breathed an inner sigh of relief as the she saw that his face held that look of childish inquisitiveness to it indicating that he was not angry.

He laid a gentle arm on her shoulder. "Now go and talk to her. I'm certain that she's rather confused and disoriented at the present. Find out what you can but don't push her too hard." He patted her on the cheek as he had always done for the hundred years they had known each other and gave her one of his large, cheery smiles. It lasted but a moment before his face set back into his more somber expression and he turned from her to walk back to his desk, the comm-link beeping for attention.

"Commandant," he computer voice announced as he approached the desk. "General Oli Gudbjartsson is here to see you on an urgent matter."

Skre frowned and his face seemed to become even more wrinkled and seemed to age several years before her eyes as he looked up at her with that expression of regret for having answered the comm-link. "It's always urgent. Let him in." He placed his hands on the small of his back and pressed firmly as the door behind Meagan opened and a tall, bulk of a man stepped into the room.

Meagan came to attention and saluted, then turned to step out, not wanting to really be in the same room as the domineering general. She was not that lucky today.

"One more thing, Meagan," Skre said as he looked out into space and the Large Magellenic Cloud once again. "Perhaps it would be best if you were not to tell her too much at the moment, at least until we can be certain what we are dealing with here. What side she leans toward, if you see what I mean."

"Of course, Sir."

The door closed behind her, leaving the general and Skre in the room alone. Neither said anything for several moments, the tense silence settling in the room like a fine layer of dust, coating everything it touched.

"What have they taken this time?" Skre finally asked as he sat in his chair, not having looked at nor acknowledged the tall, powerful general yet.

Oli Gudbjartsson could have easily passed for a Viking, his rugged Nordic looks, long flaxen hair tied into a pony tail with two, long, thin braids ending near his pectorals, and an expression of constant suppressed rage just beneath the surface giving him the robust flair of a time long past. It was only offset by his bright sky-blue eyes and jovial mouth.

"The mining colony on Io has been lost. Although the defenders managed to destroy the majority of the heavy equipment and supplies before they were over-run, it will be felt deeply. We get much of our resources from there." His voice was succinct and rich, filled with thousands of years of tradition and a deepness penetrating one's lungs and shaking them whenever he spoke. It was a rare individual who didn't cower in fear when Oli became cross and raised his voice to the pinnacle of anger he was capable of producing.

Skre steepled his fingers under his chin again as he stared out blankly through the force-field, watching the drama of the universe play out before him in subdued hues of time. "Does Mahrisa know yet?"

"I came to you first."

"I thank you for that,"

There was silence again as the general stood casually in the beam of light that always seemed to illuminate the few meters away from the doorway, waiting for the next words from the Commandant he knew were coming. They had been at this game too long, had worked with each other too extensively for Oli to not know what was coming next, what the response would be.

Skre randomly picked a nut from the cashew-filled bowl on his desk and began to slowly, methodically chew it. "I will take the appropriate measures."

"As always," Oli said as he nodded once, curtly and turned to leave. Then, as if an after-thought, he paused. "And what of the woman? The one from the past?"

Skre popped another cashew into his mouth as he answered softly, so softly that Oli had to strain to hear the words. "I believe that she will come in very handy. Very handy indeed."

*   *   *

Alexis sat on the plain, white bed that, along with the desk and table, were the only furnishings in the spartan room in which she had awoken. She had no idea where she was. For some odd reason she could not quite grasp, she had no idea when she was either, her usual impeccable sense of time dormant, or perhaps confused. She was not sure which.

She felt un-whole, as if some part of her was missing, not attached. It was the same as the feeling she sometimes felt when she lay out on the warm summer days in the vast rolling meadows behind her cabin and reached out to touch the hawks and eagles flying so high and peacefully and in that moment of mental contact, felt herself separate and apart, as if she had left the greater part of her back on the flower-strewn grass.

So it was now, if she had somehow latched onto a small portion of the future and in so doing had left the greater part of herself behind, somewhere. The world that was now around here, now presenting itself to her visual simulation, seemed distorted to her, distorted and blurred, just like the assassins had appeared to her. She felt here but not here, trapped somehow between two places at once and in that trap, unable to see either world clearly. In the few hours she had been awake and sitting in the white-washed, windowless room, however, the feeling had subsided somewhat and she had grown used to the distortion, or at least as used to it as one could get.

Her mind felt quite clear, clearer than it had in a long time and she found that very strange. She tried to think back to what had happened right before the industrial hov had crashed into her and Ian. The pang in her heart she felt at his death, a death she had seen close up and yet been unable to prevent, was intense and yet almost non-existent, as if it had happened in another time, another world and meant nothing here, in this room, in this time, vacillating back and forth between grief and indifference. But the events leading up to the crash of the hov seemed to be a blur to her, a jumbled moment shrouded in some type of fog she could not penetrate. How she had ended up here in this room, on this bed in this light, almost see-through robe she wore was a complete mystery, as much so as where she was.

It certainly was not Earth. The gravitational field she felt tugging on her body was not nearly as strong as Earth's. It was much more like what she had felt on *Stargazer I* and that most likely meant she was aboard either a Colony or a starship, both situations not very conducive to escaping. She was not yet convinced that she was being held prisoner. The door, of course, was locked and even had a null-field of some sort around it preventing her from reaching past with her mind or even pushing it aside in order to get out.

But this room didn't speak to her of prison. She had been in a few during her life and knew that they all had that something about them that spoke to the mind of confinement, of a physical as well as mental immurement. This room had none of that. This room spoke of relaxation and peace, of a friendship transcending the mere physical.

But then again, it might just be the white color.

She sat now on the far corner of the bed, her back against the wall and her knees pulled up close to her body, feeling the null-field around the door subside. With it came a plethora of emotions flooding her mind as she had opened it up completely in an attempt to find a connection with something living and she had to close down quickly else short-circuit her mind in a blaze of odorous emotions. She was able, however, to sense the inescapable presence of a person on the other side of the door, standing there alone. It was a presence she knew all too well.

It was her supposed daughter.

That was another of the problems plaguing her mind as she sat alone. That this woman believed she was indeed Alexis' daughter was not the problem. That she looked like Alexis, talked like her and even, in an odd sort of way, acted like Alexis all pointed to the fact that she was indeed her daughter. The only problem with that was Alexis had no other children besides her son, who was now dead. So how this woman could claim to be her daughter had stumped Alexis for some time. Then Alexis had realized that this woman was from the future and thus it was more than likely that Alexis had not yet given birth to her and thus knew nothing of her.

This, however, raised a whole new set of questions, the first one being that if Alexis was now here, in the future and had not yet had her daughter in the past, how it was possible that she could have had her at all. Would not her death under that hov, if she had even died at all, prevented her from having a daughter? And if she were unable to have a daughter, then this woman who claimed to be her daughter should not exist at all. It had made her head ache to think about it too much and so she had stopped.

But now the woman was standing outside the door, preparing to come in and perhaps, just perhaps, Alexis would be able to get some answers, though she was not certain if, like Ian and his discovery of her real identity, she wanted to know any of it.

The door opened and Meagan stepped in, shutting it behind her. She stood by the door for a while, just looking at Alexis, who didn't move from her position on the bed but just stared right back.

Alexis was the first to speak. "You certainly look like you could be my daughter. You have the face down pat."

"I had a good gene pool to work from," Meagan replied in subdued tones. This was the last place she wanted to be, the last person to which she wanted to be talking and it showed in her eyes. What if she were unable to carry it off? She had so far gotten away without Skre figuring it out, but her mother was far more intelligent, more intuitive and the chances were far greater that Alexis would see right through it all and call Meagan's bluff.

Alexis picked up what she thought was hate from the first moment the woman called Meagan stepped into the room and although Meagan's mind was completely blocked off, the emotion of hate and reticence was clearly visible to even the most obtuse person.

"When were you born?" Alexis asked, trying to pump her for information in a slow, logical path. If she were indeed her daughter, then Alexis would have to be very careful in the approach, for her daughter might just have the same mental abilities as herself and in that was a danger far greater than she had ever faced before. Besides, asking questions right off might just throw this Meagan off her game and transfer the pressure away from Alexis.

Meagan crossed her arms over her chest, her breasts slightly larger and fuller than Alexis', the nipples more pronounced. "2095," was all she wanted to say.

"Any particular day" Alexis asked with a slight trace of sarcasm. "Or can I just pick one?"

"Too much information, can be harmful to you and can alter the time stream. That must be avoided at all costs."

Alexis tilted her head slightly as an acerbic smile came to her eyes. "Don't you think it's a little late to be worrying about that? From what I'm gathering just in these few minutes, I'm not supposed to be here. Come on, it's just a date. What harm could it do?" Alexis could tell that this Meagan was not going to budge on that one as they stared at each other, both of their right eyebrows raised like mirror images of the same entity.

"Okay, would your name be too much to ask for then, or do I just call you daughter?"

"Meagan. Meagan Loc..." She stopped as she realized that her last name was probably a little needless.

"That's a pretty name. I've always liked it. But then, I probably gave it to you, huh?"

Meagan flashed a venomous glare as she pursed her lips. "Get up. I'm going to take you to get something to eat and some clothes to wear apart from that robe."

Alexis gave her a half-smile. "And if I refuse?"

"Why would you do that?"

"Tell me why you hate me so much?" Alexis asked out of the blue.

"Is it that obvious?" Meagan answered as she opened the door and indicated for Alexis to exit.

Alexis stayed put. "It is now."

Meagan frowned for a moment. She had walked into that one. She would have to be much more on guard around this one. It was not every day she met someone with a greater mental power than herself. "It's not important, nor is it anything that you need to worry about. Please?" She asked as she again indicated with her arm for Alexis to get up and exit the room, "We need to talk."

Alexis uncurled her legs and placed her feet on the ground, the robe revealing more than even Meagan had at first suspected, those who designed hospital gowns not having advanced much in their art over the last two hundred years.

"It's important to me," Alexis said as she stood slowly. "If you're indeed my daughter, and at the moment I'm still not convinced of it, then it certainly would be my concern that you hate me. I must have been a really suck-ass mom. I suspected as much. It's one of the reasons I never had kids."

"I don't hate you, per se," Meagan responded with a hollow tone, even doubting her own voice.

"Then what is it?"

"It's..." she hesitated a moment, not certain what her mother was trying to accomplish but certain that it was not for anyone's benefit but her own. "It's nothing. Can we please go now? I do have other things to do today."

Alexis looked down at her body, at the robe barely covering her, then back up at Meagan from under her eyebrows. "Is this the way people dress in

303

your time? It seems a little ... revealing."

"It's to keep you from trying to make a break for it," Meagan said, the lie flowing off her tongue with such ease she actually felt a pang of guilt at having told it.

"Oh really?" Alexis said with a little laugh, her bare feet on the lukewarm floor tingling with the distortion she felt emanating from her own body. "Then I'd say that your intelligence is a little faulty in that department if they seriously believe that not having any clothes to wear would keep me from trying to make an escape." And as if to prove her point, Alexis undid the sash and let the robe fall to the floor, leaving her now completely exposed. She smiled at Meagan and then walked passed her into the corridor.

Meagan could not believe that her own mother had just done that. But then, perhaps she could. The mother she had known was not a slave to modesty or to the feelings of those around her. She was, in fact, a rather dastardly bitch who would stop at nothing to get her point across or win an argument and this little stunt fit right into that image. It really didn't matter much anyway.

Meagan shook her head and followed. "You can't just walk around here naked," she said in as calm a voice as she could manage, the guards at the end of the hallway already getting an eyeful of the ravishing beauty walking toward them.

Alexis hollered back over her shoulder as she stopped before the guards and gave them a full, half-cocked smile. "Are you coming, daughter dearest? I really don't know the way to the chow-hall and I might try to escape, naked and all."

*   *   *

"Tell me how you think you got here?" Meagan asked as she watched Alexis eat her fill in the small yet comfortable room in which they now sat. Meagan had taken the hint of her mother's naked roam through the corridors and she now wore a loose fitting jump-suit, enjoying her meal immensely. They were the only people in the room and Meagan felt odd sitting here with a woman who had been, in her time-line, dead these last fifty years. She had never believed in ghosts, but if they did exist, perhaps this was what they were. Time-travelers thrown into a future where they didn't belong, forced to cope with the loss of all they once knew.

Alexis answered in-between bites, not bothering to look up. "That all depends on where here is."

304

"2250."

Alexis stopped eating for a moment, cleaned her mouth off with a napkin and leaned back. "That's a fair bit into the future, I'd say." She was beginning to suspect that, contrary to her earlier supposition, she had not been brought here on purpose. It was becoming even probable that perhaps her coming here had been an accident, a completely unexpected result of something Alexis had unwittingly done. That Meagan was even asking about it told Alexis a lot.

"Yes. It is. Now, if you could please remember everything you did to get here, it would be of great importance."

Alexis started to eat again, cutting into the flounder that fell apart like butter and enjoying the taste explosion in her mouth as it melted on her tongue, the mingled flavors of garlic and dill in perfect ratio. "My compliments to the chef on this meal. It's really quite good."

Meagan frowned again. This was not getting anywhere fast. She should have expected that her mother would be as stubborn as she was. Such things usually were passed along, usually unknown to the parent. "I'll pass on the compliments. Now, can we please get back to the issue at hand?"

"Oh yes. How I got here. Well, if you don't know, then how should I know?" She looked around, waving her food-filled fork about as if to emphasize the point. "This isn't even my time, my experiences. Hell, 2250? I'm dead already. You're the one who should know what the hell is going on."

"That's just the point, damn it," Meagan said, letting her temper get the better of her. "You don't understand what's going on here. We need to know if this was an accident or if it's something that can be repeated, that's possible all the time."

"Why is it important?" Alexis countered as she tasted the asparagus in cream sauce and found it delectable.

"Do you always answer every question with a question? I don't remember you being this way."

"Really?" She looked at this woman, her daughter, with a sarcastic sneer. "That's funny, 'cause I don't remember you at all." She eyed her daughter a moment, then went back to her eating. "I'll ask again. Why is it so important? And while we're on the subject, what the hell is all this about anyway? Why were you trying to kill me? What's that all about? Was I that bad a mother that you decided you needed to kill me off before I even gave birth to you? Is that the way things work in the future? You just go back and kill whomever it is you want, whoever pisses you off? And then you expect

305

me to just gush forth with whatever it isyou want to know after what you've put me through? You've got to be kidding. My daughter would be a little more perceptive than that, I would think."

Meagan stood and began to pace, an annoying habit she had picked up from Skre and which she wished she could shed. Just like she wished she could shed this woman who was going to be nothing but trouble, despite the other Meagan's assurances. "I can't tell you very much. I've been instructed to keep the flow of information to you as tight as possible, and as one-sided as possible."

"You mean you aren't the one in charge around here? What a pity. I would expect more from a daughter of mine," Alexis said as she drank down the last of the water, then looked toward Meagan for more. If her supposed daughter wanted to play rough, then Alexis was more than ready for a showdown.

Meagan refilled the glass and looked down at the lady who she was beginning to find more annoying than the real mother she remembered in this time-line. "We weren't trying to kill you."

"You could have fooled me," Alexis said as she pushed the empty flounder plate aside and reached for the lobster dish. "And what about all the others you so conveniently killed off? Were you also not trying to kill them?"

"That was different. Their deaths were the sole purpose of the assignment. They needed to be taken out of the time-line, for the safety of the future. They were, to be brutish about it, expendable."

"I see," Alexis said as she cracked the lobster shell open and dug into the rich, white meat of the crustacean. "Expendable? Very interesting. And who decides whom in the past in expendable? You leave a guy like Hitler alone and kill people like Kido and Dr. Dumvo." She eyed Meagan again in-between bites and saw that the woman was getting upset, was being pushed to the limits. Good. Let her squirm a while and see what it feels like. "So now we're getting somewhere. Tell you what, daughter let's play a little game here, okay? You tell me something I want to know and then I'll tell you something you want to know. How's that sound?"

"It doesn't work that way. And if you're having trouble figuring out why you're not getting full after all the food you've eaten, there's a reason behind that," Meagan threw in as a teaser, hoping to get Alexis to become a little less stubborn, get her off the deaths in her time-line and back to the main purpose of this discussion. Despite the fact that Meagan was undoubtedly the most qualified for this, she cursed Skre for giving it to her. This was opening far too many old wounds.

Alexis looked up with a big chunk of lobster stuck on the end of her fork just outside her open mouth. She put the fork back down and narrowed her eyes as she studied the form of her daughter pacing back and forth. "I'm listening..." she said, waiting for the answer to the question forming in her mind about the same time as Meagan had vocalized it. Here she had been eating for almost thirty minutes straight and yet she felt as hungry as ever, the food going down and not making her any fuller.

"I thought the game was that first you tell me something I wanted to know," Meagan countered. She was not a slouch when it came to mind games. She had, she supposed, her mother to thank for that.

"I thought you said that it didn't work that way."

"My house, my rules."

Alexis looked at Meagan and then smiled. "Okay. Not bad. I'll give you that one." She wiped her mouth with the napkin, pushed the plate away from her and leaned back. "I'm not sure how I got here. All I know is that I saw that hov coming down and knew that it meant certain death and so I latched onto whatever I could mentally."

"And..."

"And... You're cheating now. It's your turn."

Meagan stopped pacing and looked at Alexis as she leaned back in her chair. "But you didn't tell me a damn thing. That part I already knew."

"Sure I did. You just weren't listening and that's not my fault. Now, what is this about the food and not getting full? I know it's not poisoned, I can sense that much."

Meagan saw that she was not about to win this one and gave in, but only for the moment. "The food isn't really there. It's all holograms, an illusion." She looked about the small room and motioned the walls with her arms. "This room, this table, what you're tasting is what your mind wants to see, wants to understand. That's why it tastes so good to you. It's all the good things that you've eaten all your life coming back.

Alexis blinked. "I don't follow. I can taste it and touch it. See?" She picked up the lobster piece off her fork and threw it at Meagan. It never hit her. It simply disappeared as it neared Meagan's body. Alexis looked at the spot where the lobster should have fallen to the floor, then back at the table full of food. "Okay. That was different."

"You have to understand the intricacies of time and how it's possible to index into the stream and out again," Meagan said as she made the entire table of food disappear with a single thought.

Alexis raised an eyebrow. She felt the mental projections of her daughter and was impressed, as well as greatly confused. She usually followed explanations as if she were the one giving them, but what was happening around her now gave her pause. "Go on, you've got me intrigued now,,

"You aren't really here. You're mind is, that's for certain. But as for your physical body, it's not."

"Then where the hell is it?" Alexis asked in shock as she looked down at herself and found it difficult to believe that what she was seeing was not real. She even touched her thigh and found the normal resistance to flesh and muscle.

"In order for you to understand this I'll need to give you a quick lecture on the how and why of time travel as we know it." Meagan was well aware that if Skre ever found out that she told Alexis what she was about to explain, he would blow his top. But the way Meagan figured it, her mother would have to be told eventually and better to hear it now and allow her the time to digest it rather than later when time would be at a premium.

Alexis leaned back, wondering if the chair was real or not or whether she was going to fall over backward. When she hit the seemingly solid form of the metal, she smirked at her own paranoia. "Aren't you breaking some rule or other concerning how much I know by telling me this? If you can't tell me a simple thing like the day you were born, then I find it hard to believe that you can tell me how to time travel."

"The date of my birth and the fundamental mechanics of time travel are two rather different concepts. One directly affects you and decisions that you might or might not make leading up to that date. If I tell it to you, you might decide to do something to prevent the birth and that we can't have. Time travel theory is just general information that you really can't do much with your present state." Meagan gracefully sat down on the one chair in the room that was actually real and took a deep breath as she plunged in. "Knowing the day that I was born gives you a good indication of the day that I was conceived. As such, it can alter the way you act during that time and inadvertently change things. Do you understand?"

Alexis noticed that Meagan's tone had changed ever so slightly, the hostility that had been so vibrant toned down a notch. Why it was, Alexis didn't know but it was a nice change. She was certainly very curious as to why her daughter held such animosity toward her. Was it possible that she was taken from Alexis also, like Alex had been taken from her at birth? Had Alexis turned out to be a bad mother? That was most definitely a possibility, though one on which she didn't want to dwell. As for time travel and knowing the date she conceived a daughter in the future, that was straining her gullibility greatly. But she might as well play along and see where it got her. "I suppose that makes sense."

"Okay, then listen closely because I'm not going to repeat myself. The major problem that, until about ten years ago, those who believed in time travel and who wanted to devise a method to implement it faced was that they were tied to the physical world. They were always trying to move physical objects into the time-stream, whether it be a body or an apple or a machine or whatever. Because of this obsession, the concept of how time travel actually works eluded man for far longer than it should have.

"Time travel is impossible if one is talking about moving physical objects from one point to another. At least it is for us at this time. It just doesn't work that way. The key came accidentally, as happens with most great discoveries. And ironically enough, it was a truth the ancients had known all along, that they had been telling us since the Hindus and the Buddhists and all those so-called `Eastern religions' first came along. The key is the mind. Time travel is a *mental process*, basically transference from one time to another using nothing but the mind. It's gaining access to a higher plane of existence, then once in that plane, recognizing the existence of the time-stream and slipping into it, very much like stepping into a river and letting it take you where it will.

"And as with a river, it is very difficult to work across the current and almost impossible to work against the current   It's why traveling to the future has yet to be accomplished."

"Except for me."

"Except for you. You're beginning to see?"

Alexis was indeed starting to understand more now about why her future daughter wanted to know so much, was so interested in how Alexis had gotten here to the future. They were incapable of doing it themselves and they thought she held some unforeseen answer. "So what happens to your physical body while you make this astral trip?"

"We have stasis beds in which we lay while we make our indexes and in this way our bodies are protected, though one can, if an emergency presented itself, project without the protection of the stasis beds. The only problem is that if something were to happen to your body while you were in the time-stream, you would be lost in the stream forever without a base to go back to. Your body represents what you might call a home, an anchor to bring you back to your reality. Without it, you're lost, forever.

"This actually happened a few times at the beginning of the experiments, during the always dangerous trial periods. Those poor, unfortunates are still trapped in the stream, cursed to forever more wander time. Although I suppose that it could be rather interesting if one looked at it that way and didn't mind living just as a mental projection."

"So where is my body then?" Alexis was beginning to see a problem forming here that directly involved her and she didn't like the direction of the outcome.

"I was just about to get there. Your presence here, in this time-stream, presents not only a problem but a very interesting quandary. As far as we can tell, your body was crushed along with that of your companion when that Industrial hov crashed into you."

Alexis interjected. "You guys sent that, didn't you? That was your doing, the crash I mean, to kill off Ian. But something went wrong. I wasn't supposed to be there. That wasn't foreseen, was it?"

A smile corralled itself in the corner of Meagan's mouth. "You're correct, to an extent. But we're getting off the track. Let's discuss one concept at a time here or else you'll end up more confused than ever,"

But Alexis didn't want to stay on track. She saw that there was a reason Meagan wanted to stay off the subject of Ian and the deaths of the others; of Alexis' son's death and her own under the crushing weight of the industrial hov. And if there was one thing she had learned, it was that when someone didn't want to talk about an event, there were usually good reasons and it was within those reasons that the answers for which was searching lay. "I really don't care about what you want, my dear. Answer my questions or you'll never learn how I got here and thus you'll never learn how to go to the future, which is what you're after, isn't it?"

Meagan had to reconsider her mother's intuition. She was quite capable of understanding what was going on, even though she was rather far off the mark. There certainly were those who would love to have the ability to go to the future, the United Earth Command topping that list, but it was, at the moment, the least of the Colony Time Guard's problems. "Actually it's not, though that would prove to be interesting to certain people. What we really need to know is if it was an accident, unrepeatable, or an event that we've somehow missed in our theories and should be looking for, because if it is a common event, we need to know about it first, in order to develop counter-measures."

Alexis saw that Meagan was just at the edge of telling her too much and was being very careful. If Alexis went about this the correct way, she might be able to unwittingly force information out of her that would be useful, because right now she was quickly becoming swamped with concepts the likes of which she never thought possible. It was all rather confusing to an extent and one of the things she so hated was to be confused. Confusion usually leads to mistakes and then to death. Well, perhaps it was a little too late to worry about the death part, but she still hated being confused.

"Now this thing about my death," Alexis continued, her mind switching rapidly between concepts. "You just said that those whose bodies die while they're in the time stream are trapped in time and can never get out, correct?"

"Yes."

"Then how is it that I'm here and not trapped?"

"That's the problem. We don't know," Meagan said as she spread her arms out in a gesture of puzzlement. "According to all the theories we've postulated and proven correct throughout the ten years we've been doing this, what you've managed to do is impossible. Not only do you not have a body to base out of, but you should not have been able to even index into the stream in the first place. You don't have the training or the techniques. It should never have happened."

"And yet I'm here."

"And yet here you are."

Alexis looked down at the body that certainly looked like hers, then looked back at Meagan again. "But then whose body am I occupying now. It certainly looks like mine."

"What you're seeing, what I'm seeing and the guards certainly saw when you paraded naked down the corridor, is the mental projection of what you believe your physical body looks like. You happen to have a very powerful mind and can project, unconsciously obviously, what you want others to see of you. Normally, when we index into a time-stream, the people who actually live in that time-stream are incapable of seeing us or noticing us. We're able to move about freely and observe without hindrance."

"Like a ghost."

"Yes. Very much like that. In fact, most of the sightings people in your time attributed to ghosts were actually Colony Time Guards. There are some people capable of seeing us in a limited fashion, their minds attuned to ours somehow. People who are usually connected more to the fundamental consciousness of the universe. They can't really see us completely and thus rationalize us as what they think are ghosts."

"You said most of what people think are ghosts. What about the others that aren't you?"

"That's people caught in the wrong time-stream, lost travelers, indexes gone wrong. Sometimes it's even people who die a sudden, violent death and that violence somehow violates the time-stream and causes them to be

311

stuck. We can't really explain it all yet. It's part of the time traveling puzzle."

"So when you index ... is that the right word? ... what do you see of your body, or do you?"

"When we index into the stream and alight at a specific point, our mind automatically projects an image of our body as we see ourselves. This projection can be changed, if one so desires and after much mental training so that you can appear to those actually living in the time-stream as anyone you want. But most of the time, we're invisible. With you, it seems to be the opposite. Whereas those of us who are in the Colony Time Guards have to practice hard and long to be able to project an image to others, you're going to have to practice to become invisible and not project so forcefully as you're doing now."

Meagan could tell that Alexis was closely following all she said and had latched onto something that was a contradiction, another of the problems Alexis had created. "Yes," she asked Alexis as their eyes met again. "You've a question?"

"I saw all of you, all the times that you came near me, sensed you also, almost as if I could feel the distortion in time, the ripples that you were creating in your passage."

"As I said, yours is a powerful mind. It's why I've been so good at what I do. I inherited that powerful mind, not perhaps as strong as the original in your head, but strong enough. You can pick up travelers very well. There are only a few really capable of such feats, but they usually have to been in deep trances and such. That you can do it naturally is a gift, if you want to call it that."

Some gift, Alexis thought as she tried to follow along and place everything into context, into sequence and in that sequence understand it all fully. But there were still problems, half-truths Meagan was telling her and Alexis was finding disturbing. "That then brings up another, bigger question. If you've no bodies when you index, if it's all a projection, a mental image that doesn't really exist in the physical world, then how is it that when I killed your companions, both at my cabin and at the deli in Boston, there were bodies to be taken away, to be autopsied, to be buried? That makes no sense."

That one took Meagan by surprise. She had known, of course, about the others who had indexed in, who had violated the most fundamental rule of time travel and had, in that violation, caused immense ripples in the time-stream. She was also quite aware, as was Skre, that they were from the future, a future where indexing with physical bodies was possible.

If that were the case, if physical bodies were truly present then it meant that someone besides the Colony Time Guard had managed to figure out advanced time-travel and it could only be the United Earth Command. "That was not us. We were not trying to kill you. Your death was but an unforeseen accident attached to the death of Ian Montana."

"But you're from the future," Alexis said with a laugh. "How can anything that happened in the past be a surprise to you?"

Meagan leaned forward in her chair and made several strings appear on the table. She picked them up and proceeded to explain to Alexis, using the strings as props. "You making the same mistake that we all made about time." She held up one string. "In your mind, time is but a single string, where any event that happened in the past can be indexed and what happened there is fully known, no surprises." She held up several of the strings. "But what we know now is that time is made up of several strings, in fact an infinite number of them." She pulled a thread from the original string. "A time-stream can split, like this. Any event can cause this. You decide to go to work on the metro instead of in your hov and the metro has a terrible accident and you're killed. That creates a new time-stream, because you could have just as easily chosen to go with the hov and missed the accident and not been killed."

She intertwined several of the strings. "At other times, catastrophic events can bind time-streams together at specific points, making them concurrent for a few brief seconds or a few years. The first explosion of the atomic bomb was one of those points. The first super-collider that created anti-matter was another. At those places, time was bent, pulled out of its normal course and fused together so that although the same exact events may not happen, something catastrophic to the time-stream does happen."

Meagan held up the strings, holding one a little further away. "Let's say that this is my time-stream, the one we both find ourselves in now. In this time-stream, you never died and thus I was born." She held another string to the first one, at an angle about halfway along. "In your time-stream, you die and that death under that hov breaks off an completely separate time-stream, this one here, which will move along creating new events that may or may not correlate with the original time-stream from whence it broke off.

"When we indexed back into your time-stream, which had already been split off when we eliminated the first of those whom you've been investigating, we had no idea what to expect for it was a new time-stream, unknown. It's obvious now that our actions caused you to be in that location and it was neither what we wanted nor what we expected. As such, now we're struck with you here along with a rather perplexing conundrum."

"There must be someone else involved, someone who might just use this new knowledge I represent for some cross purpose, right?" She looked at Meagan shrewdly. "Because otherwise you wouldn't be pressing me so about how I got here and you certainly would not find it necessary to kill off innocent people like you did. So how do I know that you're one of the good guys? How do I know that giving you this knowledge won't cause the demise of Earth as I know it and bring about the ruin of humanity?"

Meagan sighed irritably. She had expected that question much earlier and had been rather happy when it hadn't risen its ugly head, hoping that perhaps Alexis would not go that direction. But as before, they had under-estimated Alexis Locke, a phenomena proving to be the undoing of all their work. It was also becoming a bit of a bother. Meagan was going to have to think a little harder around her mother to stay current, to stay ahead of her and predict these little spurts of prescience that she seemed so good at.

Meagan indicated for Alexis to look at the far wall as she mentally accessed the computer and asked it to open the blast shield on the main viewing aperture. The heavy, reinforced wall opened to reveal Earth lazily spinning below, the globe filling up half the visible area as the sun shined on it from behind the Colony in which they sat.

Alexis stood and walked toward the opening, protected from the ravages of space by nothing more than a force-field keeping the life-support gases from escaping. It was a crystal clear view, as if they were floating alone in space, the distance of the Colony making the planet appear about the size of a basketball. Alexis had seen Earth before from space, most recently from *Stargazer I*, but what she was looking at now was not the same Earth she had seen then, the intense blue of the oceans, the billowing white puffs of the clouds, the dominant browns of the land mass now replaced by a dismal, almost greasy mixture of grays and sooty blacks enveloping the planet in a shroud of filth. It was as if the planet she had known had been replaced by a foul orb of loathsome corruption physically manifesting itself into the very atmosphere until all that was left was ball of squalor.

"What happened?"

"Humans happened. The United Earth Command happened." Meagan shot off in short, curt, dialectic bursts of speech. "And most of all, the MTP project happened."

Alexis looked closer and saw something else, something she didn't think looked right coming at her from the filthy orb. "What are those?" she said as she pointed toward the far limb of the revolting planet.

Meagan squinted her eyes to pick out the objects to which Alexis was referring. When she saw them her eyes widened in shock. "That's trouble is what that is," she spit out as the cacophony of the main alarm klaxon began to wail through-out the Colony, demanding attention, action.

Alexis focused in on the objects as they drew closer and realized that they were small attack-craft with vicious, angular lines and what appeared to be a preponderance of weapons, their intent obvious in their manifestation and their formation.

They meant to attack.

It seems to be a common failing of humanity
to bring to whatever place they go
that brutal, vicious trait we as a species find
so revolting: pride. It has been the cause of
many a conflict, accomplishing nothing that would
cure humanity of this loathsome idiosyncrasy.
— Trent M'ås Hammerfist
Ambassador of the Tri ve Bael

24

The attack lasted but twenty minutes.

The defensive fighters of the Colony, weakened by the large battle recently fought for the possession of the Io mining systems, had fought valiantly. Yet in the end, they proved to be too few against the United Earth Command's mass-wave tactics. The main defensive armament of the Colony accounted for at least a third of the attacking ships, but it only took a few of the heavily armed United Earth fighters to cause extensive damage to *Einstein XXI*. The Colony was not built to withstand the particle weapon attacks of the kind recently employed against the Colonies.

Mortally wounded and spewing its precious gases into insatiable space, the exploded bodies of the numerous unfortunate civilians caught in the open when the main Colony dome had been penetrated, floating about the wreckage like macabre, crimson satellites, the Colony was doomed. The initial attack had not destroyed the Colony outright, but it left it to the never lessening pressures of space and it would soon collapse on its own, much to the jubilation of the few surviving ships limping back to Earth, triumphant in their mission.

Alexis and Meagan had been caught in an auxiliary area apart from the main Colony and were thus spared the rapid de-compression and painfully hideous death that would have entailed. But the multiple fires erupting throughout the Colony and the strain placed on the structure from the various explosions and explosive de-compressions rocking it to the core quickly made their position untenable.

Meagan lead Alexis to the main evacuation staging area but found their way blocked by heavy, billowing smoke and sealed emergency hatches slamming shut throughout the Colony as the damage control computers and droids tried unsuccessfully to contain the damage inflicted and minimize the secondary explosions creating so much havoc.

They back-tracked toward the main defensive staging area, a portion of the Colony Meagan knew was more heavily armored and thus stood a better chance of surviving such an attack. When they arrived, they found that it too had suffered extensive damage, the dead and the dying lying about in burnt and crushed poses of pain and distress. Several defensive fighters stood ready for launch, the crews laying about in various states of death, the pilots no where to be seen.

Meagan pointed toward the fighters as she spoke, coughing from the acrid smoke beginning to cascade into the hanger from fires quickly working their way through the oxygen rich environment. "These fighters are only single-seaters. We can't both occupy one. The controls would become confused and inoperative with two minds in such close proximity. They work on mental commands. There are no physical controls apart from a few rudimentary ones. You think of what you want and the ship reacts. It takes concentration and determination, but I know that you're more than capable of handling it. You have a far superior mind than the pilots who actually fly these things so you should have no problem whatsoever.

"Set the nav-com for *Helios Prime*. You got that? *Helios Prime*. It knows the way. I'll try to stay on your six but I might have to pull off to engage the fighters I'm certain will be coming back to finish this place off. They don't like to leave survivors behind. They think it's more effective the more of us they kill in each attack."

"Does this happen often around here?" Alexis inquired as she soaked in the information Meagan had just spewed out at her, aware that she was about to step into a craft she had no idea how to fly.

"This wasn't a regular attack. I'm not sure what's going on, but it might just be an unfortunate coincidence that they attack here, when you show up. The UEF generally stay away from the civilian Colonies. Killing innocents and all that, not that they have qualms about killing us off in more subtle ways."

Alexis watched Meagan climb up into her fighter as she offered her own opinion. "Maybe it has to do with me."

Meagan looked over at Alexis as she started to climb up the side of her own ship. "They've no idea that you're here, Alexis. Not everything is about you, mother."

Alexis climbed into the cockpit and the canopy closed about her automatically as the hanger was rocked by a secondary explosion blowing out the far wall and starting the rapid decompression she could swear she could feel against her skin, in her ears, her stomach and figured it was just an artifact of her mental powers. She surveyed the rather plain looking instrument panel accosting her. She could feel the build up of pressure in the cockpit, the quiet hiss of the life-support systems bringing the fighter interior to equilibrium as the outside world was collapsing into the chaos of space.

Meagan's voice came to her as if out of the air. *The computer can recognize most commands. Don't talk. Just think. One distinct thought at a time, otherwise the machine will get confused and just shutdown until you give it a clear command. Don't try anything fancy. Just give the nav-com your destination and tell the ship to take you there. That's it.*

Alexis looked up as Meagan's fighter rose up off the deck and then careened out into space. She frowned, not certain as to how this was going to work but willing to give it a try, as if there was really much of a choice. She thought *Helios Prime* and the air before her came alive with an intricate holographic display of the path her ship was going to take to bring her to the base that appeared to be located rather near the sun, within the orbit of Venus. Several other holographic instruments also appeared and she studied them for a moment, recognizing most but not all.

The deck beneath her ship rocked and tilted as another explosion seared the canopy, the flames roaring over her ship like a banshee. She quickly realized that this was not the place to be contemplating the state of her ship and gave as clear a thought as she could for the fighter to go.

Nothing happened.

Alarms began to wail for attention, telling her that the outside temperature was beginning to become unstable and that the structure in which they were currently sitting was about to break apart. She tried again to make the ship go but once again nothing happened.

Realizing that she was obviously doing something wrong, she relaxed and thought of all the other vehicles she had ever operated. It came to her with a rather foolish expression on her face. She thought and the main control panel came up before her. She ran through the pre-flight quickly, allowing the ship to bring the propulsion systems online. There was another explosion lifting the ship and then dropping it down brutally, down past the once existent deck as Alexis brought the engines to full throttle, brought up the main defensive shields and ordered the ship on a specific path straight out into space gapping open beneath her as the main defensive staging area blew itself into small, shiny, metallic pieces behind her.

It looked very much like a fireworks display.

Meagan's fighter came up next to Alexis' and as Alexis looked over, she could clearly see the scowl on her daughter's face. "What the hell took you so long? It's really not that difficult."

Alexis was about to make a witty reply but quickly realized that she would need to first engage the communication protocol before she answered or else the main computer might think she was trying to give commands. "You could've been a little more specific about how this damn thing works. You didn't mention that I had to turn the stupid thing on first."

Meagan's voice came back with the same tint of mockery as if she had spoken the words. "I would've thought that was obvious."

"Well it wasn't."

The two fighters made their way clear of the self-destructing Colony, the multiple fires and explosions giving the spinning cylinder of death the morbid, almost fascinating appearance of a Christmas tree with it holiday lights all aglow.

"How many people just died?" Alexis asked as she watched the structure disintegrate.

"*Einstein XXI* was one of the newer, expanded Colonies. It housed over 75,000 people. I assume most of them perished."

Alexis pulled her eyes away and stared into the empty space before her, so alive with the splendor of creation. It seemed that even in the future, she was unable to escape the wake of death and mayhem that seemed to be following her every step. Did she somehow cause a curse to be placed on her? "How long will it take us to get to this *Helios Prime*," she asked, trying to get her mind off the destruction and all the death, the tortured souls of those just killed already starting to infringe on her mind.

"Not too long. But I think we've got trouble right now."

Alexis' threat board began to light up and a small image of the fighters closing in on them was displayed for her with all the specifications and armament carried. Projections of possible maneuvers and counter-moves began to flash before her, most of which seemed far too risky for the ship to actually do, until she remembered that she was thinking like a terrestrial-bound pilot and there was no appreciable friction or gravity out here and what was impossible in atmosphere was most likely normal procedure here.

"You continue on your course, I'll take care of these guys," Meagan explained as the communications grid was shut down and Meagan's fighter peeled off to engage the pursuing attackers.

Alexis watched it disappear into the blackness surrounding her like an all-inclusive veil and was damned if she was going to let her daughter have all the fun. She concentrated a moment and tried to come up with a series of commands that would make her fighter do what she wanted. Several more screens popped into existence as she studied the specifications of her opponents.

The enemy fighters appeared to be slightly more heavily armed and protected, but Alexis appeared to have the advantage of maneuver and speed. Other than that, it appeared to be an even match. There was of course that little matter concerning the pilots in the other fighters being veterans at this type of warfare, whereas Alexis was still trying to figure out how to turn her ship around and make it go where she wanted it.

But then such minor details had never bothered her in the past, so she ignored them here also. Her fighter was violently rocked to the side and sent tumbling out of control, the damage control board lighting up in exasperation as more warnings began to blare in frustration. She concentrated and issued a series of commands that, to her own amazement, stabilized the fighter and brought her around on an intercept course with the fast approaching enemy.

She was not too happy about the sloppy job, but a new display submitting for her perusal the specifications of a missile, caught her attention, as well as a trajectory grid showing some type of projectile closing in on her.

Two projectiles.

She quickly put two and two together and realized that the missile displayed so conveniently by the computer was the same as the ones about to turn her ship into a mass of disassociated particles. She thought *counter-measures* and another screen appeared listing the various options. She choose several, not at all certain what they all did and initiated them, then heeled the ship hard over and headed straight for the two missiles.

The counter-measures activated, causing one of the missiles to explode itself in an orange shower of quickly extinguished fire. The other missile seemed impartial about the counter-measures and continued to press home its attack. Her threat panel kindly informed Alexis that another set of missiles had been launched at her, a fact striking her as somehow unfair. She didn't even know where her missiles were located, or if she even had any. She had taken a quick look at the exterior of her ship when she first climbed in and didn't remember seeing any missiles hanging down.

As the distance between the remaining missile and her fighter closed at an accelerated rate, she dove her ship hard over in a radical maneuver that the missile could not possibly copy, then launched another series of counter-measures effectively nullifying the missile's tracking ability. It flew off harmlessly into space.

As the other two missiles closed in, Alexis thought *weapons systems* and was satisfied to find that she also had a set of such missiles, with slightly different configurations. She brought up the tracking screen, found the two culprits who seemed determined to turn her into a permanent resident of space and gave a series of commands. The weapons system obeyed without a moment's hesitation and two missiles launched from the interior racks – thus the reason she had not seen any hanging down – then quickly went their appointed way...

... Into the blackness of space, nowhere near the two approaching enemy ships.

She cursed as she realized her error and quickly launched two more, this time with the proper instructions. She was politely told that the distance was now too close for the use of missiles and she would have to resort to the close-in weapons system, which consisted of four high-velocity particle cannons and a plasma weapon, whose concept she didn't even begin to understand.

The computer then began to give her tactical suggestions as to the proper way to fight and she shook her head as she promptly ignored them. She missed the old days when the computers simply talked to you but didn't have the gall to make suggestions. She wondered if she could turn the damn thing off and no sooner had she thought it than the computer voice promptly became silent.

She dodged the next two missiles screaming toward her, one of them exploding far too close for comfort, weakening her shields, spraying her fuselage with a splinter of tiny particles and sending her tumbling away again. As she stabilized the ship she caught sight of the two enemy fighters as they split up and began what they believed was the final run for the kill. Alexis noticed that the particle weapons passed through the shields without a problem, the primary purpose of the shields apparently to guard against the energy weapons and the blasts of the explosions one invariably encountered during such high-tech dog-fights.

This, of course, meant that she would have to be very careful about letting them get too close. One spray of those cannons and it could ruin her whole day. She peeled off toward the enemy fighter to her lower left and asked for more power. Her ship responded with a bone-jarring acceleration closing the distance in a heartbeat so that by the time Alexis tried to fire the plasma cannon, she was already passed her intended victim in blur of metal. She readjusted her speed by applying the braking thrusters and then re-oriented herself, watching the tracking screen carefully as the two fighters closed in again, her unexpected maneuver catching them off-balance.

She wondered how Meagan was doing.

Another screen popped into existence and Alexis was greeted with the tactical display of Meagan and her three enemy fighters as they initiated their deadly dance. It seemed that her daughter was a rather accomplished fighter pilot and a moment of pride entered her breast before she ignored it as heartburn.

A new threat warning went off and she pulled the ship up and to the right, the stream of lethal particles barely missing her left propulsion nacelle. She chastised herself for losing concentration. She was going to have to play this game a lot more seriously if she expected to survive. The two enemy fighters were lining up for another attack, coming in from opposite sides and different angles to sandwich her in-between.

She quickly analyzed the attack and concentrated on the closest ship. As the distance closed, Alexis began to re-configure the missile-arming parameters by-passing the security codes and self-arming protocols. She had an idea. It was a little risky, but it had an outside chance of working and to her, those were the best of ideas because they would be a surprise to her opponent.

She had noticed that the enemy fighters had also stopped using their missiles, which meant they were now in close-in mode, not thinking of having to dodge any missiles that might suddenly pop up. She could use that to her advantage. The only problem was that with the safeties disengaged, the missile would see her ship as just as much of a target as the enemy, a decided disadvantage.

A stream of particles came flying at her and she barrel-rolled in awkward symmetry to throw the enemy targeting scanners off as much as possible, all the while holding her tracking system tight on the tail of the enemy ship. She let loose with a volley from the plasma cannons at the last moment, highlighting the shields of the enemy fighter in a glow of bluish hue as the energy was absorbed, then activated full braking thrusters and pirouetted her ship around just as she passed close by over the other ship.

A fraction of second after the enemy fighter passed, beginning a radical maneuver of its own to break off the engagement, Alexis launched her missile. It flew straight and true, seeking the laser designator Alexis kept firmly planted on the aft portion of the enemy. It closed the distance far quicker than the other pilot could react and impacted into the fighter, turning it into a spherical pyre of orange and crimson, large pieces of the now shattered fuselage hurling off into space in random directions. It lasted but a mere few seconds, the spot once holding the enemy fighter now devoid of anything but the few scattered remnants of the ship and its pilot.

She smiled to herself at her accomplishment, then remembered that there was still another ship out there in the blackness hunting her and. She brought the tracking system back up to ascertain its location.

But it was gone.

There was no sign of it at on the scanner grid and that bothered her immensely. She seriously doubted that the other pilot would just give up and leave. As if in reply to her thought, her ship was buffeted by a series of bluish lances lighting up the interior of the cockpit in a hellish revival as the plasma bolts slammed into her shields from the far distance. More warnings began to appear showing her that the last attack had weakened her shields considerably. She strained to see where the attack had come from, the scanner screens still not showing anything in the immediate vicinity.

She immediately thought *stealth mode* and began a series of extreme maneuvers to shake the targeting scanners of her invisible enemy. A glint in the blackness, a reflection from the sun off the canopy or a shiny piece of the fuselage gave the attacker away as more lances of plasma streaked through space toward her. She dodged them successfully, only to be told that more missiles were in-bound.

She concentrated even more, getting used to the rapid response available with the thought-controlled fighter. She accelerated hard and prepared another missile as she closed in on the unsuspecting enemy who thought himself invisible to her. Although certain that the other pilot had seen her recent maneuver vanquishing his wingman, it was possible that the trick just might work again.

She let loose with a fusillade of particles slicing through the blackness and the outer weapons rack of the enemy fighter, pitching it away from the multiple impacts. Alexis followed close on his heels as the enemy stabilized and set off a series of counter-measures fuzzing out Alexis' scanners and making it impossible to guide the missile to target.

The two ships engaged in a deadly dance for several minutes as Alexis stayed on him like a shadow, alternating between plasma lances and the particle cannons in a weird and almost mystical gambol. Alexis finally picked her moment and launched the altered missile, letting it loose when she was almost on top of the enemy fighter. The target veered down and to the side in a violent action causing the missile to miss cleanly. But the missile was not finished yet. Without the safeties to disengage it, the missile continued to scan for a target and found Alexis' ship quite suitable.

She noticed this immediately and scowled deeply. She was afraid this might happen and had not had the time to prepare a defense if it did. And then an idea formed a split second afterward. She pulled her ship violently around and headed straight for the enemy who was filling the space between them with a lethal hail of particles and plasma. Her shields continued to light up with each lance of energy walloping into her, the particle's paths traced out by the tracer shells and guided by the tracker scanners missing by mere centimeters as Alexis used up every counter-measure she had available and rolled and rollicked her ship as best she could to avoid the mortal bite of the particles, closing the distance with each nano-second, the missile hot on her tail.

She was playing chicken, responding with her own storm of plasma and particles creating a hell-storm between the two rapidly closing ships. At the last second, as particles slammed into her fighter causing alarm klaxons to wail with dire intent, the life-support systems beginning to fail with the punctured pressure leaks spilling the vital gases into space, she pulled up and away, almost grazing the canopy of the other ship flaring under her in a spark-producing collision sending Alexis' fighter spinning off in fierce and corybantic gyrations.

But she was the lucky one.

The missile, almost on top of Alexis' fighter as she scraped past her antagonist, saw for an instant the two fighters as one and slammed into the closest part, which happened to be the cockpit of the enemy fighter. It erupted in a spray of fire and parts, spinning off into the void trailing a stream of glowing particles and burnt pilot.

"That's the most incredible and foolhardy thing that I think I've ever seen in my life," Meagan communicated as Alexis struggled to stabilize the ship and the damage that had been caused by the last pass. "You're certifiable."

"It worked, didn't it? Now stop complaining and tell me how to fix this thing because it's telling me that I've got a major problem." Alexis was lost as to how to properly get her fighter to heal itself, the continued warnings and loss of pressure beginning to worry her a little.

Neither Meagan nor she had the time to put on pressure suits before jumping into the fighters and evacuating the Colony, so any serious pressure loss or life-support failure would mean the end of Alexis.

"What are you worried about?" Meagan's calm voice came to Alexis as she managed to get the ship headed back toward *Helios Prime*. "Have you forgotten that you don't have a body at the moment, that you're nothing but a mental projection caught in this time stream? What do you need life support for?"

Alexis thought about that statement, forgetting for a moment that she no longer had a body that she was, for all intents and purposes, dead already.

"It works off of thought waves. Have you physically touched anything yet? No, you haven't. You've piloted the ship as it was intended to be piloted: by using your thoughts. Remember that discussion that we were having before all this happened, the one about the problem with how you got here? This is one of the benefits of time travel. You don't have to worry about such minor matters as breathable air and the like. For all intents and purposes you're a free agent where that's concerned. You can even walk under water or through fire if you wanted."

Alexis had to laugh as the computer informed her that she was dead, taking control of the fighter and continuing with its last course toward *Helios Prime*. This might just prove to be not such a bad deal after all.

"You mean to tell me that you carried out all those maneuvers thinking all the time that you might get killed?" Meagan said in amazed stupor. "You're even stupider than I thought, or perhaps more heroic."

Alexis pursed her lips as she watched the blackness outside her cracked canopy majestically display itself for her. "All my heroics are strictly on the surface. Maybe that's where they always are. Don't be so quick to praise me," she responded pithily.

"Maybe so, but it's still the damnedest thing that I ever saw."

When we index to the past and make changes
do we change our future or do we create an
entirely new future? It is this question and no
other that we must address before we ever
consider this course of action that the recent
events have proven are possible.

--- From the Cabinet Notes of
Halle van der Höhenstein,
Elder-Elect of the Ruling Council of
The UFC
5 July 2248

25

20 August 2250, 2050 hrs (CT)
Helios Prime

The medical facility was packed. Between the survivors from the recent destruction of *Einstein XXI* and the overflow from the loss of the Io mining colony, bed-space was at a premium. Skre Yellowleaf lay under the light-greenish hue of the shimmering sterilization field on one of the numerous regenerative beds, a medical droid hovering over him working diligently and simultaneously on his burnt arm and fractured leg. A nurse droid worked on his other side, assisting the medical droid and monitoring the patient's vital signs.

General Oli Gudbjartsson stood at the foot of the regenerative table, his head bandaged neatly from the cut he had received, his ribs still sore from the work performed on them but a few hours ago. He wore his same, self-assured expression, that aura of confidence hanging about him spreading to those who lay around awaiting attention or recovering from their wounds. But Oli was not a happy man. n fact, he was extremely perturbed by the recent attack on the Colony, an attack both unnecessary and unheard of in its viciousness.

It had been a long-standing agreement between the two warring factions that concentrations of civilians were not to be attacked, especially those that were the most vulnerable. The Colonies, whose intact capture was one of the highest priorities of the United Earth Forces, had never been subjected to such an intense attack in which one had been destroyed outright.

It appeared that as of yesterday, that agreement was no longer in force. Such an out-right violation changed the whole character of the war. It brought with it a new dimension to the already fierce conflict, raising the level of brutality to what it had been during the great purges and ethnic cleansings that had taken an estimated 750 million innocent lives at the hands of the ruthless dictator Emperor Huang.

"Have we heard from Colonel Locke?" Skre asked, his eyes staring up at the overhead with that expression of deep thought mixing with strained nerves, the numbness in his body matched by a numbness in his head from the death of so many people in a brilliant flash of irretrievable violence.

"Yes. She and the Alexis woman have been recovered safely. They've just arrived here at *Helios Prime* and are on their way to the med-center as we speak."

Skre nodded his head slightly, a movement causing him to receive an admonition from the medical droid to lay still. "That's good. We can ill afford to lose Colonel Locke at this point. What of the attack? Any indication of why?"

Oli seemed to hesitant, resistant to what it was that he wanted to say.

Skre picked up on this immediately. They had known each other too well. "Tell me your thoughts, old friend. What do you think provoked this unparalleled attack?"

Oli pursed his lips and looked down at his feet a moment, then back up at the prone figure of the Commandant, a man whom he greatly respected but whose recent decisions went against everything the general believed. He cleared his throat brusquely. "It's clear that the presence of the woman Alexis Locke can be the only explanation for the attack. The UEF has never attacked a Colony with such vigor and destructive power. It's completely counter-productive to their cause to destroy the one thing they want most of all, especially one of the newer, expanded Colonies. There can only be one reason."

"And you believe this reason to be Alexis Locke?" They were both silent for a moment before Skre spoke again. "How is it possible that they are even aware of her presence in this time stream? How is it that they find her presence here so disturbing that they must destroy that which they prize above all else? This, to me, is not logical."

"There's one other possible explanation," Oil said quietly as the medical droid finished with Skre and moved on to the next patient without so much as a word spoken. The nurse droid applied an antiseptic molecular coating to the wounds and then passed the skin graft acceleration over his arm. When she was done, there was no sign whatsoever that Skre's arm had ever sustained a third degree burn. His leg was currently covered in a glimmering patina of bluish hue as his bone healed itself through genetic manipulations and nano-bot intervention. The nano-bots would eventually leave the body when their job was accomplished.

"What is this other possibility, Oli?"

"That the UEF no longer has a need for the Colonies and this incident is the beginning of a campaign to destroy all the Colonies... and thus us."

Skre began to sit up but the nurse droid scolded him and placed a restraining field over him. He glared at the machine a moment, but it paid no attention to him, unaffected as it was by human emotions and complaints. Skre let out a long, slow breath of air that was as much an expulsion as it was an emotion.

"Neither of these possibilities pleases me. Both have numerous problems related to them. We must begin to find the answers." He looked up at Oli. "Bring them in here as soon as possible. And bring in Cycomeand[1] Vork... He may be able to shed some light on our problem."

Oli bowed slightly, then indicated for the guard at the door to let in Colonel Locke and her guest as soon as they arrived. Oli stayed by Skre's side, quietly contemplating what all this meant and how best he was going to counter the UEF's newest strategy.

They didn't have to wait long.

Meagan and Alexis came walking in within minutes, followed by Vork. The Cycomeand, like all those of his generation, appeared human-like in almost all aspects except for the large imprint on his forehead – required of all cyborg regardless of function – and his large, sky-blue eyes. The first generation models looked completely non-human but it was quickly ascertained that a human form was the most conducive to the mobility required and now the newest generation were almost indistinguishable from a human at a distance.

---

1 Cycomeand stands for Cybernetic Computer Enhanced Android. These machines came into existence in the year 2132 as mobile memory systems for consultations and data analysis. The Hart-Nakamura Mind Transference Protocol was strictly banned for use in the Cycomeand in the year 2140 after it was determined that such a transference constituted the creation of a new life form and was in violation of the Ramirez-Kin Conception Accord of 2106.

Meagan came to attention while Alexis stood next to her with arms crossed and an insolent look on her face. Oli returned the salute and ordered Meagan to relax.

Skre spoke, his voice slow and vibrant yet filled with an urgency belying the trepidation he felt. "Colonel Locke, it's good to see that you survived the destruction of *Einstein XXIII*."

Meagan nodded her head slightly in acknowledgment and Alexis looked at her daughter with a raised eyebrow. "Colonel? Not bad, though I would've preferred general by this stage in your life. But I suppose colonel's fine too."

All three looked at Alexis as if she had spoken out of turn during some profound religious ceremony. She looked back at them, especially the handsome and tall general bursting with energy who looked like a transplanted Viking. "Did I say something wrong?"

A frown crossed Meagan's face a moment, then she resumed her stoic gaze. "Alexis Locke, this is Commandant Skre Finehair Yellowleaf, head of the Colony Time Guards. This is General Oli Gudbjartsson, First Consul of the UFC Defensive Forces. And this is Cycomeand Vork."

"Psycho-what?" Alexis asked as she looked at the obviously non-human thing standing a respectful distance from the group and looking on with indifference to the human introductions, as if such things were beneath him.

"Cyco*meand*," Meagan clarified. "It's an android. A walking computer basically. It's harmless."

Alexis looked at the machine with distaste. "You certainly have come a long way from my day in artificial intelligence."

Vork turned his head to look at Alexis, his eyes staring at her with a passionlessness bordering on the psychotic. "The term artificial intelligence is not really applicable to my kind, Alexis Locke," he said to her in a normal, simple, mid-range voice sounding uncomfortably human but without the expressiveness common to the species. "I can be more accurately described as...."

"There is no time for this at the moment," Skre interrupted, aware that before this recent turn of events, they literally had all the time in the world at their fingertips. Now they were counting every minute until the UEF struck again, especially if they were indeed launching a campaign of wanton destruction of all the O'Neill Colonies.

The Colonies have to all be retro-fitted for the defensive systems needed to protect them and that process will take decades and it still will not be a guarantee of success. It was far too easy to penetrate the populated cylinders and render the Colony useless for habitation. "Perhaps later you can explain yourself to Ms. Locke, but at the moment there are pressing matters that need our immediate attention."

Alexis turned from the android back toward the old man who had spoken. "So you're the one in charge here? I want some answers and I'm tired of playing hide around the facts with Meagan here, who seems to think that the less I know the better off I'll be. I'm the displaced person here. I'm the one without a body who seems to be stuck here in the middle of someone else's war."

"Be that as it may, young lady," Skre began as he tried to sit up again and was restrained by the retaining field around him that the nurse droid had yet to release. "But we are in the beginnings of a dire situation here and you may hold the key to our problem."

Alexis looked around at the packed room. "And you think that this is the best place to discuss these matters? In a hospital?"

"I cannot move from the recovery bed for at least another hour so that my fracture can heal properly and I don't believe we have an hour to waste, so here is as good a place as any." Skre looked now toward Meagan. "Colonel, were you able to get any information of value from our unexpected guest?"

"None, Sir. She appears to know little to nothing of the method she used to get here to our time-stream. I also believe that she's ignorant of the problems that beset us at the moment."

Skre nodded his head as if agreeing with Alexis' naiveté concerning her own future. "Then perhaps it's time that we explained ourselves to her and perhaps in that, something will come of her presence among us."

Alexis sensed a spirit of honesty emitting from the old man, as if his words had the ability to soothe one's mind and soul and bring calmness to the world around him. "I'd like that very much, Commandant. As you can imagine, I'm rather lost and confused at the moment."

Oli, who had been eyeing Alexis the entire time with a disdainfulness and enmity pounding into the side of Alexis' head like a rock, spoke with a down-turned mouth, his words slow and effortless, as if to make certain Alexis understood every intonation and connotation that he implied. "Do you truly think that it's wise to give her this knowledge? We have no true idea of her loyalties or her moral rectitude."

Alexis eyed the general with a half-smile, half-smirk and a pair of smoldering eyes that would have cut to ribbons a lesser man. "Moral rectitude? What are you, the morality police or something? What the hell am I going to do with this precious knowledge of yours? I don't even know who the hell the enemy is. And from what Meagan here has been kind enough to tell me, I can't go back to my time anyway since my body is apparently a large smear in the grass, thanks to you. You people are really starting to wear my patience."

Oli glared at Alexis a moment, his eyes burning in a passionate hatred. "Hold you tongue, woman, else I hold it for you. You're a guest here and not worthy to partake in this discussion, so perhaps it would be best for all involved if you were to just stay quiet and listen. Perhaps you may learn something."

"Oh really, Erik the Red. You want to go outside and see who has the right to be here, because I'd love to show you the heel of my boot."

Oli bristled at the insult, filling up his massive chest like a puffer fish. "Your incorrect analogy not withstanding, you're in no condition to challenge me. I could easily take you with one hand tied — . "

"Enough of this childishness," Skre said, not raising his voice more than normal but somehow cowing those around him with an unconscious mental dressing down backing the general off as he made ready to throttle Alexis. "As I said before, we have no time for any of this foolishness. Alexis Locke is correct. There is no logical reason to deny her the information that may perhaps unlock the key to our current dilemma. We are quickly running out of options. We must take some risks."

Oli bowed and stepped away from Alexis, but his expression toward her didn't change in the least. "As you wish, Sir."

Skre smiled at Alexis, a smile from the heart. Alexis recognized that the man was sincere in his desire for her to help and she stepped away from the general who seemed to arouse something in her that was both primal and amatory. Perhaps that was why she had reacted so forcefully to what was just a simple insult, the likes of which she had ignored many times in the past. Maybe she just needed sex. She relaxed her facial expression as she listened to what the old man had to say, trying not to look at Oli anymore despite his good looks.

"There's a long history between your time and our time, Alexis Locke, a long, drawn out drama of evil that need not be repeated in your lifetime." He breathed in deeply as if in pain. The nurse droid administered a painkiller, then went back to her blank stare as she hovered between Skre's bed and the one beside it, waiting for the next opportunity to be useful.

"Perhaps this should wait until you're better," Alexis offered, but the look of exigency crossing the old man's eyes told her that there was no more time.

"No. We need to discuss this now. You must know why we deemed it necessary to interfere in your time-stream and do the acts that you must see

331

from your perspective as deplorable and ruthless." He indicated for Vork to step forward. "Perhaps it would be best if you received an accurate accounting of the past few centuries and the Cycomeand would be best for that."

Vork beamed an unnatural smile setting Alexis' teeth on edge. "No offense, but I'd prefer to hear it from a human." She scanned the android as if it were a shank of meat. "I'm not very comfortable with that thing yet."

Meagan sighed. "As you see, Sir," she said with sarcasm dripping off her lips, "this is the attitude and unreasonable mind that I've been beset with."

"Yes...," Skre uttered in a long, drawn out breath. "But it is to be expected. Her request is not unreasonable, I suppose. General, you may proceed."

Alexis turned to look at the tall man with the flaxen hair whose voice rolled off his tongue like logs down a slush pipe, bumping and jostling the words as if they were foreign to his tongue, this feat he had been ordered to do somehow beneath him.

But he spoke anyway, not looking at the woman in whom he found no redeeming values whatsoever. "On 28 June 2105, Alexander Hart, Ykaterina Godonov and Kido Nakamura presented a paper to the National Academy of Sciences on the successful solutions to the Kutuskoy Equation, a hitherto unsolvable complex of three-dimensional differential equations based on a new math form discovered in 2035 by the Russian geneticist Andre Kutuskoy. It was based on synaptic sequences and the complex wave-forms associated with their formation and disassociation. It can predict when a synaptic partnership will form, when synaptic trees will branch and how they will react to retrieval algorithms. More importantly, it comes in very handy during the critical formation process within the human brain cells when memories are stored.

"The paper that was presented gave Hart and his group the key to the project they had been working on since 2084. But the paper, at that time, was received with skepticism for both its unorthodox approach to the solutions and to the viability of its use in the future." Oli stopped here as if to allow Alexis to catch up.

She looked at him, then rose her eyebrows inquisitively, asking him if there was more or if that was all.

"I'm just making certain that you understand," he stated with a virulent tongue as if she were a small child. "I will continue, then. On 2 July 2105, the Hart-Dumvo transference equipment was presented at an informal press conference. This also was received with skepticism. But on 16 July 2105, a date that has become infamous for the day humanity began its long march into diablerie, a working prototype of the Hart-Nakamura Mind Transference Protocol was unveiled. Heralded as the beginning of a new era in human evolution and the opening of a golden age of science, the Mind Transference Protocol was a quantum leap forward in technology, for it solved the last remaining problem with the battle for longevity, namely how to re-create the mind of a human without losing all of the memories and personalities that make up that individual. The Mind Transference Protocol, and I shall refer to it as the MTP from here on out, allowed the entire contents of a human mind to be downloaded into a special computer memory buffer.   It was an astonishing feat of engineering and software design and allowed for the advent of pseudo-immortality to become a reality."

"Pseudo-immortality?" Alexis asked with a shake of her head.

Oli eyed her with disdain once again. "If you will allow me to finish, I'll explain it all to you. Are all women from your time-stream like you? Never mind. With the advances in cloning and organ regeneration, life spans had been expanded to about one-hundred-and-fifty years at the most, as you're aware. These advances had already been established in your time. The one problem was always the deterioration of the physical brain, a process that science had yet to reverse.

"But with the MTP, it didn't matter. Now, all that was needed for a person to live for as long as they wished was to have a clone created and grown. When the clone reached the proper age, your mind would be downloaded to the memory buffer and then up-loaded into the empty clone brain, thus giving the person, in essence, a brand new, top-of-the-line, genetically engineered body.

"One could even, for the right price and on the numerous black markets that cropped up, change your looks completely or change your sex, if the fancy struck you, though I can't understand why any man would want to be a woman."

"General ...." Skre admonished quietly.

Oli nodded his head, though a slight smile sat in the corner of his mouth at the barb he had been able insert. "The possibilities were endless. This pseudo-immortality became a reality on 21 December 2125 when the first successful full transfer was achieved. Of course, the moral questions that arose concerning the growing and harvesting of the clones and their rights and the contents of their minds that were, basically, trashed, opened up a series of controversial debates and anti-MTP rallies and rebellions. But the technology soon became standard."

Alexis held her hand up to stop the general in his history lecture. "Are you being serious with me? Is that what they were all working on?" She looked at the three humans and saw that there was not a trace of deceit on any of their faces. "That sounds like a godsend for humanity. What a fantastic opportunity and a legal nightmare."

"Many felt as you do," Skre added, his large eyes holding a subtle hint of anguish and lost opportunities. "But as is common with human nature, there were also those who saw this as their opportunity to gain power and fame. And one of those was Sun Liu Huang, a powerful industrialist from the Greater East-Asian Co-Prosperity Sphere. His name is a curse to all humans and I shudder to even speak it." The sudden outburst of emotion from the old man who had so far been more or less a rock as the story was related, stuck Alexis as odd.

But she could easily understand the sentiment. She felt the same way about certain people in her own time. Cav's name came to mind quickly.

Oli continued. "On 5 November 2108, Sun Liu Huang began his research on the use of the MTP for an army of combat cyborg, each genetically engineered and downloaded with the same mind, a mind of a seasoned, veteran warrior. Now to understand how Huang was able to achieve his goals, it must be mentioned that when the mind is downloaded into the memory buffer, it is possible to add memory, for it is no different at that point than any computer memory.

"The data that could be added ranged from a whole new language to how to fly the most advanced fighters. The possibilities were endless and Huang used them to create an army of soldiers who were basically invincible, each a master at every type of combat, every type of technology, every type of weapons system and with the experience and training of a seasoned veteran, each capable of understanding perfectly what the other was thinking since they all had the same mind, all acting in concord like a single, multi-limbed organism. And most important, they were fearless. They never routed, never lost morale, did whatever it was that was ordered of them.

"On 1 January 2128, Huang tested his new army against the Siberian frontier and successfully conquered it and all its riches in under a month. In July of that same year, he successfully invaded Russia and the Ukraine, and then the European Community fell the next year in a series of deadly, disastrous campaigns proving beyond a doubt the meddle of Huang's army. But it wasn't just his army that made his achievements so easy. It was also his highly successful intelligence campaign, for once Huang was able to get a hold of any top-level official or military personnel, all he needed do was download that individual's mind and then methodically pick through all the data, including troop dispositions, weapon advancements, secret bases, you name it. He would be able to get it all and he did, using his newly gained intelligence in sweeping advances that took his enemies by surprise and crushed them in a matter of weeks, if not days."

Although brutal, Alexis could easily believe what the general was telling her, the course of human events in her own past a stark reminder of what a single, megalomaniac tyrant can do with unlimited power. But what she found hard to believe was that no one rose up to challenge this Huang. "Didn't anyone in the United States try to oppose him? Try to create their own army along the same lines?"

"When Huang, who now went by the title Emperor of the first Huang Dynasty, was successful with his Asian and European campaigns, he began an intense and vicious plan to destroy all traces of the MTP technology save for his own so that no one else could do what you have just suggested. There was no longer a United States of America at this time. President Claudine Maxwell had created, when she entered office in 2086, the North American Alliance, which included all of Canada and Mexico. Hers was the only country with the resources left to oppose Huang. It was that cursed woman, may she burn in hell forever more, who gave Huang his finally victory." Oli spit the words out as if they were burning his mouth, his hatred for Claudine Maxwell apparent, a name that had become a curse among the Colonists as much as Benedict Arnold was an epitaph for treachery and treason.

And Alexis could easily understand why, without even knowing yet what the woman had done to foster such emotions. She had sensed that Maxwell was bad news the first time she saw her on the holo-vid. There was an aura about her stinking of evil and corruption like nothing Alexis had ever seen. That this woman had become some sort of archfiend to the world was consistent with what Alexis had seen in her those many years ago.

And Cav was most likely hand-in-hand with her duplicity.

"Huang approached President Maxwell with a proposal, which would allow her to become even more powerful if she were to help him destroy all the MTP devices and the attendant technology. He, of course, had no such plans. But Maxwell, hungry for power and corrupt to the bone, took the deal and helped with the destruction of all the MTP tech in the North American Alliance and around the world, leaving the only such devices in Huang's hands.

"With that threat out of the way, Huang swept the remaining forces aside in 2130, including the Indian Army, which could have easily maintained a strong position with the help of the North American Alliance but which was thrown to the dogs with the treachery of Claudine Maxwell. She was made the First Secretary of the North American Province and then ceremoniously executed by Huang for treason, a rather ironic and fitting end.

"With the entire world under his thumb, Huang," (Alexis noted that he didn't use the honorific title Emperor when he spoke of the man) "began a series of what he termed purges, which were in essence nothing more than ethnic cleansing. Basically, if you weren't of Oriental extraction, you were slated for execution. He started with the Indian subcontinent and by 2135 had wiped out the majority of the indigenous people there, repopulating the land with his own supporters and his so-called 'pure people.'

"At this point, the United Federation of Colonies, or UFC, severed all ties with Earth and began preparations for the massive influx of refugees we knew would be coming. And come they did, by the millions. Unfortunately, we were unable to support such a large influx. Each Colony could perhaps take one hundred refugees without upsetting the delicate balance of the eco-systems within the Colonies and new Colonies were not being built quickly enough to contend with the massive flow. A second Mars planet-based Colony was started as well as a Europa Colony, and that relieved some of the pressure, but millions died in the attempt to flee or in the cold of space with nowhere to go."

Alexis interrupted again, the assortment of questions flowing through her mind as the general related his tale, which was in essence the history of her future, beginning to scream out for answers. What he was describing sounded so much like the disastrous 20th century with its incessant warfare and mass killings by dictatorial rulers. She had thought that by her time individuals having the ability to rise to such unlimited power was gone forever. The European Community, the powerful Indian Democracy and the East-Asian Co-Prosperity Sphere, along with The United States of course, would never allow a single individual to arise again and shift the balance of power.

It occurred to her that during each of the periods holding such a tyrant in the past, those living then also believed that it could never happen to them either and didn't even know that it was happening until it was all said and done. It was this very belief within the complacency of the masses toward their government and ruling elite that allowed such people to arise without question. Most people had no inkling how their government worked or what went on behind the scenes to make countries powerful, either economically or militarily. They elected people who were not like them at all, almost always multi-millionaires who had no concern for anything or anyone who made under a million a year and it was these people who controlled the balance of power, who decided which country or group had to be eliminated or encouraged.

It was a common fallacy of the human species, she was convinced, that allowed them to set people above them of whom they knew very little, expecting them to hold the reigns of power in their hands and not become corrupt. It was these same people who, with the touch of single button, could have wiped the species off the planet throughout most of the latter half of the 20th century and the first half of the 21st. That great leaders would arise from the ashes of apathy was aptly demonstrated throughout the turbulent and troubled history of man on the planet and it had started with the simple rulers of Sumer and Akkad, worked its way to Alexander the Great, the Roman and early Chinese Emperors, Napoleon, Hitler, and now had apparently culminated with the successful coup of Huang, bringing the human race to the brink of its own destruction without a trace of little green men from outer space to help it along, as had always been supposed.

Alexis was thus not surprised at all by the brutal series of repressions this Huang instituted, for the pattern was always the same. It was a pattern of Human nature, to shun those that didn't fit in, those one believed to be different, whether racially or sexually or religiously or ethnically. Some went so far as to call it a major human failure.

Could it be called anything else?

Alexis suddenly realized that the general had continued with his history lesson and she had missed some of it as her mind wandered over the fallibility of humans. A small frown crossed her smooth face and she concentrated on him again, aware that the man did have some sort of charm to him that seemed to pulse out of him like a warm summer breeze. She shrugged the feeling off as the after-effects of having died.

"On 5 May 2160, Huang put an end to the exodus with massive and brutal reprisals against those who had helped the refugees and those who wanted to leave, throwing them into slave-labor camps where they were worked to death feeding the machinery of the Huang Dynasty. By this time, the resources of the Earth were nearly exhausted and Huang began to turn his envious and vicious eyes toward the Colonies, who mined their wealth from the nearly inexhaustible resources of the solar system. In a series of lightning attacks, the UEF captured several of the larger mining operations from the Colonies and the current war had begun.

"In essence, Huang wanted to gain control of all the Colonies and thus all

337

the mining consortiums, for Earth was becoming uninhabitable with all the pollution and CO_2 in the atmosphere, the average temperature of the planet having risen almost ten degrees." Oli eyed Alexis a moment as if daring her to challenge his version of the story, then fastened his eyes back on Skre. "That's the way things have stood since, the war raging on between the Colonies and the Earth for the survival of the species as a whole."

Alexis was rather subdued after the general had finished. It was indeed a history darker than any man had ever experienced and she saw clearly that these people before her believed it had all stemmed from the invention of the MTP. It was quite possible that they were right.

Skre spoke up, the color on his face flushing out more as the medications began to take hold and the healing of his body began to quicken. "On 10 November 2238, a man named Sergio Cobb, an unknown and obscure philosopher/transcendental healer, approached the UFC ruling council with a proposal for a radical new idea that seemed, at the time, beyond fantasy. He proposed a way to travel through time using not the body but the mind, releasing the mind from the body in a controlled journey that allowed access to the time-stream and thus to any time in the past. His ideas were, of course, as all such new, radical ideas are, summarily dismissed when first presented, set aside as the imaginative musings of a dreamer.

"But someone in the ruling council must have believed the quiet, unassuming young man who disappeared after he had presented his idea, to become as unknown as he had been before hand, for the project was handed to me a few months later in 2239. I was directed to begin secret experiments with the concept, and on 3 May 2240 I was able to achieve the first successful time index and the theory given to us was proven as valid. Two days later the Colony Time Guards were formed by secret executive order of the Ruling Council."

They all looked at Alexis as if waiting for her to say something, as if expecting her to perhaps balk at their tale or the concepts involved. She looked back at them blankly. Although she had numerous questions to ask, she could feel that Skre had one more thing to tell her, one more item that would be the capstone to the history of darkness she had shared in the last few minutes and perhaps, just perhaps even provide the answer to the nagging question of what she had to do with all of it.

When no one said anything, she asked a few obligatory questions to show that she was listening. "How many Colonies are still in your control?"

Vork spoke up, assuming that any question to do with numbers was his area. "There are currently four thousand O'Neill Colonies in operation and under our control, in orbits ranging from this one which is just inside the orbit of Venus, to the Colonies that orbit between Mars and the Asteroid belt. Those four thousand Colonies house 119,400,278 souls. The Planet-based Colonies on Mars, Europa and Ganymede, and mining Colonies on the numerous larger asteroids, hold an additional 80,211,096 souls for a total of 199,611,374 souls in the UFC. This does not take into account the recent destruction of *Einstein XXIII* or the recent loss of the Io Mining Colony, which actually puts the total now at..."

Skre held his hand up and Vork stopped in mid-sentence. "Such detail is not necessary, Vork. Thank you."

"As you wish, Commandant."

Alexis was stunned. She had thought that perhaps there were a few hundred thousand people living in the Colonies and half that number working in the mines, but nearly 200 million people? The numbers were numbing. "What do you do with all the newborns that must be produced every year?" she asked in awe. There was no way that they could build enough Colonies quickly enough to support that many people being born.

Vork answered her. "Each individual woman is only allowed a total of two children, after which she is sterilized. Six Colony ships have already been launched into interstellar space to establish Colonies among the stars. They were sent out in 2129, 2184, 2199, 2220, 2222, and 2245. Each carried a maximum of 100,000 souls. Each year ten new Colonies are built, each capable of housing up to 75,000 souls for a total of 750,000 new living spaces available every year. There are plans for sending out a Colony Ship every five years. Thus, the expansion of the human race within the UFC is well planned and administrated."

Alexis shook her head. It was absolutely amazing to her that all this had been accomplished in the span of only one-hundred-and-sixty-five years. Except for the destruction to Earth and the loss of the billions during the purges and ethnic cleansing Huang had master-minded, it appeared to be almost a golden age of exploration and expansion for the species as a whole, and yet the darkness that was Huang still seemed to hang over everything like a pale web of corrupt banality.

She still didn't see her place in any of it. "This is all very interesting, but I still don't see what it has to do with me and the killing of all those people in my time. What possible connection can they have had with Huang and his killings? Maybe I'm just not seeing it, but this looks like you should be thinking along the lines of killing off Huang and his whole family in the past to prevent this from happening."

All three looked at each other with that expression of quiet desperation, of guilt stemming from an action one knows is somehow morally wrong but which has to be carried out anyway for the greater good. It was a look that could be found on the faces of those who allowed the Kings of France to be beheaded, who allowed the ravages of Napoleon and Hitler and Stalin. It was that look of utter self-condemnation rising like a putrid redolence from the soul and adulterating one's moral fiber forever more.

It was a look Alexis knew all to well, for she had traveled down that road herself. With a subtle sign from Skre, Vork now spoke up, his smooth voice grating on Alexis' ears. "On 6 May 2240, Commandant Skre Finehair Yellowleaf proposed what would eventually be called the Yellowleaf Conjecture. The Conjecture is simple in its design yet holds the salvation of the universe in its embrace. In its basic form, the Conjecture stipulates that when the greater good of Humanity is in question, then the innocence of any particular individual is void and null. It states, in effect, that there are no more innocent people.

"With this in mind, the proposal begs the question of whether or not it is morally correct to change the past in order to preserve the future. With a series of vigorous prerequisites and limitations, each individual act proposed within any given time-stream is separately evaluated for its merits and the changes that it can or cannot inflict on that time-stream.

"On 1 August 2250, Time Index Conjecture #001 was finally approved after ten years of bitter debate and discussion. This Conjecture stipulated that, and I quote, `Whereas the implications of the MTP have been catastrophic for the human species as a whole, and in so much as the applications, the resultant conclusions and the immediate decline of Earth due to its inception have been well documented, it is hereby resolved with the unanimous opinion of the Ruling Council of the UFC that this conjecture be implemented forthwith and with due haste. Time Index Conjecture #001 will read as follows: All individuals with the prior knowledge of the MTP technology, its implications and its subsequent applications who can, in part or combined with others, produce the said technology or can direct said technology to be created, are to be eliminated from the time stream prior to their involvement in the advancement of the said technology by any and all means possible.' This Conjecture, with Colonel Meagan Locke in command, commenced on 2 August 2250 and has now been completed."

Alexis was thoroughly and completely shocked at what she had just heard. With this single decision, the lives of countless individuals in the past had been deemed unnecessary, perhaps even injurious to the human species, and in that momentous moment, they had been forfeited for the greater good.

It harkened back to the Nazi era of Europe, to the purges of Stalin and Mao Tse Tung, to the callous decisions of India and Pakistan to use nuclear weapons on each other. It was the decision by a single body of men to determine whether a life was worth living or not and in a single, unalterable moment of immaculate conception the world had been changed to a future that was deemed better than with that person in existence. It was a cold-hearted decision to make a change in the past with the technology of the future and with the even-tempered declaration of the cyborg, as if he were simply reciting a poem, Alexis had found the answer to the question that had started her on this odyssey in the first place.

For now Alexis Locke knew who had killed her son.

> *The history of the world is not the theater*
> *of happiness; periods of happiness are*
> *blank pages in it; for they are periods of harmony.*
> *--- Hegel*

26

20 August 2250
2050 hrs
Tianjin, China

"As I foretold, your attempt to kill her on the Colony was ineffectual, at best," the tall, broad-shouldered man said, his voice flowing like a bubbling brook, the words lilting off his tongue as if they had been born there long ago. "All your attempts will now be nothing more than small pebbles thrown into the time-stream, making small ripples that disappear with the current, affecting nothing. You should have done as I first suggested. You still can. Chan Ts'ao, chu ken."

"Stop speaking in riddles, damn you!" the Emperor spit out into the darkened corner from where the voice came, the shadows of the room like tiny eddies of light gathering in the darkness around the figure as if he were a shadow.

The man shrugged his shoulders ever so slightly, the disagreeable look on his face hidden from view, the fire in his eyes almost burning through the darkness. It was a fire born of loathing, of an abhorrence that went beyond the physical and reached into the dark realms of the irrational. "I speak but the ancient tongue, Emperor of the Everlasting." The honorific came out like a laugh, a raillery against the man who sat now in the gilded chair and thought himself master of all he surveyed. "One such as you should surely understand the hidden meaning in all that was once said."

Had it been any other man, the Emperor would have had him killed many times over for his intolerable arrogance and insults. One of the many benefits of the MTP was that torture could be sustained almost continuously for years since all one needed to do was transfer the mind to a fresh, unharmed body and torture indefinitely. Such tortures of his enemies had offered much amusement for the Emperor. But as pleasing as such a prospect was, this man he could not touch. He was immune from all that, apart from the world as the Emperor saw it and thus untouchable. The man in the shadows was likened to one of the gods of old, those immortals who toyed with man for their own amusement.

The analogy struck the Emperor as rather unsettling.

He had never believed in any of the ancient tales of the divine spirits who once roamed the land like the water, appearing at every corner, helping or hindering as they saw fit.

But now he was not so sure.

Now things were becoming different.

"I understand perfectly the meaning of the old saying you have used," the Emperor caustically intoned. "'When pulling weeds, make sure you get rid of all the roots.' It is as old as dirt and yet, what does it have to do with the situation we face at the moment? She is here, in our time, something that you said was impossible, that you said would spell the ruin of all that I have accomplished."

There was a shifting in the shadows, almost a wave of distortion, a shimmering of darkness that seemed to pulse with a life of its own. The Emperor was so tempted to rush over to the corner and pull the man out, to see his face, his physique, to know to whom it was that he had shackled his empire and his fate. But he had tried that before and ended up looking like a fool before the harem of concubines relaxing in the pool but scant meters from his dais, their glistening naked bodies calling to him for pleasures beyond mortal imaginations.

Yes, he had tried it before and come away empty handed, as if the figure was but a figment of his imagination, a shadow within a shadow within his mind, the words he spoke his own sub-conscious directing him ever onward.

The line between wake and dream was so frayed and tattered that such a possibility was not beyond him, was not all that implausible. The one in the shadows, the one who had given him his first hint of what the MTP could do, could achieve if placed in the proper hands, he was not only untouchable but unapproachable, disappearing like smoke drifting in the wind whenever danger appeared. In all these past years, the Emperor had never once seen his face. All he had to go on was that voice that seemed to flow like time itself, the calming tone of its perfect suggestions flowing like a supine spring. It was a voice now starting to appear in his dreams as much as in his waking hours, merging the two in a rush of blurred actions, decisions, sexual pleasures that lost him to all concepts of reality, his few lucid moments of silence like the seagull on the beach, sitting and waiting for the crashing wave that would inevitably appear and drive it away

Now was just such a moment, a silent tempest of unbridled perspicuity where he could see what lay ahead as clearly as what had already been. The figure was speaking again, as if whispering in his ear a history of life like Mephistopheles and Faustus, giving him the words with which he could grab the serpent by the tail and control it, or unleash it to suit his own needs. "What I said, since you seem to have remembered my words in your own fashion, was that were she to come to your time, it would spell the beginning of the end, for her presence here would mean that the barrier has been breached, the impossible obtained. I never said that it was impossible. Improbable, but not impossible."

"Was it the doing of the Colony Time Guards? Do you think that they have found the way?" the Emperor asked with feverish eyes, feeling the talons of his dream world beginning to sink into his mind, clouding it up again. "I will destroy all the Colonies and thus rid myself of this phantom forever."

"This is not known. But you cannot destroy her by destroying the one thing that you need. You can only destroy her by destroying her past ...destroying all of her past."

"But we tried that and it didn't work!" he screamed into the darkness, grabbing his head with his hands as the clouds of his torment lowered onto his mind and threatened to throw him back into the realm of fantasy, where he was incapable of making proper decisions. It was a world of knowing nothing but the bodies of those pleasure seekers and givers around him who infested his coherence like a vine around a rose bush, giving it a look of vibrant life and highlighted beauty but slowly strangling it to death, till in the end all that was left was the vine.

"We underestimated her," the voice said, barely reaching him in a murmur of wind. "We will not do so again...."

* * * *

20 August 2250, 2050 hrs CT
Helios Prime

"Let me see if I have this right," Alexis stated, her voice low and menacing, her mind reeling with the words spoken, the concepts given voice, the very darkness seeming to envelop her with its amoral justification for murder. "You decided that it was morally correct to kill all those innocent people because of something they were going to do in the future? Something that they had not even really begun to work on? With that definition, there won't be any innocents left anywhere. Everyone's guilty of something."

Vork answered for the group, as if his unemotional circuitry was the only one capable of contending with her accusations. "The people who were targeted for elimination in your time-stream were those people who had a direct contribution to the development of the MTP. It was the only logical choice that could be made. Their deaths served the greater good."

"And what about the people caught in the cross-fire?" Alexis countered, aware that she had used the same damnable justification when she had been active, had used the same lie to convince her own mind that what she was doing was correct. And now that it had been thrust back into her face, was being used to justify a decision that was not of her own doing, she saw the clear and obvious flaw in the argument, the deception and deceit accompanying it and giving it a veneer of truth that was nothing but a micro-thin layer of morality, of which the first subtle breeze would blow away to reveal the horrifying truth beneath. "What crime did they commit in the future? What about their contributions to the future? Were they expendable also? When does it stop?"

"All those that were killed were thoroughly checked out," Vork stated in flat, even tones, unaffected by Alexis' anguish. "The collateral damage that occurred due the elimination of those responsible for the MTP was insignificant to the time- stream. Their deaths affected nothing, their descendants would have affected nothing in that time-stream up till our time. All collateral damage was thoroughly investigated and cleared."

"Collateral damage? Is that what you're calling them in your time?" she looked at the humans around her, ashamed of her own species, ashamed and appalled at the lengths these people had been willing to go to satisfy their own egotistical needs. "What is a life worth then nowadays? Was there some kind of formula that you used to work your way through the time-stream to decide that person X wasn't significant? Who the hell decided what defined a significant life? How dare you believe that you have the right to decide who should die and who should live!" She was livid.

"The decision took ten years," Vork said, as if in defense.

"I could care less of if took a thousand years!" she raged back, aware somewhere in her mind that this was a hospital, that patients were becoming disturbed at her hysterics and shouting. But it didn't register over the outrage she felt. "How can you decide through generations that one person back in my time won't be the ancestor of someone who is significant? Who made you God?"

"Thorough research was done on exactly who was to be eliminated," Vork said again, as if the others had been rendered incapable of speaking about this subject.

Meagan seemed to be the most affected of the group, Alexis noted, the pained expression on her face more than the guilt of the past. It was almost as if she were sad for Alexis, as if Meagan knew something concerning all what was being said of which the others were unaware.

"Stop saying `eliminated,'" she spat at him. "Say killed, murdered. Stop making it sound like something sterile and clean, because it isn't."

Vork continued, ignoring her telling remark. "We have access to all the archival records, to all the possible contributions those individuals could have made to humanity during the time between now and then. They were deemed to be expendable."

"Expendable? So you've invested yourself with the power to decide who is and isn't expendable. Well, how fortunate for us poor souls in the past to have someone like you looking out for us and canceling our lives out when we've fulfilled our usefulness." She looked at Skre, who seemed unperturbed by the accusations flying through the air like hail. She looked at the general, who discovered that this was a good time to look at the shine on his shoes rather than meet her eyes, his objections to the same moral questions having long since faded to his sense of duty.

She looked at Meagan, who seemed to have sadness in her eyes, a melancholy expression that was misplaced, that appeared to be part of a larger problem that Alexis could not see. "Was I deemed to be expendable?" she asked, shocked beyond compare at what she was hearing, looking at those around her for an answer she didn't want to hear.

"Yes," Meagan said softly, her voice like a toxin to Alexis, startling her and forcing her to look at her daughter as if at a ghost.

"But then that would mean that you'd be never born," Alexis stated, not understanding, lost in a sea of contradictions that were pounding her relentlessly in surges of doubt. "How can that not be significant? You're the one who goes back in time and causes all the murders in the first place. If you aren't even born...?"

Skre now spoke up, his voice firm and confident, as if the decisions made affected him little, their validity secure in his mind. "Have you not noticed, Alexis Locke, that although Vork stated that Conjecture #001 was completed, nothing here has changed? Have you not noticed that even though you are here with us, pulled from your time-stream through some method that we are uncertain of as of yet, Meagan Locke, your daughter, is still standing here talking to you? Do you not find this odd?"

Alexis realized what he was saying the moment the words left his mouth. As far as she knew, she had died in that park along with Ian, smeared into the grass by the industrial hov and yet here was her unborn daughter, a daughter that she would not have for another ten years or so, standing before her. More than that, the MTP technology was still present. These people were still engaged in the life-or-death struggle with Huang. Nothing here was changed.

Alexis stared at Skre in bewilderment. She took a step back, both mentally and physically. Of all she knew about time travel, most of which had come from novels and the movies, what she was seeing should not be taking place. If they indeed had been successful in their time manipulations, then the future should have changed, changed to the way it would have been without the MTP technology. But that appeared not to be true. And Meagan, her daughter, was still here, alive, talking and thinking and breathing even though

Alexis would never carry her in the womb.

Alexis' notion that this was all a dream was beginning to grow. "What are you trying to say?" she asked, her voice now soft and low, an edge of danger to it that was not lost on anyone.

"No matter what we accomplished in the past," Vork stated in that even-tempered, easy voice that Alexis was beginning to despise, "our lives will not be changed. *Our* history will not be changed. In our time-stream, all those individuals whom we eliminated still exist. They still invented the technology. You still gave birth to Meagan. All is as it was. For us, nothing has changed. Nothing can ever change. We cannot affect our lives by anything that we do in the past. It is a limitation of the time- stream itself. "

Alexis narrowed her eyes as she looked at the cyborg, then back at Skre. "Do you mean to tell me that all the manipulations that you've done to the past do you no good whatsoever? What's the point then? Why even go to the trouble?"

Skre looked at Vork and nodded his head, as if giving penitence to them all and allowing the cyborg to purge the human's sins by the spoken word. "We do it so that those who now live in the time-stream just created will not have to endure the pain and suffering humans have been subjected to in this time-stream. It is done to help others to a better life."

Alexis' expression made it clear that she didn't understand. Vork noticed this and clarified further, giving the very secret of the time-stream to her. "The time-stream works in a very predictable and regimented way. Whenever we create an incursion into the stream, a new branch is created, split off from the main branch. Major incursions create large breaks. Minor incursions of little significance will sometimes cause new streams and sometimes will not. This detail has yet to be worked out fully.

"The major incursion we created branched off a large and new time- stream in which the MTP is never produced and thus Huang never rises to power. It is completely separate from our time-stream and yet has many of the same characteristics, most of the same people doing the same things. What it does not have is the MTP, Huang, and you. It was not done for ourselves. It can not be done for our time-stream."

Alexis gawked as if she didn't believe it, coming as it did from a machine, a fact she didn't fail to notice deep down inside, in the part of her mind that was still being objective. The humans seemed averse to speaking, to voicing the concepts Alexis found so hard to believe. The only one capable seemed to be the machine, the human construct exempt from the human failings and thus able to look at them objectively.

"So you're telling me that it's all altruistic, that everything you've done provides nothing of benefit for you. I find that very hard to swallow. It's bullshit is what it is. You decide that certain people who have done nothing wrong in their lives are expendable, insignificant I think is the word that was used; you kill them off in accidents that don't even appear as accidents, and then you have the gall to tell me you don't even benefit from it, that you're doing all this for the greater benefit of all humanity? Why do I find that so hard to believe?"

Skre spoke up again, as if her adamancy had sparked something in him. "It matters little what you believe or don't believe, Ms. Locke. The laws of the time-stream care little for what individuals think. You have not lived through the terror into which Huang and the MTP have plunged humans. You don't live with the daily fright that we in the Colonies all live with, wondering when the next attack will come, when our lives will again be changed and disrupted. And since you cannot know this terror, cannot understand under what circumstances these decisions were made, then you cannot judge us in any way. History may judge us in the future, and that is to be expected. Whether they see us as saviors or as Satan we will never know."

"Why? With the MTP and this pseudo-immortality, you can live forever and thus know exactly what history writes about your decisions," Alexis vomited back at him, her disgust with the whole thing rising up like putrid bile. "You can even write the damn history yourself if you want."

"You assume too much," Meagan said, her voice still quiet.

"Using the MTP technology would make us no better than Huang and his minions," Skre explained firmly. "its use has been banned from the UFC for generations. We live as we were meant to, perhaps as much as two-hundred standard years with the newer genetic manipulations and gene therapies. The lower gravity also helps. But as for pseudo-immortality... we want nothing of it."

Alexis frowned, her anger, that had once been so pronounced, so accessible, was beginning to fade in the face of the logical arguments and explanations she was receiving. She found it difficult to hate the truly philanthropic nature of these people before her, if that indeed was what they were. But the murder of those people back on Earth, of her son, still held a glowing ember in her belly. "It all sounds so perfect, so nice," she said in a slightly more subdued tone, though the under-currents of hate were still boiling beneath the surface. "It makes it all much too convenient, too easy to believe. But let me ask you something. If what you did back in the past created an entirely new time-stream, then how the hell can you be certain that what you've achieved will come to pass in the new time-stream?" She shook her head in exasperation, aware that she was not only unable to believe what was being told her, but starting not to care, to comprehend all she was seeing and hearing as an artifact of her death, a vicious joke being played on her by the god of the underworld.   The feeling that it was all a dream struck her with febrile fervor.

"It is possible for us to move from one parallel time-stream to the next and thus observe what has happened or what will happen," Vork answered for her.

"Okay, let's say that this new time stream is created by the death of the people responsible for the MTP. How can you be certain that the future of that time-stream pans out the way you expect it to? How do you know that the MTP technology wasn't invented thirty years later by someone completely different and the same damn thing happens anyway?" Alexis was looking for the flaws, the illogic that dreams always had, to prove to herself that it was a dream, that this was all a part of some spilt-second mental process that was occurring as her body was destroyed under the mass of the industrial hov.

Vork continued to render the explanations for which Alexis was so eager, that she seemed to need as much as she had once needed oxygen. "When we index back to a particular time, the time-stream appears to freeze in place from our perspective. We have yet to fully understand the functioning of time and time travel and its relation to what we so inaccurately call the time-stream, but from what we have so far gathered, and that has been proven, there is what would be best described as a bubble formed around the time travelers. This bubble remains intact until the time travelers index back to the time from where they came, keeping the time-stream uncontaminated from the effects of the changes until the travelers are done.

"There seems to be some sort of connection that occurs between the two time-streams, the one that the travelers are from and the one that they index to. This connection, this bubble, allows us to perform the tasks we have been assigned and then melts back into the time-stream to which it now belongs, restoring time back to a regular flow only after the travelers index back, after the incursion is over. If the travelers, for whatever reason, are unable to index back to the time from which they came, then all that occurs within the bubble is nullified as the bubble collapses, leaving no trace of the changes on the time-stream and the travelers are stuck within the current of the stream forever, neither in a time-stream nor out of one but somewhere lost between."

Alexis was trying hard to follow along but it all seemed so abstract, so senseless. "That still doesn't explain about the new future and how you can be certain that it turns out the way you want it to."

"The Dahlgren Theory clearly states that all parallel time-streams must, by necessity and due to the connection that exists between the streams, always be at the same index point along their path. In other words, each time-stream must be at the same point along the index. This date, 20 August 2250, can be accessed in all time streams that have been channeled, that have existed since the beginning or that were created by a major incursion into the stream. Tomorrow, 21 August 2205, will also be accessible tomorrow, and so on."

"You've lost me there, robot," Alexis said, aware that all three humans were keenly watching her, judging her reactions, her anger.

"When the travelers return from an index where a major incursion occurred and a new, parallel time-stream is created, they will be able to access that time-stream updated to this day, with the full panoply of history within it, as if it had existed all along. In other words, when we create a new time-stream, a fragment if you will, it is created in its entirety, complete. Although it splits off from its parent time-stream, it still retains a future that exists as truly as its past exists.

"As an example, say that Colonel Locke indexes back to your time-stream and changes the path of the bullets that assassinated President Kennedy. The first one. When Colonel Locke returns to our time-stream, she can index to the new, created time-stream and it will exist even at this time we are in now, it will have a full history created from that new break-point onward as if it had existed always.

"We don't have an explanation for why this occurs besides the fact that all the parallel streams seem to have to be equal to each other, as Dahlgren's Theory states. As such, it is easily possible to index over to the time-stream that was created with the deaths of the MTP creators and see exactly what that future entails, to judge how well our incursion worked. In this way we can also see what the deaths of the others, those not involved in the project but caught up in the process, has changed to see if they truly were insignificant."

"And I assume that you've done this?" Alexis asked, beginning to see a pattern in all this soup and having a terrible rumbling inside her, a vertiginous feeling that stemmed from the fact that her life, her contributions to history, were considered insignificant in the long run. They had just said, in no small measure, that Alexis Locke's life caused little change in the stream of life.

It was a poignant part in anyone's existence when they realized that their contribution to history amounted to nothing, living a Willie Loman life of insignificance.

"Yes. It has been checked and as of this date in the year 2250, that time-stream has not yet show any signs of the development of the MTP," Vork stated.

"Which makes our conjecture successful," Meagan added, though the tone of her voice said otherwise.

"Except for one small problem," Skre said as the nurse droid released the retaining field and he was able to finally sit up.

"Me," Alexis hypothesized.

"That is correct. Your presence here causes over three-fourths of our theories and laws and most of our understanding of how things work in the time-stream to become either invalid or subject to question." Skre looked at her with a half-smile, but his eyes held a grimness that was unsettlingly.

"But I still don't understand what the problem is?"

"There are, in fact, many," Vork stated as if counting off sheep at the market. "The most important one I shall state first. That you were able to index to our time is not that much of a problem to overcome. The theories, postulates and laws that have been formulated to date can easily account for your mind being here, with us. Since time travel only occurs within the mind, and since your mind is quite powerful, this is not such a major problem. The problem occurs with the fact that you have indexed into a future that for you is nonexistent." He paused here as if to wait for her to come to a miraculous conclusion from the data that he had provided. When she said nothing, he continued. "Indexing to the past does not violate any of the fundamental rules of either the Balakovskoya Doctrine or the Hijimura Principles. The past exists. It is part of the time-stream as much as this regenerative table is part of this medical facility. It is accessible through numerous sources. It is a simple matter to research any time in the past to determine what happened during that time and thus study it."

"But the future is unknown," Alexis said, seeing where the cyborg was headed and not liking the conclusion to which she was coming. It was a conclusion that made her belief that this was all a dream sound more and more reasonable, more and more necessary for her own sanity.

"Precisely. The future, which includes all events from one nano-second from now to a thousand years from now, is unknowable. We can predict with some measure of accuracy what may happen and humans find some measure of satisfaction in this process. But to know exactly what will happen at precisely what time is, by definition, unknowable. When the time-stream is accessed, when one of the Colony Time Guard teams indexes into the stream, there is nothing ahead. There is not even an `ahead' as we think of it. There is only the past. For us, the stream only goes one way."

The problem suddenly became apparent to her, or at least what she saw as the problem. What she gleaned from the data given might or might not be what the others saw. "Which means that I've violated that whole supposition by coming to this future here. I should never have been able to do that."

"That's one of the problems," Skre said pensively.

"But this future did exist," she complained. "I mean, Meagan came from it to kill all those people, so it obviously existed."

"Of course it exists," Skre stated flatly, with a slight trace of annoyance. "But it can't be accessed. There is a block of some sort that denies us access to our future. To us it is the past. But to you it is the future and inaccessible. You've managed to overcome that block. And we need to know how."

"Why? What possible use could it have to you?"

"That's one of the other problems," Vork interjected, as if upset that the human Skre had stolen his thunder. "We have no idea what it would imply to be able to index to the future as well as to the past. Your very presence here might be causing catastrophic consequences to the future. You are an unknown and unknowns in our business are dangerous."

She ran her hand through hair that was not there, the sensation she felt making it seem so real, as if she truly had hair there, as if she truly had a body that could feel and hurt and sense. That one little fact still was bumping around in her mind like a billiard ball, smashing into other concepts and pocketing them in an elastic collision of synapses. That she could walk through the walls, survive in space, yet still affect physical objects as if she had hands and breath and legs was a conundrum she with which was not ready yet to deal.

But all that seemed to sink to the back of her mind as the continued explanations impacted into her remorselessly. "What are the other problems that I pose, since we seem to be on a roll here," she jokingly stated, though her voice held little humor.

"The next major problem is the statement that you made to Colonel Locke concerning the presence of the three attackers in your cabin," Skre stated. "They didn't come from us. They were physical bodies, bodies that could not have indexed through the time-stream as we know it."

"But they had a poison that was far beyond our capabilities in my time and weaponry and defenses that were unlike anything that I've ever seen," Alexis countered. "If they didn't come from you, where did they come from? And what about the two who attacked the deli and took out Clovis and the others? And the missile that hit the taxi I was in that killed Fujita. If it wasn't you, then who could it possibly have been? No one else could have possibly known what it was that I was doing at those times, especially since I was operating, from what you've said, in a time bubble that hadn't yet melted into the time stream."

Skre's brow furrowed and Oli looked up at her with a start, as if she had said something untoward, something that they had not thought of before. Quick looks were exchanged that Alexis knew from experience were never good.

"It is possible," Vork began, as if analyzing the possibilities as he spoke, ignoring the stares of the humans, "that what we are experiencing at this moment is the defining epoch of a new future, a future that includes the possibility of indexing not only into the past but also the future, as well as moving physical objects through the stream. That you, Alexis Locke, during your time, were attacked by material weapons and physical bodies using advanced technology that is many, many years ahead of your future, suggests only two possible, rational options.

"One: someone from your time was able to index into the future, discover the technology that would be possible, and then have that technology constructed to deal with you. This is not very likely. No where is that technology used in either our past or in the time-stream that we created with the incursion Colonel Locke created through Time Conjecture #001, except where it naturally occurred during the proper time-stream, which is decades after the attack. This means that this option is not very valid, else the technology would have appeared much sooner.

"Two: someone or something -- for the presence of a non-terrestrial species can not be ruled out in this scenario -- indexed to the past with advanced weapons and technology that allows physical objects to be indexed along with the mind. They came back either to specifically kill you or to affect a change that involves you. What this change may be, we have no way of telling, for the change may not manifest itself until much later in either of our histories and it may have occurred in a time-stream where you don't die."

Alexis nodded her head. It all sounded so reasonable, but it was still so much like a dream. And what was worse, these people around her apparently seemed to think that the others that she encountered had actually been trying to kill her, which was patently not true. The three at the cabin, though possessed of weapons, were there, she was certain, to find something that she had, most likely the disk she had taken from Cav containing all the info on the five deaths. The two at the deli had no idea that she was even there until she killed the first one. As for the missile attack on the taxi, that one was up for grabs. They may have been trying to kill her by that point in time as she was becoming annoying.

She spoke, giving voice to her doubts. "There's only one problem with that theory. Until the taxi, I don't think that they were trying to kill me at all. They were there for something else entirely, I'm sure of it."

The looks of confusion and shock passing through the faces of the humans was contrasted sharply by the unaffected Vork, who simply looked at Alexis as if she had stated an obvious fact. Skre was beginning to quickly realize that Alexis was throwing curve ball after curve ball at them, changing his entire outlook on her presence.

"Then it would appear that we have an even larger problem than that which we first believed, Commandant," the cyborg stated as it began to analyze the new data and integrate it with the old. "It is very possible that since the two people these individuals killed were both involved, though to a very minor degree, with the MTP technology, and that these unknown time travelers were working during the same time index as Colonel Locke was, it can be hypothesized that what we are dealing with is an index from our future, at a sufficiently advanced time when they have solved the physical transmutation problem through the time-stream. Since our original conjecture was unaffected by these incursions, then it may be possible that whomever is involved was not working at cross purposes to us, but rather to assist us in some way we cannot, at the present moment, see."

Skre shook his head, the uneasiness on his face and in his eyes like gleaming shards of broken glass. "I don't like this. There's something wrong here." He turned to look at Alexis. "Were there any other times, between the time you accepted this assignment and now, that someone has tried to kill you, besides the last attempt with the industrial hov.

A smile caressed Alexis' mouth and then fell away. "Yes, there actually was another time. On the Colony, when I was running and before the HEE incident with Meagan." She shot her daughter a look of contempt for that little episode. "I was shot by someone other than the Colony guards, though at the time I suspected that it was an agent who had crossed over."

Skre looked at Vork. "Is it possible, Vork, that Alexis' death during any one of the incidents could have seriously affected the time-stream and the outcome of the future?"

"That is a difficult question to answer."

"He didn't ask if it was difficult to answer, machine," Alexis snapped at the cyborg. "He asked if it was possible." Why she was getting mad at the machine she didn't really know, but it seemed to be a handy release for her tumultuous emotions. There was so much happening, so many facts to assimilate that she was beginning to get irritated with herself for not paying more attention in physics.

"It is possible that the death of Alexis Locke could cause a severe problem in the time-stream, just as it is possible that her death could solve a problem of which we are not aware of, a problem that does not affect us and thus we are not concerned with but which affects those who want her dead. When we checked the new parallel time-stream that we created, we were but checking for the production of the MTP technology and its subsequent uncertainty for human survival. It might be of interest to make a new time index to see what exactly her death has affected in the time-stream and perhaps from there we can make a further supposition as to who it is with which we are dealing."

Skre frowned. That was not what he wanted to hear. He wanted to hear that Alexis' death had no impact whatsoever. It was a long-shot, but there was always hope. "Colonel Locke," Skre stated softly yet forcefully, that tone in his voice telling her that he wanted no opposition to the order that he was about to issue, just adroit obedience. "Please take Alexis Locke to the archives and let her look through her history. Perhaps there's something there that we've over-looked."

Meagan looked at Skre with narrowed eyes and almost blurted out an objection, that showing Alexis the future would only allow her to see what she had done to Meagan and would give her information that would be in violation of the archival access ban. Alexis seeing her own future could have nothing but unnecessary complications.

But she saw the look in the Commandant's eyes, heard the connotation in his voice. "Yes, Sir." With an arm motion, Meagan indicated for Alexis to follow her.

Alexis was well aware that Skre and the others wanted to talk without her being present and that galled her, but to be able to see her future, what she would have done had they not killed her in that park was a temptation not to be resisted. She followed.

Skre waited several minutes after Alexis left before he spoke. "Vork. Make certain that she cannot access any of the more vital information in the archives, especially concerning Meagan's birth or her life."

"Yes, Commandant."

Skre looked up at the general with that penetrating look that told Oli that they had problems. "It is worse than I had at first suspected. Did you catch what she said?"

"Yes. I did." Oli's words came out in hammered, measured beats. "Someone in the new future is indexing."

It was suggested often that the man who appeared out of nowhere and gave to us the secret of time travel was himself a time traveler indexing back from the future to specifically give us the technology. What is most disturbing about this is that it is currently an offense punishable by death to give future technology to people in the past. Was his indexing to us an accident or a purposeful act? If it was purposeful, then the question must be asked why?
— Commandant Skre Finehair Yellowleaf
10 October 2245

27

"You do realize that I must have said something that really shook them up," Alexis said with that mocking tone of hers, walking beside Meagan as she lead them to the main archive room. "Because this was just a bullshit reason to get us out of there so that they can talk."

"Yes," Meagan replied tightly, her mind elsewhere, her steps precise.

"And that doesn't bother you?"

"I do as I'm ordered. I don't feel the need to constantly question those above me." Meagan's barbed reply was not lost on Alexis, the tension emanating from her like a taunt drumhead.

"Why do you hate me so? What in the world did I do to you that is causing this animosity?"

Meagan didn't answer at first, but she did stop walking, standing in the middle of the empty corridor with a peevish look on her face. She finally turned to look at Alexis and her eyes flashed like blue icicles. "Don't pretend to be concerned about me, mother. I think it would be best, since it seems that I'm being forced to work with you, for us not to bring up the past or try to make amends for it. It's too late for that."

"Perhaps you're forgetting that it's not my past, Meagan," Alexis shot back, not willing to give in to this head strong girl who reminded her so much of herself. "To me it hasn't even happened yet so blaming me doesn't get you anywhere. I can easily see how you're my daughter. You're just as stubborn and headstrong as I am. I didn't realize what a bitch I must have been if I was anything like you."

Meagan stared hard at her a moment, as if ready to strike out for that remark, then started walking again. "Don't compare us." Her words were like poisoned darts. "We may share genes, but that's about as far as it goes."

Alexis, tired of the constant strain between them on this obviously sensitive subject, switched topics. "What do you think it was that I said that made your boss so upset?"

"That's obvious."

When Meagan offered no further explanation, Alexis spoke again. "How? I'm not seeing it."

"Then maybe you aren't looking carefully enough," Meagan replied with a blast of fire. She stopped again and took a deep breath, as if trying to control her emotions. She turned to look at Alexis, the substantiality of her body so real to Meagan's senses and yet so superficial, just like it had been for Meagan's mother in this time-stream. It was odd that it would be that way. Perhaps that was the way it always was.

Meagan took another deep breath before she spoke. "I find it disturbing that Commandant Yellowleaf has contradicted his earlier order to not give you any information pertaining to your future or my past. He's not like that. There must be something wrong that I am not seeing, something beyond the obvious that I picked up from what you've told us for him to have dismissed us with such an obvious ploy."

"I can help," Alexis offered, though it somehow sounded hollow even to herself. "What was it that you heard me say?"

"You truly don't see it. I thought you more sagacious than that."

Alexis felt like she was engaged in a game of verbal darts and she was the dartboard. "Do you think you can stop with the insults long enough to have a civil, meaningful conversation with me?"

Meagan pursed her lips a moment, an arrow of compromise flashing through her eyes for a split-second. "Does it not disturb you that there were others in your time, other time travelers, who were trying to kill you?"

Alexis narrowed her eyes. "It's an occupational hazard. And anyway, what does it matter how many were trying to kill me? You were trying the same thing. To me it's all the same. They were all from the future and saw me as a threat of some sort. I don't see how it matters. And anyway, as I say, I really don't think that they were trying to kill me until the end."

"And the darts that were specifically genetically engineered to kill you? What of them?"

"They obviously didn't do their homework," Alexis replied with an off-handed motion, "Else they would have known that such things are useless on me. Whoever they were, they certainly didn't know me all that well. They may have known where to find me at specific times and what I'd be doing, but they certainly didn't know what I was capable of. That's the one thing that's obvious to me."

Meagan looked deep into the eyes that were not really there, the emotions they betrayed but an artifact of Alexis' powerful mind projecting her image onto Meagan. She had wished many times that she had the same level of genetic manipulation her mother possessed. But the dilution from the breeding with an inferior had produced a genetic structure not quite up to par with Alexis'. Although powerful in her own right, Meagan didn't even come close to what Alexis was doing at the moment, had been doing since she had first saved herself from an instant death under the industrial hov back on Earth. "It matters because whomever it was that was trying to kill you, to take you out of the time-stream, could have come from any number of futures, even the one that we created. As a matter of fact, that's probably where they came from. How else could they have possibly known where and when to find you. It is the only possible answer."

"And...?" Alexis asked with raised eyebrows, not understanding what difference it could possibly make from where they came. They were trying to kill her and that was all she cared about. This was not her war and not her time and thus it was not any of her concern.

"In that future, as far as we can tell, time travel has yet to be discovered."

*   *   *

"She's powerful far beyond what we assumed," Oli said with that low rumble that was his voice.

"That is the least of our problems," Skre said with a deep breath. "It would appear that we have others indexing into our domain and making changes, changes that're having effects that we haven't foreseen. The last thing we need is for some other time continuum to decide they need to make changes in *our* time-streams, negating all that we've done." He turned to look at Vork. "What do you make of all this?"

"You will have to be a little more specific, Commandant. `All this' encompasses much."

"Alexis Locke, Vork. Alexis Locke," Skre said with a tinge of frustration.

"The presence of Alexis Locke in this time-stream at this time is perplexing. The very fact that she was able, without forethought or even, it would certainly appear, conscious effort, to bring herself through time attached to the mind of Colonel Locke is intriguing. That there were other time travelers not from our time nor sent by us who were operating at the same time to eliminate Alexis Locke is also troublesome."

360

Skre lay back down, tired of sitting up without a back support. "I know all that, Vork. Give me an analysis. What does it all mean?"

"The meanings that can be attached to this are numerous, though I must admit that most are trivial and thus most likely extraneous. What is most interesting is that these other time travelers were targeting people who we had determined were not a threat to the production of the MTP. Why this is, we can not know. Our determinations as to who posed a threat to the production of the MTP was thorough. The probability that we could have missed two individuals, regardless how minor, is approximately eight-hundred-and-seventy-thousand to one.

"Thus, it is unlikely that their deaths had anything to do with their connection to the MTP. But it is of interest that they died while in the company of Alexis Locke. However, the fact that the time-stream was not affected by their deaths is telling. What we need to determine is whether a new time-stream was created by their deaths and whether that new time-stream is significantly different from the one we created and if different, in what way and what it will eventually effect.

"As for Alexis Locke, there is but one deduction that can be made. Since we had planned on eliminating her from the time-stream, a fact that could be easily verified by the other time travelers, they still felt it necessary to try to eliminate her also. It can only be surmised that they deemed it necessary to eliminate Alexis Locke before we did for a reason that we don't understand nor can see. From this deduction and from the fact that she is here with us, now, having found a way to bring herself into the future, then only one logical conclusion can be drawn: the other time travelers found a major problem with her presence here in this future and strove to eliminate her before she was able to connect herself to Colonel Locke. The question we must ask is why."

Oli shook his head in doubt. "If that were true, then you'd think that they would've tried harder to kill her off and not been so damn sloppy and inept about it."

"This is an illogical assumption," Vork corrected the general.

"Regardless of whether or not the other time travelers actually succeeded does not invalidate the supposition that they wanted her death to occur before our final attempt. It is obvious that they, whomever they may be, didn't want her to appear here as she has now done, else they would have let us take care of her death as would eventually happen. It was a sure thing. It had, as far as they were concerned, already happened so why try to have it happen earlier unless there was a problem with the way it actually happened.

"This leads one to the only conclusion possible, as I have already stated. They didn't want Alexis Locke to come to our time and that means that they knew that she would come here attached to Colonel Locke. And that, of course, means that to them it is the past." Vork cocked his head a moment, then looked at Skre. "It is even possible that we will be the authorizing agency in the future sending back teams to kill her off before our current successful attempt at eliminating her from that time-stream occurs."

Oli grumbled at Vork's analysis. He could not argue with it at all and that bothered him. The cyborg itself bothered him. "What could she possibly do here? And if she does do something, how do we prevent it if we have no idea what it is? She might have already done it, for Christ sake."

"Or do we?" Skre stated from his prone position. "How do we know that she doesn't do something good, something that should happen to improve our lives? It's just a supposition that we might be the ones trying to kill her off earlier. It's just as likely that it's someone completely unconnected to the Colony Time Guard. But that's getting a little deep.

"For the most part, I agree with Vork's conclusions. What we must now determine is why they don't want her here in this time index and who they actually are. Can you draw any conclusions concerning who these people may be and where they come from, Vork, other than our own future?"

"Although data is sketchy, certain conclusions can be drawn. It is clear that they came from our time-stream. I say this because of the fact that they knew Alexis Locke's movements and positions with a certainty that can only be achieved through access to the records that the new time-stream we created can produce along with the fact that they would have no reason to tamper with the time-stream at all if they came from any other, for the simple fact that Alexis Locke exists in this time-stream in which we are currently residing. Any problems that her existence here creates does not affect any other time-stream.

"We also know that they possess technology in advance of our own in terms of time travel since they were able to index their physical bodies and weaponry. With the level of sophistication these travelers seem to possess in terms of their ability to move physical objects through the stream, it must also be concluded that they come from the distant future."

"And that makes it our top priority to find out what it is that Alexis will do here that makes her death so imperative to the other time travelers," Skre said to Oli.

The general nodded his head in comprehension. "But I do have one question. What if we determine that her presence here causes a major

362

catastrophe of some sort? How do we kill her when she doesn't even have a body anymore? I'm still having problems with that. She must have an incredibly powerful mind to be able to make herself known to so many of us at the same time. I mean, I felt as if she were in the same room as us, as if she was real. I even got a little aroused. She's certainly a feisty one."

Skre chuckled slightly. "Yes, she is one of a kind, that is certain. I'm quite positive that that's the reason that she was able to index to the future like she did. But that is a good point." He turned his head to look at Vork. "Vork, you need to start working on a way that we can, if it becomes necessary, kill Alexis Locke in her present state. Make it a level one priority and keep it to yourself. Understood?"

"Of course, Commandant. I shall begin the investigations at this very moment. But I must point out that there is another possibility that we cannot nor should not overlook. There is a chance that those who are indexing into our time-streams are not human. There is a three-to-one chance that we are dealing with what we would call intelligent non-humans. If that is the case, then it will be nearly impossible to understand what they are thinking and why they feel it necessary to prevent Alexis Locke from moving into the future as she has. It will take decades, if not longer, to understand a truly alien culture and decipher their motives."

Oli grunted at Vork. "Aliens? You think aliens did it? Have you blown a chip or something?"

"I'm functionally within parameters, general."

"He's right, Oli. We can't gloss over the possibility that it might not be humans. Just because we still haven't found any, doesn't mean that they don't exist."

Oli grunted again as if that made the arguments null and void.

"If there is nothing else, Commandant, I should be leaving to carry out my investigations," Vork asked without any hint that he found Oli's vocalizations threatening.

Skre looked at Oli, his friend for more years then either of them could remember. "No, Vork. That's enough for now. General, I have a bad feeling about all this. And for some odd reason, the stench of Huang seems to be lingering in my nostrils."

"Yes. This I smell also."

Vork analyzed his olfactory processes and found no usual odors in the air, but aware that humans had the tendency to say such things, he kept his comments to himself.

*   *   *

"This isn't the archive room," Alexis said through compressed lips as they walked into the main Colony, the large mass of the sun burning brightly in the dark sky above, slightly bigger than it appeared from Earth. Bird-song and the sound of children playing floated up to them, the smell of pine and cedar fresh in the warm and clean crisp air. This Colony seemed to have a much more country feel to it than the other Alexis had visited, and then subsequently destroyed. The houses seemed to be clustered together in little hamlets, the English thatch roof and half-timbered designs reminiscent of Kiswich, Durham and the Nuly Valley.

There was a potency here that was exhilarating to her, a life force that seemed to draw her toward it like she had never felt before and she reveled in it.

"I'm not about to take you to the archives," Meagan replied harshly. "The last thing you need is more information."

"But I thought you said that you followed orders?" Her voice was acerbic in tone.

"Not when he really didn't mean them. I know Skre and there was no way that he really wanted me to take you to the archives and let you look through them. That would be foolish. We've no idea what ramifications your foreknowledge of events could have. It could be just what those who were trying to kill you wanted to prevent."

Alexis didn't quite agree, but who was she to argue with the logic of it all. She was not even certain what was going on anyway and she might just as well let the dream play itself out before her mind finally died from lack of oxygen. The thought that out of the three Colonies on which she had stepped foot, two had been damaged if not outright destroyed, sat heavy on her mind. That all these people who were simply enjoying their lives in peace might have that peace shattered like a broken glass bothered her more than the death of people had ever bothered her before.

It was as if Clovis was in her mind urging on those lives she had taken to torment her with their agony and loss. She figured that it was probably something she ate, then realized with a frown that she didn't eat anymore because she no longer had a body in need of nourishment. That, of course, was something else that really bothered her. How was it possible for her to survive like this? She remembered Meagan saying that when a body died while they were indexing – a term that she still didn't connect with time travel – then that person's mind was trapped in the time-stream forever, unable to enter any particular time.

But that obviously wasn't the case because her body had died and yet here she was, moving about as if nothing had happened. Was she a ghost, a lost spirit damned to forever wander through the continuum of life and never feel Earthly pleasures again? She shuddered, and the sensation was so real that she almost forgot for a moment that she didn't possess a body to shudder, no nerve endings to drive the electrical impulses to the physical brain. "Is it possible that I'm a ghost?" she asked quietly, like a whisper of the night breeze.

Meagan looked at her mother sideways, her face screwing up into an expression of bewilderment. "I suppose that could be one way of looking at it. It figures that you'd haunt me even after you die."

Alexis felt the stab to her heart, the unbridled hatred of this woman for her so beyond her comprehension. It wasn't as if she had never encountered hate in her life. As a matter of fact, it was a rare individual who didn't hate her. It was just that she could not fathom what she could have possibly done that was so terrible for her own daughter to hate her so. It angered her, not knowing. It was like she was going to do something wrong tomorrow and was punished for it today, thus causing her to do the thing wrong in the first place.

It was one of those vicious cycles that time travel always seemed to create in the movies. She smiled, her eyes brightening like tiny fireflies had flown in behind them.

"What's that smile for?" Meagan asked as she watched the specter that was her mother. The idea that she might just very well be a ghost had intrigued her, started a train of thought that was leading to interesting conclusions.

"Nothing."

"Well it must have been something, else it wouldn't have created such an effect."

Alexis looked at her daughter with a mixture of bafflement and vexation. "What do you care? You hate me, remember?"

Meagan's faint smile, which had seemed to mirror the larger one on Alexis' face, vanished like a popped balloon. She looked at the woman before her a moment, then back down at the quiet hamlets below, the life in them moving apace, ignorant of the greater plans that were revolving around them. "We'd better be getting back. I'm sure that they've had enough time to contemplate your presence here."

Alexis realized that a small, fragile window had opened to Meagan's soul and she had thrown a rock through it, smashing whatever chance she might have had at making a little headway with her daughter. She followed her away from the peace of the hamlet with a feeling of foolishness for her own stupidity.

Sometimes it is the chance meeting between individuals
that are the most telling. A facial expression, a turned phrase,
a blink of the eye.... all these can decide the fate of nations,
just as the flap of the wings of a butterfly in Asia, can
affect the weather in Central America.
--- Dr. Vincent Cavalier

28

20 August 2085, 2300 hrs
The White House, Washington, D.C.

Cav looked worn out. He sat in the leather chair in the Oval Office, distraught and pensive, his usual heavy body flabbier, the rolls of flesh under the rumpled suit hanging on him like globs of gelatinous goo. The cool air circulating in the room didn't penetrate his sweaty skin, its color drained of all its vitality, his eyes deep in the sockets like lost marbles in a cushion. He stared at his hands as if they would burst at any moment, spewing plump, white maggots onto the rich carpeted floor.

The President sat opposite him in her designer suit with the high skirt line. The light gray color matched her eyes well and her cheeks seemed unusually flushed and rosy. Her eyes sparkled with a vibrancy of life, hope, success. She studied the report on the screen before her intently, reading every line twice, catching every innuendo, every subtle fact and hint. A smile barely touched her plump, red, luscious lips that her tongue continued to moisten in an unconscious motion.

Claudine Maxwell stood by the large, armored window, looking out into the darkness beyond illuminated by the powerful lights spreading their rays upon the deserted lawn in stark, bold conical patterns. The intense heat of the day was slowly waning, the humidity that had sat on the city like an oppressive quilt still unwavering in its despotism. She wore a pair of designer slacks and short coat revealing her curves in subtle patterns of sensuality, her eyes scintillating with a hidden pleasure matching the iniquitous smile touching her face like a sculpture.

President O' Rourke finally leaned back and turned off the screen, steepling her hands before her chin and looking down at her desk. Looking up would mean having to see the fat, broken husk of a man sitting across from her, and that she didn't want to do. She spoke, her voice firm and full of a conviction sending shards of broken glass into Cav's soul and ripping it asunder into jagged fragments. "I hope that this is the last of Alexis Locke, then. It's certainly about time."

Cav's eyes focused for a moment, a spark of life coming back into them in the tiniest twinkle as he slowly moved his fleshy head up to look at her.

She spoke again before he had a chance to voice an opinion. "Claudine, what have you been able to resolve with the fiasco on the O' Neill Colony? I don't want that to come back around again and bite me in the ass during the elections."

Claudine stirred from her vigil by the window and spoke. "It's being called a terrorist act. We've managed to place the blame squarely on the shoulders of a known terrorist leader and rebel. As far as anyone is concerned, there's absolutely no link between this government and the events that occurred. We're clean."

"And do you believe this report on Alexis Locke's death?"

"I see no reason not to, ' Claudine answered with authority, stepping away from the window and walking slowly over to one of the other chairs in the office. She glanced at Cav and almost felt a tinge of sympathy for the man who was clearly falling apart before their eyes. "I don't think we need to worry about any trouble coming from that avenue any more." She indicated Cav with her eyes as the President followed her visually to the chair in which she sat elegantly, using the desolated condition of the bulk of a man as proof that Alexis was gone for good.

"And you, Dr. Cavalier?" the President asked. "Are you convinced that she's dead? I need to know in no uncertain terms, sir. The time and place for people like her has passed. We're on the verge of a worldwide peace movement that'll bring prosperity and wealth to all the people and the last thing we need are rogue super agents throwing monkey wrenches into the works."

Cav didn't understand any of the words spoken at him. They were so much gibberish spoken from two faceless mouths. He might as well have been trying to understand the mating song of the cricket. That he had been responsible for Alexis' death sat on his soul like an acid bath, eating through it with a voracity that was demonic. Never had he felt so alone, so lost. It was if the floor had been pulled out from under him and he was falling, falling deep into a chasm out of which he could see no possible way out.

All his life had been tied up in her, all his hopes and dreams with her. And then, in a moment of psychotic disregard, he had listened to the voices

368

around him and betrayed the one person he had truly loved in the world. Now he no longer listened to the voices, for they held nothing but the lamentations of Satan, the mere sound of them driving him closer and closer to insanity.

"Dr. Cavalier?" the President prompted when the man just sat there unresponsive, staring at her with those dead eyes boring through her as if she were just so much dust in the air.

"I don't think we'll get much out of him for a while," Claudine offered, wrinkling her nose at the odors seeming to be rising from his sweat-soaked clothes. "He was pretty close to his pet project and her death has hit him hard."

"I can see that." O' Rourke watched him for a few more minutes, then frowned and called for the security boys to show Cav out. "I don't think we'll need to have anymore contact with Dr. Cavalier, Claudine. Make sure to take him off the authorized visitors list. And you might even want to lay some hints down at the Justice Department about illegal activities and mendacious Federal fund usage."

Claudine smiled as the Secret Service lead Cav out of the room. "I'll look into it, Mrs. President."

She walked with him out the door and both of them noticed the small Asian man sitting patiently, waiting to be shown into the Oval Office. Claudine was going to speak to Cav, try to assure him that she would make certain he was still involved, just to tease him at this stage in his life when he was utterly powerless, but instead she caught sight of the wealthy and powerful industrialist whom she had been having secret discussions with for the past year and in that recognition, completely forgot that Cav existed.

Cav's mind came alive with a brief flare as his eyes met the eyes of the small man. There was a recognition there, a moment of precognition that seemed out of place to Cav. He knew the man from somewhere. Even in his present state, it was as clear as day. And there was something in the man's eyes as well, a hint of surprise, perhaps even amusement at seeing Cav here, now, in this place, almost as if he had been told to expect it but didn't believe it until this moment in time.

He noticed that Claudine seemed to know the man also, to know him well.

A part of Cav's mind that was still functioning at a higher level took over and he stopped for a moment to re-tie the laces on his right shoe, which were quite tight already.

Claudine walked up to the small Asian, who rose and bowed respectfully to her. She smiled that smile Cav knew so well, that he knew meant that this man was someone whom Claudine was using for her own advantage, perhaps even partnered with for some devious scheme.

"Neh Hoh Mah?" Claudine said with a fluency amazing Cav.

He had never known her to possess any language skills.

The small man beamed a false smile at her and her attempt to speak his language, the superciliousness of his manner seeming to be lost on Claudine. "I speak very good English, Mrs. Maxwell. But thank you for your attempt." His voice was odd, as if it somehow didn't belong to him. It seemed to have a power in it that was insidious and deep, as if drawing from a deep well he didn't possess. It had an aura to it that enveloping the small anteroom and hush those around him. Even the Secret Service agents turned to look at him. It was almost, Cav thought as he worked slowly on his shoelaces, as if the man had an underlying power in his voice capable of mesmerizing masses of people, like other great speakers. But this power seemed foreign to the little man, as if it was not naturally his and it disturbed Cav greatly.

His escort, noticing that he was taking too long on the simple act of tying his shoelaces, requested kindly that he stand up and continue to walk and as he stood, he was able to hear the name of the man that had so piqued his interest and, it seemed, the interest of Claudine Maxwell.

Sun Liu Huang.

It was a name that would stick with him forever.

*   *   *

20 August 2250, 2305 hrs
Helios Prime

"We have a problem, Commandant," the wiry red-head stated at full attention, her bosom threatening to burst her uniform open as she thrust out her chest in an effort to make a good impression.

Skre looked up from his meal, the first one he had managed to get in the last thirty hours. His vexed appearance didn't deter the messenger one bit.

"Colony Time Guard Team Three has just returned from an exploratory index to the time stream Alpha Two. General Gudbjartsson is waiting for you in the Command Center, Sir."

Skre looked down at his half-eaten Sole Florentine with a side of pineapple-cheese salad and heard as much as felt his stomach growl in protest. He placed his fork down gently and wiped his mouth as he looked up at the stunningly beautiful girl who stood before him. "Tell the general that I'll be there shortly."

She saluted briskly, turned sharply and walked away. Skre picked up his wine glass and downed the last of the Wehlener Sonnenuhr Riesling Eiswein from the private stocks in his home on the *New Mosel Prime* Colony, then twirled the glass in his fingers for a few minutes, the delicate aroma of the dish before him tempting him to ignore the summons and just eat.

But that he couldn't do.

Oli knew that Skre was eating and would not have interrupted him if it were not of the utmost importance. And that he had sent a messenger to tell Skre didn't bode well. It meant that the general was unable, or unwilling, to leave his post. Skre rose slowly, still stiff from his recent recovery, and left his meal to grow cold.

The Command Center was not a large room, as one would expect from such a grandiose title. Five people generally worked during a shift, including the general or one of his assistants. The large holo-screens held various displays while smaller holo-systems suspended in the air held the vital signs of the team members currently indexing, their bodies safely resting in the adjacent rooms. Several other displays held a wealth of information on the various time-streams created, their history's encapsulated into manageable chunks of raw data, which could be accessed at the touch of a button or a voice command. It was simplistic in its design yet held the most complicated and advanced systems humanity had ever built and controlled the traveling that was beyond science fiction.

Skre stepped in and immediately saw that Vork and the general were standing beside each other, while a member of the Colony Time Guard, still dressed in the sleeping attire worn when they indexed, stood a respectful distance back. Oli and Vork seemed to be locked in a deep discussion before what appeared to be an unfolding history line.

"General," Skre said as he stepped up next to the tall blonde-haired man. "What's this all about? I was in the middle of a nice meal."

"My apologies, Commandant, but the situation is urgent." Oli looked up from the screen he was observing and at Skre, the look of confusion and consternation in his face obvious. "Colonel Gray-Feather has just returned from a routine index to time-stream Alpha Two and has brought back some disturbing news."

The colonel stepped forward and stood shock-still at attention, his eyes staring straight ahead but said nothing.

"The MTP has been developed in Alpha Two and Huang has gained power," Oli stated with a tight, clipped expression.

"How the hell can that be?" Skre exclaimed, stepping forward to take a look at the history line Oli had been peering at with Vork. "We just checked that time-stream and there was no sign whatsoever of the MTP being developed. Are we certain that it's the correct stream?"

"All the index markers were accounted for and the time matrix confirms that my team was in the correct steam, the same one that we just indexed to not twenty-four hours ago," the colonel said harshly.

"Then how the..." Skre was at a loss for words. This was not supposed to happen. "Vork, what the hell's going on here?"

Vork spoke in his emotionless voice. "There is only one explanation. The time-stream that we created using Time Conjecture #001 has been somehow corrupted and changed, a feat that all our current theories and laws concerning time travel maintain is impossible. Either we don't know enough about time travel to allow for the proper understanding of how it works or there is someone else indexing through the time-stream far advanced compared to us. Since we have already established that other travelers have made themselves known during the time that Colonel Locke was indexing into, then I believe we can safely say that these same people have indexed into Alpha-Two and have somehow changed the future within a single time-stream."

"But how were they able to do that?" Skre asked, the shock of what they were discussing still not completely sinking in.

"That," Oli said as he rubbed his chin, "is the problem. We don't have a clue how they did it, but they did. All the work that we accomplished, all the people we killed in the belief that we were sacrificing them for the greater good, has been nullified. The MTP has surfaced again."

"Where is Colonel Locke and our guest?" Skre asked with a sigh.

"Colonel Locke is currently showing Alexis Locke around the Colony. You do know that she disobeyed your direct order about taking Alexis to the archives."

"Yes, Yes..." Skre said distractedly. "I expected as much. It's for the better anyway."

"I believe that now we have a clue as to who is responsible," Vork interjected, standing there with his flat look, apparently impatient with the two humans for their seemingly superfluous conversation. "It has become apparent that a common denominator has surfaced between our history and that of Alpha Two. That common denominator is Sun Liu Huang. He has arisen in both time-streams and used the MTP to his advantage in both.

There is a sixty-five point two-one percent probability that this man is in some way responsible for the change in Alpha Two."

Skre and Oli looked at each other a moment.

"It would appear that we were correct concerning our little friend Mr. Huang," Skre said softly, rubbing his forehead in a vain attempt to stem the headache he felt approaching.

"The question is, Commandant, what do we do about it now."

*   *   *

"So tell me exactly how it is that you, what's the word... index?... to the past?" Alexis inquired as she stood with Meagan looking over the replica of a glacial lake in the bowl between two rolling, green pseudo-mountains. Bleached white rocks with specks of colored lichen stuck out of the mat of wild grasses like erratic teeth. Several people were having a picnic down the shoreline, their three children splashing and playing with the family dog.

"It's complicated," was the only response she received from the woman standing next to her who looked so much like Alexis.

It was difficult for Alexis. This whole time travel thing was still bumping around in her mind like loose cannons on a man-of-war, threatening to sink her at any moment with some profound revelation. That Meagan was almost ninety years older than Alexis was also a difficult hurdle to get over. Daughters were not supposed to be older than their mothers. There was something unnatural about it. And to have Meagan ignore her as she did, hate her in such a deep and profound way was tantamount to slicing her own body over and over again, the cuts and wounds appearing like some form of demonic repentance for a crime that she had not even committed yet.

But that was not even the worst of it. That she was having these feelings in the first place bothered her greatly. When she had discovered that her son was one of those killed, she didn't have nearly the amount of emotion inside her as she did now, standing here next to her daughter. What had changed? That her daughter had most likely been the one to kill her son, Meagan's own brother, Alexis was saving for a revelation at a later time. That Meagan already knew what she had done never occurred to Alexis, for that would be such a terrible reality to have to face that she unconsciously shoved it into the far recess of her mind. And why did Alexis even care what this woman thought? She was not even technically Alexis' daughter but more a stranger than anything else and Alexis had never cared what others thought of her, ever. It had just never mattered.

So why was it mattering now? What hold did this woman have on Alexis that was causing these feelings to manifest like locusts. These feelings for her daughter joined with Clovis and Fujita's ghosts and brewed beneath the surface of her emotions and yet there was a numbness to it all, like a lid on a pressure cooker allowing the contents to heat and build pressure yet didn't allow any release.

Perhaps it was not time for the release yet anyway. That time would come eventually, and when it did, she was certain that the full fury of the storm unleashed would be disastrous. She didn't want to be around when her own wall of control spanned.

In the meantime, Alexis was determined to continue trying to break through the wall Meagan had erected, the same wall, Alexis was sure, surrounding her own heart in battlements of dura-aluminum and trans-titanium. "Then enlighten me," Alexis said.

She had noticed that Meagan seemed intent on leading the limited conversations that they had down paths she chose and ignored all else. It was vexatious to say the least.

Meagan looked at her mother a moment, a fleeting gaze holding a world of meaning to it. "Why? Am I to believe that you truly care?"

Alexis slowly shook her head in frustration. "Are you this snobby to everyone, or is it just reserved for me?"

Meagan didn't feel it necessary to engage in another debate with the woman who stood next to her and thus said nothing in response. She could not say anything. Any words from her would reveal her falseness as surely as crying would reveal sadness.

"Am I still alive in this time?" Alexis asked, switching topics and seeing if this one had a more favorable response. If this had been any other person, Alexis would have long since walked away. She didn't like talking to people much anyway and to have to put up with this really taxed her. But then it was her daughter. There was some kind of unconscious draw to the woman that Alexis didn't understand and couldn't fight. She wanted to know things about her, to discover all she could about the other child she had besides Alexander. But from the reception she had received so far, her daughter might as well have been dead also.

Meagan continued to stare out over the lake, her hands clasped tightly, too tightly, Alexis noticed, behind her back. There were several small vessels on the water and Meagan's eyes negligently followed their progress as she finally spoke, her voice like a blast of cold, arctic air chilling to the very bone. "No, you're not alive."

Alexis smirked. "Well, a real conversation finally. What will I tell my friends?"

"You have no friends here." The statement was cold and harsh, spoken with a tone of hostility that would have made a lesser woman recoil.

Alexis arched an eyebrow. "Interesting choice of words," she said with derision, watching the knuckles of her daughter's hands whiten from the pressure she was exerting on them. "All this hatred inside you must be a torment to live with."

"It keeps me going forward in the face of all the death and destruction I see daily."

"Is it really that bad?"

"When you've seen what I've seen, done had I've done, then you'll not have to ask such an asinine question." She started to walk away, down the shoreline and away from the picnicking, happy family as if their ebullience for life was an affliction to her soul.

Alexis watched for a few moments, then followed. What was it that was driving her daughter on like this? What possible conflict raged inside that head so fiercely that it made her hatred so vehement? Alexis asked no more questions for several minutes, trying to fathom the woman who was her daughter, a woman who seemed to be possessed of demons that would torment Satan himself.

Meagan finally stopped by a copse of weeping willows, their dangling, mournful limbs dipping down into the quiet, still water as if they were responsible for the presence in the lake. Their stillness seemed unnatural, like a tombstone on the shore, hanging there in muted testimony to the lack of a moon to move the tides; to the decay of Earth due to humanity's depravity; to the rift existing between daughter and mother.

It somehow seemed a fitting place for Meagan to stop. There was something inside this woman that Alexis could sense but could not see. Something in there was so dark and loathsome, so filled with evil that it was destroying her. That Alexis could have done something so vile to her own daughter completely rattled her, for that was all she could think of at the moment that would explain the hatred emanating like waves from this woman.

"It really bothered you to kill all those people, didn't it?" Alexis asked quietly, her voice subdued, though holding an undercurrent of bitterness, the wanting to ask how it felt to kill her own brother strong and urgent. But the other darkness seemed to take priority and throwing that log onto the already blazing fire was not worthwhile at the moment.

Meagan unclasped her hands and ran one through her short hair, as if trying to purge the question from her memory. But she didn't bother to answer.

"I know it would have me."

Meagan's head lowered just a fraction of a centimeter, enough for Alexis to notice, to notice the throe of affliction her daughter was apparently keeping inside. There was a soft beep. Meagan seemed to stiffen a moment as the message was received in her earpiece. She turned to look at Alexis. "We're needed back at the Command Center." The relief in the eyes and voice at getting away from answering the telling question was tangible.

Without even looking to see if Alexis was following or not, Meagan took off at a brisk walk up the side of the bowl in which the lake sat. She would have to ask Skre to assign Alexis to another, for she could not take this any longer.

Her voice carried down along the sloping grass as if it were the very wind itself. "Nothing bothers you, mother. You've killed more than I ever did."

*   *   *

20 August 2575,
2325 hrs
Generation Ship *Argos*
Time-stream Alpha Two

He stood by the large, shielded transparent bulkhead, absorbing the mass of stars and nebulae that was the Milky Way, the barred spiral that was home to humans. It was a sight that always took his breath away, always inspired him with a reverence for the Creator's hand in the masterpiece that was the universe. It made him feel so infinitesimal. It was almost as much of a revelation as the first time he had seen Earth as it had been, in all its bejeweled blue and white glory, drifting around the sun in a timeless suspension. That had been something to behold, like an antique in a museum long thought lost.

Now he rarely saw Earth, that lifeless ball of dirt and stone limping about the somehow dulled star that was the sun like a lost asteroid. Of course, it was not completely lifeless. The animals still held sway over much of the oceans and there were untouched areas of wildlife still surviving without the interference of humanity and its unstoppable needs. But for the most part, it was dead to his species.

The home the God-head had given them as custodians had been dug up and mined and desecrated until even it could no longer sustain the wanton desires of a dying species bent on its own destruction. Then humans had corrupted space, as if the destruction of a planet was not enough to satisfy their greed, moving into the blackness like a virus, spreading in exponential growth and crowding the solar system with the numerous Colonies like seed spores ready to disgorge their deadly toxin.

And if that had not been enough to curse forever this vile species, next had come the interstellar craft specifically designed to spread the virus to the closest stars, to infect them with the godliness that had infected the very fabric of human existence.

And finally had come the Generation Ships, those massive constructs of metal and polymers and flesh capable of sustaining generations of infesting humans in their travels through space, infecting whatever it touched, contaminating every star system at which it temporarily touched base, spreading the human virus like a plague, like the rats of the Middle Ages had unwillingly carried to the western world their deadly cargo.

So too were the Generation Ships, unwilling carriers within their bellies of the plague of space, the deadly virus to which there was no cure.

There was not one specific event that could be turned to and pointed at so that one could say, *see, there is the turning point, there is where humanity became the monsters they always feared would come from the stars and devour them.* But if one were paying close enough attention, the development of the MTP was certainly close to the core of what went wrong. the very crux of the idiosyncrasy that was humanity and had caused the unprecedented expansion of knowledge to bring this nemesis that was humanity, to space.

Unfortunately, however, the MTP also began to assert man's self-sufficiency and to make a rift between him and the eternal truths of religion. Here was to be found the fountain-head of the tragedy of human history. God became the enemy of man and man the enemy of God. For with the MTP and its subsequent applications, man had no more need for a religion of faith, the religion of technology having risen supreme like a resurrected idol.

This was a situation that was, to him, intolerable. It was a situation requiring drastic measures and he was the man to implement those measures, whether humanity saw it as a good thing or not. Humans could no longer tell what was good and what was evil anyway. A line had been crossed somewhere wherein a grayness had fallen over the land and obscured that fine boundary between light and darkness.

The woman who leaned casually against the desk in the center of the room watched the man staring blindly into space, the blackness wherein the stars of creation shone like a backdrop to some comic tragedy that had gone terribly wrong. She knew what he was thinking, knew what it was that he was saying to himself, the self-proclaimed crusade to change the past and alter the future to his own ideals creating a bone of contention between the two ever since they had first met that fateful day.

Should she ask him what we was thinking anyway? Why bother. She didn't need a lecture right now on moral responsibility to the God-head that was his religion and his life. She thought it all so much hog-wash anyway, a waste of a fine mind and a fine body. If the God-head had wanted things to be different, it would have interfered long ago. But it had not and that was enough of an answer for her. The lack of any credible intervention – there had of course been the assorted Holy miracles and communications from the God-head from those who had received a revelation that was as much in their stomach as in their mind – had thoroughly convinced her that either the God-head didn't really care what humans did, or it didn't exist in the first place.

Either option meant more or less the same thing. Humans were on their own, as it had always been. Because of that, she would have to make the changes herself, take matters into her own hands.

But he was still useful to her purpose, despite his mis-placed beliefs, at least to the extent that he had access to the technology she needed, to the paths needed for her to see in the confused and complicated time-streams that now criss-crossed each other like intertwined snakes of perdition. And for this, she was willing to submit to his illogical faith and perseverance.

It was, if she were to be honest with herself, his very access to the God-head that allowed him the unlimited vision of the past and the future for which reason she was here, that had interested her in him in the first place and drawn her across time to this place and this index. Without that, he would be just another religious fool ready to martyr himself for a useless cause.

He spoke, his voice so smooth and full, so vibrant that it made her insides quiver in anticipation of some profound revelation in which she didn't believe but which he might actually be able to make her believe. What was it that he had that made her feel this way? "So the great rebel leader has come to me for help. It is ironic that you are in part responsible for the state in which humanity finds itself and yet ... yet now you are here asking for the very key to the Universe, nay, to creation itself for the express purpose of changing that which you yourself helped to create. It is indeed interesting how life comes around full circle, how it brings to a complete whole that which seems at the moment naught but a straight line." He turned from the window, his shock-white hair arrayed as if it were a halo about his head, his eyes white like the petals of the pure and innocent summer flowers, no irises visible, just that absorbing radiance of spirituality emanating from his forehead.

He spread his arms out as if in supplication and smiled. He gazed intently at her now, as if he were plunging into the depths of her soul, seeing the core of her existence and in that seeing, knowing that here was the key for all he had prayed.

When he spoke again, his voice was low and rough, a rumble of drums vibrating through the air like a death-knell. "Can you affect the change that is needed? Will this information achieve the end, which is what the God-head wants? For if not, then it is the Devil's work that brings you to me and I will not abide that."

"We've been over this before. You know the answer to that question as well as I do." Her voice held a hint of treason, a touch of refutation. It was the voice of a desperate rebel ready to institute desperate ends, coming to a sworn enemy because no one else would do.

"Then so be it, Meagan Locke. The knowledge you seek shall be yours, for the God-head has ordained that this be so. But I warn you. Worlds can be destroyed as easily as one kills a wasp with what you are asking. Be careful that it is used for the God-head and not the vanity of man."

Meagan smiled faintly. *May God have mercy on my soul*, was the only thought that came to her at that moment and she found that very odd.

*   *   *

2575 Common Reckoning
The planet Callibib, Ruling House of the Elrsai
Alpha Two time-stream

They stood around the marked floor in a circle. Sovereign Avis Blackhood Callibib, Supreme Lord of the Elrsai, stood reflectively at what was the head of the circle, the area marked on the floor by the symbol of the High Lord, the symbol of the power he wielded at the choosing of the other Houses in absolute sovereignty.

The First House of Skodl and the second House of Sha'qaq were also present. It was not, however, a full roost. This discussion and decision didn't require a full roost, its implications far too severe to include all the five

Houses of the Callibib Ascendancy.

Fraqaq of the House Sha'qaq spoke, his mind-voice a light lilting of song and speech commingled in a harmony that was pleasing to the mind even though the words themselves were harsh and abrasive. *We must prevent, at all costs, the humans from acquiring this. They are the plague that was forewarned. It has now reached us and we must be careful, lest we bring our own demise upon us with rash actions.*

Sha'dib of the House Skodl seconded this assertion. *The humans must be denied all access to our DNA and technology. It can be no other way. We must not allow them to subvert us. We cannot allow them to destroy us by a simple mistake. They are far too volatile.*

They both looked at the Supreme Lord, waiting for his reply, his approval of their intent and purpose. To allow the vile humans access to that which would, in the end, be the demise of the Elrsai was a thought beyond consideration. And yet, the advanced scouts had found the human Generation Ship, had seen them approaching the Elrsai systems in their monstrosity that was evil incarnate. There could be no other way. The Supreme Lord had to understand this. And if not, then they had to convince him.

He spoke, finally, after much time had passed, his thoughts firm in their conviction yet hinting at a trace of doubt, perhaps even sorrow. *It is agreed that we must not allow the humans access to our technology. In their hands, it could mean the end of all that is good.* He looked up at this point and into the eyes of the two Elrsai standing at their appropriate spots by the symbols of their Houses on the circle of the beautifully tiled floor, their plumage showing their distress. *But we can also not interfere in the past... or the future. We must allow time to take its course as it will, lest we be just as guilty as we claim the humans to be.*

They all locked eyes for a moment, thoughts of dissension flirting in their minds like summer butterflies, then disappearing into vaporous non-existence. For the Elrsai, there was no dissension.

But to allow it to happen would mean the end of us, the end of the Elrsai, our time-stream absorbed back into the main where it came from, Fraqaq pleaded.

This is a possibility, but then that may be the way it is to be. We are not to judge such things. I have made my decision. So it is, so it must be. They both bowed low to the Supreme Lord, his decision binding on them and their kin. But they knew in their hearts that it was a decision with profound implications for more than just the Elrsai. To give humans the ability to time travel would have repercussions for all species in all times, for humans had the annoying habit of destroying anything they touched.

One of the questions that must be asked,
and an answer found, is whether one can travel back to a time
and meet oneself. Is this possible? And if so, what are
the consequences of such a meeting? If we truly have a soul,
then how is it that there can be two of the same soul in
the same time and place? Will this simple occurrence
cause catastrophic consequences of its own volition?
Or is it just an impossibility whose existence
we should not even bother with? Such questions
are at the very heart of time travel.
— Prelate Ha'th Ramayana
First Vicar of the Judea-Islam Contingent

29

21 August 2085, 0015 hrs
Helios Prime

   Alexis could sense the tension in the room the moment she stepped in, as if it were a displeasing odor permeating the air with maudlin abundance. Vork, whom she was beginning to like despite her first reactions to the human-machine hybrid – the Cycomeand seemed to be the only one of the group she felt she could trust – stood speaking with Skre and the Nordic general.
   Others in the room seemed subdued in their work, as if they had overheard something that they should not have and now were despondent in that knowledge. With a little bit of concentration, she could actually pick out the surface thoughts of those few individuals in the room who didn't seem to have a mental wall in place and it was these thoughts that made her feel the most uneasy, for they were thoughts of family, home, life in such intensity as one only thinks about when faced with a mortal dilemma.

Whatever had happened had been bad.

"Colonel Locke," Skre started off as he noticed that she and Alexis had entered and broke off his conversation with Oli. "I have an assignment for you. You need to take your team and go into Alpha Two to determine when and how the MTP technology was developed."

Meagan looked at the Commandant as if he had a snake in his hair. "But Alpha Two doesn't have the MTP, Sir."

"It appears to now. The last exploratory found that the time-stream has been changed," The words were spoken gravely.

"But how is that possible, Sir?" Meagan questioned, aware that what he was saying was supposed to be theoretically impossible.

But there was strangeness in her voice that Alexis caught. It was barely there, but it piqued Alexis' interest, as if Meagan really was not surprised at all at the sudden, inexplicable existence of the MTP in the new time-stream. Was it possible that her daughter was playing both sides and that she knew more than they thought and thus had some advantage to play? If she were truly her daughter, then the answer had to be affirmative.

"We don't know," Oli rumbled in answer to Meagan's inquiry. "It appears that whoever was trying to kill Alexis Locke has now changed the time-stream and somehow managed not to create a new one. What was a non-MTP time just the other day is now a full-fledged MTP time. We need to know when the change occurred and how they did it, especially in regards to changing the future within a single time stream. Such technology is dangerous. It's the bane of all that we've been striving for."

"I'll leave right away, Sir," Meagan replied with a little too much relish as she came to attention like the good little soldier she was.

"I'll go with you," Alexis said, not realizing the can of worms she was about to open.

Skre and the general reacted with wide-eyes and a distracted wave of the hand.

"That would not be wise. We cannot determine what effect your presence will have on the time stream," Skre stated flatly. "It would be best if you just stayed here with us while Colonel Locke does what she's been trained to do."

Alexis smiled at the two men. "And how exactly are you going to stop me? If I'm not mistaken, I'm more or less a ghost with the ability to go wherever I please. I have no physical body. And besides, I'm sure that I can be helpful somehow."

"It's out of the question and not up for discussion, Ms. Locke," Skre said forcefully.

Vork spoke up before Alexis could respond to the authoritative reply of the Commandant. "It is my estimate, Commandant, that Alexis Locke will be useful to Colonel Locke on this assignment and that she should be allowed to go along. I also must point out that it is very possible that since Alexis Locke was able to link with Colonel Locke's mind at the moment that her body was destroyed, we may have no choice in letting her go where Colonel Locke goes. I would say that there is an eighty-five percent probability that Alexis and Meagan Locke are somehow connected on a mental level that will not allow them to be separated in time."

"That's not what I wanted to hear," Meagan said caustically. "Are you telling me that I can't get away from her anymore?"

"Mothers are always difficult to get rid of," Alexis answered back with a smile. "And besides, perhaps this is what I was brought here to do. Perhaps *this* is what the other time travelers didn't want me doing here in the future."

"And perhaps," Skre said with ire, his words biting into the air in response to not just Alexis' request but the entire disaster they were facing, "this is what they were trying to stop. We have no idea what it is that you do or don't do that's such a problem that you had to be killed before meeting Meagan and linking to her in whatever way you did. You staying here with us, where we can watch you, is the best possible solution."

"I am sorry, Commandant, but I must disagree with you on this point," Vork chimed in again.

Both Skre and Oli looked at the Cycomeand as if it had blown a fuse. Cycomeand were not known to disagree openly with humans. It was not built into their programming.

"I find this behavior of yours interesting, Vork," Skre said, though his eyes held more than his simple words. "Why are you so insistent that Alexis Locke go on this index? This is not like you to challenge a decision of mine."

Vork looked from Skre to Oli, his emotionless face studying them for a brief moment before answering. "I am simply stating the facts as I see them, Commandant. The data speaks for itself."

"So there it is," Alexis said with a half-smile, wondering if there truly was an ulterior motive behind the support of Vork. "Even the walking computer thinks that it's a good idea. So, when do we start?"

Skre continued to stare at Vork, ignoring Alexis' remarks. "Vork, I'd like you to do a self-diagnosis, checking specifically for any parameters or matrixes that are foreign to your initial set conditions."

"As you wish, Commandant. Though I am working at optimal performance." Vork closed his eyes for moment as he ran the self-tests on all his systems.

Skre looked at Meagan. "Colonel, you'll need to work quickly and quietly on this assignment. There's no telling how advanced our new found time travel partners are or even whether they're waiting in the stream for you. Initiate no contact. If any trouble develops, come back immediately. This is just an info-gathering index and we need the answers quickly."

"Will I be taking Alexis along or not?" Meagan asked with a disdain to her voice that to Alexis spoke of hidden agendas, something almost primal in its emotion, false in its conviction.

What is it that Meagan's afraid of? Alexis thought to herself as those around her made decisions without including her, a situation she was not used to at all, nor particularly enjoyed. *Why is she so set against me going with her? Will I see something I'm not supposed to see? Until her unplanned excursion into the future, she had always been involved in the decisions affecting her life or her missions.* Until her last mission that is, when Cav came and hauled her away from her cabin with ulterior motives almost falling out of his pants pockets. She should have said no as was her first instinct and now, because of her need to find the murderers of a son she never knew, she was stuck here with people who viewed her as so much excess baggage.

It was, in essence, becoming bothersome.

"There really isn't any need to discuss this at all," Alexis interjected into the argument. "I'm going and that's that. If you think that you can stop me, then go ahead and try. Otherwise, stop wasting time.'

Vork opened his eyes again and looked at Skre. "My self-diagnosis has found no errors, viruses or non-inclusive programming. I am clean and functioning at optimal performance."

Alexis motioned toward the Cycomeand. "See, even it says that it's a good idea. Let's get this started."

Skre let his eyes wander over to the general, who shrugged his shoulders in indecision. Skre pursed his lips, took a deep breath as if making some monumental decisions, then spoke as he looked at Alexis. "Okay. You can go. But you must do all that Colonel Locke says. Understand? It is imperative that you don't contaminate the time-stream of Alpha Two with your presence or make yourself known in anyway. I cannot stress this enough. You're an observer and nothing more. Touch nothing, disturb nothing, interact with *nothing*."

"You'll have to concentrate on toning your powers down extensively," Meagan stated as she shook her head in mock disagreement. Meagan was, though she would certainly not tell the others, glad that Alexis had convinced Skre to allow her to go. It meant that events were moving along as predicted, as foretold to her. "You have the most powerful mind that I've yet run across and you project yourself strongly onto others, as is obvious with the fact that everyone in here can see and hear you. When we index, you'll have to stay very, very low key."

"I can do that," Alexis answered back with indignation at the thought that she would be unable to control herself, though at the moment she had no idea how to tone her powers down. She had no idea how she was doing what she was doing now.

"Are you sure? Try it now," Meagan demanded.

She thought about it a moment and decided that the best way to tone her mental projections down would be to imagine herself as invisible. She tried that and felt that she had done a good job of it, but Meagan continued to stare right at her, as if she was still completely visible.

"How's that?" Alexis asked, her mind racing to come up with some way to make herself invisible both visually and mentally.

"Well, we certainly can't see you but you're still projecting a powerful presence that I can feel in my mind, like when you close your eyes but can sense someone is standing behind you. You need to try harder or else I'll request that someone else besides myself be assigned to the index. I cannot risk the rest of my team by taking you along if you're going to make yourself visible to everyone we run across."

Skre's face brightened. "That's it. How simple. Colonel, Locke, you're no longer on this assignment." He turned to look at Oli. "General, choose another team immediately and let's get this started." Skre looked at Alexis as if he had won some sort of singular victory.

Oli nodded once and then left the room.

Alexis looked at Meagan with consternation as her body reappeared for all to see. Meagan seemed quite perplexed at the sudden change of events, as if she could not understand how she had been taken off the assignment so easily. That was not supposed to happen.

Vork seemed rather perturbed also, or at least as perturbed as a Cycomeand can look. He seemed to be concentrating rather hard on something and his eyes became unfocused.

Alexis turned toward Skre. "This isn't going to work. I'm going on this mission and that's final, regardless who leads it."

"How?" Meagan asked.

"I'll figure it out. I'm pretty intelligent, you know. I came here when I wasn't

386

suppose to, didn't I?" Not wanting to hear anymore debate, Alexis turned and exited the room, leaving behind a lingering feeling of wrath in the air of the Command Center like a sweet hint of perfume.

Skre looked to Meagan with an inquisitive stare, but she had nothing to add. They all knew Alexis could probably figure out how to attach herself to another mind and index into the time-stream without a problem. What they didn't know was what she was capable of doing once in the time-stream.

Vork spoke up now after an in-depth analysis of a conjecture on which he had been concentrating. "Commandant, I would like to put forward a possibility."

Skre, wary of the Cycomeand after its unusual display earlier, nodded his head for Vork to continue. Cycomeand were not supposed to offer opinions unless specifically asked and they certainly were not supposed to contradict their superiors. Skre had only seen that behavior twice before. Once was when the Cycomeand was actually correct in its assessment of the military situation and its unauthorized behavior saved lives.

The other time was when the Cycomeand had been infected by the UEF and sent in as a foil. Skre had been present for both occasions and he was not at all convinced that either of those scenarios at this stage in their current crisis would be better than the other.

"I have been analyzing a theory that I have concerning the changing of the time-stream without creating a new, parallel stream. Such a phenomena would require considerable power and presence of mind. It would also require extensive research and the acquisition of hitherto unknown technology within a time-stream that does not contain said technology. As such, there is a strong possibility that there are but a limited number of people capable of such an act."

"Alexis," Meagan said before Vork could finish.

"Yes, Colonel. Alexis Locke has the mental capacity to alter the time-stream."

"The question is," Skre said, a bad feeling beginning to grow in the pit of his stomach at the implications starting to fall like dominoes within his mind. "Does Alexis Locke know that she has this capability and would she use it?"

"That is a valid question," Vork stated simply. "It very well may be that she is the one who changes Alpha Two by her mere presence."

"But you were the one arguing for her to go!" Meagan exclaimed, not understanding the contradictory messages the cyborg was spewing forth. "Now you think it's a bad idea?"

"This I didn't say. All I am suggesting is that she may be a valuable asset

387

to you in your attempts to correct the time-stream. Her going into the stream is a given and thus cannot be altered. There is little use in expending resources to deter or keep her from indexing. Perhaps it would be a better use of our resources, were we to use her as best we can to achieve the goals you wish achieved."

"Now that's the Vork I know," Skre said as he patted the Cycomeand on the shoulder. "I suppose that you have a way that we can use her?"

"Yes, Commandant. I do."

*   *   *

2575 Common Reckoning
Ldbli Prime: Home world of the Elrsai,
Fifth House of the Callibib Ascendancy.

Lord Dorcest Rama, Lord High Scone of Ldbli Prime and Fifth Liege-Lord to the Callibib Emperor, stood by the opening to the aviary, the light breeze barely ruffling his exquisite black feathers. His deep black eyes, holding the slightest hint of red in them, scanned the far off mountainside absently, watching the lazy spirals his hatchlings were making in the afternoon thermal. The streaks of red and green down the back of his plumage indicated that he was born of noble blood, into the House Piqaq of the Elrsai of the Callibib Ascendancy, which stretched for thousands of parsecs along the inner arms of the galaxy and had ruled firm for over twenty thousand Earth years.

He stood no more than a meter, his total body weight perhaps pushing thirty-eight kilos at the most. His wings, when fully stretched, spanned almost three meters, more than enough to generate the lift needed to soar high into the emerald green sky when he so choose. And that was just what he wanted to do now, to soar on the thermals with his hatchlings, carefree and at peace with the natural order of the cosmos, attaining inner enlightenment that came only with the freedom of flight, freedom from the shackles of the ground that seemed to draw the energy from him like a sponge, draining him dry with the ordinary problems of ruling one of the upper Houses of the Callibib Ascendancy.

Yes, to fly freely with no worries save where the next thermal might be found was what he indeed wanted now, for the troubles that Allab Yana, Duke Counselor to House Piqaq, had brought this day were indeed a heavy burden. What had been transpiring since that unwanted and unwelcome visitor had come from across space was what the forgotten prophets had foreseen eons ago. The spreading of the great virus across space was the nightmare of every Elrsai and now it appeared that his House had unwittingly helped in the virus' endemic rise to power.

Allab Yana chirped discreetly, trying to draw the attention of his Lord away from the mountains and the thermal calling him as much as it was calling Allab.

Has it been verified? Lord Dorcest Rama communicated to his Duke Counselor.

The Elrsai had developed telepathic communicative skills many millennium ago, replacing the awkward and cumbersome vocalizations that the more primitive and vulgar species still seemed to find so necessary, as if speaking out loud was a prerequisite for civilization. This was especially true of humans, that race of pirates and marauders infecting space with their virus-like expansion, spreading their diseases of the mind to all they encountered. They were a base race of primitive impulses and urges, an immature species, untrustworthy with so much as a grain of advanced technology. They seemed to incorporate such things into their megalomaniac need for weapons, war and constant bickering that was like a sickness to all they touched, as if it were the air they breathed and needed for their survival.

That their vile Generation Ships had been allowed access to the home-worlds of the Elrsai had been a mistake, a major miscalculation. That they had been trusted with access to the technology archives of House Piqaq had been ill advised, if not negligent.

It has, my Lord, Allab Yana answered with submission. *The Archivist reported that all data pertaining to the time theories of Bashar Bagnot have been downloaded, as well as the schematics and base diagrams of the advanced indexing technology. It has also been verified that our entire DNA coding was also downloaded to the human vessel.*

Dorcest Rama ruffled his wings slightly, re-adjusting them just to have something to do rather than think of the implications such knowledge could have in the hands of the immature humans. Had the Elrsai still been an uncouth military power like the humans obviously were, it would have been a simple matter of tracking down the Generation Ship and dispersing its contents throughout space, thus ending any threat the vile species offered.

 But that was no longer an option.

The Elrsai had forsaken violence as a means of obtaining solutions an eternity ago and to even contemplate such a move made his stomach grumble. He had no choice but to grant the demands of the humans else face annihilation. It was, in hindsight, a decision that should have been made in council.

Should I draft a communiqué to the First House, my Lord?

Dorcest Rama looked down toward the ground a good eighty meters below, then back up at the mountains that were so very, very inviting.

My Lord?

No, Allab. That would not be wise. He turned to look at his Duke Counselor, who stood the requisite five quants away. *Have the Techs been able to produce a human clone yet?*

Yes, Lord. Very fine quality.

Dorcest Rama nodded his head in an agitated way. *Then I will hold a roost. Perhaps we can solve this problem without the Sovereign Avis Blackhood Callibib, Supreme Lord of the Elrsai, ever knowing that anything has gone awry.*

The Duke Counselor bowed slightly and spread his wings out in the time-honored symbol of obedience.

And have the Archivists begin to research this planet called Earth from the database the vile humans were so kind to lend us. We will need to know where to begin. We will need to know with whom to begin. He turned back to the call of the openness of the air beckoning him, spread his wings out and launched himself into the relaxation of flight, aware that this might be the last time in a long, long time he was allowed to feel such freedom.

*   *   *

27 August 2575, 0200 hrs
Sol System
Time-Stream Alpha One

The small ship appeared outside the dead system almost magically, only the rapid oscillating distortions of folded-space, the sudden burst of trapped light and the gravity wave sweeping the fabric of space-time like a soft ripple indicating that a deep-traveler had arrived. The debris of the countless wars ravaging the blackness around the dark and forbidding planet that was Earth drifted about in random, elliptical orbits of patchwork chaos, morbid remainders of the senseless death accompanying the end of the 21st and arrival of the 22nd centuries.

The mines of Europa and Io, of Callisto and Ganymede still functioned on a limited scale, the deep-space haulers of the Aldebaran-Pleiades Consortium coming in once a year to carry out the last resources of a back-water system. The asteroid mines still served the plethora of O' Neill Colonies that were the only abode of human habitation in the system.

Earth was in the middle stages of The Recover, the extensive effort by the Huang Dynasty to allow the planet to restore itself to its pre-Dynastic climate, crawling along far behind schedule. The Dynasty had moved its headquarters from the wreckage that was Earth in 2250 and gone to the Aldebaran system, a much more conducive locale for the Emperor Huang and his minions.

No humans lived on Earth anymore.

After the peace treaty signed between the Huang Dynasty and the United Religious Alliance back in 2310, the direct descendant of the now defunct UFC, Earth had become the first joint project carried out by the two governments. It would take a long time for it revert to its former glory, if it ever did.

Most people viewed that treaty as the starting point for the expansion of the Dynasty, spreading in space like some anoxic virus, infecting planet upon planet in its all-consuming need for resources and living space, a limitless juggernaut whose very expansion fed its need for more and more. The MTP and pseudo-immortality made the growth of humans completely uncontained. With people living forever – unless killed accidentally or murdered and their brains destroyed beyond repair – and no inhibitions on the number of children one could pop out like candy, the birth-rate was an explosion of spores from a coral reef, millions upon millions of humans crawling over the Galaxy in search of a home, infecting all they touched with their vile and reprehensible morals, or lack thereof.

The Generation Ships, on the other hand, plied the empty reaches of space in constant exploration, building new ships as needed on their endless search for new cultures and species to exploit. Without the use of the MTP and with life spans but reaching the two-hundred year mark, the United Religious Alliance was not nearly as prolific as the Dynasty, and they didn't want to be.

The Treaty of Lar Thorssen had stipulated that the Huang Dynasty had titular control over of all planetary systems discovered by human colonization efforts while the United Religious Alliance, in their massive Generation Ships, had access to any and all resources needed, when needed, as well as the right to build a limited number of O'Neill Colonies in orbit around the Dynastic worlds. The Colonies now circling Sol had all been captured by the Dynasty shortly before the treaty had been signed, when the last of the Generation

Ships had been built from the asteroid mines and the UFC had been divested of authority by the religious alliance.

As such, the Sol system was now strictly Dynastic territory, the only allowance made for the entry of United Religious Alliance ships as stipulated for The Recover and the scientific teams constantly monitoring the slow progress. All other ships were subject to boarding and eventual seizure by Dynastic forces, the crew, if not killed outright, sent to the penal colonies over-flowing with innocents dying by the thousands every day.

The unexpected and unauthorized appearance of the small deep-traveler caused a slight bit of an alarm in the usually peaceful sector and fighters and a boarding ship were immediately sent out to investigate. Once the proper codes had been transmitted and the complement of the crew cleared as one of the numerous scientific teams to observe one of the many aspects of The Recover, all was quiet again and the small ship parked itself in a high orbit above the planet near the *Sun Tsu* Colony.

The rebel leader Meagan Locke relaxed.

She had bought the proper daily codes at a high price, including the loss of two of her better agents, and had been informed at the last minute that the theft had been discovered and the codes might be changed by the time she was able to get to the Sol System. Her fears had been, apparently, for naught.

She now looked back at her two accomplices: a tall, lanky woman with red hair and fiery green eyes holding a passion that went beyond intense, her body firm and toned, the many years of experience in warfare turning her into one of the best at what she did; the other was a short, stocky man with bulging muscles and straight, raven black hair tied back in a queue, his hardened and leathery face showing the emotionless mien of another seasoned warrior.

This was Meagan's fourth body since that fateful day when she had last been on the surface of Earth. Most of the rebels had found the use of the MTP – which was, in conjunction with the dictatorial and licentious Huang Dynasty, the prime reason for the continual wars and rebellions – very useful for their purpose, allowing the experience and inner-trust of the rebellion to continue through-out the years, fighting the guerrilla war against the far-flung Dynasty with an intensity making the Dynastic forces stand up and take notice.

Unfortunately, Meagan had slowly come to see that regardless of the resources at their disposal and the number of rebels they managed to procreate or convert, their strife was, in the end, a hopeless one. The

Dynasty was just too large, too far-flung throughout the galaxy, insinuating itself into every habitable corner like the virus it was. The rebellion was locked in a losing struggle at breaking Huang's death grip on humanity.

It was that realization, and the sudden and unexpected acquisition from the Elrsai of the key to her plans, that had brought her to this point in time, to high orbit above a planet she had not seen in over three hundred years. Here was the inception point of the virus that was humanity and the one place she might be able to make a difference.

"Are we ready?" she asked, already knowing the answer but having to voice it anyhow.

"As ready as we'll ever be," the female responded with a soprano rolling off her tongue like a harsh call to arms.

"Are we all clear on our objectives?" Meagan questioned, aware that they had only one shot at this, one chance to sneak passed the time-stream guards of the Dynasty and make their subtle changes.

Both her companions nodded their heads. The man lifted up the small container holding the DNA sample and handed it to Meagan, along with the broken-down codes and sequences that would allow the procreation of what they were hoping would be the beginning of the end for the dreaded Dynasty.

"It's a bit ironic that you're the one who will do this, is it not?" the man said, his deep rumble of a voice making the words seem even more important then they were. "The daughter creates the mother who creates the daughter."

"Paradox," the female said quietly, her eyes sparkling with an inner heat.

"The circle of life is beyond our comprehension," Meagan said as she ran her hand across her mouth, the dryness therein suffocating. "That we are allowed to play a part in it at all is an honor. May Vishnu the Preserver guide our steps."

The man and woman both touched their own foreheads with their hands. "Krishna is our pathfinder."

She looked at them for a long moment, memorizing their faces so that she could tell of their heroics later, then gave the voice command to start the index. "Now it all begins."

To be a shining light in the path is not always the best way to accomplish one's goals. Sometimes, to be subtle and discreet, to blend in with the surroundings and in that blending become one with nature, can be more profitable to one's attainment. A ghost who wanders the corridors forever, never making its presence known can usually accomplish much more than the ghost who throws the dishes about and makes a nuisance of itself. Such is one of the many paths to true enlightenment.

-- Yogi Krishnay
First Prelate
United Religious Alliance
2304 CE

30

21 August 2085, 0220 hrs
Helios Prime

It had taken a while, but Alexis finally found the entrance to the chambers where the bodies of those indexing were kept safe. She watched quietly as the team members, five in all, were dressed in skin-tight suits that were nothing more than advanced medical monitoring equipment. With their minds elsewhere once they indexed, it was the responsibility of the medical droids to keep the bodies in stasis and safe from harm, making certain that the lower brain functions such as heart-rate and respiration continued to function normally.

She was slightly surprised to see Meagan step in a few minutes later, looking like the proverbially determined soldier ready for combat, her mouth drawn down in a semblance of a frown that was more than what it appeared.

She walked right up to Alexis, even though Alexis was practicing being invisible – she made a mental note to herself that she would need more practice – and spoke. "I thought I'd find you here. Do you have any clue as to how you're going to do this?" Her voice was rough and acrimonious, filled with a bile saturating the air around them with needle pricks.

"Not at the moment, but I'm sure it'll come to me," Alexis responded acidly, starting to come to the conclusion that no matter what she did, her daughter was not ever going to melt where her mother was concerned.

"Like hell it will. We train for over four years before making our first index. It's not easy and it's not safe and it would be best if you didn't waste our time with this."

Alexis stared at her daughter, who was being helped off with her clothes by one of the human assistants. "It's not like I haven't done it before."

"And can you remember anything about it?" Meagan lashed back as she stood naked before her mother, the assistant holding out the medical suit for her. "No, you can't."

They stared at each other for several stressful moments, Alexis looking into the physical eyes of the perfectly formed woman before her and seeing in them a touch, a bare hint of something besides anger, perhaps even sympathy.

"I thought you weren't going, daughter? Or is that whole thing about following orders more bullshit?"

"Things change." She looked into the projected eyes of her mother, a woman she had grown to love over the years and now had to hate for all the wrong reasons.

Or perhaps they were the right reasons.

It was all still painfully confusing to Meagan and she knew that she could not keep the pretense up much longer, of an ire grating at her like a rusted file.

"Just tell me what to do so that this doesn't turn into a cluster-fuck, Meagan," Alexis said softly, latching onto that tiny speck of something in her daughter's eyes signaling to her there was more to this than anger.

Meagan sighed pensively, then donned the medical suit. "Okay," she finally gave in through clenched teeth, holding back with titanic forces the lash of forgiveness she was wanting to bring out. "Since you seem determined on this course of action, I might as well help you so that you don't fuck it up for the rest of us. You'll need to clear your mind of everything and start with a blank slate. From there, you'll need to imagine the time-stream."

"How do I do that? I don't even have a clue what it looks like."

Meagan sat up on the med-table assigned her. "Perhaps you should just latch onto my mind like you did before and watch as I do it. You're quick enough to figure it out as we go. Just don't get lost."

"Lost? How do I keep from doing that?" Alexis asked in surprise that such a thing was even possible.

"I don't know. It's never happened to me." Meagan closed her eyes and began her trance, as the others were doing. She was well aware that all was progressing as she had been foretold. As she had been forewarned. It just seemed so staged, so foreign to her way of thinking, working with the future to stop the past and all the while pretending to hate that which she had grown up loving.

Alexis, now worried, on top of everything else, about getting lost, reached out and touched her daughter's mind only to find her thoughts congealing into blackness, her mind calming to a state of oneness with her body, eliminating all save her heartbeat and breathing. Alexis tried the same thing, but found that there was nothing to her own self beyond the darkness onto which she could grasp, no heart pumping blood or lungs pushing air.

It was disturbing to realize that one's body truly was no longer in existence and she almost missed it when Meagan leapt out of her body and into the time-stream.

*   *   *

5 October 2020, 1100 hrs (local time)
Earth:
Sauai 'i,
Western Somoa

The subdued roar of the gently crashing waves was putting him to sleep. The cool breeze blowing in off the blue-green ocean, carrying with it a spray of salt and seagulls, cooled his body off as he worshiped the sun. The white sand around him shined like a large reflector, his sunglasses barely adequate enough to diminish the glare. His tan was coming along nicely, his body, as it reacted defensively to the ultra-violet destructiveness of the sun's rays, giving him that mis-construed healthy golden hue humans found so attractive.

His small laptop was discarded under the multi-colored beach towel in favor of the relaxation of doing nothing but watch the topless women in all their glory strut about the beach or play by the water. His own firm, hard, muscular body, in combination with his youthful and attractive face, had always been more than enough to attract his share of girls. That he was well known on the island for his generous nature and brilliant mind never hurt either. The faces of the two women he had enjoyed last night, in a spasm of passionate and meaningless ribaldry, he had already forgotten.

The sensation lingering in his body he could, however, hardly forget. He leaned his head back on the head-rest he had constructed out of the hard-packed sand and closed his eyes. The last thing he wanted to think about was the work he was supposed to be doing, but it started to intrude anyway on his erotic thoughts of Claudine Maxwell and that thong she had barely worn the last time she came to the island. He was expecting her any time within the next few days and the anticipation was making him even more aroused, their trysts in the bedroom fine examples of the art of love-making and eroticism.

He sighed contentedly as he put his hands behind his head and pushed the thoughts of genetic engineering and gene splicing out of his head and focused in on Claudine and her perfect pair of...

...a shadow fell on him and he had the distinct impression that someone was standing over him. He opened one eye to see who this interloper was, but the glare from the sun lashing out from behind her head to hide her features in a halo of shadow.

He opened both eyes and shielded them with his hand, squinting. "You're blocking my sun."

"Dr. Cavalier?" the soft and silky voice asked, his arousal immediate as she stepped to the side to reveal herself, the two perfectly rounded, firm, and young breasts with the hard, cherry-sized nibbles staring straight at him. "Why, yes, I'm Dr. Cavalier," he said with a large smile. "But my friends call me Cav."

Meagan extended her hand out in a demure gesture, smiling at him with all the charm of Alexis' half-smile, her eyes sparkling. "I have an offer for you that I think you'll find interesting."

Already interested regardless what it was that she had to say, he motioned to the sand next to him. "Please, have a seat. I'm always interested in new ideas."

Meagan sat elegantly, which was not an easy feat with thong jamming up into her buttocks both unfamiliar and uncomfortable. Why the women of this century had ever thought it a good thing to wear these diminutive scraps of fabric was beyond her. With what it covered, or didn't cover as the case may be, she might as well have gone completely nude. That, however, might have been a little too risqué and she chose to endure the discomfort of the string that seemed determined to find its own place inside her rectum.

Such luxuries as lying about on a beach and doing nothing were extremely foreign to her.

"And what's your name, my delightful young beauty?" Cav asked as he purposefully kept his gaze on her stunning blue-green eyes, knowing that he would have more than enough time in the near future to check out the rest of her body. He felt lucky about this one.

Had someone asked him about Claudine, he would have responded, *Claudine who?*

"Name's aren't important. Do you have a room nearby?"

Cav had his computer, towel, book and other assorted items in his hand within a matter of seconds as he stood and offered her his hand. "As a matter of fact, I do."

He lay strewn across the bed, every nerve of his body afire with the stimulation he just had the immense pleasure of experiencing, far overwhelming anything he had ever felt before. Whatever she was, she was most certainly a goddess, her skills in bed incomparable to anyone he had ever been with or even read about. He didn't notice when she left quietly, didn't notice the data she stored in his computer, or the small sample of DNA she left in his jacket pocket.

She disappeared as if she had never existed.

When Cav finally awoke and, after a long shower and cool drink of water, checked his e-mail, he was startled to find the following message typed onto his screen:

The data that I have given you will solve the problems you're having with the genetic code you've been working with. The DNA sample in your pocket will allow you to begin the growing cycle. Build her well. She is the salvation of the future. But be warned: build no others

*　　*　　*

The Time-stream

Alexis' head exploded in a fire of colors and images. Like the first time she had linked with Meagan on that grassy field by the lake and seen the future and the past merge into one, so it was now. At the moment of transition, she felt Meagan slipping away, the tenuous link established, fragile in its structure, weak in its content.

She had concentrated hard, grasped onto whatever she could, reached into her daughter's mind with a fury that was primal and was thrown into the time-stream in a rush of unbelievable turbulence. She no longer felt her body, as she had when on the Colony. All she felt now was a freedom that was exhilarating, a oneness with the cosmos beyond description. She saw around her what appeared to be wisps of smoke, gently floating in a mat of blackness, stretching off into infinity, moving in soft, slow undulations like a waking snake after a cold night. She could see several of the smoke trails, what she took to be separate time-streams, running parallel to each other.

To one side the trails all began to merge into one, each parallel stream eventually merging into a larger main stream until only one stream remained, thick and strong and alive. To the other side the streams continued to separate from the main stream until it was impossible to tell which was the main stream and which were the parallel streams, like an ever-growing hydra writhing and wriggling in soothing motions of pulsing energy.

Within each stream of smoke she could make out images and events, the faces of people and things and planets and stars; life and death. The whole matrix of what life was lay before her in numerous duplications only slightly different in some cases, vastly altered in others. She saw that some of the streams come to a stop long before they reached infinity, as if they just diffused out in a cloud of scattered particles, the smoke of which they appeared to be made dispersed into the blackness, those poor souls trapped in the fateful stream lost in an aborted scream of terror.

And then she realized that she was seeing the future, seeing both sides of the time-streams that Meagan and Vork said could not be seen. She shuddered with the realization, with the cognition grabbing her in a fist of iron and blood, reaching into her soul and tearing at it with the lost cries of millions. Alexis, with that start of sudden cognition shaking a soul like jelly, realized that she might just be the only one who could see this sight splayed out before her like a tempered tempest of destiny. Should she tell Meagan, reveal that she can see the future? That she had access to information that no one else did? She decided to wait, to see what developed.

She had learned long ago – did that term even apply to her anymore? – that giving out too much information on what you knew was like painting a big sign on your back that read *abuse me*. She would wait, hold this card until she could determine what was really happening, why Skre and that tall, handsome general were both so set against her going on this trip.

She also realized that she was not alone, that there were others here with her, floating in a time-less melee of lost opportunities, adrift in a sea of space without time, trapped in a time without space until all that was left was a numbness wanting release. There was a multitude of them and they all began to converge on her like vultures to carrion, the power and light of her mind drawing them ever onward to her, to touch her, feel her, be her; and in that being, escape their immurement from the streams drifting like lazy smoke upon the blackness.

Meagan's voice came to her then, her daughter's presence like a sop to the many minds converging. *You must stay clear of The Lost, for they will attach themselves to you in an effort to escape their hellish bonds, and in that attachment, keep you from ever leaving, like a drowning man drowning his rescuer in his panic.*

The others screamed silently in anguish at the presence of Meagan and then faded off into the dark shadows of time where they had been left behind, echoes of languishing spirits whose crimes were written in obscure tomes to which only the gods had access.

Alexis was horrified, the thoughts of an impending attachment of the anguished to her mind, like a gloominess to her soul. *How did all these people end up lost?*

Meagan spoke again, her tone rapid yet calm, the anger displayed before muted. *Now that I have you where we can talk without the fear of being overheard, I must explain to you what it is that you must do, for you didn't come to the future by accident. It was all planned out long ago, or actually far in the future if you want to be technical.*

Alexis felt comprehension pass her by like a train on the wrong track. *What the hell are you talking about? And what about the others? Where's the rest of the team?*

They've already indexed to the assigned stream. You and I must talk and here is the only place possible.

Alexis could sense the souls Meagan had referred to as The Lost hovering on the periphery, waiting for something she could not comprehend. It was like a feeling of misplaced keys, poking your sub-conscious in pinpricks of remembrance. *Won't they miss us?*

One of the nice things about indexing is that while we're here, in the amalgamation, the in-between time where the streams are visible, time has no meaning. Although it is strictly against the rules and procedures of the Time Colony Guards, we can spend as long as we like in here and then just index to the proper time without losing a moment. We will be able to index to the exact moment the rest of the team appeared in the stream and the other members of the team will never know the difference.

Alexis found that extremely interesting. If it were true, and she had no reason to doubt it, then these Time Guards could affect the course of history on their own, with their own agenda, and no one would be the wiser. *Doesn't that lead to irresistible temptation? I mean, what keeps you from changing whatever you want?*

Our honor. Our bond to the Colony Time Guards not to change events for personal gain. We were all chosen with care, screened for mental instabilities, psychosis. But that's not the issue. There are things you need to know, that must be explained to you now.

Alexis could feel something major about to happen, some life-altering event was about to transpire and yet she felt torn, unable to concentrate on any one, singular thing. She felt lost, as if all the time-streams were calling to her, all the dispersed streams pleading with her to help them as they scattered like chaff before the wind. She could hear the faint grasp of voices in her mind, like distant thunder on the wind. They were pleading in a pelting of passion beginning to fill her mind with a mimic of lost lives gone by.

Her daughter's voice brought her partially back to the reality of her current objective. *Many years ago, I was approached by a Meagan from the future, the far future. In this meeting, your arrival was foretold, for you were created for one purpose and one purpose only: to eliminate the MTP from the time-streams once and for all and correct the mistake that was made with its implementation.*

How the hell can I do that?" Alexis asked with a growing feeling of dread. Finding her son's killers, once her prime purpose, now seemed like spilled milk.

Because you're a free agent, one of The Lost who can, against all the rules, move freely into and out of any time-stream. You have the power to be able to affect changes in all the time-streams at once, to, in essence, bind them together in one fraction of a moment and make the changes that will affect all the streams from that point onward.

And Cav knew all this when he created me? Alexis asked, what she was hearing spinning her mind into a maelstrom of confusion. *Why do I seriously doubt that? He made me to be the perfect agent, to work for whatever government paid the highest and help secure the world from what he saw as evil and corruption. He was in it for the money and the prestige.*

Alexis could sense the rising anger and frustration from Meagan. *Can you please just listen and not interrupt. What I have to say is crucial and you need to understand it. Where do you think Cav came up with the DNA structures for you? With the altered mindsets that you and no one else has? Did you ever wonder why all his other creations that came from the same basic structures went so bad, failed? He was a brilliant man, that's for certain, but he wasn't brilliant enough to leap several hundred years into the future with his research like he did. He had help.*

Alexis knew the questions were rhetorical and didn't answer, though the issues Meagan had raised made her question all she had thought she knew about Cav, and her own creation.

You're the first product of a fusion of human and alien, a purposefully made creation from the future to fulfill a purpose in the past. Your death under that hov, with me there, was all planned. I was told where you would be and how to create the being that you now are, for no one else can do what you can do. You are pure mind, an amalgam of human capacity for creativity and alien power of thought. That you can move into this void between times as freely as I can is testimony to the perfect design that you are. You can do things that no one else can do and that's the whole point. It's the whole reason for your existence.

The whole reason? Alexis asked, unable to contain herself, to keep from voicing the terrible revelation that she, Alexis Locke, was not only non-human but also built specifically for one purpose and one purpose only. She was alien. Ian had been correct to be so wary of her.

That thought almost drowned out the rising voices in her mind like a thunderclap, almost stunning her into a submissive stupor. To be built for one purpose and one purpose only was the same as saying her life had meant nothing, her accomplishments and background null and void with a single spoken sentence. It was cold and cruel and hurt like a knife to the chest, the searing disclosure blazing into her soul like an iron, branding her with a life that was meaningless. She felt like a destitute forest that had just endured a raging firestorm, burnt barren of all that had been and left with a blackened and devastated echo of past glories.

With a single word, Meagan had stripped Alexis of her soul, robbed her of her heritage and left her stranded on the shore like a piece of driftwood, with no past and no future.

Why? Was all she could say, to vocalize in the mental exchange they were sharing.

Meagan could sense the devastation, the utter ruin that was left of the fortress that had been Alexis, and almost broke down. The sense of her mother so lost and alone was almost too much for the daughter to bear. But she knew that she needed to continue, to tell it all and in the telling not reveal her part in it or the demise that would come if Alexis was successful. *Why is not important at the moment*, was the only answer that she could make.

It's important to me, Alexis fired back, though it lacked the intensity of her former self. *You tell me that all that I've done is for naught, that my life is not only forfeit to my creators but harnessed to a higher purpose that makes all that I've ever done null and void and you say it's not important? What could you possibly say, what could I possibly do that could make up for the wasted years I've apparently spent in pursuit of a goal that's been unobtainable?*

As I said, Meagan tried to clarify, fighting back the emotions straining for release inside her and in their stead bringing forth the hatred and animosity that would make it easier on both of them.   For hating her mother was the only way she had learned she could do all this to her. *It's up to you to correct the mistakes of the past and change the fate of the future. You're whining and complaining is useless and beneath you.*

That's not good enough, Alexis shot back, the lost echoes of her past slamming into her with the need for recognition. *You've to give me more than that.*

I can't. All I can tell you is what I was told. I thought that you would have taken this a little better. This whining is most unbecoming.

Alexis felt a profusion of emotions run the gauntlet of her mind in a milli-second of utter disbelief. Whining? She's told that her life has been meaningless up to this point and all that she gets as a reply is that she should stop whining? *Why do you want me to hate you so much, because you're doing a damn good job of it.*

Your feelings toward me are none of my concern. All I care about is relaying the message that I was asked to give, that is all. Whether you hate me or not doesn't bother me in the least. I expected you to live up to your design, to your heritage, but in this, I was obviously mistaken." Meagan was dying inside, her soul tore apart in a parody of shame for the lies she was being forced to bring forth. Was it all worth the effort, the love lost, the hatred growing with each word spoken?

Alexis felt like killing. For the briefest of moments, that blackest of thoughts flirted with her consciousness and demanded action, requiring compensation. This attempt to provoke Alexis, to burn any bridges that might have existed between the two, was far too obvious, far too open and flagrant. There had to be something behind it all, something else besides this animosity that was so feral in its nature.

Meagan continued, sensing that she was getting to Alexis, that the hatred and indifference she was spewing forth in streams of savage abandon were beginning to take affect, to achieve the desired effect. *Your sole mission is to bind, for a brief moment, all the time streams together into a single time and in that time index make the changes that will be permanent in all the streams. It is all that you're to do, all that you were created for. There is nothing else. You have no life. Your life is forfeit to the greater good and there is nothing that you can do about it. Salvation is not for you.*

How? Did this Meagan from the future tell you how this was supposed to happen or did she just expect me to know? Alexis spewed back, lost to all simple reason and caught in the web of loathing that Meagan was spinning. *How do I know that this isn't just some excuse by you to get what you want done? How do I know that you aren't the bad person in all this, wanting to destroy all the time-streams for some radical position or offense committed?*

You don't, Meagan said simply. *All you have is what you've seen so far and what your conscience tells you. You've seen the near destruction of Earth, the war between humans that kills without restraints. You heard the history of my time-stream, saw all the mass murders and social disorder that came from the MTP. How can this be questioned as being anything but evil?*

I still don't know what the hell is happening to me, so for all I know, this could all be some type of dream, or even some type of side-effect of the MTP that was, perhaps, used on me and I don't even know about it. This could all be some vast, sophisticated virtual reality wherein you're trying to get me to do your dirty work for you. When it comes right down to it, I don't know jack shit. I could be lying on that grassy field under that hov, my life oozing out of me and all this could be a last attempt to gain information from me.

Meagan had expected this line of questioning to appear eventually. It was the only logical progression from the facts that could be made if one didn't choose to believe that it was all real. And the Meagan from the future had anticipated it also, had told her that it would happen as if she had been there, experienced it first-hand. It was very possible that she had.

The future Meagan had never clearly stated from what time-stream she had come and it was altogether possible that she was from the same stream and not from an alternate, parallel one. If that was the case, then it was not that far a leap to ascertain that the future Meagan had experienced this very moment in time exactly as it was panning out now, the cycle of the stream repeating over and over again as it regenerated itself and flowed in a circle of continuous renewal. It had been enough of a shock to see herself in the future – for the future Meagan had traveled physically through the stream in the innards of a ship, the technology she possessed far in advance of anything Meagan had ever dreamt possible and thus Meagan had actually been able to see the physical body of her future self, a self not much different from what she looked like now – and to know that she would live generations further than she had thought possible.

To have been cognizant enough, at such a meeting, to ask the proper questions and gain the appropriate knowledge was asking a little too much.

But the future Meagan had no advice to give her concerning the quandary now apparent. She had merely stated that Alexis would eventually balk at the whole concept and refuse to do anymore and that there would be an event that would change her mind conclusively. But what that event was, the future Meagan had not said, had not even hinted it.

Perhaps it was because to know the event would cause it not to happen. Or maybe if Meagan knew what the event was beforehand, she too would balk at the idea and in that way alter the intended outcome. The future Meagan had been very specific and forceful, even passionate about making Alexis do what it was she was created for, to bind the time-streams together and in that brief binding, when she could affect all of them at once, make the changes that would clear all the futures and cleanse them of the MTP until humans were mature enough to use it wisely.

They both felt them, mother and daughter sensing the approach of something or someone completely different than what they had encountered so far in the in-between time, in the void that was timelessness. That other travelers were here was taken for granted, moving within and between the times like tiny bacterium in the blood stream. But it was rare if not inconceivable that two such travelers, in all the unlimited amount of time available, should encounter one another in such a proximity as was happening now.

And more than that, whatever it was that was coming – for it didn't seem to either of them that it was human in any way, shape, or form – had the distinct impression of coming toward them, even at them, purposefully directing itself to be at the same point in the continuum as Alexis and Meagan.

It bothered Meagan tremendously, for the impression pushing ahead of the interlopers like the bow wave of a large ship was not one of friendship. *I think you're about to find the reason for your creation*, Meagan indicated with growing apprehension as the wrongness of the intruders seized her lungs with an iron grip.

The Rebellion formed out of the misconceptions of the religion
that took the mantle of power from the UFC
and made peace with that which was in its purest
sense evil. It is religion that shields evil with its very
presence, using evil as an excuse to exercise
its self-righteousness onto the masses and gain
control of the mind as well as the soul, and in that
control, gain pseudo salvation from its own taint of evil..
— From the Journal of Meagan Locke

31

The time-stream ...

Skral Utchu Lak of the House of Piqaq, Ward Prime of the Uhmna, Genenhums of the Elrsai, sat in the small and cramped vessel brooding over this most recent onus placed on him. The last such assignment had been a complete fiasco and because of that, he didn't hold very high regard for the success of this latest project conceived from the same mind.

As a genetically engineered human working exclusively for the Elrsai, and more restrictively for the House Piqaq, Utchu Lak, who had risen to the rank of Skral during his short service, had seen his share of botched assignments prepared by the non-militant Elrsai. This latest one, he had no doubt, would follow in the inglorious footsteps of its predecessors.

When humans had come along in their ugly and ungainly Generation Ships – more a postulant carrier of viral degeneracy than an exploration vessel – they had presented the perfect opportunity to create a race of warrior slaves for the Elrsai. All the Elrsai needed to do was procure some of the human DNA and a few volunteers for stock production. With genetic codes already intact, the growing chambers were the final touch, as well as a touch of the Elrsai DNA, to create the perfect spawn for the Elrsai dirty work: the Genenhums. And within that group were the Uhmnas, those who were the elite constructs, sent on the missions that were deemed particularly dangerous, perhaps even suicidal.

Programmed from birth to know little but what was told them and incapable of learning anything not strictly controlled by the Monitors, the Uhmna were, in effect, expendable warriors and were used with that in mind for any problems the Elrsai believed needed rectifying and were beyond the purview of the ethical morals of the Elrsai themselves

Of course, had the rulers of the Callibib Ascendancy, or even any of the other ranked Houses, found out about this little experiment, the House of Piqaq would find itself in more trouble than even the earnest-while Lord Dorcest Rama could extricate them. It was fortunate that this experiment with humans had only been in operation for a few years. Anything longer and the Ascendancy would unquestionably discover the truth. House Piqaq already had the banishable offense of their incursions into the time-stream to their credit. The discovery of their experiments with humans would only add to the problems already present.

But Utchu Lak had no real thoughts of such things. As far as he was concerned, the Uhmnas of the Genenhums had been around since the beginning of time – which for him was of course close to the truth since for Utchu Lak, time had begun the moment his consciousness had been sparked awake – and they had served the Elrsai honorably ever since.

Of course, had he known that he was one of a handful of experimental genetically grown creatures beginning with the fateful arrival of the human Generation Ship *Argos* and its crew of dirty, low-intelligent, immature sub-species, he would have perhaps had a slightly different opinion of his benefactors. But such things he didn't know and never would know, his limited capacity – specifically hardwired into his brain for just such reasons – allowing him just enough mental power to operate the equipment and carry out the assignments handed to him.

Having only been around for two years, Utchu Lak had no clue concerning what had happened prior to his arrival into life and had no interest in it either. When sent on assignment, the Uhmna had nothing but that assignment on their minds, all else nullified by the Monitors to ensure strict compliance. Utchu Lak, as most others at his high level of rank, had learned to defeat the procedures and equipment of the Monitors and retain a semblance of their former missions, albeit sketchy and vague. As such, he could tell that he had gone on several missions before and all had failed, a fact that, had he been allowed to develop as a normal human, would have weighed much heavier on his mind.

But as it was, he was just slightly concerned that he would fail again and in that failure disappoint House Piqaq, to which his utter and complete allegiance lay. He didn't like disappointing Lord Dorcest Rama.

As he reflected, his mind working overtime to form opinions that he was not allowed to have in the first place, he came to the startling revelation that it was the very limitation the Monitors placed on the Uhmnas that led to all the failures, for without the ability to change mission parameters or think independently, the Uhmnas would become confused when presented with anything not defined beforehand. The termination of those who had gone to the cabin on that frightful planet Earth, and that human female Alexis Locke, and had ended up dead before even accomplishing one of their mission objectives, was a perfect example. They had been completely surprised when the human female had been home and in that surprise, had failed to take the initiative and extricate themselves for a re-insertion at a later time-index.

Utchu Lak understood this as a major flaw in the mission parameters, though he really didn't understand how it was a flaw or what that really meant in the long run, but he did see it as a flaw and in that revelation, was fully aware that this mission on which he was currently assigned, would most likely end as had the one to Earth.

That mission, those deaths, had opened up a can of worms that the Elrsai had been trying to correct ever since. Utchu Lak had been on that assignment, or at least he had the vague feeling that he had been on it, piloting the time-jumper hovering in orbit while his companions faced their death. And now he was again in the time-stream, piloting the uncomfortable and cramped time-jumper toward the mental signal that could only be Alexis Locke, his assignment this time simple and direct: capture the annoying Earth female before she made a mess of things beyond what had already happened.

Had Utchu Lak known that the theft of the advanced time traveling technology, which made it possible for him to be traveling as he was in his time-jumper in the first place, was what led to the entire disaster building within the streams, he may have perhaps realized that he was unwittingly helping the demise of humanity. But then, for the Genenhums as a whole, humanity was not a concern. Humans in general were not much of a concern for anyone. The Genenhums only real concerns were the missions on which they were sent, working for the peaceful and benevolent Elrsai. What happened to anyone as a consequence of their success was not important. As a matter of fact, it was not even something about which they ever thought. The Monitors had made sure of that.

Then why was he experiencing such a bad feeling about what he was about to do? He must be malfunctioning. That was the only explanation he could comprehend. He should return, tell his Monitors that he was not performing at optimal levels and that another should be assigned to this mission. But he stayed his course, his programming making it impossible to turn back, to abort, to form an opinion in anyway that was not strictly within the mission parameters. And failure was not one of the mission parameters.

Then why did he feel like he was about to fail again?

When he had finally brought his time-jumper close enough to the mind of Alexis Locke to activate the containment field, Utchu Lak was only thinking about success, the only option available and the only one about which he truly cared. His other, inadvertent and illegal thoughts were quickly drowned out by his mission parameters and there was not much room left in his half-empty brain for anything else.

*　　*　　*

Grand Marshal Meagan Locke of the Rebellion punched into the void of the in-between-time with her time-jumper, fresh from her successful mission to give Dr. Vincent Cavalier the secrets to the creation of what would become her mother, and the rather interesting sexual side experience she had enjoyed more than she had in a long time. Her two companions, who had indexed to other streams to verify that certain events transpired as they were ordained, she had left behind, not wanting to involve them in the action she was about to initiate. It was bad enough that she had begun the Rebellion and helped in the general malaise permeating the galaxy with every sector in which one could find Dynastic Cruisers.

She didn't need to embroil her two friends in a scheme that would mean their certain death. Her death was more than enough to absolve her of all the evil she had committed in her long, long life.

It had always been a dream of hers to live forever, to never worry about dying because of the body failing, living to see what was around every corner and in that living, learn more and more until time ended. But the truth of the matter had been that this pseudo-immortality was not all that it was cracked up to be. She had seen far too much, had been involved in too many deaths, plagues and wars to want to see anymore. She had enough of life and all its attendant misgivings and plague-ridden vices.

Humans were not destined to live forever, else it would have been implemented in their DNA, there would have been provisions for it in the body. But human bodies had limitations and limitations meant that who or whatever had initially decided that a species such as this should exist, knew well enough not to give them immortality. The creation of the MTP was straining the very fabric of the universe. It had been a curse, a vile infection worse then all the calamities of man combined.

And she had lived to see it come to a fruition horrendous in its destruction and pitiable in its defenses. Humans were just not ready for such advancement. Perhaps they never would be. She was surprised that her species had gotten as far as it had without plunging itself into a self-imposed extinction. And if that were not enough to give her the feeling that she had lived past any idea of her own destiny, she had been forced to index to the past, to another past in another time-stream, to index to her own body and tell herself, in a juxtaposition that was ironic at best and shear chaos at worst, that she would need to get her mother to achieve a goal that would, in the end, not only kill herself but also all that she held dear.

She had to convince her own self, in the past, to make her mother hate her to such an extent that she would not think twice about doing what had to be done, in destroying the MTP utterly from the time-streams and in that destruction, nullifying her own life and that of her whole family, as well as changing the history of an entire race of aliens.

And it was, in the end, all her fault to begin with.

If it had not been so real, it would have been laughable, a comic tragedy recited by the worst playwrights. For what Alexis Locke needed to do, what she had been created to do nonetheless, was nothing short of eradicating an entire concept from history and in that eradication, collapse untold time-streams into oblivion, resetting the clock, as it were, back to a time when none of them existed in the first place. At least that was the plan, the only plan the Grand Marshal and her fellow rebels had devised as the best and only way to end the dominion of the Huang Dynasty and save the lives of countless billions of individuals with the sacrifice of one.

But then perhaps that was what fate was.

Perhaps Grand Marshal Meagan Locke was fate, coming down on the position of Alexis and Meagan's past self in the in-between-time to make one last attempt at justifying her life and her shame.

OrpPerhaps, as the United Religious Alliance had branded her, she was just a crazed heretic.

*   *   *

We must index to the stream now, Meagan stated in no uncertain terms. *Whatever is coming, I have no experience with and don't believe that they have honorable intentions.* In fact, Meagan had never met anything in the in-between-time that was an actual physical object. Until the discussions that had taken place with Alexis and the Commandant concerning the attacks on Alexis in her own time-stream, indexing through time was thought to be impossible with physical objects. That they should all of a sudden meet one now, when Alexis was indexing, was far too much of a coincidence for Meagan.

Alexis agreed and linked into Meagan's mind as she prepared to index into the proper time-stream.

Skral Utchu Lak activated the magnetic-triad containment system and fired, enveloping the two minds he now sensed – the second one much less powerful yet still strong enough to register on his scanners. He didn't care much about the second mind. He was not told anything about two individuals to apprehend, just one. But it didn't make much of a difference to the magnetic-triad system. He adjusted the power levels to compensate, made the containment field within his ship ready and brought aboard his two captives.

It was all far too simple.

Meagan tried to index and found that she was trapped, severed completely from the time-streams and her mental connection to her body, as surely as if she had never had one. Whatever it was around her was strong and solid, like a cloak draped, suffocating her mind and bringing fears of claustrophobia down on her like the blackest night. She had never experienced anything like this before, had never even heard of the remote possibility of being able to do this to a free mind. How it was possible, she could not even guess. As far as she knew, there was nothing physical to contain, nothing but her own thoughts flowing freely within time and yet here she was held like a mouse in a trap, being pulled into a physical ship in a realm where the physical was prohibited.

She began to panic, to see her whole mission, the entire fate of the future, falling apart around her. The future Meagan had said nothing of this, nothing. Was this the event she had kept from Meagan, which she had said would possibly change the course of time if she were to know about it beforehand?

Capture?

Meagan, despite her years of training, her calm demeanor when it came to missions and her constant need for control, was beginning to feel that sickening spread of panic in her stomach tasting like the vilest bile. She tried everything to escape, to break the bonds holding her consciousness ensnared in a tomb of blankness threatening to invalidate her thoughts as the wind to a candle flame, leaving nothing but a wisp of trailing smoke behind.

It was only Alexis' voice that saved her from the ultimate panic, the panic that kills. Alexis, not sure what was supposed to happen during these time indexes anyway and uncertain as to what had just transpired, seemed non-pulsed by the whole ordeal. *Is this normal?* she asked, aware of the waves of fear and panic beginning to build within her daughter that seemed so foreign to her character. For a fleeting moment, Alexis had the distinct feeling that it was someone else's mind into which she had tapped, that her daughter Meagan had gone and left behind this stranger with fear and panic rising like sweat dripping.

No. It's not normal.

I can't seem to break out of this, Alexis continued, aware that the mere sound of her voice was having a calming effect on Meagan. *I would say that we've been captured by someone from the future.*

Yes.

Alexis tried to probe outside the field, to see beyond the blankness enshrouding her, casting her alone with her thoughts as well as those of Meagan. It was like being thrown into a locked closet, all sensory organs depraved of stimulation and the mind left to wander on its own and find a peace within. *Relax Meagan. They can't hurt us.*

Meagan's thoughts flowed hard and clear, the trepidation like a damp cloth over her nose. *They weren't supposed to be able to capture us either.*

Skral Utchu Lak, satisfied with the acquisition of Alexis Locke, and the extra mind whom he could care less about, set the time index forward, addressed the main matrix, charged the polarizers and began his journey back to planet Ldbli and the successful completion of his mission.

*   *   *

Grand Marshal Meagan Locke watched in satisfaction as the Elrsai vessel captured Alexis and her past self. All was proceeding as planned, as it had occurred back when she had been the one captured. All that the Grand Marshal needed to do now to break the chain of events inexorably leading toward the mess that was her present time, to follow this Elrsai vessel to the correct place and time in the proper time-stream and then know where it was that she needed to fulfill her final act.

23 August 2075
0600 hrs.
Earth

Cav laid the vid-screen down on the small shelf next to the over-sized Jacuzzi in which he relaxed, closing his eyes, rubbing them with his fat, little fingers. The steam from the heated water rose like tendrils of seaweed into the crisp, cool air of the mountain evening. The quiet of night was punctuated only by the background serenade of the crickets and the occasional mournful cry of the wolves prowling the upper slopes and singing to each other in a communion humans could never experience. The stars overhead shone in a panoply of twinkling splendor, the cloud of the Milky Way like a band of gas spread across the desolation of the distant suns burning with the fury of a thousand fusion reactors.

Ever since his chance encounter with Huang and the closeness between them that he had seen on the face and mannerisms of Claudine, Cav had been busy. Although he had come up with little, his obsession had let him forget, if however temporarily, Alexis, and how he had let her down, killed her in his attempt to listen to the dictates of others rather than his own heart.

He had lost agents before, had even seen them killed before his very eyes; but Alexis was different. Ever since that anonymous, beautiful woman – who, in retrospect, had looked so much like Alexis, had given him the secret to her creation – Cav had held a special place for Alexis in his heart. Now that place had been ripped out, shredded with the vengeance of guilt and all that was left was a gaping hole never to be filled, which was slowly and irreversibly bleeding him to death.

The image of that woman back then, on that beach in the South Pacific, came floating back to him as he lay in the relaxation of the Jacuzzi, floating back like a leaf caught in a light zephyr, blowing randomly about until it settles on the edge of a railing and sits there, unsure whether to stay or fall, to remain attached to the firmness of the wood or return to the etherealness of the wind. In such a way did the memories of their night together come back to him, a random connection of events leading to the re-visitation ... and to the revelation.

A smile cracked his face as the pleasures she had inflicted on him re-surfaced in his mind and his groin, the smooth, firmness of her body like a tonic to his soul, to his libido. She had been more than he had ever had before and he had always imagined that that was the way Alexis would make love, with a finesse and wildness to set any man afire again and again. And she had looked so much like Alexis that now, with the memory so many years passed, it was almost as if it had been Alexis in that bed with him.

And then Claudine came to his mind, her body flashing before him as it had rode atop him so many times, almost as if it had somehow felt the other woman present in his mind, felt a jealousy making her intrude her own memories forcefully upon him to remove anything save her remembrances. *But what the hell*, he thought as he let the memories flow. *If he could no longer have her in reality, why not have her all he wanted in his fantasies.*

He remembered that Claudine had shown up shortly after the other had left, shown up in her all-over tan and sparkling eyes and ferine aggression driving him to an ecstasy almost matching that of the other, the golden hues of Claudine's inner thighs....

Cav sat up with a start, splashing water around the tub in a swirl of agitation. He reached for his holo-screen, fumbling with the slickness of his hands, cursing at his obesity as much as at his obtuseness. He activated the memory buffer and linked into the main computer in his office, downloading the complete file in under a few nano-seconds. He frantically raced to find the correct sector, the picture that would either verify his sudden revelation or dash it against the rocks of despair and convoluted memory.

He found it after several minutes of cursing and rising panic, the holo-image of the inner thigh of those who had attacked Alexis in her cabin, displayed. He blocked in on the tattoo and enlarged, the image coming before his eyes like the image before his mind, the two matching perfectly.

It had never occurred to him before, never even entered into his consciousness.

Now it all came back to him and the connection was complete. He remembered when he saw it on Claudine's upper inner thigh, right by the joint of the hip and leg, butting up against the glorious softness of her vagina. He had asked and she had answered with a spurious explanation that had, at the time, meant nothing to Cav, the pleasures of her body much more important to him than an occult tattoo she had.

But now it hit him like a brick.

Claudine Maxwell, the president's Chief of Staff, had the same tattoo as those who had attacked Alexis, belonged, it could be logically assumed, to the same group and that in itself was a major revelation. How could she be the same as them? They were advanced beyond anything Cav had ever seen, that the scientists who still talked about how they just disintegrated on the autopsy table had ever seen.

Cav had come to the only conclusion possible, apart from that of aliens, which he found hard to swallow, and that conclusion put these people into the dark realm of black ops of a powerful government. And it was not the United States. Of that he was certain. Claudine, however, was the Chief-of-staff of the President of the United States. Did that mean that she was working for a foreign government also? What a perfect double agent, what perfect placement.

Cav spent the rest of the darkness lingering in the sky doing research, tapping into any and all data-bases he could, using resources and skills he had not employed for decades. And when the sun came up to greet the new day and spread its golden rays over the land in marching columns of brilliant daylight, Cav had found his answer.

Claudine Maxwell didn't exist before her eighteenth birthday.

Although she had a birth certificate and high school transcripts and a supposed mother and father, they all turned out to be false when Cav delved deeper into their veracity. A cursory back-ground check found nothing amiss, but Cav's extensive search came up with falsified documents and computer tampering on a grand scale and accomplished with a precision only a few people in the world could match.

And armed with the identical tattoo on her as those that would kill Alexis Locke, Cav came to the startling conclusion that forced him to initiate a plan that would either bring him glory as a hero or death as a traitor, and perhaps along the way atone for a small portion of his guilt.

*　　*　　*

Lord Dorcest Rama watched as the small vessel parked itself on the elevated landing pad, the whine of the inertial dampeners and the heavy, chest-pounding thump-thump of the anti-grav boosters coming to a quick silence as the landing skids made contact with a soft thud and the egress hatch opened to a hiss of pressure. He was anxious for the successful conclusion of this particular mission more than he had ever been in the past. If this worked, then his mistake of letting the humans have banned technology might just be overlooked, if not covered up completely.

His perturbation and tumult were apparent to the other who stood with him, the Duke Counselor Allab Yama having advised strongly against such a bold and unorthodox move as the abduction of a non-Elrsai from within the in-between-time itself. If the Sovereign Avis Blackhood Callibib, Supreme Lord of the Elrsai, ever even caught a whiff of what House Piqaq was doing, it would spell the end of the long and illustrious history of this noble family.

Such intrusions into the time-streams were strictly forbidden. To abduct someone from the time-streams was not even on the law books, for the very notion was beyond consideration.

To abduct a non-Elrsai ... well, he didn't even want to think about the consequences of that fateful decision. Houses had fallen for far lesser trespasses. Lord Dorcest Rama would just have to make certain that the Supreme House never found out about this little side adventure and then he might be able to finally relax.

The Genenhum Utchu Lak stepped up to the requisite three quants from Lord Dorcest Rama and prostrated himself before the talons of the Lord High Scone of Ldbli Prime. He held in his hands a small container, its compact power-source blinking placately, the shear power of the magnetic-triad containment field within pulsing the very air around it so that it shimmered and undulated in waves of slight gravity perturbations bleeding off into the hot afternoon air, making any who stood nearby react with uneasy stomachs and headaches.

Even at this distance, the over-powering stench of the human-hybrid made Allab Yama queasy. He hated working with these primitives. It was so... uncivilized to have them around at all. That was another mistaken decision.

Were you successful? Dorcest Rama asked in his high-toned command voice, the voice all Elrsai used on the lowly and pitiful Uhmnas who served them.

"Not only was I able to capture the human-hybrid Alexis Locke, but I was also able to capture another that she was traveling with, most gracious Lord High Scone," Skral Utchu Lak answered with severe deference and obeisance. The Genenhums were purposely not given the power to communicate telepathically, the mis-trust of such a secretive utensil in their primitive minds not worth the risk. Besides, in this way, the Elrsai could discuss things when around the Genenhums and not have to worry about them over-hearing anything important.

Dorcest Rama briefly flared a head feather at the unexpected yet interesting addition of another captive. *This is good. You have done well, Skral. You will be rewarded."*

Utchu Lak prostrated himself even lower, something Allab Yama didn't think possible, then held out the containment box for inspection. Two Elrsai scientists stepped forward and took the box from the Genenhum, but before they could make it off the assembly platform, the heavy vibration of a Royal Callibib Shuttle coming up against the platform stopped everyone. The coarse gravity waves from the control pods hanging under the bulky vessel like pustule sores passed through those assembled on the platform with nauseating effect.

Lord Dorcest Rama never understood why the Royal shuttles always had to keep their anti-grav modules running at full bore when they came close to the assembly platform. It certainly was not necessary for the proper functioning of the ship or its safety. He assumed that it was for the affect of making everyone sick and weak in preparation for the advent of the great Supreme Lord of the Elrsai's arrival, thus making it that much more difficult for someone to assassinate him. Despite the fact that no such attempt had ever been made on the royal personage, Lord Dorcest could think of no other reason for the rude and nauseating behavior so common for the Royal shuttles. It was extremely annoying.

But that was all small stuff compared to the fact that the Supreme Lord of the Elrsai was arriving here, now, at the very moment when the illegal abduction of the non-Elrsai was in the final stages of completion. This bothered Lord Dorcest excessively. What could he possibly want now?

The Royal entourage spilled out of the shuttle like a nest of enraged ants, swarming over the assembly platform in a rush to reach their assigned positions before the Supreme Lord stepped out. Lord Dorcest could not help but notice that the Lords of all the upper Houses had arrived also, a rare event to say the least, especially as unannounced as this was. The Supreme Lord represented the House Callibib, First House of the Ascendancy and the current Royal House. Then there was House Sod, House Sha'qaq, and House Draak, with Lord Dorcest's House Piqaq representing the Fifth and final Upper House of the Ascendancy.

Whatever was happening, it was not a good sign when all the Lords of the Houses assembled like this.

Sovereign Avis Blackhood Callibib stepped out of the shuttle to the trumpet of fanfare and pomp, his Royal advisors following behind as if they were attached by leashes, which they might as well have been. Avis Blackhood was large, the election to the Supreme Lordship having enacted genetic glandular changes in his physique making him twice as large as the typical Elrsai, his usual black plumage now streaked with vivid hues of red and blue in striped patterns indicating his Royal birth. Of course, if Lord Dorcest's House had been chosen as the Supreme House, he also would have grown in size as fitted the Royal personage. It was one of the many genetic quarks of the Elrsai.

Avis Blackhood's head plume rose above him like a parasol, bobbing ever so slightly forward with each step like a broken sunshade as he waddled forward with pretentious abandon, the anger on his face visible in palatable waves. He walked right up to Lord Dorcest, heedless of the usual one quant space customary when speaking to a Lord, and bent over so that he could look right into the eyes of House Piqaq.

What in the seven levels of upper purgation were you thinking, Dorcest? Have you decided to just bypass all the rules and laws laid down for us? Or have you decided that the Fifth House of the Ascendancy had the obligatory right to ignore the rules and do what they pleased? Well, what is it? What is your answer? I'm waiting. Ummm?" His voice was a high whine of irritation grating right through one's skin and attacking the nerves head on.

Lord Dorcest's eyes grew wide with the shock that the Supreme Lord knew of his folly. He had never seen an Elrsai this upset before. Never. He fumbled for an answer, then decided that ignorance was the best route to take. *I don't have the faintest idea what you're referring to, I'm sure, Sovereign Avis Blackhood Callibib.*

Avis Blackhood straighten up, took a long look at the renegade Lord, then shifted his eyes to the containment box the scientists still held in their small wing talons. *And what would be in that? Do you think me that stupid that I wouldn't know what was transpiring in my own systems? Did you honestly believe that you could index into the time-stream and abduct a member of another race without causing reactive waves in the streams? Are you just making this up as you go along or did you actually have a plan?*

It was worse than Lord Dorcest had at first thought. It was beyond worse. It appeared that the Supreme Lord knew all of it. How did this happen?

Well? Have you anything to say on your behalf that might mitigate this tremendous blunder on your part and keep the House Piqaq from banishment?

Banishment!

The word hit Lord Dorcest like a body blow. It was the ultimate disgrace. All the nobles of his House would be sent to one of the numerous banishment colonies on the outer rim, never again to participate in the culture or life-style of the Elrsai, to waste away on an abandoned world where the winds blew so strongly that flight was impossible but a few days out of the year. And for the non-nobles, the retainers, scientists and servants who had nothing to do with the disgrace, who would have to participate in the banishment as well; the physical clipping of their wings – which was illegal to do to a noble – was the proscribed punishment. It generally lead to suicide within a fortnight.

Lord Dorcest, who usually was quite good at impromptu responses under pressure, only had one thing pop into his mind. *I did it for the greater glory of the Elrsai and the protection of our species.*

And how is that? How is dishonoring our entire species in any way a glorious thing?! What are you sputtering on about?

Allab Yama made to speak, but the Supreme Lord cut him off with a sharp gesture of his wing. *I will hear this answer from the Lord of the House and not his Duke Counselor.*

Lord Dorcest was beginning to feel hot, as if he were mottling right there in front of everyone. He swallowed hard, then made the reply that seemed his only logical answer. *The primitive humans stole our time travel technology as well as a sample of our DNA and this one that I have abducted is the result of that symbiosis. She is a human-Elrsai hybrid.* It was all he could think of to deflect the attention away from the personal attack on his House. That it was a slight lie was of little concern at the moment.

Avis Blackhood took a step back as his eyes opened wide, a strange guttural sound escaping his beak as a ripple of apprehension and anxiety ran through the gathered crowd of the Royal entourage. His beady, black eyes narrowed as what Lord Dorcest had just said penetrated fully. His words, when he finally spoke after the intolerable silence hanging in the air like a coiled spring, were sharp, slow, and precise. *Are you trying to tell me that you let the dirty, primitive, immature humans have access to our DNA and our technology?*

Yes, Lord Dorcest responded in utter dismay. It was not the word he had wanted to use. It was, to say the least, a bit too affirmative.

And that they have created the hybrid that was foretold?

It would appear that way.

Avis Blackhood gave Lord Dorcest such a look that would have scared the feathers off of a lesser Elrsai. *IT WOULD APPEAR THAT WAY?! Do you realize what this means? Do you have the slightest idea of what damage such a symbiosis can do?*

Lord Dorcest saw a way out in that statement, a way to make up for all that he had done wrong, with all the rules he had violated. He rose up to his full height and stood before the scowling Supreme Lord with as much dignity as he could muster. *That is why I have abducted her and have her locked away.* He felt a release with that statement, as if he had saved his House's honor with a few simple words. He was not prepared for the onslaught that was to follow.

Avis Blackhood looked at the containment box pulsing with a life of its own as if it were a cyro-dimetrix explosive, backing away from the two scientists holding it and making them quite nervous. *You brought the hybrid here*?

Of course, Lord Dorcest said with a renewed sense of vigor. *This way we can detain her as long as we need and not have to worry about her.*

Avis Blackhood clucked a few times in complete irritation, a sound he only made, his advisors noted, when he was about to do something connotating grave and long-reaching consequences, and they all mentally cowered in preparation of the next words. *Did the hybrid know of our existence or our part in her construction?*

I don't see how she could have, Lord Dorcest answered with a smile in his eyes. He was quite unaware of the hammer about to fall on him, pleased with himself for the way that he had handled this.

YOU IMBECILE!, Sovereign Avis Blackhood Callibib, Supreme Lord of the Elrsai projected as he waved a wing in the gesture meaing only one thing: banishment. *You've brought the demise of the Elrsai to our very doorsteps with this one.* He turned to look back at his Prime Advisor. *Get the containment box and prepare to leave immediately. It may already be too late. Activate the shields.*

As he walked back to the Royal Shuttle in a rapid hopping motion, his entourage following suit, the Supreme Lord never turned back to look at Lord Dorcest of House Piqaq. It was the worst thing that could have happened, for it meant only one thing: utter and complete banishment. He was ruined.

The human understanding, from its peculiar nature,
easily supposes a greater degree of order and
regularity in things than it really finds.
— Francis Bacon (1670 CE)

32

The high-pitched whine of the dischargers followed on the heels of the electric blue plasma hitting the assembly platform and turning several of the Royal Entourage into burning husks of charred carrion, feathers exploding in abundance. Lord Dorcest jumped in surprise at the attack from the handful of what appeared to him to be Ka'kach destroyers swarming in from out of the sun and bracketing the Royal shuttle with multiple charges. The angular and sinister looking warships screamed past in ear-splitting graviton vibrations rocking the platform, threatening to disturb its equilibrium and send it crashing into the thick green canopy below.

Lord Dorcest was not aware that they were at war with anyone, especially not the hitherto friendly Ka'kach, who had never indicated any resentment toward the Elrsai. But as he watched the destroyers come around for a second attack, smelt the burnt remnants of once living advisors and felt the force of the Royal shuttle's shields as they came online, he realized that it didn't matter one bit whether he knew they were at war or not. All that mattered at the moment was his survival.

He jumped off the platform and dove down toward the ground to avoid the destruction that was certain to visit the assembly platform before long. It was then he had the sudden, rather happy thought that if the Royal shuttle were to be destroyed with the Supreme Lord in it, his order of banishment would never get recorded. What a happy coincidence.

Unfortunately, it was his last thought as the destroyers laced the platform with a volley of plasma charges and its grav-lifts, losing their containment in a surge of energy spasms and massive gravity waves, failed. The huge platform crashed down into the trees below in a slow motion ecstasy of mock-flight, both the Royal shuttle and Skral Utchu Lak's small ship blasting off at the last moment and struggling for altitude with the heavy thump-thump of their anti-grav lifts hammering the air in a rending of space shedding many a tree of its entire foliage.

Lord Dorcest Rama, Lord High Scone of House Piqaq, found himself trapped in the maze of foliage that was the canopy of trees as the platform crashed down, crushing him under its weight like a small bug and ending his life in a moment of unknown bliss, his banishment order no longer a relevant factor.

The Royal shuttle broke through the atmosphere in a scream, its shields undulating and shimmering as it took hit after hit from the pursuing destroyers, bent on leaving no trace of the shuttle worth salvaging. Skral Utchu Lak's small ship they left alone to fly off toward the main defensive base on the other side of the planet, any thoughts of freedom from the slavery he was under not even entering the Genenhum's mind. He was not programmed for that.

All that the Ka'kach destroyers were interested in was the Royal shuttle and the deadly cargo it carried. That the shuttle carried the Supreme Lord of the Elrsai was also not a factor to the attackers. They certainly knew that he was onboard, but they were unconcerned. All that mattered was that the Royal shuttle held the containment box within which the future survival of the Ka'kach lay.

Had anyone on the assembly platform bothered to notice, they would have seen that the destroyers swooping out of the green sky in their rain of destruction were not of a familiar design. They would have noticed, in fact, that the Ka'kach destroyers were like nothing they had ever seen before, or would see for another four hundred years. But no one in the Royal shuttle took any notice of anything save the failing shields and the inability to jump into hyper-drive, the space around them bent and mutated in some bizarre fashion making it impossible for the navigators to find a safe path through space and into the fold.

Without any weaponry, either defensive or offense – the Elrsai had given up on such things long ago – and shields not meant to take the rapid and repeated pounding of the powerful dischargers, the Elrsai were no match for such military-minded details – it was only a matter of time before the shuttle was turned into a dispersed mass of randomly floating particles, the larger pieces of metal spinning off in all directions with the few, last bursts of electric blue plasma still encircling them as the energy from the spent dischargers slowly bled off into space.

The containment box within which Alexis and Meagan still resided, floated scorched and dented among the debris, its power source still ignorantly working away despite the abuse it had taken. The Ka'kach moved in for the kill.

The destroyers didn't notice the small ship following them that now made a run for the box under their very noses and snatched it up in a blatant display of disregard for the power and honor of the Ka'kach. Grand Marshal Meagan Locke, after making certain that the box had been safely stored aboard by the stellar-droid, activated the time matrix, dropped her shields and indexed into the in-between-time before the Ka'kach could even register that something was amiss, their late and futile discharger bursts flying off into empty space with little to no effect, their curses echoing only within their own minds.

*   *   *

She had no idea how much time had passed, or even whether time had passed at all. All was blankness. It was a blankness she had never experienced before. It was a total denial of any sensory preceptors, leaving her alone within her mind, with her thoughts and memories like some demented holo-album, nothing new to tease the eyes or the ears, the tongue or the nose, the fingers.

Nothing.

There was only Meagan and herself, whose fear and panic were like a stinking retch of nauseous echoes in the closeness of the containment box. Was this what death was like: alone with nothing but memories of the past haunting one endlessly until all that was left was a deranged, forlorn mind that knew nothing save itself, feeding off old memories like vomit?

Was this how it ended for those who were lost in the in-between-time, trapped forever in an infinite expanse that was but a reflection of one's own mind, nothing new to ever again grace the mind and the soul with knowledge? It was no wonder that The Lost of the in-between-time had gravitated toward Alexis like locust to the corn. If this was what they felt, then she could easily understand why they wanted release so desperately.

She had actually known people in the real world who had lived like this, whose lives were but a shadow of themselves, lost within their own worlds and minds and never knowing what wonders there were to experience outside their locked and sealed tombs. She could not understand how someone could live like that, with this absolute nothingness always around them in a perpetual gray of altered life that was nothing but a stark reminder of what they had done, not what they might do.

Alexis refused to believe that she was dead, that her mind had been thrown onto a trash-heap to waste away from within in a cloying blackness that seemed to soak the very vitality out of her with every intolerable, blank, numbing second passing by in a vacuum of time comprehension. And so she tried to retrace all her steps, all the clues that had led her to this place and time with a daughter she had not yet created, who hated her with a passion seeming to teeter between regret and rage. With every moment passing by, she felt the defenses of Meagan crumble, fall apart like adobe walls in the rain, slowly, inexorably until all that was left was a lost vestige of what had been, the outline stamped in the very mud that once was the wall.

And with this crumbling, Alexis sensed the despair and the confusion, the anger and the shame permeating her daughter's very existence until all that was left was a shell of broken memories signifying nothing in the end.

Will you tell me why you're angry with me? Alexis asked in an attempt to solve the riddle, to answer the one question that seemed to validate her life more than any other. That her daughter had told her that she, Alexis, was built from alien DNA and created for just one purpose was enough of a blow to Alexis' ego to ram her into a self-depreciating stupor. But there she didn't go. It would have been easy to slip into a numbness that was self-denial, but Alexis had never taken the easy path and she was not about to do it now. There was something here, something important she could learn and Alexis was damned if she was going to let this opportunity pass her by.

There was a clue here, a last piece to the puzzle started in Cav's office with the five murders and was now dumped into her lap like a misplaced old rag.

It's not important anymore, Meagan answered quietly and meekly, her thoughts such a tumble of emotion and doubt she was barely able to form coherent sentences.

What is it that I did? I must have done something horrible to create all this anger, Alexis pressed, wanting, needing to know the truth, if such a word really had any meaning anymore. She was hoping to break the final visage of the walls, to penetrate the inner mind and in that infiltration learn for herself what drove the hatred onward.

Have you ever thought that perhaps you did nothing wrong? Meagan shot back, the anger present more a product of strained passion than deep-seated ire. *Did it ever occur to you that it's not you at all, but me?*

What did the future Meagan tell you about me? What is it that's so important that I was created at what appears to be such a high cost? Alexis inquired, aware that Meagan was about to lose it, that her control was frayed and on the edge of imploding into herself in a destructive frenzy of self-chastisement.

I don't know! Meagan cried out. *All I know is that you're somehow different, special. That you're creation was the by-product of something that happened in the future, that has to do with the MTP and humanity and the aliens, but apart from that I know nothing!*

Alexis pressed harder, knowing that it was a fine line that she walked here. *Tell me again, what it is that I'm supposed to do.*

I already told you once.

So, tell me again. It's not at all clear to me.

No! Stop it! Meagan screamed out in pleading waves of anguish.

Alexis was close, so close to the truth. *Why must I bind the time-streams together? Why must I eradicate the MTP? What is it that you had a glimpse of in the future that's causing you such torment?*

Meagan's mind began to collapse in on itself in a vortex of broken dreams and shattered promises, of altered lives and needless killings. Her life had already been shattered once by the first arrival of her future self with the bizarre and unreal tales of what had been, of what she would do in the future, of what had to be done to Alexis, her mother. That she had lost her once, back in the past, back in that time when all her memories seemed to crash together in a rush of meaninglessness had already been a severe blow.

But to have found her mother again in the new time-stream, see her, interact with her, and then, in a final act of unselfishness and altruism, watch her destroy herself again was too much to ask. At the time that her future self had told her all this, had laid the plan out like a refurbished carpet, Meagan had not felt the ultimate emotions now threatening to drown her in a sea of guilt and culpability. But now, alone with her thoughts and the thoughts of her mother, the closeness between them what she had missed so much for so many years, was too much for her to contain, to control from bursting forth in a precipitance of anger and fright that risked upsetting the entire plan.

No, you ask too much! You can't know! All has to be as it was. There is no future otherwise, only past.

Alexis was not following her at all, the random ramblings like a carousel gone wild. *You're not making sense, Meagan. Talk to me. Tell me what it is that's tormenting you so. Let it all out or else it'll eat you up alive.*

NO!

Why?

For some unknown reason, Meagan's mind was still blocked from Alexis' probe, as if there was a physical wall built around her that defied penetration.

You can't know your own future! It'll ruin everything, EVERYTHING!! The suffering was at excruciating levels, the tribulation of a secret so dark that it blackened all it touched and was too much for a single mind to contain. *Don't you understand? All this has happened before and it will all happen again! The time-stream doesn't care about you or me or anything. It just is! It doesn't suffer from the restrictions of a consciousness that gnaws at your bones like a rabid dog!*

I don't understand, Alexis stated as calmly as she could, actually having no clue what Meagan was going on about. But Alexis could feel that Meagan's mind was about to snap in the air like a premonition of doom. *You aren't making any sense, Meagan.*

But that's just the thing! I am making sense. You're the one that doesn't fit, doesn't belong and thus doesn't understand. IT'S YOU! It's always been YOU!

Alexis was beginning to regret ever having brought up the subject, but she was committed now and there was no place to hide. *What's been me? What is it that I do, or did, or have to do that's so terrible?*

There was a long moment of silence, a bare whisper of something in the air telling Alexis that the moment was here, that the time had come for Meagan's mental dam to open in a flood of words and ideas drowning her in its betrayal. When it did come, it was in a stream of rapid-fire words and concepts that struck Alexis like a jack-hammer, cracking into her with a fierceness that was beyond compare.

We can't kill anyone when we index! We don't have the capacity or the power. We can affect small changes, break into data-bases, move objects around, but to kill requires a power far beyond that which any human has. Do you see it now? Do you understand the total destruction that was caused by my stupid mistake in the future that lead to your creation?

Alexis was stunned. Following the line of logic laid down lead to only one conclusion. *But the five scientists who were killed...*

YOU KILLED THEM!! It's always been you! It's what you have to do, what needs to be done to save the future and the billions that will die in the terror that is the Huang Dynasty. You did it already, in the future, just like you're about to do it again. But it never ends! I must not have looked at all the causes, checked out all the ramifications because nothing new is happening, nothing changes. You kill them off, you die and still NOTHING CHANGES!!

426

Alexis' mind reeled with the revelation. She had killed them all? Even Alexander, her son? She had been sent on a mission to find a killer only to learn that she had been that killer. *But how...*

Because of what you are, the power you possess due to the genetic alterations given to Cav by my future self in your past. You're the only one capable of doing what needs to be done. Don't you see? It's all a big circle. You've already done it, but no one knows it. Do you know what the Yellowleaf Conjecture actually was? DO YOU! Of course you don't! How could you. You're already dead by then, killed by my own hand at the instructions of my future self for a mission to your past so that you can achieve the result that you were investigating in the first place!

Do you know how difficult it was for me to have to lure you onto that field and then crash that hov on you? Do you? It ripped me apart and now, now we're trapped in this God-forsaken place and it was all for NOTHING!! FOR FUCKING NOTHING!!"

Alexis felt her world crashing down in a tornado of contradictions. There was no way that it could be, no possible way. She tried to maintain a hold on her emotions, on that terror racing through her at the moment, riding on the thought that she was the one who had killed her own son, would kill her own son for a grander purpose that she didn't even understand. She needed to stay focused, to concentrate on what Meagan was saying and glean from it some semblance of knowledge from which she could work, concentrate, focus. *Is that why you hate me?*

NO! Don't you see it? Can't you understand what it is that's going on here?

No, I don't!" Alexis yelled back in frustration, the anger she had directed at those working with Meagan, those who had supposedly killed her son now coming back around with a vengeance to crash into her own mind in a wave of self-deception threatening to blow her away.

YOU'RE THE PROBLEM! It was your creation that began this series of events that never seems to end, that leads to the MTP, to Huang, to the Dynasty, to the death of billions of humans and the desecration of Earth! And I was the one who started it all, in the future.

There was silence again as Meagan's last words faded into the darkness about them, as if it had taken all her strength to say and now had drained her to utter ruin. But she had one more statement, one more concept emitted like the last dying breath of her life. Her quiet whisper was in such stark contrast to the mental screaming that had occurred before that it was as if someone else had spoken it. *That's why I'm so mad at you, why I have to pretend to hate you. It's the only way to get you to hate me and thus do the right thing.*

It's the only way.

To do what? I still don't understand.

The silence now spewing forth from Meagan's mind was like a large storm building behind a force field, the power brewing ready to release in a torrent of emotions. But her words didn't come in a torrent. Instead, with her emotions drained and racked like a broken power coupling, her words emptied out in a bare, mental whisper.

To change the time-stream so that neither of us ever existed.

*   *   *

"What do you mean we lost them?" Skre said with harsh irritation to Meagan's second-in-command.

The man had returned to the Colony when Meagan and Alexis had not shown up in the time index and now he stood before the Commandant wondering how this was going to affect his chances at promotion. "They never showed up. We indexed into the proper time-stream but Colonel Locke and Alexis Locke were not with us. I have no explanation."

Skre dismissed the major with a distracted wave of his hand indicating he no longer wanted to talk, then leaned on the desk before him and looked at Vork, who stood silently by observing all. "Get hold of the general. We seem to have the beginnings of a major fuck-up on our hands here."

Vork nodded his head and sent out the proper requests for the location of General Gudbjartsson. "Shall I inform the trackers to begin searching for Colonel Locke?" the Cycomeand asked.

"Yes. Yes. I need to know where she ended up. I knew it was a bad idea to send Alexis with her. She probably mis-directed her to who-knows-where," Skre spewed out in his ire, trying to come up with some logical explanation for why. It didn't make any sense. Where would they have gone? Meagan was his most trust-worthy subordinate. She would never do something like this without first telling him and this Alexis was the prime culprit here.

Vork smiled, a rare and totally uncharacteristic anomaly for a Cycomeand, especially a military one. But Skre was far too involved in the problems created by Colonel Locke's disappearance to notice the anomaly.

*   *   *

428

20 December 2084,
1400 hrs.
Earth:
Verkhoyansk Mountains, Northeast Siberia

Grand Marshal Meagan Locke brought her time-jumper to a smooth, gentle landing among the frozen trees at the edge of the large expanse of forest huddling up against the foot of the snow-clad mountains as if trying to draw warmth from the Earth itself. The frozen peaks, with their jagged spires of cathedralesque grandeur rose into the clear blue sky like crystal bells. The temperature was hovering near negative thirty-six Celsius and the small frozen water crystals floating quietly in the still air sparkled like radiated fairies on the wing, falling to the permafrost after being disturbed by the anti-grav lifters of the time-jumper.

The dispersal field around the ship would keep the planet's primitive detection systems from observing her in any way, so she had no fear from that quarter; but she purposely chose this remote, cold, inhospitable sight so that no one would observe the large explosion that would accompany the destruction of the magnetic-triad field on the containment box. Such potent power sources tended to react dramatically when separated from their hosts and she didn't want to take any chances of attracting a crowd.

She expected the spy satellites and the anti-nuclear devices in orbit to catch the massive energy flux, but by the time prying eyes could be focused on the sight, she hoped to be long gone. Her release of Alexis and Colonel Locke would take very little time.

The outside air burned her lungs as she walked the twenty or so meters away from her ship. Her breath froze instantly as she reached the area where she could safely deactivate the containment field, her hair white from the hoar-frost clinging to it like tiny icicles, she remembered why she hated the cold so much. It leached through her garments as if they were not even there, grabbing her flesh in an ice-cold vise making it difficult to breath.

She laid the box on the permafrost and then walked back to her ship, drawing her energy weapon as she went. She took aim at the calmly blinking power source on the side of the box and fired. The explosion was even larger than she had expected and it knocked her back against the hard metal of the ship, stunning her momentarily as the echoes of the blast resounded through the mountains and the forest in waves of redundant booms.

She found herself sitting on the frozen ground, a pounding in the back of her head where she had hit the hull of the ship, immediate in its desire for attention. As she focused her eyes, she beheld the images of Alexis and Colonel Locke before her, scowling down as if she had been the one to capture them in the first place. She struggled to her feet, the pain increasing as she rose, her hand involuntarily going to the back of her head.

"How long have I been out?" she asked, aware that the defensive facilities of Siberia would be rushing eyes and ears to her location to identify the source of the intense and unknown explosion, which had released amounts of tachyon and chrono-particles never before seen.

"A few minutes at the most," Alexis responded, the freedom from the blankness of the box such a release that she was having trouble absorbing all the input she was receiving.

"We have to leave this place," Grand Marshal Locke said as she looked at her gloved hand to see if there was any blood on it from her unexpected impact into the hull. "Get in the ship and I'll take us to another location."

"No," Meagan said to her future self, aware now with the liberation of her mind from the secrets she had held that this was not the way to proceed. "This has to stop."

"Yes, I agree, and that's why we have to finish what we've started," future Meagan said with a no-opposition tone. "Get in the ship."

"No," Meagan said, crossing her arms in a gesture of defiance. "We have to stop making the same mistakes, doing the same things over and over again. It's obvious that it doesn't work."

Grand Marshal Locke, getting colder by the second, wrapped her arms around her chest. "It's cold here and if we don't leave this place, the local authorities will see us and there'll be an even bigger problem. We can discuss this all later, *after* we leave." She stepped into the ship and brought the thrusters on-line, the heavy thump-thump and background screech of the grav-lifts echoing into the canyons.

Alexis indicated that the future Meagan was right about being spotted. "It doesn't do us much good to sit around here and get caught in another mess."

Meagan frowned, then reluctantly agreed, her mind such a mess of contradictions that she really didn't know anymore what she was doing. Forgotten completely were Skre, the general and her mission. Now all that swirled in her mind in colliding patterns of mis-trust and guilt was how to fix the mess that her future self was trying to make.

The time-jumper lifted off the perma-frost and headed south toward the great deserts stretching to the horizon and back. It landed in a remote, sand-infested corner of nowhere in a spray of tan. Grand Marshal Locke turned in her seat to look at Alexis and Meagan as they stared at her, Meagan with a look of hatred that was supposed to be reserved for Alexis, Alexis bored and detached.

"I'm sorry about the capture by the Elrsai," she said with a true undercurrent of sympathy. "I never had to experience that. It's something new in the time-stream."

"New?" Meagan asked in mistrust. "I doubt that. And who the hell are the Elrsai?"

"Yeah, I forgot about that little detail. You haven't met them yet. They're an alien race who managed to capture you in the in-between-time. They're a rather peaceful lot, but they seem to have taken a rather peculiar interest in Alexis. It's probably something to do with the fact that it was from them that we acquired the advanced time travel technology and the extra bit of DNA that's in Alexis and makes her so special. It seems that the synthesis of the two genetic codes gave rise to a result that was, shall we say, unexpected.

"You've become some sort of fulfillment of an ancient Elrsai prophecy or something like that. I'm not sure on the details. The House that captured you was the House from which we acquired the technology in the first place and I have a feeling that they were just trying to cover their tracks by making sure that Alexis was removed from the time-stream permanently."

"And so you just went in a stole us from them again," Alexis stated flatly, amazed at the gall of the woman who was her daughter.

"No. Actually the Ka'kach stole you from the Elrsai and I in turn stole you from them."

Alexis' eyes narrowed as these new terms and words battled for attention in her mind. "What? Who are they?"

"The Ka'kach are another species who also are rather peaceful, or were rather peaceful I should say. I'm not sure what that was all about. Those that took you from the Elrsai and killed the Supreme Lord in the process, they were from the future, several hundred years I would say from the looks of their vessels and the weapons used. They wanted to strand you in space, I would think, leave you in that containment box until they could find some way to kill Alexis.

"You see, that's one of the benefits of the combination of DNA between human and Elrsai. Without it, Alexis' soul, for the lack of a better word, would have been thrown into the time-stream and re-integrated when she was crushed beneath that industrial hov. She would certainly not be able to interact as she is now and retain cognition of her memories. She's rather unique and that was the whole point. For only someone with her abilities can do what needs to be done."

Alexis, after the conversation and the release of emotions with Meagan, was having a difficult time believing that this Meagan and the other Meagan standing by her were in reality the same person, albeit from different times. One was cocky and confident, assured of her mission and purpose and unlikely to be persuaded otherwise. The other was a ball of seething emotions and contradictions, her anger and pain escaping in breaking waves. It was fascinating for Alexis to see what the passage of time could do to someone, how it could change one's personality, ones' outlook until there was no longer recognition between past and future selves.

But none of that really mattered. What mattered was that they were expecting things from her that she had no clue about, any sense of what it was she was supposed to do. "You know, I didn't ask for any of this and I really don't see why I should even do it," she stated with a calmness she didn't feel.

"It's not a decision that's up to you," Grand Marshal Locke said without much emotion. "You don't really have a choice in the matter. None of us do. Time is in charge now and other forces that we have no control over, like the Elrsai and the Ka'kach. Do you really think that they're going to stop searching for you? It's obvious that you're a real threat to them. And time's changing constantly. That's its nature. It's always in a state of flux, which is why someone like Alexis was needed." She turned to her past self with a look that speaking of sympathy, yet seemed almost fake. "I understand your anger, Meagan."

She felt so odd talking to herself like this. What was even more odd was that she had no memory of this event ever occurring in her own life. This of course meant that the creation of Alexis in the past had changed events, had opened a new time-stream that at the present was driving ever forward toward the goal for which she had so faithfully striven, planned, prepared. But would Alexis truly be able to do it correctly this time?

"Of course you understand it. We're the same person, for Christ sake," Meagan spit out harshly, as if the person talking to her were daft.

"What I mean is that you don't see the whole picture. You're reacting from data that isn't complete and that's why you can't see what it is that I'm striving for."

Alexis listened closely to the bizarre conversation between two people who were, basically, the same person. She still was not exactly sure what her role in this ever expanding drama was, but she was beginning to see more and more of the picture and she wanted to be involved less and less.

"Okay, so tell me again what it is that you're striving for, because I don't see it at all. All I see is a mess, a convoluted scheme that doesn't seem to be working at all. We're still here, still meeting as we're supposed to. The first time that we met, you told me that I needed to make my own mother, whom I haven't seen in years, hate me to such an extent that she wouldn't think twice about changing the time-stream to the point that I don't exist anymore. You told me that it was vital to the success of the mission and would, in the end, save countless lives throughout the galaxy."

Meagan stopped a moment, the anger she had directed toward Alexis, that she had faked till it felt real, now directed at herself, at her gullibility and her own cowardice for coming up with a scheme like this in the future. It was as if she had discovered that she ended up on a penal colony in the future for a stupid and ignorant act and was thus furious at herself in the present for allowing it to happen in the first place.

She spread her arms out in a futile gesture of understanding. "And yet, nothing seems to have changed. As a matter if fact, now we have alien species coming after us and a vicious paradoxical loop occurring to which there appears to be no escape. You call this planning? I wouldn't call it that. This is ludicrous. When did I become so fucking stupid?"

"You can't see the whole picture," the Grand Marshal repeated, her refusal to reveal more an inbred reaction to the consequences that knowing the future entailed.

Meagan responded in exasperation. "What picture?" She stared at herself a moment, then continued. "Let me see if I have this straight, okay? In the future, I decide that the only way to relieve the problems that are facing me and humanity, for which I seem to have become the spokeswoman, is to cause the creation of an entirely new alien-human hybrid in the past, who turns out to be my mother and who'll be able to, eventually, change the future in some strange sort of way that I really don't understand. This person then somehow gets pulled into the future at her death, a death that I have my past-self arrange, even though this person hasn't even given birth to me yet to allow me to do all these things in the first place. And then, something goes wrong in the time-stream when it isn't supposed to and now aliens are trying to kill us. Is that about the long and short of it, because that's all I see at the moment."

The Grand Marshal realized that she was not going to get anything accomplished unless she laid it all out, gave up the future of her past self and in that very act changed the future to something completely different again. It was what she had been warned, the vagaries of time and the time-streams beyond mere human comprehension. The Elrsai had been aware of it and had warned her time and again about tampering with the past. Now she was beginning to see the tip of the iceberg that was her plan, its many variations bleeding across the streams like an open wound.

"Okay, okay. I see your point. I suppose that from where you're sitting, this all seems like a mess, but there is a point to it, it all has a purpose and it appears that the only way to fulfill that purpose is to tell it all to you and hope that the time-stream doesn't change too much because of the telling."

Alexis was thoroughly confused by now. She was being treated as if she was not even in the ship, as if they were talking about someone who had once existed or that existed in another plain of existence but was not around anymore. All this talk of time-streams and changes and aliens didn't seem to fit together at all. It was as if she were but an observer to a macabre play about herself.

"In the future, in my future – for we apparently are no longer living in the same time-stream – the Huang Dynasty becomes huge, a monster. It dominates human civilization, if one can even call it that. The UFC no longer exists. It's replaced by an organization called the United Religious Alliance which is nothing more than a puppet entity controlled by Huang and his followers, who still live, using the MTP technology to expand their lives and the lives of all humans to nearly forever.

"In order to achieve this, the Dynasty must have a continual pool of replacement clones on hand for the billions upon billions of humans who now populate the galaxy like an infection. That means that there are planets populated with nothing but slave clones whose only purpose is to give their bodies, either whole or in parts, to a human somewhere so that he can live another two hundred years. They're basically mindless clones, replacement parts grown without any regard for their minds or consciousness. They're basically breed stock, treated like we used to treat our food animals regardless of the fact that they're as human as anyone else.

"The repression and brutal conditions of those who are not part of the inner elite of the Dynasty is terrible, with millions killed every year in the numerous penal colonies that populate the star systems. Those who didn't believe in the Dynasty, who wanted no part in the senseless slaughters and way of life that sacrificed one human for the sake of another, fled in the Generation Ships built as the last Colonies of the UFC were absorbed. But even these ships were eventually penetrated by the Dynasty, infected by the desire to live forever.

"It was out of these conditions that the Rebellion formed, a loosely organized group of those who had enough of both the Dynasty and the United Religious Alliance, which was in effect nothing but a mouth piece for Huang, pretending to be opposed to his intrigues and schemes and yet kowtowing to his every whim when necessary.

"I was one of the founders of the Rebellion, one of the few who saw through the sickness that was even invading the Colony Time Guards, a sickness spreading itself throughout the galaxy like a plague. The Rebellion was able to convince several of the Generation Ships to come to our side and move to the fringes of the Dynasty to plan and help bring down the evil that is Huang. But even these ships weren't safe, except for the deep-space types that managed to breach the inner halo and pass through to the other side.

"It was one of these ships that made first contact with the Elrsai, an advanced species who had technology that we could use; technology that would allow the Rebellion to destroy once and for all the Dynasty and all the evil it was spreading. That technology came in two ways: the ability to time index physically and the ability to create a human who could span all time-streams at once and bring them together at one point and time."

"That would be me," Alexis said, aware that the tale the future Meagan was spinning could be all lies, intentional falsehoods to deceive her into taking a path that would achieve goals that might be as nefarious as the Dynasty's appeared to be. Her guard went up and she listened carefully, aware that she might not have a second chance at this.

"Yes. The Elrsai have incredibly powerful minds when it comes to time travel, but because of the peaceful nature of their race, they never exploited it in any way. They were more than happy to just leave things the way they were and live their lives as they came. It was one of the Elrsai working for me who discovered that if their mental powers could be structured into the DNA of a human, then that hybrid could do things that no one else could. Could, in effect, transcend the time-streams and fix all of them at the same instant, which is the only way that they can all be changed. It was with that in mind that the Rebellion forced you to be created."

"And it never occurred to you that you were creating your own mother?" Meagan asked in shock. "Didn't you realize what it was that you were doing? That it must have been done before already and failed? How else could we be born in the first place?"

"No, as a matter of fact it didn't. As far as I knew, my mother, Alexis Locke, died of a natural death long ago and, apart from the work that she did for Vincent Cavalier, never even came close to possessing the powers that I thought our creation should have. It wasn't until after the deed had been done that we realized our error. That we realized we had perpetuated a closed time loop with the creation of the very person responsible for our existence in the first place. But even when I realized what I had done, I understood that it had to be this way, that a systematic mistake had been made somewhere along the way and that if I could but just correct it, then our intended purpose would still be accomplished."

"This is all very nice, listening to the planning of our family tree and all," Meagan said acidly, aware that there was nothing she had heard that would justify such a corrupting of the time-stream, an event to which she had sworn, taken an oath to never bring forward. How could her future self just ignore that oath? She could not even conceive of doing that. "But what does it have to do with what you want Alexis to do? How does it make what you're doing right?" The one thing Meagan had always prided herself on, that the Colony Time Guards had always held as a sacred duty and honor, was that they would never make an alteration in the time-stream that was personal, that affected themselves in anyway, either financially or emotionally or held even the slightest chance of killing someone off whose off-spring might change the world.

When the Yellowleaf Conjecture had been first proposed, there had been much debated about what Alexis rightly declared to be the forfeiting of one soul for the sake of many hundreds of souls, and the affect on the time-stream of that soul's genes no longer circulating. When the Conjecture had finally been approved and Meagan had been chosen to lead the teams that would carry it out, she had strong feelings that were opposed to the whole scheme.

But when the people she had been assigned to *re-direct*, which was the euphemism thrown around at the time, were being killed just prior to her arrival, she had been rather shocked.

It was at that time that Meagan had realized what was happening. She had seen the time causality loop that had been formed and onto which Skre's Conjecture had stumbled. When her future self had appeared to her shortly thereafter and had explained that it was her mother who was doing the killings and laid the entire plan at Meagan's feet, Meagan had, besides being vastly confused, been relieved that she would not have to kill off these innocent people, assuaging her of a guilt taking up shop in her up before she had even killed one of them.

But now, now that she was beginning to see the vastness of the plan she would create in the future, that would violate the very principles she had sworn to uphold, she found it hard to believe that the woman who sat before her, who looked and talked just like her, was in fact her future self. There was no way she could ever see herself changing in such a drastic way to first become a rebel and then to hatch such a web of alterations and time manipulation that would alter not only her own life but that of millions of others.

In fact, as she listened to her future self explain it all, she realized for the first time that she was directly responsible for not only her own birth but the creation of her own mother. One could argue that she was more than ready to carry out her orders of the Yellowleaf Conjecture, regardless her own moral position to the contrary, but that act would create an entirely new time-stream in which the depravations of the Dynasty would be absent. Her actions would not affect the lives of the people already living, would not in anyway affect all the time-streams at once and possibly destroy countless lives in the bargain.

What this future Meagan was planning, had planned and tried to carry out, was the altering of all time-streams in a grand destruction of technology and people on a scale defying logic. Even when she looked deep inside herself, deep into the black pits every one had lurking within where those thoughts one deemed too demonic and corrupt sat and waited for the will to supersede the soul, she could not see herself doing it, making changes that had echoes of Dynasty written all over it.

It was just beyond her.

That, in conjunction with the fact that the future Meagan had tried to make her lie to her mother, lie to make her own mother hate her to such an extreme that she would be willing to destroy it all without caring, now convinced Meagan that this was not her future self. That whoever this person was – for perhaps she was a Meagan from the future, just not her future – she was certainly not from the same time-stream and didn't hold onto the same belief systems. It was an impossibility that they were one in the same person.

Whoever she was, she had to be stopped, if for nothing else than to ease Meagan's own mind that she would never become so obsessed with one, driving idea, pushing aside all that stood in its way. Meagan didn't realize, of course, that she was falling into the same pattern of behavior, with the obsession to stop herself driving her onward with a fury. That was usually the way it went with humans. They never recognized the behavior in themselves that they abhorred in others.

"Make it right?" Grand Marshal Locke asked, aware of just what her past self was thinking, having been there before. "There's no right or wrong here. It isn't that simple. Nothing is. This isn't a black and white Universe where the good guys and the bad guys are easily picked out. It's obvious that to the Ka'kach, we are the evil ones, the ones who want to destroy all that is."

Meagan rose her hand up in a plea for the future Meagan to stop. "Wait, wait, wait. This is getting far beyond reality. Are you telling me that you didn't know that any of this would occur when you started, that it's all new to you. What is it that's so special about what you planned that could possibly have such far-reaching affects? I mean, why would they even know about Alexis and what you've planned and how it affects them? We don't even know them yet. In my time-stream, we're still thousands of light-years apart. This all started out as a simple mission to destroy the creators of the MTP and now it seems to have a life of its own!"

The proximity alarm startled them all with its chirp for attention and Grand Marshal Meagan turned to look at who could possibly be wandering around in the middle of this desert. When she saw the scanner traces and the sure-fire sign of a jumper coming in from the fold, she reacted instantly. She powered up the main drive systems and started the calculations for a time index, working as fast as she could without stopping to offer an explanation.

The time-jumper lifted off the sand dunes with a jerk and screamed out low over the ground, the whine of the drive-system ever increasing as the ship sped off until the time matrix and the main time-fold generator could align themselves. The ship rocked from a hit, the shield failure warning lights flashing in angry red. Several more hits bracketed the small ship, the electric blue of the plasma strikes snaking and sizzling around the degrading shields like live wires.

"What the hell is this now?!" Meagan exclaimed as the matrix aligned and the time-jumper indexed at the same time that the shields failed.

"It appears that the Ka'kach are a very persistent species," was the only reply she received from the Grand Marshal as they once again found themselves in the in-between-time.

One world, one time, one life.
This is what we are striving for.
This is the way it should be.
— Rebel slogan

33

3000 C.E.
First Palatial Estate,
Planet of HUANG PRIME,
The Forbidden Zone

To say that the estate was luxurious would be like saying that the Taj Mahal was just another tomb. With the wealth of the Dynasty flowing in on a scale unprecedented in the annals of humanity, the planet of Huang Prime was one large, imposing, opulent refuge in the center of the Forbidden Zone, where the elite of the Dynasty could relax in the extensive gardens and spas gracing the planet.

It was also the place from which the ever-reaching tentacles of government stretched out in corrupt and dictatorial procession to entangle all they touched and slowly but surely bring all that was into the folds of the vast Machiavellian fastness that was the Dynasty.

The Forbidden Zone itself, like the Forbidden City of old, was a spherical expanse of space encompassing the star system in which Huang Prime sat like a shroud of secrecy and venality. Only the cadre forming the inner circles of the totalitarian despotism were allowed access, the powerful and swift battleships prowling like junk-yard dogs along the fringes with a mesmerizing consistency. To be allowed access into the Forbidden Zone was a rare privilege, those of the Royal family and associated Houses who lived there unaware of anything outside the Zone, their lives veiled in a cloak of self-deception and decadence feeding off the labor of those who knew not of the copiousness that their work produced.

To not be one of the direct members of the Dynastic family or a member of a Noble House – there were, in fact, no direct heirs to Huang or the Dynasty, each of the off-spring inadvertently born to his numerous concubines killed before birth to curtail any power struggle for the throne, the concubine slain also as an object lesson to the others – and still be allowed to set foot on Huang Prime had occurred perhaps two or three times in the last six hundred years. Each one of those times had precipitated a major change in policy shortly thereafter.

This province of luxury and superfluities excess was an oasis of wealth where those who had caught favor in the eyes of the Emperor were cuddled and wooed and shown the results of almost nine hundred years of iron-fisted rule. Huang himself was in his fifth new body, the state of the MTP technology and the clone farms having reached a pinnacle of advancement allowing for anyone to change bodies within a matter of hours of the decision, if not sooner. Elaborate safety procedures and precautions had been in place since the beginning, making it virtually impossible for anyone, save the Dynastic Clone Farms, to clone anyone associated with the Royal family or the elite Houses, thus forestalling any impostors.

The transfer protocols were also closely supervised and overseen by Dynastic Counselors and advisors who made certain that all transferals were conducted legally and within the set limits established by Huang himself, which prohibited the MTP technology to those the government considered subversive or amoral.

A vast data-base stored the minds of all those who had used the MTP so that the Dynasty had access to the knowledge of all who lived within its ever-expanding boundaries, knowledge of the most intimate and personal kind as well as knowledge of all on which the populace was working, all their secrets and dreams and aspirations. And it was used extensively to drive the Dynasty onward and protect it from ruin, to root out those who were not following the righteous path for the greater glory of the Dynasty.

No secrets were kept in the Dynasty.

No privacy was to be expected.

With a complete monopoly on the technology and its subsequent applications, the Dynasty held a power that no other government had held before and it was one of the key factors in the smooth and perpetual life of the Dynasty itself.

Of course, there were those few individuals who knew of the Rebellion's acquisition of the MTP technology almost eight hundred years ago and their ensuing use of it on their more useful adherents, but that knowledge was kept as a state secret, the existence of the monopoly as firm in the minds of the people who lived their purposeless lives in the grasp of the Dynasty as the fact that there was no Rebellion in the first place.

Rebellions meant that the government was not in complete control, that there were those who disagreed with the policies and decisions of the elitist leaders and that was one belief that could not be tolerated. So, the

Rebellion, if spoken of at all, was referred to as myth, legend, fable. It was something people spoke of in the shadows but of which there was never had any clear evidence, the whispered rumors of the traders and the deep-space haulers digested into the power couplings of the mighty warships traversing space or the dark eclipse of the penal colonies from whence none ever returned. If the government never acknowledged the existence of the Rebellion, then that rebellion didn't exist, lost in the vastness of space and the massiveness of the Dynasty till all that was left were unsubstantiated rumors, the occasional attacks and minor successes of the Rebellion attributed to alien incursions or anything else that was not the Rebellion.

But to Huang, the Rebellion was a thorn in his side that had been bothering him for longer than he cared to remember. And as if that was not enough to cause his ulcers to burn, the name Alexis Locke continued to recur, at least once a year to his utter dismay and disappointment, her name synonymous with prophecies of doom and destruction.

Today was not any different.

Today the Rebellion was foremost in Huang's mind, foremost in the minds of the few Counselors he kept around, sitting in their small chairs along the sides of the expansive receiving hall built for no other purpose than to intimidate those who came to see the heart and mind of the Dynasty itself. Its old-style columns rose like fingers of God into the lofty darkness above, disappearing into a black void as extensive as space itself, hanging like a suffocating blanket of oppression, meant to overawe the supplicants who came to grovel at the feet of ultimate power. The exquisite artwork, stolen from the depths of Earth itself and any other civilization that had the audacity to stand in the way of the Dynasty, adorned the walls the closer one approached the penultimate seat of power. The large, genetically cloned guards towering over all others like the guardians of hell, brooded at any who approached, their nasty looking plasma weapons and swords a deterrent to even the most hardened fanatic.

The Rebellion, which had up until this point been but a minor problem, had now become a major crux, a crux festering and growing like a malaise within the plague that was the Dynasty itself. And Alexis Locke was at the very heart of the malaise, her powers and abilities unrecognized until now; until the report hovering before him in the air, its holography representation giving him the details of what she could do in the past that would affect all that was the future, and in a single moment, end it.

As it turned out, Alexis Locke dead in the future was far more powerful than Alexis Locke alive in the past. He had been warned of this and thus had never bothered to kill her off in the past. Had he but known that it was the act of her death in the presence of her daughter – that incredible vexatious Meagan Locke who seemed to persistently plague him regardless what century he chose to live – was the key to her presence in the future, Huang would have killed Alexis off long ago. He still could, of course, having all time at his beck and call, but it would be a useless conjecture since Alexis was already traveling around the time-stream in her new powerful state. Killing her off now, in the past, would be as useless as trying to kill her off in her dead state. It was one of those vagaries of time Huang found so very irritatingly enigmatic.

And so it was that the Ka'kach had been allowed into the Forbidden Zone, allowed access to the inner sanctum that, since the vast and expensive war three hundred years ago that had broken the Ka'kach civilization into mere fragments of itself, had been off-limits to their kind in any form.

That was about to change.

The three Ka'kach slowly made their way down the hallway, their eyes boring straight ahead and fixed onto the sole reason for their life: Huang. They ignored the vast hallway, were indifferent to the effect it was supposed to have on them, indifferent to all save that lone figure who represented to them their deepest and most vile nightmares.

There were three of them.

There were always three of them; no more and no less.

The Ka'kach were a rare species always born in threes, their minds forever linked together in a symbiotic relationship forcing them to always be together. If one died, they all died, bereft of an essential part of themselves as necessary as any major organ to a human. With their strong mental link, the Ka'kach were very intelligent, their prowess in the fields of technology and science legendary. Yet, that had been before.

Before the Dynasty.

The Ka'kach – with their short, one meter tall statue, their wolf-like heads and rows of sharp, jagged teeth, their four arms ending in razor-sharp retractable claws and their two stout legs and thick tail as much for balance as for movement – had once been the engineers of the galaxy, known by all the other sentient species as the ones to call when problems presented themselves or theories needed testing.

That was all before they had the audacity to stand in the way of the Dynasty, for at that time the Ka'kach were also known for their tactical military genius, the ability, with their three minds working as one, to analyze any situation and make a quick and correct choice that would assure victory.

For some reason, however, it had failed against the mighty clone legions of the Dynasty, the capacity to field army after army overwhelming the small numbers of the Ka'kach – their long gestation period a pox against rapid expansion of the population – until all that was left were isolated pockets suing for surrender lest their species become extinct at the hands of an inferior race.

All their brilliance and genius in the art of war had been for naught against the staggering and overpowering abundance of the humans, the savage and fanatical ferocity of the bipeds like nothing ever seen before. And those who were left had made the decision to surrender and wait, wait for a chance to strike back at those who had brought them to the brink of extermination in a matter of a few hundred years.

So now the Ka'kach were subservient to the Dynasty, kowtowed to the whims of the Emperor. He didn't call for them often to perform the tasks he seemed to think them best at. And he had never called them to his inner sanctum in the Forbidden Zone.

Never.

They stopped several meters from the raised dais where upon Huang sat, looking down disdainfully at a vanquished foe, mere slaves for the vagary of a human, a species at which they had once laughed.

They spoke in turns, each speaking a part of the whole as their minds worked on the problem together, a trait Huang found utterly annoying. Their voices were low grumbles of a growl, the translators implanted within their throats reproducing the sounds into Dynastic Chinese, a variant of the Mandarin that had once been the language of former days of glory.

"Bidding we come..."

"At your..."

"Most reverent Emperor, Huang."

They all bowed as if attached to the same bar, the rags they called clothes haphazardly failing on their bodies like leaves on a dying tree, their eyes burning brightly with a deep-seated yet subtly hidden hatred that would, one day, burn a hole through the very heart of the Dynasty.

Huang frowned, the smell emanating from the furry diminutive creatures like a cesspool. He had given up complaining long ago about it, his many meetings with the Ka'kach outside of the Forbidden Zone those many years ago when he had still ventured outside his secure domain, still fresh in his nostrils. "I have an assignment for you that is different than anything you've done before."

They stared at him without speaking.

He smirked a moment; rubbed his hands together. "I need you to find someone in the past. To find them and then place them in stasis so that they will not be a bother to me anymore. I need you to find Alexis Locke."

"Past go..."

"We not can possible..."

"Assignment not logical."

Huang sighed, the stilted and mixed grammar of the translators a burden to him, following the meanings behind the many-tiered vocabulary of the Ka'kach difficult at best. But it was the only translation possible, or so the technicians assured him, the language of the Ka'kach spoken on such a higher plane than the primitive grunts of the humans that it was the best that could be expected. Rendering Ka'kach into any form of human speak was akin to turning human speak into bird.

"I will provide for the means of traveling to the past," Huang stated in irritation. Although he despised working with the Ka'kach, they were the best assassins around and were completely submissive to his demands, whatever they may be. Huang had rid himself of many a potential problem using the Ka'kach talents. He had even tried to use them to rid him of that other nuisance Meagan Locke – the entire Locke family a barb in his hand it seemed – but she had been rather elusive, evading the best attempts at assassination.

When it had been suggested to the Emperor that the Ka'kach could actually be indexed into the past and used to eliminate the vexing Rebel leader at a time and place that it was known she would be, Huang had come to a much better conclusion. Why not just eliminate the mother and the daughter together, thus destroying the seed and the family line in one fell blow and save him the obstacles invariably cropping up with these things and the time-stream.

It had always been assumed that the Ka'kach were incapable of indexing to the past, their multiple-leveled mind functions and tri-mind continuance incompatible with the indexing technology. But now that problem had been solved and Huang had the perfect assignment for them.

"It will be up to you to find the time and place best to deal with the individual whom I want dealt with."

"Kill her dead..,"

"Do you why not..."

"Sense more make."

The Ka'kach stood like lost dogs as they spoke, looking up at the Emperor with that feral glare that, had Huang not dealt with it before, would have scared the shit out of him.

"Because she is very special. She can't be killed. So you must isolate her in a place where she can do me no more damage."

The Ka'kach looked at each other a moment as if contemplating the value of the assignment and its ultimate meaning to them. If she were such a threat to Huang, then perhaps they should not kill her. Anyone who was an enemy of Huang was an ally to the Ka'kach.

"Special she be why..."

"If she in past..."

"Before her deal with?"

Huang leaned forward. "Because she can't be killed. She doesn't *exist* in the physical plane. And I've just now figured out how to send you Ka'kach back in time without causing untold problems."

"Technology have you..."

"Time for long..."

"Since when?"

Too many questions. Huang didn't like the direction the questions were now taking and leaned back again, indicating for one of the few counselors to step forward. "This is not important. You will do this for me or else I will eliminate all the remaining Ka'kach like the flea-ridden pestilence they are. Is that clear?" He spoke these words with a simple yet direct power that, though his voice never rose higher, echoed in the hallway like a plasma cannon discharge.

The Ka'kach paused a moment again, but this time they stared hard and long at Huang as his Counselor stepped up next to them and patiently waited for orders.

"Do will we..."

"You order have..."

"As you say..."

"Yes," Huang said with a self-satisfied look on his face half-hidden by the revulsion he was beginning to feel toward these creatures. "Yes, I know you will." His gaze lingered a moment on the beasts before him who seemed to exist apart from the world in which humanity lived, then shifted his eyes to his Counselor, switching to a dialect that the translators were incapable of translating for the Ka'kach. "Prepare them for the index. And Chin Hi... Begin the elimination of the Ka'kach that we have planned for. I have a feeling that they will figure out a way to use the time travel technology to their benefit and that's the last thing that I need. Let them finish this one last task, and then kill them all."

The Counselor bowed respectfully and showed the Ka'kach out, but not before the three took one last, long look at the Emperor, almost as if they had understood what he had said, their eyes betraying their utter contempt for the human whom they were bonded to ... at least for the moment.

Huang watched them leave, their odor lingering in the air like an after-thought. He thought a moment, the kernel of an idea that had begun to form earlier starting to sprout into a more thorough concept. "Ping-Wei, prepare my personal yacht. I have a mission to perform that none but I can accomplish."

One of the Counselors stood and bowed before he left to ready the Imperial yacht.

The Senior Counselor, Lo Han Tsu, his hands clasped together before him, his colorful attire proclaiming his status, stepped forward. "If I may be so bold, my Emperor, as to ask what it is that requires your personal attention. This is not your usual routine."

"There is someone to whom I must speak, who I must ready for the future. He is weak and un-schooled in the ways of the future. It is time that I paid my respects to him." Huang had long wondered who it had been that had always lurked in the shadows when he had first started, who had given him the idea of the MTP and all its nefarious applications, who had, in essence, started him down the road to the power and fame he now wielded with an iron fist of fury. Now he knew.

The Emperor stood, the guards to either side coming to attention. "Yes, it is time that I make that visit. Time that I begin the process that will allow me to be where I am now. It is time that I visited myself."

*   *   *

"Do you have any clue as to why they want me dead?" Alexis asked The Grand Marshal as they sat in the in-between-time, waiting. "What did I ever do to them?"

"It's probably not a matter of what you've done but more likely what you will do, or perhaps even what'll happen as a consequence of something that you do," she answered in reluctant terms. "But it really doesn't matter what they want or think. We're not doing this for their sake. We're doing it for humanity."

"There's no way that you and I are the same person," Meagan said with disdain. "That you would disregard the concerns of another species proves that we are two completely different people."

446

The Grand Marshal turned on her past self with a snap. "When you've lived through what I've seen, then you'll understand that the righteous and pure attitude you have at the moment is bull-shit. It's bullshit! And the sooner you learn to overcome that weakness, the better off you'll be. Believe me, I know.

Don't forget that I was you at one time and the more I listen to your sniffling and whining and complaining, the more I realize what an ass I was, what a complete fool for believing in people and things that were so totally wrong.

"Skre and all his righteous attitudes were all a front, a waste of time and resources. Huang was always the one that should have been targeted, that should have been stopped before allowing him to drag humanity down with him and his Dynasty. There is but one evil in the world, one pit of loathsome foulness that reeks to high hell, and that evil is Huang and his perpetual Dynasty. There is nothing else that matters."

"I don't believe you," Meagan shot back just as harshly, not willing to let this person dictate how she should feel and act. "There's no way that feeling compassion for another species or trying to prevent the destruction on the scale that you're talking of is ever a good thing. No way! I don't know what the hell happened to make me change into this cold-hearted bitch that you've become, but I don't like it and I'll sure as hell try to prevent it from happening to me! You're obsessed with Huang. Obsessed!"

"Yes, perhaps I am, but in my time Huang is all there is!" she shot back with a shrill voice, her jaw quivering slightly. "All I once knew and loved is gone because of that evil, destroyed in a spread of plague and disease that is humanity! You can't understand because to you it hasn't happened yet! To you it's still the future, but to me it's a part of my life like a vile hole in my soul!"

"You're sick with obsession, and I for one don't plan on taking that path," Meagan spewed out in self-absorbed rage.

"Then you'll end up dead. It's that simple. The Dynasty, as you well know, doesn't have compassion and mercy and doesn't respect it in the least bit. As a matter of fact, they detest it and try to root it out wherever they can. I never realized how damn weak and pitiful I was back then! How I ever survived those lean times I'll never know!"

Meagan could not believe what she was hearing. If this was her future, then she didn't want any part of it. "Then I'd rather be dead if you're the only other choice."

"You're too stupid to even talk to."

Alexis spoke up, aware that they were getting nowhere closer to the truth of what she was supposed to be doing, what her whole purpose was. "You two are acting like little kids. It's like watching someone argue with themselves in the mirror and losing. You two are pathetic."

They both looked at her a moment, compassion passing through the eyes of Meagan, disdain through the eyes of Locke.

"You're right," the Grand Marshal said with subdued tones. "It makes no difference whether you," and she referred to Meagan with a distracted gesture, "believe in this or not. You're not the important one here. Alexis is the one who counts. She's the only one who counts at the moment. When I gave her DNA and genetic structures to Dr. Cavalier, I was preparing her for this moment in time, this place. My past self happening to be here is just an unexpected by-product."

"Yes, okay, you've told me all this already," Alexis stated with growing frustration. "What the hell is it that I'm supposed to do? Why in the world would my own daughter want me to hate her to such an extent? And why the hell are you two arguing over it?"

"That's simple," the Grand Marshal said as she looked at her past self with a slight tinge of guilt at having asked her to make Alexis hate her. "But I'm not the one who can tell you. This is something that you'll have to figure out yourself, when the time comes. I can tell you nothing else."

Alexis sighed. This was like learning to drive a hov without ever having seen one before in your life.

The proximity alarm sounded again.

"Shit, they're back," Locke announced as she spun around and began the calculations to index to the proper time. It only took a few moments, then she spun around again and spoke directly to Alexis. "Okay, now's the time for you to do your magic."

"What magic?"

"You mean she hasn't even told you even that much?" she said, looking at Meagan with a frown.

"I told her, but she doesn't have a clue how to do it, and neither do I."

"Do what?" Alexis asked. Meagan had told her so many things that she was not sure anymore what they were taking about, to what they were referring.

The ship rocked from the plasma burst scattering the rear shields and sending sparks flying from the secondary power couplings and plasma relays.

"Bring the time-streams together, damn it, bind them into one so that any change that you affect will be felt in all of them," Locke shouted out as she began to maneuver the ship away from the fast approaching Ka'kach destroyer that seemed quite determined to eliminate them from time altogether. Then she noticed the energy surge, the alarming increase of magnetic-triad waves emanating from the destroyer as if in a concerted spread. She was well aware what that was all about and just hoped that she could make the jump into the time-stream before the containment system acquired.

"Okay, how do I go about doing that?"

"Concentrate on it, think about it, make it happen," Locke said as plasma bursts scattered their volatile energy about the in-between-time and around the ship as she dodged the attacks. "You have the ability. All you need to do is make it happen, think it and it will happen."

"That makes no sense," Alexis replied back. "I don't even know what it is that I'm suppose to think about. This isn't much of a plan!"

There was a burst of light, a flash of multi-colored upheavals that seemed to concentrate into a pinprick off their bow, stretching to infinity. There was a moment of distortion, a feeling of lost time and lost consciousness blurring Alexis' vision as the ship indexed into a time-stream to escape their pursuers.

The smoky trails of the time-streams were replaced by solid, glowing balls of gas sitting in the void like flames of perdition, the lone planet hovering to their right like a dirty ball of crystallized caramel.

"Now listen," the Grand Marshal exclaimed as she stabilized the time matrix around them. "We don't have much time. I'm certain that the Ka'kach will be following us here soon. They're rather adept at things like this, though I've never known them to be assassins for hire or very aggressive. Something must have happened in my future to turn them into hired thugs. That ship registers as if it's from the future, the far future. I'm not really sure what's going on with them, but anyway .... Listen Alexis. You need to bind the streams together so that I can index you to the proper place and allow you to do what it is that you need to do."

Alexis' vision was all blurred, the blobs floating before her like smeared out watercolors. She remembered this happening the last time she had indexed abruptly, when she had awoken in the small room on that Colony in the future. Or was that the past now? She could no longer tell.

All she knew was that she was being asked to do something that she had no clue how to accomplish. And not having a clue was not something that happened often in her life. She was growing irritated and frustrated and that was never a good sign. "I can't do what it is that you're asking. Until I was pulled into the future, I didn't even know that time travel was possible, so how I'm supposed to bind these time-streams together is really beyond me."

"Have you even tried?" Meagan asked, awed at the technology the ship they were presently in possessed. To be able to index so quickly with an entire ship and all its contents was pure science fiction to her. All that she had ever learned told her that it was impossible, and yet here she had just been witness to it, had even experienced it to the extreme. Although still uncertain as to the validity of her future self's assertions concerning what it was that Alexis had to do, one thing was for certain: she could not wait to live in the time that this type of technology was available.

"No, of course I haven't tried," Alexis rapped out coldly.

"Then try it now," the Grand Marshal demanded with compressed lips. "Before we run out of time."

"How the hell is that possible, running out of time I mean?" Alexis snapped.

"Just try it, damn it!" It was said in a fulminating voice. "Stop looking for excuses!"

Alexis didn't see why she should do any of the things she was being asked to do. As far as she was concerned, it had nothing to do with her. She was dead. Her body was a smear on the grass. What did she care what happened now? It was not as if she knew anyone who would be hurt, cared for anyone who was still alive. But that was just the thing. She did care. Always had. There had always been something in her that had made her care about issues. Not that she had ever marched in a protest or anything that bold.

But she did care. And if what either of her daughters in time said was true, even just a small portion, then there certainly was reason enough to help. If the billions of people killed in the labor camps and the exterminations camps was not enough, then she didn't know what would be. Killing off this Huang person was not any more demanding than any other assignment she had been given. He was not the problem and she assumed that he was one of the first people she was obliged to kill.

What was bothering her was what her daughter was not telling her. What about the collateral affects? What of those people whose lives would be forever changed by the far-reaching plan that the far future Meagan had envisioned? Was it really in the best interests of the human species to deprive them of a technology that would fundamentally change the way they lived? Deprive them of a technology that would wipe out deadly diseases, cancer, AIDS, any and all such epidemics with the simple transference of the mind to a new body?

Perhaps the specter of the Dynasty hanging over all that humanity did was the price to be paid for advancing the human species beyond itself. The question to be asked was whether the loss of that technology and advancement was worth not having Huang and his Dynasty around?

It was apparent that the far future Meagan, the Rebel Leader who had hardened into a bare shadow of her former self through the depravations of the Dynasty, was thoroughly convinced that this was the right path, the only path to enlightenment and repentance. But just because she believed it with all her heart and soul, was it really true?

Adolf Hitler had started out as a rebel also.

"What the hell are you waiting for?" the Grand Marshal demanded. "They'll be here any moment and one or two more blasts of their weapons and then they'll be able to capture you in their magnetic containment field again like before and I won't be around to save you!"

Alexis looked at her daughter, a full-grown daughter she had not even had conceived yet. What would her actions mean for these two, for their lives in the time stream? "If I bind these streams together and affect the changes that you want, what happens to you two? How are you even born if I don't exist in any of the streams anymore?"

Both Meagans looked at each other for a moment, the same thoughts passing through their minds in the same instant, that spark of recognition appearing between two people who had known each other in the distant past making connection. They both knew the answer to that one. And for the first time since they had crossed paths, they reached a mutual agreement.

The Grand Marshal spoke up. "As I said before, we aren't the important ones in this. We're just the catalyst that makes it all possible. Our lives are meaningless in the greater scheme of things. It doesn't matter what happens to us. All that matters is that Huang never gains power, that no Huang ever gains power. And the only way to assure that is by never allowing the MTP to be produced. At least not until humans can learn to control it. At the moment, that doesn't look like it'll be any time soon."

"But it matters to me," Alexis said with suppressed emotion. "How am I supposed to willingly affect a change that I know will destroy my own children? What kind of a person do you think I am?"

"The type of person who knows what's best for the species as a whole," the Grand Marshal said with a passion she had been harboring for centuries, for just this moment. "The type of person who can see into the future and know that with this one act, all can be resolved, all can be restored."

"You can see into the future?" Meagan asked, aware of the immense implications such an ability could have. If she could see into the future, then that meant that she could index into the future.

"I suppose that's what it is," Alexis responded, confused by the compassion and vibrancy of which her daughter was capable, that she was using to accomplish this one goal, regardless of the outcome to her own life. "When I'm in the in-between-time, I can see both sides of the time-streams. I can see the beginning and the end."

"There's an end?" Meagan asked, looking from Alexis to her future self, seeing in the eyes of the woman that she would become an awareness of this fact and this ability Alexis possessed. How did she find out?

"Some of the time-streams seemed to have an end. Or at least what appears to be an end. They just sort of dispersed into nothing."

"But that's not supposed to be possible. It opens up a whole new world," Meagan said in total wonderment, finally understanding how it had been possible for Alexis to travel to her own future, and finally beginning to see what it was that her future self was striving to obtain.

"There isn't time for this," the Grand Marshal stated in consternation. "I'm showing an increase in chronometric particles and a large flux in the prevailing gravity waves. The Ka'kach are coming." She turned to look at Alexis, imploring with her eyes, with her voice. "Bind the streams together. Grab them and bring them to one point in time, to one place, together. Try it now. It's the only way possible."

This was not what Alexis wanted. She didn't want any of it but she knew that she had at least to try. If nothing else, then at least to prove to herself that she could do it. There were times in one's life when doing what one wanted was so far from the actual reality that it was a wonder humans could even imagine a different outcome.

She concentrated and found herself outside of the ship, the distortion and the undulations of her visions telling her that she was now back in the in-between-time, where the time-streams spanned the heavens like writhing snakes. She thought about what her daughter had said, about binding the streams together in one place, but nothing happened. She tried to grab one of the streams, but there was nothing on which to grab. In utter failure and contempt, she blanked her mind completely and placed all her thoughts toward this one concept, this one idea. She had actually done such things before, forced herself to make objects move, to block bullets, but it had been so long ago and it had come so simply to her that she had forgotten what such a commitment entailed.

She made a mental picture of the streams all coming together, like strands of multi-colored ribbons being pinched together at one spot, all touching each other in one place and time, merging now into one turbulent eddy of time and place and gravity, the loose ends of the streams writhing off like live wires to both sides, snapping about in their confinement, contorted in serpentine waves of energy.

She pictured this all and concentrated on it, forced it to be real, to be before her. She had no expectations whatsoever that what she was doing would accomplish anything, but when she opened her eyes and looked, she was thoroughly shocked.

She had done it.

Before her in the void of the in-between-time, the time-streams were as she had imagined, all touching together in one place. But the energy that was coming off of the crux of the bind was immense, pulsating through her like breakers on the beach, crashing down upon the fabric of space-time and bending it, smashing it, subjecting it to pressures and stresses it was not meant to take.

The Grand Marshals' voice came to her, the mental connection between the two of them like a physical bond. *Now you have to index and make the changes that will save humanity from itself. You must eliminate all possibility that the MTP will ever be invented. You have to stop it here, now, before it can affect the future.*

In a flash of present, past and future, Alexis found herself falling toward the knot that was the bind, the conjunction of all the time-streams that had been made, that would be made; a confluence of all times.

And in that knot, Alexis found her answer.

*   *   *

2575 CE
Planet Callibib,
First House of the Elrsai

The gathered representatives of the Elrsai, summoned to the First House to elect a new leader after the tragic death of the Supreme Lord, stopped in the middle of their discussions and looked around. They had felt a disturbance in time, as if a giant hand had swept through and the after-eddies of the gravity wake had passed over the assembled Lords like a slight, spring breeze.

They were silent for a moment, each lost in his own thoughts, each thought the same. As if with one mind they all pushed the holo-imagers aside and dispersed, back to their own home planets, back to their loved ones without having elected anyone. There was no reason anymore to pick a new leader.

For the Elrsai, the end was finally here.
The signs of the prophecy had arisen.

*　　*　　*

The three Ka'kach watched as the mind of the one called Alexis Locke moved into the in-between-time and bound the time-streams together in an unprecedented display of power. The human ship, with the other two humans still aboard, sat squarely in the middle of the targeting computer's sights, ready for the final volley that would reduce it to sub-atomic particles in an instant.

They saw what the lone human was doing.

Their three minds calculated the outcome of the result.

And they smiled as they understood, understood that the time that they had been waiting for had arrived. The time of the end of the dominion by the humans was over. In fact, if the Human-Elrsai hybrid was successful, the dominion would never even take place, the time-stream wherein that event lay merged into the others and never occurred.

The targeting computer was turned off.

The destroyer indexed back to its proper time, unconcerned with what Huang would do to them.

Their subservience was over.

*　　*　　*

24 August 2075:
1204 hrs.
Earth
Washington, DC, USA

Cav sat in his hov, watching the foot traffic amble by, the suits and skirts and slacks all blending into one large expanse of humanity, the oppressive heat of the mid-day sun bearing down with a vengeance. Even the flowers lining the side of the walkway seemed to be wilting under the fatiguing humidity filling the air with its vaporized moisture.

He was here to play out the last act of this drama that was his life, to hopefully atone for his wasted efforts and amoral deeds that now seemed to weigh upon him even more than the fatty tissue sagging his body under its onerous weight. He was here across from the White House to fulfill the one last mission that he saw as his destiny.

He was here to take captive that bitch Claudine Maxwell, force her to tell him who she really was, what the tattoo meant, for whom she worked. And then, when the questions had been answered to his satisfaction, Dr. Vincent Cavalier intended to kill Claudine and in that accomplishment perform his penance for the sins that he had brought onto the world and for her desire to have Alexis killed.

He realized that she would most likely not be too willing to devolve the information for which he was looking, but that didn't matter. He had ways; many, many ways of making her scream at the top of her lungs in abject horror and pain and in the end beg to tell him all he wanted if it would only stop the torture being inflicted. He had done it before to tougher victims and they had all broken.

She too would break.

A particularly attractive woman walked by. She was dressed in a high red skirt, a large brimmed sun-hat, and had a lean and sleek dog on a leash. An open buttoned red blouse, without bra, exposing a round, sweat-glistening breast to view, caught his eye as she strutted by to the beat of her own inner music. He watched her walk by the entire length of the hov and then...

...she was walking by again, as if in instant replay.

The birds that had been singing their plaintive songs against the heat were singing the same notes, the breeze was blowing the same way, the people around her were all walking at the same pace as they had before, and he had the distinct feeling of relocation, distortion, deja vu at its most extreme.

He sat up straighter and looked around him, aware that something had just happened, that the lady with the dog had just walked by moments before and then it had all happened all over again. It was as if time had skipped a beat and then started again, slightly behind itself. He felt a wave of nausea pass through him, his stomach turning over with the after-effects of the experience.

Something odd was about to happen, he could feel it.

Then Claudine's hov rose out of the enclosed parking area and headed for home... and he followed.

*   *   *

24 August 2575: 1204 hrs.
Generation Ship *Argos*:
Time-stream Alpha Two

He felt the distortion wave pass through the ship like a gentle ground swell, the inertial dampeners compensating rapidly at the unexpected undulation so that the occurrence lasted but a fraction of a second. The skip of time passing through his body felt like a cool summer breeze, refreshing in its bare glimmer of hope at the approach of autumn.

He looked out into the large open expanse displaying the field of the Universe before him in all its glory. A disturbance was forming off their port bow, a disturbance that was swirling, pulling, tugging at the surrounding space like a tear in the fabric. The massive Generation Ship buckled slightly, rent by the ever-increasing waves of gravitons pouring out of the rift, the wormhole forming in record time as the gap was bridged between space and sub-space. Wisps of the burning sphere of gas lighting up this particular corner of space began to be pulled into the rift, defining its boundaries like colored dye in a draining sink.

He spread his arms out wide in full supplication to the greater glory that was the God-head. "It has begun," he whispered under his breath like a fine wine. "The time of reckoning is here. Now the devil will pay his due."

The stress alarms drowned out his words, but his smile shined like a thousand suns.

Man is absolutely alone, with not a
single friend; and between one and none
there lies an infinity.
          – Nietzsche

34

21 December 2084: 0800 hrs.
Mars Colony *Galileo Prime*

Alexis had never been to the Mars Colony. She had of course seen the holo-images, the news features and the like, but she had never had the need to actually set foot on the main Colony and thus had no real sense of its magnitude nor its grandeur.

So it was a slight bit of a surprise to find herself here, as if she had lived here all her life, with Meagan beside her in a state of utter confusion. Alexis saw that the planet held a beauty all its own, the red hue permeating not only the ground but the sky in an intoxicating yet odd sort of way. The vastness of the open plains, with no tree to break the dusty monotony of the stark, barren, yet beautiful landscape so in opposition to the green-lined avenues of the Colony, its human inhabitants creating a slice of Earth on a planet that had its own sense of majesty.

It was, she realized for the first time, a perfect example of the way humans tended to bring with them their own sense of reality, regardless of what stared them straight in the face, changing the landscape in order to create a world in which they felt comfortable while all the while ignoring the natural beauty of their surroundings.

Maybe it was not the MTP that she should be negating, but rather humans themselves, the destruction influence they perverted upon everything they touched like a plague.

Where the hell are we and why am I here? Meagan demanded, confused and disoriented at the sudden time and position shift occurring within seconds of the time rift forming.

"*Galileo Prime* would be my guess," Alexis answered vocally, her body appearing in the deserted lab complex as if she were physically there. "And somewhere around the 20th of the December, 2084."

Meagan, her mind conditioned to mask her mental presence whenever she indexed, looked at the physical manifestation of Alexis with a revolting derision at the blatant disregarding of the Colony Time Guard regulations. The date Alexis had indicated had not yet registered with Meagan's senses despite the familiarity of the laboratory. *You need to make yourself invisible, now. You can't be seen. It's a complete violation of policy. There are holo-imagers here that are recording your presence.*

Alexis heard the door slide open, saw the attractive young red-head walk in, distracted with the hand-held computer she was intently studying. She was oblivious to the physical manifestation of Alexis. *I think it's a little too late now*, Alexis projected to Meagan. She indicated the oblivious woman with the tilt of her chin.

Dr. Godonov is here already.

Meagan looked, recognized the female from the numerous holo-images intently studied. Meagan had never had the chance to see Dr. Godonov alive and now that she did, a pang of guilt swept through her at the waste of it all, of the loss of innocence the entire concept they were about to initiate was causing.

Alexis stepped forward. She could care less about whether the redhead could see her or not. If she was going to do this, going to kill these people for reasons that were still far beyond her comprehension, then she was going to do it her way. She was done being dictated to and from this point onward, Alexis would be the one making the rules, as it had always been.

Godonov, finally noticing that there was something different about her lab, tore her eyes away from the computer screen and looked around. When her eyes fell on the visage of Alexis, she jumped back a step, the fright on her face obvious. "Bozhe moy... Zdes te ne bez perevoda. Zdes dylya slozhebnogo plochshad." she said with stuttering Russian, backing away from the stranger who seemed to emit waves of dread.

"Are you Dr. Ykaterina Godonov?" Alexis asked in English, trying to remember how this woman had been killed the last time, what the files Cav had given her had stated. Just that very thought, that this female, this human mind and soul, had been already killed in another time-stream struck Alexis as the oddest thing she had yet encountered. She had seen the holo-images of the destroyed lab, had read the coroner's report on the charred remains of the woman. That she was standing here, now, before Alexis alive as alive could be made Alexis wonder about her own sanity.

Time travel was certainly not an easy concept to grasp. And Alexis found it even odder that she had done all this before in another time-stream and that in that time-stream, in what was once her time-stream, she had been sent to investigate these very deaths she was about to commit. She wondered what the legal defense of that would sound like. *I don't care what the holo-images show, your honor, there was no way that I could have killed that person because during that time I was over fifty-two million miles away.*

"Yes...." Godonov answered hesitantly, slowly working her way back toward the door through which she had entered, to the large red panic button on the wall that would summon the guards in a heart-beat.

There's no time for this, Meagan scolded, aware that Alexis was not going to try to kill this person without first talking to her. *If you're going to do this, then it needs to be done quickly. All the work that needs to be done we have to do quickly. The binding you've induced won't last forever and the longer that we keep this up, the more problems are going to occur. Right now hundreds of sub-space rifts are opening through the time-streams as they're pulled apart from the constraining forces placed on them.*

And how do you know all this? Alexis asked as she held her hands up in a sign of non-aggression and smiled at Godonov. *And what happened to the fiery speeches you were making about not believing the future Meagan and not going along with all this and so on? You seem to have made a rather abrupt turn around here. I thought you said earlier that none of this changes anything, that all the killings are a waste because the cycle continues to repeat.*

Only if we keep making the same mistakes. The pattern has to be changed and it already has, because I'm here with you instead of showing up a few minutes after you like I remember it happening, after they were all dead. When my future self stated that you could see the future, when you stated that some of the time-streams seemed to just end, that they had an end at all, I finally understood what it was that this was all about. I finally saw what it was that my future self was trying to tell me. We aren't the only ones affected by our actions. What you're about to do, these actions you're about to under take, have far reaching implications beyond our little worlds, our selfishness.

That you can see the future tells me that you are special, that you and only you can do what needs to be done to not only protect humanity from the Dynasty and its disastrous future, but also to protect all those dead-end time-streams that should have never been created. This has to happen successfully, else we'll all just repeat the same damn mistakes over and over again and billions upon billions will dead for no reason but our failure.

And that's why we have to be successful this time, Alexis stated with a frown, looking at the frightened doctor and sighing slightly, aware that the deaths would have to start here and now, that she would have to be the one to kill these innocent people. But there was not anything to be done about it. Alexis had finally come to the conclusion that all this needed to be done, even if she really didn't understand why. She just had the sense that what she was about to do was what she had been created to do, that everything else in her life had been but practice for this moment in time, in all times and had meant nothing in the greater scheme of the order of the universe, if there was an order at all. She thought for a moment on how the explosion had occurred the first time, what the investigators had concluded. Explosion, most likely from a plasma conduit.

Concentrating on the main power coupling running behind the far wall, Alexis tilted her head and projected a half-smile filled with sympathy and pain at the innocent and unaware doctor.

Dr. Ykaterina Godonov stopped in mid-stride just as she was about to hit the alarm, seeing in Alexis' pained expression something hinting at more danger than she had first suspected. There was a terror here beyond normal human experience.

"I'm sorry it has to end like this," Alexis explained as she bypassed the primary and secondary security protocols and ruptured the main plasma conduit, allowing the eruption of mega-quads of super-heated plasma to break from the containment field and turn the entire lab complex into a blast furnace as the heat swept through the structure with the potency of a mini-sun.

Dr. Ykaterina Godonov, the thirty-five year-old genetic researcher never even felt her own death as she was carbonized in an instant, the emergency containment fields confining the discharge to the lab complex and saving the rest of the Colony from destruction.

Alexis looked at Meagan, whose pained expression matched her own in a morbid parody of sympathy. *Let's finish this before I change my mind.* It was said through clenched teeth.

*   *   *

3 March 2085
1810 hrs.
Osaka, Japan

   Kido Nakamura seated herself at the small, cozy, neighborhood restaurant in the heart of the Osaka business district. The busy foot traffic was mirrored by the copious hovs plying the airways in the overcast and dreary sky. Snow was expected by the evening, with accumulations up to sixteen centimeters by morning, unusual for this time of year. But Kido didn't care much about that. She was quite excited about the new prospects of the software she had been asked to create discreetly, secretly even; from the conversations with Ian Montana and Alexander Hart. If this idea of theirs panned out, she would be a millionaire many, many times over.
   "Suishi o kudasai," she said to the waiter who came by to take her order. She felt like eating a good plate of rare fish at this moment and relaxed back in the smooth and old wooden chair.
   She never noticed the two gunmen who came into the restaurant, who accosted the customers rudely and loudly.   She didn't notice, lost in the intricacies of the design beginning to congeal in her mind for the first stages of the transfer protocol, until the first gun-shots rang out, the distinctive high-whine and twack-twack of the hand-held projectile cannons identifying them as AK-88s, the latest in high-tech terrorist toys Alexis had projected onto the minds of those near, the intrusion of her own thoughts like a bullet to each brain in the restaurant.
   Kido looked up, startled at the commotion and noises with which she was unfamiliar and met the eyes of the two antagonists as they swung toward her position, the menacing barrels of the cannons zeroing in on her. For the briefest of moments, as she met the gaze of the gunmen, saw the blue-green eyes of a soul she recognized, with which she might even commiserate, saw a pity, a sympathy, a compassion she would never have expected from such people, almost as if they were sorry that this had to happen, that she had to die here in this restaurant on this cloud-ladened winter day.
   Kido narrowed her eyes and titled her head as she matched them gaze for gaze... ...and then in her mind the muzzles of the cannons erupted in a discharge of high-velocity rings slicing through her body as if it were made of

butter, shattering the window behind her, tearing the furniture to splinters, and killing Kido Nakamura in a spray of blood and bile and gore ripping her body apart and snuffing her life out in an instant of lost dreams.

It was a good as any weapon ever devised.

Alexis' powerful mind bent the very fabric of space-time around Kido Nakamura to tear out the life of this one individual without ever being physically present.

It would have made an assassin proud.

*   *   *

27 May 2085
2010 hrs
Stargazer I
Earth Orbit

Dr. Mbombo Dumvo sat at his lab bench and sighed, dropping the holo-imager down roughly as the images corning from the powerful electron microscope showing that the nana-bots were not constructing themselves at all as they were designed. He rubbed his eyes and leaned back, tired of the constant failures he was having with the most basic of his designs. Instead of reproducing themselves as exact replicas, the nano-bots were replicating different versions of themselves that were defective. He had no clue as to why it was happening.

It was not like they could think about what they were doing, as if they had free will and had decided that today they would construct malfunctioning copies instead of following their preset programming.

It had him stumped.

And he was late for dinner. Very late. He had not even called his wife to tell her and that made him want to go home now even less, the verbal tongue-lashing he knew was waiting for him not what he needed this night.

There was a noise, as if a test-tube had fallen and shattered on the ground, the small tinkle of glass distinctive in the empty lab. He looked up with a displeased expression, wondering who in the world would be here now, bothering him when they all knew not to. Hell, they were not even aware that he was working this late and none of his lazy lab assistants would be coming in at this time of night.

Then he realized that the sound was coming from the next lab over, from the plasma experimenters who seemed to work at all hours of the day and night and had adamant arguments every day over some aspect of their work. He was glad that he didn't have such a team working for him. He would be unable to take the constant anxiety of actually arguing with someone every day, especially when just listening to his neighbors argue was enough to give him heartburn.

He made to stretch his back when he heard the alarm, the computer warning of a containment breach, the tell-tale sound of a magnetic field collapsing and the plasma within breaching. He knew what needed to be done in an instant and made for the far door as quickly as he could.

It was, unfortunately, not quick enough.

The lab building erupted into a fireball as the primary, secondary and even the emergency containment fields were breached by the high-energy experimental plasma. Like a large road flare, the plasma erupted through the roof, saturated the entire floor plan in super-heated fury and leaving nothing behind but the disassociated molecules that had once been Dr. Mbombo Dumvo.

Alexis was beginning to become sick.

*   *   *

7 June 2085
1400 hrs
Cerro Torre
South America

Alexis watched as the man slowly yet doggedly climbed the mountainside. She had learned now how to control the force of her presence, how to make herself invisible or blue or a man or whatever she wanted and presently floated just above the poor soul who was about to die. She had the faint, almost passing feeling that what she was doing was becoming easier with each victim and it made her mind rebel at the waste of it all. What kind of a god would allow her to do all this? What person would want to?

A genetically engineered one, built for one exclusive purpose, whose life was forfeit the moment she was conceived and who had played the game of life unaware of her final destiny.

Had Alexis been able, she would have puked.

Meagan was by her side, watching, waiting, invisible to all save herself. *It doesn't seem right, does it?* Meagan projected in tones of heavy culpability, the death of the other three starting to weigh on her mind more than she had thought it ever would.

It's a little late to start having second thoughts Meagan, don't you think?

It's just that before, when I was supposed to have been the one to kill all these people, it seemed so noble and right. And now.. now when I'm actually participating in the killings, it just seems like murder.

Alexis looked at Meagan's mental projection. *Fine time to feel like that. I've said as much all along. Don't stand there and tell me, the one doing all the actual killing, that you think it's all a bad idea now. Don't you fucking dare. You no longer have the luxury of feeling superior, of telling me anything about how you feel and how all this is a fucking bad idea because you're the one in the future whose going to cause all this crap, so you've got no more say in this. This is hard enough already without you deciding that your conscience has suddenly kicked in. I call the shots now, not you and not your future self. Save all that bullshit for someone else. I don't give a crap anymore."*

They were quiet for a moment as they watched Dr. Pratali stop to rest, not wanting to look at each other. Meagan had rarely seen this side of her mother before, the self-assured, domineering bitch most people remembered her as. But she understood perfectly from where all the anger and frustration were coming. What she was doing was not easy, especially for someone who had not seen or experienced Huang, the Dynasty and the MTP.

Alexis was doing all this on conjecture, on what others told her and in that, Meagan knew that were she in her mother's shoes, she would be unable to just kill these innocents in such a callous manner. It spoke much of her mother's inner turmoil and self-conception in her own destiny.

It also spoke much of the demons at work inside her, of the demons Cav inadvertently placed within her, to be unleashed at this very moment in time. Meagan was beginning to wonder if it was all worth it, or if humans should just learn to live with the mistakes they created of their own volition.

Alexis found the first of the ice screws and broke it in half.

The line running through it snapped taut with the weight of the climbers as it whined its way through the next screw's loop at the loss of support. She snapped that one also, and then the next and the next. As Pratali looked up and saw what was happening, saw all the screws fail in unbelievable succession, Alexis made herself visible to him, floating in the air above.

He looked at her with awe, his eyes widening as she spoke, perhaps hoping to ease his transition to the next life, perhaps to ease her own guilt.

"I'm sorry. Your death is for a greater good for all humanity."

He fell with the profound epiphany in his mind that he had seen the angel of death and that she had apologized to him for taking his life.

Why do you do that? Meagan asked in consternation as the body bounced off the jagged, ice-covered rocks three-hundred meters below and continued to tumble down the icy slope, lifelessly. *I don't see the point.*

I didn't expect you to.

When were you planning on killing Alexander Hart? I noticed that you missed him in the sequence. Meagan didn't want to make this inane small talk, but she had to say something, had to engage her mind and in that engagement, not think of what it was she had forced her own mother to do.

Alexis indexed them to the next time, the next place, the ease with which she was beginning to work the time-stream comforting to her and yet disquieting, as if it had all been done before and she was remembering it subconsciously. That had been bothering her for some time. If she had indeed done all this before, had killed all these people in her own time-stream, thus leading to her involvement in the whole scheme in the first place, then why had it not been successful? What had happened to cause her first attempt to fail?

She was hoping that the answer would present itself soon, that she would be able to see where the mistake had been made and correct it, keep it from re-occurring and ending this time loop once and for all. She had the feeling that the mistake had been with Ian, that his death under that industrial hov had been a last minute addition and that neither her daughter or Skre or the handsome general of the great hair had been aware of its imminent importance.

But there was another whom she knew she would have to kill, kill at the very end after all the others, a person who she knew her daughter or the Colony Time Guards had never had on their lists concerning the MTP. It was the killing that would end the loop forever and thus it was the killing that was perhaps the mistake all the various times this had been tried already.

Meagan spoke again. *You haven't answered my question.*

I'm saving him for last, Alexis replied curtly, not ready yet to tell Meagan that it was her brother she would be killing.

Why? That doesn't make any sense.

Like I said before, you no longer have the option of questioning anything, so don't bother me with it anymore, okay? This is hard enough without you constantly questioning every fucking decision I make. You blew it the last time you tried this. Your opinion doesn't really hold much weight, now does it?

*   *   *

24 August 2085
1500 hrs
Claudine Maxwell's house
Chevy Chase, Maryland

Cav walked confidently into a bedroom to the sounds and smells of what could only be a sexual frenzy. He stood, his arms crossed as he leaned on the doorframe, watching as Claudine and the man who went by the name of Huang were engaged in full intercourse. Cav almost laughed at the spectacle. Claudine was screaming with fake grunts and groans, with which Cav had been so familiar so long ago, her breasts heaving like Jell-O with each penetration from the sweaty, small Asian who seemed totally engrossed in his current obligation, his face screwed up in priceless passion.

Cav cleared his throat indignantly.

Claudine opened her eyes and looked for the source of the intrusion.

Huang jumped off her as if she was on fire, reverting to a martial arts stance.

"What the hell are you doing, Cav?!" Claudine yelled with vexation as she sat up, not bothering to cover her nakedness, her face a mask of hatred and fury.

"Just watching a very interesting news article in the making. The President's Chief-of-Staff in bed with a wealthy Chinese Industrialist who is trying to gain major trading concessions from the government. I think they call that conflict of interest."

"Fuck you, Cav," she yelled at him as she stepped off the bed, her sweat-glistening nude body no longer turning Cav on, no longer giving him that urge in his groin. "Guards!"

"Do you really think that I'd be standing here, Claudine, if your Secret Service boys were still alive? You never did appreciate what I did very much."

She eyed him a moment, then pulled open the drawer of the night stand and whipped out the large caliber weapon. "Then I'll just have to kill you myself, you stupid fucking bastard!"

"I wasn't the one fucking, Claudine," Cav commented humorously, calmly as he raised his dart pistol and shot her in the neck before she ever had the

466

impulse to pull her own trigger. She collapsed a fraction of a second later as the rapidly acting tranquilizer kicked in.

Huang and Cav locked eyes a moment, a recognition that was not there grabbing them forcefully, as if they had been sworn blood enemies in a former life and the leftover karma still resonated within them like banked embers.

"Where do I know you from?" Cav asked in curiosity, though he could really care less. He sensed a feeling of familiarity between the two that went beyond the chance encounter outside the Oval Office. It was a familiarity touching him deep inside and speaking of another time, another place It was a deja-vu as strong as he had ever felt before, like a fading distortion of a burnt memory.

"It is not important, fat little man. You will shortly be dead," Huang replied with stiltedness to his words coming from not knowing a language fluently, his accent implacable. He had a confidence that seemed rather misplaced seeing that he was the one on the business end of the dart gun.

"I don't see how that's possible," Cav responded as he eyed the little man and saw something in him that didn't seem right, which seemed out of place as much as it seemed out of time. "And anyway, I don't have a problem with you. I just want to kill her." Why did he feel like he had said and done all this before, as if he knew what the next phrase would be?

"Then why did you just knock her out? Why not kill her outright? You Americans are so damn stupid."

Cav, the dart pistol having lowered slightly, raised it back up with the abrasive remark. "I'm not an American. And I only knocked her out because I have a few questions that need answering and the techniques I propose to use need a special place. Did you happen to notice her tattoo? Are you aware that you're her next victim?" Cav was reaching in the dark with that one, but it was worth a try. Although he had been out of active field operations for over forty years, his sense of danger was still perked up by this little man who seemed to possess a power beyond what one would expect.

Huang, having already activated his implanted security chip connected to his hidden jump-ship and sending a summons to his bodyguards in the in-between-time, was intrigued by the oblique reference and looked at the unconscious, naked female on the bed. How much did this stupid, fat man know?

Cav, seeing that the man had bit, advanced on Claudine and spread her legs open roughly, his loins completely unfazed with the sight and smells that were at his finger-tips, revealing not only the tattoo that stood out like a branding iron, but also her sumptuous vaginal mound and the essence of her recently aborted love-making session seeping onto the sheets. "See?"

Huang looked down distractedly and was shocked, both at the fact that he had never noticed it before and what it implied.

Elrsai!

Those conniving, interfering avians.

How had they done this? To him, the emperor?

Cav could see the shock in the man's eyes and smiled. "She's not who she says she is. Her background is all fake."

Huang grabbed Claudine's head in his hand and caustically turned it to the side, brushing her hair back with the other hand to look for the tell-tale mark on the back of her neck, to verify his suspicions, his fears. "Shit!" he said as he let go and stood away from the bed. "Zhè bù ke néng."

He turned to look at Cav. This man would have to be eliminated, and quickly. And where were his guards? They should have appeared long ago. Huang was beginning to have a brooding sense of foreboding hanging in the air like a cancer. He had known that making this ill-advised index was risky, but he certainly never figured on indexing right into a trap. He had made certain that this index was safe, that nothing untoward had happened to Claudine Maxwell during this time ... and now this.

Had his advisors lied to him?

No, that was not possible. They all knew the penalties associated with such a blatant act and would never dare implement it... unless of course they were certain that the Emperor would end up dead.

But by this fat little excuse for a man? Not likely.

And what was with the Elrsai Genenhum? What possible use could the Elrsai have with replacing the real Claudine Maxwell with an Uhmna? The more he thought about it, the more he knew for certain that this had not happened in this time-stream, that this time-stream was clean. He was certain that the last time he had had sex with Claudine Maxwell she didn't have that tattoo, that she completely human.

So how had he indexed to the wrong time-stream? That was also impossible. His equipment aboard his time-jumper was state-of-the-art and he had personally inputted the coordinates, seen the past in the stream, known that this was the same time-stream that he had visited over and over again.

He needed to return to his palace and his Dynasty. He had not stayed Emperor for over eight hundreds years by allowing such things to slip past his notice. There would have to be an investigation and perhaps even the purge of the Elrsai he had been planning for centuries. That blatantly interfering species with their nerve-racking peaceful intentions and constant whining about the time-streams had come to their unceremonious end.

But first, there was this annoying individual, an individual who would have been one of the first eliminated from the genetic pool during Huang's early purges. "You are a stupid, stupid man," Huang said as he advanced on Cav. "You should have left well enough alone and not mentioned this, for now I have to kill you."

Cav smiled at him and then fired a dart into his neck. Huang reached up and pulled the fuzzy little projectile out, studying it non-chalantly. It had no effect.

"Your primitive little toys will not work on this body. It has been hardened and protected by centuries of experimentation and genetic manipulations until it is impervious to such minor nuisances. You, on the other hand ..."

"But how...?" Cav had not expected that little problem. But then he had not expected to encounter any resistance whatsoever, especially not from this industrialist who was not supposed to be here at all. How could his intel have been this faulty? There was enough in that dart to take down a man twice Cav's size. Huang should be dozing on the floor at the moment, if not dead from an overdose.

He fired again, twice in rapid succession. There was still no effect.

"I suppose that since you're now going to die, there's no harm in telling you all, letting you know exactly who it is that you've tried to assassinate and the consequences this will have on your future... But I don't think so. That's just too much of a cliché, don't you think? Perhaps it would be better if I just kill you."

There was a series of distortions, a wave of energy passing over the two of them, making Cav's stomach quiver and boil. It was as if the room had turned upside down for a second and then straightened out, the sudden presence of more people in the room a shock to Cav.

Huang smiled as he saw his huge, menacing guards appear all around the room, five in all. Now he would not have to dirty his hands with the death of this idiot. "Kill him," he said as if ordering a sandwich. "And take the female back with you. She is a Genenhum from the Elrsai. An early model from the looks of it. We can dissect her slowly and perhaps gain some insight into their construction. Download her mind also. I want to look at her mission parameters."

The massively built guards looked at Cav. This would be an easy one. Two of them approached, ready to tear his head off and shit down his throat, literally.

As Cav tensed for the battle he knew he had no way of winning, the two advancing guards were thrown into the far wall as if by magic, their impact so strong that they actually broke through, plaster, steel and particle-board falling down in a dust cloud of debris, their shattered bodies dead before they reached the ground.

Cav straightened up, wondering if he had somehow done that. He had been working on his mental powers, what little he had for such things as telepathy and telekinesis, but he had not even managed to levitate a pencil, much less move two such large people.

The other three guards drew nasty looking weapons as they fell into defensive stances around their Emperor, sizing up the threat situation and trying to ascertain what had happened. The head of one of the guards exploded in a spray of blood and gray matter splattering the walls and Huang. Another guard was eviscerated in an instant, his entrails flung across the room like blood-covered ribbons, laying in tatters on the floor and across the bed. He groaned once as his eyes rolled back into his head and he fell to his knees and then his face, looking down at his empty stomach in astonishment.

The last guard was slightly worried at this point, the unseen attacker capable of much damage. Huang looked about him with a wonder barely covering his terror. He mentally tried to call more guards, his inexhaustible supply only a thought away. But there was something blocking his call, covering the house in a blanket of mental aversion that was strong, more powerful than he had ever encountered.

And for the first time in nearly eight hundred years, he was afraid.

The last guard began to fire randomly into the room, forcing Cav to fall to the floor as the plasma bursts scorched the walls in a cryptic blaze of black patterns. Then his arms were torn off as if they were made of putty, the bloody stumps left spewing their crimson life-force onto the carpet. He looked in shock at his missing appendages and then began to scream. His scream lasted but a moment as his throat was torn out next, cleanly and neatly, leaving him with a gapping hole in his neck and absolute terror in his eyes as he gurgled his opposition. He toppled over to sucking sounds as the blood ran into his lungs and suffocated him slowly.

Huang stood in the middle of the carnage, aware that this was the work of the Elrsai, who, it would certainly appear, had finally caught up with him. That Claudine had been one of their genetically enhanced humans simply confirmed the fact. He could not believe that he had been that stupid to have fallen for her charms without checking her out better, finding the flaw that the fat little man cowering on the floor had found.

Or better yet, perhaps it was the Ka'kach, possibly turned against him in the future somehow for his brutal treatment of their species. Perhaps they had won the war with the Dynasty in another time-stream and were coming back to this one to rid it of his presence also. But even that made no sense, for had they wanted him dead, he would have been the first one taken. And if Claudine had actually been planted by the Elrsai, she was certainly no assassin, for the same logic applied to her actions also. That she might have been placed here to spy on him was a thought, but an errant one, for he rarely visited Claudine in this time-stream, only when he was totally frustrated by Alexis Locke and her annoying daughter.

He didn't understand, and for the Emperor of the Dynasty to not understand was a bad thing for everyone involved. "You should not have done this," Huang stated in faltering tones, trying to re-assert his authority, speaking to the fat little man since no one else was visible. "Now I will make you suffer for an eternity for this insult."

"I don't think so." The disembodied voice filled the room with an ominous pretension and both men looked around to see who had spoken, though Cav was fairly certain that he recognized the voice.

"Alexis?" he asked in shock.

"Alexis Locke?" Huang stated with a disdain dripping off his tongue like venom. Now it was all coming together for him. It was she, the perennial thorn in his side, the Wellington to his Napoleon, Stalin to his Hitler. "Show yourself, bitch, so that I may know you in person and see your eyes as I kill you." Huang didn't like surprises, especially bad ones.

A blow struck Huang across the face. He reeled from the impact, blood flowing from the cut to his lip as he stumbled to the blood-soaked carpet. He stood, his pride and ego stronger then his intellect. "No one treats the Emperor of the Dynasty in this way! NO ONE!"

She doubled him over with a punch to the stomach, the whoosh of air as it fled his lungs audible.

"Emperor of the Dynasty?" Cav asked, completely confused as to what was happening. "What Dynasty? What's he talking about? And where are you Alexis? You were killed by that industrial hov. I saw your body, or what was left of it. What the hell's going on here?"

"This isn't the time, Cav," Alexis responded as she thought about how to kill Huang and Claudine without making it look too obvious. "Just be patient and wait a moment." With the others, it had been easy since it had already been done before. All Alexis had to do was follow the pattern that had been set up. But this was different. Now she was changing the time-stream anew, making new plans and decisions fresh and virgin, changing and creating as she went and she had no idea how it should be done or what damage she might inflict.

But then it really didn't matter all that much. It was all going to be destroyed anyway.

"Did you know that it was my daughter who gave you my DNA structure back then on the beach?" she asked Cav as she stared at the unconscious Claudine and the gasping Huang.

"How did you know about that?" Cav queried, completely beside himself with what was happening. "Are you a ghost? Are you haunting me?" Then the words stuck him that she had said. "Your daughter? You don't have a daughter."

"Please Cav. Don't be obtuse. You started a chain of events that's ending now, here. A chain of events for which I was purposely created. You were used Cav, used simply as the catalyst for my creation. And now it's time to end it all. Did you really think that my daughter gave you all that incredibly advanced information for the heck of it, because maybe you screwed her real well? Get serious. You were always a little slow where women were involved, weren't you?"

"I don't understand what the hell you're babbling about, Alexis. If you're not a ghost, then show yourself. Let me see you."

Alexis appeared next to the still gasping Huang, suddenly materializing as he had last seen her in all her radiant glory.

He almost fell over at her sudden appearance. "How .... what...?"

She looked at him a moment, a moment of almost sympathy, then brought her attention to the recovering Huang. She grabbed him by the neck and began to squeeze the very life out of him. "This is for all the billions upon billions of lives that you carelessly slaughtered for what? Glory? Power?"

His hands frantically scratched at hers, but since she was not really there physically, it was to no effect. His eyes widened in horror at was happening. He never expected it to end this way. What had happened to all his guards, to those sworn to protect him with their lives? He had over ten thousand ready and willing to die at his command, programmed from when they were mere infants to protect his life with theirs. This could not be happening. There were safe-guards against this sort of thing. No one knew where or when he indexed. No one.

He was surrounded by protection equipment that would pick up an incursion into the time-stream in which he indexed, alerting him instantly and setting him back to his time-jumper. How had she found him? How had she been able to sneak up on him without his sophisticated guards knowing about it?

"Did you really think that someone wouldn't eventually find you and take their revenge?" Alexis continued to harass him as the life drained out of him. She didn't intend to kill him outright. Not just yet at least. That would be too simple for the man responsible for so much spilled blood and terror. She had a much more ignoble end for the mighty emperor who appeared before her now, on his knees, like just another small, pathetic man.

She still had one more thing she needed to do.

"And Grand Marshal Meagan Locke says hello by the way....She wanted me to relay a little message for you. The Rebellion has succeeded."

His half-closed, listless eyes shot open in surprise at the name and its implications.

The Rebellion.

Meagan Locke.

Along with Alexis Locke, they were like acid to his senses.

How had she been able to do all this, to achieve what was supposed to be impossible? The only way she could have escaped his detection equipment was if she had not indexed and if she had not indexed, then how had she just appeared like that? How did she know about Meagan Locke and the Rebellion, a name and an event centuries in the future.

"How....?" he managed to gasped out with the last of his breath, all the latent power built into his body useless against such an attack, an attack that was mental and not physical, that was power beyond what he thought was possible.

"I'm not human, Huang. I'm half Elrsai. Remember the Elrsai? I was specially created to kill you and win the Rebellion by making it so that the Dynasty never rises to power, that you never live to use the MTP and contaminate the galaxy with the plague that is Humanity. I'm here to clean up the time-streams from your filthy touch and it all starts with you." Alexis made certain that the man understood, that he saw all that was in her existence, in the Rebellion and in his ultimate death before his eyes roiled into the back of his head and his body slumped to the floor, unconscious. "Help me get them into the bed together, Cav," Alexis said as she lifted the small Asian up and placed him.

Cav, unable to hear any of what Alexis had said to Huang and assuming that she had just killed the man, moved like a zombie as he lifted the naked

Claudine upon the bed and helped Alexis position the two bodies in an erotic position of intercourse that would leave no doubt to the investigators what these two had been doing when they died.

Alexis looked over Cav. "You need to leave now, Cav. No questions. Just go. As far from here as you can and as quickly. I'll explain it all later. I promise." She had no intention of explaining anything to him later. There was not going to be a later for the man. His death was as assured as Huang's and Claudine's.

"I..." he started, then stopped, unable to process all that was happening. "What about these two?"

"Don't worry about these two. They're going to get what they deserve. Believe me."

He looked at her a moment longer, wanting to say so much that was in his heart but unable to form the words properly. "I never meant for you to die, Alexis. That wasn't part of the plan. Never."

"Doesn't really matter, now does it Cav?" she said sarcastically.

"This all went terribly wrong somewhere."

"Yes, when you created me." She had already figured out that the death of Claudine and Huang would be easy. Some sort of explosion, something that fried both of them in an eternal embrace, ruining her reputation and her dreams all in one moment, and denying to the future the holocaust that was Huang.

Cav sighed and shook his head. He had the bad feeling in the pit of his stomach that she was going to kill him as easily as she was about to kill the Chief-of-Staff of the President of the United States and a major, well-connected Chinese industrialist. "I never meant for all this to happen to you, Alexis. I didn't create you for this. I created you to bring order to a world of chaos."

"Chaos? Chaos is the natural state of the universe, Cav. You of all people should know that. You created me for one purpose and one purpose only and now I'm fulfilling that purpose. You just didn't know it, that's all. But as I said, it really doesn't matter anymore. And besides, the less you know, the better off you'll be. Go somewhere and enjoy yourself." She could not bring herself to tell him that he would have to die also, that his death was the final link in the chain ending this vicious cycle. Although she felt a loathing for him for his duplicity and his lack of fortitude when it came down to Claudine and Ian, she just could not bring herself to hate him. He had been the closest thing to a father she had ever had in a life which now was as meaningless as the single leaf falling off the autumn aspen and turning into fertilizer.

Although there was hatred and animosity there, it was tempered by the love he had shown to her when she was young.

It was still there in her memories.

Cav hesitated a moment, wanted to reach out and touch her, assure her, comfort her as he had done so many times in the past but knew that it was too late for any of that now. He turned and left. Although he didn't understand, he did trust Alexis and if she, whatever it was that she was now, told him to leave, then that was what he would do. He had no idea what DNA structure and genetic codes were that he had received from that beautiful woman so long ago, but this was not what he had expected as the result. Had he known then, he would never have accepted it, would have tossed it all out with the garbage and let someone else deal with it.

But then that was in the past, and the past could not be changed.

Alexis looked around for a source of explosive power to drive the fire she needed to engulf the house and incinerate the two. The use of natural gas had been phased out over twenty years ago with the advent of the new fusion reactors, providing more power than anyone knew what to do with, so that route was out of the question.

"What's wrong?" Meagan asked, waiting for Alexis to kill off Huang.

"I was trying to figure out how to ignite this place. Have any suggestions?"

"Why not just ignite it yourself."

"I can do that?"

"I don't see why not."

Alexis concentrated on the holo-vid sitting serenely in the corner, thought of fire and the entire device blew up in a shatter of shards, igniting the carpet and the wall for a brief moment before the fire prevention system of the house engaged and doused the flames quickly.

Alexis frowned.

"You need to do better than that. Why not disengage the security systems and then make something bigger, more intense?"

Here she was, this master plan to fix the past and thus save the future and she couldn't even figure out how to start a fire. Five minutes later, however, the house was engulfed in roaring flames licking out of the windows and the roof, turning the entwined bodies of Claudine Maxwell and Sun Liu Huang into charred remnants, leaving just enough to ascertain what it was that they had been doing and to make the morning papers. Such an ignoble end for two people who craved power so much seemed somehow fitting.

Alexis and Meagan watched from a distance.

We have to hurry, Meagan said stoically as she began to feel the tug of the time-streams, the stress of the bind that was creating this one time-stream wherein all was, wherein all that they changed would forever be sealed into all the streams broken off. Killing Huang here, even though he was the future Huang, would kill him in every time-stream in which he had existed. It was one of the benefits of what Alexis had done. By forcefully binding all the time-streams together, she had achieved the perfect tool for what was needed. *This bind of yours will not hold for long. It'll break apart soon and leave us where we were before. It's not meant to be like this.*

Yes, I can sense it slipping already. We have but three more to finish.

Three? Meagan asked, aware of only Ian Montana and Alexander Hart. *We have but two left.*

Alexis had finally found the flaw, the one death that had been missed over and over again and that would, she was positive, fix what her birth had created in the first place. *No, we have three. We have the one person that was obviously missed the first time that this was tried. The master-mind behind the entire MTP project. If he remains, he'll just find another group to create it. That's probably how Huang was able to change your Alpha Two time-stream. He used him, the one person in this clusterfuck who no one even conceived knew about the MTP.* She should have seen it from the beginning, seen what he was doing, why he had been so adamant that she not take this assignment, so subtly destructive in his help, so ingenuous with his concern. There was only one person who could have bank-rolled this entire project, who could have had people like Kiril and Hugh on his payroll.

Meagan didn't understand how they could have missed someone so important. They had done a thorough search of all the individuals involved in the MTP and had found them all. There was no way that one had been missed, but then, since the cycle continued to repeat and since Huang had been able to change a non-MTP time-stream into a MTP time-stream, Alexis must have found a flaw in their research. *Who is this person?*

The world around them blurred and jumped, then settled back to a new surrounding, a new place on Earth. There were forests, meadows, mountains in a mixture of sublime tranquility. There was a light breeze in the air, a hint of winter in the smells rolling down from the granite escarpments and embracing the late blooming flowers of fall as the sun lazily danced across the deep azure sky.

It was not the place for a murder.

The last person is Vincent Cavalier.

476

It is forbidden to kill; therefore all murderers are punished,
unless they kill in large numbers and to the sound of the trumpet.
Then they are called heroes.
                                    – Jean Jacques Rousseau

The greatest sacrifice is to give your life for another.
The greatest tragedy is to have the other turn out to be evil.
In a perfect world, this would never occur. But then in a
perfect world, one would never have to sacrifice one's life.
Perfection has a lot going for it.
                                    — from the journal of
                                    Meagan Locke

35

4 October 2063
0700 hrs
Los Alamos, New Mexico

   The Pajarito Mountains were alive with the colors of autumn. The dark green of the Ponderosa and Bull pines in stark contrast to the spectrum of colors turning the Aspens shades of reds and golden hues mixing and merging in an exhibit of splendor repeating every year, marking the end of the warm times and the beginning of the winter, the time of life for hibernation and death.
   Snow would soon be falling on the nestled community sitting on the ridges of the escarpment, turning the thoughts of the town-folk to the thrills of skiing and ice-skating, snowball fights and sledding. It was a time of change, a time when the carefree days of summer, relaxing in the warm rays of the sun as it baked the Rio Grande river valley below, were replaced by the cold winds

tearing down from the north and capping the mountains in hats of white brilliance, the gray-ladened clouds heralding the icy touch of Jack Frost.

Most people never understood the coming of winter, seeing the dying of the trees and the loss of warmth as punishment for sins uncommitted. Most saw the cold and the snow, which coated all in the same, pristine blanket of innocent simplicity, as the coming of the hiding time, the time for staying indoors, building a fire against the deprivations of nature and waiting impatiently for the return of spring and that illogical thought of growth. People didn't see winter as a necessary part of the overall plan, the death of the leaves, the browning of the land, the barrenness of the landscape seen more for its misery and grayness than for its redemptive qualities, and necessity.

But just as Spring was a vital part of the rebirth of species, so was Winter needed to herald the advent of the new life to be brought forth, to give to the trees and the flowers and the bugs that reason for flourishing that was missing when the warmth spread over the land with the rising of the sun. Without Winter there would be no spring, for without death there was no life. Most people never saw this. But then, most people never see much beyond their own noses.

Ian Montana sat on the porch of his cabin over-looking the mountains to the east, the sun just now spilling its golden rays into the nest of shadows sitting in the nape of the undulating landscape, chasing them out as it rose ever higher in the clear sky. The warmth it had presented during the summer somehow lacking, the chill that sat in the air like an invisible phantom inhibiting. The tendrils of steam rising from his coffee filling the air around him with its potent aroma of mocha and mint, a combination he found refreshingly brisk in the mornings.

He was expecting Alexis at any minute.

They had a picnic planned today, a sojourn into the forest with nothing but a basket of cold cuts and bread, a bottle of good white zinfandel and the abundance of nature to accompany them. He had been looking forward to it ever since she had called up two days ago and suggested it. Ian was beginning to think that Alexis just might be the one, the one whom he could love as a friend and a lover and not feel guilty.

He was certain that Cav would have something to say about their whirlwind romance, but Ian didn't care. Cav could not tell him whom to date and not to date. Especially not when it felt this right. Cav could go to hell if he thought he could break them up with a simple order.

He had asked Alexis once if she had ever fallen in love before and, true to

478

form, she had responded with a sarcastic quip, stating that she had never fallen in love but had stepped in it a few times. A smile played across his face as he remembered that day, that expression on her face, the shyness that seemed to be hidden under the brusque exterior she presented to everyone.

He knew that it was nothing but a wall, a defense around her heart. He had had the same defenses at one time. Such defenses were meant to be broken.

An odd feeling passed over him then, as if someone were watching him. There was a scent in the air mingling with the mocha and mint and tinkling his senses with its subtlety. "Alexis?" he asked, the feeling of her presence like a hint of winter in the air. He stood and walked into the den, looking around for her.

Then it was gone, as if it had never been.

Warning bells began to go off in his mind, warnings that something was not right. He happened to look at the digital clock on the wall when it jumped backward in a distorted wave, then jump forward again back to where it should have been. He looked at it a moment in confusion, wondering if he had actually seen it do that or whether his mind was playing tricks on him.

A strange, strong feeling of deja vu passed over him. He felt a cold chill up his spine, the scent of Alexis wafting over him like a ghost, filling his nostrils with memories of her that were fuzzy and blurred, fresh and alive. He spun, looking about him for the source of the disturbance. The room appeared to be empty except for him.

Then a whisper in the wind reached his ear, the voice so familiar yet so distant. "I loved you more than you will ever know. Thank you."

"Who is that?" he said, an odd mixture of curiosity and fear building in his stomach like a bubble of gas. "Show yourself."

The pain started in his left arm, a searing pain running the length of the arm as if a long needle had been inserted in a vein. He grabbed it with his right hand and looked at the arm in question as if scrutinizing something that didn't belong to him. Then the pain hit his chest like a spear, impacting his heart in an icy cold grip ending his life in a heartbeat, the broken husk of his body falling heavy to the wooden floor, his eyes wide open in shock and wonderment, the mocha and mint coffee draining from the broken cup, running along the floor boards in some type of morbid parody of his death.

Meagan frowned as she looked at Alexis, feeling the waves of suppressed pain her mother was feeling at the moment. This death had hit her the hardest of all and Meagan was suddenly keenly aware that Alexis and Ian had once been lovers. *I didn't know that you knew him so well. I'm sorry it had to be this way.*

Alexis' answer was brisk and harsh, as if the wound to her heart had hardened it even more. *As you've said all along, it had to be done.* The sarcasm was tangible. *We must sacrifice the few for the many, right?*

This wasn't my idea, you know, Meagan shot back, aware that a back-log of pain and anger were building in Alexis, ready to explode if not released, implode to the detriment to all those around her. It was as if the tension building in the time-streams, from the bind holding them together in unnatural union, was mirrored in Alexis' soul, mirrored to such an extent that one affected the other in the minutest detail. Were one to break, the other would let loose also: the result would be catastrophic.

And Meagan also knew what it must be like for Alexis, to have to kill those you loved for the sole purpose of making the future worth living, for a future of which she would never be a part. Now Meagan was finally understanding why her future self had made such a big deal out of making Alexis hate her, hate with a passion that would cause not the slightest stir of regret for her own death. It was all to make it easier for Alexis to carry out a mission that had nothing easy about it.

This was all implemented by my future self, a future self that I don't even recognize anymore. She's the one that had you created, that forced you to do all this, Meagan tried to explain in vain supplications that fell on deaf ears.

Alexis took one last look at Ian, laying on the hardwood floor of his home that she knew so well, his face as serene in death, as it had been in life. She tried to feel something, to catch a glimmer of emotion at his death and found nothing.

Nothing within her deep-seated psyche even hinting at regret or loss was evident. There was a sense of loss, like at the parting of an old jacket or used sofa, but nothing that she would have called passion, grief. It was as if those areas of her mind had been sealed off, shut out from the rest of her by the alien DNA as effectively as if she had never had access to those emotions at all. It was as if he had been a total stranger, a stranger mattering as little to her as Clovis had.

And yet, Clovis had haunted her.

His death had somehow touched her in a way that none other had before. So why could she not feel anything for Ian, for the man she had loved at one time more than she ever thought she could? She also know knew that Clovis had not been the target of that assassination back at the deli, that Fujita had not been the object of the missile and the bullet shot through the window.

It had all been meant for her.

She had carried death around with her like a handbag, brought to all that she touched, talked to like a virulent air-borne disease killing on contact. She was as much of a plague on humanity as humanity was upon the universe.

In the final analysis, she didn't deserve to live.

The room blurred as she indexed to the next time and place, the next death at her hands as if she were the very incarnation of the Grim Reaper, selecting those fated to die in the past for their sins in the future. Her hands were already blooded and washing them of that blood, like Pilate, would not absolve her of any sin.

Alexis looked at Meagan's projection, at the mental image presented to her mind. A smile forced its way to Alexis' lips, hovered there a moment as if testing the waters, then left just as quickly, like an unwelcome visitor. *None of it matters anymore. I can see it all now, the future and the past like the flip-side of a coin; both a part of the same continuum; both part of the same consciousness that runs through the void like a giant hand.* Alexis had no idea from where these words were coming, from where these ideas were spawning like a mutated abstraction.

Meagan listened in fascination, wondering what in the world her mother was talking about, the vague references lost on her, the words no more than raindrops off her back.

My birth, your birth, Alexis continued as if possessed by some new found epiphany, *was all part of a greater plan, a self-realizing loop that causes my creation so that I can give birth to you, so that you can cause my creation and on and on and on. It's a bubble inside a loop inside a mutant time-stream that churns and froths like a primordial soup, just waiting for the proper time to burst open and spill its volatile contents onto the rest of time and in so doing, corrupt it.*

The time has come to end it all. Your future self took great pains to figure this all out properly, to make certain that nothing would be disturbed by our temporal presence in time. We, all three of us, are bound up together. When this is all over, when I've accomplished what it was that I was created for, all will be as if we had never existed. Our existence will never be recorded. No one will know that we ever were. In this way, the time-streams will be protected and uncorrupted. Alexis narrowed her eyes as she looked at her daughter with wonder. *Were you aware of all this? Did she make it all clear to you what would happen when we killed the last one?*

Meagan, her mind still trying to swim through the morass of philosophy Alexis had spewed out, understood this part clearly. *Yes, I'm aware of the end result. But I don't think that there's any other option, any other choice. It's either our deaths or the billions in the future.*

I see, Alexis said vaguely as she looked at the landscape surrounding them, felt the tension building around her from the unnatural binding of the time-streams, and knew that their time was almost over. *We could just let it go, not do the last killing and in that preserve ourselves. Huang is already dead. All those but one involved in the MTP are dead. Who are we to pick and chose whom to kill and whom not to kill, like some god on high?*

Meagan saw what was coming, saw the finality that was closing in on them ... and knew that this was not Alexis talking. This was whatever Alexis was becoming, the Elrsai DNA asserting itself as the end drew near in one last futile attempt to avert the disaster that would befall them. *But the time-stream has to be closed. You were made for one reason and one reason only. Your genes in the human gene pool cause a corruption that will eventually be the end of humanity as we know it,* Meagan protested, though she knew that it was in vain, that whatever it was that had taken hold of Alexis was not about to forestall the plans that were almost complete.

And that's such a bad thing? Alexis responded as she felt him coming closer, felt the connection she had felt the first time she had been near Meagan, as if an invisible string were tugging inside her stomach and pulling her closer to a place and a person she didn't want to hurt.

We can't just decide on the spur of the moment, when we're halfway through this mess, that we can change the way things are, Meagan said just to say something, to understand where it was that Alexis was headed. *As you said, we aren't gods.*

Humans made themselves gods when they sacrificed the first of their kind for a vague and ill-defined belief system, choosing the value of the community over that of the individual, Alexis stammered out in staccato bursts of passion she had never felt before, that she was pressed to find the reason behind. She didn't understand from where all the words were gushing, but she knew that was a part of her, which she had ignored for too long. *Humans made this mess and will make it again. They are a boil on the face of life.*

She could feel something awakening inside her, something that was not human anymore, that was a hybrid of two species. She felt a rise in her mental powers beyond anything she had ever known before and as she watched the raft come gently floating down the turbulent white river, she saw in a flash of insight all the time-streams together, presented before her as if she were in total control of it all.

She saw all the pasts and all the futures with a clarity born of desperation, a clarity showing her the answers to questions yet to be asked.

She saw a group of bird-like creatures in a circle, in a room, on a planet that was on the other side of the galaxy, on the other side of time. They appeared to be in a dispute, a conclave to discuss what it was that would happen in the future. They all looked at her as if she were there, their black-as-coal eyes showing a depth of intelligence that would have made any human look like the primate from which he had evolved.

Your existence was foretold, your purpose warned of, they said in voices flowing like the waters bubbling and brooking and dancing like bird-song on the wind. *The time for one such as you was not yet. But the gods have spoken and their will is supreme. End it before the streams separate. End it before it begins all over again. End it to set right what was made wrong by your very existence. Our existence is immaterial. As is yours. Fulfill your destiny and end it.*

And then she saw it all, a grand tour of the Universe in a fraction of a second, showing to her all the misery and death and hatred saturating the fabric of space-time and bending it to its own will in a tempest of jumbled time. And she saw the most important thing: she saw that humans were the cause of most of the pain, their influence and touch like a virile virus turning all encountered into a black, stinking sump of envy, pride and sloth; gluttony, lust and covetousness; and anger: anger sweeping through space like a maelstrom.

She touched the face of God in that moment and saw that he was crying, weeping for the creation that had taken control and in that control, ravaged all that had been set down so very long ago.

And she knew in that instant what needed to be done.

Alexis, are you all right? Meagan asked as she saw her mother's face take on a vague look that seemed to fade her entire projection into fuzzy, dim shades. Immense sorrow and pain swept across Alexis' eyes like a flame, followed by a cold-hard, steel-sharp determination.

I now see what it is that we're doing. Alexis' image reasserted itself to Meagan and in her mother's eyes, Meagan saw that she had reached her final decision and that Alexis was back in control. *I see now the price that needs to be paid.*

*   *   *

26 May 2085
0930 hrs
White Nile River
The Sudan

Dr. Alexander Hart was having the time of his life. He had always wanted to go on an extensive rafting trip and when this opportunity to go to Africa and raft the upper reaches of the Nile was presented to him, there was no way that he could refuse. The day was gearing up to be a hot one if the warmth of the air this early in the morning was any indication. The small, puffy white clouds drifting on the lazy upper winds would be gone before long, replaced by the resplendent deep blue of the African sky stretching across the vault of the heavens like a crystal dome.

The cute brunette with whom he had been having his wonderful romance for the last few months sat next to him on the outer edge of the raft, the large smile on her face and the laughter in her eyes mirrored in Alexander's face as they paddled with the rest of the group toward the next set of rapids, where the white-water rolled and rumbled as it made its way past unseen rocks. Her name was Maria, a name Alexander had always thought so perfect for a girl and he was certain that he was falling in love with this petite, vivacious, intelligent girl as he had never fallen in love before.

She was a biomechanical engineer who had just graduated from MIT on a full scholarship and who seemed to love all the things Alexander loved. It seemed to be a match made in heaven. And she had that oh-so-cute tattoo on her inner thigh that she was so mysterious concerning. It lent an air of eroticism to their romance that titillated him greatly. That she questioned him greatly about his work and was never satisfied when he told her that it was nothing, never sparked any real warnings.

That she seemed to think that he needed to spend his time on more worthwhile projects bothered him slightly, but certainly not enough to dim his passion for her presence.

The white-water rapidly approached and Alexander tensed himself for the thrill and fear about to grab him as the raft was maneuvered for the perfect run down the rapids. It dipped into the first well as water splashed over the bow and soaked them all through and through, the laughter and the shouts and the shear fun those paddling furiously were experiencing echoing up into the canyons like the scattering of birds.

Then the raft rocked unexpectedly, as if pulled from underneath, sucked into a vortex that was not supposed to be there. An unseen force grabbed

Alexander by the back of his life-vest and pulled him off the raft and into the water before anyone could even react, looking to all involved as if he had but lost his balance and toppled in.

He struggled as the pounding water beat him relentlessly, the buoyancy of the life vest fighting against the weight of the water... and of something else. He felt a presence with him, a presence as distinct as his brunette friend had been to him but moments before, a presence feeling familiar somehow, as if he had known it all his life. He opened his eyes and to his utter amazement beheld the face of an angel, a beautiful woman who seemed to float in the turbulent waters as if apart from them, unaffected by the rush and the pounding and the thrashing. And as he looked closer, his lungs beginning their slow scream for more oxygen to process, he realized that this angel looked like him, had the same distinctive facial features, eyes and hair.

She spoke to his mind, in a voice he knew, a voice so much like his own that he was beset by confusion and doubt. If *there were any other way to do this, then I would find that way.* Her voice held a comfort to it soothing his soul, touching him in a bliss both spiritual and inspiring. *Sometimes the sacrifice of one individual is necessary for the survival of the species as a whole. Just as I sacrificed having you and holding you at birth, so too now must I sacrifice you again.*

Who are you? he asked as his mind told him that his air was running out, that his life was about to end in a watery death in a foreign land. But none of that seemed to matter to him. All that mattered was the angelic face floating before him and the immaculate voice speaking to him of things he didn't understand.

I am she who gave birth to you. Alexis could see the genetic markers in his mind demonstrating to her once and for all that he was indeed her son, his latent mental abilities like a resting giant. *And I am she who will take it.*

But why? I don't understand. His lungs overrode his aversion and he inhaled, water flowing down into his air passageways like a fountain of death.

Sometimes there are no valid reasons. She hugged him to her, his body struggling for a moment with the lack of oxygen, the foreign liquid in the lungs. She watched, felt his soul depart into the in-between-time, into another time-stream to be absorbed and re-distributed as was the way of creation.

Then all was quiet, the body that was Alexander Hart nothing more than a broken husk of a man who had once lived. She held him a moment longer as she transported his lifeless body further downstream, where the crocodiles would get a hold of it, then released it to the vagaries of nature, a part of her soul leaving with it down the water passage that was his death.

And not a tear fell.

*   *   *

3 October 2221
0300 hrs
O'Neill Colony *Einstein XXIII*

Cycomeand Vork sat in his regeneration alcove, his systems performing the routine checks and rechecks, the problems of the day and the questions asked being worked on as his power sources soaked up the energy they needed to survive. He had only been activated for the first time a scant three months ago and was still going through system analysis and error codes to make certain that all was functioning correctly. He was only the third of his generation and the potential of this new breed was obvious from the start.

Alexis looked at him, the idea that she was now about to implement, having come to her during her sojourn through the Universe, when she was shown all that was, and had been, and would be. The vastness of what she was expected to carry out, expected to sacrifice for the sake of a people she didn't even know, was overwhelming in its far-reaching affects.

But she had seen a way around it, a way to protect herself and her daughter from the utter destruction that would come from the final killing. She touched the cold, plastitine coating of Vork that was supposed to resemble human flesh and felt a warmth to it that she knew was nothing but her imagination, or perhaps the residual heat of the energy source from which it was drawing.

Meagan was not here with her.

Alexis had remembered a small bit of information her daughter had let slip, pertaining to how time indexing worked. Meagan had already indexed to the next time and place, to the sandy beach on the island. Alexis would join her soon and Meagan would have no clue that Alexis had been elsewhere for a time, been able to index to another time and affect a change, then index back to the proper time at the exact instant Meagan had indexed.

Thus, Meagan would never know that Alexis had done anything, gone anywhere. It had to be done this way.

"You're my last salvation, machine," she said quietly, more to herself than Vork. "You will be my savior."

She used her new found powers and shifted Vork into the in-between-time, held him in stasis, in a time and place unaffected by the un-binding of the

486

streams, by the death of Cav, by the extinction of Alexis and all that she knew.

And there he stayed.

*   *   *

6 October 2020
0600 hrs
Sauai'i West Somoa

Cav stood at the edge of the bamboo balcony of his bungalow, looking over the peaceful and serene ocean stretching forever over the horizon, the soothing sounds of the lapping waters floating on the morning breeze like an invigorant to his soul. The glass he held loosely in his right hand, whose ice chunks clicked together quietly, was half empty, the potent cognac reflecting the early morning light in a soft, dark amber.

There were no souls on the beach at this time, the few tourists visiting the island still sleeping off the night's extravagances. Cav would usually be on that beach, taking his morning run, alone and undisturbed except by the occasion calls of the seagulls and the subdued crashing of the waves.

But today was different.

After looking over the DNA data placed in his computer by the mysterious, gorgeous lady with whom he had slept last night, he realized that today was the start of a whole new life for him. For within that code lay the secret to what he had been trying to accomplish, to the idea that he had been working on for years. And it was not so much how he had received it – the feeling in his groin still telling him that she had been one of a kind – as the fact that it contained non-human DNA; genetic markers that he quickly saw would increase the mental capacity of this person by a thousand-fold.

And not only that, but she would live much longer, remain young looking through-out her unnatural life without any of the typical genetic manipulations humans were beginning to use now to enhance themselves. It was a breakthrough that would have incredible consequences.

And yet there had been the warning, the warning to build but one and then destroy the data completely.

It was that very question that was keeping him from his daily run, keeping him from the normal routine he had not broken in years.

Why him? And why only one?

What was it that she had seen in him that made her give him this data, this opportunity to change the world in such a profound way? And what was it that he was supposed to do with her once he had achieved her birth?

The idea that he dump the entire contents of the file and go on with his life as if he had never seen it, had suggested itself to his mind quite early and he had taken that suggestion seriously. But he just could not bring himself to do it, to push the button that would erase the future, his future. For this data certainly made a future for him, a future that he could easily see producing wealth beyond his wildest dreams.

And power.

A power to topple governments and dictate terms.

The thought sobered him greatly. He took another swig of the liqueur and felt it burn its way down. Did he really want that kind of power? He watched a seagull fly past the porch, sailing in the wind like the expert acrobat that he was. He blinked, and the bird was back, following the exact same flight-pattern, as if it were a shadow of the one that had just passed by.

His stomach felt odd.

A cold chill ran down his back.

Something about the morning, the beach, the ocean didn't seem right anymore, as if it were out of phase, blurred, distorted. He narrowed his eyes and looked around, but no one was visible, not a soul on what seemed like his own private beach.

He turned and walked back into the bungalow, the air around charged with electricity that was tangible. He was shocked to find two women standing in his living room. One he recognized immediately. The other looked very familiar, the familial resemblance strong between them.

"I didn't expect to see you ever again," he said, amused at the reaction of the unfamiliar woman.

She looked at him with a mixture of dumfounded wonder and something that almost seem like sympathy. That he was naked didn't seem to bother either of them. It didn't bother him either. He was proud of his body and perhaps his friend from last night had brought a friend along for a three-some. Wouldn't that be something.

Alexis could not believe how good Cav looked. His firm, toned, muscular body was such a far cry from the corpulent fat of the Cav she had known that she was finding it hard to believe that it was the same person. She could easily see why Claudine Maxwell and Cav had been lovers, could easily see herself in his arms .... she shook that thought out of her head quickly.

This was Cav, the closet thing to a father she had ever had and to have such erotic thoughts about him made her physically sick.

Alexis spoke, her voice soft and calm yet with a detachment striking Cav as distant, strained. "Is all the data that you were given in this computer here?"

Cav tilted his head sideways. That was an odd question. He was not about to give out any information that quickly. "Not so fast," he said with a smile. "Who are you? You I know," he said as he pointed to Meagan with his drink, his eyes flashing with the recognition of last night. "But you I don't."

"I'm Alexis. I'm what that information you were given will eventually produce."

He looked her over and was pleased, her perfect lines and looks more than he had expected. "Not bad. Not bad at all." Then the oddness of her statement struck him. He screwed his face up, making fine lines in the forehead with which Alexis was so familiar. That was the Cav she knew. "Wait a minute. How can you be the result of this DNA structure when I haven't even done anything with it yet?"

"It takes him awhile sometimes, doesn't it," Meagan said in the realization that he thought she was the Meagan with whom he had slept. As she looked at him, the idea of bedding him didn't offend her in the least bit. Her future self had good taste.

"Yes. He was always a little slow at certain things," Alexis countered as she rose an eyebrow and tilted her head ever so slightly. "The data? Just on the computer?"

"Why should I tell you?" Cav answered back, not at all happy with the implications they were now making, talking about him as if they had known him all his life. "And that's beside the point. How can you be what this DNA creates?"

"We're from the future, Cav," Alexis explained, aware from the stirring in her mind and the feeling tugging at her insides that the bind holding the time-streams together was ready to go at any minute. "A future that has gone terribly wrong."

Cav looked at them a moment, almost believing their story. Then he smiled and looked down at the floor. "Okay, you had me going there for a moment, but I get it now. This is all some part of a joke. Did Lewis send you? I bet it was Lewis. No, no, wait. It was probably Jill! She was also the practical joker and this sure smells like her work."

"This isn't a joke, Cav. And we don't have much time. We need to retrieve that data that was given to you, all of it, including the DNA sample in your jacket pocket."

Cav's smile lasted a moment longer as he chuckled slightly. These two sure were good. "When do we get to the sex part?" he asked in all seriousness. "That's what this is all about isn't it? First she comes last night to me and gives me a night of sex that I'll never forget and now you return with a friend, maybe even a sister, to finish off the job. This has to be the work of Jill. I'll have to thank her later, that's for certain."

Alexis concentrated on the computer and it melted into a sludge of carbon and plastic fibers, the caustic stench filling the room. Cav could not believe his eyes. He had priceless work on that machine. "What the hell do you think you're doing, you stupid bitch?" he yelled as he walked over and looked at the melted amalgam of atoms that had once been his machine. "This isn't funny anymore. I'd like you both to leave ... now."

"We aren't going anywhere," Alexis said in a harsh and firm voice, the mantle of doubt and betrayal she was feeling at the mere thought of having to kill Cav making this more difficult as each slow second ticked past. "Where is the DNA sample?"

"What sample? I don't even know what the hell you're talking about anymore? And why the hell are you asking me all this when it was your fucking slut friend here who gave me the fucking thing in the first place. Damn you." He looked from his melted computer back at the two women. "And get the hell out of here before I have to hurt you."

I can't do this, Meagan, Alexis stated as she struggled with herself to end it, to finish what she had started with the death of the five innocents. It was too much for her. They were all asking too much. She was afraid that this was going to happen, that she was going to find it impossible to kill Cav in the past and thus to kill herself and her daughter in the process.

You have to, Alexis. There is no choice anymore. We've come this far. You've killed all the others and cleaned the time-streams of their contamination. If this is truly the flaw, if it's his death that sets it all right again, then you have to finish it. I see that now. Without Cav gone, the whole thing starts all over again. New time-streams will again arise wherein your son, my brother, is born and comes up with the MTP. This has to end now. Cav is the final piece to the puzzle. I understand that now.

But don't you understand that it means your death also, and mine? Doesn't that bother you in the least, that we'll cease to exist in the blink of an eye?" There was a frustration to her voice making Meagan almost agree.

Cav was walking over to a cabinet where he kept his firearm, ready to use it if these two women didn't leave. He had no idea why they were just staring at each other like that, but he also didn't care. These two were bad news.

Of course I understand it. I've understood it all along. But it's a sacrifice that has to be made, the final one to heal the time-streams and save humanity from itself. There is no other way.

Alexis smiled at that, knowing that there was another way, that she had already implemented it and that what she was about to do here, although final in its own way, was not the end of everything.

"What the hell are you smiling at, bitch?" Cav exclaimed as he pulled the weapon out of drawer and pointed it at them. "I'll say it one more time: get out!"

"We can't do that, Cav," Alexis responded as she felt the bind slip, the time-streams beginning to break free. She had to accomplish this before any of them slipped loose. They all had to be together, all the Cavs had to die at this time and place.

Images of the future flashed in her mind's eye again of the destruction and the death, the brutality of the penal colonies and the concentration camps of the Dynasty. She saw the destruction of other species on other planets, the wholesale slaughter of intelligence and culture for the simple sake of preserving Humanity from itself.

She saw that it had to be, that the Elrsai knew that it had to be, that her altered DNA was crying out to her to do it, to end the cycle regardless of the cost to her or her family. It was for what she had been built. It was her destiny, her primary purpose and that purpose had to be fulfilled.

"I'm sorry, Cav," Alexis said in such a passionate and sympathetic voice that he lowered the gun and narrowed his eyes, not certain what she had meant by that statement but aware that it could not be good.

She reached into his chest, took hold of his heart.

I'm so sorry, but there isn't any other option. And even though I barely knew you, my daughter, I'm very proud of you.

Thank you, mother. I'm scared.

There's no reason to be.

"Sorry about what?" Cav asked as he felt a funny tingling in his chest.

She stopped the electric impulses driving his heart, blocked off the pain receptors. He died quickly and painlessly, slumping to the floor as the life that was Vincent Cavalier left the time-streams forever. It was a simple death of a simple man of which no one took much notice on the island, his body sent back to the mainland for a proper burial and not much more said except how sad it was that one so young had died like that, in this day and age of medical wonders.

As his life essence left, as his soul separated from the mortal coil to which it was attached in a tenuous link of ill-defined moments and memories, this vast complex that is mind, storing within it such a wanton world of virtuous feelings and emotions, Alexis touched one, last life.

Vork awoke from his slumber, from his stasis, and was placed back in the time-stream, ready to re-integrate into a world that would be completely different from the one he had left, the data within him safe.

Without Cav to create her, Alexis Locke evaporated from existence as if she had never existed. Without Alexis to give birth to her, Meagan also vanished without a trace, gone forever from all time-streams. Without Alexis' power holding the time-streams together, they snapped apart like coiled springs, the strain they had produced on space-time beginning to relax with every passing moment.

The Dynasty ceased to exist in any form, its effects on the time-streams and the future erased as cleanly as if surgically removed. With no Huang to use a non-existent MTP technology, that future was never produced, that time-stream dissipating in a spray of molecules and haze to be re-integrated into the remaining streams like mud to water.

Without Meagan Locke and the Colony Time Guards to create it, time-stream Alpha Two snapped off the main time stream and ceased to exist in totality, all those trapped within not even memories anymore in anyone's mind. The Elrsai were one of those lost, their entire civilization, culture, species having only risen in the new, created time-stream and no where else, the prophecy that had been a part of their heritage for eons on end having come true in a flash of precognition.

They had unwittingly helped in their own destruction.

Then the time-streams settled back down, uncoiled smoothly, those that had been mutated, that Alexis had seen and felt, end in a torment of billions, simply disappeared, their reason for being, gone. In the other time-streams that were strong and complete, life continued apace without much of a difference.

Only those who were paying close attention at the exact moment that the unbinding had occurred, when those that had been killed off by Alexis vanished in the future, their lines never having started, their lives never having been; only those few individuals may have noticed a slight jump in time, a twitch, a strong sense of deja vu that would have stayed with them far longer than usual. But other than that, there was no affect, no record of what Alexis and Meagan Locke had accomplished, had achieved with their own deaths, their sacrifice unknown to history, their effect on time un-recorded.

They were, simply, no more.

EPILOGUE

It is only as an esthetic phenomenon that existence
and the world appear justified.
– Nietzsche

16 October 2221
0835 hrs
O'Neill Colony *Einstein XXI*

Vork walked into the procreation lab and looked around. The many nurses watching over the newly born, ignored the Cycomeand. It was not as if the android was going to break something or steal an infant. And Cycomeand were known to be very sterile, so it certainly would not be spreading any diseases. Besides, everyone here knew Vork and liked him, as far as one could like a cyborg, with its coldness and emotionless outlook.

This was fine with Vork, who had a driving sense inside him, as if a glitch had worked its way into his higher programming and instituted a procedure that had lead him to this place, at this time. He would rather that no one saw him anyhow. He was still trying to understand the loss of time he had sustained, the addition of memory vast in its magnitude. It was as if he had someone else's memories inside him, rumbling around and interacting with his own programs in a rather annoying and illogical way. He would be glad when this was all over.

He studied the Colony nursery and quickly found the area for which he was looking, that would be the best place to start. He walked over slowly, not

493

raising any suspicions in the least, looking down at the miniature humans for the one he knew was here, whose name had been etched in him like a memory.

Upon finding the proper name, he stopped. He looked at the holo-chart:
Daughter of Priscilla Ann Locke & Joubert Claude Locke
The infant girl stared up at him, her eyes holding that wonder only the truly innocent can have. She cooed and made little movements with her arms that appeared to Vork to be so much wasted effort. He looked back at the baby emotionlessly, not feeling anything toward the defenseless and weak creature before him and touched her forehead, softly.

The baby's eyes lost their innocence for a brief moment and were filled with a pain and tragedy no newborn should know. She looked at Vork with an intelligence Vork was not aware human babies possess ...and smiled at him, as if it suddenly knew him and was, as illogical as it sounded, thanking him for his presence.

Then it was gone, passed into the recesses of her still developing memory until the right moment to emerge.

When the transference was complete, Vork stepped away and left the room, any memory of what he had just done erased cleanly. As he walked the corridors leading back to his assigned working space, he actually wondered what in the world he had been doing in the nursery in the first place. He had no need to be there.

*   *   *

3 February 2261
1607 hrs
Earth

"Okay, one more push and it'll be here," the doctor intoned rhythmically, the familiar words flowing out of his mouth automatically as he watched the baby's head breach.

The sweat-soaked and thoroughly pissed off female pushed with all her might, her faced contorted into a mask of pain, joy, rage all rolled into one. The tall Nordic-looking man beside her with the surgical mask over his face, sweat on his brow and a more pained expression on his face than his wife's, was hoping that she would not squeeze all of the blood out of his hand before this was over, her grip like reinforced titanium.

"And again," the doctor calmly intoned as the nurse made ready to receive the new born.

Despite all the medical advances recently made, the pain associated with giving birth had remained aloof from their touch, as if the Creator had actually meant it when he said that childbirth would forever more be painful.

A wave of relief flooded the female's senses as she felt the baby push out, her pain contorted face relaxing into a frenzied smile, all the thoughts of killing her husband for causing all this passing as if they had never existed.

"You have a healthy little girl, Mrs. Gudbjartsson-Locke," the doctor beamed at her, taking off his gloves and standing up. "Do you have a name picked out for her yet?"

The female looked up at her husband, whose smile was as big as hers. The baby was placed in her arms, its cries lost to her in the joy that it represented. "Yes, yes we have," she said in ragged gasps, the lost echoes of the pain fading rapidly as she beheld her first-born child. "Oli and I have decided on Meagan Alexandra."

"That's a nice name," the doctor said as his mind moved on to the next patient he had to see. It would most likely be a Cesarean birth. "I wish you all the best of luck."

Alexis looked down at her daughter, saw the innocence in the eyes, the resemblance to that which she had once known in a time that no longer existed, and knew that this one's future was secure.

And she cried....

Printed in the United States
35493LVS00004B/100-102